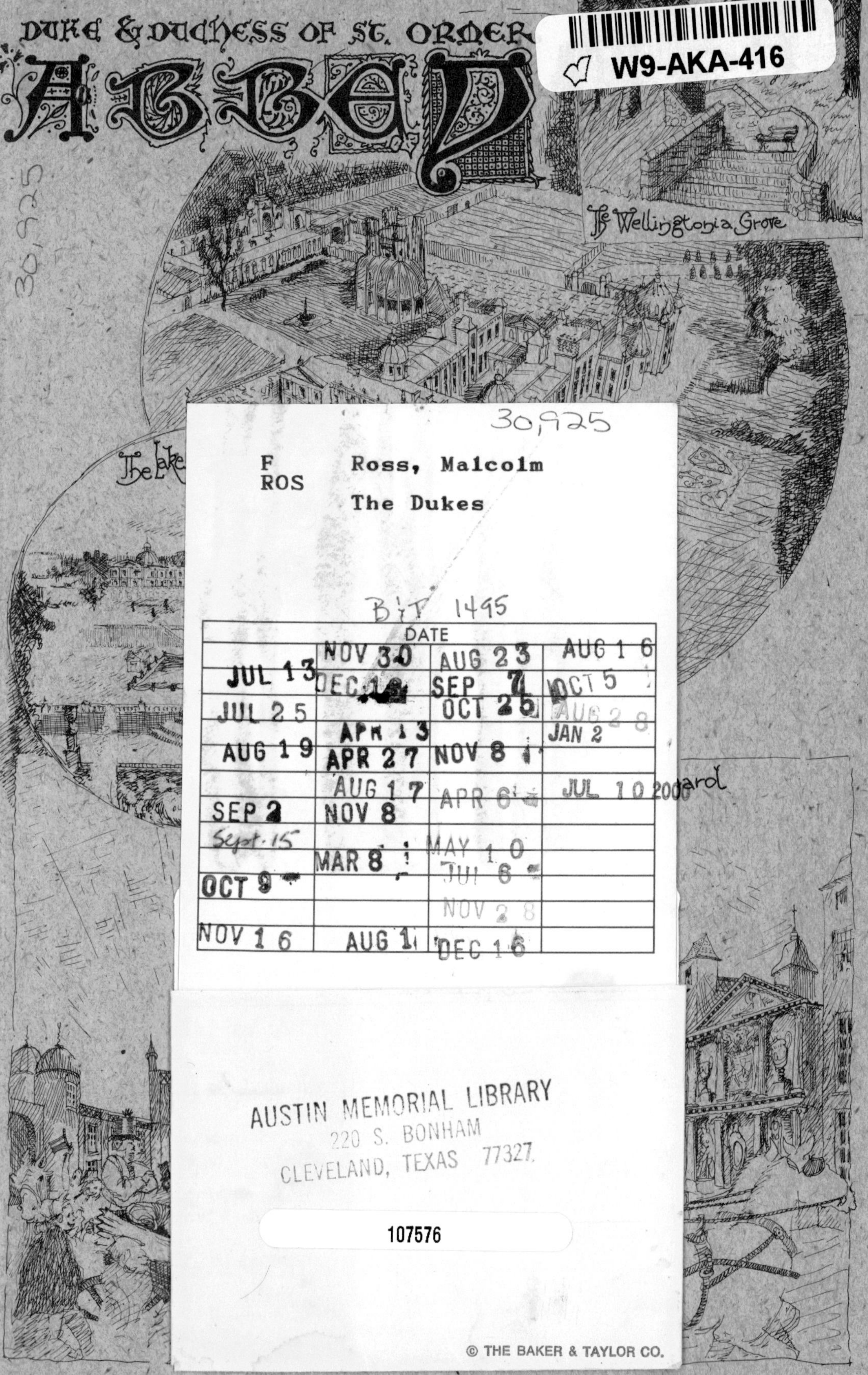
DUKE & DUCHESS OF ST. OMER
ABBEY
The Wellingtonia Grove
The Lake

A NOVEL

Malcolm Ross

SIMON AND SCHUSTER

NEW YORK

Published by Simon and Schuster
A Division of Gulf & Western Corporation
Simon & Schuster Building
Rockefeller Center
1230 Avenue of the Americas
New York, New York 10020
SIMON AND SCHUSTER *and colophon*
are trademarks of Simon & Schuster
Designed by Edith Fowler
Manufactured in the United States of America

10 9 8 7 6 5 4 3 2 1

Library of Congress Cataloging in Publication Data

——

The dukes.

I. Title.
PR6068.0827D8 1981 823'.914 80-27950
ISBN 0-671-25111-2

for
Donald and Norma Berwick
peerless in their way

CONTENTS

PART ONE

1849

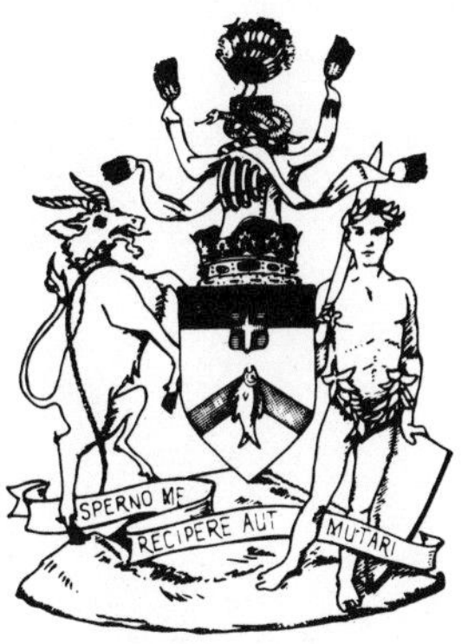
SPERNO ME
RECIPERE AUT
MUTARI

Blood Ennobles

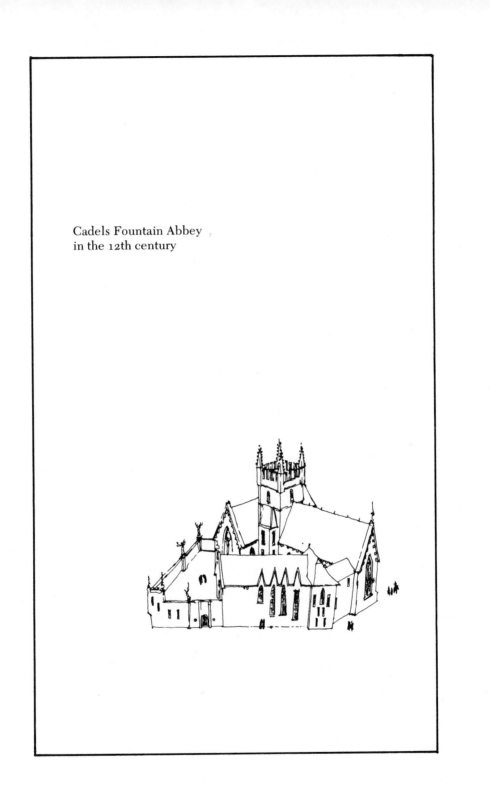

Cadels Fountain Abbey
in the 12th century

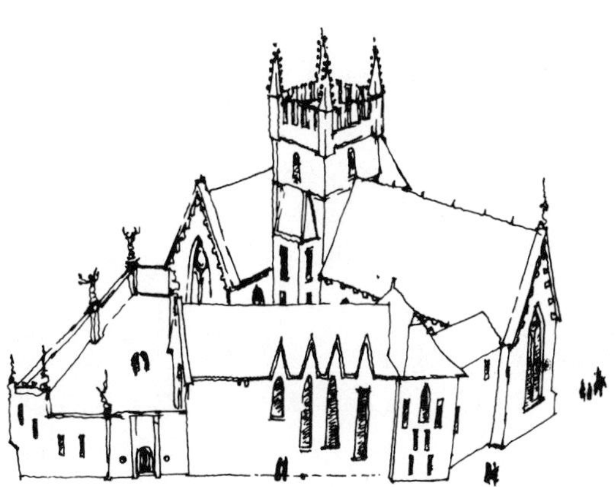

From *Debrett's Peerage and Titles of Courtesy* (1850 edition)

ST. ORMER, DUKE OF. (Du Bois.) [Duke, E. 1639.]

SPERNO ME
RECIPERE AUT
MUTARI

AUGUSTUS CLARENCE FITZSTEPHEN WROTTESLEY VEITCH DU BOIS, K.G. 4th Duke; *b.* May 19th, 1769. ed. at Eton. Hereditary Lord Marcher of the Royal Forests. High Steward of Oxford Without. Former A.D.C. to H.M. King George III and Hon. Col. (formerly Lieut.-Col. Comdg.) Berkshire L.I. (now D.St.O.L.I.), patron of thirty-five livings, a D.L. and J.P. for Cornwall, and a D.L. for Dorset; *m.* 1800, Lady Charlotte Emily, dau. of 5th Earl of St. Mawe who *d.* 1821, and has no issue.

ARMS,—Argent, a chevron sanguine surmounted by a fish haurient gold. A chief sable charged with two mullets or. Over all, in the chief centre point, on an escutcheon azure, a cross argent, thereon another cross gules. CREST,—A peacock in pride proper upon a serpent nowed proper. SUPPORTERS,—*Dexter,* an heraldic goat, armed, unguled, and tufted, ducally gorged and chained reflexed or. *Sinister,* an ancient Briton wreathed about the temples and waist in laurels, holding in his dexter hand a sword, gold, resting on his shoulder proper, and supporting with his sinister hand an antique shield, silver.
Motto,—Sperno me recipere aut mutari.
Seats,—Chalfont Abbey, Bucks.; Constantine Park, Cornwall. *Town Residence*—Knightsbridge House. *Clubs,*—Brooks's, Turf.

SISTERS LIVING

Lady Harriet Mary; *b.* 1772; was Lady of the Bedchamber to H.M. the late Queen Caroline, *Residence,*—Bracknell Park, Bracknell, Berks.
Lady Katherine Geraldine (Marchioness of Avonside); *b.* 1775: *m.* 1795 the 3rd Marquis of Avonside, who *d.* 1831. *Residence,*—10 Brook Street, Mayfair.

WIDOW LIVING OF SON OF THIRD DUKE

Fanny Wilhelmine, dau. of the late *Sir* Kesteven Charles, M.P. 5th Bt; *m.* 1st, 1802, *Lord* Henry Wrottesley St. John du Bois, 3rd son of 3rd Duke, who *d.* 1809; 2ndly, 1815, the

Hon. Rupert Carrington, and has issue living, by 1st marriage [see cols., infra]. *Residence,*—New Park, Kings Norton, Leics.

COLLATERAL BRANCHES LIVING.

Issue of late *Lord* Henry Wrottesley St. John du Bois, 3rd son of 3rd Duke, *b.* 1772, *d.* 1809; *m.* 1802, Fanny Wilhelmine [(ante); she *m.* 2ndly, 1815, the *Hon.* Rupert Carrington, formerly of Belgrave Hall, Leics.] dau. of the late *Sir* Kesteven Charles, M.P., 5th Bt.:—

Blanche Juliet, *b.* 1804; *m.* 1826, Richard Boscawen, Barrister-at-Law, and has issue living, Clarence Henry Blount, *b.* 1827.——Agatha Blanche, *b.* 1828; *m.* 1846, Col. Richard Evans, D.C.L.I. Evelyn Roberta, *b.* 1806; *m.* 1826, William Edward Wyndham, who *d.* 1830, and has issue living, Anthony Edward, *b.* 1828. Residence,—Yockenthwaite, Yorks.

Issue of Revd. *Lord* Richard Fitzstephen Veitch du Bois, brother of 1st Duke, and, by a *novodamus* of 1641, heirs of the remainder of all honours on the extinction of the direct male line; *b.* 1622, *m.* 1643, Grace Harvey, eld. dau. of Sir Geoffrey Hartley of Fingest Manor, Berks.:—

Godfrey Henry du Bois of Fingest Manor, *b.* 1645, *m.* 1670, his cousin Lady Anne Wrottesley, eld. dau. of the 1st Duke, and had issue, William du Bois, *b.* 1671, who later took the style of William Boyce and *m.* 1698, Margaret Champion and had issue of three sons, Orlando, *b.* out of wedlock, 1697, Henry, *b.* 1699, and John, *b.* 1702; Orlando's eld. son, Oliver (who styled himself Boyes), *m.* 1750 his cousin, Chastity, eld. dau. of Henry; John's only son, Harold, *m.* 1755 his cousin, Piety, younger dau. of Henry who *d.* 1740 without heirs male; the issue beyond this generation (who stand in the relationship of 3rd cousins once removed to the pres. Duke) is unclear. Pending resolution, the title will fall into abeyance among the other colls.

PREDECESSORS—[1] *Sir* CLARENCE du Bois, *K.G.*, one of the founder knights of the Order of the Garter: *b.* 1340, *m.* 1361, Anne Harley; *d.* 1412; *s.* by his son [2] CHARLES, *b.* 1410, *m.* (3rdly) 1486, Matilda Veitch, Lady of Marlow; Sir Charles was summoned to Parliament in right of his wife as *Baron Marlow* (peerage of England) 1486. His natural son was Clarence Fitzbois, *b.* 1434; appointed Hereditary Lord Marcher of the Royal Forests, 1490; cr. *Baron of Stonor* (peerage of England) 1492, he *d.s.p.* 1506, when his titles passed by Royal Favour to his legitimate half-brother [3] RICHARD VEITCH, *b.* 1490, who had *s.* his father in 1494. He commanded the English cavalry with great distinction at Flodden and was cr. *Earl of Brompton* (peerage of England) 1513. He was attainted for treason under Henry VIII of England and beheaded in the Tower; *d.s.p.* 1538. The evidence at his trial was supplied by his nephew [4] GODFREY, son of Sir William du Bois and Margaret Knowle, son of Charles [supra]; *b.* 1522; was cr. *Earl of Belgravia* (peerage of England) 1539 and received all his cousin's titles as reward for his testimony. He served the 1st Duke of Somerset and, on acquiring estates in Cornwall, was cr. *Viscount Constantine* (peerage of England) 1542. He escaped Somerset's disgrace and later greatly enlarged his Cornish estate. He also acquired and rebuilt Chalfont Abbey in co. Buckingham; *d.* 1591; *s.* by his son [5] CHARLES CLARENCE VEITCH, who, falsely suspected of complicity in the Lopez plot to poison Queen Elizabeth, was attainted and forced to flee to Spain in 1594. In 1596 he supplied information that helped Lords Howard and Essex to sack Cadiz, and for this was restored to all his dignities and estates and cr. *Marquis of Knightsbridge* (peerage of England) 1597, *m.* 1578 Lady Pamela Wildwood, dau. of the 2nd Marquis of Westwell; *d.* 1621, *s.* by his son [6] WILLIAM CLARENCE, 2nd Marquis; *m.* 1600 Jane Seton, his cook; played a leading part in organizing the Hampton Court Conference, which was responsible for the King James Bible; *d.* 1624; *s.* by his son [7]CLARENCE WILLIAM Henry, *K.G.*, 3rd Marquis, then a minor; cr. *Duke of St. Ormer* (peerage of England) 1639, the oldest surviving uninterrupted dukedom, the remainder of which, by a *novodamus* of 1641, may pass, together with the other honours, on the extinction or abeyance of the male line to the hs. of the 1st Duke's eld. dau. Lady Anne Wrottesley; *b.* 1641 (she having fulfilled the necessary condition that she marry a descendant of her uncle, Rev. *Ld.* Richard, by marrying her cousin, Godfrey du Bois, in 1670) [see colls supra]; founded big estates in the American colony; he was later a patron of the consortium of London Merchants who profitably farmed the entire English customs duties until 1671 and was able to add tens of thousands of acres to the Berks. estates; he deployed the Berks. Yeomanry, of which he was C.-in-C. first in the royalist cause, later for the parliamentatians; he was a brief supporter of Monmouth's Rebellion in 1685 but in 1688 was of the Whig faction that invited William of Orange on to the throne; *m.* 1638, Jane, eld. dau. of Sir William Wrottesley of Watling Hall and widow of the 4th Earl of Farnham, thus returning the estates at Marlow and Henley to the family; *d.* 1702; *s.* by his son [8] HENRY VEITCH WROTTESLEY, 2nd Duke, Col. of the Berks. Yeomanry, who *d.* in circumstances of utmost gallantry at Oudenarde, 1708; *m.* 1700, Pamela, *Baroness Yeo* in her own right, dau. of 4th Baron Harwick of Bledlow, whose estates at Bledlow passed into the du Bois inheritance; *s.* by his son [9] WILLIAM WROTTESLEY VEITCH, *K.G.*, 3rd Duke, then a minor; on his majority he was successively Lord-Lieut. of Ireland, Ambassador to Spain, and a member of most Whig administrations until his death; *m.* 1768, his cousin at one remove, Stephanie Anne, dau. of John Tainter of Bledlow Manor; *d.* 1770; *s.* by his son [10] AUGUSTUS CLARENCE FITZSTEPHEN WROTTESLEY VEITCH, the present peer, who is also Marquis of Knightsbridge, Earl of Brompton, Earl of Belgravia, Viscount Constantine, Baron Marlow, Baron of Stonor, and Baron Yeo.

CHAPTER ONE

HE DOCTOR may bleed the duke now," the duke said.

The valet turned to the shadows beyond the reach of the single candle. "You have his grace's permission to bleed his person," he said.

The doctor cleared his throat and came awkwardly into the light; he held the kidney bowl and scalpel in such a way that they could not touch—for fear the rattle of the one upon the other should betray his terror.

When the duke stood to bare his forearm he presented a vast cliff of damasked brocade; his bald head, at the top of that unscalable height, gleamed like samite. He clearly was not ill. The bleeding was a simple precaution against a plethora.

The doctor pressed the kidney bowl to the pale flesh of a once-powerful forearm. The knife flashed a nervous silver as he sought among the scars of recent and more ancient bleedings. He drew breath to speak.

But the duke, watching those tremulous lips, was ahead of him. "Don't prattle to me of your leeches, damn your sides," he said, as if the doctor had already spoken. "Is it sharp this time?"

"It is, your grace." Again the doctor cleared his throat. "And clean."

"A pox to your clean, sir!"

The valet smiled, glad to be out of the firing line for once.

The blood snaked hot down the duke's forearm and fell, dark as old wine, into the bowl.

"What's in that blood, sir? Tell me that," the duke commanded.

"Why, your grace, er, iron . . . ah . . . calcium . . . er . . ."

The duke laughed. "Little you know. Little learning and less sense! 'The midwife laid her hand on your thick skull, With this prophetic blessing—*be thou dull!*' " He put his mouth conspiratorially close to the ear of the doctor, who stared with terror out into the titanic blackness of the unseeable bedchamber.

"Now listen, sir; hark'ee well and tell me truly. What does ten thousand firkins of ale leave in a man's arteries, eh? Tell me that. Or a thousand hogsheads of fine claret? Eh? Or a hundred tuns of brandy. Mmm? When a man sees a pleasing wench, what juice passes from his eyes to his blood that gives him no ease, no peace, till he tops her? What's the liquid that riots in our veins when a thousand guineas rides on a single card or a thoroughbred filly half a furlong out? Or when Charley Fox breaks from covert and the scent screams and the going's firm. Eh?"

"Why, sir, such excesses must leave *some*thing in our veins, that's certain. But what it may be . . ."

The duke was not listening. "Tell me what, Mr. Quack, Mr. Leeches, tell me what irrigates every corner of a body as big and fine as this"—he squared his shoulders—"yet leaves it barren!"

The valet turned to nip a smoking lump from the candlewick. The doctor bent low over the kidney bowl. Neither man could face that terrible self-accusation.

There was no sound in the room but the fury of the duke's breathing.

"Riddle me that, you pretender to the crown of science!" the duke jeered.

When they withdrew, he lay back between his cold sheets, pressed the swab fiercely to the new clot on his forearm, and wished he had not lost the gift of easy tears.

"No heir," he said aloud to the deathly black around him. He thought of Charlotte, his duchess, who had died in childbed long ago, telling him her stillborn son was fathered by another—Charlotte whom he had cursed and harried, year in, year out, for her supposed barrenness, when it was only her faithfulness to him had made her so. He thought then of the wasted years, pumping his sterility into numberless trollops and girls of every low degree, any one of whom he would have married if she had presented him with one undoubted heir. But none had.

Not so long ago any one of these memories would have been enough to release his tears, and, with them, the soothing balm of grief. Now, even on each other's heels, they had lost that power.

He turned then, as he always did, to the memories of his young manhood, when the dukedom of St. Ormer had seemed as secure as the Tower of London and its extinction was unthinkable. He remembered the days in the field, the evenings at Brooks's, the nights in the boudoirs. There was a zest in those memories that had vanished from this vile, modern country.

Nowhere now could you smell a winter hedgerow quite so sweet as then; no modern horse would leap as rashly or with half such heart as those mounts of long ago; the very foxes and hounds were palsied weaklings when set beside those red-streaking demons that webbed the landscapes of his memory, and the baying packs that flowed like portions of a magic river, at liberty to stream uphill as easily as down.

Where now was laughter as innocently wicked as the gusts and gales of it that greeted the turn of their cards at Brooks's? Where now were the men who could command such storms, where the raffish and sinister Henry Frederick, Duke of Cumberland . . . where Charles James Fox, the unlaundered epicurean and tender cynic, or—above all men—the peerless Prince of Wales? Where was he? The world would never see their like again.

"Oh, my prince!" the duke whispered, an ancient man lost in those most treacherous lands of all.

And at last there was the narcotic of tears.

They woke him at four next morning; from dreams of cataclysm and apocalypse they tapped and pinched and "your-graced" his full-blooded mind back into its newly anemic body.

"Devil take you!" he shouted, blinking at the dark.

"Your grace! Sir!" It was McKay, his secretary.

Scoby, the valet, slipped a shawl around his shoulders, plumped up the down of his pillows, retrieved his nightcap and pulled it back over his head, and passed him a watered brandy, all in one movement. In one further movement he was holding a candle at the duke's right shoulder.

In its light he saw that McKay was presenting a salver; the letter upon it bore the seal of Elliott & Polkinghorne, solicitors.

"Mr. Polkinghorne's found the lost line of the family, sir," McKay said.

The duke grunted angrily, to conceal his joy. The lost line of the family—*found!*

But how did McKay know? The duke peered closely at the seal to check that it had not been tampered with.

"Mr. Polkinghorne wrote to me too, sir," McKay said.

The duke frowned.

"To be sure to wake you, sir."

The frown deepened.

"Your instructions, your grace, were, no matter what the hour or occasion, day or night—"

"Don't plague me, you ill-kept loon!" the duke thundered. "Don't serve me my own words. I know what I said." He stared at the letter on the silver tray. "It'll keep!" he barked and, blowing out the candle, hurled himself back beneath his counterpane. Over the hammering of his heart he barely heard the secretary and the valet go blundering out into the dark.

He was capricious with them, partly because it was a lifetime habit to be capricious with his inferiors but mainly to hide his terror from McKay and Scoby. While the hunt for the lost line of the family was on, there was all the excitement of drawing a new fox covert: Would it prove blank, or would the foxes break from it like startled crows? And what sort of fox would the ultimate quarry be—valiant or a coward, stouthearted or a misery? What sort of man would be heir to Augustus Clarence Fitzstephen Wrottesley Veitch du Bois, Fourth Duke of St. Ormer, Marquis of Knightsbridge, Earl of Brompton, Earl of Belgravia, Viscount Constantine, Baron Marlow, Baron of Stonor, and Baron Yeo?

Until now, all things were possible of this lost line. Was it the line of John, younger brother of the First Duke, who had fled to Scotland and then to France during the Commonwealth, there to marry into the powerful de Boisigny family? Had part of that line escaped the Terror after all? Or was it the line through Stephen, the bastard son of his grandfather, the Second Duke, who had been brought up at the Hanoverian court and whose son had married a Hohenzollern? Had they indeed been legitimized on the accession of George I to the throne of England?

Or was this all just so much wishful thinking? Would his heir turn out to be no more than a petty baronet—a toadying lickspittle like his neighbor Sir Duncan Kinnaird, bankrupt through four generations? Or even worse—a mere squire? Perhaps with a northern accent and pig dung on his boots? Or had Polkinghorne found descendants beyond those damned third cousins, the detestable Puritan Boyces?

The answer to these and a thousand like questions lay in the stout parchment that he still clutched between his trembling fingers. He could tolerate the suspense no more. "Scoby!" he roared.

At once Scoby came in, bearing the relighted candle; after long years of service this capricious master had become as predictable as the tides at Greenwich.

In a fever of anticipation the duke broke the seal. He hammered the parchment flat and read the neat, crabbed handwriting.

After two paragraphs he stopped breathing. What blood the doctor had left him drained from his face and limbs. He stared at the words on the page.

He looked again at the seal, suspecting a hoax. It was genuine.

He peered at Scoby's impassive face, seeking the merest hint of a telltale smile. In vain.

He read to the end, hoping the later half would contradict the opening one. It did not.

One by one the alternatives vanished. One by one the teeming horde of possibilities, from imperial Hohenzollerns down to simple squires, took their leave, until there lurked on that once-vast stage the single, solitary—and hitherto quite unsuspected—figure of . . .

The duke, Augustus Clarence Fitzstephen Wrottesley Veitch du Bois, lay back upon his pillow, closed his eyes, and said in utter disbelief: "Alfred Boyce, manufacturer of lacquered metal boxes!"

CHAPTER TWO

"DEVIL TAKE YOU, girl!" shouted Alfred Boyce, manufacturer of lacquered metal boxes. "Because a man stays the night away, does he pay less for his room? He does not! So should he get the same service as if he stayed? He should!"

The maid looked around in bewilderment. "But the bed is made, sir. The ewer's dry. The room's as tidy as I left it yesterday."

"We'll see about that," Alfred said. And he rumpled the bed, kicked the rug all of a heap, and then, pouring a liberal splash of water into the ewer, threw off his shirt and washed himself.

He did not need a wash, for he had done the same ablutions at four o'clock that morning—only three hours ago—at the Cross Keys in Hanston, fourteen miles away. Nor was he customarily as mean-spirited as these actions made him seem. He liked the bustle of servants. He liked being waited upon. But today, more than ever, he needed to feel he was still the master *some*where—if only in this narrow, otherwise unlettable room over the coaching entrance of the Midland Hotel in the Cokeley district of Birmingham; for today, unless he could achieve some extraordinary feat of commerce (quite against his recent form), today Alfred Boyce's little manufacturing empire was going to fall apart. The very girl—Eileen—whom he now ordered about with such uncharacteristic spite would soon, without adding a penny to her name, be a thousand times richer than he. So he seized these last few chances to show what mastery remained to him.

"You're out of your usual good humor, sir," Eileen said cheerfully as she bustled about, setting the room to rights.

"Hold your tongue! Have I had any visitors yesterday or last night?"

He almost forgot himself and said "creditors."

The girl went on with her business in sullen silence.

Alfred, invigorated by his wash, made a new resolve, realizing it would do him no good to show the world how bad his affairs were . . . and servants have tongues.

"Ah, come on," he said. "Give us a kiss." His laugh was so vast and deep you'd imagine he was built around a bass organ pipe, except that he was short and slight enough to vanish comfortably inside such a tube.

The maid was shocked. Mr. Boyce had never before suggested such improprieties. His gleaming eyes and the wet mouth that lurked inside his full black beard frightened her as she saw him in the new light of his suggestion.

He laughed again. "It was a jest," he said. "If I'm out of humor, it's because that new mare of your master's rushes at every rut and puddle, shows her heels at every starling, and thinks the dogs between Soho and the Bull Ring came straight from the forests of Africa. Bring me porridge and a nice kipper or three, eh?"

Reassured, Eileen smiled. "You had two callers last night. A Mr. Polkinghorne, solicitor, who will wait on you again today."

"Solicitor!" Alfred said, laughing even as his guts slithered down to his boots. "I hope it's that legacy at last."

"And there was Sir Eric Newbiggin . . ."

"Sir Eric!" Alfred was stunned. "In person?"

"Yes, and very eager to see you, too. He left you word—there on the mantelpiece."

Alfred followed the dart of her eyes and saw the envelope propped between two lacquered metal boxes, samples of his wares. As in a dream he crossed the room and took up the paper. *Midland Hotel* was stamped upon it.

"This is not Sir Eric's notepaper."

"He came expecting to find you in, I suppose." She was lingering now, to see his reaction. Suspicions kindled.

The letter ran:

My dear Boyce,

Too long I have put off writing to you. I was overhasty, not to say brusque, at our last Meeting, when you

> were kind enough to favour Me with the Suggestion of a Private Business Arrangement. I have thought more of it since and have come to realize the Great Merit of your proposal . . .

This is a hoax, Alfred thought. *It can be nothing else.* "Did you yourself see Sir Eric?" he asked the girl.

"No, sir."

"Does anyone else here know him?"

"I'm certain they do. Everyone in Cokeley knows Sir Eric."

"Aye, and so do I."

His eye fell to a later paragraph: "My daughter Hermione tells me she has for some time been aware of your Glances in Church . . ."

That's a good one, Alfred thought. He had become a Unitarian for the sole purpose of meeting and forming an acquaintance with Sir Eric. The love that burned within him for Hermione, undeclared and unrequited, had come later, and not as a welcome bonus. She knew of it, he could sense that. And, though she was impossibly beautiful and impossibly beyond his humble reach, she had responded sufficiently, with a glance here, a smile there, to sustain the barest hope. "If she were only free of her parents . . ." was a daydream that lulled him to sleep most nights.

And Sir Eric knew of his feelings; there was no doubt of it. He had even sneered about them at their last meeting. And what was he saying now in this letter? ". . . in your altered circumstances no possible objection could be put in the way of . . ."

Oh, of course it was a hoax! "In your altered circumstances"? What? A euphemism for "now that you're about to go bankrupt"! It was very likely that the richest man in rich, rich Birmingham should say, in effect: "I know you've got your eye on my daughter. Well, now you're going bankrupt you'll have lots of time on your hands, so why not come up to the Hall and court her every day"!

No, it was a hoax, timed with unintentional cruelty by drinking companions somewhere about their fifth or sixth pint of ale. He took up a pen and wrote, "Well tried, sir!" in a large hand, right across "Sir Eric" 's neat lines.

"Give this to Sir Eric—*if* he returns," he said, handing the letter to the maid with a knowing smile. He did not even bother to fold it back into its envelope. "Now, where's the porridge and kippers, eh?"

By lunchtime everyone at the Midland had read the letter and marveled at Alfred's cavalier reply.

"Was he drunk?" asked Tom Austin, the landlord.

"He was a bit strange," Eileen said. "But not drunk."

"Something's afoot," Tom Austin said, for at least the thirtieth time that morning. "That solicitor cove, he still here?"

"He's not even tooken off his coat," she said.

"Something's afoot."

CHAPTER THREE

BY THAT SAME lunchtime Alfred had half-saved his tottering business. "Not but what 'half-saved' isn't the same as 'half-lost,' " he glumly told himself. To complete the job he needed every hour of the day that remained, and now here was this Polkinghorne barring the way to his room where all his notes and formulas were kept. He should have taken them this morning, except that he could hardly have expected to be faced with such a fabulous order.

"Fifteen thousand," Mr. Bird had said. "And more to follow if those go well."

Never mind what's to follow, Alfred had thought to himself, a nice order for fifteen thousand would be something to wave in the face—the increasingly odious face—of Josiah Pringle, his banker and chief persecutor. Perhaps he could even confront this Polkinghorne and his summonses then.

Thank heaven he'd never shown Mr. Bird around his "factory." The man would have seen at once that he'd never make fifteen thousand metal boxes there—not even plain-colored ones, much less fifteen thousand enameled with golden Chinese lions.

He turned the corner of Railway Row; his factory was, in fact, one of the railway arches, blocked off at each end. Beneath those bricks, which oozed soot-stained water every time it rained, eight scrawny, laughing city girls toiled and gossiped under the tolerantly watchful eye of Widow Garter, who also managed the outwork.

"Fifteen thousand," Alfred said to himself aloud. "You haven't the faintest hope of doing it." Even as his stomach fell (its only predictable movement these days) he grinned. Something within him needed just that sort of challenge to keep alive.

"You sure?" Mr. Bird had asked. "There's only one box-printing machine can handle that pattern and quantity, so far as I know, and that's a Boulton & Pethwick Imprimatur. Have you got one?"

"Well, it's been on the temperamental lay just these last few weeks, Mr. Bird." (Alfred, remembering this rashness, giggled—for, of course, he owned no machine of any kind, much less a mighty Imprimatur.) "And I've been so busy with the plain boxes. But for fifteen thousand it might be worth tinkering with. Get it going again. We'll see. I'll bring you a sample tomorrow. Oh, I might change the design slightly."

"That design's not to be touched, Mr. Boyce."

"I think you'll like the changes I make, Mr. Bird."

That was a test sentence, of course, to see how desperate Bird was. And when he grudgingly answered, "They had better be good," Alfred knew he was very desperate.

Birmingham Metal Box and Lacquering Manufactory: the plaque above the brick arch was as bright as the day it went up, ten months earlier. He still felt a tingle of pride at it. Sir Eric Newbiggin might sneer, but he, Alfred Boyce, had come farther in his twenty-three years than Sir Eric had in fifty, or whatever he was. (For Alfred everyone over forty might as well be ninety.)

Alfred was not entirely without resources and ideas for meeting this impossible challenge. Just around the corner, in Railway Cuttings, was a wood-block engraver who also made blocks for wallpaper and chintz printers; Alfred had seen those blocks and was sure they would do for printing his designs. He wouldn't need the costly Imprimatur, if he was right—and if his other idea turned out to be workable.

It, too, had not been tried before on any scale. It was for a mordant, or glue, that would stick "gold" powder to lacquered tin. True, there were a dozen or more such mordants on the market already, but most of them let the powder rub off on anything it touched. The rest had to be baked at temperatures that damaged ordinary lacquers. Alfred had been brought up after his parents had died by an uncle who was an apothecary; from him he had learned the joy of fiddling about with "formulas and things." He had fiddled about with mordants until he found one that would bake in a moderate oven, a temperature that lacquers would tolerate. At which point debts and creditors had brought the experiments to a hasty stop. Now the same debts and the same creditors were about to put them back into headlong operation—except that the formula was in his papers back at the Midland. Once again he cursed Mr. Polkinghorne and all the tribe of solicitors.

Carefully and quietly Mr. Polkinghorne once again cursed young Alfred Boyce. Didn't the fellow know the meaning of the words "to your advantage"? How long must he wait in this wretched inn with its almost undrinkable ale?

Of course he *would* wait—a week if necessary. Alfred Boyce was only twenty-three; he could be the Fifth Duke for the next fifty years, the rest of the century. Mr. Polkinghorne wanted to deliver the good news in person; he wanted young Mr. Boyce to know and trust him from the start. A duke with such prospects and fifty thousand acres of prime land, to say nothing of town properties, was worth even a week of waiting if it confirmed him as a client.

But that did not make the beer more palatable nor the serving maids more attractive.

At nine that evening Alfred had his wood block and, by dint of sandpapering its "flocked," or velveted, printing surface to the thinnest downy layer, he found it printed a wet mordant onto lacquered metal without spreading it, not even into the finest parts of the design—the lion's eyes and his delicate, forked tongue of flame.

The trouble was the mordant—his special one, the one that baked at low temperatures. He had to have the formula from his room. And he had to have it soon or the apothecaries would all be closed.

Ten minutes later he was standing in the biting March rain in the shadows to one side of the coaching arch of the Midland. If only he occupied the room on either side, he might stand a chance of scaling up to it. But he could see no possible way of going the last few feet to his own window, right over the center of the arch. Quiet as a shadow he stole indoors.

There, tantalized by the comforting reek of stale beer, cabbage, and beef fat, he drew himself into a bricked-up archway, perfectly shaded, and waited for one of the servants to pass by.

Out of the mêlée of voices from the bar his ear picked that of Tom Austin, the landlord. "Coming, Mr. Polkinghorne, sir!" it cried in response to a summons from the private bar, which lay just beyond the partition on the opposite side of the passage.

"Any new-new-news?" That was obviously Polkinghorne, a solicitor with a skinful by the sound of it.

Tom Austin must have shaken his head: no.

"And you're sure no one knows where this factory place is?"

"It's near the station, I'm sure of it," said another voice—and it was some moments before Alfred realized, with shock, that it was the voice of Sir Eric Newbiggin. Come to protest that forgery, of course. Everything that happened in Cokeley was carried at once to the Hall.

"He's a tenant of the Midland Railway. That I know," Tom Austin added.

"Which isn't much assistance on a wet and windy night," Sir Eric said. "Well, I must be off. You'll bring our young friend up to the Hall as soon as you've broken him—"

". . . the good tidings," Sir Eric had been going to say, but Polkinghorne cut him short with tipsy dignity: "*I*, sir, shall hardly be in a position to dictate his movements."

No! Alfred thought. *That'll be up to the turnkey at Marshallswick, or whatever debtor's gaol you take me to.* He flung himself back into the shadows just in time to let Sir Eric, who in the dark was no more than a whiff of brandy and bad breath, pass out into the night. *I'll slip up now and get those papers,* Alfred thought. Polkinghorne seemed set to drink himself into a stupor.

He reached his room without discovery and it was then only a matter of moments to find the papers, even in the dark. He was tiptoeing back along the passage when he heard the voices of Polkinghorne and the landlord at the foot of the stairs. They were making heavy labor of the ascent, and Tom Austin was assuring the solicitor (truthfully, as Alfred knew only too well) that from his room, right next door to Alfred's, he could hear every sound in that end of the hotel. "Not a mouse could go along that corridor without your ahearing of it, sir," he said.

Alfred proved it as he fled back to his room; every floorboard sang a Hallelujah Chorus, off-key.

"I'm the first you've ever admish, admitsch, admitted it to," Polkinghorne laughed—and but for that laugh he would have ended his quest that minute.

Alfred looked glumly out the window. What had seemed impossible from below looked suicidal from above. While precious minutes ebbed away he stood and waited for noises which might indicate that Polkinghorne was going to sleep.

Water slopped into an ewer. Then there were sounds of washing, not as a man might wash in order to wash himself but in order to sober up: the sounds of a hippopotamus going down or of a walrus coming up. Under their cover Alfred began the quietest possible move along the corridor, inching his right foot along the right skirting, his left along the left—a technique for minimizing floorboard squeak that he had perfected in creeping up to the maid's room at his uncle's. The things we learn at fifteen are with us for life.

He was almost back to the stairhead when Eileen appeared, bearing a baked brick in a towel for the solicitor's bed.

"Why, Mr. Boyce!" she began.

Alfred fled, sending her sprawling.

"Something's afoot," Tom Austin said when he heard of it.

"The fellow's unhinged," Sir Eric said when the news reached the Hall.

"He is the duke's heir," Mr. Polkinghorne said. "His very behavior confirms it, I'm afraid."

The iron spikes that seemed to have invaded his ribcage brought Alfred to a breathless halt at the corner of Railway Row—at which point he remembered that he ought, in fact, to be going to the apothecary's in Trafalgar Place. When Alfred arrived the man and his family were at evening prayers, but ten minutes later Alfred was on his way back to Railway Row with the proper ingredients for his special mordant.

All through the night he worked, producing some four dozen boxes—as many as he could carry and more than enough to convince Mr. Bird that he could fulfill the order.

The longest watches of the night came as each batch was baked in his meager oven. But the *gold!* It was superb, as sparkling and fine as the gold on porcelain. No one had ever laid such a gold before. It would be the wonder of the whole japanning and lacquering world. It would make his fortune.

As the later batches went through there was all the time he could want for imagining that bright tomorrow. The day-to-day details were necessarily vague, but he had a clear view of a vast factory belching smoke over the entire town. There was another picture of himself in aldermanic robes, leading a procession somewhere. And in a Freemason's apron; they were the fellows to join! And going into a dainty boudoir, where lay a vibrant, incandescent woman—*his!*

That would be the reward, all right. He wouldn't need to fear them any more: beautiful women. No more Widow Garters.

Though . . . *be fair,* he thought, she had served him well.

Three or four times a month he went to Josiah Pringle, his banker, in Willenshawe, twenty-five miles away—far enough for no gossip to stray back to Cokeley, where he represented himself as an heir of some considerable endowment merely dipping his toes into commerce "to see how it suits me and whether or no there's a fortune in it."

"My dear old uncle Harvey, who made a dozen fortunes shipping Bristol gin—you must have heard of him," he said, "—my dear old uncle Harvey always said, 'Start small, my boy. Think of the oak and remember the acorn.' I bless him every day though he left me not a penny."

Everyone commended the wise head on such young shoulders. And how sensible, too, to take such modest rooms. "I'll spend not a penny more than the business justifies," he said—with absolute truth, for there was not a penny more to spend. So he lived in a room some of his factory hands might despise and yet enjoyed the reputation of a gentleman with a ten-servant house and a park about it.

Which took care of all his problems except the problem of women. Alfred adored women, and with a splendid impartiality. There were none too old, few too young, none too lean, nor few too fat, too plain, too common, too dull, too cross, too frightened, too remote—all could (at the very least) quicken his interest. Most of them, from the average upward to the sublime, had the power to obsess him, to absorb all his waking hours and torment all his sleeping ones. And therein lay his trouble.

If he had been unsuccessful in that direction, his problems would have been small. He could, like most men, have resigned himself to a mute and distant adoration while getting on with the practical business of life. But Alfred had a way with women. They took one look at his short, powerful body, or caught one glimpse of his shining, coal-black eyes as he smiled at them, and something within them was already moving toward a humor that might turn into a mood that might harden into a disposition that might flower into a determination to say yes to propositions that were still hours away (or days, or weeks, or minutes, depending on circumstances). He could not help it. He did not deliberately provoke it; he knew no way to control it. He could recall scores of times when he had been as surprised as anybody to find himself lost in a delicious fumble with a woman he scarcely knew—in clothes cupboards, graveyards, alleys, woods . . . and once in a vestry.

It was no way to build a business, of course. Women could ruin it, not by meaning to, just by being. Hence the Widow Garter. He and she, or, rather, his and her needs, were made for each other. She, missing the comforts of a husband; he, a potential serf to every soft lip, dark eye, tender neck, heaving bosom, curly lock, and slender wrist that caught his eye.

Several times a month Widow Garter took butter and eggs to

her father in the almshouses over at Heriton; one of those days, quite at random, always coincided with a visit of Alfred's to Josiah Pringle of Willenshawe, not too impossibly far away. On their respective journeys back they always contrived to meet at an inn (as at the Cross Keys in Hanston last night) or at the house of some complaisant laundress, there to exorcize the demons that might otherwise grow too powerful.

He looked at the golden lion and grinned at the black-bearded face he saw reflected within it, already grinning up at him. "Fourteen thousand nine hundred and fifty two to go," he said. "By heavens but you're a lovely gold!"

"It's a lovely gold, Mr. Boyce, I grant you that. And your box—as a box—is much the handsomer. No doubt about it. But . . . the lion." Mr. Bird sucked his teeth and shook his head.

"The lion, Mr. Bird?"

"Aye. It doesn't say *tea*. You've completely altered the design."

Alfred looked at Mr. Bird's original design and then at his own variation. His innards did their hourly turn, aided now by over twenty-four hours without food or rest: The original lion undoubtedly belonged to a box of China tea; his own, though far more splendid, belonged to . . . what? Anything. A magician's box. Pandora's box.

"But the original is quite wrong, Mr. Bird. Quite wrong."

The best method of defense.

"Wrong!" Mr. Bird thundered. "Damn your impudence, sir!"

Alfred had to go on, of course, but what could he say? He had changed the pattern to make it possible to print by wood block, but he could hardly say that. Nor could he attack it for being something it wasn't, or something they could argue about. He had to attack it for being precisely what Mr. Bird said it was.

"I repeat—*wrong*—Mr. Bird. And it's wrong for exactly the reason you give. It says *tea*. I never saw a lion say *tea* louder than what that lion says it."

Mr. Bird's anger was overwhelmed by his surprise. "And why shouldn't a lion on a tin that holds tea say *tea*, may I ask, Mr. Boyce? It seems a very natural and proper thing for such a lion to say."

Alfred had no idea what he was going to reply until he heard the words fall from his lips. "And how long will it hold tea, Mr. Bird? A month? Six weeks? And then? Why, for years—maybe for a lifetime—it'll hold buttons, old letters, the rent money, ribbons, string . . . packets of herbs . . ." Alfred grew excited as the argument took hold of him. He could see that Mr. Bird was being swayed by it, too. "Now *your* customer, Mr. Bird, is a tea merchant—so naturally he wants a tin that says tea. But *his* customer wants no such thing—what! A box that screams *tea* to all the world, when all the world knows it's full of buttons! No, she wants a box that's handsome. Something she can leave about the place with pride. And as you said yourself . . ." He waved his hand over the two boxes and let Mr. Bird's memory of his opening compliments do the rest.

But a fleck of doubt still troubled the man's eyes, even after he had absorbed and granted the argument. Alfred, suspecting that the tea merchant was the difficulty, shot his final bolt: "The merchant who buys that tin, Mr. Bird—and I don't care whether he fills it with biscuits or comfits or buns or fancy sugar—the merchant who buys that tin could fill it with seaweed and sell it to fishermen's wives, or with snow and sell it to lady Eskimos, or with sand and . . ."

"Very well, Mr. Boyce, you've made your point." He smiled a goodbye of a smile. "I'll let you know what my customer says."

"No, Mr. Bird. That won't suit at all, I'm afraid. I'm all set to produce now. I've cleared half the workshops. I'm putting in two new ovens this very minute. I must go from here with an order for fifteen thousand."

"No, sir, you shall not."

"Then I'll make and sell on my own account."

"But it's not your design."

"That's not what you said just now."

"Yes, but that was . . ." He looked at Alfred incredulously, and with a tinge of respect, too. "Are you deliberately trying to make me withdraw, young man? Have you found a customer? Want to cut me out?"

"No, Mr. Bird. The only one who can cut you out is *you*. Either you're in or you're out. You can decide now." He smiled his most engaging smile. "But not tomorrow."

Mr. Bird leaned back in his chair, put his fingertips together, and blew out through his moustachios. "Is it true," he asked, "that you're going to be a duke?"

For a moment Alfred thought this was an inscrutable move in the game of bluff and counterbluff. Then he thought he must have heard wrong. "Duke?" he asked.

"Yes. That maid Eileen from the Midland was here with a message for you. There's a solicitor called Polkinghorne there, mightily anxious to see you. Something about your being made a duke."

"Dupe, more likely." Alfred laughed. "Come on, what d'you say?"

Mr. Bird bit his lip in furious indecision. "You have a persuasive tongue, Mr. Boyce. What d'you say to ten thousand?"

"Say? I say fifteen, Mr. Bird."

"Oh, come now! You overreach. That's not good business. Twelve and a half."

Alfred forced anger into his face then replaced it with a smile. "A hard bargain, Mr. Bird. But it matters little—tomorrow you'll beg me to double it—and then I'll tell you who else is after me for orders."

He was on the point of leaving, with the signed order for twelve and a half thousand, when Mr. Bird said, very casually, "Whose gold enamel is that, by the by?"

And Alfred, equally casually, said, "Oh, it's me own."

Mr. Bird could not disguise his sudden greedy interest. Alfred could have kicked himself—he had followed the wrong hare.

"What's the secret, then?" Mr. Bird laughed. "As if you'd tell me!"

"Oh, I'll tell you," Alfred said. "It's no great secret." He opened one of the boxes and felt inside. "No, it's all baked off," he said. "I thought there might be a bit left. I paint the inside of the box with a special coating. Lacquers bake off from the back, you see, the metal being a better conductor than the air." *How plausible it sounds,* he thought. "When the inside coating has baked off completely, the enameling is done."

It was so convincing he began to wonder if he might not have the germ of yet another enameling process.

"And no one else knows this coating of yours?"

"Of course not."

"Mr. Boyce, I'll pay you a thousand pounds if you'll agree to sell that particular enamel only through me."

Alfred began to feel a little lightheaded. "A thousand pounds a year," he said, wanting to test Mr. Bird's estimate of the market.

Mr. Bird exploded with indignation. There was a long argument that ended with a draft agreement for a thousand pounds down and a three-year exclusive contract, with numerous conditions for licensing and royalties.

Alfred had springs in his heels all the way back to the Midland. At last he was on his way! That upward leap from the level where all businesses fail to one where a few might prosper . . . he had made it. *Come Polkinghorne,* he thought. *Come creditors all! You hold no terrors now!*

Fifty-seven pounds, eighteen shillings, and threepence farthing—what a paltry sum! How could it ever have driven him to skulk in shadows and tremble at the mention of solicitors?

CHAPTER FOUR

MR. POLKINGHORNE was overjoyed to see him.

"Lord Alfred!" he cried. "At last! At long, long last!"

Alfred, more lightheaded than ever now that his astonishing good fortune was beginning to sink in, snatched the sheaf of documents from the lawyer's hand, tore them in two, and scattered them to all corners of the four-ale bar.

"Mr. Polkinghorne—*that's* what I give for your threats, sir!"

Tom Austin, shocked to the marrow, darted about the room, pounding on papers and trying to reassemble them. But Polkinghorne began to choke of an apoplexy. Outrage rooted him to the floorboards. He stood, sucking wind, staring about him at the ruin of years of patient genealogical sleuthing.

Alfred, realizing that his own euphoria had possibly carried him a little far, said in the most placating tones he could muster, "They will all be paid, sir. Have no fear. Every last one and every last farthing."

"Paid?" Polkinghorne said weakly, comprehending nothing.

"My creditors," Alfred said.

"What are they to me, my lord?"

Now it was Alfred's turn to be baffled. He looked at Tom Austin. "My lord?" he echoed. "Is he drunk?"

The landlord held up fistfuls of torn paper. "His grace the Duke of St. Ormer's crest, eh?" he said. "Family trees . . . copies tooken out of parish registers . . . birth susstificates . . . marriage lines. And where do they all lead? Why, bless us, they leads to you, Mr. Boyce. To you and you alone." Then, finding himself caught between an old familiarity and a new deference, he added a half-embarrassed "my lord."

"What is all this?" Alfred asked, staring wildly about the room. "Why d'you both call me 'my lord'?"

"Why, sir?" Tom Austin handed the mutilated papers back to Polkinghorne. "Why? For a very good reason, sir. That's why. For no other reason than that you are, as I've just told you, the future Duke of St. Ormer. That's why, sir."

Alfred looked sharply from landlord to solicitor several times. "This is surely some trick," he said.

Polkinghorne, seeing now that the damage to the documents was not half so extreme as the exuberant violence which had caused it, permitted himself a condescending smile. "If you had not . . . ah . . . disarranged these papers, sir, I could prove it to you. But no mind. I know it now by heart as well as I know the Lord's Prayer. Pray be seated. Good landlord, bring this gentleman some brandy."

He turned to Alfred. "Your father, sir, was one Arthur Boyce of Saffron Walden, who married a Felicity Bell in 1825?"

Alfred, not a little surprised, nodded his agreement.

"A year later you were born. Two years later your mother died, followed in 1830 by your father, leaving you an orphan. You were brought up by your mother's brother, William Bell of Coventry?"

Alfred's mouth was now dry enough for the brandy to sear it like fire. He nodded again but could find no words.

"Did he tell you of your family history? On the Boyce side? For instance, that the name was originally du Bois?"

"No, sir."

"And that you are descended through twenty generations from William the Conqueror?"

"There!" Tom Austin, himself vastly impressed, was disappointed at Alfred's paralyzed reception of this intelligence and tried to coax him into something more lively. But Alfred relapsed once more into a fit of speechless head-shaking.

"Well, you are. You are of the *blood!*"

"The Blood Royal," Tom Austin said portentously.

The lawyer looked wearily at the landlord and resumed his tale. "Your grandfather was John Boyce of Stoke Mandeville. His father was Harold Boyce of Pevensey. I must say I never knew such a wander-prone family as yours. Harold was the son of John Boyce of Wythenshawe, the youngest of three brothers; Orlando, who was born out of wedlock . . ."

"Near Derby," Tom Austin said. "Oh, no—excuse—that's Matlock."

Polkinghorne's lips vanished. A tightness invaded his recital. "And Henry was the elder of the two legitimate brothers."

"It's amazing what a clever lawyer can find out," Tom Austin said. "I'd wager my shirt they did their level best to hide them facts from everyone. And how long ago was this now, Mr. Polkinghorne?"

"A century and a half," Polkinghorne said, pride breaking through his stiffness.

"A century and a half!" The landlord was most impressed. "Why, that's before I was born. Or you, I daresay. There now!"

"Henry had two daughters, Chastity and Piety. This is where it gets difficult."

"It usually does with those two," Alfred said, beginning to recover.

Polkinghorne shook his head, impatient of these constant interruptions. "Orlando is illegitimate, so the title descends through Henry and falls into abeyance between his two daughters, the aforesaid Chastity and Piety."

"Is there a drop more brandy?" Alfred asked Tom Austin, who still held the bottle in his hand.

"You listen to this, young sir," the solicitor warned. "Your entire future life hangs on it."

"I'll try," Alfred promised. "But I've a lot of important things on my mind at the moment." He took a sip from his replenished glass.

"A lot of . . . You've . . . !" Polkinghorne's apoplexy returned redoubled. "We are talking, sir, about a Dukedom!" (He pronounced it so.) "The first rank of the kingdom's peerage!"

"I'll listen!" Alfred promised, and knit his brows so fiercely and stared so wildly that the solicitor was a little taken aback.

"The title—this is back in the seventeen-fifties . . ."

"A hundred years ago," Tom Austin told Alfred helpfully.

Polkinghorne glared at him and continued: "The title falls into abeyance between Chastity and Piety Boyce, daughters of Henry. And there it would rest to this day if both of them had had issue."

"Issue of blood," the landlord explained, remembering the Bible story.

"Landlord!" Polkinghorne roared. "Will you go and boil your . . ." Inspiration struck him; he turned to Alfred. "Are you hungry, sir?"

"I could eat a horse."

"Name your wants, pray. His grace of St. Ormer invites you to dine."

Alfred needed no second bidding. "Porridge and cream," he said. "Deviled kidneys. Kedgeree. Fat bacon and eggs. And a pint of the best stout to wash it down." He turned to Polkinghorne to explain. "I'll get no sleep or food these next three days, see? It's make or break with me."

The solicitor nodded uncomprehendingly; as soon as the landlord had reluctantly departed, he continued. "If Chastity and Piety had had children, the title would be in abeyance until one line or the other died out."

Alfred sipped again and nodded.

"To make matters worse, both girls married cousins. Chastity married Orlando's only son, Oliver, who for some reason, almost certainly criminal, changed his name to Boyes. Or perhaps it was a mishearing by some legal clerk. Almost all records of him are from courts or prisons. And it was the same for their only son, William, who, we have lately established, died unmarried in his eighteenth year, 1770, on board a prison hulk in the Thames awaiting transfer to a penal ship bound for Australia. That was the end of Chastity's line. Which leaves Piety."

He smiled at Alfred as much as to say, *See how well it's all turning out for you.*

Alfred was wondering whether, if he played his hand right, he could get this Polkinghorne to write out a full legal agreement for Mr. Bird to sign—something on which he could raise a bit of wind.

"Piety married Harold Boyce of Pevensey, your great-grandfather, which is how the title comes down to you. His grandfather was William du Bois, a Puritan fifty years after it was fashionable for *anyone* to be a Puritan. He adopted the style of Boyce. His father was Godfrey du Bois of Fingest Manor. He married Lady Anne du Bois, his cousin and the eldest daughter of the First Duke. It is through her that the title descends to you. Godfrey's father was the Reverend Lord Richard du Bois, younger brother of the First Duke of St. Ormer, who was the great-grandfather of the present duke, Augustus. He has no heir and is now most unlikely to achieve one. His only brother who lived to maturity died, leaving only female issue. So, improbable as it may seem, you, young man, are the heir presumptive."

Alfred, wondering how it was going to affect his business, nodded intelligently and tried to look grave.

The porridge and cream arrived.

"You're paying for this?" Alfred checked before he tucked in.

"Of course." Polkinghorne smiled. Beneath this young fellow's lower-class speech and behavior there was a great deal of the du Bois manner and attitude. His utter self-absorption, too, was most characteristic.

Alfred was grateful for the food but his heart sank at the rest of this news. It was all so complicated. His father's father's father's . . . how did it go? And all these cousin marriages and things falling into abysses or whatever he'd said. And everyone changing names. It meant nothing to him beyond the fact that it looked like consuming the one commodity he could now least afford: time.

"This has come at a most inconvenient time," he told the lawyer.

Polkinghorne behaved as if Alfred had dealt him a blow in the solar plexus. "You're a du Bois all right, my lord," he said when he recovered himself. "Any slight lingering doubt I may have entertained (not to say cherished) now deserts me. Ah, dear—how to make you understand?"

The kidneys and the stout arrived. "You're sure you're paying?" Alfred asked again.

"Yes, yes! Perhaps you'd better tell me what is so important to a young man who lives in a rathole and flees from every lawyer—what is so important that the inheritance of fifty thousand acres of land and rents over two hundred thousand pounds a year—to say nothing of the most beautiful palace in England and other houses and land in London and Cornwall—to say nothing of the rank of duke—what, I say, is so important that all this comes 'at a most inconvenient time'?"

Alfred fished out the draft agreement he and Mr. Bird had got up an hour or so earlier. "Cast your eyes over that, Mr. Polkinghorne. No, *feast* your eyes on it!"

Polkinghorne glanced through the document and saw yet more du Bois in it. This young man was clearly nobody's fool. He had this Mr. Bird neatly trussed up, all right—not unfairly so, but Bird would find it hard to be unfair to young Boyce. "Very good," he said, handing it back.

But Alfred warded it off with a playful jab of his fork.

"What's this?" the lawyer asked.

"You obviously want me to throw in my hand up here and come back with you to London."

"Of course."

Alfred looked at him calm and level. "I won't do it," he said.

"You have no choice."

"Why? What'll happen to me?"

"You'll meet the duke. You'll see your inheritance. You'll be presented to the queen. You'll take your rightful place at . . ."

"That's if I come, Mr. Polkinghorne. What if I don't?"

"But that's unthinkable."

Alfred went on eating.

"You can't possibly mean it!" He was whining now; it was the note Alfred was waiting for. With his most generous, expansive smile, he said, "Tell you what. I'll come if you do me one slight favor in return."

"Oh?" The man's legal mistrustfulness returned swiftly.

"Aye. You sit there and, while I finish my lunch, you turn that draft into a copper-bottomed, double-indemnified, steel-tipped, legal contract with, as the watchmakers say, jeweled movements. Then give me three or four days to"—he almost said *start my business* but realized it would sound too provocative—"to . . . er . . . wind up my affairs. *Then* I'll come south with you."

"If you're going to wind up things here, you won't need this contract."

"I may find there's nothing in the duking line of business for me. I may want to come back."

"Ye gods! Will you stop talking and thinking of it as a *business!* His grace will have a fit!" Polkinghorne collected himself for one last effort. "Listen to me now, sir. I shall try one more time. In the long history of our country, fewer than four hundred people—out of all those millions—fewer than four hundred have been entitled to call themselves *duke*. Indeed, it may be closer to three hundred than four. Most of those titles are extinct. And until you were found, the dukedom of St. Ormer looked all set to join them. Only twenty-seven now survive. Yours is the third-most-ancient surviving dukedom, dating from 1639. And because Norfolk and Somerset, the two older ones, were attainted at that time, yours is the oldest continuous dukedom in the realm.

"If you consider the surviving lines, your position is even more exclusive. If you were to succeed to the title of St. Ormer tomorrow, you would be the one-hundred-and-forty-fourth duke in a surviving line. The hundred-and-forty-fourth *ever!* In all of England's long history. You would stand next in rank to her majesty, you and your twenty-six peers; she would address you formally as 'right trusty and entirely beloved cousin.' Other peers, even marquises, are all leveled under the common title of 'lord.' But a duke—never! A duke is always a duke, as a prince is a prince and a king a king.

"You would be absolute monarch of a large part of two counties; on you the prosperity and welfare of thousands would depend. Your regiment, the Duke of St. Ormer's Light Infantry—the famous 'Stormers'—which has already covered itself in glory, would add yet more luster to our country's honor in battle. You would be entrusted with one of the finest and most beautiful houses in England—indeed, in Europe. You would have patronage that would have made a Tudor monarch die of envy. You would, in short, hold a large part of the government and well-being of this country in your hands."

He seized Alfred's wrist and, clutching tightly, concluded: "Don't you understand now? The question is not whether there's enough in 'this duking business' for *you;* but whether there's enough in you for the duking business!"

In his innermost heart Alfred knew he was beaten. With deep sadness he contemplated the loss of the bright new enterprise which, just two hours ago, had filled his universe. He would not yield without a fight, of course; but it would be a rear-guard action and he would be retreating all the way.

"I have obligations," he said sullenly. "Up here."

Polkinghorne sniffed surrender, but he knew the du Bois spirit well enough not to try to land this fish at once. "I can see that," he said. "Look. I'll play my part if you'll agree to turn the running of this business over to a manager—"

"What manager?"

"Never mind that. Good managers are not nearly so difficult to find as most people think."

At that moment Sir Eric Newbiggin came bustling into the bar. "My dear Boyce," he beamed, dry-soaping his hands. "Or should I say Lord Alfred?"

"So it seems," Alfred said diffidently.

"I'm delighted. We're all delighted. Dear little Hermione, I may tell you, is in an ecstasy for you. A Unitarian duke! It's what this country has long needed. Now tell me how we may help you. I can think of a thousand ways. You'll dine with us at the Hall tonight, of course. And the whole west wing is at your disposal until you make more permanent arrangements of your own."

Alfred stared at his plate, too frightened to meet Sir Eric's eyes —frightened not of the man but of the glimpse of power this little speech had opened. Polkinghorne had not lied. Perhaps he had been too hasty in rejecting the duking business. With a great effort he gathered himself together, looked up, and said, "Thank you, Sir Eric. You're most civil and kindly. I'll dine with you . . . what's today? Tuesday. I'll dine with you Friday and move up on Saturday."

Polkinghorne watched this brief exchange with intense interest. Alfred's speed of readjustment and the cool grace of his acceptance surprised the lawyer, even though he had already seen the young man's nimble wits and resourcefulness at work.

He suddenly realized how impossible it would be to convey

Alfred's true character to Duke Augustus. The duke had to see him up here in Cokeley, on his own territory. Take Alfred down to Chalfont Abbey, with its hundreds of rooms and servants, where he'd be making a mistake a minute, and the old man could misjudge him disastrously, in a way that might take months, or years, to mend. And time was not on anyone's side.

Somehow the duke *must* be induced to come up to Cokeley to meet his heir.

CHAPTER FIVE

"WOULDN'T COME?" the duke thundered. "Wanted to build a *factory?* The dog! the scum! What did you say to him?"

"I told him everything, your grace."

"Did you tell him I wanted to see him?"

"I told him you commanded it, sir. But . . . ah . . . he is a du Bois. An undoubted du Bois." He looked at the family motto carved on the mantelpiece and sighed.

The duke stopped in mid-tirade.

He pondered a moment.

He smiled. He chuckled.

He laughed. He roared with mirth.

"The young scoundrel leaves us no choice," he said, wiping his eyes. "The mountain must go to Mahomet."

When Alfred's feet touched ground again, which was at about three o'clock on the afternoon of that first great day, he realized that the six hundred pounds he had raised were not going to build him new premises. His "new factory" therefore consisted of the five railway arches adjacent to his original one.

By the Friday afternoon, production was up to five hundred boxes a day, and the orders were flowing in for more. Every user and buyer of fancy metal boxes who saw the new gold had to have it.

Alfred mixed the secret mordant himself, disguising its nature by putting it into empty cans of Potter's mordant, one of the trade standards. As a further disguise he mixed a harmless concoction of kaolin, clove oil, and white spirit with which the inside of each box was painted before baking; it fell to a fine powder that could easily be blown or tapped out when the box came from the oven.

The whole operation was in full swing that evening when he left and walked up Cokeley Rise to the Hall. He had to ring at the gatelodge and wait for the porter to come and let him through. The man looked him up and down in the light of his oil lantern and, though he clearly did not think much of what he saw—battered hat, threadbare coat, muddy boots, and all—he had been told to admit a "Lord Alfred Boyce" and that was what this ill-turned-out creature claimed to be.

The drive was immaculately graveled and as smooth as a croquet lawn. Easter was just over a week away, and the moon, almost full, picked out every manicured shrub and laid a silver outline on each bare branch. It even dignified the Hall, a plain and, to Alfred's eye, rather dull pile from Georgian days; now, with its silver columns and pediment, all crisp in blue and black, with the warm candlelight streaming out of its principal windows, it looked a home that even a duke might envy.

For a moment it held Alfred in a kind of paralysis. The immense solidity and graceful assurance of the place, its suggestion of a dignified permanence at the heart of human affairs, its supreme aloofness from the poverty and struggle that lapped the foot of the hill on which this lovely garden stood—these suddenly struck him in an entirely new light: not as part of the "furniture" of the world—something always there, like mountains and rivers—but as attainable goods. He had no idea what Chalfont Abbey might be like, and for the past few days he had been far too busy to think any more about it, but now, seeing the Hall like this in the moonlight, so graceful and assured, unlocked unexpressed thoughts all at once.

He set this sudden vision alongside his earlier dreams of wealth—factory chimneys, aldermanic robes, kept women—and saw immediately what naïve and tawdry symbols he had gloated over.

"The truth is," he said aloud, "you didn't think at all."

Those symbols were merely the ones nearest at hand. Any street urchin would pick them out as signs of wealth; they were a way of avoiding any serious thought for people to whom serious thoughts would be a delusion and distraction from the harsh business of survival.

But now, for him, there would be no delusion in such dreams—indeed, even to call them dreams was wrong. If Polkinghorne was any sort of a judge, he, Alfred, might soon become the owner of a mansion far grander than this—a palace. *And* fifty thousand acres! A light sweat broke out over his body. What did fifty acres look like, let alone fifty thousand? It was unimaginable. To own more land than you could walk over in a year, more fields than you could ever commit to memory . . . to own villages of houses you'd never set food inside . . . to forget how many barns and cattle sheds you could lay claim to—it was terrifying.

Things could be stolen whose loss you'd never personally feel: "Caught him, your grace. With forty of your rabbits!" "How many rabbits does that leave us, gamekeeper?" "About three million, sir."

What would he feel like if something of that sort happened? Would it bother him like the theft of a penny did now? Until now he'd lived with the thinnest skin between himself and a hard, malevolent world. Without it he could never have survived. And he had grown to love that rawness, to relish the speed of reaction it allowed him to every little change in circumstance. But to try to preserve that same fine and instantaneous contact with every part of his life and living when it had expanded to a vast palace on fifty thousand busy acres—that would drive him mad.

Sir Eric was actually at the door to meet him, as if to meet royalty. "My dear fellow!" he exclaimed warmly.

"D'you own all these trees, Sir Eric?" Alfred asked.

Sir Eric cleared his throat as he peered out into his fifteen moonlit acres. "I suppose I do," he said. "Though I didn't plant them and shan't live to see them felled. But what an extraordinary question. Why d'you ask?"

Alfred, at a loss himself, said, "It seems such an odd thing to say, 'I own that tree.' In a way it's like a flea saying, 'I own this dog.' "

Sir Eric, not knowing quite what else to do, laughed too heartily and guided Alfred indoors. "Except that a dog's of some use to a flea. A tree's only useful when it's turned into timber."

"You've hit it, Sir Eric," Alfred said earnestly. "You've put your finger right on the point."

"I'm so glad," Sir Eric replied, wondering how well the young man had fortified his nerves before climbing up to the Hall. He gave him a very small pale sherry.

"Yes," Alfred said, looking round. "Use and beauty, you see." It wasn't quite the subject he wanted to raise but it might prove a useful stepping stone. "How d'you tell the value of a thing when its value is beauty? Carpets, pictures, knicknacks . . . that sort of thing."

Sir Eric stared at him shrewdly. "Worrying you, is it, this inheritance? Yes, I suppose it's bound to. Well . . ."

"The only worry," Alfred said, "is how it's going to interfere with my real life. I've made a great advance this week, as I'm sure you know. Nothing happens in Cokeley but it's through the front or back door of the Hall in ten minutes."

Sir Eric smiled and swelled visibly.

"And I'm sure that in five years I'll be master of the biggest metal-box business in England. And not only metal boxes but all sorts of lines in which fashion makes for quick change. There's a hundred fortunes to be made out there and I want to make half of them."

Sir Eric was thoroughly alarmed at this outburst. It ran absolutely counter to his plans for the young heir's future—and he had planned that future right down to the size of the bouquet his daughter Hermione should carry on the day of her wedding to young Lord Alfred, or even the Fifth Duke, as he might then be. And "Hermione, Duchess of Metal Boxes" did not remotely figure in those plans.

He smiled indulgently. "Perhaps his grace will be able to persuade you that being Duke of St. Ormer is not an utterly ignoble fate when set beside the exalted rank of Metal-Box King."

Alfred's spirit fell; no one was ever going to understand. Why, when all the world but he was panting, so it seemed, to be made a duke, or even to shake the hand of an heir to a dukedom, why had fate singled out him so capriciously for the honor?

"Ah!" Sir Eric beamed as he turned toward the door. "Talking of beauty . . ."

He meant Hermione, but for Alfred she was dwarfed by the intimidating appearance of Lady Newbiggin bearing down on them like a galleon with a full head of sail; the acres of crisp silk that hung about her swished like (and indeed generated) a stiff breeze. The very candle flames bowed and brightened as she passed.

"Lord Alfred Boyce, my dear," Sir Eric said. "Lady Newbiggin."

"My *dear* Lord Alfred! It was *so* kind of you to honor our invitation."

"Was it?" Alfred asked, kissing her hand. "I mean *is* it? I would have thought the kindness was entirely yours, Lady Newbiggin."

She laughed weakly, looking a little perplexed. "Yes . . . well . . . something of that sort, anyway."

I made a mess of that, Alfred thought. Not that it bothered him.

A silence fell. Alfred smiled at Hermione, who blushed prettily.

"Oh," Lady Newbiggin said. "Of course you've not met. Yet we've seen each other so often at church . . . Hermione, my dear, allow me to present Lord Alfred Boyce—our daughter, Miss Hermione Newbiggin."

"Miss Newbiggin." He kissed her gloved hand. Here at least was a situation where he'd never be at a loss. He did not take his eyes off her face. Lord, but she was lovely! Even from afar—across two dozen pews . . . stepping into a carriage . . . spied on a high balcony at last summer's garden party before they threw him out—she had seemed ethereally beautiful. But close-to, with the glow of the firelight on her neck and the luster of the candlelight in her eyes . . .

At last she plucked her hand from his and looked awkwardly at her parents. He too glanced at her mother, guiltily expecting a gaze of tight-lipped disapproval. But all he saw, in both her and her husband, was a bland fondness bordering on delight. The meaning of it was not lost on him, of course, and, as understanding dawned, he looked back at the young girl in a kind of wondering terror at the possibilities. Like the moonlit Hall, she was now "attainable goods."

He knew beyond doubt that if he proposed to her on the spot, all three Newbiggins would go into raptures of acceptance. They probably had a contract ready waiting in one of the bureaux that stood here and there about the room.

"You must be one of the loveliest young ladies in the whole of England, Miss Newbiggin," he said, testing again.

"Oh!" Daughter and mother collapsed onto the sofa in delighted embarrassment.

"Did I say something wrong?" Alfred turned to Sir Eric.

He laughed. "Of course not. A man may tell any woman of her beauty."

"But I meant it," Alfred said. "I've always thought she was beautiful but I've never got near enough to be sure."

"Perhaps," Lady Newbiggin trilled, "you are a *little* more direct than is quite the custom nowadays, Lord Alfred."

"You see?" Alfred said with an exaggerated shrug of despair. "On every side, in everything I do, I meet the strongest arguments against having anything whatever to do with this duking business."

"No!" All three of them chorused it.

"Indeed!" Alfred was enjoying himself behind his lugubrious mask. Hermione really was unutterably lovely—in laughter, in blushing, in bewilderment, in consternation. He'd better stay off the drink at dinner or he might forget himself and exercise this exciting new power of his by proposing to her. "Indeed," he said, "I can't even respond to the simplest remark or situation without making a great pool of blushes and silences."

"Oh, but you're wrong, Lord Alfred," Sir Eric said with a hint of desperation. "Isn't he, my dear?"

"Yes! Quite wrong. Quite, quite wrong!"

"How?" Alfred asked innocently.

Lady Newbiggin looked trapped. It was Hermione who came to their rescue.

"Your instinct is right, Lord Alfred," she said. "Indeed, when one thinks of your lineage, how could your instinct be otherwise? 'Blood ennobles,' after all." She was quite calm. In fact she was so self-possessed he thought she might even have the measure of him already.

"Instinct?" he asked.

"Yes, Lord Alfred. When mama said how kind you were to come you said the kindness was hers. Your instinct was impeccable; but the words you chose were not the ones normally chosen in Society—that's all. And when we were introduced you paid me a quite undeserved compliment. But it was exactly what any other gentleman would wish to do—the instinct, you see, was correct. The choice of words, however . . ." When she smiled tc soften the unspoken thought, she won his utter devotion on the spot.

Her parents' delight was almost boundless.

"What should I have said, Miss Hermione?" he asked, merely to have the excuse to go on looking at her face and listening to her voice.

She stood. "Mama," she commanded. "A little charade! Greet me!"

How masterful she could be! How unattainably upper class! He *had* to have her. Not just for her sexual beauty but for that absolutely indefinable quality of . . . of . . . *upperness.* It was something beyond mere superiority, beyond mere assurance, beyond that massive aloofness; it permeated everything she did—the way she held herself, the tilt of her head, every little inflection of her voice, every casual glance of her eyes. He had to master and possess that boundless conviction of supremacy, even if it meant giving up forever his dreams of being Metal-Box King.

Lady Newbiggin, regal beside her husband, said to her advancing daughter: "Lord Alfred, it was so kind of you to honor our invitation!"

Hermione, bowing and kissing her mother's hand, said, "Lady

Newbiggin. On the contrary, it was you and Sir Eric who honored me with so kind an invitation. I trust I find you well?"

After a few more pleasantries she turned to Alfred and, fixing him with her great, luminous eyes—as he had gazed at her on their introduction—she kissed his hand and said, "Miss Hermione, I cannot begin to tell you how long I have looked forward to this meeting—nor how small was my hope that it would ever come about."

She spoke with such sincerity now that he understood the charade had finished the moment she turned to him; these words were hers, from her heart. He was too full of wonder to reply.

She broke contact and, to rescue him, laughed as she said, "You blush very prettily, miss!"

"Hermione!" Lady Newbiggin was afraid her daughter had gone too far.

Alfred leaped to her defense. "Oh, Lady Newbiggin, what a teacher you have here! Why, in her schoolroom I should learn the whole of etiquette in an hour. Though I would be foolish indeed if I did not spin it out to a thousand hours—or"—he turned to Hermione—"a lifetime?"

For a moment their eyes dwelled in a wholesale reassessment of each other and the situation. Her voice was light but level when she answered, "What a very *fast* pupil you would make! Already you can turn quite a pretty compliment."

On their way in to dinner the butler quietly handed him a pair of white gloves. "It's a lesson-a-minute school," Alfred said to Lady Newbiggin on his arm.

From behind him Hermione, on her father's arm, said, "All schools are finally judged by their pupils."

"Oh, dear!" Alfred laughed. "What responsibility! I should begin to look for alternative employment if I were you."

"D'you know, Lord Alfred," she said—and without turning around he thrilled again to the lightly mocking smile he knew was on her lips—"I rather think I may already have begun."

The whole of dinner passed in that same glorious vein; the only jarring note came when Sir Eric revealed that the duke was staying with his late wife's cousin, Lord Francis Gaugham of Wellington Hall, and would be driving over tomorrow, Saturday afternoon, to see his long-lost heir.

But Alfred was so overjoyed at his newfound rapport with Hermione that tomorrow was five years away. Late into the night he lay awake finding arguments to restrain himself from creeping along the ten miles of corridor that separated his room from hers—the chief argument being that he did not yet know where hers was.

By a curious irony, that was one of many similar thoughts which kept Sir Eric and his wife from their sleep, too, that night.

"It was a mistake to put him in the west wing," Sir Eric said. "His room should be next to hers."

"Eric!" his wife exploded at the impossibility of such an arrangement.

"Well—on the same corridor, anyway."

"Listen, I'm as anxious as you to see our daughter a duchess, but this little man? A joke of a duke he'll be. And he's so common."

"Oh, believe me, my dear, he's far from common. Ignorant, I grant. Ignorant of Society, ignorant of business (though he thinks he's not), ignorant of the law . . ."

"He's not ignorant of women," Lady Newbiggin said. "You can take my word on that. A most dangerous man."

"That's beside the point."

"Is it? Where Hermione's concerned I would have thought—"

"I mean it's beside *my* point—and your original point—which is that despite all his ignorance he has a talent for getting his way and for persuading others to do things his way that . . . why, only today Bird was telling me of a contract that young Boyce . . . and look how he twisted Polkinghorne round his finger . . . and you yourself heard that banker of his, Pringle, on the subject of Boyce. No, my dear, 'common' is not the word for him. You imply he has some power over women. I think it's a power over people—which to an extent, of course, includes women."

His wife drew breath to speak.

"What's more," he overrode her, "I believe young Boyce himself is only just discovering this power. But when he's got the measure of it, he'll be a hard man to check. If Hermione's to get ahold of him, it must be now."

"I don't disagree with what you say, Eric—"

"I'm glad to hear it, my love."

"Nevertheless, I think we still need to know more of this particular dukedom, St. Ormer. The present duke's reputation is hardly . . . *well!* Is it true he's bankrupted the place? Everyone talks of his debts. And didn't he try to revive the Hellfire Club?"

"But Hermione would have a dowry of at least five hundred thousand pounds, surely—"

"Oh, Eric, Eric! You are so blind where that girl is concerned!"

"I want to see her a duchess."

"And so do I. But she'd spend the bank empty. And he'd let her, he's so infatuated with her. *And* he's arrogant enough to think he could make as many fortunes as she needed, all by himself. You know how she can spend money, even with the two of us pulling hard on the reins and brakes. And that's *Miss* Hermione. Just think what *Duchess* Hermione will be capable of! No, I say the St. Ormer estate must be put in a condition to support her extravagance. Otherwise"—she glanced slyly at her husband—"they'll come back on us and bleed us white. They'll have us all in Carey Street."

He was silent at that, while she delivered a number of trivial "filler" arguments: "Anyway, getting her into bed with him might be disastrous—until we're sure he understands the obligations of a gentleman toward seduced girls of good class. And we don't even know whether a duke would be obliged to subscribe to that code. A prince certainly wouldn't be—he'd marry her off to some complaisant commoner and get the queen to make the man a baronet. How do we know a duke wouldn't be able to do the same? A duke may look down on a baronet as we look down on a stable lad."

"Oh, I doubt that," Sir Eric said, catching this last point from the waterfall of her argument. "We're all part of the same hereditary class, dukes down to baronets. The great divide comes between us and the lower orders—knights down to stable lads, as you say. Or metal-box manufacturers! Talking of which, I wonder how the duke and his heir will take to each other tomorrow."

CHAPTER SIX

THE DUKE ASKED to see Alfred alone. He made it clear that his was not a social visit, so it would be out of the question for Sir Eric and Lady Newbiggin to introduce Alfred to his kinsman—and so be able to claim intimacy with the duke ever after. His secretary did all the talking for him. The duke did no more than raise his hat a bare inch and nod in grave silence at Sir Eric and Lady Newbiggin. In silence they conducted him to the ballroom, the grandest room in the Hall, where they left him pacing like a hungry lion while they went to find Alfred and prepare him for what now had all the elements of a blood sacrifice.

Alfred understood, without the need for words, that the "old grandee," as Sir Eric jokingly called him, had everyone terrified.

Fear was in that great house like a fire. He was prepared for an ordeal of some dreadful kind.

But nothing had prepared him for the towering bulk of the solitary figure who stood at the far end of the magnificent ballroom, looking out over the terrace and gardens. The great window was all of fifteen feet high but he seemed to fill it. He wore a severely cut frock coat and still kept on his tall stovepipe hat, as if he were at his club rather than in a private house. He did not stir at the sound of Alfred's entry.

The door closed behind him with a soft, oiled click, and the two were alone. Alfred waited to be summoned closer to the Presence.

After an age the duke turned to look at him. The scrutiny was long and silent, conveying nothing to the young man except an understanding of Sir Eric's and Lady Newbiggin's fear. Curiously enough, the duke, too, was afraid—not of Alfred but of all the awful things this awful young man might prove to be. He had dreaded this moment ever since they had woken him up that night to read Polkinghorne's letter. For a few minutes longer it was possible to preserve the delusion that he would yet find some redeeming feature in this . . . this *artisan,* this *mechanical.* Soon he would have to beckon the creature over. Then it would open its mouth . . . and his last shreds of hope would evaporate. But he need not do that just yet. He could stand here a little longer—especially as there was such a ravishingly pretty girl walking about in the sunlight on the terrace . . .

But the nature of intense fear—as distinct from anxiety—is that it is quite short lived. After two minutes of respectful silence Alfred found that his heartbeat had returned to normal; in another minute his flushes had ceased and his fingers no longer trembled. A minute later and he was becoming distinctly bored. Shortly afterward he drew breath and shouted: "I'll just duck out for a newspaper, your grace." And he went, too.

He found no newspaper in the morning room but soon came back with a copy of *Punch,* which he began to read with absorption, leaning against the door.

The duke watched him impassively and then turned away to hide a smile. Polkinghorne had been right: there was something of a du Bois about this fellow. It was time they met, time to test him a little. Looking out the window—where the pretty girl was still walking up and down with, presumably, her mama, Lady Whatsername—he extended his right arm behind him into the room and snapped his fingers.

In response young Alfred whistled, as at a dog, looked behind him, and cried out, "Come up, sir! Can't you hear your master wants you? Come up, you cur—wherever you are!"

The duke laughed then. "Come here, cousin," he commanded jovially.

As Alfred walked the length of the ballroom he was astounded to feel all his original terror returning; despite the duke's apparent good humor there was something *essentially* frightening in his very presence. And the nearer Alfred came, the more physical was his fear.

But thank heaven for Hermione. She did not merely distract the duke, she was the only sight that could, at that moment, save Alfred from abject collapse; but for her he would have run without stopping until he was safely back in the Birmingham Metal Box and Lacquering Manufactory.

The duke turned to look at him and then followed Alfred's gaze back toward Hermione.

"What d'you think of 'em, young fellow?" he asked.

"Them, your grace?"

"Women."

"I hate 'em," Alfred said and gave his astonishing deep laugh—this time from sheer nervousness.

The duke was astonished.

"The power they have!" Alfred explained. "You could waste days and nights just thinking about them. I hate 'em."

As soon as the duke grasped his meaning, he burst into laughter and clapped Alfred on the shoulder. The young fellow was as common as clay, had no sense of respect—nor of dress, nor speech—yet there was about him something that suggested he had the makings of a possible successor. There was a long, hard way to go, of course, but not a hopeless one. He felt not nearly so despondent as he had only moments earlier.

"Well," he said, letting Alfred out of his grasp, "third cousin four times removed! Eh?"

"Is that what we are, your grace?"

"Call me 'duke.' Yes, that's what we are. And I'm told you don't like it."

Alfred swallowed hard. "Is that what Mr. Polkinghorne said, duke?" he asked.

"Mr. who? Oh, Polkinghorne. There's no need to call *him* mister! He's only a bloody clerk. Call no one mister except commissioned officers and the sons of peers. Yes, that's what Polkinghorne said about you."

"Well, it's true, duke." Alfred was himself again. The duke's offensive language did a great deal to restore him. "I didn't dance much of a jig when he broke the news."

"Tore his papers!"

Alfred nodded. "I thought they were bills, you see."

The duke chuckled. "Is that what it was? How much for?"

"Fifty-odd pounds." Alfred smiled.

The duke was astonished. "Do people really press such trifling debts?" he asked.

"The point was, sir, I'd just that morning made a thousand pounds. That's why I did it."

Up went the duke's brow; his eyes had more than a hint of admiration. "A horse?"

Alfred looked disgusted. "No!" *The very idea!* he thought. "No, sir." He tapped his cranium. "I sold an idea. A new way of . . . doing something. An industrial process. Something I invented. No one else can do it."

He went on adding these afterthought-explanations because it was clear that the duke was having some difficulty grasping the notion.

The old grandee knew, of course, that money was intimately associated with industry and trade, but he assumed it was all arranged and regular, like a ploughman's wage but on a greater scale. He knew, too, that fortunes were to be made in commerce, but surely only on the gambling side of it—stocks and shares, partnerships in vessels, floating railway companies . . . that sort of game. The notion that a mere mechanical could make money out of an idea was . . . bizarre.

"A thousand pounds?" he repeated. "In one morning?"

"And that's only a beginning, duke. I'm convinced of it. I don't know what *you're* good at, but *I'm* good at ideas like that. And I can sell them, too. The man I sold that one to began by turning the whole thing down. Flat! Outright! An hour later I'd talked him over. He gave me a contract worth a thousand pounds and an order worth over five hundred. That's what I live for. That's what I relish. Now tell me, sir, tell me true: Is there anything in the duking line that would suit *me?*"

As he watched young Alfred speak, saw his eyes glow, and felt a borrowed excitement rise within himself, the duke began to understand that this was no simple fellow to be won over with some mixture of bluff, flattery, and bluster.

Alfred had, obliquely, wondered what the duke was good at. The answer was: people. He was lazy about it, of course, as careless as befitted an aristocrat. He was always brusque, often arrogant, and sometimes cruel; but he was never insensitive to the effects of this behavior. If he depended on a person (and he depended on a great many people), he knew exactly how far he could nudge him or her before resentment erupted into rebellion. He was "good" at people.

He saw at once that he was going to have to be very good at young Alfred.

"Polkinghorne tells me there's going to be a new aristocracy in years to come," he said. "An aristocracy of commerce and industry."

Alfred nodded impatiently, waiting for an answer to his particular question.

"Polkinghorne says in *that* aristocracy you'll make yourself a duke."

Alfred, taken aback, laughed in embarrassment.

"Is it true?" the duke pressed.

"If not, it won't be for want of trying, sir."

"Hm!" The duke looked at Alfred awhile; he did not miss the way the young man's eyes kept straying to the pretty girl on the terrace. "I'd like to see how such a novel form of a dukedom might begin."

Alfred smiled. "I've told you, duke. It isn't a place. It's here." He put both index fingers to his temples. "And it's here." He flexed all his fingers at once. "But you'd be welcome to see its first small fruits, if that's what you're asking."

The duke bowed with mock (but not mocking) courtesy. "Your grace would do me great honor." Even when he bowed, his head was still above Alfred's.

The duke straightened. "If," he added, "you'll do me the equal honor of letting me show you *my* dukedom!"

From the look on Alfred's face the duke guessed that the pretty girl was at that moment finishing her walk and going back indoors.

"Sir Whatsthename, your host here—rich, is he?" he asked.

"They say he is, duke. They say he's one of the richest in the Midlands."

"Hm. He may yet need to be." He transfixed Alfred with those lazy, lethal eyes. "All heiresses are beautiful, remember. Don't do anything foolish in that direction, my boy." He nodded a fraction of an inch toward the terrace. "There's no maidenhead in all the world worth this dukedom of ours—not without money."

CHAPTER SEVEN

A MAIDENHEAD of a different kind was, at that moment, the chief source of all the duke's worries over money—the Maidenhead, Bourne End, & High Wycombe Railway. Though it had received its enabling Act of Parliament in 1846, four years ago, the railway mania of '47 and the subsequent commercial crisis had led to the suspension of all work, not just on the MBE&HW but on hundreds of similar branch lines throughout the kingdom—and even on some main lines.

The duke could not understand where his money had gone. As the district's chief landowner he had naturally been a heavy investor. "Not lost," they had explained, "but swallowed up. When the line is built, and the dividends start to flow, it will all be there again—capital and income."

And when would that be?

They smiled and shrugged. From time to time gangs of ruffians would appear with surveying tools and shovels; a few test holes would be dug; and then they'd vanish again, leaving the country littered with cleft sticks spiked with white paper and, months later, a further littering of bastard children; but the railroad itself got no further.

Meanwhile eighty thousand pounds of the duke's money was "swallowed up," and his best efforts had not yet devised the right emetic to make this Railway Beast disgorge. Still, he was better off (if only by a hairsbreadth) than the Duke of Buckingham, who had actually been bankrupted in the mania—that is, he had actually run out of creditors.

The duke explained this history to Alfred as they traveled on the main railway line from Paddington, in London, down the twenty-odd miles to Maidenhead. They had stopped in London just long enough to acquire a new suit of clothes for Alfred and to measure him for half a dozen more—a town suit, a country suit, evening dress, morning coat, riding coat and breeches, and "something to go out ratting in." He had met none of the duke's friends and had been warned that he was unlikely to do so until he had done something to mend his accent. After that he listened hard to the duke and picked up a pronunciation so grand, so old, and so whiggish he had to unlearn it all during the next five years. But the duke liked to hear him say *Lunnon* for London, *goold* for gold, *yaller* for yellow, *laylock* for lilac, and *Roosia* for Russia; and he liked to *obleege* his kinsman to play at *cyards* or to walk in the *gyarden.* And Alfred, hearing the foreign sounds, first in his mind, then—shyly—on his tongue, began to think himself a *dooced* fine fellah.

At Maidenhead they descended from the duke's carriage while the porters manhandled it off its flatbed wagon and hitched it to a team of horses brought down from Chalfont Abbey. The duke took Alfred to the stationmaster's office, where he handed his watch to the stationmaster to wind.

"Never wind your own watch when you're the duke," he told Alfred as he led him to the back of the room, where a large one-inch Ordnance Survey map, showing the sanctioned line, decorated one wall.

"Give me your hands, my boy," the duke commanded.

Alfred stretched out his arms as if for a handcuffing.

"No, no. Put them up here on the map, just here between High Wycombe and Henley and out toward Oxford. That's it—stretch out all your fingers . . . more! Can't you stretch them any more than *that?* Oh, you'll have to grow, I'll tell you now." He stepped a dramatic pace backward. "Do you know what you're holding in your hands?"

A tingling sensation, part fear, part excitement, stiffened the hair on Alfred's neck. A slow smile of wonder spread over his face. "I have a very good notion, duke."

The duke spun on his heel and strode toward the door. "Come on!" he barked, taking back his watch as he walked past the stationmaster. "They keep the best time in England, these railway people," he added. "They have it sent down from London every day."

Gingerly Alfred lowered his hands from the map and looked at the territory they had covered. So that was what fifty thousand acres looked like! It was a subtly different young man who followed the duke back to the waiting carriage.

It took almost an hour to drive from Maidenhead to Chalfont Abbey, in the heart of the duke's estate. They set out first on the road to Great Marlow, and as they rattled along the duke pointed out the estates of his neighbors. The one that seemed to interest him most was not, in fact, visible from the road—Cliffden or Cliefden, hidden among its trees high on the farther bank of the river and away to the east.

"They had a bad fire there last November," the duke said.

"Burned to the ground. The poor old Duke of Sutherland—only bought it a few months before." He laughed heartily. "It used to be the summer residence of the Hanoverians; they rented it from the Fitz-Maurices, the Earls of Orkney. They can inherit through the female line, you know. If we could do the same, you wouldn't be here. Anne had it from Lord George Hamilton, her father. That was the second Anne, the one who married the Fourth Earl of Inchiquin, William. She let it to the Prince of Wales—not *the* prince, mark you, but Frederick, father of George the Third. It burned down while they had it, too." He laughed again. "Back in '95. It was the fault of a maid servant reading a novel in bed. Take my advice—get rid of any lower servant who can read. Sir George Warrender rebuilt it twenty years ago. And now it's in blackened ruins again. Sutherland's rebuilding it using the designs from Somerset House, the old Somerset House, of course. He thinks it's going to be the grandest place, but it won't hold a *candle* to Chalfont Abbey." He laughed uproariously at the joke he was about to make. "In fact, that's the one thing it had better *not* try—considering the history of the fucking place!"

He dissolved in an apoplexy of mirth, slapping his own thigh and Alfred's indiscriminately—so much so that he failed once again to notice Alfred's shocked distaste at his language.

As his intimacy with Alfred had increased, his language had grown coarser. At first Alfred had thought it was a self-conscious effort on the duke's part to use lower-class language and so make him, Alfred, feel at ease. He, for his part, had tried to show the duke that such crudity of speech was quite alien to him. And then it dawned that this was, indeed, the duke's natural way of talking among his intimates. Somehow that was doubly horrifying. He had thought of the queen and her court as conversing in a flowery English, a blend of Shakespeare and the King James Bible.

What made it more difficult was the duke's vast store of bawdy experiences. Alfred had put up a fair score of his own in that line, but the duke, with a fifty-nine-year lead, could outdo him twenty to one, if not two hundred to one; and Alfred's enjoyment of *those* stories was full-hearted. If only the duke could learn to steer that difficult but essential line which divides a genuine, good old bawdy tale from mere smut and foul language—how famously they would get on!

"It must be marvelous," Alfred said when the mirth had died.

"What, Cliffden?"

"No. History. To have the history of England as your own family history. I mean—you talk about these things the way friends meeting at an inn for a pint of ale talk about their own day-to-day goings-on. But it's the history of England. I mean—the Duke of Sutherland, well that's just like old Pa Sutherland down the street at number four to you, isn't it?"

"Number four? What are you driveling about, my boy? How does *four* come into it?"

Alfred sighed. "Never mind, duke."

"I sometimes wonder, Alfred, if you are quite sane."

"Yes. I imagine you must, sir."

The Thames at Great Marlow sparkled in the spring sunshine. It was now early April and new green was everywhere. Fleecy clouds dappled an azure sky, driven by a light, dry breeze. The duke was delighted; his lands would never show to better advantage.

As they drove through the town, Alfred noticed that everyone in the streets turned and faced them; the women curtsied, the men doffed their hats, the children bowed low. Halfway up the main street the duke rapped the roof with his cane. The coach stopped and he descended, beckoning Alfred to follow.

He strode forward, towering over the people around. There was not exactly fear in their eyes, Alfred saw, more a kind of guarded reticence masked behind smiles of the warmest welcome.

"Widow Hobbs!" the duke said to a youngish woman at the door of a shop. "No more trouble with that boy of yours?"

"All thanks to your grace." She curtsied.

"I knew he wasn't really so vicious. Tell him we're all pleased."

A laborer came up and began to mumble something about a leaking roof.

"Thursdays!" the duke barked. "You know that."

He leaned confidentially to Alfred and said in a voice that would vie with the town clock: "Any fool can collar you here. The only complaints I entertain are from those who'll take the trouble to walk eight miles to make them." He laughed. "At five in the morning! Admiral Hood's trick."

He hooked a finger at a shopkeeper, who hurried to him. "Welcome back, your grace."

"Thank you, Lamb. If you and the vicar will do me the honor to call this Thursday morning, we may sort out this vestry business once and for all. Come at eleven."

And so it went, all the way up the street. He had a word for everyone, a question, a suggestion, a command, an answer. The house at the corner was fronted by a pocket handkerchief of a garden. Only the duke was tall enough to see into it. "Nurse Morgan!" he said. "Nan?" It was the first time Alfred had heard the slightest note of deference in his voice. From beyond the hedge came an eldritch cackle.

"Bless me if you aren't prettier every day."

The cackle renewed itself.

"You'll have me begging to marry you yet. You know I always wanted to."

The cackle was redoubled.

The duke looked up at the windows of the house; those on the ground floor still had their shutters drawn, but at a first-floor window a woman gazed down at them. He smiled at her. "Remarkable," he said. "D'you think she knows me still?" It seemed to matter to him.

"Oh she does, your grace," the woman said. "Of course she does."

"Gus!" the old lady cackled in confirmation. "Gussie!"

"I first proposed to her," the duke told Alfred on their way back to the coach, "in the year 1772."

"What did she have that was worth a dukedom?" Alfred wondered aloud.

"She deserves more worlds than I can lose," the duke said, his eyes far away. "She was my nanny. D'you know, she was born in the same year the Jockey Club was founded!"

"How does the town manage when you're away?" Alfred asked as the coach set off once more.

"They discover the most amazing reserves of initiative and self-reliance." He chuckled. "Good for 'em, too. The thing is to strike a balance between doing everything for them—down to wiping their arses with your own fingers—and leaving them to the none-too-tender mercies of each other and the law. Not easy. They *need* us, you see. But only some of the time."

All the way to Chalfont Abbey he pointed out his many farms, naming each farmer, saying whether he was a tenant or a yeoman, giving the size of each farm, the number and age of its buildings, the quality of each man . . . his willingness to learn new methods . . . and other, more personal idiosyncrasies.

Alfred was astonished. "I thought you said you left all that sort of thing to your agents and bailiffs?" he said.

"So I do," the duke answered. "Quite right. It doesn't do for us to mingle in such affairs too closely. For myself, I don't know a bloody thing about farming." He looked at a passing farmhouse.

"Now this fellow thinks he's the world's master at dairy farming. But I'll tell you, he knows as much about milk as a cow turd stuck with primaroses!"

Then he drew Alfred's attention to a large beech forest away to the north—part of the original primeval forest that had once clad the Chilterns from horizon to horizon. Now, apart from pockets like this and the large forest at Burnham, and a few hundred carefully tended patches of fox covert, the whole country lay under plow or pasture—today a smiling richly green landscape of gentle hills and sweeping views. Almost all of it was part of the duke's estates.

By drawing Alfred's attention to the northerly view, the duke managed to distract him from the other window of the carriage until it made the perfect frame for Chalfont Abbey.

"Oh, there it is," he said—as if the buildings had the strange habit of moving from valley to valley at unpredictable times.

Alfred turned—and gasped.

Nothing he had ever seen in his life—and nothing he had more recently imagined—had prepared him for such a sight. A house, he had thought, is a house. It would be a large, decorative pile of stone and plaster. The Hall at Cokeley, perhaps on an even grander scale. But this!

It was a palace! It went on and on. Nearest them was a castle tower that abutted an ancient hall, which then rose into a miniature townscape of clifflike walls, studded with great windows, enclosing a courtyard and, on its southern side, farthest from the coach, bursting out into two wings, each with triangular pediments far greater than those of Cokeley Hall, and each, in turn, dwarfed by the even greater pediment in the central section. And still on it went, meandering back to create an outer courtyard, guarded on one side by the castle and on the other by the strangest building Alfred had ever seen—a collection of fantastic, onion-shaped domes and minarets, each tapering upward into grotesquely globed spires and gilded pinnacles.

"Well?" the duke asked, though he had already seen his reward in Alfred's face.

"That building, across the courtyard at this end . . . all those domes and things," Alfred said. "What is it?"

"That's where I live."

"And the rest? Who lives there?"

"No one. Well—I do too, I suppose. But we don't use the rest of it much."

"But those domes! It's not like any other house I've ever seen, sir."

"Then you've never been to Brighton?"

"I've never *heard* of Brighton."

The duke implored the heavens at such ignorance. "Brighton Pavilion?" he asked. "The Prince of Wales—Prinny? The master spirit of his and every other age? I copied him." He gestured at the building just as it passed out of view, where the drive turned directly toward the Abbey. "Line by line. Stone by stone."

In fact, the duke was—as so often—exaggerating. What he had done was to take the Elizabethan north flank—built in the 1560s by Godfrey du Bois, father of the First Marquis—and replaster the exterior to resemble Brighton Pavilion, sticking on a dome or a minaret wherever the original had a tower or a bit of flat roof to carry such an ornament. Inside he had put up Chinese wallpapers and replastered the ceilings; even so he had only partly succeeded in disguising the bluff, foursquare Elizabethan solidity of the original.

"And it's just you living there, duke?" Alfred asked, still unable to take in the vastness and grandeur of the place, which now began to rise all around them as they drew near the mighty entrance arch.

"*And* an army of carpenters, plumbers, stone carvers . . ."

"You're building *more?*"

"No—just keeping it going. Guess how much lead alone there is up there?"

"Several tons?"

"No! *Area.*"

"Oh . . . two thousand square feet?" Alfred plucked out of his imagination the largest area of factory space he had ever seriously dreamed of renting.

"*Fifteen* thousand!" the duke said (quoting the actual roof area, regardless of whether it was lead, stone, or slate). "Getting on for half an acre."

Alfred gestured the hopelessness of comprehending such numbers. "I shan't sleep tonight," he said. "Knowing what's poised above me."

"We'll ride around the place after luncheon," the duke promised. "You ride?"

"I've sat on horses and gone from town to town," Alfred said.

The coach drew to a halt and pulled broadside to the mighty entrance arch. As they descended onto the ancient flagstones the huge, iron-studded gates of oak swung inward, on shrieking hinges, to reveal a courtyard thronged with people. In two massed ranks they stood, servants on one side, tenants on the other, stretching from the entrance almost a hundred yards to the portals of the main house.

"Damn!" the duke said. "I was feeling hungry."

Alfred learned later that this annoyance was pretense. It would have been unthinkable for his tenants, servants, and neighbors not to greet his return. He was the patron of the whole countryside.

Preceded by the butler and the steward, followed by valets and secretaries, they walked at a solemn pace, nodding right and left, receiving the bows or curtsies of farmers and their wives, servants, grooms, gardeners, cooks, and maids. Alfred, at a quick count, estimated a hundred on the servants' side and half as many again on the tenants'.

More eyes were on him than on the duke; they all knew who he was, of course, and wanted to size him up—or, in this case, down, for only the smallest maids were shorter. He could almost hear their minds at work: *Count No-account, the half-hour gentleman!* The thought struck a chill on his mood. Since his meeting with Polkinghorne he had felt that the inheritance of the title was as inevitable as death; but these daunting ranks of his potential servants and tenants reestablished all his former resolve to remain an industrialist.

So he smiled back, confident that this would be his first and only meeting with most of them, wishing he could shout it aloud.

"Cheerful little fellow," they said to one another that evening in taprooms and sculleries. "You'd think he'd be afeared, walking in the Old One's shadow—but not a bit of it. And they do say as what he knows of farms and farming could all be held in a footless stocking with a missing leg!" And they chuckled and nudged each other in anticipation of the good times ahead.

Near the end of the line stood a gentleman who was clearly neither tenant nor servant. The duke saw him and stiffened. A hush fell. The gentleman miserably waited for an invitation to speak. The duke stared at him, then spun on his heel and strode indoors.

"Sir! Your grace!" The unhappy man thrust himself through the doorway in front of Alfred and fell to his knees before the duke, barring the passage. "I yield, your grace! I yield utterly. The man shall have a pension for life. I have the papers here." He waved a bundle of documents in the air.

"And compensation?" the duke asked calmly.

"And compensation. And I shall meet the surgeon's fee."

After another cool survey, the duke said, "Well I don't pretend to understand matters of that sort. I leave it all to my secretary." He stepped around the man.

"And I, sir? What of me?" His eyes implored the duke.

"Oh . . ." the duke hesitated as if the matter had not occurred to him before. "Well, if my secretary says all is in order, I'll put it about that you're not a blackguard after all."

The man's relief was monstrous; he began to fawn with the most abject gratitude.

"Just a bit of a bloody fool," the duke cut him short and walked away.

"What did you do to that man, duke?" Alfred asked when he had caught up.

"I?" The duke looked back with hurt innocence. "Nothing I'm aware of . . . unless"—he looked distant, as if trying to recall something too trivial to register—"I do seem to remember calling on Lady Harriet, my sister, you know, just as that fellow was leaving, and I may have indicated my surprise that he was admitted there. I don't remember doing so, but I may have."

"And this other business, sir? Those documents he brought?"

"Oh that's just estate business. No connection whatever with the other matter." He chuckled. "But didn't he just look as though the devil had shit him flying!"

Of course they were connected; even a fool could have seen that. So Alfred later found an opportunity to ask McKay, the duke's principal secretary, what had really happened. McKay, after a moment's hesitation, told him everything:

The gentleman, a certain John March, a neighbor of the duke's, had been driving a dog cart too fast along a narrow lane and had been unable to avoid one of the duke's herdsmen. The man had lost both legs below the knee and would never work again. John March, presumably because he was driving and did not want to admit himself at fault, had refused to pay any kind of compensation or pension. And the duke, on hearing this, had said quite loudly at one of his sister's drawing rooms that he was surprised to see that John March was still entertained there.

"And that was *all?*" Alfred asked.

"All!" McKay said. "When a duke passes sentence of death, my lord, he needs no black cap or other trumpery."

"Aren't you exaggerating? 'Sentence of *death*'?"

"You saw the man himself, sir. He wouldn't call it any exaggeration. No house in England was open to him, thanks to that one remark of the duke's."

CHAPTER EIGHT

LUNCHEON WAS LIGHT—a buffet of cold meats, pheasant pie, coddled quail's eggs, and Stilton cheese.

Alfred ate whatever was put in front of him, indiscriminately, without obvious relish but with no sign of distaste either. He looked around the room, at the soaring walls with their intricately laced blue and gold Chinese patterns, then at the ceilings with their delicately rococo moldings . . . It was all too big, he felt. He would never be comfortable—*at home*—in such halls of rooms. He would always feel that at any moment the servants would come in and ask him to leave while they brought in the benches and seats for some public meeting due to begin in an hour or so.

The duke watched him closely. "Food's food, eh?" he said at last.

Alfred looked puzzled.

"Can't make you out, young Boyce. There's two characters run through our family. Come out time and again. Libertine and puritan. I don't mean politically Puritan, of course. That was William du Bois, who took the name Boyce instead—your great-great-great-grandfather, who was my great-grandfather's brother's grandson. I mean Puritan in spirit. Tight with money. Wear hemp as easily as silk. Eat gruel as heartily as truffles. Sleep on stone as heavily as on goosedown. Not notice whether the fire be lit or dead . . ."

"I'm a bit like that, duke," Alfred said.

"A bit, aye! But if I sent up a maid to warm your bed tonight . . . ?"

Alfred's brows shot up; the place had amenities! The duke saw his alertness and laughed. "Yes. That's the other side of the family. We belong where polygamy's no sin. That's the point where we meet: Clarence, the First Duke, and his brother, Reverend Lord Richard—my great grandfather and your fifth-great-grandfather—libertines both, in an age that understood the joys and the glory of libertinism. The age of Dryden. Not like these poxy times, I may say. But how much of it's still in you?"

"I'll try and take the best of both, sir."

"Ha! Like Henry, the Second Duke. 'Mask of Steel' they called him. He died under Marlborough at Oudenaarde, a soldier to his toenails. But he left the country littered with naturals. 'Wide as his command, he scattered his image through the land.' That laborer in Great Marlow, fellow with the leaking roof, he's descended from one of them. So was the groom on our carriage. So's my valet. And a couple of the gardeners. Dozens of 'em. One of Henry's natural sons, Stephen—by a girl of good class he was—he went to the court of Hanover and married a Hohenzollern woman. At one time we had hopes that line might be the line of inheritance. But . . ."

"It would have suited us both, duke," Alfred said. "Are you sure they're ruled out?"

"Entirely!" the duke snapped. They finished the meal in silence.

"We'll go through the place century by century," the duke said. "There's something in the du Bois nature that won't let anything go, you know. Others tear down their seats and rebuild them. We just add. And we look after it all, too. You'll find no beetle and no rot here. There's everything from the beginning back in 1150—or almost. You'll see."

They were walking across the Great Courtyard, where three infantry battalions could have drilled without conflicting. The servants had returned to their business; the tenants had taken their due of ale and departed home. Pigeons and rooks strutted over the cobbles, pecking at morsels no human eye could discern; two cats stalked them without hope. A couple of pensioned hounds lay basking in the sun. For all its grandeur of scale the scene suddenly struck Alfred as being essentially domestic.

"I meant to show you our coat of arms," the duke said, turning suddenly to their left.

A one-story arcade had originally connected the two Elizabethan wings, closing off the inner courtyard. It still served those functions, but the Third Duke, the present duke's father, had "grandified" it by adding two blind arcades above in Georgian style, surmounted by a great pediment. At its center stood the family arms, sculpted in high relief. The escutcheon had a number of heraldic devices—stars, a chevron, a crescent, and a miniature escutcheon with the cross of St. George on it—but its chief feature was a leaping fish of gold. The crest was a peacock over a knotted serpent. The right supporter was a heraldic goat, the left was an Ancient Briton with a gold sword and silver shield. Between their legs wound the motto, *Sperno me recipere aut mutari.*

"It tells everything," the duke said. "We're proud as peacocks, cunning as serpents, randy as goats, and fearless as those Ancient Brits who saw off the Romans."

"Whoever designed it even thought of me," Alfred said, pointing to the escutcheon. "The fish out of water."

The duke drew a sharp breath and Alfred prepared to flinch from his anger. But he mastered it and said, "I hope it *is* you, my boy. That's the golden salmon, the bringer of wisdom from afar." He laughed.

"What does the Latin mean?"

"The books say, *I will neither retreat nor be swayed.* Our enemies probably have a different gloss: *I am foolhardy and shit-stubborn.*"

He led the way past a large manorial hall to the castle at the northwestern extremity of the Abbey. At the great vaulted doorway he pointed to some wasted bits in the stone. "Been some fighting here, I daresay. I wouldn't think this spot was too healthy round about the time of the Wars of the Roses. It wasn't ours then, of course. The Herberts owned it through their descent from John of Gaunt and Catherine Swynford, which would put them in the Tudor camp. So if it was artillery did that, it must have been Lancastrian." He spoke these last words almost as if the events might have happened while he had been away in Cokeley the previous week.

Immediately inside the door of Herberts Tower, as it was called, a narrow spiral stair descended to a crypt. "We're all down here," the duke said, fishing a small key from his pocket. With it he tried to open a small cupboard let into the wall, but the lock was rusty and yielded only after several thumps. The hinges were so corroded they acted more in the way of springs, forcing the door to close by an inch or two whenever it was let go.

"Good God!" the duke said, and, reaching into the cupboard, he drew forth an ancient toy horse, a crude, spotted bit of carving about six inches high. "I lost that when I was four! In 1773—the same year I first told Nanny Morgan I'd grow up and marry her! Well, I'm damned! And hello again, Caesar! How long have you been there?" Clutching this ancient treasure to him, he reached back into the cupboard and took out a massive key, which he handed to Alfred as he said, "See if you can open the door, my boy."

As Alfred put in the key, a large spider slipped out by a hole in the bottom of the lock case and fell by a thread to the stone floor, where it scuttered quickly away. The ancient lock opened more easily than the one on the cupboard. He pushed at the heavy door; it, too, moved easily and in silence.

"Gentleman—your heir, Lord Alfred Boyce," the duke announced. And to Alfred, completing the introduction, he said: "Our tribe—God Almighty's gentlemen!"

Alfred thought he was jesting but one look showed that the old man was quite serious.

A dim light filtered down through half a dozen small openings high in the walls on three sides. The entire room was lined with wide marble shelves, some thirty inches apart, and on them stood upwards of forty coffins of stone or lead. Instinctively Alfred sniffed, but there was only a trace of dampness on the seldom-stirred air.

"Sir Clarence and his lady are down in the church in Marlow. And there's an effigy of Richard there, though no one knows where his remains are. He was the First Earl of Brompton. Beheaded in the Tower of London by Henry the Eighth. But from Godfrey on" —he patted the coffin next to the doorway on the lowest shelf— "we're all here. Going round in strict order of date. Death's a leveler. In some families they put peers above, commoners below. But we say Death's a leveler."

Alfred nodded agreement, gazing around at the coffins dimly looming out of their recesses between the shelves.

"Godfrey built most of what you now see at Chalfont. He was the First Earl of Belgravia. Made a fortune under the Duke of Somerset and somehow escaped the ax. His son, Charles"—their eyes passed on over a dozen coffins—"was the First Marquis. They thought he was in the Lopez plot to poison the queen. Queen Elizabeth. Poor fellow had to flee to Spain. But we haven't got that nowled serpent in our crest for nothing! If he hadn't made such a thorough study of the naval defenses of Cadiz, Lords Howard and Essex wouldn't have made so easy a job of sacking the place. That bit of treachery to his hosts won us the marquisate!

"But there"—he gestured toward one of the corner bays, where the children's coffins were racked—"lie most of the sons who should have followed him. One of mine is there, too. Born a shapeless lump—like anarchy." There was a moment's silence before the duke continued. "So the Second Marquis was Godfrey's youngest boy, a little weakling who married his own cook, Anne Seton, and spent his life translating the Bible. Not an ancestor to swell one with pride, what! Thank heaven *his* son"—he patted another coffin—"brought us back on course. Clarence, the First Duke. My great-grandfather."

"The libertine," Alfred said, remembering their lunchtime conversation.

"Yes!" The duke was delighted. "But a nasty sort of a fellow for all that. Or so I imagine." He patted the coffin in a conciliatory way. "Sparing your presence, great-grandfather most noble," he said to it. "He made a fortune out of tax farming. Most of the land we'll see from the top of this tower, and everything we drove through today, was added by this fellow. He led our regiment, the Stormers, first against Parliament, then against the king—his greatest friend! The monarch to whom he owed his dukedom! Then, to show he meant it, I suppose, he supported Monmouth's rebellion for a week—that was June 1685—but in 1688 he was suddenly an ardent Whig and helped invite William of Orange over here. We've been Whigs ever since, of course."

"Another serpent?" Alfred ventured.

"Well, he was quite open about it—about being a shit. He must have had quite unbelievable charm to have survived. He's the one I'd most have liked to know. His diaries are all up in the muniment room. In one of them he wrote a short epistle in praise of civil war. He says it tests the supreme quality of a general, which is not knowing how to inspire your men, nor where to deploy them, but when to carry them over to the other side—and how to manage it without a mutiny!"

Alfred looked at the coffin with a new respect. "And he managed it twice!"

"His son Henry," the duke announced, patting yet another coffin. This one was of lead, decorated with low-relief battle scenes and effigies of the god Mars.

"The Steel . . ." Alfred said, urgently fishing, angry that he could not remember. How much more real these people became when you could actually pat their coffins! "The Steel Mask—no, the Mask of Steel!"

The duke, pleased again, nodded. "We used to imagine, my brother Henry and I, that he was actually buried wearing a mask of steel. He was brought home from Oudenaarde pickled in a brandy barrel, you know. We spent hours down here trying to pry off the lid."

"And never . . . ?"

"Never."

Alfred gave a tentative heave at the lid, but it was cemented too firmly.

"Which brings us to his son—my father." He patted another coffin, near the end. "William, the Third Duke. He took down the southern end of the Elizabethan house and built that vast Georgian wing in its place. You'll see it later. We're still paying for it, I may say." He dropped his voice and watched Alfred closely. "For that, and for my Brighton folly."

"And the upkeep," Alfred said, not knowing whether he was expected to press this point.

The duke rested his hand on the first bit of empty shelf. "This space is for the Fourth Duke," he said. "Level in death with his two brothers. Then it'll all be your worry." He put the toy horse on the space and left it.

Alfred said nothing.

The duke turned abruptly to a coffin about two thirds of the way along the sequence. "We're forgetting your branch," he said. "This is the Reverend Lord Richard du Bois, your fifth-great-grandfather." He bent forward and reached his hand in between the shelves, saying, "I wonder, now . . ."

There was a clatter of stone on stone as a part of the coffin fell away. "Yes!" the duke was triumphant. "Look, you can see a bit of him."

Alfred peered in and saw what could have been a piece of ancient leather or bark. Nothing remotely human, anyway.

"My brother Henry discovered that piece of stone was loose," the duke added. "Touch your ancestor if you wish."

Alfred did not in the least *wish* to touch these moldering remains, yet something within him, a force too strong to deny, impelled his hand into the blackness, while he watched with imprisoned fascination. The thing inside the coffin was cold, and hard—not like stone but like a gnarled tree root. And quite dry.

The duke's voice was insistent and low. "You reach and touch across seven generations," he said.

The hair stiffened on Alfred's neck.

The duke took his arm gently and pulled it free again. "There's a splendid barbarity in the tie of blood," he said. "It's noble and yet it's savage. It's noble when we use it justly. It's savage when we turn upon it and abuse it."

Alfred hardly dared to breathe.

"Say what you will"—the duke continued what had become a kind of incantation—"we live by blood. And our blood is different. Our blood *is* an ennoblement."

He smiled—a grimace of victory—and held wide his arms. Alfred, bereft of all will, moved into that vast embrace—and simultaneously stepped over that invisible boundary which separated the Boyce from the du Bois.

His final glance around the room, as they stood again at the door, measured the difference: These were now *his* ancestors, too —or, rather, his antecessors; but that was a distinction he could not then make.

• •

At the top of Herberts Tower, out in the fresh air, his head cleared and he began to regret the impulses that had moved him down in the crypt. The rational parts of his mind rejected all the commitments his actions might have implied. *I'm still free,* he told himself.

"A man is to be cheated into passion, but to be reasoned into truth," the duke said, still breathless from the climb. "So—to reason!" He pointed to the southwest. "The county boundary runs just beyond that wooded hill there—Coldharbour Hill. From the French, *col d'arbre*—always been wooded, you see. Our lands are roughly one third in Oxfordshire, two thirds in Buckinghamshire. We call the two divisions 'Oxon' and 'Bucks,' you see. Then Bucks is subdivided again. There are a few hundred acres over the Thames in Berkshire, too."

He let this sink in before he resumed, "You asked me last week, that day we first met (was it only last week!) you asked me what there might be for you in the 'duking business,' remember?"

Alfred nodded warily.

"There it is." He waved an arm most of a full circle. "All you can see and ten times more."

He watched with keen, hooded eyes as Alfred looked glumly around. "What's the matter?" he asked.

Alfred could not meet his gaze. "I feel bad," he said. "I must be a great disappointment to you. Any other man would be on his knees with joy and gratitude. But I look at all that land"—he studiously avoided looking at it—"and I tell you I feel nothing but . . . terror."

"Terror doesn't last," the duke said. "And you may count yourself fortunate to feel it now. I was the opposite. I grew up knowing how utterly superior I was, knowing I was born to manage these lands, knowing I could do no wrong. And I made every mistake a landowner can possibly make. If I hadn't been a peer and above the common courts, if the lands hadn't been entailed to the last rod, pole, or perch, you'd be inheriting nothing but a boxful of old papers. Even now . . ." He chose not to complete the sentence. "My terror began late in life, when I realized what a prick I'd been all those years."

"I don't feel terror all the time," Alfred said. "But I do feel . . . let down. I must be honest with you, duke. I like you too much—and respect you too much—to be anything else. Most of me still wants to be back there under those railway arches, worrying about pennies . . . doing it all by myself." He looked at the duke but those eyes stared him out. "All this," he added lamely, feeling that more words were needed to plug the silence, "is just . . . served up on a salver. I'd feel a fraud to accept it. Blood or no blood." He thought, but did not add, that he also wanted to be where Hermione was.

No change showed in the duke's demeanor, but he clenched his fists and held his breath in sheer delight. At the same time he cursed his lack of insight—thinking he understood this young fellow! He had understood everything except the single most important thing: He was a du Bois from his scalp to his socks! Most men might dream of having wealth and honors shower upon them like rain; but not this one. This one wanted nothing he hadn't himself achieved. *Well, now,* he thought, *here's a challenge!*

"On a salver, eh?" he echoed mockingly. "Well, your frankness touches me, my boy. And"—he darted a furtive glance at Alfred—"shames me."

"Shames!"

"Yes." He pretended not to be able to meet Alfred's astonished eye. "Let me confess to you what I hoped to conceal until after . . ." Instead of completing the sentence he turned to the battlement, face into the sun, and stared out over his lands. "If by the time you stand here with *your* successor and talk of handing over—if by that time you own it, *truly* own it, you can tell him you bought it all yourself, field by field. Tell him you owed nothing to me. Not a twig."

Alfred laughed in disbelief.

"Oh, yes," the duke insisted. "As I said, if it wasn't for the fact that peers can't be pressed for debt in the common courts, and if it wasn't for the fact that every last acre is entailed, I'd be Duke of the Deep Blue Sea. You're inheriting *nothing!* Except the chance to buy it all back from the bankers and Jews."

"Jews!" Alfred was horrified.

"Oh, yes. Don't despise the tribe of Benjudah. If truth were told, there's more honor among them than you could squeeze out of the entire British peerage and all the Protestant bankers put together. And never slight them, either; they never forget an insult—just as they never forget a favor. You needn't go so far as to invite them to your dinner table. I don't mean that. But there's no need to treat 'em like most Englishmen do."

He was delighted to see a new glint in Alfred's eye as he leaned out over the battlement and looked again at the pastures and woodland all around. "How much is owed, duke?" he asked.

"It was the enclosures," the duke said, struggling to inject an unfamiliar whine of self-justification into his voice. "The Polkinghornes of this world made a fortune, I may say—as when do they not? Half of it went in legal and parliamentary fees. Like the fucking railways—there's another thing . . ."

"Yes, but how much?"

"Have you any idea what hedgerows cost? Gates? What would you shell out for a mile of mortised posts and rails, eh? Or for a hundred thousand quicksets—half of them lost in the drought of '22? And that's before a single brick was laid or a single new barn was built."

"All in all, then, duke, it came to . . . ?"

"Fifteen pounds an acre, some of it. Of course we doubled the rents, but it's still a case of spend now and get it back in thirty years."

"How many acres did you enclose, duke?" Alfred hoped he could calculate the size of the debt that way.

But the duke was ahead of him. "Enclosures weren't all," he said. "Look, my boy. I don't want to frighten you off with all this talk of debt. We'll go into it all another time, eh? And the whole management of the estate. If you have a hankering for industry, I may tell you that's quite a little industry in itself. Let's look at the rest of the house."

He turned to the stairway entrance. Alfred, who had hardly been able to look at the land that stretched all about them when they first came out, now lingered far longer than was polite. As his eyes traversed field and hedge, copse and village, his jaw muscles chewed vigorously though his teeth were tight clenched.

The duke, in the dark of the stairhead, watched him in triumph—and felt the first stirrings of a new sensation. He did not pin it down until they were back on the ground floor, by the door to the crypt. Then he knew: It was the feeling of being able to contemplate death without flinching.

CHAPTER NINE

"UP, MY BOY! Dear God, when I was your age I could leap into a saddle from falling ground," the duke challenged.

Alfred was learning that the word "thoroughbred" means more

than just a certain nobility of head and elegance of line in a horse; it also means, for example, a sensitivity of the spine so exquisite that a good horseman can steer his mount and change its pace entirely through his own seat.

This thoroughbred filly of Alfred's was used to such horsemen. He, by contrast, was used to old hacks and screws hired out by innkeepers, beasts with mouths of iron and backs of oak. Every move he made sent the filly into paroxysms of nervousness; she pawed the cobbles and yawed in tight circles. Every adjustment to the reins made her chuck her head, her eyes wide and her nostrils flaring. It was going to be a disaster, he knew it. As soon as she saw a bit of prairie, she'd be off and no holding her. She was sweating even now.

"Tighten that martingale," the duke told the groom. "Lead her for a bit. Let loose your reins, Alfred."

To Alfred's surprise the old man rode at once indoors—into the medieval Great Hall that abutted Herberts Tower. The groom led him inside, too; the door was high enough to admit him without the need to duck, even if he had been standing on the horse's back.

He found himself in the Abbey kitchens. The hooves rang sharp and strangely hollow on the giant limestone flags. Two stable lads, with shovels and buckets, brought up the rear.

"Used to be the monks' refectory," the duke said. "Then it was the washhouse. Full of hand looms in my father's time. I turned it into kitchens when I built the Brighton wing."

Alfred, grateful for the groom's hand at his mount's head, looked about them. Pointed-arch windows, glazed with rather simple motifs in stained glass, pierced both walls, letting in light from horizontal to near vertical, wherever the filth that grimed them did not obscure it altogether.

A chef, several undercooks, kitchen porters, and scullery maids looked up in only moderate surprise at the two horsemen and watched them all the way to the far door—beneath which Alfred had to duck.

He rose to a different world: Elizabethan rather than medieval. There was oak paneling on the walls and stiffly ornamental plaster on the ceilings. A threadbare drugget that had once been highly colored ran the length of the corridor floor, which was boarded in oak.

"Now we're into the part built by Godfrey—the first coffin, remember?" the duke said.

"The one who escaped the ax."

"Fortunately for us." He looked about him, nodding self-agreement. "All these rooms must have seemed very grand in their day."

To Alfred they seemed very grand still. The doors were tall enough to be seen through without stooping as they rode past. Relays of servants ran ahead to throw them open and stayed behind to close them. In many rooms there were fires set and kindled.

"It keeps very dry," he said to the duke.

"We light the fires by rota, you know. Twenty each day. Most rooms get a fire once a week that way."

Carved cupboards and stout chairs, stained black with time, stood in every nook and corner. Alfred had impressions of leaded-glass bookcases gleaming along some of the walls; of stout refectory tables scarred with knives, swords, and no doubt horses' hooves; of an old globe, all elm, brown plaster, and brass; of delicate tapestries, the maiden tribute of decades of needlework; of stiffly formal portraits whose sitters stared back at him in nouveau-riche arrogance and uncertainty.

"These are all minor people," the duke said. "That's Helena Giles, sister of the Katherine who married Charles du Bois, Godfrey's brother. They had a manor at Stonor which fell down long ago. You're seeing the meanest part first. The rooms above are all much grander."

But instead of going to the rooms above, they pressed ahead into the Georgian wing, the vast southern addition built by the duke's father. Even by itself it would have dwarfed most of the great houses in the kingdom.

If Alfred had imagined any of the rooms he had been in so far were grand, he now changed his notions entirely. For here, where the architect left off the painter and plasterer took over, creating halls of infinite perspective. Gleaming parquet floors (on which their horses' hooves rang out like castanets being played inside kettledrums) stretched to far horizons of baroque plaster. Massive pillars twisted and soared to cerulean acres where goddesses and nymphs, cherubs and satyrs sported in flamelike profusion over the empyreal ceilings. Cornucopias of fruit and triumphal swags poured down over cornices and spilled back into walls, where shepherdesses and swains, peruked and beauty-spotted, plucked lutes and wild roses, embarked for Cythera, danced at fêtes galantes, and swooned at fêtes champêtres, made sheep's eyes at each other over well-laundered flocks of sheep and amid haycocks combed as neat and dainty as a pet dog's fur.

"These are the state rooms," the duke said. "Not much in demand these days, of course. Her majesty can't bear them—too *ga-*

lantes for her Prussian-provincial taste." He laughed mockingly. "Suggested I get in a few gross of fig leaves and employ a drapery painter. But I'm buggered if I will."

He led the way to the next room, which was equally grand. Its walls were lined with books, imprisoned behind glass and a mesh of bronze. "Fifteen thousand, someone told me," he said. "My father, I think. I've not looked at them—mostly sermons, I believe. I'll show you what to do about sermons on Sunday. By the way, talking of her majesty, I can't present you until the House of Lords has looked at all the papers. It's a foregone conclusion, of course—or you'd not be here now, I may tell you. But we have to follow the form in these things." He paused and looked around the room. A new light crept into his eyes. "I say—rather a splendid notion. When it's all signed and certified, we'll ask her majesty to stay for a few days and give a grand ball here. In May I should think. Yes! She can grant you a private drawing room on her first day." He grinned hugely. "Then I'll get her to grant you the style of Marquis of Knightsbridge, heir presumptive. Yes! We'll invite everyone who could possibly be of any use to you—right down to cabinet ministers! Oh, it'll be grand to see these rooms in proper use again!"

He was so delighted he urged his horse to a trot, out into the next room, which proved to be the great marble staircase and hall at the center of this whole southern wing. Alfred's filly, fearing to be left behind, broke free of the groom and went after the duke at a smartly extended trot. This had the unfortunate effect of bringing her smack in line with the start of the staircase, which swept up in a generous arc to the first-floor gallery.

Alfred, who had swept up the reins in panic, breathed a sigh of relief, not for one moment imagining that this spirited little lady would attempt the ascent. To his horror she broke into a canter just two strides off. He barely had time to give her back the reins and clutch at her mane and neck for dear life and even dearer limb.

You'd think she'd done it every day, he always said when he told the story later. She was one living ripple of muscle, an equine eel slithering upward as if the air were her true medium. She paused at the three-quarter landing and would, he was sure, have turned and picked her way down again as surefooted as a goat, if the duke had not at that moment recovered from his surprise and, giving a great whoop of joy, spurred after him at full canter. The filly was off again like a dart, but the duke's bigger horse gained enough for them all to arrive at the gallery above simultaneously.

"Well!" the duke laughed, breathless with excitement. "I had intended to do this on foot, but once again, my lord, you shame me. Stay near the walls, won't you, in case she pisses. It turns all the blue on the ceilings black for some reason."

"It must be a copper salt in the pigment. It would turn to cuprammonium-something—probably black."

"Forget it, my boy," the duke said earnestly. "No good can possibly come of knowing things like that. Clear your head. You'll need all the room you've got up there for the things you're going to learn these next twenty years." He walked ahead and then looked back sternly. "Beginning, I may say, with how to sit a horse decently. You're worse than an infantry corporal."

He led Alfred the length of the gallery—the Thornhill Room, he called it—and back, past all the principal family portraits. It was the perfect counterpoint to the time they had spent in the crypt. For here, painted by all the masters of their day, from Hilliard and Holbein, through Kneller, to Gainsborough and the duke's own portrait by Romney, were those men and women whose bones still moldered in that stone-dry, stone-cold room below the tower.

"Next best thing to living flesh," the duke said.

And it was. Alfred now felt he knew them so well that they seemed on the point of climbing out of their frames, stretching their limbs, and speaking to him: Godfrey, stocky and cunning, trying to look as mighty as a Roman and as humble as a Christian, and succeeding only in looking like a minor god with the wind up; Charles, his son, one half of whose face conspicuously failed to match the other, his left side being sardonic and observant, and his right pure self-regard and feigned indifference; and Clarence, the First Duke . . .

"Jove!" the duke cried at the sight of Clarence. He reined in and turned to stare at Alfred. "Don't you see it, my boy?"

Alfred stared at the painting; it was by Van Dyck and had all his insouciant freshness and élan. Stare at it long enough and you'd swear it moved; but however long Alfred stared at it, he saw nothing which might have made the duke call out like that. Clarence was a short, handsome fellow with deep-set eyes. They radiated a fearlessness that amounted to contempt—but playful rather than arrogant, a contempt devoid of moral judgment. His smile, as Van Dyck saw it, was tolerant; but the painter had managed to convey that it could quite easily change to something harder. Clarence, you would guess, had not been one to suffer fools gladly.

Alfred looked quizzically at the duke.

"Not familiar?" the duke asked.

"Perhaps," Alfred said, out of politeness rather than conviction. "Is he like someone we saw downstairs?"

The duke roared with laughter and rode on. "You'll see it one day. Then you'll remember this."

Alfred looked keenly at the Reverend Lord Richard, Clarence's brother, and at Richard's son, Godfrey, but could see no likeness to himself. The duke shook his head and, to Alfred's puzzlement, said, "You may have more right to this place than I, my boy." But when pressed he declined to explain.

Alfred dismounted and let the groom lead his horse back down the stairs; the duke, also on foot, led his own. At the bottom of the stairs they went out through the large side doors and onto the terrace. The duke handed over his horse to be led away. He and Alfred walked to the balustrade; the terrace was broad enough, and long enough, to hold a full-size market.

"Always meant to add a fountain here," the duke said. "That's something you could do. I daresay you'll not go in for any building."

Alfred laughed, partly in delight at the idea of making a fountain and partly at the thought that anyone might even consider adding one more stone to this vast, sprawling pile of a palace. For a while they stood in silence looking down the pool-strewn valley, with its carefully wooded sides, running due south from the terrace.

"He had a sense of drama, my father," the duke said. "If you thought the Abbey impressive from the northern approach, you should see it from down there!"

He led Alfred down a flight of stone steps, in order (Alfred imagined) to show him this view; but the old grandee had a far more serious purpose.

"My boy," he said as they set off at a measured pace around the nearest and most ornamental of the lakes, "I don't want you to think, because I'm the mildest and most decent fellow as was ever made by God and English ale, that all dukes are as good. Truth to tell, they're a pretty scurvy lot at present. We live in an age of cant and false appearances, which brings out the worst in everyone, especially the aristocracy. Most especially dukes, who have no one to keep them in order. So if you're going to turn out a good sort of fellow, a true du Bois, it'll have to be by your own effort. Roman generals had slaves to whisper 'you're only a mortal' as they rode in triumph. We really ought to have the same sort of fellow every day. Except we'd lose dignity by it. But every now and then listen for that whisper. Supply it yourself if need be. And profit by the example of two dozen dukes who don't. Beginning with the Norfolks.

"The only decent Norfolk was old Jockey, the eleventh, who could drink even me under the table—and then go on to another house and do the same all over again. Never washed. The present one goes about like a vagrant. Besides, they're Catholics. Forget them.

"Somerset is preposterous. He was born Seymour and changed his name to St. Maur out of sheer romance. Abolished flogging in the navy. Writes *books!*" This was clearly a worse crime than winding one's own watch. "He married one of Hamilton's daughters and thinks leg of mutton and boiled potatoes a great feast. The chef was a shepherd.

"Hamilton himself is mad, of course. Fancies he's a Scotch king though all the world knows the true claimant is Lord Abercorn. He's hired a hermit to live in his park. And he paid eleven thousand for an Egyptian sarcophagus from Thebes to be buried in—though they'll have to lop off his feet before he'll fit.

"The Beauforts are good squires, bone from the neck up, mud from the knee down, and nothing but simple appetite in between.

"The Bedfords never talk to each other, even in health, which they rarely experience and never enjoy.

"Cavendishes are only happy when they've got their nose in a book—except the Fifth Duke of Devonshire." His eyes softened as a happy memory stirred him. "And Georgiana. Now there *was* a woman! Not beautiful, but she bubbled like a fountain of life and gaiety. Between them they made Devonshire House the only house in London. She had all the Villiers blood you could wish on anyone. The court of Charles the Second and the court of Prinny are the only two happy courts in our history—and the only two decent courts we're likely to have, I'll wager."

He turned to Alfred. "Now here's a funny thing. Charles the Second lived in tolerable harmony with his wife and all his mistresses, one of whom was Barbara Villiers. And there was Georgiana Spencer, full of Villiers blood. And who, may I ask, was her dearest friend? Why, her husband's mistress, Bess, Lady Elizabeth Foster, the Earl of Bristol's daughter! Lived under the same roof, children shared the same nursery. Now she *was* a beauty, Bess."

"Can a duke do that?" Alfred asked. "How could he keep it a secret?"

The duke laughed. "Everyone knew—though of course no one ever discussed it with him. A duke can do anything, my boy, anything he wants. And not the sovereign himself—or herself—can do a thing about it. We can commit felonies and the courts may not arrest us. We can run up debts and laugh at our creditors. We can put whom we want in Parliament. And in our own estates we have absolute power. When you inherit you can turn into an unwashed, drunken, lecherous shit, a tyrant, a recluse, a bookworm—whatever you will—and not a soul in all the world can say you nay!"

"Even an industrial manufacturer?" Alfred asked.

"By proxy, of course," the duke answered evenly, not being drawn. "If you tried it in person, you'd be cut out of good society—you'd be like a general who'd been denied any military intelligence. Useless. You may think Society's just a lot of snobbery and quaint rules. Well it isn't. It's about information . . . mutual assistance. It's the horse against the inside fence." He cleared his throat in satisfaction with the arrangement. "As to your personal behavior, you'd have to be a monster of cold-heartedness, like the present Newcastle, before you'd be cut out of Society—and even then there'd be hundreds who'd owe you obligations and couldn't cut you. And thousands who'd curry favor for the sake of some patronage." He fell silent a moment and then added, "Of course, Lady Bess had to go to France to have Devonshire's children. Even that age drew its limits. Today"—he snorted—"I suppose she'd have to go to China! Where was I? Devonshire. Ah, yes, the Argylls.

"You may ignore all the Scotch dukedoms. A vile lot, the Scotch. The Argylls were created out of falsehood and cowardice, and never rose above it. They're Campbells, which means 'twisted mouth.' Their finest hour was when they murdered their hosts, the Macdonalds, at Glencoe. And that was only a century and a half ago. The Murrays, dukes of Atholl, never knew who was lawful sovereign. The latest one didn't even know he himself was a duke; died in a padded cell in St. John's Wood. The wife of the present duke, the sixth, is a great friend of the queen's, so that shows you what sort of people *they* are! The Roxburghe dukes were librarians up to about 1800, the end of the Drummond line. Now, with the Innes line, they've turned into soldiers—a dry, cold lot. Nothing against them. Nothing for them. The only good Montrose was the first—though the present duchess and Lady Sarah Ingestre led the booing and hissing against the queen at Ascot after her majesty hounded poor Flora Hastings to her death, so there's *one* thing in their favor."

"I can't wait to meet all these nice people, duke," Alfred said.

The duke laughed. "Oh, you will. *And* take their part, because, naturally, we've all got to hang together."

"Also I gather you don't much admire her majesty?"

The duke cleared his throat and *almost* spat. "A nasty, small-minded little prude," he barked. "Ah, you should have been alive and young under the old monarchy, the Hanoverians! Now they *were* monarchs. These Saxe-Coburgs will be the ruin of England.

You'll live to see it. Who comes after Montrose? Scotch, I mean. Ah, yes—Sutherland, though he's as Scotch as the river Thames."

"Is this the one who's rebuilding Cliffden?" Alfred asked.

"Yes," the duke said and, without a trace of a smile, added, " 'Old Pa Sutherland at number four' to you."

It was Alfred's turn to laugh. "I see," he said.

"They're the most recent creation—1833. Before that he was Marquis of Stafford. He and his wife own the entire county of Sutherland, right up in the north of Scotland. One million three hundred thousand acres of . . . nothing! That's what it was forty years ago. Not a road, no mails, one sheep bridge. And ten to fifteen thousand wild Highlanders with their goats and crops, living quite beyond the reach of money. First he kicked them out—evicted them by the thousands—and planted English sheep farmers there. And then he built four hundred miles of the best roads in the kingdom, and over a hundred bridges."

"But surely, sir, that's a great improvement?" Alfred said.

"The inhumanity of it!" the duke said angrily. "Those were his tenants. His *people*. What of his duty to them? His rents are over three hundred thousand a year. What would a bit of decency have cost him? Our people here are like our family, from shepherd to forester and carpenter to kitchen maid. You saw them all this morning—that was a family greeting its head, if you didn't realize it. When each of them came into the world, we paid the midwife. We paid their schooling. When they're sick we pay the doctor and the hospital. They marry on our purse. We buy their clothes. We lodge and feed them. We pension them. We even pay for their funerals and gravestones. Not only here but London too. And down in the Cornish estates. Costs us forty thousand a year if it's a penny. And that's before we spend a farthing on ourselves."

Alfred nodded. At the start of this catechism of dukes he had only dimly glimpsed the old man's purpose; suddenly it had become very clear. "That finishes the Scotch dukes, then," he prompted.

"A wretched lot," the duke went on. "And the Irish. Leinster—the present one, anyway—is a mild fool. Creevey used to say he'd brush your coat for you if you asked him kindly. But his father, the second duke, was a fine man. He saw that Ireland will one day go the same way as America, if we don't profit from that lesson—and it will. He's one of the few dukes I'd give you more than twopence for.

"The worst thing we ever did was make our generals dukes. Marlborough knew no cause but himself and betrayed every monarch and country that ever employed him. His wife was a devil. And when they married into the Spencers they united with the least principled family in English life. The fourth duke didn't speak to a soul for three years, and now the fifth wants us to turn all marquises into women. Tscha!"

When he saw Alfred's bewilderment he added: "He wants to stop spelling it m,a,r,q,u,i,s and spell it m,a,r,q,u,e,s,s instead. Don't ever let him do that to us. I'll tell you now, this country's going to rue the day it ever let the brood of Sir Winston Churchill rise above the rank of baronet—which is where they belong. And as for Wellington! Well, he can't last long now. Then you'll see a heartless, bloodless dynasty unroll!

"Who's next? Dorset. Well, they're extinct anyway. Died out six or seven years ago. Northumberland, the Percys, nice people, any one of them would make a good squire. But too soft and bookish to be dukes. That's my humble opinion, anyway. And Buckingham's broke! The family name is Temple-Nugent-Brydges-Chandos-Grenville." He laughed. "If they'd coined money on the same scale, they'd be out of Carey Street by now."

"The Rutlands are good to their people. Good hunting, too. But they live only for themselves. There's nothing worse than a *pompous* epicure in my view."

Alfred laughed. "Are there no really good dukes?" he asked.

"Only the ones I've left out."

"Oh." Alfred had not believed this catalogue could possibly have omitted any duke.

"Except for Portland. I forgot Portland—which is the best one can do with them. Water colors left out in three days of rain would be stronger. No, my boy, the best dukes are all bastards—from the best king we ever had. One of the two best, anyway. The second Charles.

"Buccleuch ought to be king now, if there were justice, which of course there never is. Charles did marry Lucy Walter, and Monmouth was the rightful successor. Dreadful man, but never mind. Buccleuch is Monmouth's heir and ought to be on the throne at this moment. He's a capital fellow. One of his predecessors, 'Old Q,' had every woman worth having in London."

Alfred laughed.

"Oh, yes! Sat on his balcony in Piccadilly, ogling them all. Built a special staircase so that his man, good Jack Radford, could fetch the victim up directly. Generous, too. Died with ninety letters from women unopened on his bed. The fifth of Buccleuch's very decent, too. They keep open house at Drumlanrig for three months every year. Anyone may come, retinue and all. Stay as long as you like. Just write and say, 'I'm coming'; that's all the invitation you need. Richest man in Europe. Talks to his shepherd just as he'd talk to you or me. Or the queen.

"The Graftons were got by Charles out of Barbara Villiers, cousin to the second duke of Buckingham. There's Villiers blood in all of us—you too, young Alfred. In the Churchills, the Murrays, the Hamiltons, the Cecils, the Russells—and most of the royal families in Europe."

"And Georgiana Devonshire," Alfred said.

The duke was pleased that the memory had stuck—not then knowing how much the story of the Fifth Duke of Devonshire, his wife, Georgiana, and his mistress, Bess, had appealed to Alfred.

"But there's more of Charles than of Villiers in the Graftons—amiable, tolerant, lazy, pleasure-seeking, simply furnished in the top story, hate fuss, love to be loved, and they spread bastards like thistle seeds. You'll like Grafton, I know.

"The Beauclerks, dukes of St. Albans, are from Nell Gwynn."

"Ah!" At last Alfred heard a name he knew.

"Her blood, too, runs pretty generously—Loders, Capells, Cavendishes, Maynards, St. Clair-Erskines, they've all got it. She was the nicest of them—too nice. And it's the same with the St. Albanses. Nice to the point of idiocy. But they live long, like us. The one who just died was only the third. Married Coutts's widow, Harriet Mellon, the whore. She was sixty-something. St. Albans was twenty-something. But the family was silly. Despised her. When she died, she left St. Albans two houses and ten thousand, but she left the rest—nearly two million—to Angela Burdett. That put the smile down in their boots!

"But the best of all are the Lennoxes, their graces of Richmond. The only line of dukes that has been popular and loved from the first to the present day. Charles to a man! It's living proof of the survival of blood and breeding—all his bastards show it, but none so much as the Richmonds, and the third of Richmond was the man for my money. Beautiful fellow. Dignified. Charming. Loved the women. Bit wild in his youth. Brought in a bill for universal suffrage above the age of eighteen! But he had the right idea."

Alfred looked at him in amazement at this opinion.

"Of course it's the right idea," the duke insisted. "In the end the people must govern themselves—as long as the aristocracy has its hand on the rudder, of course. Another amazing thing—Richmond was one of the few members of the nobility to support the American colonists. Justice, you see. That was his passion. Yet everyone liked him. Detested the ideas. Loved the man. That's the Richmonds. That's Charles's blood.

"The present Richmond is the fifth. Ignorant as pigshit. Thick-headed as a doornail. Drones on like a bagpipe. But a good fellow. Frank and easy as a summer's day. His tenants worship him. He's another one you'll like."

They had now walked one and a half times around the lake, but Alfred had been so absorbed in the catechism of dukes and their qualities (or lack of them) that he had barely glanced up at the Abbey.

"Ah!" the duke exclaimed and, gripping Alfred's arm, wafted his free hand across the whole field of view.

Alfred was speechless. The entire panorama was filled by that mighty façade. The newly scythed lawns rose to the mellow limestone walls of the terrace, whose front, patterned with blind arcading, was interrupted only by the two sweeping diagonals of the great stone stairways, by one of which they had descended. And above . . .

It's like the duke himself, Alfred thought. Majestic, austere, vastly self-assured . . . and yet, for all its grandeur, it contrived to be both domestic and welcoming.

"That's what artists call the *sublime,* my boy. One day I suppose our only claim to fame, my father and I, will be that we employed an architect called John Nash." He laughed to show he was exaggerating. "He designed Brighton Pavilion, you know. And rebuilt Buckingham Palace—which, by the way, is thirty-seven foot shorter than that. And that's another thing her majesty don't like." Again his hand waved across the panorama, possessing it. "Come on, there's still half of it you haven't seen yet."

Together they walked back toward the house. The duke began to list the treasures yet to come—furniture that had belonged to Marie Antoinette, gold plate from the Medici, sculptures from the Guelphs, and paintings by Rubens, Rembrandt, Veronese, Vermeer, Canaletto; almost every master of European art was there.

"Lady Tempest says it's a better collection than Lady Susan Hamilton brought to his grace of Somerset—or left behind," the duke added.

"She's the one who thinks boiled mutton a great feast," Alfred said.

The duke laughed, delighted. "That memory will do you no harm," he promised.

By the end of their tour, when they had arrived back at the Brighton wing (which now seemed charmingly *small* in scale),

Alfred had such visual indigestion (from a surfeit of clocks, bookcases, paintings, chairs, escritoires, bureaux, jardinières, barometers, sculptures, superports in low relief, four-poster beds and half testers, Adam fireplaces, Elizabethan plasterwork, gilding, ormolu, boule, Turkey carpets, Dutch marquetry, English silver, and French porcelain) that he would gladly have spent the night in a charcoal burner's hut.

The duke had one more surprise for Alfred. After dinner, which was heavy rather than sumptuous, the old man lighted him to bed, a vast four-poster in the east wing.

"Room for four mistresses," Alfred said hopefully, remembering their lunchtime conversation.

"They cost more than you'd imagine," the duke said. "Believe me!" He was on the point of going when he turned back. "Talking of which," he added. "Money, I mean, I've got you an assistant secretaryship at one of the ministries. There's no necessity whatever for you to take a dole from me when you can earn it by the sweat of your own brow. It's worth fifteen hundred a year. Only a beginning, of course."

Alfred stared at him in barest comprehension but, as always, the duke paid no heed. "You'll be gazetted tomorrow, but I shouldn't think there's the slightest need to turn up in Downing Street until the autumn. The important thing is we've got our toe in. Next election you'll go into Parliament and then we can soon cobble together a few offices worth about ten thousand between them. Learn to manage on a pinchpenny income like that and the dukedom will be simple. Eh? What?"

"Ministry?" Alfred said at last. "What ministry? What do . . ."

"What ministry! Does it matter? The War Office, I think. I left the arrangements to McKay. He'll tell you. I don't concern myself with such pettifogging details. Sleep well!"

But Alfred did not sleep at all well, not for several nights. He awoke at three with violent stomach cramps, nausea, and diarrhea, which stayed with him the best part of a week.

"The Chalfont squitters," the duke called them, saying that they afflicted everyone sooner or later. He'd be over them very quickly, healthy young twig like him.

At the end of the week, the day before Alfred took groggily to his feet again, the duke received a letter from his late wife's cousin, Lord Francis Gaugham of Wellington Hall, near Cokeley. It told him all he needed to know, and all he had feared to hear, about Hermione Newbiggin. Beautiful or no, heiress or no, she was not on any account to become the future duchess of St. Ormer.

Let Alfred be infatuated, besotted, heartsmitten with any

woman, or any *hundred* women, provided they had no legal access to his inheritance. The woman who *could* get her hands on that money—the duchess—should be a good, solid, sensible type of gel, preferably plain (no temptations to philander, whatever Alfred himself might do in that line), preferably of a spendthrift family (she'd be disgusted at any extravagance), preferably from the ranks of the gentry or lower peerage (she'd know the correct social form and, even more important, she'd know when *not* to apply it—unlike the daughter of a new *industrial* peer, who would have got it all up from books and would apply it willy-nilly), and preferably from a family that littered a high proportion of heirs male.

Of course! The duke could have kicked himself for not having thought of her before.

CHAPTER TEN

SINCE HER FIFTEENTH birthday Flora Kinnaird had known that if she left her future for her parents to arrange, she'd end up a nobody married to a nonesuch and possessed of nothing. Like hanging, it had concentrated her mind wonderfully. She had inspected herself in her looking glass and sensibly decided that her beauty would advance her, if anything, even less than her parents' genial neglect. Of her own wit she could form no judgment, having no scope to give it exercise. Such talent as she had, then, she reasoned, had better be trained toward making herself an agreeable and useful person. If, on her way, she also made useful connections and acquired useful knowledge, so much the better.

Certainly she would achieve neither at home. Her parents were charming souls who could concentrate on nothing above five minutes. As a drunkard walks a chalk line, they lurched along that fine division which separates insolvency from outright bankruptcy. But they gave good dinners, kept an excellent cellar, could put the crustiest colonel or the most neurasthenic old maid at ease, never said a malicious word, always kept a confidence, and above all they smiled. Thus they also kept themselves like the dog with an appetite for fleas—nose just above water.

When her parents broke into her money pig to buy ribbons for her fifteenth birthday (laughing and saying wasn't it a dreadful thing to do), she knew she must find her own salvation. She was a whole week older before she devised a plan and put it into action.

Her father's heavily mortgaged lands marched with—indeed, were entirely surrounded by—those of the duke, actually bordering on the Abbey demesne and home farm. Flora had always been at liberty to ride through its deer park, fish its lakes, climb its trees, and sketch its picturesque corners. Not since she was nine had she fallen from a horse, so she was badly out of practice when she came off just seven days after her fifteenth birthday. Her screams could be heard from anywhere in the Georgian wing—which was not surprising since she was rather close. And, of course, the servants carried her indoors and, of course, Mrs. Kerns, the housekeeper, herself took charge of the bathing and bandaging and soothing—for Flora was, after all, a baronet's daughter.

Mrs. Kerns was flattered at the interest the child took in the house. "You keep it so beautifully," she told the housekeeper. "So *beautifully.*" And the hint of tears in her eyes moved Mrs. Kerns to pity; she knew well what a slatternly home the girl came from, for all its carefree warmth and gaiety. Naturally she had to stay the night, for though the ankle did not *look* swollen (thanks, as Flora herself said, to Mrs. Kerns's care and skill), it was clearly too painful for her to use.

"Poor mite," Mrs. Kerns said to Miss Lucas, her assistant, as she left the girl's room that evening. "There's an innate *niceness* in her as that family will spoil."

And when Mrs. Kerns helped Flora dress next day, and when Flora was still full of admiration for the beauty and neatness of the house, and when she went on to wish with a sigh that *she* might learn such domesticated arts, and when, finally, she added, with a cheerful laugh, that wasn't it funny how in the old days the young sons and daughters of gentry were sent off to fine houses where, under a great lord's protection, they learned all those skills they'd need in life—and weren't we silly nowadays to think all a girl needed was to be good at the piano and with her paintbrush . . . when she said all these things she seemed merely to voice thoughts already in Mrs. Kerns's head.

And then, when her ankle had recovered—a matter of some hours only—it seemed quite natural for the girl to follow her about . . . and then to help in little ways. And she really was helpful, too. And so attentive, and obliging, and diligent. Mrs. Kerns was quite glad to see her return the following day, and the next, and the next

. . . until, it seemed, Flora had become the one indispensable person in her household.

There was nothing she wouldn't do; within a year there was nothing she couldn't do. When a spark burned a hole in an old tapestry, she mended it with stitches identical to those done three centuries before. When Mrs. Kerns was ill and got behind with her accounts, Flora brought them to her bedside and, after only the least instruction, got them up to date.

And she never wasted a moment, either. Always asking questions—which would be annoying in another but not in her, she was eager to know and listened with such respectful attention. She'd even ask the little scullery maids how to scour pans and scrub floors. And she wasn't above rolling up her own sleeves when the occasion demanded—no false pride in her. Flora was always there where she was most needed, doing anything from baking the bread to stretching the linen. She could also count out the silver and rack the most delicate wines, for she was every bit as helpful to Mr. Williams, the butler, as she was to Mrs. Kerns.

In time she even did things beyond Mrs. Kerns's capacities. Once, for instance, when the housekeeper was buying linen for sheeting, Flora—in her nicest way—stepped into the bargaining and got off another three halfpence a yard. And although she was the sweetest and gentlest girl, there were times when an innate robustness asserted itself—as when a sleeping dog was run over in the Great Courtyard and the gardener hesitated to put it out of its misery; it was Flora who picked up a bootscraper and dashed out the poor dog's brains, though she wept for an hour after.

Nor did she confine her help to the domestic side alone. Once she was in a corridor upstairs in the east wing, near the duke's business room, doing a little sketch of the plasterwork there, when Mr. Dubedat, the duke's principal land agent, came out. His somewhat condescending smile faded the moment he actually looked at her work.

"That's quite powerful," he said. "Most girls do very weak, wishy-washy sort of things." And he went away looking thoughtful.

Next day he was back with some architect's plans and a few not very convincing thumbnail sketches. "His grace can't read plans," he said. "And I'm not much good at these bird's-eye views. Do you think *you* could . . . ?"

She not only could, she did. Sometimes it was necessary for her to ride out and see the setting for these new farm buildings with her own eyes, because the duke was keen that they should blend harmoniously with the surrounding countryside. Mr. Dubedat himself would escort her, and he found himself looking forward to the trips more and more, for the girl paid such flattering attention to everything he said, and showed such an intelligent interest in the business of managing so vast an estate.

Mr. Dubedat envied the gentleman who took her to wife. Few young girls nowadays were so hard-working, so intelligent, so competent—and yet so ladylike. He almost wished he had the courage to ask her himself, though of course he knew that she, being a baronet's daughter, was destined for a higher sphere.

Flora herself knew something of the high opinion in which the others held her—and it made her want to flinch from her very skin. She knew what she was like *inside.* And there she was far from being the resourceful, cool, level-headed young miss that Mrs. Kerns and Mr. Dubedat and the others thought they saw in her. Inside she was a prey to passions that only a will as strong and a necessity as abject as hers could hold in check.

She had her sights on a husband, of course—not a particular husband, but any husband of a certain standing and income: a man of the professional or landed classes (provided his land was unencumbered). Without a husband a woman had no place in society, could not entertain, could not even receive calls, and had to be accompanied everywhere. Anything she might do in life, therefore, had to start with the acquisition of a husband. Why, then, did she fall so unreasonably and so passionately in love with all the most unsuitable people? With stableboys. With her brothers' married friends. With young noblemen who, though they were bachelors, were far beyond her reach.

She would sit at her sewing or some other little task to help Mrs. Kerns, talking all the while of Domestic Economy, knowing that Mrs. Kerns was thinking *Ah! The innocent little treasure!* and, all that same while, her imagination—a creature utterly beyond her interior will—was rioting after the gorgeous, darling inamorato whose face and form currently haunted her every unguarded moment.

The hypocrisy of it plagued her (for she did not then know it was the hypocrisy of the entire female world to feign incurious apathy where the heart was wounded deepest) and kept her head from being turned by the praises she could not help earning.

Even the duke, who noticed only pretty girls, they said, would stop from time to time and press her hand or pat her head, saying things like "Whate'er she does is done with so much ease, In her alone 'tis natural to please," or " 'None but the brave deserves the fair!' "

She understood then—for she recognized the last quotation—that he was quoting the poet Dryden whenever he said slightly flowery things like that. She took to reading Dryden herself, at first merely in order to have something to quote back at his grace, but soon she was reading for the sheer pleasure of it.

It was not long before the duke found out her interest. He came upon her one day straightening some tapestries. The dust of ages upon them had made her fingers grimy. "Tut, tut," he said. " 'Too black for heav'n,' miss."

And she, laughing, turned them so that the clean backs of her hands and fingers showed and said, " 'And yet too white for hell,' sir!"

Delighted that she had caught the allusion, he took her off to his library and made her read from Dryden for half an hour. From that time on she had read to him almost every week.

She had become so much part of the furniture of the place, it was no wonder he had failed to think of her as the possible next duchess. But once he had thought of her in that light, he could think of no one else. The very next day he sent an invitation to Sir Eric and Lady Newbiggin and their daughter Hermione to visit Chalfont Abbey.

A social murder had to be arranged.

CHAPTER ELEVEN

WHEN THE SERMON was exactly ten minutes old, the duke's gold hunter watch rang a loud alarum. The only people it startled were Alfred and the Newbiggins—and the visiting preacher, who glared at the duke as a schoolmaster might glare at one of his charges. The duke was no more accustomed to such treatment than the Reverend Dr. Grenville was used to having his sermons curtailed by members of his congregation.

At the eleventh minute the duke produced—with a great deal of huffing and flapping—a large white handkerchief into which he blew his nose, to the accompaniment of a brontosaurian turnout of his windpipe and larynx.

The Reverend Dr. Grenville glared even harder, but went

doggedly on with his sermon. The congregation sat tense as a gunspring, hardly breathing.

At the twelfth minute the duke seized a poker and rattled it in the hearth of the old iron stove at his left. The fact that no fire burned within only made it ring out the louder. Dr. Penn, the incumbent minister, reached up through the carved screen that separated the choir stall from the pulpit and tugged at the visiting preacher's surplice. The Reverend Dr. Grenville plucked his garment free of the vicar's clutch and waited furiously for the duke to cease his rattling. He continued his sermon at exactly the point in mid-sentence where he had left off.

"All sorts going into the church these days," the duke said loudly to Alfred.

The atmosphere was now so strained it could have been cut into blocks and sold to a foundry. Again the vicar tugged at his preacher's surplice, but to no better effect.

"This church," the duke went on, looking about him, "cost me the extraordinary sum of sixteen thousand pounds. Ugly, what? I regret it now—the old place was very pretty. And the sermons much more to my liking, I may say. Short."

The preacher was pointing at him. "You, sir! Yes, *you!* If you are not instantly silent—"

He had no chance to complete the threat before the duke rose to his full height and bellowed: "Organist! Hymn one hundred and nine." Then, turning to the congregation: "Hymn one-oh-nine."

They were on their feet and clearing their throats before he repeated the number. The organist, too, was threading out a weak and wavering chord well before the bellows boys had pumped up the reservoir. He had to begin by picking out the tune in single notes.

They sang in relief. They sang to contain their laughter. They sang loud enough to drown out the Reverend Dr. Grenville, who, after one or two futile sentences, marched angrily off into the vestry. He had entirely quit the parish before the first worshiper came blinking out into the bright sunshine.

"You see," the duke said with Olympian calm. "No matter how tactful and pleasant one is, there's always some damfool who needs a blunderbuss fired into his ear trumpet before he takes one's meaning."

On the journey back from Great Marlow he halted the landau just beyond Frieth. "Why don't you young people stroll home from here across the fields?" he suggested. "Perfect day. Do you all good. Miss Kinnaird knows the way. Used to do it meself in younger days. Often."

And so Alfred found himself walking his beloved Hermione the two miles home, chaperoned by the agreeable, self-effacing little Flora. Their path was an old pack-horse trail along the gently sloping hill crest leading first up to the wide, bright sky and then down to the Abbey, approaching it by the Brighton wing.

The day was warm, lulled by a southern breeze, heady with the scent of new grass and new-green woodland. The ground was soft and dry underfoot. The rustle of silk and the swish of crinolines made Alfred's blood race. He offered an arm to both of the girls, because he could not, of course, offer one to Hermione alone. How different they were! Hermione managed to use every bump in their path as an occasion for a little extra squeeze, while Flora positively radiated her indifference through her touch. He was relieved. Once or twice lately he had caught a fleeting hint of interest—and more —when Flora's eyes had met his unawares.

"Well, Lord Alfred," Hermione said as they paused to look down at Chalfont Abbey, sparkling like a city in the sun. "And are you not a little overwhelmed by it all?"

"A *little*, Miss Hermione?" he laughed. "Utterly. I was protected from it at first because I was determined, as soon as possible, to get back to Cokeley and resume my former life."

"Oh? You've changed your mind then?" She was obviously delighted to hear it. "What brought that about, may I ask?"

"I don't think I should say."

"Debt," Flora said.

Alfred turned on her. "Miss Flora! If you know, I don't believe you should—"

"Oh, his grace won't object. He's open enough about it. In fact you made him very proud, Lord Alfred."

"Debt?" Hermione repeated anxiously.

"If his grace chooses to talk about it," Alfred insisted, "that's his affair. But it doesn't give us—"

"Oh don't be so unutterably middle class, Lord Alfred!" Hermione laughed. "What do you think an aristocracy *is* if it's not a high 'change of privileged information? How d'you think we survive?"

Alfred melted. How commanding she was!

Flora studied Alfred's response minutely.

"You were about to add, Miss Flora?" Hermione prompted.

"The duke is saying that Lord Alfred must be unique among heirs in that he wasn't remotely interested in the estate or its inheritance until he discovered it to be encumbered with debt."

Hermione's tingling laugh of disbelief stung Alfred. "It's true," he said. "Where's the merit in inheriting fifty thousand acres? But to free them of debt! Aye—to earn them back and pass them on. Free! Eh?"

Flora was so moved at his earnest enthusiasm that she had to draw several deep breaths to calm herself. She was sure now that he was the most marvelous man she could ever hope to meet.

Hermione laughed again. "Well! It's very noble, I'm sure. But you must also know it's quite unnecessary. The debts are the duke's, not the estate's. When he dies you may laugh in his creditors' faces; you'll owe them nothing."

"But the land—" Alfred began.

"The land is all entailed. Everything's entailed. Silver . . . furniture . . . everything. Even you won't own it, Lord Alfred—not in the sense that you could sell it—unless you can get a clever lawyer to break the entail. But you'll enjoy the income. And the duke's rent roll alone is over two hundred and fifteen thousand a year!" She closed her eyes in ecstasy.

"Did the duke not tell you, Lord Alfred?" Flora asked.

Alfred shook his head. "It seems so . . . well . . . dishonest."

"Pshaw!" Hermione said. "The lenders know it well enough. It's a risk they take—why else do they charge forty percent and more! Believe me, Lord Alfred, they've been paid once over already, if not twice. Besides, a lot of them lend with no expectation of being repaid. They'll lend a duke ten or twenty thousand and the duke will get their son a position as envoy somewhere, or as secretary at some ministry."

Alfred's ears burned.

"Is it true that the creditors can't sue?" Alfred asked.

Hermione smiled sweetly. "I've said enough, I feel. I'm sure Miss Flora is more adept in matters of *that* sort."

Flora laughed, a tinkling sort of laugh she had just that minute learned from Hermione. "Come, Hermione," she chided. "I may call you Hermione, mayn't I? And I positively insist you call me Flora . . ."

When Hermione looked put out at this, Flora went on. "There now! I'm wrong, I know. It should be you, as the *older* of us, who ought to lay aside formalities (except that I am the daughter of a much more ancient title). But we are going to be such friends, the three of us. I feel it in my bones."

What Alfred could feel in his bones—and flesh—was Hermione's suppressed fury. Part of him (the part that loved Hermione) was angry, too, with Flora; but another part (the part that loved all women, their company and their ways) rejoiced at little Flora and her quite unexpected show of spirit.

"What I was going to say, Hermione dear," Flora went on,

"was that we mustn't assume that because Lord Alfred *is* Lord Alfred, he has somehow magically acquired knowledge that is commonplace (and even tedious) in our sort of circle. For instance, Lord Alfred, Hermione was just now good-naturedly teasing me about the fact that my family is quite irresponsible, not to say reckless, about money; indeed, we have been smashed and restored too often to count. But I'm sure the joke passed right over your head. Did it not?"

Alfred gulped. "I'm sure Miss Hermione would not jest . . . er . . ."

He forced Hermione to rescue him. "Oh, Flora, my poor dear! I had no idea things were so *bad.* Lord Alfred, let me appeal to your sense of chivalry. Could you not ask the duke to grant poor dear Flora some small stipend . . . some pocket money, even? She is such a . . . a . . . a *use*ful person." She smiled. "To him, anyway."

"Nor," Flora went on evenly, "may we assume that Lord Alfred is aware of the many different ways in which a peer can make his money. In recent years there have been some baronets who have come into it by way of *trade* and stock exchange speculation! And though they are universally looked down upon, I believe they are by no means the worst of us."

"No, indeed," Hermione interrupted, "for at least they pay their way."

"Exactly!" Flora said—and with such delight you'd think agreement with Hermione was her life's dearest wish. "And that's why it's so noble of dear Lord Alfred to insist upon paying *his* way, and meeting the duke's obligations. That's why the duke, and I, and everyone who hears of it, are *so* proud of you, Lord Alfred."

Hermione was, for a moment, too furious to trust herself to speak. Flora, pretending to take her silence for agreement, said, "There now! I knew we should soon find ourselves in perfect harmony."

CHAPTER TWELVE

"YES, BUT CAN HE be talked out of this madness?" Lady Newbiggin asked. "I don't think he's the sort of person you could talk out of *anything*."

"Let him pile up a few debts of his own," Sir Eric said. "It won't require much talking then to change his tune."

"Oh!" Lady Newbiggin said crossly. "So like a man! You rush into things you know nothing about, with all the confidence in the world. You can't possibly know Lord Alfred well enough to be so sure."

He drew a deep breath and pouted.

"And now," she went on, "you're going to sulk and go on doing exactly what you intended doing all along. I don't know why you bother to discuss it with me when all you want is my silent agreement."

"Silent!" Sir Eric snorted as he left to go and talk with Hermione.

That same hour the duke had an interview with Flora, who, shortly afterward, went in search of Danielle, Hermione's pretty black-haired, blue-eyed French maid.

Alfred slipped between the two acres of embroidered linen that covered his vast bed, blew out his candle, and fell at once into the sweetly aching void where his stomach used to be.

She had kissed him! And he had kissed her! Again and again and time and again. He had brushed his lips, thistledown lightly, over the soft, perfect skin of her face. He had felt her lips breathe his name in an ecstasy of yearning upon his eyelids; close-to they had parted like some sweetly yielding, coral-colored sea creature—flesh of oyster, with teeth of pearls: "Oh, Alfred!" they had murmured. "Dearest, darlingest man! My Alfred, my own!"

My own! "Oh, Hermione . . ." he said it now, aloud, from within the sheets, conjuring her from the black-folded night. "Hermione, Hermione, Hermione . . ."

He had been within an ace of proposing to her but felt it would somehow devalue the moment by externalizing it. Spiritually they were already man and wife. The heat of their passion affirmed it, and left no stain of doubt or accusation. To propose would have been to invoke the world and its suddenly alien ways, the world of lawyers and endowments and settlements. His celestial union with her filled the universe and quite crowded out such temporal flummery.

"Oh, Hermione," he murmured again.

"Yes, my dearest?" she said.

The bed yielded to a gentle, but decidedly unethereal, weight. A faint, warm light flickered into the deep-mined cavern of his sheets, shedding a fitful gleam on its linen-fold walls. He had been lying in a crouchback huddle; now he straightened with a crisp friction that swished in his ears. The night air was a sudden chill on his forehead and cheeks.

But night itself had fled, banished by the candle whose gold lay tender and revealing on that slim neck and that most beautiful face, beautiful above all earthly beauty . . . Hermione's.

"Were you looking for me down there?" she asked, smiling archly. "Well, then . . ."

She almost dropped the candle on the bedside cabinet in her haste to climb between the sheets. "Brrrrr . . ." she shivered, and reached for her beloved.

What she embraced was an armful of bolster, hastily thrust between them by a chivalrous Alfred. His head appeared shyly over the top of it, offering a chaste pout of a kiss.

She clenched her fists in disappointment. "You think I'm very wicked," she said in sullen tones that might have come at the bitter conclusion of a long, fierce argument.

He was astonished. "No," he protested.

"I said I'd be with you all night."

"I thought you meant in *spirit.*"

She began to weep. "Oh, you must think me awful. How I despise myself now . . ."

"Of course not."

"I thought our love was so marvelous. I thought it would sanctify anything."

"It does! Oh, darling, it does, it does. *Anything!*"

"I wish I was dead. I feel so wretched."

Miserably he reached a hand across the bolster. It touched a silken jelly, a glancing caress that sped his fingers six inches northward to the firmer roundness of her shoulder. He squeezed with passion.

Her crying ceased. "Darling?" It was an ambiguous whisper, trembling with dread and husky with promise. A shiver tingled his neck, ran down his spine, and produced an erection.

"Yes?" Now the shiver was in his voice.

Her fingernails began to rake his arm, up and down, a slow and gentle provocation. "We are free creatures, you and I. Nothing we do can bind us. You understand that, don't you? Our love is perfect freedom."

He pulled his arm away, not understanding the drift of her words but aware that she was so calm again he had no further excuse to touch her.

"We are free to do just what we want," she insisted.

"And you, dearest, what d'you want?"

She sighed heavily. "Oh, Alfred, I'm afraid I'm not at all the nice sort of person you think I am. Yes, yes!" She stifled his objection with a soft finger, barely touching his lips. She caressed his lips. The hardness of his erection began to hurt him. "I *know* myself, my dear. I love luxury to distraction—almost as much as I love you. I love to spend money. If you knew what a pleasure it is to have a whole succession of milliners and haberdashers attend on me all day . . . oh! And if I had a *house!* What a horde of painters and paperhangers and carpet layers I should see! And how I should haunt the sale rooms! My father says give me my head and I'd empty the Bank of England . . ."

"Hermione, my most precious, why are you telling me this?"

"I want you to know, darling."

"Ye-es?"

"I mean—why I wouldn't—why we couldn't—why it would be impossible for our love to develop into . . . why we cannot bind one another by anything we do. Oh, Alfred, you are obtuse at times!"

"You mean . . . not marry?" He was aghast.

She slumped and nodded glumly. "It's out of the question, dearest."

"But . . . oh, Hermione, there's nothing I want more in all the world."

Alfred was not being entirely truthful. There was, in fact, just at that moment, one thing he wanted more. The pain of it was beginning to dominate his thoughts.

"But if you're determined to meet other people's debts," Hermione went on. "And, of course, I think it's most terribly honorable and noble of you, and I admire you for it more than anyone, more than the duke does, more even than dear, sweet little Miss Flora. But I just know I'll never match your goodness. I've told you what I'm like. Our worlds could never meet; yours all thrift and duty, mine all vanity and extravagance."

Alfred stared at her in misery; he seemed on the point of despairing agreement with her.

"But," she quickly added. "I love you so much I'm ready to give everything for one glorious night with you; my honor, my virtue, my name. Oh, Alfred, I do love you so!"

"But what will you do afterward?" Alfred asked, astonished at this degree of sacrifice.

She closed her eyes and lay rigid; her lips moved as if in prayer.

"You must think of that," Alfred said.

"I shall find a man who *can* support me," she said flatly.

He closed his eyes on his misery.

She, unseen now by Alfred, glared at him. "Or . . . several men, perhaps."

"No!" he cried, coming to life again.

"I won't think of that now," she said, relaxing joyfully. "All I want to think of is you—*us*. Tonight! All that exists is tonight. Forever." She reached out her arms.

"Hermione?" He fought his surrender. "Are you sure you cannot change?"

"Oh, quite sure."

"Impossible?"

"Utterly."

He almost choked on the words, but he said them at last: "Then I shall. For you I'd do even that. You shall not sacrifice your honor —I will sacrifice mine." He looked at her shyly and tried out the word: "*Bugger* the duke's creditors!"

Her eyes grew wide but he saw it was in delight, not horror. She hauled him over the bolster faster than he, impeded as he was, could squirm.

At the last moment a look of panic came into her eyes. "I have never . . . " she faltered.

He caressed the hair off her forehead, trapped in a light beading of sweat. "You'll see how gentle I can be," he promised. "I shall be gentle at the beginning and a gentleman at the end. Shall I put out the light?" He snuffed the candle before she could reply. Then, with trembling patience, he began to ease the silken nightdress from her body.

In the corridor outside, the duke waited until the noise of their congress grew rash; then he nodded encouragingly at Danielle. The little French maid dowsed her candle and opened the door, whose hinges the duke had ordered particularly to be oiled that very afternoon.

She slid noiselessly into the black and crossed the nine well-rehearsed steps to the great bed. Under cover of their rutting she slipped gently in beside them—if a six-foot gap can be called "beside"—and lay still as a night creature. Long after the other two had fallen asleep, she reminded herself of the rewards she had been promised if she could sacrifice this one night's slumber and remain undiscovered until it was time to be . . . discovered.

CHAPTER THIRTEEN

"Duke!" Sir Eric's delight at seeing the duke—fully dressed, in the corridor, slap-bang outside Lord Alfred's room—was unfeigned.

"Thursday morning," the duke said. "Tenants' complaints. See them at five, keeps the congenital moaners away. What's your excuse?"

"Excuse?"

"Yes. Why are you here?"

"Oh. Well—I left a book in my daughter's room. Then, happening to wake early, I went to get it—only to find her bed deserted."

The duke's eyes narrowed. He looked at Alfred's door and frowned. "Housecrawlin'?" he snapped. "Is that what you think?"

Sir Eric drew back alarmed. "Of course not, sir. Naturally not. I was . . . ah . . . merely . . . er . . . looking for an empty room on this side whose windows would give a view of the formal garden. Hermione has taken such a liking to it, I thought she might have gone for an early walk in the dew . . ."

"Let's see." The duke opened the door to the empty room beside Alfred's and strode to the tall windows.

Sir Eric was at his heels. The two men stared down at a formal garden they both knew would be empty of Hermione. Sir Eric looked at the dividing wall to Alfred's room. "It never even crossed my mind, sir, but . . . er . . . you don't think . . . ?"

The duke's face turned a plethoric purple. "I'll horsewhip the scoundrel if that's it," he roared.

Sir Eric wrung his hands. "Careful, sir. Careful. Let us be careful. Lady Newbiggin and I have no more desire to be ruined than you wish to be embarrassed."

A rare compassion softened the duke's face. A moment later he conferred an even rarer privilege. "My friend," he said, "it shall not come to that. If there's been any . . . ermhurmmm . . . the House of du Bois will know where its duty lies. You may be sure of that!"

Sir Eric found it hard to disguise his joy—until the duke, half turning away, added in tones of equal reassurance: "What! If we couldn't find her a goodish sort of baronet somewhere." Then, catching sight of Sir Eric's alarm, he added hastily, like a traveler scraping out his last penny for a highwayman, "Or a *viscount*. Yes! Why not!"

He chose not to see Sir Eric's dejected response to this magnificent promise; instead he led him back to the corridor—just in time to see Hermione making a bad job of a clandestine exit from Alfred's room.

She darted back into the doorway, hesitated, looked wildly up and down the corridor, and burst into tears.

The duke was suddenly filled with good-humored envy for Alfred and this night past; whatever else she was, Hermione was also a most beautiful woman. The feeling was colored, too, with sadness. It would be so easy to be lost in love with such beauty; poor Alfred was in for a hard time of it.

But—he squared himself—it had to be done. In *this* world, the world of inheritance, estates, and titles, she was just another maidenhead with a price on it. And in her case the price was unacceptable. "What's this, young lady?" he asked, his sternness modulated by a suggestion of suspended judgment coupled with respect for her tears.

"Oh, Papa! Papa!" She moved toward him but he, miserably playing out a farce he now suspected to be pointless, repulsed her. "Wretched creature!" he said, with seven out of ten for conviction.

Before either daughter or duke could adjust to this lackluster performance, they were all halted by the unmistakable trill of a very feminine giggle through the partly open door to Alfred's room, followed by his utterly unguarded: "What the devil!"

Hermione's tears ceased at once. A look of wild alarm replaced them as she half-recognized the voice behind the giggle. She stared at her father. His eyes seemed unable to focus on anything; his tongue heaved in pointless spasm on the floor of his slackly open mouth.

"Yes!" the duke agreed. "What the devil?" And he strode into Alfred's room. Hermione was hard behind. Sir Eric, still stunned, drifted in more slowly, in time to see a lithe, young, naked female dive beneath the covers beside a still-astonished Alfred.

"Danielle!" Hermione shrieked.

The duke crossed to the bed and threw back the covers.

Alfred sat up in outrage.

Danielle, prone, squirmed like an eel, as if she might find some trick of sinking through the sheets and feather mattress.

The duke roared with laughter. "Mistress and maid! Well now, don't that put a different complexion on things!"

Alfred, crabwise, put some space between himself and Danielle. "She . . ." He gestured at her wriggling body. "I didn't . . . we never . . . this was no . . ." and a dozen other forms of denial crowded one another to the point of incoherence.

"Alfred! Oh, Alfred!" Hermione wept with a fervor that could only be genuine.

"What's the meaning of this, sir?" her father demanded of Alfred and the duke impartially.

Lady Newbiggin strode into the room. Her eyes took in the scene with one sweep. She turned in sour triumph to her husband. "Meaning, Sir Eric?" she sneered. "Why, sir, it means you've been trumped! Trumped, finessed, outplayed, Machiavellied, and fainagued. We must save what we can." She turned from her husband. "Duke, I trust we may rely on your discretion? No word of this must go beyond the six of us now in this room. I presume you have some arrangement with *that* creature." She tilted her jaw angrily toward Danielle.

"Duke!" Alfred cried in a mixture of anguish and fury. "No!"

The duke pulled a heavy coverlet from the bed and threw it over Danielle. "Go now," he told her before he turned to Alfred. "No, what?"

"Not you!"

"Don't you see, my boy? It was a plot between them to fleece us; they were all in it."

"No!" Alfred implored Hermione.

Her eyes fell. "I still love you," she said defiantly.

"And I you!" He turned back to the duke. "It makes no difference," he said. "I still love her, and I'll still marry her."

"So you shall, my dear fellow," the duke said evenly, as if Alfred had just passed some kind of secret test.

Hermione and her father exchanged an involuntary glance of hope, which she swiftly transferred to Alfred.

"On one condition," the duke added. "The estate will be entailed, of course, and the income put in trust for your heirs. You will have an allowance from it of . . . let us say, forty thousand pounds."

"No!" Hermione shouted.

"Darling!" Alfred said. "Surely forty thousand will be more than—"

She stamped her foot. "Oh, do be quiet, Alfred dear. You know nothing about it. I need, I mean *we* need at least another . . ." She turned to her father. "Papa—to have a daughter a duchess, that must be worth . . . would you allow two hundred thousand a year?"

The man was at bay.

"Yes, dear," his wife said. "It was worth her honor, but is it worth two hundred thou? Here's a nice balancing."

"Darling!" Alfred said. "We can manage on only forty. As long as we have each other. Surely that's the . . ."

She did not seem to be listening, so intently were her eyes fixed on her father's face.

At last he came to a decision. "We shall do a lot better," he said, "than this three-farthing dukedom."

Hermione gave one cry of anger and ran from the room.

"Darling!" Alfred shouted as he leaped from the bed. And though he was not more than a few seconds behind her, she had already bolted her door by the time he reached it. Dejectedly he returned to his own room. As he drew near he heard Sir Eric saying, obviously to the duke, "Oh, yes, sir, we shall be counting on something a hundred times more reliable than your honor and discretion. Indeed! We shall be counting on your sense of self-preservation. You shall learn, sir, that a man with a debt has a ball and chain at his ankle, be he commoner or duke. And whoever agrees to pick up that burden and carry it awhile has a dozen chances a day to tweak the chain and make the wearer's life a misery. Be he commoner or duke!"

PART TWO

1849-1850

SPERNO ME
RECIPERE AUT
MUTARI

Love Conquers All

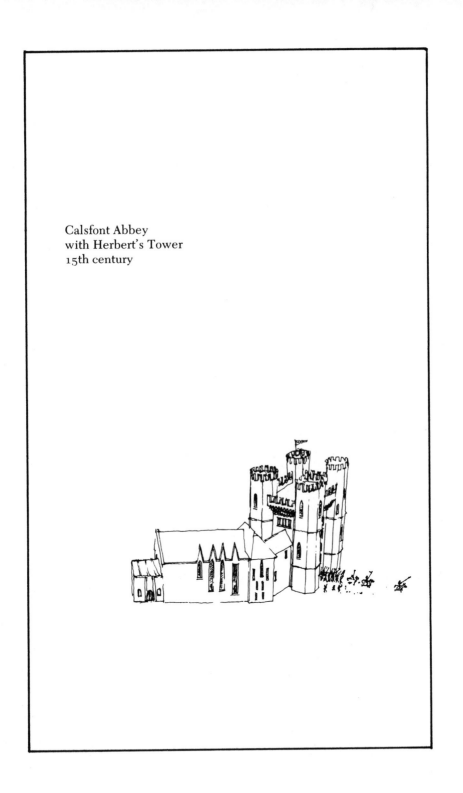

Calsfont Abbey
with Herbert's Tower
15th century

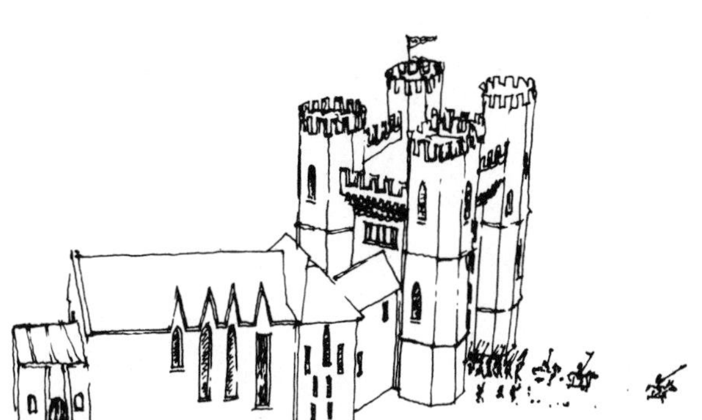

CHAPTER FOURTEEN

OVER THE FOLLOWING weeks the duke allowed Alfred no time to mope—nor to escape. When Alfred insisted he must go back to Cokeley, "just for a day or so," to see to his business, the duke sent instead for Willerby, the agent he had put into the firm to manage it; the man gave Alfred the supreme disappointment of learning that the business was thriving better than he had dared to hope even in his most arrogant moments.

"But how?" Alfred asked in amazement.

"It's the secret of all great enterprise," the duke said. "You've hit upon it earlier than most, that's all. Believe me, I've seen a score of firms ruined by proprietors who simply could not delegate their powers and leave a good man be." He laughed. "It's the secret of 'the duking business,' too," he added.

Alfred was thrown then into the business of the estate and household as if the world ended at the boundaries on Mr. Dubedat's maps. He learned the elements of sitting a horse and the simpler movements and paces, not on any of the duke's thoroughbreds but on a tolerant, good natured half-bred gelding hunter whose stall plate read "Napoleon" but whom everyone knew as "Boney."

He was fitted out in gentleman's clothes by the duke's own tailor, the hunt tailor in Great Marlow. And he was kitted out by Meyer & Mortimer in full dress, undress, and mess dress as a major in the Stormers.

"Naturally," the duke explained, "if there's a war or foreign tour of duty, you'd resign and let some eager young professional take your place."

Alfred watched the duke command a couple of ceremonial parades before he himself was put to inspecting massed ranks of broomsticks, pails, rakes, and ropes doing duty as platoons of infantrymen and officers—all under the vigilant eye of Color Sergeant Treadwell from the regiment. Between drills he learned the details of regimental life, from the duties of each rank to the role of the light infantry in the army as a whole. From there he soon progressed to the regiment's history and battle honors.

"Though the one who could tell you most about that would be Miss Flora," Sergeant Treadwell said. "She copied it all up for the duke something lovely, with all them shields and colors and little pictures and battle plans and all."

From Mr. Dubedat he learned how the estate was managed day to day. The fifty-thousand-odd acres were divided into "Bucks" and "Oxon" divisions, about two-thirds being in Buckinghamshire, and one third in Oxfordshire (plus those few hundred acres over the Thames in Berkshire). The larger Bucks section was again divided into Bucks I and II, giving three roughly equal divisions, each of about seventeen thousand acres.

Each division had its own agent, under Mr. Dubedat, responsible for supervising the gamekeepers, water bailiffs, farm bailiffs, and a corps of masons, plumbers, carpenters, hedge builders, fencers, drainage men, and lumberyard workers. Alfred was amazed at the depth and extent of the man's knowledge of all the estate's tenants, but Dubedat himself pooh-poohed it: "The one who really knows them" he said, "is Miss Flora. Her family, of course, has been here for generations and they're greatly liked. Not respected, I wouldn't say, but vastly liked. You go into Great Marlow on a market day. If she's there with Sir Duncan, her father, you'll see every farmer there'll stop and pass the time of day. There's nothing they don't get to hear of, and all in the most amiable way."

That evening, when the ritual of reporting his day's learning was done, Alfred asked the duke to tell him more about young Flora, whom everyone seemed to hold in such high regard.

"Oh . . ." The duke was dismissive. "Just a useful little body. Nothing more. Plain little thing. No dowry. She'll be lucky to make a match with a good farmer. Why?" His eyes riveted Alfred, cold with amusement. "Not thinking of *her*, I hope."

"No, no!" Alfred said hastily and fervently. "All the same, the people around here appear to hold a very high opinion of her."

The duke seemed astonished; then he was thoughtful. "I'll say one thing in favor of a plain gel. Advantage over a pretty one. A pretty gel will want all your time and attention, but a plain one, if she's any sense in her—and little Miss Flora and common sense are all of a piece throughout—knows that men are but children of a larger growth. She knows our eyes, and more, must wander from time to time, and she's a good deal more complaisant about it than your Cleopatras." The duke watched him closely. "Still," he added,

"I fancy we'll do a great deal better for you than Miss Flora, what!" And he laughed hugely at the promise.

"Indeed." Alfred laughed too, never having thought of Flora in that light. Later he was less sure he liked the idea that the duke was fishing the matrimonial waters on his behalf.

It was curious how Flora's name kept cropping up. When Mrs. Kerns was showing him around the house and explaining its running, it was: "Miss Flora knows the history of that. . . . Miss Flora can tell you all about Sèvres porcelain. . . . Miss Flora mended that for me."

And even Mr. Williams, when he was showing Alfred the cellars, explaining the management of wines, and allowing him to taste a few, said, "The one with a real palate for wines now is . . ."

"Let me guess," Alfred interrupted. "Miss Flora!"

"Ah! She can sniff a corked wine at ten paces."

Alfred began to wonder how the duke could dismiss her so lightly.

Since Hermione had been tricked out of his life, he had been too busy to think about her by day, and usually too tired to think about her for long at night. He knew that she had tried to trap him into marriage, yet he could not believe it had all been faked. She had loved him as much as he still loved her. He was sure of it. But then, with his growing awareness of his future responsibility, he found it difficult to maintain the simplicity of his adoration. Common sense told him to think forward, to think of the dukedom and its responsibilities, to think of himself fulfilling that role, to think of the sort of woman he would need as duchess at his side. Less and less did it amount to Hermione; more and more, especially as he talked to those most intimately concerned with the house and estate, it added up to . . . Flora.

He tried to think of Flora lying in bed beside him and was astounded to find that he could not. A curious and quite new sense of shame erased her image in the moment he achieved it. For the first time in his life he felt *unworthy* of a woman.

The phantom that crept in instead was of a lithe young body wriggling over him, swinging two swollen brown nipples a warm half-inch from his face and giggling in a French accent.

Danielle! At last he found a simple acre in the new map of his emotions; a bit of terrain that looked reassuringly like the Old Country. But what had happened to Danielle?

CHAPTER FIFTEEN

"I HOPE I DID RIGHT, my lord, in bringing Miss Flora along?" Mr. Dubedat asked.

"Good heavens yes," Alfred assured him. "She's an ornament to any outing." He smiled at her. She smiled vaguely back but obviously had not caught his words above the clatter of their horses' hooves upon the cobblestones. He leaned forward and shouted to her. "I say you're an ornament to any outing, Miss Flora."

She smiled but held up a finger to warn him she would dissent from this opinion when she could be heard. Soon they passed around Herberts Tower and onto the softer gravel walks of the west gardens, making for the woodland rides on that side of the demesne.

"It's kind of you to say so, Lord Alfred, but"—she patted the satchel that hung to the right of her saddle—"today I am a maid of work."

"The day Miss Flora confines herself to being an ornament," Dubedat said, laughing, "I mean, of course, a *mere* ornament, this estate will grind to a halt."

"Oh, come, sir!" she chided.

"It's the truth," Dubedat answered. "I don't know how we ever managed without you."

"You see, Lord Alfred?" she said. "The servants of the aristocracy are born flatterers."

"I believe you, Miss Flora. They even practice it behind one's back—at least in your case they do."

She blushed and tossed her head impatiently. "Those are our lands." She pointed to some fields across the valley. "Do you see a difference between them and the duke's? We'll get a clearer view when we come out the other side of this woodland."

The trees were in full summer leaf now, turning the broad rides into high naves through a vast cathedral of green. Birdsong fell upon them from the minstrel canopy of foliage. Like all Chiltern woods, this one was almost exclusively of beech. The delicate silver fawn of the smooth trunks and branches seemed to glow with an inner light that made the air warm and only half real. Here and there earlier landscape gardeners had cut dells into the light-denying upper story of the beech and there they had planted other trees and shrubs to control and direct the otherwise infinite perspective of trunks and sapling stems.

They had imported boulders, too, and peat by the ton, to succor rhododendrons and azaleas, now at the very peak of their blossom. From time to time all three riders were forced to halt and stand in silent wonder at the pink and orange and purple flames that burned with supernal brilliance through the green gloom.

"Travel the world over," Dubedat said, "you'll find no one who understands landscape like the English. We've brought home the best from everywhere, and we've blended it better than anywhere."

They broke out again into open country through a grove of Wellingtonias, brought from America and planted by the duke about twenty-five years earlier; now almost thirty feet tall, they made a brash contrast with the gracefully mature woodlands behind them.

"You may live to see them rival our beeches, sir," Dubedat told Alfred. "And you, Miss Flora. But not I."

Flora smiled at Alfred. There was something comforting in the thought that his life and hers were yoked to such a slow and steady pacemaker as this grove of young trees.

"There now," she said, pointing at the stream that ran along the foot of the valley, which was now only half a mile away over a stretch of open deer park. "Our land. The duke's land. See the difference?"

"Yours is much the darker," he said.

"Come and see why. Let's canter."

Side by side the three of them cantered over the springy turf to a broad and shallow ford where the horses had to pick a fastidious way among the pebbles. Alfred took a fearful bumping.

"Whoo!" he said, breathless. "I wouldn't want to do too much of that."

Flora drew breath to speak, then paused. "Poor Lord Alfred," she said at last. "You must be tired of all the world telling you what to do and what not to do."

"Go on," he said. "If there's a way of cantering without producing headaches, I'm the most willing of learners. I hate doing things badly, anyway. I mean to be the best horseman in the Home Counties before I'm done."

So she told him how to sit back, and sit deep, giving with the horse's movement.

Alfred followed the advice and found an instantaneous improvement. They cantered up a low rise to another stretch of woodland. Lazy smoke drifted among the trees until it was teased to wisps by the stronger breezes at the open edge.

"They're burning some loppings here," Dubedat said. "I'll just see they've been sensible about it. No need for Boney to come in; he's a bit wary of fire and smoke." He rode alone into the wood.

"You didn't tell me what causes the difference between your land and ours, Miss Flora," Alfred prompted.

"In a word, Lord Alfred: drainage. Did you notice how firm the going was, even beside the river?"

Alfred nodded. She had a lovely voice, he thought.

"In our fields we could hardly have *walked*, let alone cantered. You look at our lands and you'll see what the duke's were like twenty years ago."

She broke off and looked shrewdly at Alfred. "May I be very bold, sir, and ask what you think of him—as a landlord, as a proprietor of land?"

"He pretends to know as little about it as I."

"Ah! So you know it's a pretense with him?"

"When all the books you see in his study and beside his bed are on husbandry and cereals and breeding and rotations and drainage? Why does he pretend, I wonder? Is anyone deceived by it?"

"It was the style of his youth. He belongs to the age when the worst you could say of a man was '*enthusiast.*' To be stoic, calm, and aloof was all—except in their amusements, of course. There it was *comme-il-faut* (even if it bored them to distraction) to show all the enthusiasm they shunned in their genuine interests." She looked keenly at Alfred. "It was a style. I'm glad you're not deceived by it, sir. So many young aristocrats today have taken it as a kind of gospel text. They really do know nothing, and care less."

Her gaze did not falter; in the end it was Alfred who looked away. What a powerful sense of conviction she radiated. He could quite understand why everyone talked of her as a sort of touchstone of competence and calm assurance. He liked it—as he liked all excellence.

"It must have cost a lot," he said, nodding toward the land. "All this drainage and enclosure. All the improvements."

"It still does," Flora said and pointed to her satchel. "This site we are on our way to see, this new farmhouse, is one of forty or more the estate has built or is building."

"Do you think he might have overextended the estate?"

"A peer—especially a duke—can extend himself as far as he likes. Or as far as his creditors will allow. Dear Miss Hermione was right there. What a very *nice* girl she was, by the by. I do hope she comes on another visit soon?"

"Yes, indeed," Alfred lied with blithe earnestness. "Next month, I believe. For a much longer visit. But, to get back to what we were saying," he went on, "there *was* the Duke of Buckingham, you know."

"Ah, but he really did go crash. That was railway speculation. A very different thing altogether. In twenty years, when the St. Ormer debts are paid off, this will be one of the most profitable estates in England."

"As long as agricultural prices hold."

She smiled. "What? With two railways running through the estate, and all London to feed? And Birmingham?"

He frowned; he knew of no railways. There were none on the maps, except the main line through Maidenhead and Reading, neither of which towns was within the estate.

"Oh, they'll be built," Flora said confidently. "There are those who question the duke's wisdom in investing so heavily in those lines—especially after his grace of Buckingham's experiences—but . . ." She shook her head in disagreement.

To press her further Alfred persisted. "It's still all agriculture, isn't it though? Feeding London. Feeding Birmingham."

She merely smiled, half turning away.

"You don't think so, Miss Flora?" he asked.

"What does a mere girl know, Lord Alfred?"

"Come now. You're playing the duke's game, pretended ignorance."

She laughed then. "Look behind us," she said. "What do you see?"

He followed her gaze. "Trees . . . smoke . . ."

"Nothing else?"

"Undergrowth . . ."

"No chairs? No tables? Not a single dresser or wardrobe? Beech is a beautiful wood, you know."

"Ah!" He understood then and looked again at the wood with new interest—and at Flora.

She gazed calmly back at him, still with that cool smile on her lips. Then, with an air of laying all the cards of a very good hand on the table, she added: "And if timber still seems a mite too agricultural, I may mention the hard chalk and limestone to the north of Bucks I. They are only hand-worked quarries at the moment, but a nearby railway could make them highly profitable. And, of course, there's sand and gravel everywhere."

He knew then that, if he was to be the next duke, Flora had to be the next duchess. There was no quality or qualification for the part that she lacked.

Could he love her? Could he learn to love her, in time? Did it even matter, when so much else about her was perfect for the role? The dukedom was the thing—its prosperity, the service it could give the whole countryside, the general good. What was one man's love beside that?

And there was always Danielle, if he could find her.

Or a hundred like her, if he could not.

Yes, he thought, pleased at his self-sacrifice for the sake of the dukedom, Miss Flora would do very well. Very well indeed.

CHAPTER SIXTEEN

"DUKE? Why are you always so dismissive about young Flora?" Alfred asked that evening.

"Never mind Flora," the old man answered eagerly. "I have just the wife for you, my boy. The Marquis of Morne's second daughter. Name of Gertrude. Not the young man's vision exactly—nor, I may say, is she much of an old man's dream. She looks like one of Lord Derby's great red deer. But she'll soon fatten. They all run to fat, her tribe—or waddle if they're already past running. But never mind; their purses are even fatter. She'll bring a dowry that will all but clear the estate of debt. A million and a bit! Say?"

"I said, why are you so dismissive of Flora?"

"*And,*" the duke tumbled on, "they litter males like enchanted rabbits. You'd have a platoon of sons about you in no time."

"Flora, duke."

"Damn Flora! She's as much use to you as a fart to a bronze horse. But Lady Gertie's worth a Jew's eye—think of that."

Alfred closed his eyes wearily. "Very well, sir, I'll see your Lady Gertie—if merely out of courtesy, I suppose."

"The only thing against Flora is her family. Met 'em yet? Met her pater, Sir Feckless himself?"

"I've not yet been invited."

"Invited!" The duke laughed. "Do what the rest of the county does: turn up. But don't go before midday, unless you've forgotten how pigs live and sleep."

Alfred looked at the duke levelly. "I think I might do that, sir."

When he had gone the Duke clapped his hands and chortled heartily. His scheme to make Alfred marry Flora was unfolding well.

From the deserted and partly unroofed gatelodge, two large Berkshire sows stared up at him with nervous curiosity, grunting by turns. Alfred looked again at the gateposts. One read "Rodings," the other "Hall"; even though they were obscured by ivy, the letters were unequivocal. But the rusted gates had clearly not been opened in years. Nor could any horseman, much less a carriage, have negotiated the drive, whose surface was a patchwork of mud and mending, whose canopy was hung with low branches of many years' growth, and whose edges were invaded with brambles and docks of the same vintage. There must be another way in.

He urged Boney along the lane that skirted the demesne of Rodings Hall. The boundary wall, or ex-wall, was reduced to a string of stone heaps and cairns. After a quarter of a mile he came to a larger break, where the land was poached with many hooves and rutted with carriage wheels. Beyond, a makeshift lane wound drunkenly among the junglelike regrowth before it burst in surprise on the remains of a carriage sweep.

A horse was trotting somewhere nearby, behind an unkempt thicket of rhododendron. On the far side of the sweep Alfred had the fleeting impression of a large, dirty house, roofed in a mixture of thatch, tarred canvas, and broken slates.

"Hold her, will you!"

A breathless young man about his own age came running up behind a mare on long reins. "Whoa!"

Alfred leaned over and caught her by the bridle. She shied, almost unseating him from Boney; but she settled as soon as the young man came up and caught her head on the other side.

"Thanks." He began to fiddle with the reins.

He was dressed in riding breeches, a gorgeous red waistcoat, and a fine cotton shirt with its sleeves rolled up.

"I'll lunge her for a while." He grinned at Alfred, who took to him at once. "She's going to make our fortune, this filly."

Alfred, looking at the house, said, "Not before time."

"No!" He laughed. "You must be Lord Alfred Boyce, eh? The long-lost heir."

"I never felt lost," Alfred said.

The young man paused and looked at him. "No, of course you didn't." They both laughed. "I'm Ian Kinnaird, by the way." Holding the martingale traces in his left hand, he reached his right across to shake Alfred's. He was one of those magnetic, instantly friendly characters. Alfred took to him at once.

"Look, I shan't be long at this but do go in if you wish," Ian said. "Wander around. You're bound to meet someone."

"May I stay and watch?" Alfred dismounted and tied Boney to a stake that may once have supported a shrub.

"By all means."

Ian lunged the filly until she was in a fair lather, then he relented and released the martingale straps. When Alfred watched her stretch, his own muscles felt grateful for the relief. He had not realized to what degree his body had identified itself with the beast.

A groom, carrying a rug, came running from the house; moments later he was leading both horses away.

Ian looked toward the front door. "Care for a stroll?" he asked. "Or . . . er . . . did you come here to see . . . ?"

"Oh, let's stroll," Alfred said.

Ian changed direction immediately, leading Alfred toward what had once been a formal garden. "You're lucky it's a dukedom," he said.

"So I keep being told. You've no idea how isolated it seems up there."

"Be thankful for that."

"Why?"

"You're so far above the reach of people's barbs that most won't even bother to aim them."

"Barbs?"

Ian cleared his throat uncomfortably. "Well . . . you know, surely. You're a decent fellow, anyone can tell. But if you'd jumped suddenly into a low peerage—a barony or viscountcy, even an earldom—any of the bottom three—there'd be plenty who'd consider you within striking distance. And even though you can't help your origin, they'd hold it against you. You know what people are like."

When Alfred did not respond, he asked anxiously, "I've not offended you, I hope?"

"No, Ian," Alfred said thoughtfully. "But you must believe me to be an awful fool."

"Good heavens, no! Why?"

"It's never occurred to me I had an *'origin'* in the way you said it."

"And you grew up in *England?*"

"Oh, I've always known about the class system, of course. I just never thought of it as applying to me."

"Good God!"

"I mean, I always knew I was going to make a fortune somehow. It wasn't an ambition, or a hope, or a dream. I *knew* it. It was a destiny. I was sure of it, you see. So I knew that when I'd made my money I'd be as good as anybody else. No better, no worse. As good as. So in my own mind, you see, I was *already* as good as the next man. The world had to wait to see it, but I didn't." He laughed.

"Well!" Ian grinned and shook his head. "It explains a lot, I must say. It explains how you've managed to stay so cool-headed. The duke couldn't fathom you at all. Not at first."

"Oh, I see! He has the measure of me now, has he?"

"So we hear."

"Perhaps I am not the only one to be protected by delusions."

Ian's smiling nod allowed that such indeed might be the case; but a fleeting narrowness of his eyelids conveyed equally that it might not.

"Dukes certainly aren't above the barbs of other dukes, though," Alfred went on. "You should hear St. Ormer's opinions of his peers. He—"

"I don't believe I should," Ian warned. "If his grace confided strong opinions to you, it was as a future duke yourself. If he'd heard you'd shared them even with a marquis, he'd have your balls for breakfast."

"Oh." Alfred closed his eyes and shook his head. "Yes, it's a field set with ten thousand traps."

"What?"

"The aristocracy. All your alliances. All your secret knowledge. That vast unspoken-about web of gossip and intrigue you all carry about with you, ready for immediate use. Like a second set of instincts. Like sheathed claws. I'll never fathom it."

The jungle around had now grown so thick that further progress was impossible. They had to turn back.

Alfred paused, debating with himself. "See here, Ian," he said at last. "I may as well confide in you. Do you mind?"

"I'd be honored, old sport."

"You're the only fellow I know. You don't think our acquaintance is too . . ."

"Please!"

"Well . . ." Alfred drew breath and straightened himself. "The truth is . . . the fact is . . . the duke wants me to marry some dreadful fat heiress, Lady Gertrude Something. And I don't want her—not even if she brought ten millions. When I'm duke, there's only one lady I want at my side. And that's your sister, Flora."

If Ian had been carrying anything, he'd have dropped it that instant.

Alfred looked at him in dismay. "Am I being too presumptuous?" he asked.

Ian laughed weakly. "Presumptuous! Good God alive, man—"

"I'll withdraw the suggestion if . . . I mean—I haven't . . ."

Ian closed his eyes tight and put tension into all his muscles. "Calm! Eeeeasy! Easy!" He spoke to himself just as he had spoken to the lathered filly. Then he relaxed and opened his eyes again. "Tell me once more. You want to marry Flora?"

"Yes."

"And you were coming here to ask her?"

"Her father. Your father."

"Ah!" Light dawned. "Ah! You've already asked Flora?"

"No. I thought the proper thing would be to ask Sir Duncan first."

Ian's eyes narrowed. "Did the duke tell you to do that?"

"No! Good God, no! He wants me to marry this awful Lady Gertie."

"So this would be against the duke's wishes?"

"I want it all signed and sealed—and open to an action for breach of promise—before word of it gets back to him."

Ian was silent awhile. "Tell me, Alfred, have you not mentioned Flora to him at all?"

"Often. But every time I do, he keeps dismissing her and praising this Lady Gertrude . . . I wish I knew the family name. The title is Morne, the Marquis of Morne. But what's the family name?"

"Aren't they in *Debrett*, or *Burke's?*"

"No. It must be a new marquisate, you see. The duke's editions are both twenty years out of date. He says nobody worth knowing about has been born since then."

Ian began to laugh.

"What's so amusing?" Alfred asked.

"Oh . . . ah . . . I don't know, Alfred. All of us go about in fear and trembling of your Duke Augustus. And here you are . . ." Words failed him; he shook his head in admiration. "You must already know that nothing touches the aristocracy so closely as questions of marriage, money, breeding, and inheritance. The mildest, milkiest-wateriest baronets have turned into foam-in-the-mouth slayers when threatened from those quarters. And here's the duke wants you to marry a marquis's daughter worth millions, and here's you getting set to engage the penniless daughter of a spendthrift baronet!" He patted Alfred on the back. "I hope you have your gallows speech ready. You certainly deserve every medal going."

Alfred stood irresolute for a moment but then framed himself to the decision. "No," he said firmly, "I have to back my judgment against his. Flora is the duchess for me. And she'll be the best in the kingdom."

Ian's admiration was genuine. "Well," he said, scraping the barrel for comfort. "The duke has an eye for courage."

"It isn't courage, really," Alfred said. "Dukes and marquises, earls and viscounts and barons—they're still like children's games to me. Make-believe. I've lived in a world where, for all practical purposes, they just don't exist."

"Don't exist!" Ian was scandalized.

"Too remote, you see. It's different in the country. I was amazed when the duke walked through Great Marlow and everybody bowed and scraped. I've never seen the like of that. You'd never see that in a city, not in Birmingham, anyway. The only peer I knew was Sir Eric Newbiggin."

"A baronet isn't a peer," Ian said.

"Well, near-peer then. Anyway, it was his money that was important, not his title. So"—he grinned at the shock which still showed in Ian's face—"no courage involved, you see. Just plain ignorance."

Ian was plainly going to contradict this, but they were now in sight of the house again and something more urgent deflected him. "Look," he said. "Don't tell the pater or he'll fall down dead with joy. My advice is to go straight to Flora. Leave her to tell the pater."

"Is she not here?"

"No. She's at the Abbey—as always."

"Tscha!" Alfred stamped in annoyance. "You could hide an army in that place."

"Or a mistress?" Ian grinned.

Alfred was momentarily embarrassed.

"Come on!" Ian urged. "We can't live entirely for pleasure. A man, especially a duke, needs a mistress to remind him of life's deeper and more solemn purposes."

Alfred still did not know what to say. Ian was, after all, Flora's brother. He gave a lopsided smile.

"I wasn't brought up to this sort of attitude at all," he said.

Now it was Ian's turn to be slightly uncomfortable. He

shrugged one shoulder, then the other, and looked aimlessly around.

"I mean," Alfred added, to help him, "I was brought up believing there's a wild-oats time and then—you know—a respectable time."

"Ah!" Ian understood at last. "But a mistress isn't what you'd call 'wild oats.' "

"No?"

"No! A mistress is quite different. Look, no decently brought up young woman wants a husband about her every night. She'd find it grotesque—and so ought he. So the answer, you see—if you can afford it, and have any respect for your wife—is a mistress. There's tons of surplus women apparently, so you also have the moral satisfaction of keeping at least one of them out of vice." He nudged Alfred and grinned. "Or two? Lucky beggar!"

Alfred laughed in astonishment to hear all the morality he had ever learned stood on its head.

"Just one tip," Ian added, serious again. "No one would care much what manner of girl you keep now. As heir presumptive, I mean. But there is a sort of feeling that a *duke's* mistress ought herself to be of good class, a daughter of the aristocracy. Some dukes keep commoners' wives or daughters, but I think it's generally agreed they lose caste by it. One of them keeps an archbishop's daughter. That's about as low as you could reasonably sink."

Alfred trotted away from Rodings Hall filled with one old determination and one new: to propose to Flora immediately, and then to find Danielle.

From the dark of the lane he saw Flora and her groom before either saw him. He pulled in by the rusted and long-disused gate to wait for them. The two large Berkshire pigs scampered back into the ruined gatelodge.

"Miss Flora," he called when she was within earshot. "I wish you'd send your groom on a bit. I have something particular I want to ask of you." His heart started to thump wildly. He wondered why. This was not to be an emotional moment but a serious and rational one. His heart ought to be calm.

She made no reply until she was close enough to speak without raising her voice. "I hope you are well today, Lord Alfred?"

"And you." He was impatient. "I want to ask you something."

"Have you visited Rodings Hall? Oh, I did so hope to show you round there myself."

"Send your groom on, do."

She nodded at her groom but turned warily back to Alfred. When the man was a little way away she said, "I hope you understand the risks I take, sir."

He shrugged impatiently. "Miss Flora," he said, annoyed at his own nervousness. "The duke has some notion to get me married to a fat bearer of sons and gold. I, for my part, have no intention of . . ."

His voice trailed off as he noticed the look of anger on her face, where he had never seen any mood but happiness and serenity.

"Has his grace favored you with this lady's name?" she asked, with an equally unwonted sharpness.

"Er . . . yes. Lady Gertie Something. A daughter of the Marquis of Morne. I don't know the family name."

"Marquis of *where?*" she interrupted him.

"Morne. It must be a new marquisate. They're not in his old, out-of-date *Debrett* or *Burke's*. She has a dowry of a million. But forget her! I have no intention of complying. And he knows it."

She pricked up her ears at that. "Careful, sir! You may not understand what you are saying. One of the Marlborough heirs was handed a list of girls whom his parents considered suitable wives and he picked the first one that began with the letter *C*. That's how duchesses are made."

"Not mine!" Alfred said firmly. But then his firmness evaporated. He began to fidget. He ought to have prepared himself better.

"Lord Alfred, I cannot advise or encourage you to go counter to his grace. Especially in so important . . ."

"It's not your advice I seek, Miss Flora," he said.

"Oh?"

"The duke's impatience is forcing me to a speed I would far rather not . . . In the normal course I would have hoped to say these words to you sometime next autumn. And not . . ." He looked around. The two Berkshires sows had left the sanctuary of the lodge and were now staring up at him through the disused gate. "I mean . . . in a drawing room. And we should then be able to look back on a summer of picnics . . . rides . . . conversation. A growing intimacy of mind and spirit. And perhaps even of heart."

All her outward composure had now returned. She gazed at him with her cool, gray, unblinking eyes. In the leaf-dark lane they seemed almost to burn with an internal fire. She wasn't all *that* plain, actually, he thought.

"And now I must ask you—I must implore you, Miss Flora—to

assume that such a summer is, indeed, behind us. We have, I venture to hope, the beginnings of a friendship between us. I certainly could not feel warmer to you at that level than I already do. And my respect is as high as it ever could be. On those foundations I beg you to accept a love that is still too green to burn. And to say you'll be my duchess."

Flora surreptitiously tickled her horse's flank with her spur, so that its agitation would mask her own. Deftly she guided it through a full circle on the spot, patting its neck and saying, "Eeeeasy, easy!" in the tones her brother had used earlier.

Alfred, deceived into thinking her quite calm, now relaxed a little himself. "Everything's telescoped, you see, Flora. I'll tell you where matters stand. I *know*—no question of it—I know you'd make the best duchess this estate is ever likely to have. There's no quality of grace, or sense, or wisdom, or understanding of our people, of knowledge of . . . I tell you, the prospect of being duke without you as duchess by my side is . . . terrifying. I will not even think of it while the hope is there that you . . ."

He wished now he had not picked so dark a place—nor one where every hesitation was punctuated by the grunting of pigs. He was making rather a lot of hesitations. What was she thinking?

"You cannot ignore the duke's wishes, Alfred," she said. "Has he any notion of this?"

"He's no fool."

"And that's no answer."

"Well, I keep telling him what a marvelous duchess you'd make."

"And?"

"He just grunts. Like these two ladies." He pointed a toe at the pigs. "Says you've no money. And then he praises this Lady Gertie to high heaven."

A new look stole into Flora's eyes. "When did he first mention her to you?" she asked.

"I think it was the very first time I told him my opinion of you."

"The old . . . !" She laughed.

Alfred asked why.

"I know the lady in question now," she said. "*That* Marquis of Morne. How could I have forgotten!"

"What's the family name? I must look them up."

After some thought she answered, "I believe they're called Nimmo."

"That's a strange name."

"No more strange than the family, I assure you. They're Italian, I believe. Came over with the Guelphs and Hanoverians. I'm sure the original name was Nemo. If it wasn't, it certainly ought to be." She laughed again and spelled it for him: "N, e, m, o—an old latin tribe!"

Alfred grew impatient again. "Flora, it isn't just my courtship of you that has been telescoped, you know. Can you assume, for your part, that you've already told me how sensible you are of the honor etcetera etcetera. And that I must give you time to consider. And that it all happened a month ago. And here I am, panting for an answer."

She was serious again. "But you *must* give me time," she told him. "Not for the usual reasons of coyness. But you really do not appreciate the difference between marrying with the duke's blessing and marrying without it."

"Assume the duke's blessing," he pressed.

"And the legal title to the moon!" She looked about them. "I cannot stay here," she said. "Or I shall be so compromised that you will in any case be obliged to marry me to restore my honor." Then, seeing a mischievous hope in his eyes, she added, "And what a poor start that would be."

"I'll escort you home," he said.

"To the gap in the wall."

He accepted the limit—and marveled that she could get a horse to walk so slowly.

"What if this love that is 'still too green to burn' should fail to mature?" she asked.

"Our life would still be agreeable," he said calmly. "We like each other well enough. We both know that already."

"Like?"

"And admire. At least, *I* admire *you*. I think you're a marvelous person, Flora."

"But?"

"What d'you mean: 'but'?"

"It sounded as if that was going to be your next word."

He thought a moment. "Shall I be honest?" he asked.

"Oh, dear," she answered. "Yes. Perhaps it would be best."

"There is a feeling that afflicts men which you could call instantaneous love. It afflicts me, anyway. It is a love for . . . beauty. Superficial beauty. Beauty of skin and feature. It plays havoc with me. It's only fair to tell you this."

Flora understood exactly what sort of warning shot Alfred was firing. "You seem to know how *superficial* a thing it is," she said.

"Utterly."

"Then one would be wrong to make much of it," she told him with a lightness she did not quite feel.

They reached the gap. "I think I'll walk the rest of the way," she said. "Will you help me down?"

He sprang from his saddle and cupped his hands for her foot. As soon as her other foot was on the ground, he straightened, intending to put a little distance between them. But her eye, only inches away, held him.

"You may," she said. And waited.

Impelled more by her will than his he lifted her face lightly in his free hand and moved his lips toward hers. They were soft. Their warmth was generous. She was young. She smelled young, too—a pale, milky smell that was heady in his nostrils.

Her breast and shoulders trembled. She fell against him with a little cry. He put his arm about her. She gasped and broke their kiss, burying her face against his neck. Her breath was a furnace.

"When shall I have my answer?" he asked.

She gathered herself a moment before she slipped from his embrace. Then she turned and walked quickly to her horse's head. "You say I am a marvelous person?" she said.

He nodded.

"You ask me to be your duchess?"

He nodded again.

"I'll give you your answer when you can truthfully say I am a marvelous woman. And when you ask me to be your wife."

CHAPTER SEVENTEEN

HE COULD NOT find Nimmo in *Debrett,* or *Burke's Peerage.* He drew a blank with Nemo, too. Then, on impulse, because Flora had spelled it so particularly, and because the Latin dictionary was on the shelf below *Debrett,* he looked up the name in that, and found his answer:

NEMO -inis, c. no man, no one, nobody.

Then he understood the game the duke had played with him. He looked up a few more words in Latin and left the library wearing a smile of quiet determination.

"Duke! I've decided—"

"Never mind that, young man. We've had the most splendid news. The judicial peers of the House of Lords have examined all your papers and have declared you to be the heir presumptive to the dukedom. There! Everything's confirmed."

"Well, that's marvelous, duke! Marvelous!" Alfred's delight was sparked more by the old grandee's joy than at the news itself. In his own mind this confirmation had been a foregone conclusion, just as, in an earlier existence, he had always been assured of his ultimate fortune.

"Even better, my boy. Her majesty has granted a special warrant allowing you the style you'd enjoy as an eldest son."

"The Marquis of Knightsbridge!" Alfred said.

"Not *the* marquis. Not formally, anyway. Just marquis. It's a courtesy title."

"Ah, yes. Of course. That's very kind of the queen."

"Kind!" The duke snorted. "She needs her aristocracy more than we need . . . well, never mind that. Now—Lord Knightsbridge—what were you going to tell me you'd decided?"

"Shall we have our grand dinner and ball now? And invite the queen and court?"

"Of course, of course. In August, I thought. Remind me to tell Mrs. Kerns. It'll all be in the *Gazette* tomorrow. What's this decision of yours?"

"Could we announce my engagement at the same time?"

"Engagement?"

"Yes. To your Lady Gertie. I've talked it over with Flora and she's persuaded me to see matters from your point of view."

"The devil she did. What?"

"My heart may be hers but the title must be Lady Gertie's." He bowed his head in contrition. "I submit, sir. Entirely to your direction."

"Eh? Damme! Well . . . hum . . . very good of you, my boy. Fact is . . . been doing a bit of thinking myself. Possibly a bit hard on you. Arranged marriage is one thing, forced marriage another. Don't like it, never did. Got carried away, perhaps. In short . . . er . . . you may . . . dammit." He breathed like an exasperated bull. "Take my meaning?"

"I'm afraid I don't, duke. But in any case let me assure you, from the bottom of my heart, I am reconciled—more than reconciled—willing—nay, *eager*—to embrace Lady Gertie and her gold."

"You are?" The duke was nonplussed.

"It would not be fitting in a son to cross your will and spurn your most solemn advice. How much less, then, in me, who know so little and am dependent on you for so many—"

"Damme, Alfred! Did Flora put you up to this?"

"Put me . . . ? No, she was quite forlorn. As indeed was I. But we are, as I say, reconciled to it now. You may write to Lady Gertie tonight." He smiled at the duke. "A million pounds is a splendid sweetener, I must say."

The duke clenched his fists and stared about him, trapped. "Damnation, sir! You can't marry the girl."

"But why not? I thought you said—"

"Because you can't. And there's an end on't. Say no more."

"I hope she is not ill, sir?"

"Ill!" He turned and strode toward the door. "She's exploded. The whole family's exploded. By anarchists."

"What a dreadful outrage! But surely you mean it is the work of *nihilists?*"

The duke stopped but did not turn. The tilt of his shoulder and the length of his hesitation told Alfred that he now understood everything. The old man was trying not to laugh. "Marry your Flora!" he barked. "I can't stop you. Never could. I know that."

He stamped out but Alfred ran after him. "With your blessing, sir?" he asked breathlessly as soon as he caught up.

The duke turned and looked at him. "Blessing?"

Alfred nodded.

"What's it to you?" There was no laughter in him now.

"It means everything to me, duke. And to Flora. Neither of us would consider it without your approval. Surely you know that."

The duke was too moved to trust himself to speak. He nodded. He placed a fumbling hand on Alfred's shoulder and squeezed hard. Then he turned abruptly on his heel and strode off down the passage. When he was what seemed like half a mile away he turned and roared: "Don't get carried away, my boy. You've a long road to trudge yet. Ask Flora to call on me tomorrow."

He was out of sight before Alfred realized he had forgotten to ask about Danielle.

"Stearns," he said to his valet that night, "you don't happen to remember a young French maid, name of Danielle? Got left behind after the Newbiggin visit. Not still hanging around the place, is she?"

Stearns believed he might have seen her once or twice.

"Well, if you happen to see her again—no hurry, mind, just if you happen to see her—tell her I'd like a word with her. There's a good fellow."

Ten minutes later, while Alfred was memorizing the names of all the collateral branches of his grace of Newcastle—the families of Pelham-Clinton and Fiennes—he looked up to see Danielle standing uncertainly, in nightdress and gown, at his bedside.

"Like the month of March," he said, "you always come in like a lamb."

She was shivering though the night was warm. "You are not angry?"

"Not any more." He pointed to the part of the bed she had occupied previously. "You didn't wait for an invitation last time."

"You see, you *are* angry."

"I'm not!" He laughed to prove it.

"You are. Otherwise why do you talk of that?"

Carefully he closed his *Debrett* and placed it beneath his bedside candlestick. Its warm light suited Danielle, with her coal-black hair and ice-blue eyes.

"I mention it," he explained, "because at this moment the only thing we have in common is the fact that we once shared the same bed for an entire night. It was, I now realize, much too short a time to allow us to make a proper acquaintance, so what better way to renew it than to take up where we left off?"

"But"—she gave an eloquent Gallic shrug—"it's different."

"Oh, very." He smiled and patted the bed again. "This time, I hope, I shall be with *my* mistress instead of yours!"

She could not help laughing at that; and laughter helped her to raise the covers and climb in beside him. He slipped across the bed toward her, but before he reached her she put her arms outside the covers and pinned them firmly to the mattress, cocooning herself and excluding him. "No!" she said.

"What is it?" He was more amused than annoyed.

"Is this love?" she asked. "Or"—she did not know the word—"whatever."

" 'Whatever,' I would say."

"I am not doing it before."

He stroked her forehead. The closer he got to her, the more beautiful she seemed. She was still trembling. "But I have," he assured her, "I know how to be gentle. So gentle. You'll see. Trust me."

"Not that! I mean . . . moh-nay."

It was a few baffling seconds before he deciphered *money*.

"There again you must trust me, Danielle. This isn't an arrangement for one night. I hope it'll last at least a year or two."

"And if children? There must be, how you say, *une disposition?*"

He laughed without disguising his impatience. "Dearest Danielle, they would be the children of an English marquis. It's unthinkable they would not be provided for. And you too. But unless you lift your arm and let me near you, there'll be no cause to provide for you. And certainly no children to provide for, eh!"

The casualness of this proposition, its very English vagueness, shocked her tidy French mind. She would have liked the whole question to be settled at the outset, so that she would have some bargain to fulfill; then she could have thrown herself heart and soul into the arrangement. Now she needed to be coaxed to it. Alfred drew near again, trying to force a way beneath her arm.

"*Encore* no!" she said. But this time she smiled mischievously.

"What now?" he asked wearily.

"Talk to me first," she said. "Tell me about me."

"What about you?"

"Tell me why you want me. Tell me what you think when you look at me."

"Dammit! All I can see is your face."

"That will be enough to start. If you please me, I let you see a bit more." She turned her head to kiss the hand that was starting to caress her hair. "Perhaps," she added.

He sighed; but the way ahead was now familiar enough.

He brought his face close to hers and stared deep into her eyes. He moved aside her hair and considered her ear. In a voice hypnotically low and insistent he said, "Your ear . . . yes, your ear, I would say, is a little too sharp for elegance. Your jaw"—his caress was the lightest touch of his fingernails; she shivered violently—"your jaw is a trifle too wide for grace. Your chin"—he played a single finger over the light down on her skin there—"your chin is a mite too determined for my comfort. Your lips"—he felt them as a blind man might feel sculpture, and she sighed—"yes, your lips are a shade too generous for my peace of mind. D'you understand me?"

"No. But you have a lovely voice. You must learn French. Go on."

"Your nose"—he ran the outer edge of his little finger up and down it—"your nose is a touch too long for delicacy. And your eyes, Danielle, yes, your stunning blue eyes." He stretched with infinite slowness and kissed their lids, first the left, farthest from him, then the right; in closing, each squeezed out what was almost a tear. "They are the perfection that masks . . . that *glorifies* this" —he took her face between both hands—"this perfection of imperfections."

She reached up both arms then, to pull him down into her surrender. The games were over with that first long, soft kiss. He broke and drew breath to speak but she laid one delicate finger across his lips, shook her head, and pulled him to her once more.

"Good God!" the duke said at breakfast. "You look as if you were found in two parishes and stitched back with a hot needle."

At their very first breakfast Alfred had said, "Would you kindly pass the cream, duke?" and the duke had glowered at the footman who ought to have tended to such matters—and then had spat at Alfred the words, "Chatter, chatter, chatter!" Since then all their breakfasts had passed in wordless silence.

So this outburst would have left Alfred speechless even if he had spent the night in the deepest and most healing slumber.

The duke murmured something to the footman, who went to the far end of the room and muttered to another footman, who left at once.

"Good, was she?" the duke asked. "A quart pot of bliss, I'll swear, what?"

He would not accept Alfred's noncommittal smiles and shrugs but had to have it told. He had to turn it into a tale from Casanova or Boccaccio. Later, when his wits were less raveled, Alfred understood why: The old man had wanted to devalue the events of last night; to nip in the bud any romance that might grow between him and Danielle.

The second footman came back with a small tissue-paper packet on a silver tray, which the first footman then brought to the duke, who left it casually on the table. He toyed with it, teasing open the paper as he spoke: "Difficult creature to manage, a mistress. She's no whore, yet she's no wife either. Difficult. Ah, you may smile. You'll see!" The paper was tearing rather than folding open. "Aye, difficult. There's feeling on one's own part, you see. Can't help loving them a little. Glorious thing, a woman's body. Work of God, of course." He sighed. "But mustn't love 'em too much. Mustn't *love* 'em. D'ye see? Lord Henry Seymour once told his mistress to put his boots outside the door. But she was an uppity thing. 'Why should I?' she asked. And he answered: 'Because one day they'll do the same for you!' See? Got to find little tricks to stop yourself."

He lifted the paper. A pair of diamond earrings fell out and rolled across the table toward Alfred.

"If she was a wife, you'd give her the pair."

Alfred picked them up and gasped; they were superb.

"But she's not a wife. She's a mistress. So give her one. Tell her she'll get the other when she's been a good girl for a bit."

Alfred smiled.

"See what I mean, eh?" the duke pressed. "It's a small difference—why, you'd not slip a rasher of wind between 'em. But"—he tapped the gleaming mahogany of the table three times with the tips of his fingers—"but vital!"

Alfred began to thank the duke, but the old man had not finished. "Now," he said, "you'll need a good allowance to keep a fine young piece of flesh like that to yourself. Otherwise someone'll nip her away from you. Done it meself, so trust me."

He thought a minute. "I have it!" he cried exultantly. "There's a fellowship going at Eton. I'll get that for you. Nominally it's only worth ten pounds, but what they do, you see, is renew all the rents on the properties the college owns in London at fifteenth-century rates—five shillings, that sort of thing, which goes to college funds—then they levy fines on the leaseholders to bring the rents up to modern levels."

"And that money doesn't go to the college?" Alfred guessed.

"Of course not. They divide it among themselves. It's about eight hundred a year. Each."

"Each!"

"Yes. And they have the gift of about thirty-five benefices. You could get one of those, too. The whole thing would be worth, say, eighteen hundred a year. That ought to do." His face clouded. "You ought really to be in holy orders." Then he brightened again. "Still. We'll find a way around that." He patted Alfred's hand, closing it over the earrings. "Remember this, m'boy. In England there's always a way around. Never go head-on at anything."

Not for several years did it strike Alfred that his own use of this money (intended by the pious Henry IV to be applied for the benefit of poor and indigent scholars) to buy instead the tender favors of Danielle was—not to mince words—almost scandalous.

CHAPTER EIGHTEEN

IF THE DUKE had had his way, Alfred and Flora would have been married within the week; he wanted an heir—and damn Flora's scruples. But Flora did not come to the Abbey, neither that day nor the next. Three days after his hasty but businesslike proposal, Alfred returned to Rodings Hall determined to settle matters with her.

The first person he saw was Ian, once again exercising his favorite filly. "You've set the cat among the pigeons," he said.

"Have I?"

"The pater's threatened to lock her out of the house—and he would, too, if we could only find the keys, and if there weren't so many unhinged windows and other holes she could get back in by."

"But why?"

"Why? For not marrying you on the spot, that's why."

"Where is she?"

"One of the servants found a rusty old key in the barn and, after a morning spent in oiling the locks and trying it in each door, the old man finally discovered which room it fitted. She's locked in there until she sees sense."

"Which room is it?"

"The extraordinary thing is that she's spent every waking minute of the last three or four years turning herself into *exactly* the sort of person you'd want as a duchess, and then, when it's offered to her, she hesitates over trivialities. None of us can understand her."

"But I do. She's absolutely right—as always."

Ian's relief was vast. "You don't mean it!"

"I came here to tell her."

Ian threw his lunge whip in the air and was so excited that he failed to catch it on its return. "We were sure you'd begin to look elsewhere. I mean, one just does not say 'give me time' to a marquis and ducal heir. Congrats on that, by the way."

"Thanks. Where is she?"

Ian picked up his whip and leveled it like a musket at a small window at one end of the house on the upper floor. In the same instant Alfred saw her. His heart lurched. He waved. She waved back.

He looked at the heavy creeper growing up—and in places through—the old stone walls. A lean-to laundry house at that end of the main building would give access to the first floor, from where the creeper would afford a series of holds to her prison window.

"Give us a buck-up onto that washhouse roof," he said to Ian.

Ian laughed. "No need for that, old sport. Come inside. They'll even sweep the corridors for you—something they otherwise do but once a year."

"Ah, there's something romantic about this, though—climbing up the ivy. Come on, give us a hand. Then you go inside and unlock us."

"If you're alone with Flora at all, you'll be obliged to marry her for the sake of her honor."

"I've thought of that, of course. Call it prudent insurance."

When he was alone on the roof, after Ian had gone inside, the idea did not seem quite so bright. The wall stretched much farther above him than had seemed possible from below; and the creeper, though its foliage was thick, had disappointingly thin stems. Still—it would be something to tell their grandchildren.

"Alfred!"

He looked up. She had thrown open the window and was staring down at him, aghast.

"Fly down, my love, and I will catch you," he called.

"Don't be so stupid! Get down and come inside."

Laughing, he grasped a handful of creeper and swung himself up off the roof.

"Alfred!" she almost screamed. "Go down! It's not safe!"

He found a toehold, then another handhold . . . a heave . . . a foothold in a missing brickhole . . . another handhold . . . another toehold. It was easy really, once you got the feel of it. He took a brief rest on a first-floor window sill and noticed that Flora was still begging him to go back; but at the same time she was now laughing.

Spitting fragments of leaf and creeper from his lips, he grinned up at her and launched himself once more on the ascent. He was almost within grasp of her window sill when a pigeon flew out of a leaf-lined crevice right in front of his face. Instinctively his right hand rose to ward it off.

He hadn't a chance. For one long instant of mounting terror he held on to the creeper with his left hand, vainly scrabbling with his right for a firm stem, but all he grasped was leaves and twigs—which came off as easily as butterflies' wings.

His frantic joggling began to loosen the creeper stem in his left hand; he *heard* its rootlets sever from the wall—a noise like bubbles bursting.

He was no longer parallel to the wall but leaning out and back at an ever increasing angle. An ever *accelerating* angle. *I'm going to die,* he thought. He saw Flora's face, her mouth frozen in a scream he did not hear. He saw a broken length of gutter come away and hurtle past him. There was a rattling shower of bits of creeper, ancient crows' nests, and rotten soffit boarding. Then he was free! Free and light as thistledown.

"I love you," he shouted. "Flora!"

He fell hard, full length, on the slate roof of the washhouse. Absurdly it sank and rebounded several times, like an overstretched hammock. Then with a splintering of wood and a rattle of slates it gave way under him and shot him through to the floor below.

It was very dark, all but the blinding light of the hole he had made. There was a shattering of slate sherds all around and on him.

But that wasn't the blinding light. The blinding light followed him wherever he looked. Yet he could look. This way. That way. He wasn't dead then.

But something was wrong. A pain.

Breathe!

He was fighting for breath. Black flying worms showered upward to obliterate the blinding light, eating into its edges. *Breathe!* He couldn't. He was paralyzed, then. That was it.

An astonishing calm invaded him as he lay paralyzed and watched the black worms devour the edges of the light. What an impersonal struggle, dark against light! And how impersonal death was, after all. Like waiting for another door to open.

He looked around—not outside himself but somehow inside —for that other door. He almost knew where it was. Just a bit more thought, a bit more effort, and he'd remember.

A bit more effort. There was a mighty rushing of wind. A cold stabbing in his chest. An ache of emptiness inside, which the wind came gushing in to fill. *That* door! He knew now. The wind rushed out. In again. Out again. Pain. *Pain!*

He gasped his breathing to silence, listening for other sounds. There was none. He was alone in the universe.

He'd have to get up. There was no help but himself. He rose on one elbow. Now he was just panting, no longer gasping. But where were his legs? Nothing was there but a vast, warm, sensory void.

He lay down again and touched his chest. He could feel that. His abdomen, the upper part. He could feel that. His navel. Yes. He could feel that, too. His lower abdomen . . . His lower abdomen?

His lower abdomen! His fingers said, *all there;* but his brain held it in a . . . a what? A nothing. A limbo. Sensation ended at his navel. When he pressed below it he felt only the stretch of the skin above it, six inches away.

I'm paralyzed from the waist down, he realized.

Was that worse than death? In a curious way the answer didn't matter. That serene calm descended on him again. He lay there, neither warm nor cold, weightless, and worked out all the changes this paralysis would force on the rest of his life.

By the time Flora's desperate cries had alerted the others to what had happened, and by the time they had broken their way from the house into the old washhouse, he was able to say, "It's a confounded nuisance but I'm afraid I've broken my back. You'd better get a stretcher before you try to move me."

Ian stayed with him while the grooms ran for a stretcher.

"You're a cool cove, Knightsbridge," he said.

"Something else to tell our grandchildren!"

"You may not be paralyzed, you know. I've seen this happen in the hunting field. Fellow was back on his horse in two hours."

"I can't move a thing. Nor feel."

"Nor could he."

They moved him gingerly onto the stretcher. There was a warmth at the small of his back. That was a good sign, surely? Below the waist.

"Christ! That can't have been too comfortable!" Ian pointed to a roof truss, knotted with lath-nail heads. "You were lying right on it."

They carried him indoors and laid him on a large oak table, hastily swept free of boots, riding crops, dog leashes, and other sporting bric-à-brac.

"Where's Flora?" he asked. "Did someone tell her? I'm sure she thinks I'm dead."

"The pater's forgotten where he put the key. They're searching for it now."

"I can feel a tingling in my feet. Aiee! It's like the worst pins and needles ever!"

"Shall I rub them?"

"Do *some*thing—please!"

Flora came running into the room, frantic and tear-stained. "Oh, my darling! My dearest darling Alfred! Are you hurt?"

He reached out and grasped her arms, pulling her to him. She kissed him without thought until, realizing that everyone was watching, she pulled away in embarrassment.

"Too late!" Ian laughed. "We all saw. No room now for your fine scruples, miss! When's the nuptuals?"

"Oh, he gave me the assurance I wanted," she said. "Now it can be as soon as he likes."

"I can move my feet!" Alfred pushed against Ian's massaging hands.

"Why?" Flora was all anxiety again. "Did you think you couldn't?"

"I thought I was dead."

"Oh! So did I, so did I." She kissed him again.

There was a commotion. Servants and—presumably—other members of the family had been gathering in the hall where Alfred lay. Suddenly their ranks parted. The duke came striding in.

"What's this? What's this, sir?" He was wearing his hat—and the most intensely worried expression Alfred had ever seen.

"I'm all right, sir," he said. "Fine! In a moment or two I'll be right as rain." He tried to sit up, to show how well he was, but the pain defeated him. "Anyway, I'm not paralyzed," he said, and wriggled his feet.

A servant came with some brandy, half of which the duke put down his own throat—and was more refreshed by it than by Alfred's dubious assurances.

He turned sternly to Flora. "And you, young miss. You're the cause of all this. I was on my way here to set you straight."

Flora looked as if there were a dozen good answers she could make, but she just managed to hold her peace.

"Have a care, duke," Alfred said with mock solemnity. "You speak to the future Marchioness of Knightsbridge."

Flora smiled and took Alfred's arm. "But even more important than that . . . ?" she prompted.

Alfred added apologetically: "To my future wife."

The duke took off his hat.

"Found it!" Sir Duncan Kinnaird came triumphantly into the room, bearing aloft a key that was brown with rust and dark with oil.

"You may embrace me," the duke told Flora.

Her head reached no higher than his chest; he picked her up and plonked her on a chair. Over her shoulder he smiled at Alfred, the smile a sea captain might make on tying up at his home port after a voyage of epic duration. "Be married next week," he said gruffly. "No reason to delay, is there?"

Then, still with an arm around Flora's waist, he said, "My boy, let me present Sir Duncan Kinnaird, your father-in-law to be. Sir Duncan—Lord Knightsbridge, Alfred Boyce."

CHAPTER NINETEEN

IN FACT IT WAS closer to six weeks—the height of summer—before all the arrangements could be made. The wedding was to take place in the duke's own church in Great Marlow, successor to the ancient church in which most of the du Bois had been married since the time of Sir Clarence, father of the First Baron of Marlow.

Most of the time was consumed in the making of Flora's dress and those of her eight bridesmaids; Alfred was to wear his uniform, so that was no difficulty.

And then they were to travel back in a magnificent landau drawn by eight grays; this carriage had had no outing for forty years and needed respringing, to say nothing of lacquering and gilding. On top of which, Alfred's and Flora's own arms were to be painted in miniature on one of the doors, as a memorial of the occasion. Six weeks was hardly time enough.

To be helpful the duke decided on a small wedding, with fewer than three hundred guests—"if possible," he added ominously. In the event it proved impossible, and five hundred were invited, of whom only fifty or so had to decline. "Still small enough," the duke said. Whether Mrs. Kerns agreed he did not trouble to discover—for, of course, small or large, it was still far too many to be accommodated at Rodings Hall.

In fact the poor woman nearly drove herself to distraction over the preparations that had to be made, so much so that Flora had to ration the time she could spend nursing Alfred back to health and devote the rest of it to rescuing the housekeeper.

But Alfred was young and fit, and, what with Flora's tender ministrations by day and Danielle's gentle visitations by night, he was up and about again within two weeks.

Every country house for ten miles, great and small, was packed with guests, who may have been no more than fourth cousins or friends of friends to the householders but who had that coveted social badge, an invitation to what the *Drawing Room Companion* had called the "double-fairy-tale" wedding. For if Alfred's discovery and "rescue" had all the elements of a fairy tale, so did Flora's probable elevation to the rank of duchess. Dukes had married whores before, and rich widows or heiresses, but a commoner who was not in either of those categories was considered to stand no chance of such a match. No one could remember when a duke had last married a mere baronet's daughter. And had any duke ever married one who was penniless, especially when his own fortunes were none too healthy?

In all ways this was going to be one of the most talked-about weddings of the decade. The festivities were to last two days, with a grand ball on the first evening and a medieval jousting tournament got up by the officers and men of the regiment; and on the afternoon of the second day the queen and Prince Albert were to drive over from Windsor to see the finals of the jousting and to grant the duke a private audience at which he was to present Alfred and Flora.

The day of the wedding, Tuesday, August 20, 1850, was dry and bright. Overnight rain had passed, leaving a trail of thin cloud shoals and blue skies. The air was warm, even at half past six of the morning; without the breeze it would have been hot.

Alfred was in his uniform by eight, two hours before he had to be standing in church. He surveyed himself with dry approval in the looking glass—dark blue trousers with gold-lace stripes, pink tunic with scarlet facings, a high crimson collar embellished with oak leaves in gold, huge gold epaulettes, and a white buckskin sash resplendent with stars and tassels.

"Look at that," he said. "You'd think I was born to it."

"And so you were, my lord," Stearns, the valet, told him. "You just didn't know it, that's all."

Alfred chuckled nervously. "Yes, you could put it like that. Where's my coal scuttle?"

The "coal scuttle" was a tall cap of that shape, bearing a large gold star surmounted by a plume of feathers and a scarlet "pom."

"How do I hold it, now?" he asked.

Stearns showed him—in the crook of the arm on the hilt of the sword. "And gloves carried, not worn, sir. Her ladyship will have no gloves, neither, till you leave the church."

It gave him a start to think of Flora as "her ladyship," yet that was, of course, what she would be after the wedding: Marchioness of Knightsbridge.

He went down to breakfast. Just before they entered, Stearns coughed and said, "Sword and gloves left out here, sir."

Even the duke was a little taken aback to see how splendid Alfred looked in uniform. He made him stand by the window, walk this way, walk that, go out and make his entry again . . . before the duke spoiled it by slipping a long apron over the uniform.

"The last Marquis of Knightsbridge," he said (meaning himself), "got married dead drunk and in torn trousers. We look to you to start a better tradition."

There were about eighty guests staying at the Abbey, from the duke's sisters to cousins almost as remote as Alfred himself—plus a few cronies from "the days when England was ruled by a *real* monarch." None of this latter group had worn so well as the duke himself. They hobbled around with three dozen teeth between them, reliving ancient conquests and glories.

" 'Thrice they routed all their foes, and thrice they slew the slain,' " the duke commented sardonically to Alfred. "There's a time to go, all right!"

Alfred knew that many of the family found him slightly amusing—the printer's son, the apothecary's stepson. He knew they were wondering what sort of duke he'd make when his time came. It would take more than a pretty uniform to settle their doubts. Yet he could not honestly say that their opinion worried him all that much. He had over these months formed a very clear idea of what he wanted to do with the estate; and with Flora to guide him he had no qualms about managing the outward obligations of the dukedom, either.

"Nervous?" the duke asked as they set off for the church in the closed carriage—the landau having been sent to Rodings Hall for Flora.

"Not greatly," Alfred said, thinking the truth—that he was not at all nervous—might sound smug.

"Bloody well ought to be."

"It's something I want, sir, very much—this marriage. I'm more excited than nervous."

For a while they both sat staring out of their respective windows.

"It seems half a lifetime, duke, since you brought me this way first," Alfred said.

The duke did not at once reply. "Be good to her, my boy," he answered at last. "Little Flora . . . she's of the best."

"Of course, sir."

The duke laughed absently, "She won't remember it now, but we often used to meet, she and I. This is when she was five or six.

When the last king was alive. And she'd come awalking round the gardens with me. She'd slip her little hand into mine and say she was my lady—my duchess! I told her I already had a duchess and it made her sad. So I told her I wasn't just a duke—I was a marquis as well. And she could be my marchioness."

"The Marchioness of Knightsbridge!" Alfred said in delight, thinking this was the point of the story.

"God no! She'd have let that slip out sometime. It would have been embarrassing for her people. No, I invented a special marquisate for us. It's extinct now, of course." He smiled wickedly. "Exploded by nihilists!"

It was roasting in the church. As soon as he entered, the duke commanded that all the doors and every possible window be opened. The relief was palpable even though the breeze thus produced was tiny.

The hubbub of conversation and laughter was loud; people clearly thought of this occasion more in the light of a social than a religious event. So Flora's arrival, which brought a sudden, astonished hush, was made doubly dramatic—and then trebly so by the gasps of admiration that followed.

She was transformed. *No!* Alfred thought as he looked at her, she was transfigured.

She wore a simply cut dress of white satin, trimmed with delicate chatelaines of orange blossom, myrtle, and bouffants of tulle with Honiton lace. On her head was a garland of orange blossoms over a headdress of Honiton lace. Her train was of silver moiré antique with bouquets of roses and silver thistles tied with gold cord. It was carried by eight bridesmaids, dressed in white tulle over a white glacé; each wore a wreath of blush roses and white heather with long veils of tulle falling from the back of the wreath.

Few in that church—and certainly not Alfred—had ever seen a spectacle to match it for sheer beauty. The nine young girls seemed to have floated in from a higher, more ethereal world than this. A radiance shone out of them, touching everything and everyone with its sparkle.

The marriage vows, when he came to make them, were never more solemnly felt, never more fervently spoken. And as he placed the ring on her finger, the whole universe, or his entire awareness of it, seemed to fall inward . . . inward—a dumfounded spiral centered on that bright circle of gold. *It was done!*

She was his as he was hers; they were one. It was a marvel the flesh of their fingers did not fuse.

Outside, in the blinding sun and the merciful breeze, they

faced a guard of honor formed by the officers of the regiment, sabers drawn. As the couple approached, the first sabers went slowly up to the traditional position, then the second pair, and the third and fourth, marking the couple's progress beneath them in a stately flashing of silver and gold.

At the gate the regimental band, augmented for this occasion by drummers (which are not usual in light infantry bands), played "Rule Britannia." On the pavement opposite the gate stood the children of the duke's schools, the girls in green cloaks, the boys in navy blue. And from the church right down to the center of Great Marlow, ten deep on both sides and spilling into the roadway, stood as many of the citizens and duke's tenants as could squeeze in.

Flora and Alfred, followed by the bridesmaids, then by the duke and the rest of the congregation, walked the thronged quarter-mile smiling to left and right, deafened by the cheers they received in return. This was their family, too, now.

Alfred remembered the first time he had walked among them, across the Great Courtyard of Chalfont Abbey. What a gulf separated him now from that callow know-nothing!

And the chief engineer of that change was, he knew, the marvelous, radiant, joyful woman who was now, and always would be, at his side. His heart overflowed with gratitude for her, with happiness for himself, and with good will to all the world.

The vast, iron-studded oak gates were thrown wide open as the landau drew near. All the way home every hamlet, crossing, and junction had had its little quota of cheering, waving people, who would see no such sight again in a lifetime. And now the Great Courtyard was thronged with wedding guests, all eager for a glimpse of the young man and woman of whom they had heard and read so much.

There was a slight disturbance as the couple and the duke and his sisters descended. Alfred had a hasty impression of a small man, out of place in that elegant company, a man in a felt hat of the "wide-awake" or bowler pattern, being bundled away without ceremony by three men wearing the duke's livery. Few others seemed to notice that anything untoward had happened at all.

The wedding breakfast was served as a buffet in the two great state rooms overlooking the terrace, but Alfred and Flora were unable to eat until all the guests had been presented to them and had given their congratulations; and by then it was almost time for the speeches and the cutting of the cake. These ceremonies were to be conducted out on the terrace, where a dais had been set up to enable everyone to see the actual moment. Small tables and chairs had been put around for those guests who wished to sit; servants passed among them with dishes of strawberries and cream and glasses of champagne.

Only Alfred and Flora and Dr. Penn, the clergyman who had officiated at the wedding, went up onto the dais. Alfred's heart began to beat violently at the thought of addressing that vast multitude. What power they collectively represented—and what a weight of tradition! Every rank of society and wealth was there, from cadet branches of the royal family to the sons of sons of peers and members of the government.

Flora, perhaps guessing what was going through his mind, said, "They are all there, you see. Fops and imbeciles, the ambitious and the almost extinct, little henpecked husbands and pretentious, fleshy wives, empty noddles and empty purses, apes and misanthropes . . ."

"Oh, dear!" Alfred laughed.

"And, of course, *nice* people. Most of them are nice—merely nice, and not half so interesting."

Dr. Penn spoke a few words of the kind known as "well chosen"—well chosen to soothe, to find every corner of the hearer's mind and there to lodge, forever unmemorable.

The greatest part of Alfred's ordeal in replying was in his opening, which had to be exact: "Your royal highnesses, my lord archbishop, prime minister, my lord privy seal, my lord chamberlain, my lord master of the horse, your graces, my lords, ladies, and gentlemen—and, after this day, I hope too: my friends."

It was a daring addition but he had the coolness (outwardly at least) to carry it off; there was a small ripple of applause but it did not become general. He then went on to make the conventional speech, saying all the right things and thanking all the right people in the right order and omitting nothing—exactly as he and Flora had written it some evenings earlier. But while he spoke, his nervousness increased, for he was drawing ever nearer to the point where he would, if he had the courage, slip in a few words of his own devising.

It had occurred to him that this was the first and possibly the last chance in his life to address such a gathering, and it was a chance his ambition could not refuse. He had no intention of becoming a mere private duke, like Buccleugh or Beaufort, devoted to his tenants and estates; he had seen what power and patronage the old grandee wielded and he was determined to wield it too. This was not, in him, an ambition of the self-glorying kind, but part of his very nature: He could no more leave such power lying idle than the average man could walk past a pile of guineas or the average woman past a milliner's in spring. No! He was going into public life. But he could make no mark there if he was to be constantly sniped at behind his back as the apothecary duke.

Somehow he had to nail those sneers now; no better chance would ever come his way. He took a deep breath and prayed he would not fall on his face.

"I cannot finish," he said, "without some passing reference to my own somewhat unusual situation."

There was a buzz of interest, a tension in the air, as the program lurched from its expected course. Flora, especially, was alarmed. In taking her hand to comfort her, he drew courage for himself. He saw the duke looking up at him in consternation. He risked the merest hint of a wink; the old man smiled and settled at ease in his chair. That more than anything gave Alfred the courage he needed.

"You all must know how strange a path in life mine has been until this year—strange that is, by standards that I daily find to be less foreign. Some months ago I'm afraid I shocked that gentleman who today became my brother-in-law and best man by telling him that I had grown up in a world where the aristocracy, for all practical purposes, simply did not exist—and that world was no remote and heathen isle but the heart of a great English city."

His how-could-I smile and his tone of self-belittlement defused any possible anger at what might, given a different tone and demeanor, have seemed a studied insult.

"I meant it then as a way of showing him I was too ignorant to be overawed by all that had lately befallen me. However, I have increasingly come to see that my impudence contained, nonetheless, a truth that is profoundly shocking: The great majority of those who live in our cities—and that may soon be the great majority of Englishmen in general—are growing up deprived not alone of green pastures and wholesome air and bright sunlight but, worst of all, of the paternalistic benevolence of aristocratic government. It is a benevolence for which the counting-house hand of the factory master is no substitute, you may believe me."

They were silent now, intently so. But he could not tell whether they were beginning to resent his arrogance in daring to lecture them or whether they were captured enough by his words to come another pace or two with him. Only the duke smiled proudly on.

"You may think this a strange sort of speech for a man to make on his wedding day. And so it is. A wedding is above all a joyful time. Well, I hope our life may have its full share of zest and well-earned happiness. But a wedding is also a solemn time. A time for taking stock and mapping out the new kind of life before one. It has pleased God to call me to a station far above that in which I was reared. That of itself is a trivial event, for who am I?"

Despite this modest tailpiece there was a ripple of disapproval at his choice of words.

"Far more important is the man God chose to place over me, first as kinsman, then as mentor, and latterly as friend."

They saw his sentiment now and, in silently approving it, relaxed a little.

"Far more important, too, is the woman whom God has now put at my side." He linked Flora's arm in his. "Today her qualities are known but to a few. Yet if we are spared, you may be sure those same qualities will one day shine like the brightest beacon, far and wide."

The words rang out an undeniable challenge. Their attention was rapt once more. A sort of power, something he had never felt before, seemed to pass from them to him.

"It may be there is no purpose in all this. Yet I do not believe that. It may be I am here by the sheerest accidents of chance, I and many besides. Yet I do not believe that. If there *is* some purpose, however obscure it now may seem, if I am at any time, in ways that are now unfathomable, to be called upon to do that for which I was not born, for which I was not reared, I will do it the easier, the better, the more joyfully, for having felt the example, the support, and the love of these two people."

He bowed and, leading Flora behind the giant cake, placed her on his right, and drew out his sword.

His meaning became clear to them then, and they cheered him until the stones sang with echoes. He had told them, without even the most oblique hint at the death of the present duke, exactly what sort of duke he would one day be: a serious man for a court and a Parliament that themselves grew more serious by the year; a dedicated man in an age that cherished dedication; a deep man in a nation grown weary of its old frivolities; and a compassionate man among a people whose conscience was more tender than its heart. There was nothing in him they could not applaud; and applaud they did.

He waited for a hush before he cut the cake. When it fell, he looked at the sword, which Flora was preparing to grasp with him, and it suddenly seemed too barbaric a thing to be holding at such a time. So he brought its hilt to his lips and kissed it before he let

Flora take her hold. No one had ever done that before, but the act was so perfectly suited to the occasion that it seemed more like a revival of some ancient ritual than one new-minted. There was an *oh!* and a gasp of approval, which turned to yet more applause when the cut was made.

"He has an instinct," the duke muttered to his sister, Lady Harriet.

"Did you know that speech was coming?" she asked.

"Not a word of it."

"It went down very well."

Not too far away Lord John Russell leaned toward Benjamin Disraeli and said, "It was a capital little speech."

"And interesting," Disraeli said.

Alfred had certainly not fallen on his face.

CHAPTER TWENTY

WHEN STEARNS TOOK away the shaving water Alfred told him he would not be needed any more that night.

"Good night, my lord," Stearns said, as if it were any other evening.

But it was not any other evening. Alfred stood in his nightshirt and fidgeted with its buttons, wondering if Flora would call when she was in bed.

It ought to have been a different bed, in a different room—not the one he and Danielle . . . He should have thought of that before. Anyway, he didn't want to do *that* with her, not in such haste, not as if the whole process of courtship and all today's ceremonies had been mere preliminaries to a few moments of thrashing between the sheets; it would devalue everything she meant to him and everything he hoped for.

He just didn't want to do it—not tonight, anyway. He wanted to work up to it, woo her gently to it. Besides, he was exhausted; it wouldn't be any good. And on top of that, they had a hard day tomorrow, too, with the queen and prince coming. It would be even harder than today.

He had wanted today; he wanted the marriage. But he didn't

want to meet the queen. The very thought of it terrified him, even more, he thought ruefully, than the notion now of opening his dressing-room door, going into the bedroom, and getting into bed beside Flora. He stood patiently and waited.

Flora lay in bed, combing out her hair, wondering if she ought to call out to Alfred. Would that be too forward of her? Probably. She'd give him another moment or two. And then?

Her mother had been vague about that, bristling with warnings that sounded like promises. "Don't show surprise . . . try not to cry out if it hurts . . . he may embrace you very, er, *vigorously* . . . lie back and think of the inheritance . . ." and so on. But it hadn't left her with a very clear picture of what, exactly, Alfred was going to do.

She knew it was something that men enjoyed, not just with wives, but with any woman or girl they could. Alfred had enjoyed it in this very bed with Hermione. That brought a little smile of triumph! Alfred knew what to do; that was a great comfort. He was a marvelous man, so clever and so good. Really, she needn't worry. She could leave it all to him and—as her mother said—do exactly what he asked of her.

There was a gentle tap on his dressing-room door; she came to with a start, realizing she had half fallen asleep. My, but she was drowsy! She hoped Alfred's enjoyment didn't take too long.

"Come in," she said.

He had never seen her hair down before. There were masses of it, tumbling down all about her. His insides turned over. She *was* lovely—not beautiful like Hermione, not pretty like Danielle; just lovely. Then he saw the fear that passed across her face, clouding its inner loveliness; and he knew, without having to tell himself in so many words, exactly what would be possible tonight.

He lifted up the bedspread and got beneath it, beside her except that she was between the sheets. She showed no surprise.

"You're lovely, Flora," he told her.

She put down her comb and pouted a shame-on-you pout through her smile.

"I may tell you that now. I may tell you anything," he reminded her. "We are one flesh now."

She lay back at full length and sank into the pillow. "Yes! Tell me anything. As long as it's something like that."

He moved beside her, still with the sheet and blanket between them. She snuggled up to him supple and warm. He lay on one elbow looking down into the depths of her eyes, dark in the candlelight.

"You are lovely," he said. "You may not think so; your family may doubt it. But you are. You have a lovely face, lovely eyes, lovely hair. You have a lovely smile, lovely voice, lovely laugh. You are a lovely person."

"Woman!"

"And I love you, Flora. That's the miracle of it. When I first knew I had to make you my duchess, I liked you well enough. Even when I proposed, I liked you well enough. But I didn't love you. Now I do. And I pity that poor idiot self who proposed to you so coolly, because he couldn't see all the things about you which are so crystal clear to me."

Her eyes were brimming with tears now; she could not speak.

"Do you think you could . . . in time, I mean . . . ?"

She reached her arms out and pulled him down to kiss her. "Alfred," she murmured, blinking the tears out onto her cheeks. "Oh, Alfred, you are such a . . . such a . . ."

"Fool?"

"Yes, but such a nice fool. Dear Alfred, I have always loved you, from the hour that we met. There could never have been anyone else for me."

"You did?"

"Of course I did."

"Why did you hide it, then?"

"I don't know. Why does one hide anything? Because it's precious."

He kissed her then, her forehead, her eyelids, her cheeks, her lips. He played with the tip of his tongue in her ears and at the bend of her jaw. He raked his fingernails through her hair.

She shivered at the luxury of it.

He shivered at the maiden-milky smell of her, and the pressing closeness of her small, soft body.

He undid two buttons of her nightdress and ran his lips over her collarbone and kissed her shoulders. Then he did the buttons up again.

"Snuff out the light," he said.

When it was dark he lay beside her to sleep.

"Is that all?" she asked.

He grinned. "Why?" he teased. "What more do you want?"

"I want to go on kissing all night."

He kissed her. "And so do I. But I also want all my faculties about me when we meet the queen tomorrow."

"Of course," she said. "You're right."

After a minute or so, however, she said, "Is that really all?"

"No," he said. "There's lots more. Lots and lots. More than I know of yet."

"Oh."

"And we've got a lifetime to discover it all, together."

She sighed and settled in his arms again. Moments later they were both fast asleep.

He awoke in full vigor at six, slipped from the bed, and went to his dressing room, where he rang for Stearns.

"Where's my bath?" he asked as soon as the man came.

"Cold bath today, my lord?" Stearns was taken aback.

"Today as every day."

Ten minutes later, Stearns had organized the maids into relays to fetch twenty gallons of ice-cold water from the pump.

"I'll ring when I need you again," Alfred said. He stepped into the water with a cry of pleasure-pain at the coldness of it. Moments later a still sleepy-eyed Flora slowly opened the door.

"Sorry!" She shut it as if she had seen a man-eating beast.

"No, no!" he called out. "Come in."

Slowly, red with embarrassment, she came in. He stood up, facing her. She looked briefly at him, down his body, and then rooted her eyes to the floor.

"You can soap my back," he said.

She obeyed, glad to get somewhere where he couldn't see her blushes. She liked his back, she found. It rippled with fine muscles. She loved touching it with soft, soapy hands, too. Her heart began to beat faster and she felt hungry.

When he had rinsed off he stepped from the bath and began to dry himself. She took another towel and dried his back. His bottom was hard and *tiny*. She giggled because she wanted to bend down and kiss it, like a baby's. He hastily threw a dressing gown over himself before he turned to face her again.

"Now your turn," he said.

That stopped her giggling! "No!" she cried, clutching her nightdress to her.

"I command it," he told her sternly.

She looked at him uncertainly and toyed with her top button. "Cold water?" she said.

"Summer and winter."

"I'm going off marriage. *Must* I?"

"I told you—I command it. You've seen me. It's only fair."

When she had two buttons undone he laughed. "I don't actually insist. You don't need to unless you really want to."

She suddenly realized that she did want to. She wanted Alfred to see her body.

Yet she pulled a resigned face and said, "No, no. You insisted. You're the one that's forcing me to it." She pulled the nightdress right up about her head and then spent a long time pretending to struggle with the buttons at the cuff while her heart stilled itself a little.

She was ready to say something trivial when she finally threw off the nightdress, but the mixture of joy and adoration in his face stopped her. "You *are* lovely," he said. "I told you."

She screamed as she stepped into the cold water, then collapsed in a fit of shrieks and laughter. Stearns, sitting in the passage outside, raked the ceiling with his gaze and murmured, "Lucky *sod!*"

"Now you can soap *my* back," she commanded.

Later he dried her back, as well. And he, too, wanted to stoop and kiss her bottom, but not like a baby's—and the thought did not make him giggle. "You're lucky," he said. "All women are lucky. To have such beautiful bodies."

She turned to face him.

"When I look at you," Alfred said, "it thrills me with delight. Now you can't honestly say that when you saw me step out of the bath just now, you were thrilled to the marrow."

"No, but you're close."

"How close?"

"*Chilled* to the marrow." She laughed and flung herself into his arms. "Oh, Alfred! I do love you!"

CHAPTER TWENTY-ONE

ALFRED WISHED that the duke had picked a salon on a somewhat more domestic scale for this presentation to the queen; but, of course, the old grandee had to stage it in the Thornhill Room, the biggest room in the place, just to remind her majesty that the southern wing of Chalfont Abbey was itself larger than the front of Buckingham Palace.

"Nervous?" the duke asked Alfred as he led him to the door.

"This time I am," Alfred admitted.

"No need for it, you know. One day you'll be vastly more powerful than she could ever dream of being."

Alfred tried hard not to let his skepticism show.

"It's true," the duke said. "If I want a place for someone, I have a word in Russell's ear—or whoever's prime minister—and it's as good as done. But let *her* try it! She could do it once but not twice, or there'd soon be a mighty huffing and puffing and reminders of the meaning of *constitutional* monarchy." He put one hand on the door and then paused again. "Also remember this: She got off to a very bad start with her lords. She wants to be nice to us now—not only wants to, *needs* to." He turned the handle and opened the door a crack, then pulled it shut again. "Remember—never call her 'your majesty,' except on formal occasions like this. That's for the lower classes. Always 'ma'am.' "

He opened the door and led Alfred and Flora into the room.

It stretched before them in an infinity of polished parquet, tall mirrors, gilded candelabra, and acres of sculptured and painted naked flesh.

"Damn!" Flora said under her breath as they clanked across the echoing room. "You might have told me, duke."

"Told you what, my dear?"

"Look at her dress. And look at mine."

"Well they're both blue, but as there are only seven colors in the rainbow and seven thousand ladies of fashion, it must happen a thousand times a day."

The prince and the duke were in velvet court dress, and Alfred was in full military dress again; they would all change back into something less formal as soon as this presentation was over.

The queen was in a gorgeous crinoline dress of blue silk, dark and lustrous. Flora was in blue taffeta, equally glossy. Both dresses were trimmed with flounces of lace.

The queen did not turn to watch them. She, Prince Albert, and a few attendants stood by an open window at the far end, pointedly looking out at the overdressed crowds below, who were, in turn, studiously not looking upward, as much as to say, "We see the queen every day."

The duke's encouragement had led Alfred to expect a nervous, nondescript sort of woman; so that actual sight of the queen, as they drew near her, was something of a shock. She was . . . there was no other word for it but *regal*. An aura of power and dignity seemed to swell the air around her. There could be no doubt that she was the natural focus of everything in the room; everything in it, at that moment, existed *for* her. There was something chilling in such majesty. All Alfred's former nervousness returned.

She kept the duke waiting a few seconds, until he sucked a

tooth, rather loudly, in his vexation; then she turned to them with a remote kind of smile. It was just enough to temper the sternness she had displayed in profile, but it was still forbidding—especially when she caught sight of Flora's dress. The duke cleared his throat.

"Your majesty, I have the honor to present my kinsman's wife, Lady Flora Boyce, Marchioness of Knightsbridge, who was presented to you at a drawing room last year as Miss Kinnaird, daughter of Sir Duncan Kinnaird."

Thus Flora's transfer from the protection of her father to that of her husband was notified to the queen. Flora took the queen's hand and curtsied.

"I also have the honor to present, ma'am, my kinsman Lord Alfred Boyce, Marquis of Knightsbridge, a title you graciously permitted him by a recent warrant."

Alfred took the queen's hand and bowed from the neck. Then they moved on and were introduced to Prince Albert in the same silence.

"Well!" the queen relaxed suddenly, and smiled, as if she had been holding a pose for a photographic exposure. "We have heard a great deal about you, Lord Knightsbridge."

"All to the good, I trust, ma'am?" His voice quavered, though her relaxation had done much to calm him.

Her smile grew mischievous, "And what is now your opinion of 'the duking business'?"

"Oh, you heard that!"

"It was the joke of the court for a week."

"Then your jester, ma'am, has a sinecure." He was gaining confidence by the second.

She frowned, until Albert's laugh told her it was funny. She was very quick then. "If the office still existed, Lord Knightsbridge, its holder would tremble to hear you. I am told Lord John Russell already quakes at the thought of your giving another speech."

Alfred laughed. "Your majesty is kinder than she is well informed."

"How so?" Prince Albert asked.

"Since my change in fortune, sir, I have conceived many ambitions, but . . . to give the country its first Quaker prime minister? That was never one of them!"

They all laughed heartily, the queen and the prince even more than Alfred, and more than the lightness of his words justified. He had the fleeting suspicion that they had expected to find him vulgar and uncouth. There was more than a hint of relief in their merriment. At all events they relaxed still further.

"We have heard of your speech yesterday, Lord Knightsbridge. Its sentiments were _most_ gratifying to us," she said.

"I spoke in the abstract, ma'am, because I had not then the honor of this presentation, and to have spoken of you as the living embodiment of those sentiments might have seemed presumptuous. I wish now I had not been so"—he sought for a word—"cowardly?" He offered it for her judgment.

The queen was now so delighted with this that she did the almost unheard of thing: She patted him on the arm for reassurance. "It was not cowardice, Lord Knightsbridge. It most certainly was not that, it was a most _fine_ discrimination." She withdrew her hand and smiled at both of them. "And when shall you go away?"

"Tomorrow, ma'am," Flora said.

"We go by railway to Plymouth and then by carriage to the duke's place in Cornwall. For a month," Alfred added.

"Constantine Park?" She turned to the duke.

"Indeed, ma'am."

"Oh, it's a treasure of a house. In so much better taste than . . ." She looked about her. "You'll be _so_ happy there."

"There and everywhere, ma'am," Alfred said.

By now he could do and say no wrong. "You are so perfectly right, Lord Knightsbridge. A happy marriage, which Prince Albert and I wish you with all our hearts, is the key to everything good in life." She turned to the duke. "And now let us see the jousting, duke," she commanded.

As they went out, she asked Flora if *that* were her going-away dress.

"My uncle has given me a most beautiful Kashmir shawl, ma'am," Flora said. "With your permission I shall send for it now. It completely covers me and it is a marvelous deep *brown* in colour."

"I should like to see that very much, Lady Flora," she said.

The prince asked Alfred what he had meant by having "conceived many ambitions" since his change in fortune.

"Most of them, sir, were passing fancies; but some, I trust, will endure."

"In particular?"

Alfred felt just a little uncomfortable under that searching, earnest gaze. "If I am ever a member of the peerage, which I hope will not be for many years yet, I shall be the only one with first-hand knowledge of life as it is lived by ordinary people in our teeming cities. It would be wrong not to put such knowledge to some use, I feel."

"Ah? And in what direction?" He was not going to let up.

"I believe, sir, that aristocratic patronage and guidance could be extended to small manufacturing industries exactly as it is now extended to agriculture. Why should agriculture be the sole industry a peer may patronize?"

"Agriculture? An *industry?*"

"It's becoming one, sir. It grows more scientific every year. One by one all the old crafts are turning into industries."

The prince was thoughtful for a while. Later he asked Alfred to call upon him after the honeymoon, "in connection with this great exhibition in Hyde Park next year."

"Quite the courtier, aren't you!" the duke said when they were alone for a moment.

Alfred looked at him in surprise. "Are you annoyed, duke?"

"No." He sounded dubious. "No." He repeated the word several times without sounding a whit more convinced. "Don't go out into the world too soon, though, my boy. You have a lot to learn and secure here, you know. First rule of successful command: Secure your base."

CHAPTER TWENTY-TWO

THAT NIGHT there was only the sheet between them. The difference caused by the removal of one woollen blanket and one cotton was thrilling for both of them. It revealed the sharpness of hips, knees, ribs, and shoulder blades, and all the softness in between. They lay side by side, enjoying these new sensations, but they talked of other things.

"The queen likes you," she said.

"And I like her."

"And the prince."

"He's very serious. I wouldn't like to live on the laughter that surrounds them."

"He was the one who laughed at your joke."

"It wasn't really a joke, now, was it. More of an elegant saying. Did I tell you what beautiful eyes you have?"

"I think you could become quite a favorite at court. Because that's exactly it—they don't like jokes. Not *jokes.* But they do like people who can put things elegantly, the way you did."

"I like your eyes. I can see me in them."

"We should be prepared for invitations to the court, or at least to dinners, when the season starts."

"I like your hair, your brow, your cheeks"—he kissed and caressed each as he named it—"your lips, your chin, your neck, your shoulders . . ."

He undid the top buttons of her nightdress.

"I'll have to get some more clothes. I can't appear at court with the mmmnhh . . ."

He stopped her with a kiss as he slipped his hand onto her breast. With a deep sigh she yielded to him. There were many sighs then, and no words. She turned herself so that her other breast came into his hand. He turned himself to her so that she might know that what she had seen that morning, shriveled by cold, had another incarnation, too.

After a while he withdrew his hand, did up her buttons again, and gently caressed her neck and the back of her head. "Douse the light," he said. "We have an early start tomorrow."

In the dark she snuggled against him. "Can I?" she asked.

"Can you what?"

"Get some more clothes?"

He moved a little apart and propped himself on one elbow. "Listen," he said seriously. "You are not a beggar woman. You are the Marchioness of Knightsbridge. What is proper to your station you shall have by right. Whatever we may do in life—surely you understand this—all the important things—we shall do them together. I need you, my darling. I need you at my *side,* not at my beck and call, not at my command."

"You mean you trust me?"

"With my life. With everything. You know yourself even better than I do. You know you're not like Hermione. You won't spend a farthing more than you need. And you'll get a penny's value out of every farthing you do spend."

She was silent for a while, as if this new information needed quite some digestion. He was almost asleep when she said in a trembling voice, "Alfred?"

"Mmmm?"

"That other thing we're going to do together . . . ?"

"What other thing?"

"You know."

"You mean . . . babies?" He reached a hand out and stroked her shoulder. She lay with her back to him.

"Is it . . . you know how . . . well, I mean, I've seen . . . what I mean is, is it like horses?" She giggled and, greatly daring, thrust her bottom into him.

"Ouch!" he was taken by surprise.

"Sorry!" She spun around. "I didn't mean to . . ."

The pain was momentary. "To answer your question," he said, pushing her gently on her back, "it's more often like this."

He eased himself half onto her and then fully. With a gasp she strained to him, undulating slowly. They both trembled. Their breath came out in shivers.

Now! he thought. *This is the right moment.*

He began to ease away the sheet that still separated them. Suddenly she burst into tears. Her body was shaken by huge, soft sobs. He moved to her side, took her head in his hands, and kissed and kissed her salt-wet cheeks.

"What is it my darling?" he whispered, perplexed. "What's the matter?"

"Oh, Alfred, I love you. I love you so."

"What's the matter?"

"I don't know. I'm just so happy I'm going to be all my life with you."

She fell asleep very quickly after that; but Alfred lay long awake, wondering if her tears were of fear or (as she claimed) of love. You could never tell with women. They didn't even understand themselves, not really. But he did know one thing: He couldn't pass another night in continence beside her.

CHAPTER TWENTY-THREE

THE ENTIRE HOUSEHOLD and about sixty of the guests were there to see them off. Once again the Great Courtyard was packed with a cheering multitude, carefully graded by rank, so that the first grains of rice to strike the young couple were thrown by red-raw-handed scullery maids, the last by the noble fingers of two dukes and a duchess.

The duke himself stopped the carriage and clambered briefly

inside. He put his head between theirs, one hand on each, at the shoulder, already chuckling at what he was about to say.

"Go *to!*" he laughed. "And come back *three!* What! Eh, eh?"

Their laughter followed him back outside. An hour later their carriage was put on the train to Plymouth.

Not for nothing was the Great Western Railway, or GWR, also known as the Great Way Round. For though Plymouth is southwest of Reading, the first part of the journey actually went north, to Didcot, before the line meandered roughly west to Swindon, Bath, and Bristol. Only there did it seem to remember where Alfred's and Flora's destination lay, for it plunged abruptly south to Exeter, then west to the terminus at Plymouth. It was a long, tedious trip, with two changes of train, atrocious coffee at Swindon, and rather dull scenery at least until Exeter. But the broad gauge of the GWR tracks made for a very comfortable ride; and Flora's knowledge of the social geography of southern England helped greatly to pass the time between kisses.

They arrived at Plymouth at half past four, with four hours of coach journey still before them, first by ferry, then through the narrow, winding lanes of Cornwall. They were both asleep as the carriage bowled along the final stretch into the Roseland peninsula.

The coachman leaned down and shouted through the windows. "That's her, my lord. That's Constantine Park!"

It was early twilight. They looked out into the fiery red ball of a dusty sun, sinking over Land's End, twenty miles away as the crow flies, but twice as far by Cornish roads. The intensity of the light at first prevented them from seeing the house, which was in any case only half glimpsed among the trees.

It stood near the top of a long stretch of gently rising ground, facing south. The rise began at a creek of the river Fal and continued more or less upward, in a rolling, tilting, Cornish way, for over a mile, where it fell abruptly to another small creek. The main stream of the estuary, where ocean-going ships could anchor in over ten fathoms of water, formed the western edge of the deer park. To the east lay the thick belt of trees, mostly oak, through which threaded the mile-long entrance drive. The trees curved around to the north of the house, clad the steep hillside where it fell to the creek, and petered out along the bank. But the only trees in front of the house were deliberately sited specimens, now of magnificent size.

From the principal windows of the house one group of trees hid the straggling village of St. Just, a mile or so away to the south; others intruded cleverly on the view of Falmouth, eliminating the gasworks and part of the docks but leaving fully visible the peninsula of Pendennis with its splendid Tudor castle, and all the finer houses on the upper terraces of the town.

Constantine Park was, as the queen had promised, "a treasure of a house." Georgian to the last block of granite, it had the same quality as Chalfont Abbey—the appearance of floating, despite its monumental proportions. Indeed, it looked very like part of the south wing of the Abbey, with a great triangular pediment resting on massive pillars crowned by simple Doric capitals. The setting sun, falling aslant them, showed their full relief. In the dark spaces between them, tall, discreet windows glowed with lamplight.

"Smell the sea?" Alfred asked.

"Oh, darling," she said. "Let's just have a small supper in our room. Then we needn't dress. I'm exhausted."

For a moment he was tempted, but the duke's precepts won. "None of your Kinnaird ways here, young madam. The Boyces have always dressed for dinner."

And, indeed, everything was ready laid out. Stearns, who had come on ahead the previous day, had Alfred bathed, dressed, and spruce in half an hour. Edwina, Flora's new maid, took a little longer.

"His grace asked me special to give you this, my lord." Stearns handed over what was obviously a wine bottle, wrapped in several layers of paper. It was a bottle of Imperial Tokay. There was a note attached, sealed with the duke's own crest. "My father laid this down in '83. It's the best thigh-spreader in the Abbey's cellars. Don't ever waste it. Go to, my boy. Yrs. affec. Augustus."

They put down the whole bottle at dinner. For once the duke was not exaggerating. Flora, when he came to join her in bed, held the sheets open for him, a bud turning into a flower.

"That was kind of the duke, that wine," Alfred said, getting in.

"He's a different man since you came into his life."

Alfred took her in his arms. "And what of me?"

"I don't think you're different at all. You remember you told Ian how you'd always known you were going to make your fortune? That it wasn't hope but destiny?"

"Mmm." He nuzzled her ear.

"I believe in things like that. I believe deep inside yourself you really did always know you were going to be a duke—don't do that, listen to me—"

"Did I ever tell you how much I love you?"

"So I don't think you've changed at all."

He chuckled. "Here's something that's changed. Give me your hand."

A moment later she said, "Oooh, Alfred!"

"Oh . . . Flora!"

"I'm frightened. Does it hurt?"

"You lie on me." He shivered violently with anticipation.

"Rely on you?" She trembled, too.

He lifted her in a rolling-clasping embrace. "So." He eased his nightshirt and her nightdress upward. "And . . . so."

It hurt very little; what followed was so thrilling and joyful that she forgot it hurt at all. And though she wept again at the end, it was for the sheer brimming over of her happiness.

That morning they went for a ride in the park. Alfred thought he might begin to hunt that autumn. With a little daily practice his horsemanship had improved enormously. No ordinary jump could now deter him and he was beginning to learn what was safe and what was foolish to leave to a horse's own judgment.

"The duke has let his hunt go a bit," Flora said. "A lot of people prefer to ride with the Old Berkeley or the South Oxfordshire, or even the South Berks. Ian says it's such a shame."

"I've been thinking about Ian. I've been thinking about all your family, in fact."

Flora ducked to pass beneath an overhanging bough and then eased her horse out into the center of the ride. Alfred executed a neat half-pass to make way for her. "My!" she said. "You are getting good." Then she pulled a face. "My family. Yes. A bit of a millstone."

"They don't need to be."

He waited for her to take the bait.

"Well, they've done nothing for four generations," she said, "except totter on the verge of bankruptcy."

"I think it's rather a case of they've been given nothing to do."

"Darling—when you say 'nothing' like that, with the 'o' like in *took*, it's about the only time you still show your origins. Otherwise your accent has got very good. It's the people you're now associating with, of course—hem-hem! D'you mind my telling you?"

"No! Please do."

"It's not *noothing*, it's *nuthing*."

"Nuthing," he said precisely. "How . . . *luvly*."

"Yes, not *loovly*. Go on about my family. What d'you mean they've been given *nuthing* to do?"

"What would Ian like to do? Given an absolutely free choice?"

"Breed horses."

"Exactly. And why shouldn't he? And not just any old horses either, but Derby winners?"

Flora laughed; this was a pipe dream.

"The stables at Rodings Hall, cleaned out and reroofed, are quite big enough."

"But the land! You've seen it."

"I've seen what drainage can do. And proper husbandry. The land is there. Anyway, *we've* got the grass. And the rides."

Flora grew thoughtful. It was somehow less of a pipe dream. "Oh, but the duke will never agree. I'm the only Kinnaird he ever had time for."

"He'll have to see it. We can't just leave your people to rot."

"Anyway, what about my father? And Hector and Dougall."

They were her other brothers.

"And Grace and Mary?" she added.

"We can marry your sisters well enough when the time comes, just if you take them under your wing for a bit. Your father—don't you think he'd make an excellent master for the hunt—our hunt? The Duke of St. Ormer's?"

Flora gave an incredulous laugh.

"It's not so stupid," Alfred insisted. "Who loves the chase more? Who knows the country better? Who is on better terms with the farmers whose land gets damaged? Who's more affable and good-natured?"

"And who'd make a bigger disaster of the kennels?"

"Hector wouldn't. We could make Hector and your father joint masters, giving Hector special charge of the hounds. Which only leaves Dougall."

"Yes," she said heavily. "Dougall."

"I don't know him too well."

"That's only because you're not a field girl or a plowman's daughter. They *all* know him too well."

"You're suddenly very knowing about Men."

"Oh, I've put a lot of thoughts together this last day or two, a lot of half-thoughts, a lot of impressions, a lot of guesses. Things have suddenly become very clear to me."

They went for long, slow walks along the seashore, as they called it—for, though it was strictly speaking still a river estuary, the bay was so wide and the water so thoroughly salty that it looked for all the world like any other stretch of the coast. And they decided to take up sailing, which was becoming quite a pastime among certain sections of the upper classes.

They made new paths among the oaks on the northern slopes and decided to take up landscape gardening, too.

Life, like a dance program, was filling in very nicely.

In the second week they began to receive cards from neighbors too tactful to leave them earlier; many of them they returned with calls. They learned who was who in the county and who was no longer who. They heard which tin mines were doing well and which were played out. They were brought up to date on the progress of the china-clay industry. And they were told which fishing ports and dockyards were making the heaviest investment in the future. None of this information was imparted in so many words; rather it oozed out in asides and hints, or sandwiched between items of gossip fit to singe the eyebrows. Alfred began to understand the true value of being "in Society," and why access to it was so jealously guarded. For many of its members this kind of information spelled the difference between failure and survival.

During their third week they began a tour of the ducal estates. Flora also found time to check the housekeeping accounts and look through the linen and silver.

In the midst of it all, word came that the duke was dying.

CHAPTER TWENTY-FOUR

BY THE FOLLOWING evening they were back at Chalfont Abbey. The contrast with the gay, bustling house they had left just three weeks earlier could not have been more stark. A funereal summer mist hung over the Great Courtyard. The hundreds of windows were dark; one or two fitful lights gleamed in the Brighton wing. It was a palace of ghosts.

McKay met them at the main door. "His grace is hanging on," he said. "I believe it's only the hope of seeing you is keeping the breath in him."

"What was it?" Alfred asked. "The message said nothing."

"*Anno domini*, my lord."

"It must be something particular."

"He was so hearty," Flora said, "when we left."

McKay sighed. "The doctor told him he'd live for years if only he refrained from driving out. So his grace ordered his carriage—the open landau—and drove right around the estate. Fourteen hours he was out. He was dying when he came back. I told him so.

'Aye,' he said. 'But like a gentleman, eh!' I suppose the truth is he was ready."

The duke was asleep when they tiptoed into his room. Alfred raised his eyebrows; the doctor shrugged his shoulders. Yet the old grandee looked as fit as they had always known him; there was no labored breathing, his cheeks were not sunken, his color was good —almost too good.

After twenty minutes or so he awoke. At first he blinked uncomprehendingly around him. Then he saw them, but it was still several seconds before he recognized them. When he did, however, he smiled fit to crack his face. He reached a hand toward each, one to the left and one to the right of his bed. "How do your graces?" he asked.

"Most nobly," Alfred said with a lightness he did not feel. "We shall laugh at this yet, sir."

"You will, my boy. I shan't." He closed his eyes and seemed to fall asleep again.

Alfred and Flora sat on the bed, one on each side of him. He awoke again. "I had something to tell you," he said. Then he seemed to fall asleep once more.

After another long silence he spoke again, this time without opening his eyes. "Oh, yes! 'All empire is . . .' " He faltered.

"Yes, duke?" Alfred prompted. " 'All empire is . . .'?"

Flora, who by now knew her Dryden as well as the duke, supplied the rest: " 'All empire is no more than power in trust.' "

A seraphic smile spread across the duke's face. He squeezed Flora's hand and shook it weakly.

A long, fitful vigil later he opened his eyes for the last time. He looked at Alfred and tried to speak; only a croak emerged. With immense effort he cleared his throat. His eyes held Alfred's in a trance, almost as if they implored him to do nothing to break the slender thread of concentration that now united them. Everyone there could see that he was sinking fast.

" 'Farewell,' " he said, speaking to Alfred alone.

"Come, sir . . ." Alfred began with forced heartiness.

But the duke, shaking his head with impatience and clasping Alfred's hand as if life alone were there, stopped him.

" 'Farewell,' " he tried again, " 'too little and too lately known, whom I began . . .' "

There was a long silence. Then his breathing, already shallow, fell to a whisper . . . fell to nothing. His fingers ceased to grip either of them. Again Flora completed the quotation the duke had begun: " 'Farewell, too little and too lately known, whom I began to think and call my own.' "

Alfred took the limp arms and folded them over the duke's chest. The doctor held a small looking glass to the slightly parted lips and confirmed what they already knew.

Alfred knelt at the bedside and overflowed—rather than burst—into tears. Flora came to join him.

McKay and Mrs. Kerns allowed their grief its scope. Then the housekeeper said, "I must lay him out now, your graces."

On the duke's tongue the words "your graces" had seemed an irony; when Mrs. Kerns spoke them she sealed off more than half a century. It was a verdict—or at least a finding—of death more absolute than either the doctor's mirror or their own intuitions.

Alfred Boyce, the printer's son, the ward of a humble apothecary, was now the Fifth Duke of St. Ormer; and Flora was duchess. They went to their own room but knew they could not sleep. Alfred took the candle and together, hand in hand, they wandered through the rooms of the Abbey, mute bearers of bad tidings to those echoing, shrouded darknesses.

"He was the last real duke," Alfred said. "I'll only be a kind of counterfeit."

"Don't say such a thing," Flora told him. "Don't think it, either."

Alfred did not respond.

Flora went on: "He was a duke for *his* age. No one can deny that. But equally no one can deny he was increasingly out of joint with *our* age. He didn't understand it. Industry and things like that. But you do." She squeezed his arm. "You'll be ten times the duke he was. For *this* age."

"We'll see," he said.

"You will," she insisted. "A duke isn't like the rest of the nobility. He is the pioneer. He cuts the path through the forest. He puts the blazes on the trees. Even more than the sovereign, he is the spirit of the age."

CHAPTER TWENTY-FIVE

THE DEATH of Duke Augustus was not a national affair. His brand of Whig politics had long ago played itself off the national stage. So the presence at his funeral of the prime minister and some of the cabinet, as well as a few lesser royalties, was more formal than felt. The nation noted his passing; no more than that.

The true grief, the authentic loss, was local. As the gun carriage bearing the duke's coffin set off from the church, on the last journey through Great Marlow and out to Chalfont Abbey, Alfred, at the head of the funeral escort from the regiment of which he was now colonel-in-chief, looked long and hard at the faces of those who lined the route. There was grief in them; and the grief was more personal than public. Time had ceased for the man who had always spared time for them. Cantankerous he may have been, even downright rude, but he never ignored them or treated their worries with contempt. A once-assured part of their collective future was once again at hazard—at the whim of the new man.

Alfred, as stiff and upright as his sword, turned neither right nor left; the compulsions of military ceremonial effaced his private grief. He made one exception, and one only: Opposite Nanny Morgan's, where the old grandee had stopped that first day in Great Marlow, he halted the cortège and saluted. The ancient nurse, at the first-floor window, nodded gravely and dabbed a handkerchief to her eye.

Arrived at Chalfont Abbey the cortège wound across the Great Courtyard to the huge, iron-studded oaken doors of Herberts Tower. Here the ceremony changed character, from public to private. The escort was dismissed; the men joined the tenants for a funeral tea held in the two big tithe barns bordering the stable yard and the officers joined the gentry for a buffet in one of the larger rooms in the Brighton wing. Only Alfred, Flora, the old duke's two sisters, Lady Harriet and Lady Katherine, and McKay were left.

Block and tackle had been fixed to the vaulted arch above. With its aid gardeners and estate workers lifted the simple oak coffin from the gun carriage. A boy took the flag, the duke's own colors, to the battlements and raised it to half-mast, beside the Union Jack, which had flown there for the past three days. The gun carriage was trundled away and four flagstones were removed to give access to the crypt below. The vicar spoke the solemn words of interment—earth to earth, ashes to ashes, dust to dust—and the coffin was slowly lowered into the black of the pit.

Lady Harriet was calm but Lady Katherine needed the comfort of Flora's arm about her. They turned to walk out into the Great Courtyard.

"I'll see him properly placed," Alfred said and headed for the door to the crypt stairs.

"There he is now," one of the gardeners was saying. "Equal with my old mam and dad." His voice echoed crisply off the stone all around.

" 'Death's a leveler,' " Alfred said as he stepped into the crypt. His scarlet uniform seemed absurdly festive in that world of black and gray. The laborers shuffled respectfully.

"What d'you do now?" Alfred asked.

They showed him how the body, wrapped all over in a winding sheet, even the face, was set to lie on a pallet of oak inside its temporary coffin. With the block and tackle they lifted it out, pallet and all, and laid it inside the stone sarcophagus which the duke had commissioned over thirty years earlier. It took all six of them to hoist the lid into place and then to inch the sarcophagus off its trestle and onto the marble shelf that was to be its permanent resting place.

"There's been a slipup, your grace," the master mason said. He placed a tablet of marble in front of a space on the coffin that was obviously designed to hold it. "Cut too short, you see, sir?"

"Yes, I see." The tablet, which simply read *Augustus Clarence Fitzstephen Wrottesley Veitch du Bois, 1769–1850 Fourth Duke of St. Ormer,* was four inches short.

"I'll recut another, shall I, your grace?"

Alfred, after a moment's thought, said, "No. Find a piece to fit the space—a piece of black granite would look nice—and carve upon it the words 'All empire is no more than power in trust.' He'd have liked that. By the way, was there a child's toy down here, a little wooden horse?"

One of the men reached onto the shelf above the sarcophagus and brought down the toy the old grandee had called "Caesar." He handed it over.

Alfred waited in silence until they had packed up their tools and tackle and gone. The four flagstones grated back into place with a resounding finality. He was alone—not just in the crypt but in the world.

It was one thing to make idle plans for the estate and his trusteeship of it, knowing that the duke, the real arbiter, was there to sanction or refuse them; it was quite another to take the responsibility for those plans on his own immature shoulders. The sheer size of the undertakings he now faced appalled him. For a fleeting instant he was angry with the old man, whose death seemed a kind of desertion. Then he was ashamed of his anger. He possessed the only thing that mattered, the blood of the du Bois. Everything else —social skills, ability to manage the estate, command of people, good form—these were not merely secondary, they were quite trivial in comparison. The blood was all. He was one of God Almighty's gentlemen.

"Farewell," he said, laying his hand on the sarcophagus. There were no tears left to shed, but his grief was unabated.

He left the horse where the old duke had found it first, in the cupboard where the keys were kept.

The last of the mourners had gone, but Lawyer Polkinghorne remained. All afternoon he had been twitching with impatience.

"Is he to read the will?" Alfred had asked Lady Harriet.

"There's nothing to read," she said. "There are a few bequests to servants of the estate and to old Nanny Morgan, people like that. The residue is left to you. Augustus agreed it with meself and Kate some months ago."

"Oh." Alfred was a little embarrassed. "If you want some memento of him . . ." he offered.

"Well, now . . ." She eyed a Holbein portrait on the wall, one the duke had bought in his own lifetime, not part of the entailed property.

"Any of his personal effects," Alfred added hastily.

She had taken a tortoise-shell brush and comb. Katherine had taken nothing.

He was alone with Polkinghorne in the duke's—now *his*—business room. "Lady Harriet has told me the main provisions of the late duke's will," he said to the lawyer.

"Matters have changed, your grace," Polkinghorne answered gravely.

"Oh?" Alfred's heart gave a lurch.

"D'you remember the day of your wedding, sir—an obnoxious little upstart in a wide-awake hat who was bundled away as you and the duchess descended from the carriage?"

"Ah, yes." Alfred had forgotten the incident until now. "Who was he?"

"A nasty bit of outdoor work on the part of his parents, sir. A writ server by the name of Swope."

"Writ server?" Alfred was amused. "He wanted to serve a writ on a duke?"

"No, sir. On *you*."

"Ah." Alfred was suddenly thoughtful. "Let me guess now. Sir Eric Newbiggin has some hand in this?"

Polkinghorne was surprised. "The late duke said you weren't to be told, sir."

"I wasn't. I overheard. That day Sir Eric left in such an ill temper, I heard him tell the duke that a man with a debt has a ball and chain, and whoever picks up that ball can make its wearer twitch and dance . . . something like that. Is that what he's trying? He's bought up the estate's debts and now he's going to press me for them, is that it?"

Polkinghorne nodded; he was disappointed to find that half his tale was anticipated.

"Can he, Mr. Polkinghorne? Duke Augustus always said we may laugh in our creditors' faces, if it so please us."

"In practice, yes. That is quite true. A rich man who cared little what it cost him, and who cared even less for Society at large, could . . . well, let us say, make a nuisance of himself."

Alfred rang for McKay. "Ask her grace to be kind enough to join us," he said.

"In the *business* room, sir?" McKay was shocked.

Alfred stared angrily back. McKay left hastily; he would not question his new master so swiftly next time.

When Flora came, Alfred asked Polkinghorne to begin again.

As she listened, Flora's face grew longer and longer. At last she stood and walked about, wringing her hands. "Debt!" she said in an agonized voice. "Debt, debt, debt! How I loathe and detest that word. Oh, Polkinghorne, what are we to do?"

Polkinghorne glanced primly at Alfred. "Perhaps," he answered, "if your grace would leave it to the duke and me."

"Be calm, my dear," Alfred said, recovering from his astonishment at Flora's collapse. "In the first place, it isn't our debt, it's the late duke's. I'll pay it, right enough, but as an act of grace and favor, not as a legal obligation. And I'll pay it in our own good time. I didn't ask you here to puzzle over finances."

"Oh . . . what then?" she asked, only half pacified.

"We have a *social* nuisance to deal with—this Newbiggin fellow. To treat him as a legal nuisance would be absurd."

Polkinghorne smiled approvingly. "And dangerous, sir."

Flora relaxed at that. A social nuisance. That was *her* ground. She laughed. "For a moment it seemed as if I were home again." She turned to the lawyer. "Well, Polkinghorne, a social nuisance he may be, but his attack will be a legal one. Now tell us how. What process? He can't use the ordinary courts, surely?"

"No, your grace. He has to use the House of Lords, the only court empowered to try a peer. Technically, it sits as the Court of the Lord Steward."

"And is the procedure the same as in the lower courts?"

"By no means, ma'am. Exactly what the Lords' procedure is, I'm not certain. I don't think anyone is, least of all their lordships. I cannot find a single case—certainly not in the last century and a half—when a peer was successfully pressed for debt. There have been several actions but they have on every occasion fallen to pieces because of errors in drafting, errors in service, errors in procedure. In the end the litigants have seen that it's a bit like a steeplechase over sheer mountain crags at night without a moon. In short, they've all thrown in the towel."

"But, as you say," Alfred reminded him, "a rich man . . ."

Polkinghorne nodded absently.

"What are you thinking?" Alfred asked.

The lawyer smiled. "Perhaps I'm the last one who should say this, sir, but, ah, the fact that England has no written constitution and no Bill of Rights means that judges enjoy enormous discretion. They would deny it strenuously, of course, but in fact they are quite free to invent new law as they go along. Especially in a field like this, where no case has ever gone the distance—no modern case, anyway."

"Is that hopeful?" Alfred pressed.

"Indeed it is, sir. I shouldn't think their lordships would welcome a successful suit for debt by a commoner against a peer. It would open the sea wall to a monster flood of similar actions. Why, the House could be tied up in litigation for debt until the end of the century."

"So we needn't worry about the possibility of Newbiggin's success?" Flora asked.

"He could still be . . ." Polkinghorne sought the right words.

Flora found them: " . . . a *bloody* nuisance."

"As you say, ma'am."

"But of the social variety," Flora went on. "I wonder what his wife thinks."

"She disagrees with him over nearly everything," Alfred said.

"Anyone who pursued what was obviously a vindictive action like this—especially against a duke—would certainly be cut absolutely from good society." Flora was thinking aloud. "Lady N. won't be happy at that, I'm sure."

Alfred, watching her and half guessing what was in her mind, smiled. "So?" he prompted.

"Divide and conquer," she said. "I shall write to them at once."

She stood; the two men stood. Polkinghorne was worried. "I think, if I may suggest it, your grace, that, for the moment, anyway, all correspondence between your graces and the plaintiffs should go through me—in as much as . . . er . . . that is to say, in so far as . . ."

"Nonsense, lawyer," Flora said. "We are not 'in so far,' nor are we 'in as much.' I shall write to Lady Newbiggin inviting the duke and me to stay at the Hall, Cokeley, for"—she looked at Alfred—"ten days?"

"*Stay* with them?" Alfred was astounded.

Polkinghorne was aghast.

"Yes." Flora was calmly amused. "What baronet's wife could possibly close her doors to a duke and duchess?"

"What if Newbiggin commands her to?" Alfred asked, still not grasping the point.

"Why, then," Flora said, "we shall have at least two allies, the wife and the daughter, beneath his roof."

And she left them savoring the elegance of it.

"Jove," the lawyer said. "It's a master stroke. Either way it puts Sir Eric in a most uncomfortable position."

He and Alfred then went on to deal with several other legal affairs concerning the estate and the inheritance—not least being the need for Alfred and Flora to draw up their own wills. All the while Alfred was aware that something still agitated the lawyer. "There's something still on your mind, Mr. Polkinghorne," he prompted.

The man gave an insincerely light laugh. "I don't even know whether it's worth mentioning it, your grace."

"Let me judge."

"Well, we received a letter the other day. From Australia. From solicitors in Victoria. They represent a man by the name of Bruce Boys, who claims that his grandfather was one William Boys or Boyes"—the lawyer spelled both names to make the distinction clear—"who was transported from London in 1770 on a convict ship."

"Yet we have documentary proof that he died that same year on a prison hulk in the Thames," Alfred said.

"And Messrs. Marcus and May, the Australian solicitors, claim they have documentary proof to the contrary."

"Yet we have a death certificate."

Polkinghorne looked around. "There should be a copy somewhere here, sir. The late duke insisted on having a copy of everything I turned up."

McKay was sent for and quickly produced the relevant box.

The death certificate clearly bore the name of one William Boyes, and the date 1770. The cause of death was given as "black bile." His age was entered as eighteen, which, as Polkinghorne pointed out, was exactly right for the William Boyes who was the son of Oliver Boyes and his cousin Chastity, neé Boyce (whose sister, Piety, was Alfred's father's father's mother).

Alfred turned the certificate over in his hands; it seemed very new. "Is this the original?" he asked.

"No, sir. A copy. The original is at Somerset House."

"A modern copy," Alfred said, "by a modern clerk—who knew you were seeking the death certificate of a William Boyes?"

The lawyer's forensic mind saw the implications at once. "Sir, you are not, I trust, suggesting—"

"I'm suggesting nothing, Mr. Polkinghorne. But I would like to be clear as to what happened. Exactly what happened?"

"Well . . ." The man was unhappy. "This is a modern certificate compiled from the old Bills of Mortality, in this case from the Office of General Gaol Delivery, now among the Home Office records."

Alfred felt reality melting like water in sand. "What was the very first actual record of William Boyes's death? The first written notification of it?" he asked.

"There were two, sir. We can't say which came first."

"I would like to see some kind of facsimile, by an artist, or even by some photographical means, if that were possible."

Polkinghorne searched through the papers again and pulled forth a couple of pale brown sheets. "These are by calotype," he said. "They are of the two original entries. This from the turnkey's log. This from the Bill of Mortality."

"You were very thorough, Mr. Polkinghorne."

"His late grace insisted on it, sir."

"Surely the turnkey's log came before the other?"

The lawyer shook his head. "One can't be sure of *anything* where the jails of the last century are concerned, sir. The turnkey might have sent in the names of the dead on the backs of old butchers' receipts—and then made up his official log at the end of each month, backward, as it were, from the Bill."

Alfred looked at the two facsimiles. The entry in the Bill read

but that in the log read

"It could be William Boges or Buges or Bogis or even Bugis," he said.

"But the Bill is unequivocally *Boyes*, sir. And none of those other names is known in England."

Alfred sighed. For the first time he began to worry. "I'm sure you see the point, though, Mr. Polkinghorne. It appears most unlikely that the turnkey made up his log 'backward.' But there is a possibility that the clerk who drew up the Bill either misread the log or—like you—refused to believe that Bogis-Buges-etcetera could possibly be intended and so wrote Boyes."

The lawyer nodded unhappily.

"And our Australian would-be kinsman, Bruce Boys, that's definitely without the *e*?"

Another nod.

"Just to make matters easy! Now tell me, when their lordships determined that I was the heir presumptive, which of all these documents did they see?"

Even more dejectedly the lawyer picked up the modern copy.

"Nothing else?"

"Nothing else, sir."

"What a web!" He pondered for a moment. "See here, Mr. Polkinghorne, we must immediately discover if the names Boges-Bugis-etcetera appear in *any* other records—births, marriages, prisons . . . debtors . . . workhouses . . . any and all records. Also the name Boys. Leave no list unsearched now, d'you hear me?"

"It shall be done, your grace."

"And now let us assume, for a moment, that Bruce Boys is, indeed, my—what would he be?—my third cousin. What then?"

"Why then, sir, the line through Chastity is not extinct and the titles fall into abeyance among the heirs general until the issue is clear. Except the Barony of Yeo, which can descend in the female line and has already passed to Lady Harriet du Bois."

A new thought struck Alfred. "I have read that the sovereign can end an abeyance in favor of any of the parties at any time, by Royal Warrant."

The lawyer nodded doubtfully.

"I am quite a favorite of her majesty," Alfred said.

But Polkinghorne shook his head. "You have powerful neighbors, too, sir, who would not be heartbroken to see this estate broken up. The late duke has created some of the best farmland in the kingdom here at Chalfont Abbey. You have a hundred neighbors and rich tenants who would love to pick up the pieces."

"But the entail?"

"An entail is hard to break if the inheritance is clear. However, if the titles are in abeyance and . . ."

The full horror of it suddenly struck Alfred. "But," he said in a faltering voice, "that would leave me a commoner again—and open to Sir Eric Newbiggin's action in the ordinary courts!"

It was a very worried and dispirited solicitor who left Chalfont Abbey that evening to return to London.

As Alfred watched him go, he felt a sudden intuition: This coming struggle to retain the title and estate, and fight off the claims for debt, was *not* at heart a legal battle! It might, at this moment, present itself in those terms; but that was a red herring. The real battle was elsewhere—in the hearts and minds of everyone involved. In the heart and mind of the queen, of his neighbors, of the Newbiggins, of his fellow peers in the House of Lords. If he could win that battle first, the legal victory would follow. Hadn't Polkinghorne himself said it: The Lords can make up the law as they go along!

There was a new jauntiness in his tread and a new zest in his spirit as he went in search of Flora. He had once told the duke that he wanted nothing he hadn't personally earned. Fate herself must have smiled to hear the glibness of it!

CHAPTER TWENTY-SIX

SUCH AN UNMANLY affliction, migraine!" Lady Newbiggin said crossly in a voice that certainly carried up to her husband's window from the terrace, where she, Hermione, Flora, and Alfred were sitting. Nobody agreed or disagreed.

It was a golden autumn. There was a delicious coolness on the air and the light was somehow more tenuous than it had been in torrid July and August.

"It will be neurasthenia next!" Lady Newbiggin added even more loudly.

Again only birdsong and the play of fountains answered her.

Alfred was in a light sweat, not so much because of the pleasant heat but because of the even more pleasant closeness of Hermione, as radiantly beautiful as ever. He remembered every curve and softness of her. Just to look at her made his pulse race once more;

naturally, he looked at her quite often—brief, lust-fired glances that, literally, glanced off her and onward to Flora, who was nearly always looking back at him in what he imagined to be an adoring fondness. Caught *in flagrante inspectatione,* he felt such a swine.

He loved Flora, worshiped her; in her arms he experienced ecstasies of a depth and magnificence he had never known with anyone else, not even with such rare beauties as Hermione. Why, then, did that not satisfy him? What was left unfulfilled to lust after other and much lesser women—Danielle and Hermione, to name but the most immediate two—as hotly as ever? It was beginning to dominate his thoughts in the most dangerous way.

The extraordinary thing was that Hermione and Flora had now become such firm friends. The icy charm that used to permeate every corner and moment of their relationship had melted to a genuine warmth. The pair of them spent hours walking around the garden together, going to the shops together, singing or playing duets, and planning imaginary tours to all the countries of the world.

These hours had been squeezed into one of the most punishing social programs imaginable. Everyone who was anyone within a hundred miles was invited to either a dinner or an at-home "to meet Their Graces, the Duke and Duchess of St. Ormer." Those who were not away shooting or fishing, or still recovering from the excesses of last season at some Continental spa, came. They made a good-sized party every afternoon and evening. Tiring though it was, Alfred and Flora were delighted. The more firmly they were identified as Sir Eric's guests in the minds of his neighbors (especially neighbors who were themselves among the gentry and nobility) the less possible was it for him to begin *any* litigation against them—especially an action for debt; not even the worst cad in the social register would dream of such treachery. Flora estimated that they had bought at least three years' peace, if not five.

Small wonder that Sir Eric had taken the least part that politeness dictated in the whole proceeding, and retired to his room with "migraine" or some such affliction whenever possible.

The reprieve had really been won at the first dinner—indeed, even before that, when the first invitations had been issued, marking the duke and duchess as friends of the Newbiggins. The rest was just so much cement and reinforcement. The thought nagged at Alfred.

"We must do more," he said one night to Flora. "We've borrowed five years, let's say. But it *is* borrowed time. The clock is already ticking. We need to do something more permanent."

"Become a Mussulman convert," Flora, so sure of his love, teased. "Then you could marry Hermione, too."

He took her tenderly in his arms and said, "Are you sure now? Are you sure you wouldn't mind?"

He expected her to laugh and push him away and so end the little comedy. To his surprise she merely hugged a little tighter and then stared back at him with a strange, almost experimental, mixture of love and truculence in her eyes. "Well . . ." she said at last. "I wonder if it would really be so dreadful."

That night in bed, he had just begun to caress her when he heard her stifle a yawn.

"Hey?" he said.

"Oh, I'm sorry, darling. But I'm so tired."

"Ah." He withdrew his hand.

"Well," she said, tenderly reproachful, "we have rather gone at it a lot."

"But we're still newly married."

"Nearly two months!"

"That's very newly married. I think I'll still feel newly married to you a year from now. Ten years even."

There was a catch in her breath, a suppressed gasp.

"I learn so much about you every time—I mean, all the time. Every day."

She snuggled up to him. "Go on then," she said, half-inviting him with her voice, half-fending him off with her sigh.

"No," he said politely. "Not if you're tired."

At once she drew a little away, pecked him with a kiss, and flung herself completely on her own side of the bed with her back to him. "You're the most wonderful husband," she yawned. "A true gentleman."

He was, perforce, a wonderful husband and true gentleman the next night, too.

And the following day, Sunday, was the day they sat out in the autumn sun, while Lady Newbiggin shouted insults up at her husband's window, and Alfred shivered at the nearness of Hermione.

No, he thought, not nearness, but *propinquity!* What a thrilling word, propinquity—awash with suggestions of pinkness and softness and (because it sounded more Latin than English) of delicate upper-class sin. Oh! To enjoy propinquity with Hermione again!

"Bullen-Chetwynne will be here in an hour," Lady Newbiggin said. "Tedious man. We really ought to go and dress for evensong."

Bullen-Chetwynne had been one of the dinner guests a few nights earlier. He was returning tonight, though it was a Sunday, because he was, potentially at least, "of the family." He had not actually proposed to Hermione, but that was merely because theirs would not, in any case, be the sort of marriage that was proposed —more the kind that was arranged.

In many ways he suited Hermione admirably. He was a middle-aged bachelor who lived for his hunting and shooting. In the dead months between seasons he was either slaughtering tigers in India, bagging polar bears in Greenland, or dropping anything that moved in Africa. The walls of Bullen Towers, his country house, were crammed with heads—horned, fanged, antlered, or tusked; spotted, striped, blazed, mottled or burnished—from five continents. On every shelf, in every niche, birds and fish were frozen in glass boxes. Every room was a Museum of the Moment of Death.

Bullen-Chetwynne had, naturally, always been well off; but a few years ago on the death of an uncle he had come into a huge fortune, nearly two million pounds and a thriving business in the Baltic Exchange. Most men would at once have sought out a country estate and put down roots—got a seat on the local bench, founded a dynasty, and so on. He knew that was what he ought to do but it was so different from what he actually wanted that he was damned if he saw why he should. He went so far as to buy some rough shooting in Scotland and the salmon rights on one of the best stretches of the Shannon in Ireland; but he found himself so mercilessly fleeced by poachers and by indolent gamekeepers and bailiffs that his appetite for real estate, or estate of any kind, quite vanished. From then on he behaved as he had always done, living well within his former means, which had, in any case, been more than ample. The money, in government stock, had gone on steadily accumulating; the trading business, thanks to an excellent general manager, had continued to thrive under the benign neglect of its proprietor.

But, though the lack of an estate, wife, and position did not trouble him, the absence of an heir did. There was no one else to leave his money to. He devised a charity that would have taken poor young slum boys on the verge of manhood and given them a cracking fine shooting holiday in Africa or Scotland—something they could look back on with pleasure all their lives—before returning them to the soot and poverty. But the lawyers and other people he talked to, people who would have to run the thing after he had gone, were so lukewarm that he dropped the idea. That was when he went wife hunting instead.

He hunted her like any other quarry: as a trophy—though one

to grace his household rather than merely adorn its walls. Hermione, reputed to be one of the most beautiful women in the country, was an obvious choice. And she was not as averse to the idea as she might have been just a year earlier. An instinct that had matured only lately within her told her that "Bull," as everyone knew him, would not bother her much; indeed, for most of the year he would not be there to bother her at all. He was almost indifferent to money; his fortune, augmented by her dowry, ought to be more than enough for even her needs. All in all, the prospect of becoming Mrs. Bullen-Chetwynne was not unpleasant.

Unfortunately, Bull was stalking other quarry, too: a Miss Maude Overton. She was no beauty, but her family, the Overtons of Broughtonside, had held out the prospect of being able to secure Bull a baronetcy through the influence of a cousin of theirs who happened to be an earl. Bull was a simple fellow but no fool. No hunter of tigers and polar bears can possibly be a fool—no *surviving* hunter, anyway. He had put the whole matter straight to Sir Eric and Lady Newbiggin: He would be proud to marry Hermione but even prouder to die as Sir Redvers Bullen-Chetwynne and leave the title to an heir.

He said no more than that, but he knew that their friends the Duke and Duchess of St. Ormer were due on a visit. He told Lady Newbiggin there was no immediate hurry. Lady Newbiggin had related the entire story within moments of their arrival.

Alfred discussed it with Flora; they agreed in a general sort of way that it would be splendid to help raise the Newbiggin bid for the prize Bull, but Alfred was so ashamed of his continuing lust for Hermione that he was afraid to be specific.

He edged a little nearer to the point that Sunday evening, while they were dressing for church. "I can't just offer him a viscountcy or something, out of the blue," he said. "It would seem so crude."

"No. Offer him something else and tie the viscountcy in with it."

"But what? What do you offer a man with two million pounds?"

She took up a necklace and went toward her dressing room. "Obviously it will have to be connected with the slaughter of things in fur and feathers and scales, since he hasn't the remotest interest in anything else on earth."

Hunting? he thought. Had she forgotten they had earmarked her father, Sir Duncan, as M.F.H. of the St. Ormer? "You can't mean hunting," he said through her door. "Surely?"

"Oh, Alfred. It's man's business all this. You'll think of something."

Offer Bull something? To do with the estate? That would imply his moving down near Chalfont Abbey. With his wife, Hermione. There are twenty-eight miles of sweat glands in the human body; every inch of Alfred's gave a sudden and delicious ejaculation at the thought.

Bull read the lesson in church. He stood off, four feet from the lectern, and addressed it as if it were a large public meeting in a hall with bad sound propagation. He spoke exactly the same way at table, aiming his intensely blue eyes in a frank, unseeing gaze down his long, delicately aquiline nose, and bellowed at the same public meeting, now crowded between the candelabra and a dish of grapes and pomegranates. "Much fishin' your way, duke?"

"Our main river is the Thames," Alfred began.

"Ruined!" He became concerned. "Don't know how you're goin' to live, what! Your predecessor let the St. Ormer go hang. Went shooting every blue moon—no covert left worth the name. Hemmed if I know how you'll live."

He spoke as if the provisioning of Alfred's table were utterly dependent on what could be shot, hooked, or netted.

"I'm proposing to revive the fortunes of the St. Ormer," Alfred answered into the dying echoes of Bull's voice. "But here's a thing that's just occurred to me. We're going to build a railway from Maidenhead right up to the north of our estate, connecting into the other main line at Princes Risborough. Now there's a lot of country up there, roughly between the Old Berkeley, the South Oxfordshire, and the Whaddon Chase. It's not hunted at all at the moment except for a few commoners' packs. The railway, you see, would change all that."

Bull's mouth hung open. His forkful of *selle de mouton* and *pommes duchesse* was slowly lowered again to the plate. A new hunt! And in such superb country—for, naturally, he knew the neighboring hunts well.

"I'd call it the Stokenchurch, which is where I'd build the kennels." Alfred laughed modestly. "I rather thought I'd be my own master. Even though I've not actually hunted yet. And even though I'd not be able to spare it too much time. But one could probably manage in an hour or two a week, don't you think?"

Bull emitted a strangled noise deep in his throat and fixed Alfred with an angry stare.

Alfred could not resist adding, "Perhaps we wouldn't hunt actual foxes the first season, just drag a box of kippers about until we know the country."

Bull went purple. Alfred began to be alarmed; surely the man must be rupturing vessels all over the place.

"Blasphemy!" came the bellow at last. "It's an outrage, sir! Why you . . . you . . ."

"Bull!" Hermione cried in alarm.

"I'm sorry, sir." Alfred was suddenly most conciliatory. "As I told you, I know nothing about it. But I'm most eager to learn. Please tell me." His smile sparkled. "Please? You are obviously just the man to enlighten me."

Bull's sporting good nature reasserted itself, if only just. He was still trembling as he began trying to convey to Alfred all that had to be done in building up a new hunt with a new pack in new kennels in new country. It was twenty years' work for a dedicated man just to get the foundations—a lifetime's work to make a first-class hunt.

"Ah!" Alfred let understanding show in his face. "Perhaps I'd better postpone the idea then. Where could one find such a man quickly? Unless"—inspiration—"you might care to help me, sir?"

Bull, panting with delight, roared that it would be an honor. Alfred asked where it would be best to advertise.

"Advertise?" Bull was aghast.

"For the right people."

"*I* am the right people! That's what I meant. I'll set up your hunt for you, duke. The best hunt in the south!"

"You!"

"Yes, me! What did ye think I meant? Don't you understand," he bellowed. "It's the sort of thing one *dreams* about." He grinned. "I don't care if you *are* the Duke of St. Ormer, you couldn't stop me now if you tried."

"Well," Alfred said, "we must do something in return. We can't just . . ." Inspiration: "What about a viscountcy, eh? The best hunt in the kingdom ought to have a viscount as its M.F.H., what? Lord Bullen-Chetwynne? It has a ring. What d'you say, Hermione?"

She smiled and looked casually down at her fingers. "An undeniable ring, duke."

The future Lord Bullen-Chetwynne looked at her, at Alfred, at Flora, at Sir Eric and Lady Newbiggin. He too smiled; and he did not need to hear the full terms of the bargain.

Sir Eric, defeated now on all fronts, stared hard at his hands. They were empty.

CHAPTER TWENTY-SEVEN

BULLEN-CHETWYNNE was not able to come down to Chalfont Abbey until the New Year; twenty-seven Polish bison, forty-one Swedish elk, sixty-five Irish salmon and forty trout, and countless capercaillie in Scotland all had the prior claim. It was a valedictory tour of northern Europe's killing grounds by one who would see little of them for the next five years.

That autumn and winter Alfred and Flora went to several dinners at Buckingham Palace and Windsor; they also attended a formal drawing room and a levée. Alfred was made Lord Lieutenant of Buckinghamshire and a Deputy Lieutenant of Cornwall. The latter post was something of a sinecure but the lord lieutenantship was a position of real power. In theory no one could build a house in the country or marry someone outside it without his leave. These days a lord lieutenant was chiefly responsible for recommending all the justices of the peace in the county and for manning and running each petty-sessions division. This required the closest co-operation of all the gentry. Alfred learned that at this level the official life of the county was much more federal than hierarchical in nature. He had to be scrupulous in respecting the opinions of every squire and magistrate, and to avoid giving offense by leaning too much one way or the other. Flora's intimate knowledge of most of the families involved was invaluable to him.

The common bond between them all lay in the game laws and game preservation. No single act of the new duke's could have done more to win him the approval of country gentlemen, from the highest to the humblest, than his decision to found a new hunt in the northern part of the estate and to take a more active interest in his pheasant manors. The old duke's enclosures, they all agreed, had gone part of the way by removing common lands and making the management of game birds possible. But only the new duke could turn that possibility into fact. In 1823 twelve guns had brought down 525 pheasant in a single day at Ashridge, in country not too unlike the Chalfont Abbey estates. The bag still stood unbeaten.

"We'll top that Ashridge record yet," Alfred said.

He was almost universally accounted a sound man.

That winter, too, he was elected to Brooks's, the Whig club—almost the family club of the du Bois—and to the Army and Navy (the "Rag and Famish," as it was nicknamed). The great advantage of the British club, as Duke Augustus had once told him, was that "a man could make a damfool of himself and no word of scandal would ever go out-of-doors." Nevertheless, Alfred soon got a reputation as a man who made up his own mind when he wanted to.

He now knew what ducal power was and acted accordingly. One of the parsons appointed by Duke Augustus began to give trouble shortly after Alfred succeeded to the title. A hunting-shooting man, this parson had never devoted more than a few hours a week to his parish duties; now he refused to do even that much. He went fishing all day every Sunday. No services were held unless a vicar or curate came over from a neighboring parish. Not even the Bishop of Winchester could get the man to do his duty; he was secure in his living and could do just as he pleased until he died.

When Alfred heard of it, he went to the parsonage the very next Sunday, arriving just as the man was setting off in a dogcart for a day's fishing.

"It's Sunday," Alfred roared at him.

For a moment the man seemed about to shrug his shoulders, but something of Alfred's well-controlled fury and hardness of spirit communicated, eye to eye. "Good Lord, your grace, I thought it was Saturday!"

Alfred, who had been ready to roast the man, decided to give him a further chance: "I know, vicar, that in the course of business you're obliged to believe in many things that are even more improbable than that, but I tell you it's Sunday."

The man mistook the humor for weakness and gathered his reins.

"So if you don't go at once to your church," Alfred went on in that same light but deadly tone, "I shall horsewhip you to within an inch of its door—and your life."

The astonished parson looked for support to the parish beadle—for what Alfred proposed would be a criminal assault. The beadle walked away, whistling "For He's a Jolly Good Fellow."

It was a dispirited cleric who trudged his way to church and conducted his first matins for several weeks. On the next four Sundays, the duke and duchess led the congregation at all three services. There was no further trouble.

That autumn, too—that same busy autumn—he was introduced to the House of Lords. A peer's Parliament robe is a gorgeous affair—a full-length tunic and cloak of close-woven pure wool, dyed a rich scarlet. It is open half way down each side and edged with miniver, the winter fur of the ermine or stoat. The wide, round collar is of the same fur, tied to the scarlet cloak with great flounces of silk ribbons. The right half of the robe, from the center front all the way around to the spine, is trimmed with three-inch-wide horizontal bars of miniver, topped by two-inch bands of gold lace; two bars for a baron, two and a half for a viscount, and so on up through earl and marquis to four magnificent bands for a duke, the first spanning his breast, the fourth at the level of his knee. With their graces of Bedford and Richmond to his right and left, also in their Parliament robes, they made a formidable wall of scarlet, white, and gold.

Duke Augustus had been the last duke to carry the tricorn hat at his introduction; now only the Lord Chancellor kept the old headgear. Alfred and his sponsors carried the fore-and-aft cocked hat brought in from France during the Directory and made fashionable by the Duke of Wellington.

The small group assembled in the lobby outside the peers' chamber, preceded by Black Rod, the servant of the Lords, and by Garter King of Arms, the principal herald of the kingdom in his gorgeous medieval tabard, quartered with the arms of Britain, bearing in his left hand the white and gold scepter of authority and in his right the patent of the creation of the dukedom of St. Ormer. At the appointed moment they advanced down the center of the chamber, beside the cross benches, toward the Lord Chancellor in his black gown and full-bottom wig, crowned, on this occasion, by his black tricorn hat.

As they moved from the dark of the lobby to the relative lightness of the chamber, Alfred felt a corresponding lightness of spirit. In a way, he had suddenly ceased to be himself and had become instead an actor in an endless national pageant. He felt his own person submerge into the impersonality of a number—"The Fifth" —and a cypher—"The Duke of St. Ormer." Even more, he felt himself as that number and cypher, knit into the great tapestry of English History. Here he was, part of a ceremony that went back in many forms but in one unbroken tradition (for even the Commonwealth of Cromwell had invested its Lord Protector and Lord High General) to the Black Prince at least. His flesh tingled at the realization, which made him at once both proud and intensely humble —proud that fate had singled him out, humble at the thought of the hundreds of truly great men who had trod this ceremony before him.

In that way he also understood the immense inner value of the ceremonial itself. It was for the participant himself, to quicken his sense of dedication; it was to humble the heretic, invigorate the lethargic, calm the splenetic, and (as with Alfred) to elevate the ordinary. It was a magic.

They fanned out and stood before the Lord Chancellor, who remained seated on the woolsack, the ancient symbol of the country's wealth. Three times they reverenced the empty royal throne before Garter read the patent of creation. Alfred then stepped forward, handed his writ of summons to the Lord Chancellor, and took his oath of allegiance. Then he was escorted, as before, to the ducal benches on the government side, where he and his two sponsors put on their cocked hats. Three times they removed them; three times the Lord Chancellor doffed his tricorn in acknowledgment. And then it was over; the Fifth Duke of St. Ormer had been *Introduced* to his sovereign and peers.

Only then did he dare look up into the peeresses' gallery, where the first face he saw was Flora's, burnished with pride for him.

The menace of Mr. Bruce Boys seemed as remote as the man himself.

They spent a few days after Christmas with the royal family at Osborne, on the Isle of Wight. Alfred had by now unlearned most of Duke Augustus's prejudice against the new Saxe-Coburg dynasty. He found Victoria, who was no taller than himself, to be shrewd (rather than clever) and gay-spirited (rather than witty). All the royal amusements were very simple—indeed, away from the necessary formality of court, they liked their life to be as simple and unceremonious as possible. On later visits to Balmoral, which was then no more than the pepper-pot castle of a small squire, Alfred was to see her majesty going in and out of cottagers' homes, talking with wives and husbands and helping with their troubles, like the wife of any modest gentleman. Osborne, being a somewhat grander house, imposed a slightly greater formality, but she was still at heart the same simple, dignified woman.

She, her maids of honor, and Flora spent an hour or so each day learning the intricacies of Highland dancing, which had given the Court some trouble at the Gathering of the Clans at Braemar the previous summer. Prince Albert and young Bertie, the Prince of Wales, then just turned nine, went for walks each afternoon, whatever the weather. They passed the time naming the birds they saw and the plants they picked. Alfred, one of whose boyhood passions had been geology, fascinated the young prince with the story of the chalk and flint and sandstone whose cliffs reared so majestically from the foreshore.

But the entire royal family seemed impervious to cold. The house was barely heated. Their bed might have been of single width for all the distance Alfred and Flora put between them—and even then it needed a good tot of whisky to get the temperature up to begin with.

On the 30th of that December the queen learned that the Crystal Palace, the home of Albert's inspired vision of a Great Exhibition was complete, ready to hand over to the painters and finishers. The contractors, Messrs. Fox and Henderson, had moved onto the site on July 19th, at which time not a bar of iron nor a pane of glass was made. And now, just over five months later, it was finished. Twice as wide as St. Paul's Cathedral and four times as long, with twenty-one acres of exhibition space, using a method of construction never before attempted on such a scale—it was finished!

Nothing that the Egyptians or Romans had done came anywhere near it, to Alfred's mind. *This* was the age to live in, the age that made all things possible to anyone with sufficient vision, daring, and enterprise. When Prince Albert asked him to chair the exhibitors' committee, he accepted with pride.

But he was even more proud that evening, when Flora told him the queen's physician had just confirmed that she was expecting their first child.

CHAPTER TWENTY-EIGHT

AMONG HIS MANY oddities, Bullen-Chetwynne had an odd way of entering a room. He would come in with puckered-up eyes, make four quick strides, head thrust forward; then he would halt and begin to look around him—searching, Flora always said, for that public meeting he carried with him wherever he went.

Four strides did not get him very far into most of the rooms at Chalfont Abbey. He would stand marooned for a moment; then he would clap his hands and dry-soap them vigorously, and begin to advance in a series of crablike lurches, saying things like "What, what!" or "All the jolly jollies!" When he had arrived at more or less the position he intended to reach, he would subside onto his heels, then rock himself back and forth like a man expertly dodging assagais by mere fractions of an inch. Bullen-Chetwynne was not at ease in most ordinary rooms.

So his behavior in Herberts Tower was all the more impressive. To say he walked into it as if he owned it would be an understatement; he walked as if every one of those gloomy, echoing, stone chambers had been his birthplace.

"Jove, duke," he exclaimed a dozen times. "Here's a jolly sort of a place, what! A fellow could really breathe here, eh? And don't those walls just *beg* to be hung with trophies!"

Alfred's purpose had been to take Bull up to the top of the tower and show him the country. But when the man waxed lyrical about the chambers and vaults they passed through on the way, a new idea seized him: Bull could make his quarters in Herberts Tower itself!

They had not yet discussed the question of a dwelling for Bull and Hermione, but Alfred had assumed he would either have to find or build a country house for the Master near Stokenchurch, the site of the intended kennels. But that was only just over four miles away to the north. Why not billet the man here, in the Tower, instead?

Hermione was why not. But Hermione was also *why*. He shivered.

"You like this place, don't you, Bull," he said.

"Like it, duke? Well, who wouldn't, eh?" He slapped a vast stone wall, streaked with slime and moss. "By jove! You're a lucky dog."

"Tell you what, I'll have it taken down stone by stone and reerected near the kennels."

"Oh, but you'll want it for yourself, surely? Can't for the life of me understand why you haven't moved in already. You could shoot geese from the battlements every evening." He closed his eyes, blinded by the ecstasy of it.

"I say, d'you really like it that much, Bull?"

Bull looked at him like a boy who's detected the forthcoming offer of a fiver from a rich uncle who has never before given a farthing.

"Why not move in here? Think of it as a tied cottage—goes with the job."

Bull's jaw dropped. "I say, duke!" He looked around in wonder at the twenty-foot-thick walls and the vaulting designed to withstand months of the best that medieval cannon could rain down. "I say!"

"Hermione won't like, of course," Alfred said casually.

Bull's face fell.

"But we can build her as decent a modern house as any woman could want. Butt it against the tower, you see. On that side. Give you a nice garden over there, too. You could grow superb fruit on this face of the stableyard wall."

"Up as far as the old falconry?" Bull fished, happy once more. "Get that going again?"

"I daresay. And in the meantime—what?" Inspiration: "Why! You could have as much of the first floor of the west wing as you want. There's an old gallery runs the full length of the original abbey. We could panel that off to link the west wing and the tower in complete privacy."

Bull was once again in ecstasy. "Jove, duke, you're a white man!"

Alfred smiled. "We're moving over into the west wing as well," he added, still casually. "The duchess isn't too fond of the Fourth Duke's Brighton folly. So we'll be on the ground floor and we'll probably take two or three of the first-floor rooms for bedrooms. But you may have the rest. It'll be more company for Hermione when you're away. She and the duchess get along so famously, don't you know."

Bull's ability to register gratitude was now so overloaded that Alfred feared for a moment he might burst into tears. But he gathered himself and squeezed Alfred's arm, Roman-manly style. "You don't know it, sir, but you've just eased me mind of its greatest burden. A chap isn't taught to think these things out properly. I mean, wives are all very well but what does one *do* with them, eh? Getting heirs and that sort of thing is ten minutes' work; what does one do the rest of the time? I can't see Miss Newbiggin doin' much with breedin' the hounds, and the kennels in general. Nor lookin' after guns. And she don't hunt." He snorted. "You sometimes wonder what keeps people alive."

Alfred, now thoroughly alarmed, said, "You're not going back on your promise, though? Of course, you aren't."

"Was goin' to put it to her. How miserable she might've been. But don't need to now, what! Jove, I've not been so happy since I brought down an imperial stag near Ballinteer on Wednesday the fourteenth of November eighteen-thirty-two. A fifteen-pointer he was. Stalked him with one round loaded, none in the pouch. Ah, he's a gentleman-in-antlers, your stag. That was some sport, I may tell ye." He chuckled at the memory.

On their resumed climb to the battlements Bull said, "D'you know, duke, I could almost say I'm looking forward to this marriage now. I was afraid it might be one hell of an interference. But now I can do the necessary, then go back more or less to me own ways—and knowin' the little woman'll be happy."

"Never fear, Bull," Alfred promised. "We'll see to it. She'll be happy down there"—he wafted a gesture toward the west wing, its mellow old stone glowing warm in the thin sunshine of that January afternoon—"if I have any part in it."

Seven weeks later to the day he was lying beside Hermione, in *her* bed, in *her* bedroom, in *her* part of the house.

"Who's the clever man?" she whispered huskily in his ear. "Who's a clever duke!"

"No cleverer than the fifth of Devonshire. Some more of this Imperial Tokay? It really is very good, isn't it."

"The Fifth Duke of Devonshire?" she asked. "The one who married the Spencer girl, Georgiana?"

Alfred grinned and poured her the wine anyway.

"So I'm to be your Lady Elizabeth Foster?"

"There are worse fates, surely."

Hermione giggled. "In later years, you know—or didn't you know?—Bess Foster became Duchess of Devonshire."

Alfred's frown showed her he had not known. She went on. "Nor, I suppose, did you know that Duchess Georgiana had a daughter by Charles Grey? She was over thirty at the time, too. No silly little girl."

Alfred scowled; the old duke had not mentioned these details.

Hermione laughed that tinkling laugh which at some times could be like a burst of stars and at others was like a dozen sharp headache throbs delivered in quick time. "Never mind then!" She kissed him consolingly. "Cavendish forgave her utterly. In the end."

He sipped his wine and stared moodily at his toes. "What was Bull like?" he asked.

"Like?"

"On your honeymoon."

"Oh."

Silence.

"Well?" Alfred prompted.

"You're not going to make me disloyal to Bull, Alfred." She clutched the opened halves of her nightgown a little less open.

"You may find this . . . we both may find this a trifle bizarre, but I have developed a great respect and even affection for my husband. He's a good-hearted man, utterly without malice, reliable . . . affectionate in his own way—"

"A sort of cross," Alfred said, "between a horse, a hound, a setter, and a terrier."

Hermione suppressed a smile, almost. "No man more loyal works for *you*," she said.

At that, Alfred accepted the rebuke. "I don't mean to talk the fellow down," he told her. "In fact I'm most fond of him too. Who could help it? But from the way he was talking before you married, I wondered how on earth he was going to manage it."

"Oh, so you discussed me, did you!"

"Not you. Surely you know him too well to believe that. And me. No, we discussed the general business of getting heirs. He spoke as if it were going to be the most frightful ordeal."

"Hm!" She was only half pacified. But then, after a reflective silence, she giggled and said, "He apologized, you know."

"Apologized?"

Another giggle. "I suppose it's disloyal even to say that. But, oh, it was so *funny!* He came at me in the small hours, it must have been about three. I'd only just got to sleep, what with that relentless, *bloody* waterfall! He came at me from behind. And when he felt I was awake, he said, 'Sorry, old girl! I thought you might stay asleep. Lie still, there's a brick. Be brave. Soon be done.' And there was no contact between us except . . . well, the obvious. And then afterward he said, 'Awfully sorry about that, old thing. Has to be done, though. Let me know if it didn't work. Then I'm afraid we'll have to put up with it again.' And after that it was just fishing, fishing, fishing, the whole damned fortnight."

She shivered. "I thought I'd grow scales myself by the end of it!"

"Didn't he enjoy it?"

"Fishing?"

He looked witheringly at her.

"Oh! D'you know, I don't believe he did. I think he found it highly distasteful—judging by the fervor of his apology."

Alfred felt an extraordinary upwelling of relief. He lay half upon her again and kissed her. "Aren't you lucky, then!" he said.

"No. You're the one who's lucky."

He flung himself on his back and gave a contented sigh. "I think you're right," he agreed. "A year ago tonight I was lying sleepless in that awful bedroom in the Midland Hotel, Cokeley, desperate for two things. One was to be in bed beside you. The other was to scratch together fifty pounds to start me in business." He snorted. "I haven't thought about that business for more than ten minutes put together since then, and yet, I hear, it's become the biggest lacquering business in the Midlands. They're going to go into metal-box manufacturing next." Another sigh. "What a year it's been, eh! What a year!"

PART THREE

1854-1876

SPERNO ME
RECIPERE AUT
MUTARI

Noblesse Oblige

Chalfont Abbey
as rebuilt c. 1600
by Charles Clarence, 1st Marquis of Knightsbridge

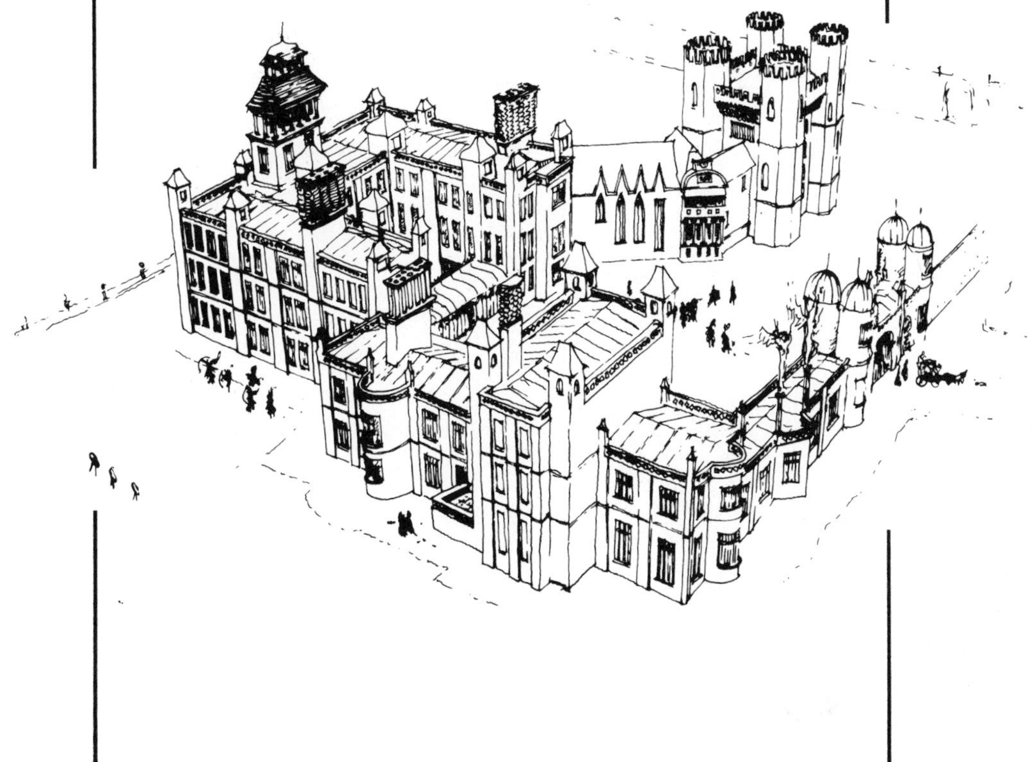

CHAPTER TWENTY-NINE

THE RAIN TURNED to sleet and finally to snow before Alfred and Bull and their escort had gone half a mile from Balaclava. The misery, waste, and chaos they had seen in the port was nothing compared to what they now met on the four-mile slog to the lines before Sebastopol. There was no road; there had never been more than a rough track through the clay. The constant passage of men, mules, and horses—to say nothing of the siege mortars and cannon and the tons of heavy shot for them—had turned it to a knee-deep mire.

Exhausted horses died where they fell; and hundreds had fallen. The most their drovers could do was get the harness and traces off them and leave them where they were. The smell of putrefaction was appalling. Man was the commonest beast of burden hereabouts. In uniforms that had not dried out for six weeks, with bellies that had not been properly filled in six months, some without soles to their boots, all without socks, they staggered north from the port carrying barley, hay, bullets, biscuits, trenching tools, salt beef, unroasted coffee, sugar, and Bibles. If they fell, they rose at once, uncomplaining sculptures in mud, and continued their nightmare journey. No one cracked a whip over them, no one shouted, "Come on now, step lively!" No one, it seemed, was in command of them at all.

"I never saw such spirit, duke," Captain Jenkins said. He was the adjutant of the D.St.O.L.I. and had been put in charge of the duke's escort. "They're dying of cold and starvation and cholera and scurvy and everything going—"

"Except enemy shot," Alfred interrupted.

"A few even die of that. The only medicine we have, for all complaints, is tincture of opium. Yet they'll struggle on like this, knowing that what they fail to do one of their comrades will have to shoulder as an additional burden."

Alfred, pulling his collar tight against the driving snow, urged his horse around the bloated corpses of three donkeys and marveled.

"And fight at the end of it," the captain added. "Wet, starved, and exhausted, they'll fight like terriers. There's a man in my company called Layard—you may know the family, sir?"

"From Fingest? The father's a carpenter?"

"The very one, sir. He had both legs broken by grapeshot. In a skirmish last week, this was. D'you know, that man apologized to me because they hadn't managed to capture the enemy's redoubt!"

"Do we deserve such men, captain?"

Bull, slightly ahead of them, reined in and gave a roar of outrage. Alfred followed his pointing finger and saw, a hundred yards off, to one side of the track, upwards of eighty horses, tethered almost hock deep in mud. Bull turned off and rode toward them, unable to believe what he saw; Alfred and the escort followed.

Forage had been thrown down on the mud but not a tenth of it could have reached the horses' bellies; they were all starving, as wet and exhausted as the men.

"My god!" Bull said. "If any bearers of mine treated horses like that, I'd shoot them. Why are they down here in the mud? Why not put them on the higher ground up there?"

The captain smiled condescendingly. "We're not a rabble, my lord. A military camp is laid out in a certain prescribed manner."

"But you could dig shelters up there and cover them with sailcloth."

"It's not the military way of doing things, sir."

"But where's the point?" Bull asked angrily. "Not one of those horses could carry a man to church, let alone to battle. Who's in charge?"

"Lord Lucan, sir. But he won't be here. Lord Cardigan has immediate command."

"Well, then—" Bull began.

"But you won't find him either, sir. He lives on his yacht down in the bay."

"Come on, Bull," Alfred intervened. "We must get up to the regiment."

Reluctantly Bull rejoined them.

"There's generally a good reason for the military way of doing things, Lord Bullen-Chetwynne." The captain was conciliatory. "Horse lines are a set distance from the tent lines because of the flies, you see."

"Flies," Bull said, looking contemptuously at the now thickly falling snow.

"Yes. I'm told they were dreadful in the Peninsular campaigns."

The way narrowed through a rocky defile and then broadened to about twenty tracks, all deep in soggy clay, twisting among boulders and cairns of partly cleared stone. Alfred and the lieutenant of his escort were separated a little from Bull and the captain.

"Where's your home, lieutenant?" Alfred asked. He had been introduced as Lieutenant the Hon. Geoffrey de Lacy Somers; but Alfred could not place the family.

"In Cumberland, duke," he answered. "It's not unlike this sort of country."

"So you don't miss it so much? Compared with—say—if you were in India?"

"War is a soldier's dream, sir," the lieutenant replied, gently letting Alfred know that "missing home" was not a topic for a theater of war.

"A very proper answer, Somers," he said. "I suppose you won't think of home until *Sebastopol* is added to the regiment's battle honors."

"That's right, sir," the lieutenant said.

At the top of the long upward track, about two miles from Balaclava, they came to a fine old farmhouse which served as the English headquarters.

"The Duke of St. Ormer and Lord Bullen-Chetwynne to meet Lord Raglan," Captain Jenkins told the guard, who at once presented arms.

Lord Raglan looked tired and ill, and though he received them with great courtesy, his mind was—understandably—elsewhere. For a while he confused St. Ormer with St. Albans, another dukedom, but recovered adroitly enough. They talked of corn prices, the prospects for the remainder of the hunting season, the queen's health, and similar matters. Alfred and Bull left a card on their way out. The snow had eased but more was nearby in the northern sky.

The Stormer lines were in front of the Redan, the mighty earthworks that guarded the southeastern approaches to Sebastopol. Each day the Russians were adding to the fortifications in the rear of the Redan, so that even if it fell to the English the victors would only find themselves faced with another and then another bastion, each of which would cost them lives they could ill afford. The captain explained all this as they picked their way over the battlefield to the Stormer headquarters.

Grapeshot scarred the ground, making it look as if a mad ploughman had been let loose upon the hills. "Are we safe here?" Alfred asked.

"We are at the moment, duke," Captain Jenkins told him. "There's an armistice to gather the dead and wounded from this morning's attack." He pointed to the white flags flying over the English and Russian lines; a half-mile away to the northeast, around that other great defensive redoubt, the Malakoff, the French and Russians were exchanging sporadic rifle fire.

"Would you like to meet some Russians, duke?" the lieutenant asked. "There's some tolerable fellows among them."

The snow suddenly began to fall heavily, filling the air with a strange light that seemed to filter down from all four corners of the sky. The flags of truce, visible only moments earlier, vanished. The sharp crack of muskets from the Malakoff was muted. The world closed in to the little valley along whose bed they picked their way, twisting and turning, up toward the Redan.

But it was only a shower. By the time they reached the group of caves known as "the Ovens," from the heat of the skirmishes that had won them many times for each army, it had passed.

The Russians were magnificent—tall fellows in immaculate uniforms and polished boots, the officers all with gleaming swords and white kid gloves. Lieutenant Somers said they kept these men especially to parade during such armistices and so intimidate the English, who looked what they were—wet, ragged, exhausted, and starving. But not dispirited; indeed, they kept up a friendly badinage with the Russians. One favorite chant was "Johnny English!" To which the Russians shouted back "Bono!" Then "Johnny Frenchie!" "Bono!" "Johnny Russki!" "Bono!" and finally "Johnny Turk!" And they would all shout, "No bono!" and laugh.

A Russian officer, obviously known to Captain Jenkins, approached the duke's party and was introduced; they exchanged cards and offered each other cigars.

"You took your time putting up the white flags," Jenkins complained. "Some of those wounded have lain there six hours. In *this*." He gestured at the mud and snow.

"It was an administrative error," Captain Plisetski said with a mocking smile. "But there's no need to explain to an English soldier about administrative errors!"

"Nor courage," Bull said angrily. "I see all the officers' bodies are right up against your rifle pits."

"They are dragged there, my lord, by our brutal and degraded peasant soldiers, who want to cut off the gold epaulettes and loot the pockets while it's dark. They are flogged for it, naturally. Well." He turned to the two officers. "And are you going to capture our Redan soon?"

"Soon or late, we'll capture it, never fear," Jenkins said.

"Do it soon," Plisetski advised, still with that superior smile.

"Before your artillery has made it quite impregnable. They're filling those walls with so much iron and steel that before long no army in the world will be able to break them down." He walked away with a laugh and a wave of his white-gloved hand. "Meanwhile," he shouted back over his shoulder, "convey to them our deepest gratitude."

"If I had a pistol, I'd drop him now," Bull said with angry restraint.

Alfred saw that he was trembling with fury. His eyes flickered this way and that over the Russian defenses, the rifle pits, the earthworks, as if he were about to volunteer himself.

"We'll report to the colonel," Alfred said.

There were no officers' messes in the lines closest to the Russians. The Stormer tents were beyond the reach of musket fire and mostly hidden from the Russian cannon by a maze of low ridges. Where the military necessity to keep the tents in straight ranks exposed one or another of them, temporary earthworks had been thrown up as a shield. Colonel Stockwell's tent, surrounded by those of his officers, was in a deeper gully on the enemy side of the camp. Alfred and Bull pitched their tents and those of their servants in the same gully, a little way off. They dressed for dinner at once, though it was only three of the afternoon.

Alfred knew Stockwell only slightly. When they last met, he had been a major in command of one of the companies. The colonel at that time had been the younger son of an earl, but he had had no stomach for such a campaign as this and had gone to a levée at the Horseguards to resign as soon as war was declared. He had lost the purchase price of his colonelcy, of course, and Stockwell, a professional soldier who could not have afforded the eight-thousand-odd pounds, had received the command by assignment. Slowly war brought the best to the top, regardless of wealth or aristocratic connection.

The duck and potted shrimps Alfred had brought up from Balaclava were most acceptable. The officers and men had eaten nothing but salt pork or beef and dry biscuit for weeks. Bull was uncharacteristically withdrawn, even morose, throughout the meal, however, and retired to bed as soon as politeness allowed.

"Hope he's not sickening with cholera," the colonel said. "It's rife at the moment, despite the cold."

Stockwell was a tall, stooping man with craggy eyebrows and deep-set eyes that rarely came to rest. His mouth was fixed in a grim smile, softened only by the twinkling restlessness of those eyes. It was a face precariously balanced between sternness and compassion; it conveyed an integrity that went beyond mere honesty or frankness, a power of decision that was both wise and absolute. *If I were a common soldier,* Alfred thought as he observed and listened to the man, *I'd follow you to Hell's gates and through.* He was everything Lord Raglan ought to have been and wasn't.

One by one the officers withdrew, until Alfred and Stockwell were alone. The colonel eased his collar, drew off his boots, and sent for his pipe and slippers. Alfred followed his example but lit a cigar instead.

"It's very good of you to come out here, duke," Stockwell said. "The men have been different ever since your landfall was confirmed."

"It would have seemed wrong not to come."

"They need to know that someone *cares.* That they're not just a forgotten rabble." He looked as if he were about to say more, but no words came.

"The news was so bad," Alfred went on. "Since the Battle of Balaclava everything seems to have gone wrong."

"Long before that, sir. We planned for this siege to be over last summer."

"Oh! Is that why there's no winter clothing for anyone?"

The colonel drew breath to speak but then pursed his lips and maintained his silence. Alfred looked around at the mess servant. "I don't think we need keep this fellow from his duties," he said.

When they were alone Alfred turned to the other. "See here, Stockwell, I thought to find things bad out here. I thought one can't expect an army that hasn't fought for forty years to go into a big campaign like this without some confusion . . . waste, and so on. But this is more than that."

Stockwell nodded guardedly.

Alfred continued, "Let me be frank with you—because I hope you'll be equally frank with me in return. This is more than mere pardonable confusion. This is bungling and blundering to a degree that borders on the criminal."

Stockwell puffed at his pipe, thinking seriously; his eyes never strayed from Alfred's. At last he said, "I think you put it very mildly, duke." But he waited for Alfred to speak again.

Alfred puffed at his cigar. "It's asking a great deal, I know," he said carefully. "If a captain or even a major came to me with a complaint about you, I'd have his balls for breakfast. A commanding officer has a right to expect the loyalty of everyone who serves under him. No one can take away that right except himself. The question is, how far do things have to deteriorate before that right is forfeited?"

Stockwell nodded.

"What d'you want to know, duke?" the colonel asked.

"The truth, colonel. Why, for instance, are you all in such unsuitable clothing for this dreadful cold?"

"I wish I knew, duke. The clothing is there. It's been down in Balaclava for six weeks but the quartermaster won't release it without authority, and that authorization is waiting its turn with ten thousand others." He relit his pipe. "I'll give you an incident, by no means the worst, but you could take it as typical. A ship arrived off Balaclava before Christmas. No one troubled to find out what she contained. The port was full. There was no berth for her. She had to anchor out in the roads. The French harbor at Kamitsch Bay has room for twelve hundred vessels. It's only four miles away and the roads are on dry, hard ground. We never needed Balaclava as a port. But no, we have to have our own place. A week later, a civilian of the commissariat comes on board with a requisition. The ship is to sail at once on a secret mission to Constantinople. Three days out, nearing Constantinople, the civilian, greatly daring, breaks secrecy and tells the captain his mission: to buy boots that are desperately needed by the army. The captain laughs in despair. 'Did no one tell you my cargo, sir?' he asks. 'It is boots. This ship is full of boots!' " The colonel did not laugh. "The ship, I may say, put about at once, but it has still not been unloaded. It's still down there and we are still as you see us!"

Alfred shook his head at the enormity of it. "I happened to read Lord Raglan's dispatches to the Horseguards before I left," he said. "He writes of nothing but the weather."

"Weather *is* important."

"So is command."

"It would be wrong to blame Lord Raglan for everything," the colonel said carefully. "You put your finger on the wart, duke, when you pointed out that we've not fought a war for forty years. Let me tell you exactly how bad things are. The entire English army is out here; there are no reserves at home. All fifty thousand men are here. Yet I doubt if five thousand are fit to fight. Did you see the cavalry horse lines on your way up?"

Alfred closed his eyes and nodded.

"The Light Brigade, after making up the losses of that celebrated charge last October, had four hundred and twenty mounts. I'm reliably told that three hundred and fifty have died since then for want of stabling, and there are fifty more that can never be saved. The Heavy Brigade is almost as bad. Four hundred out of seven hundred gone and over a hundred more beyond saving."

He shook some spittle from his pipe and puffed it back alight. "If it weren't for the French, we should have starved to death. The Russians could have walked through our lines in their nightshirts. We English are the most arrogant, stupid race alive, if you seek my candid opinion. The French, before they came out here, spoke to every French consul, merchant, or traveler who knew the area; and then they made their plans. We came out here and ignored the simplest and most obviously common-sensical advice. We applied every last letter of a military manual that was out-of-date even during the Peninsular Wars—and that could never by any stretch of improvisation have been made to apply to Russia in winter."

"What's the answer, Stockwell? You've obviously thought about it."

"We have the answer down there in Balaclava, duke. You must have seen it—the new railway?"

"Oh, yes?" Alfred was puzzled.

"They've been here five days. Two-hundred-odd navvies. And in that time they've built nearly a mile of track in the port and have put up their own hutted camp. Their overseer, Mr. Beattie"—he stressed the *mister*—"tells me they'll build forty miles of railway, to all parts of our lines, in the next four weeks. It will carry two hundred tons of material up here each *day*. They don't wear pretty pink uniforms. They don't drill to perfection. I'd like to see any man try to flog one of them. The clothing they've been issued is more sensible than you or I brought, I daresay. They aren't starved. And by God, if they weren't so valuable, I'd arm them and we'd take the Redan in an hour and Sebastopol in a day!"

"You mean the men—" Alfred began.

But Stockwell was too eagerly launched now. "Mr. Beattie tells me that his employer, Mr. Brassey,"—again there was that stress on the *mister*—"has sixty thousand such Leviathans working for him in England, France, Argentina . . . Sixty thousand! He has not the slightest difficulty in feeding and supplying them, however remote they may be. And here's the British army at its wit's end to keep a mere thirty thousand from starving and freezing to death. No sir! England does not lack the ability. The native ingenuity is there, if it could only be applied. But there is an iron wall around our army that keeps it out: *Lord* Cardigan, *Lord* Lucan—the horse killers—and *Lord* Raglan, the . . ." He did not complete the thought.

"You mean—the aristocracy!" Alfred was appalled that he had

been led, step by logical step, to this conclusion. Yet now that he faced it he wanted to resist it with every ounce of will.

"I mean the supposed divine right of leadership, duke. In practice it means a commander like Lord Cardigan, who sits in his yacht for weeks on end. You're lucky to have seen Lord Raglan today; I've not seen him for a month. I'd swear not a hundred common soldiers would recognize him, out of the thousands who've been out here with him for the best part of the year. We tend to blame the commissariat for a lot of our troubles, but the real blame, in my view, lies with the barons and viscounts and earls who find it utterly impossible to communicate directly with the officials of the commissariat because they are civilians and—even worse—they are *tradesmen!*"

Alfred absorbed this thought in silence. It ran contrary to everything the old duke had told him and everything he had come to believe.

"And now, duke, I must place my resignation in your hands," the colonel began.

"It is not accepted, colonel," Alfred said curtly. "I'll retire for the night now, if you'll excuse me. You've given me a great deal to think about."

Alfred was still deep in thought, despite his fatigue, an hour later, when there was a scrabbling at his tent door flap and Bull came bursting in.

"Duke!" he roared. He was a very different man from the morose, withdrawn fellow who had left the mess two hours earlier. His eyes gleamed, his red cheeks shone like pippins. "Want to see a sight to warm the cockles?" he asked.

He was already rummaging in a flour sack, which he produced from the folds of his long overcoat. "There!" He upended it with a magician's flourish.

Something fell out, hitting the duckboard floor with a dull thud. Alfred first had the absurd thought that it was a turnip. Then he saw beyond doubt that it was a human head, severed at the neck. One of its eyes was open. One of *his* eyes, for it was the head of the Russian Captain Plisetski. He appeared to wink in ghastly collusion at Bull's atrocity.

"He'll never sneer at England again, duke, what!" Bull said.

Alfred lowered his head into his hands. "Oh, Bull!" he whispered. "Bull!"

"Something wrong?"

"We must bury it at once," Alfred said. Then, seeing the look on Bull's face, he asked, "Why—what did you intend?"

"Intend, duke? Trophy, of course. Herberts Tower. Pride of place."

Alfred almost succumbed to laughter. Where could reason and such insanity meet? "Put it away, Bull, there's a sport. Someone may come in."

Bull obeyed. "You wouldn't bury it, though, duke?"

"No." Alfred thought better of it. "If they find it, there'll be all hell to pay and someone in the regiment will be blamed. How did it happen?"

"Happen?" Bull was puzzled. "It didn't happen, I did it."

"But how?"

"I just walked through their sentries. Showed them that card he gave me. Kept asking for their officers' mess. Found him. Called him out. Told him to put up his fists. Knocked him out. And took my trophy. Had to use a bit of bushcraft on our side, though. Dodge our chaps. I tell you, a good deerstalker could get in there and come out with Prince Gortschakoff himself. Good mind to volunteer."

"Bull—you know this is murder?"

Lord Bullen-Chetwynne fidgeted. "Technically, I suppose," he allowed. "But dammit, duke, the fellow was insulting England under a flag of armistice. He put himself beyond the bounds of civilized protection. Surely you can see that?"

"While you were over there did you identify yourself at all?"

"Of course I did. To him. I'm no—"

"But to no one else?"

"Don't think so."

"What language did you speak?"

"Russian, when I had to."

"I didn't know you spoke Russian."

"Hang it, duke. It's not the sort of thing one boasts about. I happened to pick up a smattering when I was shooting bison in Bialowiecz a few years ago. Year we met. Always helps to know the native lingo in case of mutiny." He chuckled. "I think their sentries took me for one of their spies. Kept grinning and slapping my shoulders."

Alfred was baffled at this utter lack of moral awareness in Bull. The Russian had insulted England, so that put him beyond the human pale and turned him into fair game for a crime that, in England, would have earned a life sentence in a criminal asylum. How could one begin to explain?

"What did you think of doing with it?" he asked.

Bull, sensing victory, smiled. "Get salt. Put it in a trophy bag, of course."

"And carry it home?"

"I was hoping you'd put it in your trunks, duke."

"Oh, you were!"

"Yes. The customs will hardly search your things."

"So you are aware that what you've done is wrong! That it would lead to the most fearful stink!"

Bull shrugged uncomfortably. "It could be a trifle awkward," he admitted.

"We'd better leave tomorrow," Alfred said, "immediately after we've seen and talked to the men."

Alfred hoped that his pride showed in his face as he walked up and down the opened—and severely depleted—ranks of the Stormers. England had done little to deserve such men. The hardship and neglect they had suffered would have driven any other army to mutiny, or at least to desertion under fire; yet this was the rabble that even the Russian war correspondents spoke of with awe. *If we could but organize ourselves better,* he thought, *what power could withstand us?*

"I'd like to see them about their ordinary business," Alfred said. "I'd like to walk among them and talk with them."

Captain Jenkins was astonished. Lieutenant Somers, Alfred could see, was scandalized. Dukes did not mix with common people. But Colonel Stockwell approved.

And so the Duke of St. Ormer did the unthinkable. He walked among common soldiers, told them their queen and country were proud of them, that no man who gave his life out here need fear for the provision of his loved ones at home. He even shook the hands of a few whom the colonel singled out for exceptional bravery.

On their way down to Balaclava, Alfred and Bull came upon the navvies laying the new railway. In the thirty-odd hours since Alfred was last here they had pushed the line out almost a mile from the port. They would even now be pushing it farther if some sort of fracas had not developed with the military.

A young cavalry officer of the Eleventh Light Dragoons—part of the Light Brigade commanded by Lord Cardigan—surrounded by a motley pack of mongrel dogs milling in and out of his horse's feet, was parading round shouting, "Bring him over here! Tie him on that cartwheel! Where's the cat and drummer?"

A small picquet, consisting of a corporal of horse and four troopers, was trying to isolate one of the navvies and do as their lieutenant commanded. But the other navvies were resisting them. It had not come to open fighting yet, but many of the navvies were armed with pistols and were brandishing them; the situation was on the verge of an explosion.

"What's going on?" Alfred, who was in civilian clothes again, asked the foreman.

"Young madman, sir"—the foreman pointed out the lieutenant—"came ahunting through here with that pack o' dogs. Told us to get out o' his way. We of course said no. He struck Harvest Hog with his whip. Hog flung clay back at him—which I agree he shouldn't ought to of done—and now your man wants to flog him."

Had Alfred not already been three days in the Crimea he would not have believed it. He spurred forward and drew up opposite the lieutenant. "You, sir," he shouted over the din, "will report at once to your lines. You will consider yourself under open arrest until I have spoken to your commanding officer, Lord Cardigan, I presume." To his dismay he heard how his anger was robbing him of his newly perfected upper-class accent.

The lieutenant, unaware that he was speaking to a duke, snapped, "Commissariat lackey! I am Lieutenant the Honorable Gerard de Talbois. How dare—"

"Have a care, you puppy!" Bull cut in with a roar that must have reached the Russian lines four miles away. "You are addressing his grace the Duke of St. Ormer. And I am Lord Bullen-Chetwynne."

De Talbois was clearly insane with anger. What had started out as a bit of upper-class high spirits—a mock hunt with a pack of stray dogs—had somehow become a matter of honor. He was not so mad as to persist in the face of this warning, but he was mad enough to "explain" to the corporal of horse as he left that their departure was merely to oblige "the gutter duke and his head gamekeeper."

Alfred, hearing this insult, was too livid to move. Bull was quicker. He spurred his horse to the lieutenant's side and struck him a light, token blow across the cheek. De Talbois checked at once.

Bull spat out his challenge: "His grace could not demean himself to answer you, you cur. But you will answer me. You will do me the honor of—"

"No!" Alfred cantered four strides and thrust his mount between them. He urged his horse into a sideways walk, pushing Bull away from the officer. "There will be no dueling," he commanded. His lower-class accent was firmly banished again.

Bull protested but Alfred was adamant: "It is against the law. It is against military discipline. It would be *murder*." The last word, spoken in earnest for the second time in twenty-four hours, penetrated Bull's anger and made him pause.

Alfred turned to the lieutenant. "And you, Mr. de Talbois, may tender your apologies now and we'll put the whole affair down to the strain of . . . to the heat of the moment."

The young officer's lips vanished in a new burst of anger; his nostrils flared.

"Or," Alfred said, as if offering a concession, "you may wait until Lord Cardigan commands you to do so."

De Talbois breathed like a man about to attempt ten minutes under water. "I apologize," he said at last.

Alfred stared at him; in the game of ascendency he had his fingers over the summit ledge while the other was now looking for an easy way down.

"What I said was unpardonable . . . your grace. You will"—he stumbled, speaking slowly as if just learning a new branch of his native tongue, which no doubt he was—"permit me to tender my profoundest apologies, trusting your grace will accept it as an action . . . as the result . . . as something said in the heat of the moment."

Silent and unsmiling, Alfred reached across a hand to shake that of the lieutenant. He turned to the navvies. "Who's Harvest Hog?" he called.

A tall, burly fellow in a stocking cap came shambling forward. Alfred, to his astonishment, saw that the man's fly buttons were undone and that his penis, long as a horse's and half swathed in filthy bandages, was dangling loosely out. A great laugh went up from the rest of the navvies.

Alfred had to speak sharply to prevent himself from laughing, too. "Why are you dressed like that? Or *un*dressed?"

The man shrugged a truculent, grinning embarrassment. The overseer stepped quickly forward. "Er, he was, er, taking horizontal refreshment, your grace, with, er, one of the local virgins, er, on a heap of cold cinders, and, er—*missed!*"

Alfred winced at the description.

"I thought the fellow was insultin' me," de Talbois said.

"And so he did." Alfred turned to Harvest Hog. "You threw clay at this officer." It was not a question.

The navvy nodded, surly.

"That was an unforgivable insult."

The navvy shrugged.

"This gentleman and I have just shown you how civilized, Christian people may behave when insults are traded."

The man did not move.

"He set you an example," Alfred almost shouted. He looked over the man's head to the group of navvies beyond. "He set you all an example."

The overseer turned. "Come on, Hog. Say it."

"I apologize . . . sir." Hog had the same difficulty with the words that the lieutenant had earlier experienced. "I shouldn't never ought to of cast clay at 'ee."

"Accepted!" de Talbois barked. There was clearly no question of a handshake here. The four vertical feet that separated the officer and the navvy could as well have been four thousand.

De Talbois saluted Alfred and spurred away to his lines. The dogs, who had dispersed among the navvies and the surrounding rocks, streamed yelping after him.

In the ensuing silence Alfred leaned confidentially over toward Harvest Hog, the barest suggestion of a smile on his face. "Doesn't it get cold?" he asked.

Hog looked down, grinned, and looked up again. "Be healed in a day or two, sir. I calculate I'll find some way o' warmin' un up again then, see!"

When Alfred and Bull resumed their way down to Balaclava, the overseer called for—and got—three rousing cheers for his grace the Duke of St. Ormer.

CHAPTER THIRTY

THE CHILDREN of dukes rarely mingle with their parents. Indeed, there was one Eldest Son who had no idea he was heir to a dukedom until he was sixteen, when a rare playfellow happened to blurt out the fact. And there have been dozens, eldest and youngest, sons and daughters, who never exchanged more than formal pleasantries with their parents in all their lives—and then only on the infrequent occasions when they could not avoid meeting one another.

But Alfred's children, by Flora and by Hermione, were brought up differently.

By 1860 there were nine children, five by Flora, four by Hermione. (There were also two by Danielle, who was set up in a smart house across the park in Bayswater with the surname of Fitzbois: Frances, then six, and Grenville, just two.) To be sure, Hermione's four sons—the Hon. William Redvers, nine, the Hon. John Cardigan, six, the Hon. George Raglan, four, and the Hon. James Lucan, two—might conceivably, so to speak, have been sired, in his customary apologetic fashion, by Bull; he himself entertained no doubt of it, not knowing there was any doubt to be entertained. And it was certainly he who, in the country phrase, "put the names on them." No one looking at those names could doubt *that*.

Of Flora's five, Lady Emily was nine, Lady Louise seven, Richard, Marquis of Knightsbridge and heir apparent, six, Lord Charles four, and Lady Felicity, just past her third birthday. To Alfred it had seemed incongruous to look down at a helpless, barely coordinated baby in a cradle and call it "Lady Emily" or "Lord Charles." Not that he or Flora saw their babies very often; life made too many other demands. But once they passed their fourth birthday and could engage in elementary conversation, they graduated from the goodnight-kiss-and-tea-on-Sundays to the "Paddington Station breakfasts," as Hermione called them with a shudder.

Actually, they were very unlike Paddington Station. The children had their cold baths at half past six each morning, breakfasted at seven, and half an hour later came up to their parents' breakfast room to stand in order of precedence along one side of the sixteen-foot dining table. Alfred sat at its head, Flora at its foot, and Bull had the whole side opposite the youngsters to himself. One by one, beginning with the young marquis and ending with the Hon. John Cardigan, each child summarized what he or she had done yesterday and hoped to achieve today. Achievement was the keynote.

These breakfasts were also courts of summary jurisdiction, where transgressions reported by nannies and servants were dealt with, as well as confessionals. For instance, if one of the boys had been caught boiling up blackberries to make "jam," any other child who had recently indulged in the same forbidden activity was expected to own up, as a point of honor. The punishments were discussed openly among the parents, so that the children could see they were facing Due Process rather than Arbitrary Authority. In limited ways the children could even join in; for example, one or two of them might "go bond" for the future good behavior of a wrongdoer, sharing the punishment if the wrongdoing was repeated.

After breakfast there was fifteen minutes of "ambulation"—

strolling on the terrace, if fine, or in the Inner Court, if wet. Here individual children could be taken aside and reasoned with—the most serious punishment in the ducal judicial armory; other punishments ranged from Warnings to Banishment for a Day. But such takings-aside were rare; in general, this was a chance for parents or children to discuss their individual activities, wishes, or achievements. When the older ones wanted to add a new section to their museum, when William wanted to study chemistry and geology, when Emily wanted to go to the National Portrait Gallery, when Knightsbridge (as Richard was known) wanted to go to the kitchen and "help chef make lots of chocolate fudge," all these notions were first bruited at ambulations.

In summer there was an hour's riding before breakfast, four days in the riding school, two days out hacking in the deer park; then ambulations took the form of the walk back from the stables.

But there were many things to interrupt this neatly ordered routine. From autumn to spring Alfred had his parliamentary duties, including those of privy councillor. Bull stayed down at Chalfont Abbey, hunting the Stokenchurch packs six days a week. "He doesn't really need the seventh for heaven," Hermione used to say. "That's where he is the other six." And in spring and summer Flora and Hermione had the Season.

During the Season, Flora opened up Knightsbridge House, near the French Embassy. Hermione stayed there as well, and gave two magnificent balls of her own, the first of which came in the course of time to mark the beginning of the highest part of the Season, just as Flora's ball in July came to mark its end. "The Duchess of St. Ormer's" thus performed the same function for nighttime upper society as the Duke of Richmond's Goodwood Races performed for its daytime incarnation.

In winter they hunted only on Fridays and Saturdays—except Hermione, who did not hunt at all. One day was with the Duke of St. Ormer's, the other with the Stokenchurch.

There were, too, the summer holidays. The Bullen-Chetwynnes generally spent a month at Bullen Towers up in Staffordshire; Alfred and Flora usually managed a week with the royal family at Balmoral, three or four weeks on the Continent, and two or three weeks at Constantine Park down in Cornwall, where for ten days or so both families were reunited. Those were days of glorious freedom for the children, when they could scamper freely through the woods, run pony races in the park, stroll at perfect liberty along the foreshore, and even stand and paddle beneath a sunshade held by one of the footmen. In the early morning, before the sun rose above the hill that shielded the beach, all except Hermione went swimming in the crisp, cold, deep, salt water—of which they each drank a medicinal tumblerful. And they were only occasionally expected to collect specimens for their pressed-flower books and their museum.

Most of the summer Bull was usually to be found fishing or shooting in Ireland or Scotland. But he always turned up in Cornwall for these children-together holidays, though he spent half the time there fishing for basking sharks off Falmouth. The children adored him because he could tell them things like how to build a hide of branches so cunning that you'd fall over it before you saw it, and the rain would never come in, or how to filter muddy but otherwise drinkable water by pouring it lengthwise through bundles of long grass. He knew hundreds of "traveler's tricks" like that, to turn a rather tame part of Cornwall into the wild plains of Africa or the rocky wastes of Greenland. In his and their innocence he also told them how to keep their clothes dry in a tropic downpour, and thus the Roseland district was treated to the sight of a giggling gaggle of juvenile lords, ladies, and honorables, all naked, each sitting on a tight bundle of clothing while the rain poured down.

When time was so valuable, when demands on it were so insistent and came from so many quarters, these few inviolable weeks in Roseland became inexpressibly precious to Alfred and Flora. Quite ordinary events took on an extraordinary color, as they do for people in love. It might be young Charles coming up with an empty crab shell, wanting to know who had stolen the crab; it might be something as simple as a daisy-chain competition—all such occasions became, as it were, pressed in a special album of memory that could be opened at treasured moments during the rest of the year.

On a few nights each summer a strange phosphorescent creature, too small to be seen by the unaided eye, would multiply in the waters of the estuary. Then, in great excitement, they would all embark in rowing boats, taking flasks and sandwiches, and row out on a pool of cold fire. Wherever the oars dipped they scintillated and left behind eddies of glimmering. The children trailed their hands and sculpted green swirls of brightness on the face of the sea. Once William slipped off his clothes and dived overboard. He was a lithe, natural swimmer and they could follow him down for several fathoms—first an aqueous comet trailing a wreath of luminescence, then a fiery rocket hurtling back to the surface and bursting through it in a great foaming of light.

In the summer of 1861, when they were all down in Cornwall

again, John Tregembo, the duke's local agent, casually asked Alfred if he'd ever considered "doing anything about the old house."

"What old house?" Alfred asked.

"The old manor, your grace. Rosevean. The old place of the earls of St. Just—and where your family lived before they built Constantine Park."

"Never heard of it."

"Over on the other coast, your grace, not far from Trewithian."

Light dawned on Alfred. "Are you talking about that big ruined house above the cliffs, near Pednvadan Point, where that fellow Polglaze farms?"

John Tregembo nodded.

"Is that ours, too?" Alfred said. "I often wondered about it."

They all went over for a picnic the following day, and Alfred could not help laughing as they threaded their way among the abandoned azaleas and rhododendrons, some as big as a good-sized vicarage, up a broad flight of granite steps that must at one time have joined two levels of garden, and onto a carriage sweep that had shrunk to a sheep path. For more than ten years he had *owned* this place—and no one had bothered to tell him! What else was there, he wondered? Come to think of it, he hadn't ever looked at all the London properties. A duke couldn't easily go strolling down London streets, outside certain parts of Mayfair and Westminster. There was a whole patchwork of freeholds down near Fleet Street and Ludgate Circus and up toward Mount Pleasant, for instance. He'd never seen them. There were chalk and gravel pits at Notting Hill, and farms all the way down to Shepherds Bush and out toward Acton. Dubedat had once pointed out a few bits of them, visible from the railway line, but the rest he had never seen. He really ought to do that this autumn.

"Not as ruined as it looks from a distance," Bull said. He put an imaginary shotgun to his shoulder and blasted away at the jackdaws and choughs who were Alfred's tenants-in-chief. The children supplied the noises of the explosions.

"Ooh, not so much charge!" Bull cried, pretending the recoil had hurt his shoulder.

The children laughed at his antics; he could mime things like that so well, you'd really think he held a gun. The children had made him ten years younger than he had been when he married, so that at sixty-three he could behave and feel like forty.

Bull had been right. The place wasn't in nearly such bad shape as it appeared from a distance. Most of the roof had gone and where that had happened the floors below had quickly rotted and fallen. But the walls, three feet thick, had been built in granite carved by a master. The thinnest knife blade could not have been inserted between the stones, and both interior and exterior walls were of dressed stone built in courses. Rain and wind would never shift those walls; only an earthquake could topple them.

The children had never before seen a house anatomized in this way. In one room, where half the roof was intact, parts of the two floors below it had been preserved, too. Where the rest had fallen away, they could see the sockets in the stone for the floor joists; a little farther down, the first of the rotted joists not to have fallen; then the lath, then the plasterwork in all its Jacobean ingenuity. On one wall three stone fireplaces stood one above the other, incongruously floating. The chimney stack reared into the sky above them like a giant frayed bookmark. It was a primer of how to build a house.

From that day the children could never walk through any upstairs room at Chalfont Abbey without being queasily aware that a great cavernous box of the same size hung, as it were, between their feet and Mother Earth.

Alfred decided it would be a shame to let the place deteriorate any further; the brickwork was vulnerable to the weather, even if the stone wasn't. They could probably restore the entire house and grounds for under ten thousand. And now that the railway bridge at Plymouth was open, London was only seven or so hours away; they could probably get quite a good rent for the place, enough to cover the restoration, anyway.

Flora, ever inclined to penny-pinch (she had once tried to make the coachman wear gardeners' gloves dipped in whitewash), was less certain. There were so many other calls on their money. True, they hadn't needed to pay more than forty-two thousand pounds to Sir Eric, thanks to Hermione, who kindly let it slip that her father had picked up the old grandee's debts, over a million, for no more than that—from delighted creditors who had known the old duke was at death's door anyway. But everything they saved on that, and in other ways, was immediately swallowed by the insatiable demands of the estate and the dukedom itself. It was a Moloch that would devour them all.

The restoration of Rodings Hall had cost a fortune, to say nothing of the virtual rebuilding of the stables, doubling their size, so that Ian could breed his Derby winners. Bloodstock wasn't cheap either; all dealings in horseflesh seemed to be in thousands of guineas. Then there were the Stokenchurch kennels for the new hunt. Bull had gone out and bought the best hounds from Lord Henry Bentinck, legendary bitches like Harlot and Helen by Sir Richard Sutton's Hercules out of Purity, and stallion hounds the caliber of

Tamerlane by the Duke of Rutland's Comus out of Twilight; they and their management certainly did not come cheap.

And the new farms weren't bringing the expected rents. It was no use saying that agriculture was depressed everywhere; that only made it easier for farmers to get the farm of their choice. And when an intending farmer heard how strictly the game was now preserved on the duke's lands, it was no wonder he went and looked elsewhere. Alfred's answer had not been to relax the rules—he wouldn't even let the tenants take rabbits. Instead he had gone out and sought capital to build the long-awaited railway from Maidenhead up through the estate to Princes Risborough. More expenditure—in this case nearly nine hundred thousand, not all of it Alfred's—and though the line was paying a good dividend, it had not earned back much of this outlay.

Then there were other pet schemes, like the new wood turnery in High Wycombe, the stone quarries at Water End, the great glasshouses at Rotherfield Peppard, the Grimsdyke Ironworks at Nuffield . . . no doubt they were all highly commendable undertakings; no doubt, too, they'd all earn handsomely in time and repay their outlay manyfold; but at the moment it was *all* outlay, just as it had been with the old duke and his enclosures and farms, only on a much bigger scale.

The Birmingham Metal Box Co., as it was registered, had been the one good breadwinner in the stable until recently; but then Alfred—who, naturally, held his majority shareholding in the firm by proxies, for a duke could not conceivably engage directly in trade—had decided, together with Willerby, the general manager, to go in for all kinds of hardware manufacture—hinges, screws, bolts, and fastenings of every kind. So all its income, plus money the company had yet to earn, was now applied to this expansion and was not available to the ducal coffers.

As a result, though they had paid off Sir Eric, the estate's debt was now well over the million level which had marked the old grandee's high tide. Alfred's answer to any problem seemed to be to throw a few thousand guineas at it and see what happened.

It could not go on. It was the only bone of contention between Flora and Alfred. She knew exactly what moved him. She watched him in the hunting field, urging his mounts on to ever bigger, ever more daring raspers of fences. His brush with death the day they became engaged had given him a false sense of immortality. He now carried it into everything he did, believing it would be equally charmed.

The maddening thing was: Until now he seemed to be right.

CHAPTER THIRTY-ONE

FATE QUIETLY picked up the marked deck of cards one day in 1862. She took more than a decade to deal the entire hand; but that was the day she began. The devious, twisted manner of it would be worthy of an opera, if anyone can imagine an opera beginning over a cesspit. Or, to be exact, over twenty-six cesspits.

Hermione had "gone medieval." Her clothing was of the aesthetic, Pre-Raphaelite inspiration, all loosely flowing, brilliantly dyed, and tied below the breasts; and since Hermione's breasts had been untouched by even one of her four baby boys, they were still among the most beauteous in England—to say nothing of her slender waist, undamaged by four pregnancies, and now lovingly caressed by silken-tasseled cords of russet, carmine, alizarin, and all the other favorite aesthetic hues. Hermione thought it a shame that such a magnificent, and genuine, medieval treasure as the old Great Hall of the original abbey, Cadel's Fountain Abbey, should be demoted to the status of kitchen.

Flora, who liked to be medieval at home, *en famille,* but who felt she ought to cleave to convention in public, agreed. The two women pictured themselves in the restored Great Hall, sitting in chairs that Barbarossa himself could not have broken, listening to a strolling lute player, drinking mead from crudely jeweled goblets, throwing trenchers among the rushes for the mastiffs to brawl over, and feeding morsels to hooded falcons on their wrists. They could also ride bicycles and play real tennis in there.

Alfred hadn't a chance. The kitchens had to go elsewhere. "But the expense!" he tried. Flora, extravagant in this if in nothing else, was adamant.

"The building is unsafe," he said. "Flowing water has undermined it."

"What flowing water?" both women sneered.

"From the fountain. 'Chalfont' comes from 'Cadel's Fountain.' The Herberts stopped it up and it's been steadily washing out the gravel ever since."

He strutted around the kitchen, jumping hopefully on the giant flagstones, and—to his own great surprise—actually found one that rocked. What was more, it gave out the most hollow sound imaginable. One of the kitchen porters told him there were many such flagstones—more than twenty; not all of them rocked, but they gave out a melancholy hollow boom when struck hard enough.

Then, of course, there was great excitement. What did the flagstones conceal? Roman baths, perhaps; were there tessellated pavements, fluted pillars, and lost carvings by Praxiteles awaiting just a few hours of archeological labor with block and tackle? Or monks' graves; were there catacombs below, lined with pious skulls and saintly thighbones, the theologically essential ossary on Judgment Day, and emblazoned with defiant ejaculations of faith? Or medieval dungeons; would block and tackle reveal a more grisly cousin of itself, perhaps still handcuffed to the skeleton of some wretched, long-forgotten varlet, or would they stumble over the steadfast bones of a valiant knight, crushed by the *peine forte et dure?* The block and tackle was sent for at once.

Block and tackle revealed an early-nineteenth-century cesspit. Two early-nineteenth-century cesspits. Three . . . Four. They tried no further for the moment. The famous "Chalfont squitters," which still afflicted every new visitor, were at last explained.

"But the old grandee *knew* about these," Alfred marveled. "They must have been in use in his time. Yet this is where he put the kitchens!"

Naturally, then, the kitchens could not remain there another day. Fortunately, Herberts Tower had a disused kitchen, and within a week Alfred had got a second-hand railway contractor's dormitory with a cast-iron frame and fitted it out with a regimental field kitchen borrowed from the Stormer depot. These temporary kitchens stood in the Great Courtyard; but the problem remained of where to site the permanent ones.

An architect was summoned and recommended enlarging the cellars below the west wing and digging an underground tunnel between them and the stables. Still rooms, pantries, ice rooms, and larders could all be let off this tunnel.

That was when Alfred got the idea for gas. It would be possible to build a gasworks beyond the stables, even on the far side of Coldharbour Hill, and run the main into the house by means of this tunnel. They could cook by gas, so no messy coals would need to be trundled into the cellar kitchens; and they could light the entire house by gas, too. At present, one servant was employed full time just to trim the colza-oil lamps and see to the candles, and for the hunt ball or any grand affair at which Alfred, as Lord Lieutenant, was host, it took five servants merely to keep the candles changed.

It was a splendid idea, and it only cost—kitchens and all—a

mere thirty-thousand pounds. Flora's heart sank and her stomach churned as she saw the bills come in. And, in the way that one thing leads to another, it did not finish there.

Alfred was awakened one morning by a most glorious smell—a smell from his childhood, the smell of the lower part of Cokeley. It was something like turpentine, something like pitch, something like a linctus his apothecary uncle had once painted his throat with when he suffered from squill. It was a *rich* smell.

He dressed quickly and walked out over Coldharbour Hill to the gasworks, the source of these heady aromas. The works was of medium size, for it served the villages of Turville, Frieth, and Fingest, too. The gas was collected in the usual way—in a holder floating in water, or, rather, in water that slowly turned to a rich chemical liquor, which needed changing from time to time. This morning was such a time; hence the glorious aroma that had awakened Alfred and brought him hurrying here.

Any other gasworks would have discharged its liquor straight into the nearest stream or river; but the only stream hereabouts ran through the duke's park and woodlands, so, of course, such a pollution was unthinkable. Instead they had dug a big pit in the gravel, where they left it to soak into the earth or evaporate.

Perhaps the childhood memories stirred by this elemental stink had, in their turn, stirred another early longing of Alfred's, an adolescent longing to know what things are made of. By lunchtime two slick, black, oily, aromatic gallons of the liquor were brought up to the Abbey. By evening Alfred was back from London with four of the very latest fractionating stills. He was up all night.

The largest fraction was the easiest to identify—ammonia, or an ammoniacal compound. He kept a small bottleful and threw the rest out of the window. One week later the intense green and astonishing growth of the plants there told him he had found a most efficient fertilizer. But what of the other fractions? They were, he knew, far beyond his chemical learning; they belonged in this new branch of chemistry known as "organic."

That same evening he was sitting in his carriage outside the chemistry department of University College, London, watching the gaslights put out one by one.

"Er . . . may I ask your grace," McKay ventured, "whom we are waiting to see?"

"I don't know yet," Alfred answered. "But it won't be long now."

At last only one room remained lighted. "We have our man, I think," Alfred said as he descended from the carriage.

"Your grace!"

"Yes, McKay?"

"You are surely not . . . I mean . . . let me go in and fetch the fellow out here."

"Oh, McKay!" Alfred answered. "You'd deprive me of all life's pleasures. I'll never take you to a brothel. Come and announce me to the gatekeeper."

The man let them through with astonished deference. The door to the chemistry laboratories was open. Their boots clanked on stone floors and they walked between walls of institutional stone in a wash of multiple echoes, their eyes fixed on the one door at whose foot peeped a line of gold.

The burner of the midnight oil, alerted by their approach, was more curious than surprised. A short, chubby young man with a cheery face and receding hair, slightly more shortsighted, Alfred guessed, than his glasses compensated for, he watched them thread their way among the apparatus toward his bench in the corner. The smell of the place, to Alfred, was of heaven.

"Good evening, sir," he began. "I am the Duke of St. Ormer." He offered his card. "Who, if I may ask, are you?"

"Frisch," the man said. "Wolfgang Frisch." He pronounced the name as if it were English rather than German.

Alfred held out a hand. "German?" he asked.

They shook. "My father was, sir."

"Do I interrupt anything important?"

"If I may just make two or three more notes, you may have my undivided," Frisch said.

Alfred strolled slowly about the room reading *Conc. Sulph. Acid, Fuming Nitric Acid, Mag. Sulph, Hydrate of Lime, Ac. Hydrochlor* . . . on the bottles. The colors and smells, the neat separation of compounds that were so hopelessly mixed and confused out there in nature, the sense that great wonders could be achieved with these purified and separated substances—these were so redolent of his youth that he would gladly have waited half an hour, tired as he was. The thrill of the work he had done last night lay precisely in that: He had taken one of nature's hopeless mixtures and, by chemical skill, extracted and refined its separate constituents and capped them neatly in a dozen bottles.

Every now and then, from the corner of his eye, he watched young Frisch—unhurried, methodical, and a meticulous maker of notes. A dedicated man, he was just what Alfred had been looking for.

"Now, sir, I am yours," Frisch said as he swilled some reagents down the sink and washed his hands.

"Have you dined, Mr. Frisch? Let me invite you to dinner. My carriage is outside. We can go down to Simpson's in the Strand. Fancy a nice saddle of mutton?"

Frisch looked dubious. "Don't really want anything heavy," he said. "I want to be back here by six tomorrow morning. Don't think me rude, sir, but the Duke of Grafton serves a very good steak and kidney pie."

"You *know* his grace of Grafton?" Alfred was astonished.

Frisch merely looked confused.

McKay came to their rescue. "The Duke of Grafton, your grace, is a . . . er . . . a public house."

Alfred laughed. "Have they a supper room?"

Frisch nodded. "They are just up the street."

"Then let's go there." McKay was scandalized but Alfred ignored him. "I want you to tell me all about coal gas and the heavier distillates of coal."

Two hours later he had more than doubled his by no means limited store of chemical understanding. Frisch, being an enthusiast, was also the very best kind of teacher, talking too fast, getting everything in the wrong order, putting conclusions first, making great leaps of logic, bristling with asides, darting after every fascinating side thought—and *every* side thought was fascinating. He kept Alfred's mind so stretched that the information simply poured in and lodged.

Alfred learned that the liquids he had distilled were just beginning to interest certain manufacturers, especially those making dyes and those making explosives. Ever since a chemist named Perkin had made "mauve" from anilin, one of the constituents of coal tar, the hunt had been on for other dyes. A good scarlet and a good range of blues was everyone's goal, especially if the dyestuff itself could be slightly acidic; that would make the dyer's life a great deal easier.

Even more interestingly, Frisch said that if he had sufficient capital, he'd leave academe and invest in a small factory devoted solely to distilling gasworks liquor and selling the products in the trade. Ten pounds' worth of liquor could, with the expenditure of a further ten, be sold for eighty to a hundred pounds. But even that sort of profit was nothing compared with the money to be made out of one good, patentable dye compound.

Alfred told him that if he could write a good prospectus and a schedule of costs, he, Alfred, would be interested in putting up the money. "And tomorrow," he told McKay on their way home to Bayswater and Danielle, "I want you to arrange with Dunlop to take me on this long-postponed tour of our central London properties; there must be a good site for our new factory among them."

He leaned back against the soft West of England cloth. "It's a long way from our twenty-six cesspits, McKay, but if we hadn't found them last year, we wouldn't be here tonight."

"No, your grace!" McKay's voice implied that it had been a sorry business from first to last.

They found a site in the Clerkenwell Road, near the railway goods yard, which would be handy if they ever expanded their catchment area beyond the range of horse and cart. The firm, the London Distillate Company, was nominally owned by Wolf Frisch but was really the subject of a secret partnership agreement between them. Alfred put up two thousand pounds to buy the plant and earmarked a further four thousand for working capital, to tide the business over until it was in profit.

Both Flora and Hermione had the deepest misgivings about this venture. The duke's other dabblings in industry—the turnery, the ironworks, the gasworks, and so on—was already resented in some local quarters; but at least they could be seen as, like the railway, promoting the general good of the estate. They were all within its bounds and they all employed the duke's "own people." But this London Distillate Company—and, indeed, the Birmingham Metal Box Co., if word of that ever leaked out—would be a very different matter. They were both pure trade. A fourteenth duke might just get away with such disgraceful doings as a kind of eccentricity; but a duke who had been a commoner? Never.

"But I must do it," Alfred told Flora. "Because I believe it's right. If only Prince Albert hadn't died! We had so many talks about this. The future of England isn't in land, where the aristocracy is now so firmly rooted. It's in industry. That's what the British said to the whole world with our Great Exhibition. Remember what Duke Augustus said: 'All empire is no more than power in trust.' That's right. Industry is the new power, and we, the aristocracy, must take it and hold it in trust."

"But, Alfred dear. Industry is so . . . *grubby*."

"Exactly!" He began to get excited. "Because look at the grubby men who direct it! Men of absolutely no breeding. Disraeli says we're two nations, and so we are. Not *his* two. Not rich and poor. But rich and rich. A rich aristocracy, confined to rents and agriculture, and a rich new class of industrial magnates who hold the real future in their dirty, philistine hands. Truly, if the aristocracy doesn't take its rightful place at the head of industry, if it doesn't direct industrial progress and shape the future along less squalid lines than at present, we shall all deserve our fate." He paused before he asked. "Do you know what it will be?"

"What, Alfred?"

"We the aristocracy will all be lined up in a fairground side-show. 'Walk up! Walk up! Shake the hand of a real, live duke, the last of his line!' " He laughed. "Belted earls will vie with one another to tour America and be gaped at. And we shall deserve it, if we let this opportunity slip from our grasp."

Flora sighed, not convinced. "I wish you knew the aristocracy as I do, dear," she said.

"Flora, people complain on every hand that industry is inhuman. Well, who can humanize it? The Civil Service? It was the Civil Service that organized the death by starvation of millions of Scotch and Irish in the Famine. Or the workingmen themselves? A cooperative? What surgeon ever amputated his own leg? No! It can only be the aristocracy. And I'm going to show them how."

"But the aristocracy exists only for leisure," Flora objected. "Even those who are supposed to work. Look at that Foreign Secretary—the only way they could get him to sign important treaties with foreign powers was to dash out into the street and stop his carriage on its way to the opera or dinner. I wouldn't trust the aristocracy with a lost-property auction."

"They're not all like that. Anyway, someone must make a start."

"That's what the first man said who ever fell off Mont Blanc!"

Alfred laughed, to show he was not provoked. "I'll promise you one thing, my darling: I shan't go at it head-on. I'll find a way around. Duke Augustus said many profound things, and that was one of them—never go at anything head-on. In England there's always a way around."

CHAPTER THIRTY-TWO

IF ANY BOY could survive the Eton of the 1860s (we will leave Fate and the half-dealt hand of marked cards for the moment), if any boy could survive the Eton of the 1860s utterly unscathed, it was Richard Boyce. The fact that he was Marquis of Knightsbridge cut no ice there, where titles were ten a penny; nor did the fact that since the age of three he had been a major in the Coldstream Guards, drawing full pay and emoluments. What really cut the ice at Eton was that Knightsbridge was *tough*.

As a "jew" (or new boy) he had endured without complaint initiation ceremonies that left most others scarred in some way for life. They dragged him from sleep by a cord looped over his big toe; they upended his bed before he rose from it; they tossed him in a blanket and broke open his scalp; and they "put him into play" —that is, bandied him about like a shuttlecock inside a ring of upper boys seated on bedsteads and lashing out with their fists or boots until not an inch of unbruised flesh showed. As a fag he was kept up until one or two of the morning making tea and frying sausages; but when, next day, he did not know his lessons and was flogged, he took it all philosophically.

In time Knightsbridge grew quite hardened to the birch. Once, when the praepostor burst into his schoolroom at the dread fifteen-minutes-to-noon to drag him to the Bill (on no fewer than three tickets from three beaks), they found, when they stretched him over the block and bared his buttocks, the words HA HA painted one on each cheek. The Head broke two birches before he drew enough blood to wash out the challenging legend; but he gave the boy a glass of port, as a mark of admiration for his pluck, next time they met on a more social footing. From this incident he got his nickname—which he rather liked—of *Ape*, from the phrase *a posteriori*.

During his first half, an upper boy sneered at the plebeian origins of the present Duke of St. Ormer. Knightsbridge at once cried, "Ring! Ring!" and challenged the fellow to a fight under Prize Rules, even though the other was more than twice his size. They had actually traded a few blows before someone in Library came and told them to stow it. Knightsbridge demanded—and got —an apology before he would agree to obey this order. There was a vicious, unyielding glint in his eye that compelled it. No one who saw it, indeed no one, ever again raised the matter of his father's origins.

To say that Ape grew hardened to flogging would be to tell only the half of it. He actually became quite the connoisseur. His favorite was a flogging from a beak called Starling, whom the boys, naturally, called Eagle. He was a small, cadaverous man with a shiny scalp and long, lank snow-white hair hanging from the sides and back of his head, right down over his collar. From time to time he accidentally tucked bits of it into his cravat and would then jerk his head around as if trying to shake water out of his ears.

Eagle had once been married but his wife had left him. The story was that he had come to his Dame one morning and said, "She's gone."

"Why?" the Dame asked.

"She said I didn't allow her space enough for her clothes."

"And how much space did you allow her?"

"She had an ottoman. The same as the boys."

His own clothes never changed. The parts that should have been white were black with grime; those that should have been black were green with age.

But Eagle was a master of flogging—always in the evening just before lockup, always in his own rooms. He used to dab the boys' necks and faces with eau-de-cologne first, so that the sensual awakening of it would sharpen their nerves the more exquisitely to the pain. Once Ape came in and found him fondling a lady's shoe. There were half a dozen on his table, all beautifully polished and very dainty.

"Do you know, Knightsbridge," he said distantly, "there are some shops in London with entire windows filled with ladies' shoes. Did you know that?"

"No, sir."

"I love to look at them, don't you?"

"They are very pretty sir."

"Hold that one." He threw Ape a high-heeled, knee-length boot with a patent shine and lustrous black tassels. "Keep it in your hands while we take the chill off this raw winter's evening. Hold it, and think of . . . well, never mind. Think of the Empire. Hold it where I can see it."

Ape was not the most imaginative of young boys, but these nocturnal encounters with the instruments of sensual pleasure and of pain were to have a profound effect upon him.

He was also a very idle boy; if he had been less so, he would not have been flogged so often. Those punishments were really quite easy to avoid. The first three marquises of Knightsbridge, who had all been Eton Collegers, would have been shocked at the low standards to which classical learning had sunk by the 1860s. They, or any grammar-school boy of the sixteenth and seventeenth centuries, would have been able to give impromptu orations in Latin on such high themes as Free Will or Predestination; but Ape and his fellows were simply required to learn a few dozen jingles to sort out the pronouns that govern the accusative from those that govern the dative . . . and similar mysteries; there was even one jingle to distinguish between the genders of *frons* a brow and *frons* a leaf. As to Latin oratory, not one in twenty of them could stumble through the simple (not to say simple-minded) story of the scholar who chided the snails in a pan of boiling water for singing when their houses were burning. Any boy who *could* manage it they dubbed a "sap" and turned his life, like Shelley's more than half a century earlier, into a kind of hell.

Eton's masters, having little learning with which to plague their pupils, and being as fond of leisure as any other well-bred men, birched them through the obligatory jingles and coached them in the necessary cribs, then gave them the other twenty-two hours of the day to do as they liked.

It is said that no one who did not live in sixteenth-century Florence can possibly know the full meaning of the words "intrigue" and "treachery." In the same way no one who was not at Eton in the 1860s and '70s can have the remotest idea of the full richness of the words "leisure" and "idleness." As a training for his future in the Coldstream, it proved invaluable to Ape. Long periods of leisure—of poaching in the royal parks at Windsor, of badger baiting, of foxhunting, of cat and duck harrying, of driving around in smart gigs and tandems flicking the whip at errand boys, of shoplifting, of lying smoking in the long grass near Sixth Form Bench, of fighting, of gambling, of swilling, of boating, of swimming at Cuckoo Weir and later at Athens, of beagling for hares on Dorney Common, of breaking out at night and meeting Old Boys and driving in their flies to Maidenhead for supper and dalliance with actresses—alternated with brief flurries of intense, painful, and dirty activity. Could anything more aptly describe the military life? Small wonder that, as Wellington himself said, the Battle of Waterloo was won on these playing fields.

The parallel runs even closer. For just as a soldier proves his honor and earns his esteem during those flurries, rather than during the long periods of enforced leisure that separate them, so at Eton did a boy's honor and esteem depend on how he acquitted himself in the Etonian style of war: the Wall Game, the Field Game, and, for a dry bob like Ape, Cricket.

In the Wall Game it was Ape who perfected the technique of "knuckling" his opponent's face with the inside hand—a foul (one may knuckle only with the outside hand)—and then, when the fellow started to appeal, plugging his open mouth with clay held ready in the outside hand. It was Ape who pointed out, and took advantage of, the fact that though the rules permit a player to kneel on an opponent's back they are silent as to whether the knee may first be raised eighteen inches or so and then brought down with such aplomb as to leave the opponent in no doubt as to its exact moment of arrival.

The Wall Game may be regarded as a preparation for the more barbarous sorts of skirmish in a soldier's life—with cannibals and fuzzy-wuzzies, say. Cricket, at the other extreme, was for gentlemanly, set-piece battles between exclusively European armies who honored a common code. Somewhere in between, representing, say, war with Orientals or Americans—people with a different, inferior, comic, but nonetheless worthy code—came the Field Game. Ape excelled at all three.

In due time he reaped the reward of such excellence—election to the elite Eton Debating Society, or "Pop." Its days of serious debate were long gone, so it would be hard to say which name was the more quaint. Pop ruled Eton. One could almost say that the members of Pop were the dukes of the school. They were allowed to lounge on the old stone wall by Upper School. They could fag lower boys in the streets. They could walk with rolled umbrellas. They could walk on the left side of the High Street, where nannies and children, vicars, girls, common people, thieves, and beaks—the whole rich tapestry of English life—could otherwise be sure of never meeting an Eton boy. The privileges heaped on members of Pop baffle description. They could even display the Rules of their Society on the walls of their rooms—framed in a fantastic melange of blue ribbons and miniature canes.

But the greatest privilege of all was that of carrying a popcane, a supple, knobbly cane that could reduce a trouser seat to shreds. A victim of a poptanning was always told, in his written summons, to wear an old pair of trousers (and he was stretched over a window sill with his head in the courtyard and a window jammed down on his back to attenuate his screams); fifteen strokes was a lucky minimum.

Having taken it heartily as a "jew" and a "tug," Ape now dealt it out heartily as a member of Pop. He especially liked the privilege of tanning the pretty lower boys—though any boys would do. No one was more assiduous at catching smokers in the long grass, or poachers in the park, or boys mobbing in the High Street, or drinking in one of the pubs, than Ape, who had excelled at all of it.

Yet it was not dreams of juvenile buttocks that purred him to sleep at night; it was a dream of the bottom of Miss Walberswick, the Dame of his house—a young and surprisingly pretty Dame, too.

At first he dreamed of dressing her in trousers and stretching her over the Pop Room window sill. How he would tickle her with his popcane before each stroke! And how sweetly her giggles would turn to shrieks as the rod descended and cut into that delicate flesh!

But then an extraordinary reversal occurred. It came about one evening when she lanced a boil above his knee. The pain of it had been ferocious but he had not cried out.

"Doesn't it hurt, Knightsbridge?" she asked in surprise, being accustomed to the roars of others for whom she had ministered in the same way.

"No, it don't, ma'am," he answered in a voice that hardly shook. "For you are so tender and gentle." Then, in a rare lapse into the first person singular, he added: "I hope, ma'am, that if you should ever have the misfortune to suffer this affliction, you'd let me show what tenderness and gentleness I've learned from you. Especially"—he stroked her neck—"were it above the knee as well."

She blushed and—eventually—pulled her head away from his caress. "You are a dreadful boy," she said. "And just for that I'll really make it hurt." Yet, though she attacked his boil with every appearance of ferocity, she was as mild and careful as before.

But the effect on Ape! Her words, her pretense at cruelty, transfixed him. The pain became exquisite; it seared his soul and savaged his manhood. "Oh, ma'am, I love you!" he cried, and fled.

From then on his dream reversed. It was he who lay pinned and friendless over the Pop Room window sill, she who ignored his pleas for mercy and tanned him fifteen times fifteen. To complete the reversal, he wore the petticoats; she was dressed in his gray-check trousers and gorgeous waistcoat—except that she wore high-sided, high-heeled boots in patent leather with lustrous black tassels. In the mature form of this fantasy she kicked them off and made him hold them; she also splashed his face and neck with eau-de-cologne. Outside in the courtyard, old Eagle usually contrived to pass by with a cheery nod and grin of approval at the furore of Ape's shrieks.

Toward the end of that summer half—Ape's last before he made his speech, sang his *Vale*, paid his five pounds, took his inscribed copy of Gray's poems, and joined his regiment—lower boys in the house would hammer in vain upon Dame Walberswick's locked door for their senna; she and Ape were within, spooning and giggling—and quite heedless of juvenile constipation.

In August, Ape took leave and went to shoot over a friend's estates in Ireland, near Limerick; coincidentally Dame Walberswick took her annual holiday from Eton. Letters sent to Ape, care of his Irish friend, were forwarded to Chalfont Abbey, as if the friend believed he had already returned home—which was not the case. Dame W., by contrast, was never seen at Eton again—indeed, she was never seen in England.

When Ape rejoined his regiment all he would say was, "I thought I'd play the gypsy for a bit." And he smiled a smile of peculiar satisfaction. When Dame Walberswick failed to return to Eton next half, tongues naturally began to wag, having almost twenty-four hours each day in which to do so. And when Coldstream officers on duty at Windsor Castle dropped by with the news that Ape spent every spare minute dashing over to Dublin, it was not long before the whole of Society had Ape and Dame secretly married in Ireland and starting a family.

A mere baronet's son might have maintained such a secret for a year; but the heir to a dukedom had little hope of spinning it out more than a month or two. At length, and thanks to "a damned good-natured friend," even Alfred and Flora got to hear of it. Alfred taxed Knightsbridge with the tittle-tattle at once.

Ape admitted no more than that the former Dame was his mistress, that she was lodged in Dalkey, south of Dublin (and within walking distance of Kingstown Harbour, where the ferry docked), and that she was with child by him.

"But there's no marriage?" the duke insisted.

"Of course not, pater!" Ape gave every appearance of honesty.

"Then why all this secrecy? Why keep her so inconveniently far away?"

"Patricia prefers it. We both prefer it."

"What about money, young man? How old are you now? Twenty? I may say I was twenty-*three* before I had the luxury of a mistress. Still, I'll wager one thing hasn't changed in the last quarter of a century: money. Mistresses aren't cheap."

"Dammit, pater! One knows one's duty."

Alfred grew impatient; Knightsbridge was always so literal. "I don't mean that, my boy, I mean can you manage her out of your allowance?"

"Oh!" Ape grinned sheepishly. "The turf is doing one rather nicely at the moment. The gee-gees all run just as uncle Ian says they will."

"Well . . . remember: There can be no question of a marriage.

Your regiment wouldn't allow it anyway, at your age. But when the time comes your mother and I will give you a list of girls to choose from."

The following May, Flora was summoned to Dalkey by a most disjointed and distressing telegram from Knightsbridge. Patricia had died of childbed fever; the baby, a boy, survived.

The funeral was over by the time Flora arrived. Her heart went out to her son, a forlorn figure in black, set apart by his grief from the other welcomers on the quayside. Then, with slight consternation, she noticed he was in *full* mourning.

She was naturally first off the boat. "My poor darling!" She rushed to comfort him; but he was so tall and strong, and she so small, that it seemed the other way about. His valet joined her maid and footman in seeing to her luggage. Meanwhile, the day being fine and warm, with just enough breeze off the sea, Flora and her son walked along the sea front.

She stole a glance at him: so solemn—Knightsbridge who was usually cheerful and lighthearted. This death had obviously meant a great deal more to him than she had assumed.

She was torn then between her impulse as a mother, to comfort her son in his bereavement, and her duty to Alfred and the dukedom. She could not do that duty if she followed her maternal impulse and took this death as solemnly as Knightsbridge was taking it. She wanted to say something light, to set the tone—yet not unfeelingly light. Something to let him see this business as the world would see it. But what could she say? Perhaps: "Knightsbridge, dear, I think you shouldn't wear more than quarter mourning for a mistress. Or even just a black band."

And what would he reply? He might take it utterly seriously. He had no humor where social form was concerned. Everything by the rules; go by the book. He would even send Emily back to her room—Emily, who was three years older and engaged to be married—if he found her in the corridor still pulling on her gloves. "And never leave your room undressed again!" he would shout after her.

She sighed.

The noise startled Knightsbridge from his reverie; he had been politely waiting for his mother to break the silence.

"Terrible thing," he said.

"Yes," she agreed.

"No. I mean, to be a woman. Terrible thing."

In this laconic, inverted sentence she divined all the torture he had suffered. "Oh, Dickie," she said, using his childhood name. "Poor man. Was it terrible?"

"One wouldn't want to go through it again."

"Oh, my darling."

"There now, it's over, mama. It's over and done with. The question now is . . ."

Flora stopped to dab the tears from her eyes. She passed her small reticule to her son, who, knowing what she wanted, immediately scrabbled through it for her smelling salts. They revived her.

With military bluntness Knightsbridge then said, "The important thing now is the boy."

"He'll live?"

"Live!" He laughed and pointed at Killiney Hill, towering above them. "He'll run up there and back before breakfast by the time he's two. There's a very good Protestant family who'll take him in and rear him."

"As their own? What are they?"

"As if he were their own. But one doesn't want to abdicate one's own responsibility. Want to see him from time to time—as and when possible, don't you know. Put one's own name on his birth certificate—that sort of thing."

"You *can't,* Knightsbridge!"

"Of course one can. Nobody will ever dare mention it. I mean, one doesn't mind one's own sort tattlin' about it; but no newspaper will ever dare print it, or they'd face the law of *scandalum magnatum.*"

"You mean you've already done it?"

"As a matter of fact, yes."

She sighed and looked out to sea. White horses were chasing each other inshore. "Oh, Knightsbridge. Sometimes you're so very young still."

"Young! Not too young to . . ." He left it unsaid.

"Well, even that was very juvenile. Fancy not taking the most elementary precautions—or behaving like a gentleman if you couldn't."

He was too embarrassed to answer.

They paused and leaned against the sea wall. "I truly loved her," he said. "I would have married her properly when the time came, I swear it. Regardless of what you and the pater might have said. I don't know how I'm going to live without her. She was the most . . ." He choked.

He visibly regained a grip of himself. "Still, what's done is done. One mustn't make too much of these things, what! Better grieve early than late. Sorrow shared is . . ." He laughed a little wildly to cover the tremor in his voice.

Flora would have enjoyed the luxury of tears in a more private place—and the closeness to her son they would have earned her. "Practical things," she said firmly. "You must find another mistress as soon as you return to your regiment. A proper one this time. Not a lover."

He was aghast. "Steady, mater!" he said.

"Oh, don't be tedious, Knightsbridge, or I shall go back to treating you as not quite grown up."

"But, I say, it's hardly . . . well . . ."

"I'd say it's overdue, this conversation. You don't seem to realize you'll be a duke one day. A long time yet, I hope. But one day you will be. And that makes you different. Don't ever let yourself forget it. Dukes *are* different. Especially in matters of this sort. It's all very fine now to say you'd have married this woman. No doubt you would—no, let me speak my piece now. No doubt you would. But you don't seriously imagine you and she would have been allowed to remain married, do you! I promise you, within a year of its coming to light, the whole business would have been annulled. You cannot marry whom you choose, any more than your father could."

He looked at her in amazement.

"There now." She smiled. "You want to be grown up. Listen to some grown-up truths. Ordinary men may marry whom they please. They may be as careless with their hearts as they please. If their passions are too strong, why, they must either govern them or find some secret release. But you are in a different case. Dukes and monarchs—and their heirs—are at liberty to make public and open provision for their passions. Look at Bertie, the Prince of Wales. *You* know the form. There is a form for these things. If you want a woman of good class, we'll find a complaisant husband for her and use our patronage to the necessary degree. If the woman has no class, an allowance and pension will suffice."

"Jove!" was all he could get out.

She laughed. "You thought I knew nothing of these matters? Only the fast young ladies in your set can talk of it, eh? Well, it's simple prudence, my boy. And we dare not let prudery stand in the path of prudence, eh? Too much is at stake."

"S'pose not," he said in a more customary drawl.

"Why don't you have a good talk about it with the duke? In my view, there's no one manages these things better."

"The pater!"

"There you go again, dear. Every time I begin to believe you've grown up at last!"

"Jove!"

As they turned into Albert Road, where his "very good Protestant family" lived, she said, "By the way, one doesn't wear full mourning for a mistress. Most people of refinement would consider quarter-mourning quite sufficient."

"Oh . . . thanks," he said. "One did try to look it up but, as one would expect, prudery took the precedence: The books remain absolutely silent on the subject."

"Not a bad policy," she said solemnly.

The humor had gone by the time she reported this encounter back to Alfred. "This kind of love," she said, "which feeds on guilt, remorse, and death, is the most dangerous kind of all."

"Dangerous?"

"Yes. It freezes itself. I'm afraid Knightsbridge is going to build a shrine to Miss Walberswick and dedicate his whole life at its altar."

"But—the dukedom, dammit!"

"That's what I mean by dangerous. It's so easy to idealize the dead. They aren't around to receive the tarnish that life all too easily applies to the rest of us. And the military life is so satisfying—especially to an Old Etonian. I'm afraid he won't be able to resist the temptation to combine it with sacrifice and worship."

"But it never seemed to me that he was so deeply in love with her."

"Perhaps he wasn't. But what I'm saying is that it hardly matters now. The easiest woman to love and idealize is one who's no longer there. And if the fault for her death can be laid at his door—rightly or wrongly—you have all the ingredients for . . ."

"Well, he can still do his duty by the dukedom. Broken heart or no."

"I hope you're right."

"Travel. That's the thing. He must take some leave and go to South Africa."

"It might work."

"It must. And he must understand that love and remorse are all very well, but the Duke of Saint Ormer is the Duke of Saint Ormer!"

CHAPTER THIRTY-THREE

WHO IS THE REAL DUKE OF ST. O.? ran the headline in the *News of the World.* It was the rest of Fate's hand of marked cards, dealt in words of one syllable. Mr. Bruce Boys, out in Australia, had obviously tired of the Law's endless delays—twenty-five years having passed since his first letter to Elliot and Polkinghorne—and had decided to make the matter public. Polkinghorne—first the father, who had broken the news of the inheritance to Alfred, then, more recently, the son—had done a magnificent job of spinning a mighty legal web around the simple business of whether or not William Boyes (Boges/Bogis/Buges/Bugis?) had died while in the care of the Lords of Oyer and Terminer and General Gaol Delivery on a prison hulk on the Thames in the year of grace 1770. Like all good legal cobwebs it had since gathered prodigious quantities of legal dust. There had been costly and exhaustive searches under all the possible names; and it had proved successful.

There had, indeed, been a William Bugis on the same convict hulk that had temporarily housed William Boyce. But William Bugis had survived. He had served his seven years, returned to England, married—and there all record of him ceased. No deaths had been returned under the name "Bugis" for the whole of the next century. There was a birth certificate for a Frederick Bugis in 1780, but he too vanished with no further trace.

A second costly search had unearthed an old cattle drover in Spitalfields who remembered that when he was a lad of ten he had worked in Smithfield market for a butcher called Bugis who had suddenly vanished one day. "I couldn't svear to it, mark'ee," he said, "but I do seem to recollect as vot the vife and boy vos left to die in the Spitalfields Work'use."

Then came the purely legal questions: Was the clerk's unequivocal "William Boyes" authoritative despite the ambiguities of the turnkey's hand? If the title was in abeyance, did the findings of the House of Lords end that abeyance? If not, did her majesty's warrant of 1850, permitting Alfred the courtesy style of Marquis of Knightsbridge, end it? If not, did his writ of summons to a seat in the Lords end it? If not, had the writ of summons unintentionally created a new peerage? Once the Lords had adjudicated on the validity of the evidence—they being the supreme court of the kingdom—could that evidence be challenged if no new point of law was involved? Did William Boyes's felony, which, if he *had* inherited the title, would have been grounds for confiscation by attainder, *ipso facto* and *ergo* and *propter hoc* and *a posteriori* and all the rest of it, end the abeyance?

Every plum of jurisprudence that could be grafted onto this frail stock was grafted and left to ripen. Every opinion, to no one's surprise, came down most firmly in favor of the present duke, possession being, in this case, *ten* points of the law. No one wanted to see the grandson of a convicted felon at Chalfont Abbey.

None of this was even hinted at in the *News of the World* article, according to which William Boyes had successfully navigated half the globe and sired a new line which, if their lordships had not been so careless, would have to this day maintained the title and dignities of the dukedom of St. Ormer in abeyance. But it was cleverly written; there was no hope of an action for *scandalum magnatum.* Alfred himself was nowhere personally impugned.

Of course they had got it wrong, and of course they could be forced to print a retraction. But that wasn't the point. Alfred made the point when Polkinghorne, Jr., came tumbling posthaste down the line to Maidenhead to see him.

"Tedious bastard this Boys," he said.

"Indeed, your grace."

"And a bloody tedious sheet this *News of the World.*"

"But clever, sir. This is a very cleverly put together article."

"Have you heard from Boys's solicitor in Melbourne? Is this part of some bigger opera?"

"Not to our knowledge, sir."

"Then what d'you advise, Mr. Polkinghorne?"

The young man looked uncomfortably around. Being a first-class lawyer, he didn't want to get to straightforward advice yet; he would have preferred to trample the ground back and forth for half an hour until it was knee-deep in Norman French. Then, like a savior, he'd weigh in with the advice.

Alfred pulled out his watch. "Be so good as to give it a wind, would you?" he asked. "Then tell me your advice."

The poor lawyer had no chance. "I believe, your grace, it would serve best if I were to go and see the editor of this . . . alleged newspaper. He clearly has the wrong end of the story. I shall put him straight and demand an apology, a retraction, and damages—which, naturally, we shall pay to charity."

"What I think you should do," Alfred said, as if he had given the matter deep thought, "is to go and see this editor person, and tell him exactly what you've just told me."

Polkinghorne rose to go.

"Just one thing," Alfred added.

"Yes, your grace?"

"Ask for the damages *first*."

Unfortunately, Polkinghorne overdid it. When he had left the *News of the World*, the editor turned to Royston Dart, the journalist who had done the offending piece, and said, "What d'you make of that?"

"They've certainly gone to a great deal of trouble with their searches and opinions," he answered guardedly.

"That struck me too."

"They took counsel's opinion on every conceivable line."

"Isn't it interesting?"

"Not the sort of thing one does, sir, unless one is unsure of one's own case."

"As we ourselves know only too well. I'll tell you what, Dart, I don't think we'll be publishing that apology just yet. Let his grace learn something of the Law's delays. Meanwhile, let us get out our spades and go digging among the public records."

Four Sundays later a much more accurate version of the Boyce fears (and the Boys hopes) was blazoned across the pages of that paper—facsimiles of the turnkey's and clerk's entries and all. The *News of the World* was offering fifty pounds for anyone called Boges/Bugis/etc. who could trace his ancestry back to 1750 in England. The *Spectator* dryly commented that it would add a prize of five guineas for any one called Bogus, confident of being able to hand it to the same claimant. The *Times*, on the same day, made almost the same point: "However the winner may spell his patronymic, whether it be Bugis or Buges, Bogis or Boges, we may already be sure of its pronunciation: *Bogus*."

That, in general, was how Society chose to treat the episode: It was a cheap and nasty trick to boost the paper's circulation. "We are not in the regular habit of perusing this particular specimen of the gutter press," wrote the *Morning Post*, "preferring to remember the Commandment to keep the Sabbath holy, but it does now seem to us that the offending articles step so far beyond the bounds of decency that we must begin to ask why the Lord Chancellor or the Lord High Steward has as yet issued no writ under the ancient and honorable law of *scandalum magnatum*. The authorities must now teach them that they have tweaked the lion's tail once too often."

In a calmer vein there was an article in the *Nineteenth Cen-*

tury, signed "A Leading Law Correspondent"—but he might as well have signed himself "A leading Garter King of Arms" for all the secrecy there was about his identity among the upper ten thousand—in which the whole law on the abeyance of titles was set forth with great clarity; and, by amazing chance, the body of every counsel's opinion Alfred had ever paid for was worked into its text, sometimes word for word.

The *News of the World*'s fifty-pound trawl netted many a Boggis, a Buggins, a Bowyers, a Bags, and a Badgers; nothing distorts the human vision quite like hope. There were, too, of course, a thousand Boyces, and Boyeses, and Boyses—all with great expectations that the dukedom's foundations were now so thoroughly shaken, one or two bits of the falling masonry might roll in their direction. But not one Boges, not a Bogis, nor a Buges, nor . . .

The editor yawned. "I have never been so heartily sick of anything in my life, Dart," he said, "as these wretched names. Why on earth did we begin this nightmare?"

"It looked very promising, sir. You recall?" Dart said apprehensively.

"It's been nothing but trouble. Remember this, Dart, and remind me if I ever look like forgetting it: We shall never again dabble in matters of inheritance and the descent of titles unless we have a dozen counsels' opinions behind us first."

A month later, in deepest Berkshire, the rector of Woodcote, the Reverend Mortimer Boyle, wrote in his journal: "The Lord has heard my prayers and answered them. The Lord be praised! The matter's dropped and there's an end on't. *Certes* I should never have survived here had the tale of grandfather Bugis or Boyes "come out," and in the *News of the World* of all rags! Now it is buried, for Ever, let us hope."

And back into a pile of papers, indistinguishable from two dozen other piles of other papers, he stuffed those venerable parchments which the scholar within him had never allowed the respectable clergyman to destroy. And the respectable clergyman longed to destroy them for they told a tale of infamy and shame.

But for a misreading by a workhouse dame, whose failing eyesight had not been helped by the guttering taper she held dripping over the workhouse rolls, the Reverend Mortimer Boyle would be known by his true name: Boyce.

But "Boyle," the old lady had said to his father, who later became the Reverend Frederick Boyle—"See here, young Boyle, here's your new parents come to take yer. Treat 'em respeckful now and don't go showing off yer rotten horigins, d'ye hear!"

And the Reverend John Stowker, vicar of Diss in Norfolk,

smiled and let the name stand out of kindness to the lad—though from the dying confession of the youngster's mother he knew full well it was Boyce or Boyes. Only later, when Frederick, on approaching manhood and holy orders, seemed in for a lifelong attack of spiritual pride, had the kindly vicar reduced him to human scale by revealing that confession: His, Frederick's, father had been a felon, by name William Boyce or Boyes. While awaiting transportation for life to the penal colony in Australia, he had murdered (or taken advantage of the death of) a fellow prisoner named Bugis, who was to serve only seven years. Somehow Boyes had impersonated Bugis and so returned to England after serving only seven years. He had married one Sarah Cotehele of Diss, Norfolk—Frederick's mother. Then after only three years, when Frederick was but a year old, he had suddenly vanished and was never heard of again.

When Sarah had been taken into Spitalfields Workhouse she had given her husband's true name, which she had spelled Boyce. And there, on her deathbed, she had told this shameful story to her old vicar and family friend; she had added that she thought her traitorous husband had gone back to Australia. She also said that he had several times spoken of a great legacy which the Duke of St. Ormer had stolen away from his family, the First Duke being his great-great-great-grandfather. He was a bitter, violent man. " 'Tis my belief he was often mad," Sarah said.

She had also made the Reverend Stowker promise to take young Frederick back to her own people in Diss. The vicar had not the heart to tell her they were all dead of malaria; instead he adopted the boy and brought him up as his own, letting the dame's misreading of Boyle for Boyce sever him somewhat from his past.

From the moment the *News of the World* had begun its search for Bugis and variants, the Reverend Mortimer Boyle had walked in terror that his family's shame might be revealed to all. Now, God be praised, the paper had dropped the business. It could all sink back into oblivion. Never, never again would he, or the Duke of St. Ormer, or the duke's heirs be troubled with it.

But even so he could not destroy the parchment wherein it was all recorded and witnessed.

At the height of the fracas the duke and duchess went to dine at Windsor. Though Prince Albert was all of fourteen years dead, the queen was still in full mourning. She "went about" not at all. But she liked to meet those who had known Albert intimately; she liked to talk about him and remember all their happy times—the simple times in Scotland, the holidays in the Isle of Wight. Even Alfred's and Flora's wedding celebration had been transmuted to a golden memory, a medieval feast of jousting and minstrelsy. Like everyone else, Alfred and Flora found it most wearing to be constantly picking over the past; but their annoyance was softened by a tender sympathy for the poor lonely woman at the heart of it.

Before they went in to dinner, the Prince of Wales took Alfred aside. "I'm sorry to hear of your annoyance with this dreadful newspaper, uncle," he said.

Alfred smiled. "Thank you, A.E. You're a good friend. We'll survive it, I think."

"Of course! That's not in doubt at all. But it's a devil, what? Not being able to make any public riposte."

"You suffer—your family, I mean—you suffer a great deal more from that than any of us."

"But we're brought up to it. Look at the dreadful things they said and wrote about father, and how manly he always was about it."

"He is, of course, one's chief example," Alfred said, slipping easily into the Windsor house style. "God rest his soul."

"But I believe a gesture is needed, uncle. We must do something that the world can read as a sign. Mama must do it."

"What are you thinking of, A.E.?"

The prince smiled as if to say, *You'll like this.* "A lot of us believe it's time you got your Garter," he said. "There's a vacancy at the moment. The annual Chapter and Service is almost upon us. What better time?"

Alfred, who had longed for his Garter ever since becoming a duke, was delighted. "What does one say, sir—it's already been said: You're a true friend! One of my ancestors, Sir Clarence du Bois, was a founder Knight of the Order."

"Of course the Garter is really in the Prime Minister's gift. But mama retains some influence—if she is careful to use it but sparingly." He chuckled. "You don't realize how lucky you are to be a duke, even at a time like this. You wield so much more *real* power than any constitutional monarch could hope to grasp."

"Duke Augustus once told me the same thing, A.E. I didn't believe him, either!"

They were careful to modulate their laughter before they rejoined the company. In return for acts of friendship like this, Alfred used to pass along little tidbits of information picked up in the Privy Council, information the queen would share with the marble bust of Prince Albert but not with her royal son.

Conversation at dinner was heavy—as expected. Even in the lighter moments, as when they discussed the extraordinary antics of "Goosie" Blandford, wife of George Spencer-Churchill, Marquis of Blandford, and a future Duke of Marlborough—even then it was, "how *he* would have laughed!"

Goosie Blandford, daughter of the newly created Duke of Abercorn, suffered from intense boredom, like many an aristocratic lady of limited mental horizons (and equipment). Her chief diversion lay in an endless string of practical jokes. In that taste she was not alone. Apple-pie beds and tottering inkwells on doors were daily fare in most stately homes, whose marble floors and high ceilings rang with braying laughter as the sheets tore and the inkwells tumbled. But Goosie Blandford was in a class apart. The poor marquis (or "marquess," as the Churchills affected to spell it) would lift the cover off his breakfast tray to find, not the expected poached egg, but a grinning little celluloid baby. Live toads croaked at him from his wash-hand basin; dead ones slimed his pockets. Messages came from dying tenants who turned hale and hearty the moment he answered their summons. And Goosie's laugh could peal down a marble corridor like a donkey imitating thunder. She was making poor Blandford's life a hell.

They did not know it, but their decorous laughter around the royal table was the overture to a scandal that was to imperil the prince's very survival.

CHAPTER THIRTY-FOUR

THE *News of the World* sensation—the Bogus Scandal, as it was called—faded away. For the upper classes it had never been more than a passing trifle; and there was greater agitation at the impertinence of the editor than at the duke's discomfiture. For the middle and lower classes there was soon to be much stronger meat to devour: Colonel Baker's alleged indecent assault on a young governess on a train from Petersfield to Waterloo.

The only people who had not forgotten the Bogus Scandal

were Alfred's creditors. He was stretched to his very limit at the banks and had long ago turned to that obliging, smiling, obsequious, and damnably expensive fraternity who haunt Paternoster Row and its purlieus—*News of the World* readers to a man. Talk of an abeyance in the title worried them. There was no more money forthcoming after that.

Of course it would pass. When he got his Garter, for instance, their confidence would return. But meanwhile the duke was thrown back on his own rents and dividends.

It could not have come at a worse time. Eighteen months earlier Wolf Frisch had passed the day-to-day running of the London Distillate Company to a manager and "retired" to the Brighton wing of Chalfont Abbey, part of which Alfred had fitted out as an organic-chemistry laboratory. It was the only place secret enough to conduct their experiments. Alfred had managed to devote several hours each week, and sometimes each day, to this work and had even published a few papers (as plain "Alfred Boyce"). Just recently he and Wolf had perfected a whole range of blue dyestuffs that were as acidic as any dyemaster could wish, and as cerulean, as cobalt, as hyacinth, as lavender, as marine and ultramarine, as peacock, as Prussian, as turquoise, as azure, and as royal as any lady of fashion could desire. They called them Ultra blues in their patent.

The research had cost nearly a hundred thousand pounds. To set up a company that would be able to occupy a significant part of the market would cost more than twice as much again. To keep control of it Alfred and Wolf had subscribed to sixty percent of the shares. The first big call was now being made on that subscription.

What could he do? There was nothing he owned outright, or nothing whose sale would not cause the most almighty stink. So much about a dukedom was a matter of external show. A duke who economized in ways that could be seen had already lost whatever it was he was trying to preserve. If the Grosvenors had had to be given the dukedom of Westminster last year simply because they were much too rich to be left as mere earls, then what of the converse! A pauper duke was a creature infinitely more pitiable than a pauper commoner.

It was so unfair. Next year, he was sure, every one of his investments would have turned a corner and he, quite apart from the estate—he personally—would be worth a prince's ransom. But just at this moment, and largely thanks to the Bogus Scandal, he couldn't raise enough wind to lift a horse's tail.

"Ask Bull," Flora suggested when Alfred confessed his difficulties to her. She was still worried about something Knightsbridge had said, something that had not struck her until after they parted: "I would have married her properly."

What had he meant by *properly?*

Alfred did not mention his trouble even to Hermione—much less to Bull.

The very next day a most disturbing letter was delivered to Alfred's club at breakfast. It was from Polkinghorne the younger informing him that a Mr. and Mrs. Horace Walberswick were going about claiming that their daughter Patricia, lately deceased, had been secretly married to the Marquis of Knightsbridge and that the son she had borne on her deathbed was rightly Earl of Brompton and heir to the heir. They were not able to produce a marriage certificate nor a certified copy of any entry in a parish register, so no newspaper, however low, had touched the story; but it could gain a wide verbal currency and could only harm Knightsbridge and the duke.

The Walberswicks, the lawyer added, were coming to wait upon him that very morning.

The duke sent a message telling Polkinghorne to bring the pair to his room at the House of Lords; he had thought at first of suggesting a hotel in Paddington, but what would look more hole-and-corner than that if it ever came out? He sent another messenger to the Horse Guards, desiring Knightsbridge kindly to attend him in the Lords at noon.

Shortly before that hour, Mr. and Mrs. Walberswick were ushered in.

Mr. Walberswick had, in fact, been called to the Bar, though he had never practiced as a barrister. Instead, he had retired on a modest private income, and devoted his life to the natural history of Studland Heath, near Poole in Dorset. He had wrestled long with himself before allowing his only daughter, Patricia, to become an Eton Dame; but had been swayed by the thought that she was far more likely to find a husband there than on a remote Dorset headland. Not a future duke, of course—the Walberswicks' sights had not been raised so high—but a good sort of professional man; a clergyman, say, or a career officer in the army; even a housemaster. That she would instead become the mistress of a young aristocrat and die bearing his child had never entered their remotest speculations.

"Mr. and Mrs. Walberswick." Alfred rose to greet them. "Please accept my deepest condolences on the . . ."

"We will not accept them, your grace," Walberswick said. His wife nodded tight-lipped agreement.

Alfred's heart began to pound. He hated this sort of confrontation—especially as, in this case, his own "side," if it was to be thought of in those terms, was in the wrong. He drew a deep breath. "Your anger and bitterness are readily understandable," he said. "And you have my sympathy, whether you accept it or not. But rancor will serve no one's purpose, certainly not yours. For if you want to make out a claim that your grandson is a rightful heir to my title, the last thing you ought to do is fall out with me." He smiled his friendliest.

Reluctantly, Walberswick conceded the point, apologized, and accepted the duke's condolences.

"Now what is the basis of your claim, Mr. Walberswick?" Alfred asked.

"It is this, sir." He produced a sheet of paper. "These are copied extracts of three letters from our daughter last year. The originals are in our lawyer's keeping, together with other letters from her."

The first extract ran, in part:

> I am to be married on Saturday next! I am sorry to have kept it a secret from you until this, but read on and you will see why. Richard, my own dear darling Richard, is a Marquis! The Marquis of Knightsbridge and heir to His Grace of St. Ormer. But more than that to me, he is the most marvellous man who ever lived and breathed. A Child still in some ways, but a Man, oh! a Man in so many others. It is to be a secret wedding, here in the house, but to be done by an ordained clergyman of the Church of Ireland (which is the Anglican Church with a brogue, you know). I wish you could both be here, and little Cissie, but it is surely small sacrifice to have your daughter a Marchioness and, one day, a Duchess! . . .

The second:

> It is done! What a very simple and yet moving ceremony is our Solemnization of Holy Matrimony when stripped of its churchly trappings and performed in a small parlour. Richard so manly in uniform and I so plain in my everyday clothes. But what matters it? We are man and

> wife in God's sight and are all the world each other needs. . . .

The third:

> Oh how I wished to tell you this marvellous secret while you were here! Every mealtime, every walk, every moment we sat by the fire, I was bursting with it. But I was not sure then—and, anyway, I wished my dearest, dearest husband to be the first to know. And now I *am* sure of it, and Richard is beside himself with our shared happiness. I am to have a son! How do I know, you laugh: a *son?* Well I am sure of it, and so is he. As soon as the child is born, next May, he says he will tell the duke and duchess—and the whole world—of our marriage, resign his commission (being too young to marry according to the military, but how wrong they are!), and we will set up house together, properly. . . .

Knightsbridge himself arrived while the duke was reading this final extract. He had been given no warning of the purpose of this meeting and was shaken at the sight of Patricia's parents. An icy politeness masked their hatred of him.

Without a word the duke passed his son the paper. He read a few lines and said, "This isn't Patricia's hand."

They explained. He read on. Tears welled in his eyes. Angrily he wiped them away, staining his white kid gloves. When he finished he dropped the paper and ran to the window, staring out while he fought for mastery of himself.

"How much of it is true, my lord?" the duke asked sharply.

Knightsbridge started at the cold formality of his father's question.

"My lord?" Alfred insisted.

"All of it, your grace," he said quietly.

The Walberswicks sighed grimly and resettled themselves.

"You married Miss Walberswick? Are you saying that?" the duke pressed furiously.

"No, your grace." Now it was barely a whisper.

The parents sat upright again, looking in bewilderment from duke to marquis, suspecting collusion.

"No?" The duke bellowed in a voice that would have harvested an acre of ripe mustard.

"It was . . ." Knightsbridge looked around and caught sight of the lawyer, apparently for the first time. "Must Polkinghorne be here?" he asked in something closer to his usual drawl.

"Shame sets no conditions," the duke snapped. "Mr. Polkinghorne will stay. Now will you tell us, my lord, one way or another, the truth of this. Did you marry Miss Walberswick?"

"She . . . that is . . ." He looked desperately about him. "She *thought* I did, your grace."

Walberswick stood up angrily. "This is some charade!"

But the duke motioned him to be seated once more. "Explain yourself, sir!" he barked at his son.

The young man stared at his boots. "It was a trick," he muttered.

"Speak up!"

"A deception. I got her by deception. But I *loved* her!" He looked around in anguish. "Afterward! I truly fell in love with her. And I would have married her. I *swear* it!"

In the stunned silence Polkinghorne said quietly, "And the clergyman, my lord? Who was he?"

Knightsbridge was dumb.

"Answer!" the duke commanded.

"Must I?"

The duke just stared at him.

"It was a fellow from the regiment. Look! It was a joke, then. It only grew serious later. God—don't think one hasn't regretted it, and regretted it bitterly, a thousand times since."

"It would have been more honorable for you, my lord, to have killed yourself beside her deathbed," the duke told him.

"Does your grace think it didn't occur to me—that my hands didn't itch to end my wretched, disgraceful life? Does your grace think I wanted to live one moment longer in a world from which *she* had been snatched? No! Yet the fact that I am here, confessing these dreadful things, is the best witness I can offer that I loved her as I have sworn."

The improbability of the connection pricked their curiosity.

"The boy!" he shouted. Now it was he who seemed angry. "He is her flesh, too. He is all in this world that unites us. I know . . . I know . . ." His voice began to tremble. "One is supposed to hate the baby whose birth was the cause of its mother's death. But it isn't so. It isn't so. I love Neville every bit as much as I loved her. That's why I am alive still, and it's the only reason. To do all I can for him. To do it for her sake."

At this Alfred felt the first stirring of sympathy for his son. There was some good left in the boy.

Walberswick was not in the least moved. He rose to go. "You speak your lines well, my lord. And you, your grace. But we are not deceived. The clergyman exists. The ceremony was lawful. One day we shall prove it. We may lack your power. We may have none of your influence. And we certainly do not have your money. But we shall not rest until we have restored our dear girl's honor and our grandson's rights."

The duke shrugged. "You will only succeed in making your lives miserable."

Knightsbridge, seeing that they were about to leave, said, "You may have every facility to visit Neville, sir. And later, in his holidays, you may have him to stay for as long . . ."

The man's smile was sarcastic. "Your lordship is too kind! But you cannot on the one hand claim not to be the husband and, on the other, reserve the legal rights of parentage."

"Nor, with respect, sir," Polkinghorne cut in, "can you claim Lord Knightsbridge *is* the legal husband and yet deny him those rights!"

"My own name is down as father on his birth certificate," Knightsbridge said, quietly ending the argument.

The announcement caused a small sensation; only the duke, who had it from Flora, knew of it. For the first time Walberswick looked irresolute, as if the news was forcing him to reassess all of Knightsbridge's protestations.

But his wife was made of less yielding stuff. "You *aristocracy!*" she sneered. "You *nobility!* You *upper classes!* You should all be swept away and leave the world clean and fresh for decent, honest people." She was shivering with fury. "You, you and your damnable Prince of Wales, your gambling, your drunkenness, your ruining of decent women like Patricia—you are loathsome and despicable. You are an affront to simple decency. I hope this Colonel Baker is given ten years with hard labor for what he did to that poor innocent girl on that train. It's what I'd give to the lot of you! You are not fit to breathe the air of this dear land. I'd sweep you all down the nearest sewer, which is where you belong. You think of nothing but your own immoral pleasures."

"Come, dear," her husband said gently.

When they were gone, the duke sighed. He stared at his son; no softness or sympathy showed. "You must resign your commission, my lord," he said. "The Coldstream is an honorable regiment." Then, seeing his chance, he added, "Why not travel, my boy? Go to Africa, eh?"

"I shall go to a levée next week, sir. The only thing that's kept me has been to see that Neville settled well with the Powells."

"And then?"

"If one is ever to be rejoined with her, one must somehow regain one's honor. I'm sorry, your grace, but you will understand that I can never marry."

"Africa, my boy! It'll work wonders on you."

When he had gone, Polkinghorne cleared his throat and said, "We must get a signed and sworn statement from the officer who pretended to officiate at that mock wedding, your grace."

The duke was silent. "Do you think," he said at last, "that even a lifetime given in the service of his country, even if he covers himself in military glory, do you think it can wipe out the stain of this dishonor?"

"Your grace would know more of such matters than I."

"And Mrs. Walberswick—is she right? She's a decent, God-fearing, moral person. Thoroughly middle class. Is that what the middle classes are saying about us?"

The lawyer cleared his throat. "I'd have no opinion as to that, sir," he said diplomatically.

"Then, dammit, you're no bloody use to me," the duke said angrily.

"A section only, your grace." Polkinghorne leaped to mend the fence. "Only a section would support her views."

"Hmm!" Alfred pulled at the little goatee beard he had lately grown in homage—though he'd never have admitted it—to Disraeli. "She's no radical, you see. Not a political corpuscle of blood in her veins, I'd say. Yet—sweep us all into a sewer! Strong stuff, Mr. Polkinghorne. Strong stuff! I hear the thunder of the tumbrils."

"She was under great stress, your grace."

"Aye, and so was he. The question is, what do people under great stress do next, eh? What would you do?"

"I'd go back to my lawyer, sir."

"Spoken like one of them!" He laughed angrily. "No, I think what they'll do is go to the *News of the World*." To Alfred, not knowing how heartily sick the editor was of the dukedom of St. Ormer and its succession, this was a most alarming prospect.

"D'you think so, sir?" Polkinghorne asked. "They don't really seem the sort."

"In *their* mood, anyone's the sort," he replied. "Yes. I think it's time I paid that editor a visit. You'll accompany me."

When the duke's coach turned off Fleet Street and into the lane where the *News of the World* was produced each Sunday, the lawyer said, for the third time, that the visit was most unwise.

But his grace was not really listening. He was staring out the window. Then he broke into a smile.

"I shan't be needing you after all, Mr. Polkinghorne," he said. "You may take a cab back to your office. But first be so good as to step inside and tell the editor his grace of St. Ormer desires him in his carriage."

Polkinghorne was dubious.

Still Alfred smiled. "You may also let slip the fact that his grace of St. Ormer is the landlord of this building!"

The editor came like a shot off a shovel. He entered the carriage a worried man. But after half an hour or so of aimless driving —aiming, that is, only at returning to its point of departure—it was a relieved man, full of smiles, who stepped down and bowed himself backward into the building. The duke had merely wanted to know the ins and outs of owning and managing a newspaper. He had not even mentioned recent *News of the World* articles—but then, as landlord of the property, he hadn't really needed to.

From these incidents the duke learned two lessons. The first was to ignore the advice of the Polkinghornes to keep himself aloof from his affairs. Henceforth, like any good general, he'd see the ground, test its firmness, and feel the flesh, for himself.

The second, following the next issue of the newspaper and the sudden willingness of the moneylenders to float his debts once more, was a mighty respect for the influence of the press.

Two lessons? No, three. The third was the folly of living as he had on the very margins of solvency. For a year or two the coachmen could wear gardeners' gloves dipped in whitewash.

CHAPTER THIRTY-FIVE

FLORA TOOK Lord Knightsbridge's departure for South Africa very hard. The boy had done wrong—very wrong. But why did he have to blight the rest of his life, throwing it away in one wretched little war after another until he got killed? And there could be no doubt he would get killed, because that, after all, was his purpose. He'd made it quite clear in his final words: "You'll look after Neville if anything happens to me, won't you? Send him to Eton and get him down for the Foreign Office." A suicide note could not have been plainer.

All their hopes were transferred to Lord Charles, now in his final year at Eton. Had Charles been less brilliant he would have been marked down as one of the most stupendously idle fellows who ever passed through that Academy of Leisure. Had he been less good at games, he would have been a byword for shirking. In fact, he did his studies—and did them brilliantly—only because he could achieve in ten minutes what others managed, with difficulty, to do in an hour. He excelled at the Wall and Field games because he had a natural aptitude for sports and because to apply that aptitude was the line of least resistance. Indeed he *was* one of the laziest and least ambitious of boys; but even his laziness surpassed the hard-won achievements of less gifted contemporaries.

Unlike Ape he was a wet bob. Cricket consumed a whole afternoon, a cricket match an entire day; rowing occupied a mere hour —more strenuously, it is true, but it left the rest of the time free for doing absolutely nothing.

And so, in a different manner yet no less successfully, he too passed through the school relatively unscathed.

What he would do next no one had the slightest notion, least of all himself.

"Why should I do anything at all?" he would ask. "There's so many unemployed who need the tin it seems immoral to work when one don't have to."

If pressed he supposed he'd go up to Oxford, to New College or Balliol, and hunt and learn rugby football, and take a double first. He'd keep his captaincy in the Grenadiers because that might be useful. What he'd really like, he thought, would be a post at some exotic legation like Constantinople, or Vienna, or even Paris.

Until he left Eton he was also a page of honor in the queen's household. Almost his last duty was to hold the train of the Prince of Wales, deputizing for his still-mourning mother in the annual chapter and service of the Most Noble Order of the Garter—*Honi Soit Qui Mal y Pense.* It was the ceremony at which his father, the duke, was to be installed as a Knight Companion of the Order, the highest order of English chivalry and the most ancient and coveted order in Europe.

Since his introduction to the Lords, more than twenty-five years earlier, Alfred had developed quite a taste for uniforms and robes. Apart from his colonelcy-in-chief of the Stormers he was also Colonel-Proprietor of an Austrian regiment, a Past Zerubbabel of a

Royal Arch Chapter of Freemasons, an honorary Doctor of Laws of the University of London, an honorary Doctor of Literature of Trinity College, Dublin, a *Colonel-Chasseur* of the *Grande Armée de Provence*, and, after a visit to the Khan of Turkestan—where he had really been interested in ancient dyestuffs—a Sham of Kazat. All these uniforms, and many of lesser distinction, hung in camphor (a product of the London Distillate Co.) in the ducal robe chamber at Chalfont. All of them, even his unused coronation robes, were demoted one peg to make room for the Garter regalia.

One fine May morning, the morning of St. George's Day, Alfred rose from his bed in Windsor Castle, threw wide his window, sniffed the air off the Thames, and called for his shaving water. After a quick cold bath and breakfast he put on full-dress uniform and awaited his summons to the antechamber of the Throne Room. It came shortly before ten o'clock.

At any time of the year the Throne Room of Windsor Castle was one of the most magnificent rooms in the kingdom; on the day of a Garter installation it was no longer *one* of the most, it was *the* most magnificent. The gilded roof and walls were blazoned with the arms of long-gone knights; the throne, beneath its splendid Canopy of State, stood at the head of steps which were, for the occasion, carpeted in the royal blue of the Garter.

At the start of the ceremony the Prince of Wales had been escorted to his throne. Before him were assembled all the officers and Knights Companion of the Order. Around the throne and at intervals around the room stood the Queen's Bodyguard of the Yeomen of the Guard in their Beefeater uniforms. Everyone there was in full state robes, levée dress, full-dress uniform, or other regalia; the white ostrich plumes of the Knights shimmered like a sea. It was just the sort of pageant over which Prince Albert Edward loved to preside.

Alfred walked erect between his two sponsoring Knights, their graces of Norfolk and of Richmond and Gordon, the full length of the Throne Room and up the steps, where he knelt for the accolade of knighthood. Then, following the solemn ritual of the ancient ceremony, the Garter, gorgeous in its blue and gold, was buckled below his left knee. Then he was invested with the Mantle of dark-blue velvet, lined with white taffeta; to its right shoulder was attached a crimson velvet casting hood; on the left breast was embroidered a white, or "argent," shield with the red cross of St. George, surrounded by a gold-embroidered garter with buckle and the motto; at each shoulder, too, was a knot of white silk ribbon; the whole was secured by tasseled cords of blue and gold. Next came the Collar and George, fashioned from pure gold, and, finally, the Hat, a black velvet affair, Tudor in style, with a wide brim and a great plume of white ostrich feathers stiffened at its center by a black tuft of heron's feathers.

Alfred felt like a king of creation as he took the oath of the order and then assumed his place among his fellow Knights Companion.

After luncheon in the castle he was installed in the Chapel of St. George. The procession wound its way down from the castle in the Upper Ward to the chapel in the Lower Ward. The first part of the route was lined by the Foot Guards, magnificent in their scarlet tunics and black bearskin hats. The last part was lined by dismounted troopers of the Household Cavalry with drawn sabers; they were resplendent in white buckskin, gleaming breastplates, and flashing plumed helmets. At the head of the procession walked the Governor of Windsor Castle, leading the Military Knights in their scarlet tunics. Then came the Heralds of the College of Arms —Windsor, Richmond, and Somerset, Lancaster, York, and Chester —and the Pursuivants—Rouge Croix and Blue Mantle, Rouge Dragon and Portcullis—all in their tabards. Behind them were the Knights Companion, a sea of blue, gold, crimson, and black with the ostrich plumes forming stately waves upon its surface. Behind them came the Register and Secretary of the Order, followed by the Chancellor and Prelate.

A little way apart followed the sovereign's procession, headed by Garter King of Arms and Black Rod. This year, as in every year since his father died, the Prince of Wales walked alone. Behind him, holding the train of his dark-blue velvet mantle, were the two pages—one of them, Lord Charles, looking very dashing in his scarlet livery tunic and white knee breeches. Bringing up the rear came the Yeomen of the Guard, all scarlet and black and gold, carrying their tall, broad-bladed partisans.

The entire procession mounted the west steps leading up to the entrance of St. George's Chapel. They passed between the ranks of the State Trumpeters, who raised their trumpets and blew a fanfare as the Prince of Wales entered the chapel.

The old knights went straight to their stalls. Alfred waited in the aisle for his summons, which came after "God Save the Queen." The queen herself watched the whole ceremony from the seclusion of Catherine of Aragon's closet above the aisle. Those in the body of the chapel had an occasional glimpse of her stout black-clad figure, relieved only by the blue of her Garter sash.

"It is our pleasure that the Knight Companion be installed," the prince said in a firm voice.

Garter King of Arms led Alfred to his stall and unfurled his own banner before him. After the service it would be raised to hang above the stall, where it would remain until Alfred's death.

The ceremony did not move Alfred as his introduction to the Lords had done; but that, after all, was not its purpose. Its purpose was to show the world what he, Alfred, already knew: He had arrived; and now he was unassailable.

CHAPTER THIRTY-SIX

THAT EVENING there was a dinner and ball at Windsor Castle. Bull and Hermione were, naturally, in Alfred's party, which formed, as it were, a sort of crossroads between the sporting country element and the smarter town set, much as the prince did in his own life. His circle, the Marlborough House set, was thinly represented; only those whom the queen could hardly avoid inviting were present.

The queen ate in her own apartments and did not show herself at all. Toward the end of the evening she sent for Alfred. She saw him in the Green Drawing Room; two ladies in waiting were technically also present but were far out of earshot at the other end of the vast chamber.

The queen had put on weight lately; yet she looked frail. Tonight she also looked tired, and more than a little petulant. Alfred's heart fell.

"Alfred!" She forced a smile.

His heart fell even further. She called him Alfred only at times of great friendship—or awkwardness.

"Come and sit here by me and bring me some *cheer*." The smile became genuine. "You look well. And so you *should*, today of all days. *Dear* Flora was *radiant* as usual. You are *so* lucky, both of you."

Alfred knew what she meant—lucky to have each other. "Lucky in our time, ma'am," he said. "And lucky in our sovereign."

She sighed away the smile. "I'm tired, Alfred. Fourteen years' tired."

"I know." He smiled wanly.

She fixed him with a stare. "I believe you do, Alfred. I believe you're one of the few people who does know. Just as I believe you are one of the very few who can exercise a good influence on Bertie."

"He is my prince . . ." Alfred began.

"Oh, dear, that has an ominous ring! When the previous Duke of St. Ormer said 'my prince' like that, he meant my awful uncle."

"That was no more than a charming affectation," Alfred told her. "He had neither time nor patience for your uncle as king. I'm sure he never said 'my king' as he said 'my prince.' "

"Hmm," she said. "What d'you think of Bertie's visit to India?"

Alfred was, in fact, enthusiastic about it—about anything that involved the prince in public affairs—but he knew better than to say it outright. Instead he looked dubious enough to bring a smile of pleasure to her face. "Constitutionally," he said, "it's very awkward, ma'am. He can't be your representative—that's the viceroy. Yet he can't just be a private individual. He's heir to the throne, after all. I suppose if he went as the viceroy's *guest* . . . ?"

She was half pacified. "That's what Salisbury says, too. It avoids complications. Most complications, anyway."

Alfred knew very well what Lord Salisbury thought; they had exchanged views at their last Masonic meeting.

"Alix wants to go too," the queen said, a touch of vexation in her voice.

"That could give it the appearance of a court," Alfred replied. "I think it most inadvisable."

The queen smiled radiantly. "I can always rely on you, dear Alfred, for the most sensible counsel."

"I'm sure Bertie's against it too, you know," he risked telling her, for he knew that Bertie was determined not to take his wife. "He has a good diplomatist's instinct in these matters."

"Hm!" The opinion did not please her. "I'm surprised you say that, Alfred. Look at the people he's taking along: Lord Aylesford —or 'Sporting Joe,' as I hear him called—who stands on his carriage roof driving at full gallop through London, pelting the people with bags full of flour. Now is that a fit companion for a future emperor to take to India? And Lord Carrington and Lord Charles Beresford—what can they do? Shoot, I suppose. And ride without falling off."

Alfred nodded all through this outburst, as if agreeing with every word. "And yet," he said, half reluctantly. "And yet."

"What?" she asked, suspicious of any qualification.

"Suppose, ma'am . . . suppose he took instead an entourage of scholars and statesmen. Might that not lend this visit the very weight . . . the importance we are trying to deny it? Whereas, a party of . . . good lightweight companions . . . ?" He left the rest unsaid.

She was both attracted and enraged by the argument.

"Besides," Alfred went on. "I'm sure he's determined not to take Alix, which is bound to strain their relations for a while. In those circumstances it might be unwise—it might even be disastrous to send him out in a bad humor with a party of people quite uncongenial to him."

She nodded glumly, seeing what sort of bargain she was going to have to accept; she must have been hoping for his unequivocal support, Alfred thought.

He thought that, having failed to get her way, she was about to dismiss him. That would be her usual form. Instead she looked sharply at him, in a way he had come to recognize as especially dangerous, and said, "People have been telling government secrets to Bertie. And Privy Council secrets."

He knew she was accusing him, or at least working up to such an accusation. To head her off he said quickly, "To do so would be to violate a sacred oath, ma'am. It would be a treacherous and scandalous act."

She stared at him with those unblinking, penetrating, coal-black eyes. "Hm," she murmured.

"If only she weren't so insanely jealous," Flora said when Alfred told her of this encounter.

"Jealous?"

"That's what it is, dearest. I know she dresses it up as best she can in all sorts of constitutional plumage. But that's what it boils down to—plain jealousy." She snuggled against him. "I know you're horribly torn by your devotion to both of them, but I'm afraid there are aspects of her majesty's character that don't bear close scrutiny."

"Jealousy?" Alfred was still testing the idea.

"Yes. Why shouldn't the future king play a substantial part in public life? Especially if the present sovereign chooses to play no part at all? Why shouldn't he be privy to the business of the government? You know what a good diplomat Bertie is when he's given the chance—you've always said he'd make the best ambassador we've ever had. And *she* knows it too! So why does she go to such insane lengths to keep him out in the cold and the dark? Why does the court set spend half its time trying to find out what the Marlborough House set is up to, and the other half trying to stop them? Poor boy—no wonder he wastes his time on frivolities."

"I wonder if you're right."

"Of course I'm right. I'll tell her so to her face one of these days."

She laughed at his alarm. "You're soft about her," she said.

"I wouldn't go that far. I have a soft spot for her, I'll own."

She pouted.

"And for you, of course. I've a big soft spot for you."

A mischievous look stole into her eyes. "I can feel it," she whispered. "Can't you make it harder?"

He beat his forehead in mock despair. "Trapped again!" he cried. "You insatiable woman." He began to ease up her nightdress.

"You're as convincing," she went on in that same husky whisper, "as the soldier caught in the nurses' home." A moment later she added, "That's more like it!"

Then the joking was over. Their one flesh was at its familiar, marvelous riot.

CHAPTER THIRTY-SEVEN

"I FELL IN LOVE with Alfred here," Flora said.

She, Hermione, and Alfred were strolling among the Wellingtonias Duke Augustus had planted around 1820; now, getting on for sixty years old, the tallest of them were already two thirds the height of the beech trees whose solid ranks formed the backcloth to the stately grove.

"And you still remember!" Hermione marveled. "I've quite forgotten where it happened to me."

"It's happened so many times," Alfred told her. "You're forever falling in love with me." How he wished he could take them both to bed, especially in the middle of a warm afternoon like this—but it was a suggestion he had never quite summoned enough courage to make to either woman.

Flora threw herself down in a rustic seat in the center of the grove. "I've always felt that our lives are somehow bound up with these trees. Measured by them." She pointed out a sequence of increasing heights. "They were only so high when Alfred and I first saw them together. There when Knightsbridge was born. There when he went to Eton. There when Louise married Michael . . ." She hesitated, seeing Hermione's smile. "D'you think that's funny?" she asked.

Hermione grinned even more broadly. "A bit, yes."

"Why?"

"Well, here you are, in Chalfont Abbey, with permanence engraved in every stone. And yet you choose to measure out your life against"—she waved her hand—"trees!"

"D'you know, you can punch these trees as hard as you like," Alfred said, "and you can't hurt yourself. The bark is so springy, though it looks quite hard."

"I didn't know that," Hermione said.

"It's how they survive forest fires," Flora said.

"William didn't know it either," Alfred went on. "I can understand your not knowing it—but William! You'd think a boy who grew up here would discover it, somehow."

"Where is William?" Hermione asked. "He vanished after lunch."

"He said he'd help Felicity school her new mare."

"Oh?" Flora's eyebrows shot up. "He's taking quite an interest in Felicity lately, don't you think?"

"She's no more than sixteen." Alfred laughed. "He's more like an uncle to her, what? Twenty-four? Twenty-five?"

"I suppose he must be about that," Hermione agreed. "Isn't time going fast these days?"

Flora said impatiently, "He'll be twenty-four this December. Good heavens! You'd think *I* was the one who bore him, not you. And Felicity, by the way, is eighteen. So!"

"I was close," Alfred congratulated himself.

"Closer than usual," Flora allowed.

"She's a very mature eighteen, too," Hermione said. "In fact she's always been what you'd call a mature sort of person. I don't mean she's never done childish things, but she does even those in a mature kind of way."

"I always felt," Flora said, agreeing, "that she resented being a child. One has always been able to talk to her as to an adult."

"She's you all over again," Alfred told Flora. "Next year she'll ride over to Windsor Great Park, break a leg, and get taken on as full-time, unpaid assistant housekeeper to the queen. And in due time she'll marry Prince Eddie." He turned to Hermione. "It's a family tradition you know."

Flora withdrew herself from his nearness with dignity.

Hermione laughed and then grew solemn again. "It wouldn't be anything serious though, would it?" she asked. "William and Felicity? That could be awkward, I must say."

"Doesn't he show an interest in anyone?" Flora asked. "I thought the Howard girl—what was her name? Effie!—I thought she was most suitable."

Hermione, still frowning, shook her head. "Most awkward," she repeated.

"What does he want to *do?*" Flora went on.

"Nothing out of the ordinary," Hermione answered. "The same as Bull, really. Hunt. And a spot of shooting and fishing. He's no taste for politics, anyway, or any kind of public life. He wants to live at Bullen Towers, since we go there so rarely."

"Why would it be awkward?" Alfred asked.

"It wouldn't be awkward at all," Hermione said, slightly puzzled. "I only wish he would. He'd like to breed horses, too. And what better place could he wish for than Bullen—"

"No!" Alfred interrupted. "I mean awkward for him to take an interest in Felicity?"

The two women sighed and exchanged glances. "What Hermione means, dearest, is that since you are quite possibly William's father, too, the degree of consanguinity possessed by the pair of them falls within the scope of those prohibitions in the Book of Common Prayer. And don't tell me it hadn't crossed your mind."

"In fact," Alfred said, "it hadn't. But even so, those rules aren't meant to apply to *us*."

"Of course they are!" Flora laughed, though she was slightly alarmed.

"Nonsense!" Alfred said in a lofty manner. "They're for common people. Otherwise the most dreadful things would be happening down in the cottages."

"But it's inbreeding," Flora said.

"Of course it's inbreeding," Alfred told her. "That's what we're talking about."

"Well then!"

"Well what? You talk as if it were the same as incest."

"It is incest."

"But how can that be?" Alfred said patiently. "Incest is a legal thing. William and Felicity have no legal relationship at all. Not of the remotest kind. He's a Bullen-Chetwynne. She's a Boyce. Legally."

"Even so!" Flora was astonished he could not see it.

"Even so, nothing. You were right the first time. Inbreeding. That's what it is. Nothing to do with incest."

"But isn't inbreeding . . . harmful?" Hermione asked.

"It rather depends on the stock," he told her. "Our *Potentate* was sired by a son on a mother. And he won the Derby, the Oaks, and the Guineas in the same season. You can't get much nearer perfection than that. And how do you imagine we get our eight-hundred-gallon cows? Inbreeding, of course. How does Bull get his hounds with the right pads and wind for this country? Inbreeding again. If the stock is right." He turned to Flora. "You don't look convinced?"

"No. It still seems wrong to me."

"Well, it may never come to anything. But if it did, think of this: Their children would have the blood of fifteen baronets, ten dukes—I mean five on each side—"

"But it's the same five," Flora objected. "Through *you!*"

"It's still double the helping anyone else would get. Plus two lords bishop, fourteen marquises, and I don't know how many earls and viscounts and barons. And, of course, a king. William the Conqueror on both sides. Why, there'd be as much noble blood in each of them as in the three of us *put together.* If you'll pardon the phrase."

Now! he thought. *Suggest it! You'll never get another chance half as good.*

"Speaking of which—" he began.

But Hermione had started a fraction ahead of him. "Well, we must just hope nothing ever comes of it. We certainly couldn't explain to either of them why they oughtn't to marry each other."

"I'm much more worried about Charles," Flora said.

Alfred sighed. The moment had passed. "Charles?" he asked.

"We were talking the other day about the trouble the queen has keeping Bertie out of state affairs. With Charles we seem to be having a trouble of exactly the opposite kind. He'll take no interest whatever in the estate. It's quite obvious that Knightsbridge intends to die gloriously in some battle or other as soon as possible. We have to treat Charles as the heir apparent."

"But he's such a nice boy," Hermione said, "certainly the most charming, easy-natured boy one could hope to find."

"And he knows it," Flora said. "He'll charm his way all through life, if we don't stop him. And *idle!*"

"Oxford will change him" Alfred said soothingly. "That and a spell at some legation abroad. I'll get Salisbury to select him a hard taskmaster."

Flora laughed. "Oh, he's not idle out of . . . well, out of sheer idleness. It's a sort of philosophy with him. He sees idleness as the duty of the leisured classes. You ought to talk to your son Charles."

Alfred nodded. "I think I shall."

"And this is our tribe," Alfred said. "God Almighty's gentlemen!" He cleared his throat. "Gentlemen," he said. "Your heir—Lord Charles Boyce."

"Steady, pater!" Charles said, peering around with distaste at the dry, musty vaults. "You speak as though Knightsbridge is already dead."

"We must behave," Alfred said solemnly, "as if he were. You especially, Charles my boy. You are the one who will inherit everything these men—and I—worked for. We are trustees for you, just as you are a trustee for generations yet unborn. But even wider than that, we are trustees of our people—those thousands who now say with pride and gratitude, 'I'm the Duke of St. Ormer's man!' We're trustees for them, too." He smiled with a hint of apology, self-consciously. Out in the world he could play the real duke well enough; but here he'd always be, at best, the stumbling novice.

Charles, thinking his father's unaccustomed shyness was due to him, smiled reassuringly.

Alfred gathered himself, determined not to disappoint the old grandee. He cleared his throat. "But any two-a-penny baronet may say as much," he went on. "We're trustees, we dukes, for more than our own people. We're trustees for England. There's only twenty-seven of us—twenty-seven dukes. Everyone's eye is on the queen and the court, and the prince, but that's a delusion. *We're* the ones who really count. We have the real power. We do the real work—out here in the shires and counties. We set the tone. I myself have been responsible for the appointment of more people to positions of trust and responsibility than her majesty."

Charles, eyes glowing, nodded; fascination with his father's theme was possessing him.

"And if we do it well or ill, it's because of this." He gestured at the ranks of coffins all around. "Of these great men and women. Our ancestors and antecessors. You've seen their pictures in the rooms above. Now here they are. Beginning"—he hammered a fist on the stone coffin nearest the doorway—"with Godfrey, who, as you know, built most of the Abbey. His son, Charles, your namesake"—another thump on another coffin—"bought a lot of the Bucks land. But *his* cousin, Clarence . . ."

And so on. It was an abridged catechism because, of course, Charles—indeed, all the children—had been brought up on the family history.

When he came to their own ancestor, the Reverend Lord Richard, Alfred paused and looked up at his son (all his grown-up children, by Flora, by Hermione, and by Danielle, were taller than he). "What sort of man are you, I wonder?" he asked.

Charles grew uncomfortable under his father's scrutiny.

Alfred eased aside the loose piece of marble. "There!" he said speaking barely above a whisper. "Your sixth-great-grandfather. Touch him."

Charles was as reluctant to obey as his father had been twenty-five years ago; but, like that earlier Alfred, he was mesmerized by the awe of the moment. He, too, had no choice.

"You reach across two centuries of English history," Alfred said. "Your touch links eight generations!"

He had to nudge Charles's arm to break the spell. "And here's Duke Augustus, the old grandee himself." He chuckled. "I'm sure we've mentioned *him* to you."

Charles laughed, glad of the relief. "From time to time, pater. From time to time!"

At the door Alfred cleared his throat like a man about to make an embarrassing confession. "Here's a thing now," he said. "From the sublime to the ridiculous. It must never go outside the family. Tell it only to your own heir." He wet his lips and looked about them. "When we visited the Crimea, your uncle Bull and I, we—that is, he, uncle Bull—got into an argument with a Russian officer."

He told his son the full story right up to their smuggling Captain Plisetski's salted head through Customs in a trophy bag.

"At first we buried it in quicklime, but then I read some chemistry and discovered that, far from consuming flesh, quicklime actually mummifies and preserves it. So we dug it up again and . . ."

He turned uncomfortably and nodded toward the Reverend Lord Richard's coffin.

"It's in there!" Charles said.

"We pushed it in as far as we could. Where else could one successfully hide a mummified human head?"

"Good Lord!"

On their way up to the battlements they passed through Bull's trophy room, where musk ox and caribou, Highland stags and Siberian tigers, wildebeeste, zebra, and lion—all in improbable promiscuity—stared back at the visitor through serene and sightless eyes of glass.

"Your uncle Bull wanted to put the Russian there." Alfred pointed to a still-empty spot, the pride of place, above the keystone of the Gothic-arched fireplace. "Of course that was when we were still in the Crimea. As soon as we got back to England he saw the enormity of it."

"What's he keeping that space for, then?" Charles asked.

Alfred sighed. "You know this new song of Sullivan's, 'The Lost Chord'? And the idea that there's a lost Shakespeare tragedy somewhere. And a lost continent beneath the waters of the Atlantic."

"And lost tunnels connecting Chalfont Abbey and Great Marlow!"

"Yes. Well, your uncle Bull has the feeling that there's a 'lost trophy' somewhere. Not mislaid, you see. But undiscovered. A creature half-man, half-ape in the Himalayas. A giant in the Great Gobi Desert. Something like that. The trouble is, he's getting on for eighty, and it's not the sort of age at which you start mounting expeditions for—"

"Is he really, sir?" Charles was astonished. "Lord, but he's wiry, then. And tough!"

Up on the battlements, walking with the measured tread of sentries—where sentries must have trod in earnest four hundred years ago—Alfred asked Charles what, if anything, he thought of the future.

"It'll be more of the same, I suppose, pater," the young man said guardedly.

"More *what* of the same *what?*"

"Well—once every street in England was dark at sunset; now there's no real night in any of our towns and cities. So I suppose a hundred years from now there'll be lights in every lane in Europe. That sort of thing."

"But nothing really new? Is that what you're saying."

Charles shrugged. "Daily steam balloons to Biarritz and Marienbad and Naples, I suppose. Lots of things like that."

Alfred gave a humorless laugh. "There's a bit of tittle-tattle going round this family that you're one of the idlest fellows who ever lived, Charles. That you haven't a thought in your head and, what is more, have no intention of letting a thought lodge there. Until this moment I've refused to believe it. What, to come straight to the point, is your view of the future of the aristocracy?"

Charles halted and, leaning against a finial on one of the battlements, wedged himself among the stone ribs—an extraordinary, though probably unconscious, miming of a trapped man.

"We'll exist, I suppose," he said.

"What for?"

"To show people . . . things."

"Show them Chalfont Abbey? Tuppence a go? Is that what you mean?"

Charles laughed at the absurdity of it. "No, pater! Show them what's what. How to behave. How to enjoy being leisured. That's what we're *for* now, isn't it? Set an example."

"Is it? Why?"

"Hang it all, pater—God's purpose, don't you know. Ours not to reason why." When he saw this did not satisfy his father, he added: "I mean, we show the lower classes that moneygrubbing's not everything. When we go into government, we don't look for a salary. We do heaps of things free. And we also show that leisure needn't be simple debauchery, as it is with the lowest classes, but sport and travel and yachting and breeding horses. And art, of course, for those who like it—history, scholarship, bug hunting, scrabbling through ruins, sketching in the Holy Land, looking for rivers in Africa . . ." His list petered out for a moment. Lazily he looked about them, scanning the duke's acres, seeing little. He sniffed the summer air. "And philanthrophy," he said. "Getting the women and children out of coal mines and things like that. It's all been done by the aristocracy, with the help of some good middle-class draft horses."

"And where, may I ask, where in this great spectrum of noble activity do you see yourself as fitting best?"

Charles sniffed again and gave a contagious smile. "At the moment, pater, I think the answer to that is probably waiting for me in Oxford."

"It had better be so, my boy. Because either you tell me what you're going to do in life, or I'll be telling you. I hope that's understood?"

Charles looked out over the landscape, drenched now in the sunshine. "Knightsbridge is a bit of a hoick, isn't he? Turning his back on all this—just because of some woman!"

CHAPTER THIRTY-EIGHT

"WOMEN!" Alfred gave a wry laugh. "Haven't the Hindoos and the Arabs got the idea of it?"

"*You* can't complain," Hermione said. "You of all people." She pressed herself to him and kissed his cheek. "You have a more than adequate seraglio."

He shivered for her. "No, I don't complain. But neither do I mean *that*. I'm not talking about the polygamy. I mean purdah—the locking away."

"With Bertie in India now, I'll bet they've doubled the locks!"

"Yes. Except that the trouble isn't there. It's here. And it isn't Hindoo wives, it's 'Sporting Joe' Aylesford and his darling Edith."

She stroked his face, looking at his worried eyes. "Trouble?" she echoed.

"Could be big. Could be nothing. It depends how discreet and tactful we all are. Can I ask your advice?"

"Tell me." She settled on one arm and lay beside him.

"You know the gossip from Staffordshire all this winter? Edith Aylesford going up to live in Packington Hall, and Blandford moving all his hunters to some nearby village, and hoof prints in the snow to the side door?"

Hermione nodded.

"Well, it's all true."

"Adultery?" Hermione laughed. "Is that the 'trouble'? And it's so uncommon these days—especially in the Prince of Wales's set!"

"She wrote to Aylesford in India, saying she and Blandford were going to elope."

Hermione swallowed and turned pale. This was no mere escapade, padding along country-house corridors in the dark. This would become *public*. To be sure, all Society knew of the adultery already. But that was not the same thing as having the whole affair made public. An elopement would reach the newspapers.

"But they must be prevented," she said.

He nodded vigorously and sighed.

"And you've been asked to prevent it?"

"I've been asked to help. God, if only the prince wasn't away in India! Or if only he hadn't taken Aylesford along. The queen's going to crow over this, I know. She was dead set against Aylesford and Carrington going—though they've behaved with perfect dignity. Aylesford's ruined, of course, whatever happens."

"The important thing is to stop this elopement and then to stop Aylesford from suing for a divorce."

Alfred nodded glum agreement. "It's gone further than that, I'm afraid, dearest. It seems that Bertie once wrote some slightly indiscreet letters to Edith Aylesford—"

"Was *she* one of his?" Hermione was intrigued.

"I don't think it was ever an *affaire*, you know. But he admired her. No doubt of that. And you can imagine the generous sort of note he'd write. And how his little compliments and friendly expressions could be read in quite a different way. The trouble is, she gave these letters to Blandford, and he . . . God! I'd have thought that of all the tribe of Spencer-Churchills he'd be the one to have more sense. D'you know him?"

"Only slightly. He's a marvelous conversationalist."

"A charming man altogether. You'd never take him for the next Duke of Marlborough."

"But Bertie's letters?"

"Yes, and what does he do with them but give them to his younger brother!"

"Randolph! Oh, my God!"

"Exactly! You might as well hand a bomb and a matchbox to a child of four. Randolph sent a cable out to Bertie in India, didn't like the reply, and now he's gone to Alix and involved her. He's told her that if these letters are published, Bertie will never sit on the throne of England."

"Oh, poor dear. When did this happen?"

"This afternoon. What I want to know is—what do I say to Alix when I go and see her tomorrow? Dizzy wants me to see her, then the queen, and then try and reason with Blandford."

"You can safely leave Edith Aylesford to her sisters. There's four of them married into the peerage. They'll put a flea in her ear."

"That's what Flora says too."

"You may depend on it."

"But what do I say to poor Alix?"

"People misunderstand His Royal Highness, ma'am," Alfred said. "Even those who know him well. They think he's impressed with success and money. But Bertie's always at his best when people are in trouble. That's when true friendship is revealed. And that's when his generosity shows best—"

"I don't quite see the connection, though, uncle," Alix interrupted.

How beautiful she is, he thought! Superficially it was the same sort of beauty as Hermione's—flowerlike and remote. Yet underneath, Hermione was as earthy and passionate as a gypsy girl. But Alix? He would never know. How could one ever discover that sort of thing?

He knew very well how. One approaches them in time of trouble. One offers an arm to lean on, a shoulder to weep on. One slips the arm about their waist . . . *No!* He took a grip on himself. Banish the thought! Yet . . . she was so beautiful . . .

But Bertie was a friend.

But that didn't stop Bertie from sweeping his own friends' wives into bed whenever he wanted.

Oh, women! Why was the pursuit of them so all-consuming? When would he be at peace from them?

"I mean, my dear, that Bertie is *essentially* generous. He doesn't make it conditional on a good return. Look here—here are some little notes he's written to Flora over the years. Thank-yous and invitations and simple bulletins written for no other reason than that he just happened to think of us and wanted to say something. Listen." He began to quote isolated sentences from them, passing each note to her as he finished. "Your dress was quite the loveliest of any woman's there . . . your beautiful hands as you played the Chopin waltz . . . the sound of your lovely laughter lingered on long after . . ." He looked up at Alix. "You see? Everyone knows that Flora's no conventional beauty. But her hands are beautiful, and her laugh. And she has an eye for a good dress. So he singles out these things. Flora was naturally delighted to get these little notes. She'll treasure them always. But just imagine how sentences like these, wrenched out of context, would look in a newspaper! I'm sure it's the same thing with the Lady Aylesford letters."

Alix had involuntarily placed a sympathetic hand on his arm when he said, "Flora's no conventional beauty." Now she gave a squeeze. His insides turned over, yearning for her. "Dear uncle," she said. "You're so comforting. You've no idea how isolated one feels . . ." Her voice faltered.

"I'm sure I speak for all your friends," he told her, putting a hand over the hand that squeezed his arm. "The quarrel is between Aylesford and Blandford. It's monstrous of Blandford and Randolph to try to blackmail Bertie, who has no part in it at all. Those Churchills always were a sour, arrogant, pigheaded tribe. Ye gods, Alix, if I were Bertie and you my wife, I don't know where I'd find the time to write notes—however kindly—to any other mortal, man or woman!"

Nothing in her demeanor changed, except that she raised her head a little, which had the effect of offering her lips in a most ambiguous invitation. "What is unforgivable," she said, "is that we've always considered them, both Blandford and Randolph, as among our most intimate friends. Bertie will be so wounded."

While she spoke, he leaned slowly forward, bringing his lips ever closer to hers. It was a move that could be reversed at any moment—for instance, at the slightest sign of alarm in her eyes. He saw none. She watched him closing the gap between them with a kind of detached curiosity.

He kissed her, a kiss that was gossamer gentle. Her eyes did not close. She did not melt. The pace of her breathing did not alter. It was like kissing a lily. "Thank you, uncle," she said with a dazzling smile that ought to have shattered him utterly but that had the paradoxical effect of restoring him, instead. What strange things were happening! He sat up again and patted her hand, as avuncular as her courtesy title had made him seem.

"You may always count on my devotion, Alix. You know that."

"I know." She stood to walk him to the door. "We shall cut them, of course—the Churchills—and expect all our friends to do the same. Thank you so much, dear uncle, for putting my mind at rest."

As he set off for Windsor he wondered what on earth had happened back there at Marlborough House. Had it been, for her, the kiss of a courtesy uncle? An embarrassed act of kindness, half-forced? A first-time flirtation with the very idea (it hardly amounted to an act) of infidelity? The more he thought about it, the more inflamed his curiosity grew. What was an ice maiden like once she was roused?

No sooner was the thought achieved than he realized the absolute folly of trying to find out. A light flirtation, perhaps even one or two incandescent moments, with a good friend's wife—that was one thing. But an all-consuming passion that would sweep reason and decorum before it—well, wasn't that the sorry business on which he, the prime minister, the court, the Foreign Office, and half the upper nobility were now in one way or another engaged?

"None of those Owen girls was ever the <u>slightest</u> bit of good," the Queen said angrily.

"That's a little sweeping, ma'am," Alfred said. "The Owens are neighbors of mine at Great Marlow. I'm not even sure I'd lay all the blame at Lady Aylesford's door, and she's the only one who—"

"Your generosity speaks well for you, Alfred. But *of course* she's to blame."

"Well, people will call Goosie Blandford the 'innocent party.' Yet think of the appalling series of practical jokes, so called, she's played on that poor husband of hers. Would he have looked at Edith Aylesford, even, but for that?"

The queen, somewhat calmer, ceased her pacing and sat down, looking at Alfred with a mixture of admiration and pity. "But, *dear* Alfred, the origins of this passion have no bearing. Their very *existence* is what we must condemn. We know that men—some men —cannot easily control themselves. But that excuse can *never* be advanced for a lady. She must always control them—which Lady Aylesford has *signally* failed to do. And for that she must now be *forever* cast from Good Society. But what about these letters, eh?"

"I'm sure they're innocent, ma'am," he said. "And Alix thinks so too."

"You are a *dear* person, Alfred," she said at last. "A dear, good person. Bertie, I'm sorry to say it, does not deserve such good, loyal friends. But I'm afraid your loyalty blinds you. We all know what a *roving eye* he has. And more than an eye! After all"—a familiar note of sour sadness invaded her voice—"it's what killed my *poor*, dear Albert." Her hand automatically rose to her locket that hung around her neck. "That dreadful Curragh business with that slut of a Dublin actress."

"Oh, no, ma'am," Alfred said firmly. It was one subject on which he—and many others—would never defer to her.

She tossed her head angrily and looked away. "The point is, people will believe it if these letters are ever published."

"Then they must never be published, ma'am. Disraeli will see to it, I'm sure. And as for Blandford, I'll see him myself. I think I know how to approach him."

He was relieved to see the beginnings of a smile on the queen's lips. Yet still she could not avoid giving the dagger a twist. "They say Bertie had his eye on Jenny Churchill. At least it'll put a stop to *that*!"

"Once we've brought Blandford and his brother to heel," Alfred said, remorselessly keeping her to the subject in hand, "we must stop Aylesford suing for divorce."

She snorted. "He's so *unsavory*, he'd never dare. Think what would come out in open court!"

"Even so, ma'am, he faces a six-week voyage home from India. He'll be stewing in his resentment all that time. It's very likely he'll be in a towering rage, and quite beyond reason, by the time he arrives. I believe someone should have a word with him. Lord Hardwicke, perhaps."

The queen nodded her agreement and rose to show the audience was near its end. "Oh, Alfred," she said, all warmth again, "how we are going to need such cool heads as yours." She paused and looked at him dubiously. "Perhaps I may confess this to you now—after so long a time. When we first heard that the Fifth Duke of St. Ormer was to be an orphan from the lower middle classes, you may imagine our feelings. But how wrong we were! We should have trusted, you see, to the blood! We talk about it, but we don't trust it. You are the living proof, dear Alfred, that we should."

"I hope I never do anything to betray that confidence, ma'am."

At the door, as if it were an afterthought on her part (though Alfred knew full well it was not), she paused and said, "What about the poor Marlboroughs, though? I assume that even if Aylesford agrees not to divorce his wife, he'll bar the door to her. She's already lost the children—they've gone to Aylesford's mother. In those circumstances, even Blandford, though he may be 'the biggest blackguard in England,' as Bertie calls him, even he can hardly turn his back on her."

"No—hardly."

"What, then, will the Marlboroughs do?"

"They must retire with what dignity they can from metropolitan life, ma'am. Indeed, they must retire altogether from English life, in my view." Inspiration struck him. "Offer him a viceroyalty somewhere—Dublin, perhaps?"

The queen gave a start and then looked slyly at him. "Why, Alfred! There's a touch of Machiavelli about you, I'll swear. Dublin!" She laughed.

When she saw that his bewilderment was genuine, she prompted: "Who's the present viceroy?"

He beat his forehead. The present occupants of Dublin Castle and the Viceregal Lodge were the Duke and Duchess of Abercorn, Goosie Blandford's parents!

"I'll say one thing to her credit," Flora said later, when Alfred told her what had happened. "She's obviously decided not to interfere in a private matter between Blandford and Aylesford. She'll do what's right, rather than what's merely expedient. Even at some risk to herself and Bertie."

In the end, because they all kept their heads, the affair turned out as Alfred had predicted. He and Dizzy managed to din some sense into Blandford and Lord Randolph. Lord Hardwicke prevailed upon Lord Aylesford not to divorce Edith, who, now an outcast from all Society, went to live with Blandford. Goosie separated from and (years later) divorced her husband just before he became the Eighth Duke. The Seventh Duke and Duchess sold a few paintings to be able to afford the heinously expensive office of Viceroy of Ireland, took a moving and tearful farewell of the queen, and quietly withdrew from English life. Lord Aylesford went to raise beef in Texas. Blandford, as a future duke, could not easily be cut from Society; but for eight years neither Bertie nor Alix would enter any home that also entertained Lord Randolph and his pretty young wife, Jenny.

PART FOUR

1879-1888

SPERNO ME
RECIPERE AUT
MUTARI

For Queen and Country

Chalfont Abbey
in the 18th century
showing the south wing
added by Duke William

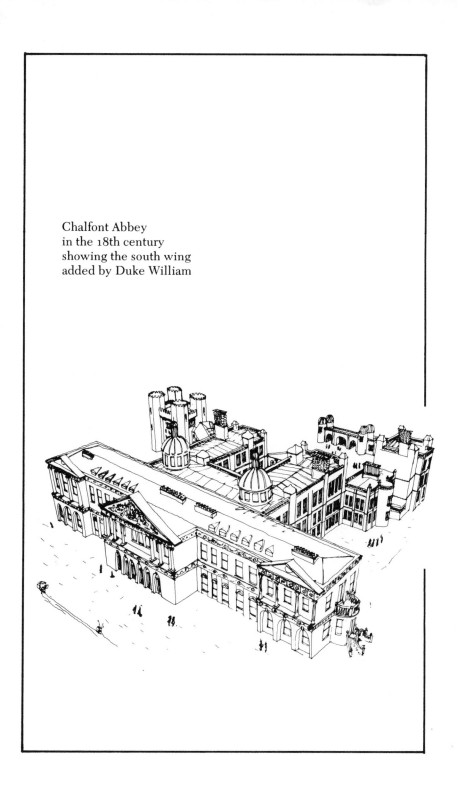

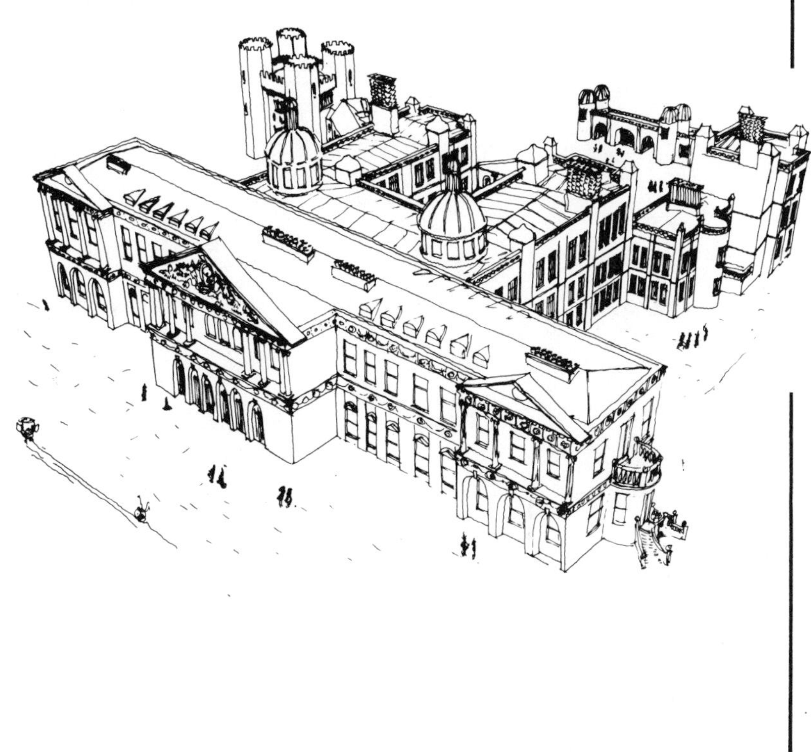

From *Debrett's Peerage and Titles of Courtesy* (1870 edition)

BULLEN-CHETWYNNE, VISCOUNT. (Bullen-Chetwynne.)
[Viscount U.K. 1853.]

REDVERS POLEBY BULLEN-CHETWYNNE, 1st Viscount, only son of the late Rear-Adm. Horatio Bullen-Chetwynne C.B; *b.* August 4th, 1798; ed. at Harrow; was Captain, 1st Coldstream; is a J.P. and a D.L. for Buckinghamshire; Founder and M.F.H. of the Stokenchurch; *m.* 1851, Hermione, dau. of Sir Eric Newbiggin, of Cokeley, and has issue.

ARMS,—Quarterly: 1st and 4th gules, a broken wing argent, *Bullen.* 2nd and 3rd or, a boar's head erased argent, *Chetwynne.* CREST,—A boar passant quarterly or and sable. SUPPORTERS,—Two stags gules gorged with a collar or, attired with fifteen points or.
Motto,—A sound mind in a sound body.
Seats,—Bullen Towers, Staffs. Herberts Tower, Chalfont Abbey, Berks. *Clubs,*—Guards, Travellers, Carlton.

SONS LIVING

Hon. WILLIAM REDVERS, *b.* December 14th, 1851; ed. at Harrow
Hon. John Cardigan, *b.* 1854; ed. at Harrow.
Hon. George Raglan, *b.* 1856; ed. at Harrow.
Hon. James Lucan, *b.* 1858.

CHAPTER THIRTY-NINE

AT HALF PAST FOUR that afternoon a cry came from the lookout on the Oskarberg: "They're coming! Black as hell and thick as grass!"

Lord Knightsbridge (incognito as "Ensign Boyce" of the Second Battalion of the 24th Regiment of Foot) looked at Lieutenant Bromhead and said, with a smile, "That's it, sir!"

The last sack of indian corn, or "mealies" as the Boers called it, had been piled on the western defenses of the little mission station and hospital, where the fortunes of war had dictated they make their stand. The previous day (though this news had only just reached them), six companies of the regiment—21 officers and 581 other ranks—had been killed by the Zulus at Isandhlwana, ten miles to the north. And now more than three thousand of those same warriors, "black as hell and thick as grass," were come to complete the massacre. Against them stood a hundred men of the 24th, commanded by Bromhead; one solitary sapper and his officer, Lieutenant Chard; and Surgeon Major Henry Spalding, in charge of the thirty-five sick and wounded men in the little thatched-roof hospital.

Twenty minutes before the lookout's cry, this tiny garrison had been joined by a hundred well-armed Kaffirs of the Natal Native Contingent, with European officers and NCOs. Half of these were posted as vedettes along the approach road the Zulus would have to take; the rest were at the mission station, helping to complete the "fortifications"—a wall of mealie bags extending roughly a hundred yards along the north side of the compound, at the crest of a rocky shelf which fell to a strip of scrub and stone bordering the wagon trail.

These reinforcements, though they merely brought the odds down from thirty to one to fifteen to one, greatly strengthened the spirit of the 24th.

"Put your tunics back on and break out the ammunition!" Bromhead ordered.

"Listen!" cried De Witt, the missionary.

For a moment all they could hear was the silence of the veld. Then it was overlaid by the most eerie, bloodcurdling sound Knightsbridge had ever heard. To hear it was to know you stared death in the face. It was the deep-throated chant of several thousand full-blooded Zulu impis, in the prime of their manhood and already half-intoxicated with the approaching battle. To the rhythm of this chant they danced forward like angry carnivores whose appetite only blood would satisfy.

The missionary ran to his horse and, without a word of farewell or even a backward glance, galloped off down the road to Helpmakaar. His dust had not settled when a streaming horde of Kaffirs—the entire NNC contingent that had been sent forward as vedettes—plunged after him, closely followed by their cursing NCOs and officers.

Within moments the rest of the NNC, those who had stayed in camp, had mounted and fled after them. Their commanding officer, a Captain Stephenson, had the grace to apologize for their desertion before he too mounted and rode after them.

The death-march music of the Zulus now filled the air. The lookouts came galloping back to camp and took the shoulder-high wall of mealie bags in one bound. Those horses had never in their lives jumped half the height, but the terror of the Zulu chant was on them, too.

"Form squares and stand firm the Twenty-fourth!" Bromhead gave the order. Though he shouted the words, there was a calm authority in his voice that braced every man in the company. "Mr. Boyce!"

"Sir?"

"Take a party of men and build a further wall out from the storehouse."

"Sir!"

There was no need to explain. The hundred remaining soldiers could not hope to defend the three hundred yards of perimeter defined by the mealie bags. Somehow during the coming battle they would have to move the thirty-five sick and wounded from the hospital to the storehouse and fall back on the seventy-yard inner compound he had just been ordered to complete.

He had barely marked out the line of it when the first attack was launched—not from the north, where the scrub gave plenty of cover, but, incredibly, over the open ground to the south. And it was launched directly against the stone walls of the storehouse, to the east, and the hospital, to the west. During the previous ninety minutes—which was all the warning the mission station had received—the men had used their bayonets to cut a dozen loopholes in those outward-facing walls, from which there now rained a withering fire. Of the first wave of Zulus no more than a handful reached the scant shelter of the cookhouse and ovens, which were still a dozen yards short of the defenses.

Then came the first attack on the rest of the perimeter—on the hundred-yard length to the north and the much shorter flanks to the east and the west. There must have been four hundred spearmen in that first wave. It seemed impossible for the defenses to hold out. While the attack lasted, Knightsbridge abandoned the almost completed wall and formed his party into a line, joining the two squares, one under Bromhead, one under Chard.

Shoulder-to-shoulder the 24th stood, and fired point-blank into the Zulus who breasted the wall. Those who were missed and came on were quickly dispatched by bayonet. Within five minutes several dozen Zulus lay dead and not a single defender had yet fallen. It began to seem as if a miracle were possible—that a hundred could hold out against three thousand. Knightsbridge felt a sharp pang of disappointment: He was no longer certain of death. In anger he cast aside his revolver, picked up a discarded Martini-Henry carbine left behind by one of the deserters, and began blazing away like a demon at the next wave of attackers.

On they came, wave after wave, leaping like antelope the dead and dying bodies of their comrades, but always brought up short by the rocky ledge and the ramparts of mealie sacks. Together the twin barriers were too high to be leaped. The sacks, now crimsoned with blood, had to be scaled. Not one Zulu in ten got even halfway over.

"Boyce!"

Bromhead's shout was just loud enough to penetrate the bedlam all around.

"Sir?"

"See to the evacuation of the hospital."

"Sir!"

Walking crabwise the fifty yards to the hospital, he still fired at any head that topped the wall, reloading as he went. Fortunately, Bromhead had had the foresight to break open a large number of ammunition boxes. No one was more than a few yards from a reloading point. Knightsbridge grabbed a box and dragged it across the veranda and into the easternmost room of the hospital, the room nearest the storehouse. The plan already forming in his mind was to evacuate the sick into this room and from there across the thirty yards of open ground to the storehouse—the final refuge of the whole company. It was the only room in the hospital that could be defended by covering fire from the storehouse compound.

In that most easterly room, and the one adjacent, there were twenty-four sick, defended by two privates, Robert and William Jones—not related.

"How is it?" Knightsbridge asked Robert Jones.

"We've kept them off this end, sir. But I can hear them hammering at the door the far end."

"Can we get into that room from the veranda?"

"No, sir. Only from the outside."

"Through the door the Zulus are trying to break?"

"Yes, sir."

"Who's in that room?"

"John and Joseph Williams, sir, and five sick."

Knightsbridge looked around at the sick in this room. "You and William Jones take it in turns to get these patients over to the storehouse compound. I'll go out and distract these housebreakers."

He ran along the veranda and into the room next to the inaccessible westernmost room. Surgeon Major Reynolds was there, tending the wounded. Knightsbridge persuaded the doctor to fall back to the storehouse with a half-dozen who could hop or limp. An equal number of "walking wounded" stayed behind to defend the hospital while it survived.

"I must fall back soon, Mr. Boyce!" Bromhead yelled. "Or we're all lost!"

Knightsbridge waved acknowledgment. Beyond the lieutenant he saw an ominous sight: Fires were being kindled in the scrub near the wagon trail. And the hospital roof was of thatch!

He ran back into the room he had just come out of. One of the men was hacking at the west wall and had made the first breach. "Williams!" Knightsbridge shouted through the hole. "Will you do it in time?"

"It's touch and go, sir. They've almost got that door down." He returned furiously to his work.

For a moment Knightsbridge was at a loss. Should he go and look for a proper pickax and help enlarge the hole from this side?

Suddenly he knew. Pausing only to check that his ammunition pouch was full, he ran back to the veranda, leaped down onto the dusty floor of the compound, and made for the western end of the hospital. He looked over the mealie-bag rampart and saw no Zulu was near; they were all working at the door, which was just around the corner.

Stealthily he leaped the fence and, with a creeping sort of tiptoe run, hastened to the corner.

He reached the corner, drew breath, and leaped out with a savage yell that rent the air and rang off the hills around. Seven Zulus turned and stared, momentarily stunned at his appearance.

His carbine barked six rapid shots, for at this range he could reload and fire without aiming. Six wiry black bodies writhed in the dust or lay still. The seventh man, recovering from the shock, ran across the intervening ten yards, leaped for him, and grabbed at his rifle barrel.

For years the British soldier had complained that the Martini-Henry barrel grew too hot to handle after a few minutes in action. Today it was the Zulu who complained—with a yell that outdid Knightsbridge's war cry. A moment later a bayonet thrust stilled him forever. Knightsbridge did not see who threw the assagai that slammed into his left shoulder and sent him reeling back around the corner. There an instinct far deeper than his wish for death impelled him back over the mealie-bag wall, back toward the hospital veranda.

The last defenders of the outer compound were just withdrawing over the inner wall as he ran back along the north side of the hospital. And the first of a new wave of attackers was scaling the outer defenses, clambering over mealie bags and the sprawling dead. The hospital was now isolated from the main body of defenders; and there were still . . . how many?—a dozen? a dozen and a half sick and wounded men to evacuate. And no more than four or five able-bodied privates and himself to do it.

As he leaped back up onto the veranda a swarm of assagais clanged off the stone and thudded into the wooden shutters over the windows. He turned and loosed a few rapid but well aimed shots at the oncoming hordes before a voice behind called, "Quick, in here, sir!" It was Private Hook.

Knightsbridge fell back through the open doorway behind him. The door was slammed and barred just in time to receive a further hail of assagais, which landed with a sharp but muted thunder. There was, oddly, no pain from his wounded shoulder, though the quantity of blood pouring down his arm and side astonished him.

Williams—thanks to the few moments' respite won for him by Knightsbridge's sortie beyond the perimeter—had enlarged the hole sufficiently to get one of the five patients through. He was just dragging through a second one when the outer door gave. The other Williams, defending it, fired into the attacking mass before it overwhelmed him.

Their situation was increasingly desperate. Attackers were busy on the door and windows on the veranda side. They were, in any case, all around the hospital. At any moment now they would surely fire the thatch. The only chance of escape was to hack another hole in the next wall—and hope the neighboring room had not, meanwhile, been overrun. With the two patients Williams had managed to save, there were now ten to be got to safety.

Knightsbridge nodded at Williams and pointed to the dividing wall. It was all the order the man needed. The ring of bayonet on stone punctuated the shots that Knightsbridge and the others pumped through the doors and loopholes. It was the longest fifteen minutes any of them had lived through. Pain was just beginning to radiate from Knightsbridge's left shoulder when Williams finally achieved his breakthrough.

The next room, the central one of the hospital, was intact. It contained a single soldier, a walking patient named Waters. He was limping desperately from loophole to loophole firing at attackers crossing the open ground to the south; every now and then he turned to shoot through the wooden door, which the Zulus on the veranda were trying to break down.

Again that door was their only access to the compound. Again Williams, blood now weeping from his blistered hands, attacked the stone of the next party wall. Knightsbridge and Hook managed to drag all ten patients to safety; Hook was just in time, killing the first three impis who burst down the door before he dived through the hole himself.

It was hard to gain an accurate picture of what was happening out there; to put an eye to a hole was to risk being transfixed by an assagai. But they all had the clear feeling that the pressure from the veranda was easing.

But now a new urgency was added. The thatch had been fired. The acrid smoke of burning mealie stalks and leaves, added to the fumes of cordite and powder, was making this sanctuary an untenable hell. There was a water barrel in the corner, only a quarter full. But it proved useless. The fire was outside, on the ridge, and eating its way down. It was too high to reach by throwing the water at it from pails; and merely wetting the underside of the thatch did nothing but increase the density of the smoke.

Soon the smoke was maddening—quite literally so, for it drove out all thought except the blind thought of escape. Fortunately, Williams was now helped from the other side by the two privates, Jones and Jones, who had earlier managed to evacuate all their patients and had returned to the empty eastern room, which held the only feasible means of escape—the window facing directly toward the inner compound in front of the storehouse.

Coughing and spluttering, they dragged the ten patients through the hole to the relative and temporary safety of the final room. It was free of all smoke except the tolerable smoke of gunfire; but the thatch at the ridge was just beginning to catch. This time no Zulus poured into the abandoned room. Falling clumps of blazing thatch would achieve all their ends for them.

Knightsbridge, gasping for air, ran as best he could to the window and burst out the frames with his rifle butt; the last shards of glass fell to the ground, six feet below.

"We're coming out!" he managed to yell on his third attempt at speech. "Cover us!"

A "right-ho!" and a wave of a hand in a once-white glove was all the answer he needed. He raised himself painfully to the sill and slid like a drunkard to the ground, sagging at the knees before he regained his stance. The pain from his shoulder was now shattering. It filled his universe.

A pair of torn and bloodied boots dangled into his field of view. The first patient. He braced himself and let the man slide down him, using the one good arm to prevent him from falling. The fellow was barely conscious.

Somehow they reeled and staggered across the open space, littered with Zulu dead and dying, to a prepared slit, one man wide, in the mealie-bag wall he himself had helped to build.

"Water!" he croaked as willing hands pulled the patient through.

Miraculously there was an enamel mug of it in his hand.

"You can't go back there, sir," Sergeant Cawley said. "Not in that condition. Let me go."

The power of the water was supernatural. It cleared his head, made the pain of his shoulder bearable. "I heard no change in orders, sar'nt," he said. "I have mine and you have yours."

He left the cup on top of the wall and marched—actually *marched*—back across the gap to the hospital. He was vaguely aware of forays toward him across the open ground by parties of Zulus. Now and then one even came within yards of him. But accurate and deadly fire from the inner compound always brought them down.

Only on this return journey did he notice Corporal Allen and Private Hitch. For the previous half hour these two had stood with their backs to the hospital wall, defending the window that was now the only usable exit from the building. Between them, ensign, corporal, and private, they got all the wounded across the no man's land without the loss of a single further life. Three trips they made in all. Three nightmare walks in hell.

Knightsbridge was drunk with pain and fatigue by the time the last of the able-bodied men made the crossing—Williams with his black-blooded hands and triumphant smile.

"All out?" Knightsbridge asked.

"Only poor delirious Sergeant Warriss, sir. He just won't come. Nearly knocked me out, he did."

Without further word Knightsbridge set off on one last trip to the now-blazing hospital. He chose not to hear Bromhead's order to return to the inner compound. Somehow, despite the searing agony of his shoulder, he managed to pile one ammunition box on top of another and climb up to the window. Waves of pain were making the scene before him go dark and light, dark and light . . . Or was it the smoke billowing ahead of the roaring flames?

The sergeant was still now. If the man was unconscious, there was a chance. He fell into the room and exploded in a riot of pain as his shoulder hit the floor. Everything was red, a red miasma. Red mists swirled about him. He crawled through them to the prostrate sergeant.

The sergeant, too, was red. *Wet* red. A scoring of assagais had ended his delirium.

The door flapped shut, then blew open again, slammed again. Billows of fiery smoke roared down and curled upward. The door was their plaything. A new pain joined him, and the stench of burning flesh. His? The sergeant's? A nest of hornets on his neck said, *his*.

What was left of his will crawled him to the door. Now he was so awash with pain, with so many different pains, he was somehow outside them. Mad thoughts had found a new way into reality. The fresh air beyond the wildly slamming door had the reek of eau-de-cologne. Then he knew that Eagle—old Eagle in his green-mold top hat and filthy tails—was waiting beyond. And Dame Walberswick . . . Patricia (was she the same one as Patricia?) held a red-hot poker to his neck to pin him down.

When he finally rolled off the veranda he saw them all. And they had all melted, in the fire of his agony, into one. Patricia was the Eagle was the Zulu standing above him with the assagai. He laughed for the sheer joy of seeing them again in this improbable place. He laughed and laughed, even as they stabbed and cut, letting out all his evil.

That strange, eldritch cackle puzzled the Zulu, made him pause. For him that pause was fatal. He fell stone dead, half his head destroyed by a bullet, on top of the dying Marquis of Knightsbridge, heir to a dukedom. In his last moment of vision the young man saw his beloved Patricia, her head entire, floating down toward him until she was upon him and they were united at last, flesh and blood, in one eternal body, far beyond the tortures of life.

He was still dying when, by the fitful gleam of the now-smoldering hospital, Corporal Redditch and Private Boon pulled the Zulu off him and said, "Blimey! He's still alive."

He was still alive, still dying, when, four days later, he briefly recovered consciousness in the hospital at Helpmakaar, the farthest anyone had dared move him.

He was still alive, and no longer dying, when, ten days later, his delirium ended and he was able to hold down some broth.

"Is the war over?" he asked.

"All except for a bit of fighting," they told him. "You've got the V.C."

"I tried," he said.

They thought he meant no more than that he had tried to do his duty.

CHAPTER FORTY

THE FACT THAT "Ensign Boyce" was really the Marquis of Knightsbridge could not help being revealed once the Victoria Cross was awarded him. Among those most interested in the deception was the army's adjutant general, Sir Garnet Wolseley, who, even before Knightsbridge was fully recovered, recruited him into his own "gang." There were then two gangs in the British army, Wolseley's and that of the Duke of Cambridge, the queen's cousin and C-in-C.

Both generals loved the army. The duke loved her as she was; Wolseley saw a thousand ways to improve her. His recruitment of Lord Knightsbridge was—apart from the "capture" of an obviously first-rate officer—an attempt to win the support of the Duke of St. Ormer, whose access to the queen was second to none.

Wolseley restored Knightsbridge to his former brevet rank as colonel in the regular army—all Guard officers then had an army rank two degrees above their regimental rank, and Knightsbridge had been a major in the Coldstream—and seconded him to his own staff. Knightsbridge went to staff college, where he discovered a quite unsuspected military talent and completed the two-year course in just over fourteen months. He was therefore free again for service in good time for the next "little war"—Wolseley's own campaign in Egypt—and another chance to get himself killed.

This Egyptian campaign was immensely popular with the imperial class in England. British rule had taken the benefits of Christian civilization around the globe, and now in Egypt a handful of nationalist zealots, led by a Colonel Arabi, had gained control of the government and were demanding the expulsion of all foreigners. Everyone with the slightest military experience or connection, from the Prince of Wales down, applied to Wolseley for inclusion in his expedition.

As a chance for *anyone* to get killed, whether he wanted to or not, the Arabi War of the late summer of 1882 was a dismal failure. That was because it was in every other way a stunning success, by far the most brilliant campaign of the whole century. The entire Egyptian army, 25,000 strong, in the heavily defended fort of Tel-el-Kebir, in the middle of smooth desert sands that gave a clear line of fire for their guns (which were the latest thing from Krupps), was routed at the cost of fifty-seven English lives—half of them Highlanders who might not have been so entirely sober as later official inquiries suggested.

Knightsbridge returned with Wolseley having lost no more than his right ear. For two hours he had fought hand to hand with the fiercest troops on the Egyptian side, the Soudanese. His left arm, ever since the Rorke's Drift battle, had been virtually useless, so he ran more than twice the risk of others; yet Death passed him by a score of times on those battlements. He lost nothing but his ear, a finger (but that was on his useless hand, so it hardly counted as a genuine loss), and that bit of his left cheek which was eventually replaced by a livid scar from ear to nostril. For his valour at Tel-el-Kebir he was made a Knight Commander of the Order of Malta and St. George.

To the seven-year-old Neville (now with new guardians) and his juvenile playmates, with whom Knightsbridge now spent most of every Sunday in Kensington Gardens or on the Serpentine, this strange, remote, brooding, mutilated warrior had all the romance of a pirate and highwayman sewn together. Those paternal Sabbaths and his Friday-night antisabbaths—when a bored, strapping lady in corsets, in a house in Meard Street, Soho, bound him to a chair and whipped his buttocks, while another stout Amazon toyed with him, whispered "Ape!" in his ear, and dabbed on the eau-de-cologne—were the only recreations in a life that was now devoted to the army and to the ultimate glory of death.

He saw his parents and his old friends only by accident or in passing, at some public or court function. Then he smiled as pleasantly as any man with a strapped-up arm, a teacup head, and a face meshed with scar tissue may smile. He wrote warm, witty letters to his parents and siblings, but never mentioned or inquired about the estate or anything connected with the dukedom. Each year, he knew, would bring a war; sooner or later he must win—by losing—his own game with Death.

CHAPTER FORTY-ONE

WHEN THEIR SON got his V.C., Alfred and Flora were sure he'd now think his honor was vindicated and so feel able to come home again and take his rightful place as heir. Their hopes were renewed after he gained his K.C.M.G. in the Arabi War. When such hopes were dashed for the second time, his parents understood once and for all that the young man was determined on death as a career and that nothing this side of the grave could stop him. They turned all their attention toward Charles—who squirmed in such limelight.

That he was brilliantly gifted no one could doubt. He fulfilled his own lethargic prophecy and took a double first at Oxford, in history and law, without taxing his brain too much at all; at the same time he plied an oar and hunted the otter and fox with the best, to say nothing of cards and wenching *en passant.* He had neither plan nor intention to apply either—or any—branch of learning in his life.

If that was annoying enough to Alfred, worse was to follow.

The Brighton wing at Chalfont Abbey was now a regular, full-scale organic-chemistry research laboratory. Wolf Frisch and two dozen assistants, many of them graduates of Leipzig and London, worked there daily, perfecting new dyestuffs and other coal-tar derivatives—first artificial fertilizers and, since 1881, explosives. The Ultra Dyestuff Co., now renamed Ultra Chemical Industries, had become one of the largest and richest such companies in Europe, rivaling German giants like Haber and Bayer. Its "Brighton wing" researchers lived in a little academic enclave, a model village, built in a clearing in the woodlands to the southwest of the Abbey; in the symmetry of the park it lay on the side which balanced the grove of Wellingtonias to which Flora was so attached.

One summer vacation young Lord Charles strolled into this village and engaged one of its graduate inhabitants in aimless chit chat which, over several pints up in a real village nearby, ranged over practically the whole of chemistry . . . and women . . . and Life. Next day Charles wandered idly around the Brighton wing asking simple questions, sniffing things, appearing to take in very little—in fact looking more than somewhat bored.

Then there was a week of good weather, during which he could be seen lolling around in swings, or the branches of trees, or drifting on one of the lakes in a bicycle-paddle-boat. A casual observer would not have been able to distinguish him from a hundred thousand other young men of independent means that hot, lazy summer week. But a less-than-casual observer would perhaps have raised an eyebrow at the thickness and weight of the tomes he was reading.

A week later he was again wandering around the Brighton wing; but the questions he now asked were far from simple. By the end of that summer he had suggested a new way—and, chemically speaking, a much more elegant way—of restoring a "poisoned" platinum catalyst to its original purity. In the next year alone it saved the firm several thousand pounds.

Alfred was delighted. "I'm so glad you're taking an interest in chemistry, my boy," he said.

But Charles just gave that broad, winning smile which endeared him to everyone and answered, "I don't think I am, you know, pater. Sorry and all that."

"Does it bore you?" Alfred was crestfallen.

"Oh, no!" Charles answered eagerly, as if his next words would be an avowal of utter fascination.

But there were no next words.

It was the same with his nonintellectual pursuits. Most young men of normal proclivities would look forward to an incandescent hour with an actress, or any willing young woman, with an anticipation close to feverish. And as that hour approached, nothing but the death of a blood relative, or a mortal wound to themselves, would deflect them from the assignation. Not so Charles. He might easily set out for such a rendezvous, meet an Italian organ grinder, realize it was simply ages since he'd used his own knowledge of that country's language, and spend the rest of the evening with the man, in public houses, remedying the oversight.

If anyone taxed him with his utter lack of direction he smiled and said, with that obscurity which clouded half his utterances, "Oh, it's all music, don't you know. It's all *music.*"

One thing did appear to interest him more consistently and for rather longer than usual, though the fact brought no joy to Alfred or Flora. It was the intellectual development of his little niece Georgina, the daughter of his youngest sister, Felicity, and William, Bull's eldest son (or, to be quite precise, the oldest son in Bull's family). They had married in 1878 and their first child, Georgina, had been born ("possessing neither horns nor tail," as Alfred pointed out) later that same year.

Charles's amiable and infinitely tolerant ways had always made him a great favorite with children. His eldest sister, Emily, had married Mervyn Gaspard, Fifth Marquis of Keyhaven, in 1875; Henry, George, and Lucy had followed in '76, '78, and '80. His other sister, Louise, had married even earlier, in 1871, to Michael Lambert, Viscount Mannin and heir to the Thirteenth Earl of Roundstone; their children, Tarquin, Fabia, and Portia, had arrived a little belatedly in '75, '78, and '80.

For all of them, at the appropriate ages, Charles had been a bear for hunting, a tiger for being frightened by, an elephant for shooting tigers from, a dog for feeding biscuits to, a monkey for laughing at, and Uncle Charles for telling stories—bizarre, wayward, exciting stories that attracted as many grown-ups as children.

"You ought to write them down," his sisters scolded him.

"I often think of it," he would say—and it was true.

But little Georgina was the one who really fascinated him. From the time she was a year old, hardly a month went by but Charles was off to Bullen Towers ostensibly to hunt or paint or shoot or dig up old tumuli, but really to monitor the progress of his little niece. Georgina was a self-aiming, self-powered experiment that nothing could stop.

If she wished to sleep, no distraction could wake her. If she did not, neither fatigue nor gin could fell her. If it was time to cry, no comforting would still her. If she wished to be lifted to look out of the west window, the east window would only make her howl and close her eyes. Later, if she had set her heart on a cake, her lips would shut tighter than any clam against chocolates or cookies; but if a cookie was the thing, no cake could be forced past lips and teeth.

Georgina never crawled, for she had determined to walk or nothing. At ten months she could half-totter-half-fall halfway across the nursery. At a year she could walk, and the mild nightmare of her upbringing turned to sheer hell.

No wonder Charles was fascinated, he who was so sparsely endowed with any tenacity of purpose in any department of life could not believe in this day-long, night-long outpouring of relentless self-will long before there was an intellect to direct it. Every wile and trick in the Victorian armory for breaking a baby's spirit was tried; every one of them failed. New nannies would tut-tut to see the child being given her head; within a month they were far more likely to be seen tiptoeing from the nursery, closing the door with infinite care (and with eyes turned heavenward in prayer to all the gods in creation, Christian and pagan alike), and heaving vast sighs of relief at the temporary peace which reigned—because Georgina, not they, wished it so. One might almost say that her peace "rained," for she was the internal climate, a new kind of indoor weather, of one entire wing of Bullen Towers.

It was six more years before Felicity and William repeated the experiment and got a brother to Georgina. They called him Frederick, which means "ruler in peace." Two years after that, in 1883, William succeeded to the title and became the Second Viscount Bullen-Chetwynne.

CHAPTER FORTY-TWO

THE DEATH OF Bull was the only shadow across the 1880s at Chalfont Abbey until the end of the decade. In every other way those years saw the crowning of all Alfred's and Flora's work since they had been plummeted into the dukedom thirty years and more ago.

Bull died, as he had lived, in a hunting seat—not a house, not a saddle, not even a shooting stick. It was a seat that no one could have predicted for him, yet a seat of which those who knew him said, on hearing of it, "Of course! Where else?"

The tale of it began a year earlier, when Bull and Alfred had been looking around the trophy rooms in Herberts Tower. Bull, pointing at the still-empty pride of place, said, "I've failed, old friend. I never filled that hole, and now I never shall."

Alfred, more as a joke than anything, answered. "You've hunted everything on land, air, and water—except the Great White Whale. What further trophy could you want?"

To Bull, who had never read any books but *Debrett* and *Burke*, and who had certainly never heard of *Moby Dick*, the joke had all the force of a revelation. From that day on he was impervious to reason, argument, cajolery, or blackmail; nothing would satisfy him but that he must now spend a fraction of his vast fortune equipping a whaling expedition to capture the trophy of trophies and complete his display at Herberts Tower.

A luxurious ocean-going steam yacht was purchased and adapted as a whale killer, bristling with harpoon guns on every quarter. At first Bull wanted to bring home the entire whale as a trophy; but reason (relatively speaking) prevailed and three guest cabins were converted into a refrigeration locker where the hide and the quartered skull of the head end could be preserved.

The rational arguments against his going were not as strong as they would have been for almost any other man in his mid-eighties. Bull was still as hale as he had been in his forties. He could still outride any member of the hunt. He would still break the ice on his bath rather than forgo his early-morning dip. He could still see a fly where it struck the most purled of rushing waters on the dullest of wet evenings. If he took along a doctor and two nurses, a good cook, a good staff, a good cellar, and all the hunt diaries going back over the last quarter-century—what could go wrong?

It was a glorious September day, with the smell of ripe corn on the late-summer air, when they took a train down to Bristol for the first sea trials of the *Hermione,* as Bull had rechristened the yacht. She lay in a wet dock by the Bonding Yard in Hotwell, where the port of Bristol ends and the estuary of the Avon begins. Even to Hermione, who naturally had the strongest misgivings about the whole venture, her namesake looked reassuringly vast. And when they went below, she was reassuringly luxurious, too, with her marble bathrooms, paneled staterooms, thickly carpeted decks, velvet curtains, and ornate brass lamps on gimbals.

"Let's *all* go on this trip!" Alfred said, voicing a thought that occurred to each of them at the sight of such comforts.

The hiss and thump of her engines was reassuringly powerful as the *Hermione* nosed out into the river and began the six-mile journey down to Avonmouth and the Bristol Channel, where they intended to steam the twenty or so miles to Wales, and back in time for tea. Through the steep-sided narrows of Clifton Gorge, Bull amused himself—and frightened the ladies and the sea gulls—by banging away on the harpoon guns, firing ropeless harpoons at targets he had caused to be painted on the cliffs the previous week. The wrought-iron shafts whanged against the stone and, for the most part, bent double before falling with a further clanging to the narrow, rock-strewn river shore.

"Not bad, what, duke!" he shouted triumphantly. "A little more practice and it's Great White Whales beware!"

"A little more *powder*," Hermione said as she and Flora went below, "and it's Great Land of Wales beware!"

But the Welsh were in no danger, for Bull ceased firing when they reached open water. Instead, they sat out of the sun on the afterdeck and lunched on duck, ices, and champagne. They spent a fabulous afternoon putting the *Hermione* through her paces in the Channel and then headed back for Hotwell. As they steered into dock, Alfred noticed that the blank end wall of the Bonding House had a target painted on it, too.

"Just one last shot!" Bull said as the rest made for the gangway. And with the spirit of a two-year-old filly, he cavorted forward to the bow harpoon.

The roar of it went like runaway thunder around Hotwell, Clifton, and the farther bank of the river. With a ringing clang the harpoon lodged in its target. "Bull!" they cried, for that was his score.

He did not move. The harpoon gun had been furnished with a seat in case the long vigils Bull anticipated up there should tire his legs; he sat in this chair and seemed to contemplate his marksmanship.

"Bull?" Alfred called.

Bull raised his hand and let it fall—a characteristic gesture. They breathed their relief from an anxiety they would not have admitted to. Bull repeated the gesture.

"I'll see if he wants anything," Alfred said.

Flora and Hermione, no more than slightly worried, followed him up to the prow.

Bull was white as a sheet, and trembling.

"M . . . m . . . muh . . . muh . . ." His lips barely moved, his voice barely sounded.

"Are you all right, Bull? Wait, I'll get help."

Alfred was stopped by Bull's forefinger, urgently beckoning. Bull raised his lips. Alfred lowered his ear.

Bull whispered "Hank . . . you . . . for . . . 'mione."

"Say?"

He half-repeated: "Hanks . . . for H'mione."

Alfred knelt then and, taking the older man's head in his hands, stared deep into his eyes. The last flicker of life there was a twinkling, sardonic kindliness. The smile, which lingered, was of peace.

He was an enigma to the end—a man of violence who had never once questioned his purposes and so had lived at perfect peace with himself—a peace that even his own death could not ruffle.

"What did he say?" Hermione asked in a small, forlorn voice. From Alfred's behavior she knew her husband was dead even as she drew near.

"He said, 'Thank Hermione.' That was all he said: 'Thank Hermione.' "

Hermione went to the rail, wept a little, and then was herself again. Bull's final words, as relayed to her, were a great balm to a conscience that, for more than thirty years, had never been absolutely easy.

He was buried in Stokenchurch, at the heart of the country he had made, and made his own. In his honor Alfred renamed the hunt the Bullen, wishing he'd had the imagination to do it years earlier.

The night after the funeral Hermione came to Alfred's and Flora's bedside, weeping.

Flora lifted the sheets, "Come in, dear," she said.

"I'll go," Alfred volunteered; but he moved so slowly that Flora had time to settle Hermione before she reached over and grabbed him by the wrist. "No, stay," she said.

Moments later she added with mock asperity, "Don't tell me it's not what you've always wanted!"

Hermione giggled through a sea of salt and then, hating herself for the levity of it, cried all the louder.

Bull's death apart, those years brought Alfred the fruit of all he had worked for. The Birmingham Metal Box Co. had become a leading maker of screws, threaded bars, bolts, padlocks, locks, hinges, and fastenings of every kind. The railway, now the Maidenhead & Princes Risborough Railway, though it did not live up to its forecast (what railway ever did?), paid a good, steady dividend. The London Distillate Co. now handled almost a quarter of all the coal-tar distillates traded in England. And the estate enterprises—the quarries, the turnery, the ironworks, and so on—were all thriving. Even the rents, going against the general trend, showed an improvement, for the Ground Game Act of 1880 (brought in at last and after bitter rear-guard opposition from Alfred and fellow landowners in the Lords) had removed the most important disadvantages of tenant farmers on land where preservation was fierce; so that the estate rents, for so long depressed by Alfred's insistence on having abundant game to shoot, now rose a little.

In any case, ever since the repeal of the Corn Laws in the 1840s it had been clear that cheap North American grain was going to hurt the English cereals farmer; so Alfred had steadily encouraged his tenants to move out of all cereals except malting barley, for which there would be no good foreign substitute.

In the same way, when he went to the Vienna Exhibition of 1870 and saw Windhausen's patent ice machine turning out 30 cwts of ice an hour at no more than a shilling a hundredweight, he realized that the days of the English sheep farmer were over. It would not be long before an enterprising shipowner fitted out a vessel with some such machine and brought lamb by the thousands of tons from Australia and New Zealand.

But Windhausen's ice machine changed Alfred's life in more ways than the agricultural. Grenville Fitzbois, his son by Danielle, had grown up with all the ambition Lord Charles seemed to lack; and Neville, Knightsbridge's son by Miss Walberswick, was another of the same stamp. As if illegitimacy was a spur or goad, their blood was restless for achievement in a way shown by none of the legitimate brood. At various times Alfred had shown Grenville over most of the ducal properties and enterprises. The lad had been conventionally impressed by the Abbey, but what had really set his eyes glowing was the sight and sound and smell of the London Distillate Co. works at full blast.

Alfred knew exactly how he felt. He remembered when he was a boy of ten and the railway had come to Birmingham. Of course the engine of that day would look no more than an amusing toy now; but what a monster it had seemed then! How terrifying was its belching of fire and smoke—and what power it expressed! And when it had gone clanking by, what strange and heady smells of smoke and hot grease and steam it left on the air! If ever there had been a moment when his soul was diverted toward industry, the inaugural run of the London & Birmingham Railway had provided it. Forty years on, the retorts and stills and reverberatory furnaces at London Distillate kindled an 1870s variant of that same industrial ambition in young Grenville. Alfred could see it.

Back in 1878, at the age of twenty, Grenville had taken a diploma in civil engineering at the University of London. Until he was twenty-two he worked in various capacities first at London Distillate, later at Ultra Chemicals—to the entire satisfaction of his superiors and his ducal father. In his spare time, meager though that was, he experimented, as chance would have it, with various kinds of refrigerating machines, which he built himself.

At first, because the chemicals were to be had for the asking, he used ether (which had been used in ice machines since the 1830s), sulphuric ether, and carbon bisulphide. Then, dissatisfied with these, he tried ammonia, methylic ether, and sulphurous acid, this last of which he had to buy. Alfred, alerted by the foreman, invited himself to the lockup shed his son had hired to see the machines for himself.

A good piece of engineering *looks* right, even to someone who may not know its purpose. To Alfred, whose eye for engineering was as good as any, these machines of Grenville's had all the right qualities—a fitness for their purpose, a harmony of their parts, a wholeness of their design. Half an hour's close questioning convinced him that the young man had a solid future in this field. All he needed was the backing.

Alfred was on the point of offering to put up the necessary capital when a sixth sense told him it would not do. This young man needed to triumph alone. Instead he said, "I've always told you, my boy, that you may rely on me for introductions and patronage, but never for an income. I'll give you an introduction to a merchant-banker friend of mine who, if I know him at all, will leap over his desk to invest in your machine."

And that was where they left the matter. Alfred was astonished, some weeks later, to learn that the arrangement had been turned down, not by the banker but by Grenville.

"But why?" he asked the young man.

"I don't have enough capital of my own, sir."

"But the other fellow would put up a hundred percent."

"And own ninety! I'm not having that."

Alfred grinned. "How big a share *do* you want?"

"More than half, anyway." He was very positive.

"How much can you scratch together?"

Grenville shrugged. "Ten percent? A hundred pounds."

"I'll lend you the rest," Alfred said. "Another four hundred." The young man began to smile. "For a mere ten percent interest," Alfred added.

The smile vanished. "But then I'd still only own forty percent."

"Don't you trust me."

"With my life, sir. But not with my business."

Alfred roared with laughter—and approval. "Dammit!" he said. "You're too bloody good to pass by. Forget the banker. I'll put up *twelve* hundred—for you're bound to have forgotten something—and you can have fifty-one percent. And if I haven't got the whole investment back inside two years, we're neither of us as clever as we think."

Within two months Grenville had produced a full-scale machine. It made ice for exactly the price he had estimated, ten shillings a ton. Within twelve months they knew they had a success; even more important, Alfred knew that his son was a businessman first, an engineer second; and Grenville knew that he had a minority shareholder who was a partner first and a father second.

The Pure Ice Refrigerator Co. Ltd. was the first limited company to which Alfred publicly put his name; steadily throughout the 1880s he came out from behind his nominees and aliases to reveal himself as the major shareholder in all the other ventures, too. It was not only that his social position was now impregnable; Society itself had changed. By the end of the century more than a quarter of the nobility were publicly listed as being directors, chairmen, or board members of every conceivable kind of company. The relative decline in the value and status of land ownership had accelerated a process that would, in any case, have been inevitable. From medieval charities to limited-liability companies, the nobility had always possessed an eye for a good thing.

Alfred now took every chance he had—in the Lords, at public dinners, and in private conversations—to promote his deeply held belief that aristocratic participation in industry would lead to a blurring of the terrible divisions that had sprung up between worker and master. Firm but kindly patronage would replace grinding exploitation. The laborer's money wage might not rise—indeed, it might even fall to nothing in the ideal future—but the amenities around him, the housing, the education, the cradle-to-grave protection from want and starvation, the parks, the libraries, the concert halls, the gymnasia—these would all so vastly improve the quality of his life that he would hardly miss the jingle of coins in his pocket. Alfred was sure that his model villages, together with places like Saltaire, Port Sunlight, some of the Quaker employers' housing estates, and—in Europe—the Krupps' township, were the vanguard of the future.

The queen took a great interest in Alfred's theories and was sure he would prove a surer prophet than those dreadful socialists, who seemed to think they were the finest invention since clairvoyancy.

"I'm not against class distinctions, Alfred," she told him. "In all societies, and even among savages, there have been different classes. But I am bitterly opposed to class antagonism and class hatred. Yet who can blame the laboring classes when they see the arrogance and frivolity of the upper class today!"

That was a dig at Bertie, of course. Alfred let it pass. "The aristocracy should not have stood aside, you see," he answered. "We shouldn't have left the business of this century to the money-grubbing middle classes. They have no vision, most of them. Can't see further than the daily balance sheet. The extraordinary thing is that those of us who treat our workmen like human beings actually make better profits than all the Josiah Bounderbies in the realm.

"Albert would have agreed so!" she sighed. "How like is your mind to his, dear Alfred!"

She reached for his hand and his comfort, as she always did when she mentioned the Prince Consort to him. He sat beside her and stroked her arm.

There was silence. She leaned her head on his shoulder. "I still miss him so," she said.

"Of course you do, my dear."

He straightened his leg. The ligaments of his knee joint cracked like dry twigs. "Oh—age!" he said.

"We'll see out the century," she challenged.

"Think so?"

"It's a Royal Command!"

"Ah, that's good." He chuckled. "Queen Canute!"

CHAPTER FORTY-THREE

STEAM, AS ONE of the more thinking railway pioneers pointed out, is a great leveler. So is rheumatism. Both influences were hard at work in the hottest room of the Turkish bath at Marienbad, where Alfred found himself beside a genial, bearded patriarch of a man. Through the mists their eyes met. There was a twinkle of fellowship, the mild rapport of mild suffering, voluntarily undergone.

"These Dutch doctors," the patriarch said with a rueful shake of his head. He was an American. "The same the world over, I guess. Two weeks behind their rich patients, three ahead of their poor."

Alfred laughed. "That's the size of it, sir. I was cured ten days ago, I'm sure."

They introduced themselves. The man was Ebenezer Graham of the Columbia Stock Yards, Chicago. His brother, John Graham, owned the Union Stock Yards; they were both in a big way of business. Alfred and he spoke of beef and then of corn, not being aware that to one of them the word meant yellow nuggets the size of peas while to the other it was a kind of bloated grass seed like wheat and barley. Then, without confusion, they passed on to what Alfred called "tins" and Eb Graham "cans." The American thought it odd that the duke knew so much about the working and tinning of sheet steel—more, he thought, than any English duke had a right to know—but Europe was full of surprises. Then the showers and masseurs separated them before either could develop the theme.

It was the sort of intense encounter that permits the exchange of deep secrets amid the steam but of no more than a distant nod at any later meeting. And that was all they exchanged when they and their wives found themselves at adjacent tables for tea. Again a genial twinkle in Graham's eye held open the promise of a further conversation. In fact, Alfred heartily wanted such a conversation. An engineer at Birmingham Metal Box had devised a new process for making tins without a seam in their sides; the opinion of an American canner on such a product would be invaluable. But how? An English duke in one of the most fashionable watering places in Europe could hardly risk such a conversation where it might be overheard. To own industrial shares was one thing; to understand an industrial process was quite different.

"Who?" Flora asked, looking nonchalantly from the American and his wife to Alfred.

He told her.

"And the very handsome young gel they have in tow? Their daughter, I suppose."

"I imagine so."

At the end of the tea hour the two parties happened to leave together, by two separate parabolic paths that brought them to a mingling point in the foyer.

"After six weeks on quail and crayfish," Graham said beneath his breath to Alfred, "a fellow gets to kind of hanker after a plate of cold crow."

His wife, who overheard, whispered something vehement, of which the only word Alfred caught was "barbarism."

Alfred decided then and there that, seamless tins or no, Mr. Eb Graham's turn of phrase would vastly relieve the tedium of this place. "I generally take a stroll at this hour, Mr. Graham," he said, vowing to himself that henceforth he would. "I'd be honored to have your company."

"Barbarism," Graham explained mischievously, just loud enough for his wife's ear to catch as he and the duke walked off, "is a Chicago word for the honest way we speak in my home state of Missouri."

"Your first visit to Europe, Mr. Graham?"

"First with Mrs. Graham and Helen, er . . . duke? I call you 'duke'?"

Alfred nodded. "Your daughter?"

"Our last, or the last still to be placed."

"She's very beautiful," Alfred said, then, remembering how fundamentalist many Americans were, he added diplomatically, "though beauty is only skin deep."

Graham chuckled. "Why, that's right where any reasonable man'd want to find it. You yourself, duke, if I may say so—you're the first live duke I ever met, and you're off the top of the sirloin."

"Meaning?"

"Meaning you don't signal the orchestra to start on the stately marches every time you say something."

"It's good of you to say so."

"Are you in any line of business, duke?"

"Family business," Alfred said lightly and, looking carefully around, drew conspiratorially close to Graham. "Might you be interested in a tin formed without a seam? A seamless can, as you would say?"

"Could be," Graham said, instantly adopting his best poker-playing voice.

That evening after dinner the three Grahams called by invitation on the duke and duchess and they played gin rummy for pennies. Both families had intended going to a recital, but Alfred's report of his conversation to Flora had led her to issue the invitation instead—just as Eb Graham's corresponding report to his wife had redoubled her delight in accepting.

Graham said he was glad to be missing the recital. "Never did think much of this Society bug," he said, ignoring his wife's signals of alarm. "I meet enough stray fools by day to want to sit up nights by the watering hole and catch the main herd."

"You're very censorious, Mr. Graham," Flora challenged. "You must *have* a Society in America, surely?"

"We sure do, duchess," Graham agreed. "Why, there's men I know whose fathers got rich selling bad whiskey to Indians who now have such fine, discriminating noses they can sniff pork the instant they hear my voice in the next room."

"Father!" Helen scolded.

Mrs. Graham's face put a dozen miles between her and her husband.

"Gin," he said, and laid down his cards.

For a while he and Alfred stood on the balcony and discussed the problems of town planning; the women looked at Flora's album of photographs, marveled at Chalfont Abbey, and thrilled at the sight of so many lords and ladies—not to mention The Queen and other "royalties"—all caught between one set of covers. Flora had a little detail or story about each of them. "That's the late Lord Rolle," she said, "who fell when he was presented, and *rolled* down the steps! . . . That's Lady Jeune. She used to eat donkey meat but gave it up because she said it made her stink."

Mrs. Graham could not suppress a gasp, but Helen, as Flora was quick to notice, betrayed her surprise by the merest fleeting change in her expression.

Later the girl sang to her own accompaniment on the piano; she also played some Chopin nocturnes, "almost *too* well," as Flora afterwards said to Alfred.

When the Americans had gone, Flora wondered how rich they really were.

"Nobody poor can stay here," Alfred said. "Or dress in such style."

"Yes, but is it all on their backs? Or all in . . . what did he call it—futures? What are futures?"

" 'Men selling commodities they don't yet possess to other men who buy with money they haven't yet earned!' He has a splendid turn of phrase, you must admit."

"I'm more interested in his other possessions. And in that daughter, Helen."

Alfred looked at her in amazement. "Jove, you're serious!"

"Never more so, my dear. I think she may do admirably for Charles—even if they have no real money to speak of. Though of course"—she spoke as much to herself as to him—"it would be very much better if they could throw in a thumping dowry."

When she saw his incredulous frown she explained, "I know it seems most unlikely that Knightsbridge will ever marry, but if he does, Charles will need an income separate from the estate. It would be providential if this young girl could supply it. That's all. Anyway, here's your chance to put into practice all the fine things you've been telling Lord Salisbury about the importance of an Anglo-American connection. American heiresses were made by God for English second sons."

"I hadn't thought of her as a Lady Charles Boyce. You really think so?"

"Yes, if they prove to be—what did you say he called it?—'off the top of the sirloin.' Can you find that out from here?"

Next morning a cable went to Alfred's stockbroker in the City instructing him to gather what financial and social information he could on the Columbia Stock Yards, Chicago, and its founder-owner, Ebenezer Graham. The young telegraph clerk smiled like an angler sensing a nibble; ten minutes earlier he had tapped out an almost identical message to the London office of the Columbia Stock Yards; in both cables the only substantive change was a direct switch of subject and signatory.

In slack moments through the morning the same young clerk sent out messages on his own account to news editors in Chicago, London, Paris, Vienna, Berlin, and Rome. There was a further spate of telegrams to those same news editors when, the replies to the original queries having been satisfactory, the Grahams left Marienbad in the duke's party and traveled to England in Alfred's private railway car.

In London they separated for a week while Alfred caught up on political and estate business and Graham, who had traveled over from America with three hundred steers, looked into the profitability of on-the-hoof exports.

On the appointed day for their visit to Chalfont Abbey, the Grahams were a little surprised to be greeted on the very apron of Paddington Station by a man claiming to be a high official of the Great Western Railway, who offered to escort them to the duke's carriage at platform three.

He was most affable . . . escorted all His Grace's guests . . . and was it to be a large house party? . . . and had they known his grace long? . . . Oh, Marienbad! And who else had been there? . . .

At this point Helen had a brief word with one of the station officials. Then she fairly ran to her mother's side, just as her mother was about to launch into a coyly smiling confirmation of the man's surmise that Lord Charles would be of the party. With her umbrella

Helen did a most unladylike thing to the kindly questioner, but it was done so swiftly that even her mother went blithely on with the answer, not noticing that her interlocutor, bent almost double, was ten yards behind and being assisted by two laughing porters. They, like her father, were among the few who had seen what happened.

"That was quick thinking, Helen," said her father. "I'd just formed the same opinion."

"What . . . what?" her mother asked vaguely.

"That was a reporter, ma," Graham told her.

"Oh." She was at first disappointed that they had not been honored with an official GWR escort. But then she was delighted. "Oh—a *reporter!*"

"Well, don't take it like that, ma," Helen warned. "The duke and duchess will be very hot when they hear it."

"Then they mustn't hear it."

"Of course they must. It'll be in the papers now, anyway. And they'll know that none of their own people would give the time of day to a reporter. Unless we tell them exactly what happened, they'll think we called that fellow in and told him everything."

"The girl's right, ma," her father confirmed.

"Fortunately," Helen said, "he was American, so it may be a week or more before anything gets into the English papers."

"How d'you know he was American?" her father asked.

"Yes, dear," her mother chimed in. "He sounded English to me."

"He sounded English, but he said 'baggage' instead of 'luggage,' he said 'visit with' instead of 'visit,' and when I said we'd be staying a *fortnight,* he looked blank for a moment."

"My!" Her father's admiration was undisguised. "The House of Graham may be about to lose its greatest asset. When did you learn to be so smart? We could use you."

Helen laughed, not altogether kindly. "What's your word on that, pa? 'Never hire a woman—hire her husband and get both of them working for you.' "

"I hope," he answered, a little miffed at her independent tone, "that the House of St. Ormer knows what a thirty-karat asset it's angling for."

"Pa!" his wife scolded.

"Well, let's be clear on it," he told both of them. "That's what this visit's all about . . . this"—he grinned at Helen and spoke in a plummy accent—"this *fortnight!*"

CHAPTER FORTY-FOUR

LORD CHARLES BOYCE did not at all impress young Helen. "He is," she wrote to one of her friends that first evening, "six feet two of handsome, charming, inaccessible inanity. He is what the Newport and Manhattan dandy would so dearly love to be and never can, because along with *his* million dollars came the middle-class American get-up-and-go that built such a fortune. Lord C. has *none* of that!"

She tried to imagine a life with this pleasant, utterly unambitious man, and felt . . . nothing . . . neither dread nor pleasure. The prospect was a blank. *Still,* she thought, *it's only the first day.*

He showed her over the house. He certainly knew a lot about it; he could almost have been a historian—or a gossip, for he knew the history of his tribe at that level, too. When he showed her a piece of furniture, he pointed out all its esthetic and stylistic qualities and then, with exactly the same degree of interest (or detachment, rather) he'd turn it upside down, or pull out a drawer, and show how it was made. With the paintings too, he was equally well informed about composition, sentiment, technique—and equally remote from them all. It was as if knowledge was a way of avoiding attachment.

Helen, who was materialist enough to believe that you got to know a person by knowing the things around him and the things that interested him, was baffled. *Still,* she thought, *it's only the third day.*

Her bewilderment increased when he showed her over the laboratory in the Brighton wing. He was as much master of the work being done there as he had been among the furniture, the marbles, and the paintings.

And to walk through the grounds with him was an introductory course in horticulture and landscape gardening. Yet he was so affable and charming about it that their stroll felt more beguiling than instructive.

"You *are* getting on well," her mother said, greatly pleased.

And Helen had to allow it was so—though she felt no closer to Lord Charles than she had at their introduction.

Still, she thought, *it's early days yet.*

That evening after tea Flora suggested a game of hide-and-go-seek. The butler rounded up all the guests in the house—a meager thirty—and the hiders went off in pairs.

Charles and Helen chose the duke's Garter wardrobe because, he said, his parents (the seekers) would never imagine that anyone could have the effrontery to hide there.

Safe in the camphor-laden dark he chuckled.

"What?" she asked.

"Here's a thing that'll baffle historians yet unborn. We are watched and chaperoned at every turn, and yet, when it comes to hide-and-go-seek, in country houses all over England we go off in our pairs for hours at a time. It'll make them wonder, surely."

"Wonder what?"

In the dark he smiled. She knew what he was talking about, of course. Most girls would pretend utter ignorance, fearful ignorance. "Will it?" they would have said. But not Helen: "Wonder what?" It was more of a prompt than a question.

"Wonder if we didn't . . ."

He stroked her hand, then her arm. He put his own arms round her, scarcely touching, and gave her the quickest and lightest of kisses.

"Or this."

A firmer kiss.

"Or this."

A lingering kiss.

She found it pleasant. Indeed, very pleasant. She responded.

He began to tremble; her heart fluttered; she sagged into his embrace. He held her effortlessly. For a long time they exhausted a variety of kisses.

"Or this."

He put a hand around her breast. She stopped sagging at once.

"You're not supposed to do that."

"I know."

There was silence. She wished she could see his face. The dark and the silence were oppressive, whereas what he had done had been . . . not oppressive.

"Do it again," she said.

Now that she knew she could stop him, it was all right.

Again his hand closed and caressed gently where no man's hand had ever caressed before. It was stupendous. But part of the glory, she had to admit, was to realize that she had at last found something which stirred this languid, lackaday young lord. Suddenly it became important to her to test how deep the stirring went—more important even than prolonging these delicious sensations.

Forcing herself to speak with a flat, calm tone, she asked, "What're you going to do in life?"

His caress went limp. "Ah," he drawled.

His hand fell absently. "The next few years anyway I'll be in the diplomatic service. I've just passed the exam. We're all very democratic about it nowadays, except that I'll get Paris, Berlin, Vienna, and St. Petersburg while Hodge the Hedgetrimmer will be stuck in Paraguay or Washington."

She laughed; only she knew how near she was to hysterics.

"I think it's pretty amusing too," he said. "But then the thought of me doing *anything* in life is absurd."

"Ah, Charles," she sighed. "Dear Charles! You really are a most extraordinary fellow."

"A lot of people say that, so I suppose there's some truth in it. But I've tried to think about it objectively and I honestly can't see it."

He spoke as he might have spoken about his inability to see the constellations of the southern hemisphere.

They were deep in conversation about the diplomatic service when Alfred and Flora jerked open the closet doors. Charles didn't even break the flow of his sentence as he and Helen stepped owlishly into the candlelight.

"D'you think he's normal?" Alfred asked Flora and Hermione that night.

"Or," Hermione teased, tickling his ear, "did you reserve it all to yourself!"

Alfred need not have worried. From the moment they emerged out of the closet Helen knew she would marry Lord Charles. Love hardly came into it, though she did not doubt that a kind of love would develop between them. Extraordinary she had called him, and extraordinary he was—far too extraordinary to walk away from and leave for someone else to discover.

The following afternoon, when they were walking about the terrace, he asked, "Do you *like* music?" He knew, of course, that she played and sang at a professional standard; but that wasn't, to him, the same as liking it.

Had he been any other young man, she would have given the conventional answer—even to Charles himself only a few days earlier. But now they were beyond that sort of convention. She looked at him, a shade disappointed. "Do *you* like climate?" she asked in return.

He saw what parallel she was drawing and nodded approvingly: No more conventional conversations. For twenty minutes they talked about music; she, to her chagrin, discovered that he, who had made no study of it at all, knew as much about it as she, whose life study it had been.

She sighed. "I'm just going to have to discover something I'm better at than you."

"That's a very American sentiment," he told her. "You'll find it'll wear off in time."

They paused at the balustrade and looked down over the lakes and shrubberies.

"Hah!" she gave a cry of sudden discovery. "I've been wondering what's wrong! Do you realize there's not a single flower in all your gardens? It's all shrubs—shrubs and roses."

"Flowers are bourgeois," he said. "Masters at Eton grow them."

She laughed.

He looked behind them at the great blank windows of the southern wing, pale with reflected sky. "The upper classes have blooms of their own to cherish," he added. "We leave the laurel and the privet to our gardeners while we cultivate our four native flowers—pomp, vanity, license, and scandal."

Laughing, she took his arm and hugged it, wondering if the warmth she felt for him—a tender, protective warmth—was, indeed, love. For a moment she had an intuition of him, prompted by a bleak undertone to his humor: She saw him not as a languid, aloof, dilettante sort of person but as a man lost in the very richness of his own knowledge and of all the possibilities it and his wealth and his breeding laid at his feet in tribute.

It hardly mattered, the certainty of it. Far more important was the certainty that from now on life was going to be a lot more interesting than she had dared even to dream.

Watching from behind those daylight-shrouded windows Alfred said, "Well, if there were a barometer for love, I think it would stand at Set Fair."

Graham nodded contentedly.

"To me it's the eighth wonder of the world," Alfred said. "What does she see in him that we've all missed?"

The other looked puzzled but ventured no opinion.

"There are three things," Alfred went on, "generally held to be the pinnacle of uselessness. One is a step ladder on a racing yacht. The second is a naval officer on a racing yacht."

"And the third?"

"I can't decide between a naval officer *on* a step ladder on a racing yacht . . . and Lord Charles."

Graham laughed. "How long have you been burying him, duke?" he asked. "All his life?"

"We've come close to it a dozen times."

"Well, there's nothing stops a funeral faster than a corpse who sits up and takes nourishment."

"Thank heaven the women take a sentimental view."

"There's one who doesn't," Graham said. He fished out a dollar and showed Alfred the image of Columbia. "She's the one we ought to be talking about."

"Then let's talk." Alfred sat in the window seat. "Bring some cordial," he told the footman.

Graham sat facing him. "Whenever we sit down to discuss Lord Charles, duke, you talk about his Tribe. I ask how sweet the ham is and you give me the pedigree of the hog farmer. Now I believe in blood-will-tell as much as any man. But I also believe the only things you'll find in a pie are what you yourself put into the making of it. A man's only as good as he makes himself, or about half as good as his father thinks he made him. So when this young man's father tells me he's the world's third most useless object, naturally I—"

"Hold on," Alfred interrupted. "Are you talking about how *good* Lord Charles is, or how useful?"

Deep furrows rutted the American's forehead. He gave a dry laugh. "I'll be darned, duke. I never thought there was much of a difference."

"Well there's all the difference in the world. The Old World, anyway. Are you asking if he'll make her happy?"

"No, sir, I'm not. That's one item I'll never accept a note on—happiness. When it comes to payment, the note won't be met. I'm asking will he treat her right?"

"Which is like asking a horse dealer, 'Will this horse ever die?' " Alfred smiled.

Graham was not satisfied. "A woman here gets dealt a hand she'd refuse to play in America. A woman's pride here, it seems to me, has as much chance of survival as an egg-sucking hen in the fricassee season."

"Ah, that was true twenty years ago, under the queen. Things happened then that no well-bred woman was supposed to recognize. So they pretended not to. They bit their lips, swallowed their pride, and made sure they saw nothing. The rule in polite society was, 'Hear, see, and speak no evil,' like the three apes. But for the past twenty years, Society has been ruled not by the queen but by H.R.H. And he's changed all that. No woman suffers in silence *today.* Well—middle-class women still do, of course. But not women of our class."

Graham was sadly amused. "I'm not concerned, duke, with suffering in silence or suffering out loud. I'm concerned with suffering at all."

Alfred found it hard to grasp. "I see," he said slowly. "Well, form is at least as important as substance in English society. As long as young Helen understands that, she need not suffer at all." He smiled his relief. "I'm glad we've cleared that up. I must say, I admire your American ways; plain speaking, eh!"

Graham shrugged. *Plain speaking!* he thought.

"Mind you," Alfred said, afraid the American might misunderstand, "there's public and public. Complaints mustn't go farther than one's own circle. Helen should study the fate of Lady Henry Somerset, who was quietly intending to live apart from her husband, until her mother, Countess Somers—a ridiculous, squawking Frenchwoman—boiled it up into a court case. That was ten years ago, but if Lady Henry lives another century, she'll never be received in any good house in England."

"She was the innocent party?"

"Innocent in the matrimonial sense, but guilty in every other! Guilty of revealing to the lower orders things that ought never to be revealed."

"Well!" Graham shook his head and chuckled. "It's a sure-fire cure for boredom, duke, I'll say that much. But let's get back to Helen and Lord Charles." He drew breath. "We old fellers, duke, when it's time to close up the shop, we like to know that someone with the same name is going to take down the shutters next morning. Am I right?"

"Meaning?" Alfred was wary.

"Meaning, I know about Lord Knightsbridge—him not marrying and so on. I know what store you set by Lord Charles's marriage and children. So the first thing I want to assure you is that on both Mrs. Graham's side and my own the proportion of males to females, born and reared, is mighty pleasing."

"Ah, yes," Alfred said. "So I understand." (In fact, he could have told Graham the exact proportion to two decimal places.)

"Where will they live?"

"For the next ten or twelve years I imagine they'll take houses wherever he's accredited. Berlin first, I'm afraid. But then Vienna, Paris, and Petersburg—though not necessarily in that order."

"You can be that sure, eh?"

"Otherwise there'd be little point in being a duke, would there."

"And then they'll come back . . . where? Here to Chalfont Abbey?"

"Part of the year. For the shooting. Will you buy them a place? Is that the way you'd like to lay out a dowry?"

Graham smiled shrewdly. "If I do, it'll be settled on her and entailed on the children."

"With a remainder to Lord Charles?"

"Well . . ." Graham was not demurring, he had just not considered the point.

"Never mind," Alfred said. "There's such a thing as having too much damned property, especially country houses. I'll give them a place. Rosevean, down in Cornwall, an old Elizabethan manor we rebuilt. And a lease on a house in Belgrave Square. It'd be best if you stick to a dowry in cash. How much were you thinking of?"

"Eighty thousand?"

"Guineas?"

"Dollars!"

"But that's only twenty thousand pounds!" Alfred said. "That'll last them only a few years. I thought you were a millionaire."

Graham chuckled. "The poorest folks on earth are a millionaire's kinsmen—or ought to be. Duke, you'll have to forgive me. I grew up in a world where a ten-cent shave and a five-cent shine could land a thousand-dollar order. And I'm still old-fashioned enough to see a certain rightness in the arrangement."

"I've no doubt," Alfred answered. "But, if I may borrow your idiom, this is no fire sale we're at."

Graham laughed.

"Helen will take to the ways of the English aristocracy," Alfred said. "I've been watching her. She's quick to notice things. Quick to learn. She may make mistakes, but never twice."

"I'm ashamed to say it, sir, but I've only just remarked the same thing myself. I haven't seen too much of her until this Europe trip. But I've seen enough now to be sure that if I backed her with a million, she'd still be worth more."

"Ah! A million! Now *that's* more like it."

Graham shook his head admiringly but flatly refused to consider such a sum.

"Your daughter will be a duchess," Alfred reminded him. "Your grandson an English duke."

"I'm not in the market for pride, sir," Graham answered. "I had a heap of it once, along with a twelve-grain dose of cant. But my ma had a trunk strap, and she never heard of gently reasoning a child out of the error of its ways. So I'm not too taken on whether Helen's an English duchess or an American missus, just so long as she's well fixed up and content."

"Talk it over with Mrs. Graham," Alfred advised, knowing well which Graham was keener on the aristocratic connection.

The sparring went on for days. Graham swore he'd be left with "a fortune that would foot up to a million in the newspapers and still leave his heirs in debt to the lawyers who wound up his estate"; but in the end he agreed to an eight-hundred-thousand-dollar dowry, half of it in Columbia Stock Yards stock.

The announcement of Helen's engagement to Lord Charles was in the *Times* the very day that copies of the *Chicago Inquirer* were landed at Liverpool, full of accurate details about both families, their meeting at Marienbad, and the Grahams' invitation to Chalfont Abbey, where, all being well, their daughter's engagement to Lord Charles would be announced. Chicago readers were even told that the Duke's heir, Lord Knightsbridge, was a confirmed bachelor and that Lord Charles's heir would most likely inherit the St. Ormer title.

Alfred's anger was tinged with admiration. "How did they discover so much?" he asked. He knew what the Grahams had told him of their encounter at Paddington, but that would have provided only a small part of this story; where had the *Inquirer* got the rest? "Why, some of these facts I didn't know myself until a few weeks ago," he said.

"Same here, duke," Graham agreed. Then he looked up shrewdly. "Marienbad?"

Alfred nodded.

"Sent a cable?"

Another nod.

Graham's index finger jabbed the air. "That cable clerk! Why, I'll stake what little Columbia stock I still own that he's in the pay of half the newspapers in Europe and America!"

Alfred accepted the explanation and stored the fact away.

CHAPTER FORTY-FIVE

JUST AFTER CHRISTMAS, Lord Charles and Helen were married at St. George's, Hanover Square. They had a brief honeymoon—no more than six weeks—at their new house, the restored Rosevean, down in Cornwall.

For most of their engagement Helen remained at Chalfont Abbey, and so did her mother. During that time great changes were begun or planned. Helen herself had nothing to do with those changes—in the sense that she uttered no word of criticism nor even cast a pained glance at existing arrangements. With great forebearance she managed to still her tongue before it curled around one syllable of the phrase which rose to her throat a dozen times a day: "Now in *America* we . . ."

Yet Helen had everything to do with those changes, in the sense that if she had not been there and if the others had not been aware that she was, in effect, the future duchess, they would not have looked about themselves so critically and found so much that was wanting. In fact they realized how many improvements had been put off during those years of pennypinching and debt.

"Dear me!" Flora said, sweeping her gaze around one of the drawing rooms as she and Helen happened to be passing through. "Some of this furniture is positively immoral. No woman can live among Aubusson carpets and Louis Quinze writing tables and remain virtuous. Virtue goes with walnut davenports and flower-painted purdoniums. I should have done something about this long ago."

So the Aubusson carpets were rolled up with mothballs in oilcloth and stuck among the rafters in the coach house. The Louis Quinze—and a lot of other elegant French furniture—was relegated to rooms that were used only a few times a year. The Chippendale chairs and tables were given several good coats of paint and sent up to the servants' quarters, where the Hepplewhite and Sheraton soon joined them.

In their place came Persian carpets from Axminster and furniture carved from elephantine blocks of teak and mahogany.

Alfred joined the fun by taking out all the elegantly thin ("spindly," as he called them) Georgian windows and replacing them with solid, light-denying frames of teak, filled with polished plate glass. The Georgian frames, being of oak, were too good merely to smash. They were stacked away in a disused tithe barn until someone could get around to adapting them as cold frames for the garden.

The garden had always been more Hermione's province than Flora's. She had no time to think of cold frames because she was busy commissioning ninety thousand square feet—or more than two acres—of hothouse. Part of it took the form of a winter garden and palm court running around the southern and westernmost faces of the foot of Herberts Tower. The rest filled almost a quarter of the walled garden. From a place without flowers at any time of the year, Chalfont Abbey was, from next season, to be transformed into one festooned in blossom through all twelve months.

Helen watched these changes in admiration tinged with bewilderment. Why did it not occur to anyone that what Chalfont Abbey needed more than anything was *one* good water closet? Even her mother could only just remember the old "earth" closet, as the English called it. Yet here all the upper classes used them—even the queen when she visited Chalfont Abbey. At least Windsor Castle had a few proper water closets, though they emptied into the rainwater gutters and often left offensive piles wreathed in houseflies and bluebottles on the lower roof leads. Neither Windsor Castle nor Chalfont Abbey had a single plumbed-in bath. Every day the duke, his family, and their guests stepped into devices that, to Helen, seemed like a ridiculous cross between giant wine coolers and soup tureens.

Water closets and plumbed baths with charcoal geysers were the first alterations she insisted on at Rosevean. Privately Flora and Hermione tut-tutted at these innovations, which struck them as wretchedly middle class—as if one could not afford the servants to empty the earth closets and to bring water in jugs "the proper way."

In the week that Lord Charles and Helen moved into Rosevean, the effects of the late Reverend Mortimer Boyle were moved out of the vicarage at Woodcote by his son, Ralph, and Nancy, Ralph's wife.

"I don't believe he's thrown away a single butcher's bill or note from a sick chorister in fifty years," Nancy said as she looked with dismay at the mountains of paper that filled his study.

Already, in carefully picking apart the stacks of books that dotted the floor and tables, they had come across lost tobacco pipes, two pairs of spectacles, cups stained with what had once been tea, and two tankards of sour, flat, refermented ale.

"Let's have one big bonfire," she suggested.

"No!" Ralph protested. "There may be things of value in here. Bring it all. I'll go through it methodically over the next few years and get it in some sort of order."

"Order!" Nancy laughed despairingly. "You can't even keep your own papers in order. You're every bit as bad as he was."

"Nevertheless, bring it all," he commanded. "Nothing's to be burned until I've seen it."

He began to sweep up fistsfuls of paper and stuff them into drawers. By chance, the bottom-most papers of the first pile he seized were the documents tracing the family's descent from Orlando Boyce, the great-great-great-uncle of the present Duke of St. Ormer. By chance, he put them into a drawer that had remained empty since a maid relined it many years ago. By chance, the newspaper with which she had relined it was the very copy of the *News of the World* which she had shown to her master and which he had returned, saying it was "of no significance."

Ralph and Nancy thus carried back to their home in Poole, Dorset, the paper ingredients of an almighty social explosion.

"Oh, it's so . . . so . . . *permanent!*" Helen said, looking up at the old granite walls of Rosevean, glistening wet against the leaden Cornish sky. "I'm glad your father restored this place instead of letting it go."

"The Boyces, and the Du Bois before them, never let *anything* go," Charles said. "Look how my father has stored those Georgian windows. If our fifteenth-century ancestors ever put up notices announcing 'archery practice this afternoon,' I'll bet they're preserved somewhere in the muniment room."

Dressed in fishermen's oilskins, they were strolling in the steady rain about the restored gardens, relishing their isolation in the landscape. Raindrops falling from pergolas of winter roses sparkled on Helen's nose and cheeks, giving Charles a pretext for kissing them away.

"Talking of the muniment room," she said, "I think I've discovered how Clarence, who was only the Third Marquis of Knightsbridge, managed to elevate himself to duke."

"Oh?" Charles was interested. Helen had spent weeks in the muniment room and had at last managed to prove the family's ancient (but until now legendary) claim to descent from William the Conqueror—or at least from Adelaide, his sister. Her work was now being verified by the College of Heralds.

"Yes. There's nothing definite there but, reading between the lines, I get the strongest feeling that Charles I—and therefore, I presume, a lot of other people—was just plain scared of him!"

"Scared!" Charles laughed.

"Oh, yes indeedy! You know that the Jane Wrottesley he married was in fact a commoner?"

"I didn't know that. She's always been called Lady Jane in the family."

"And by everyone else, even in her day. Clarence simply bullied the king into granting her the courtesy style of a countess, because he couldn't bear the notion of marrying a commoner. And though all the world knew she was just plain Miss Jane, they called her 'countess' too. I'll bet anything he bullied the king into granting the dukedom."

"Are you sure of this?"

"It's pretty clear to me. Why? Is it so incredible?"

"For those days, yes." He shook his head with the remnants of disbelief. "So Charles I was frightened of old Clarence, eh?"

Helen smiled shrewdly. "Just as Queen Victoria is frightened of the present duke," she said.

Charles's incredulity returned.

"It's true," she asserted. "I've watched them."

"She respects his opinion, and I'm sure gives it great weight. But no one frightens this queen."

"This duke does, I tell you. Perhaps he isn't fully aware of it, but he has some kind of power over her."

"I must watch them more closely next time."

"I *hope* he has, anyway!" She laughed. "I don't think she likes *me*."

"She takes time to get used to people. She'll like you well enough in a few years."

"A lot of people are frightened of your father. I bet he'll bully the editor of *Debrett* into printing your Norman ancestry, even if the College of Heralds disallows it."

Their aimless stroll had brought them back to the pool-mottled granite flagstones of the terrace. Up there the distant thunder of the sea was no longer muted by hedges of fuchsia and escallonia. The sharpness of the roar, and the vast reaches of cold, storm-swept ocean it conjured up, made them glad to hurry indoors by the French windows, drop their oilskins on the carpet, and hasten to the great log fire that crackled merrily in a hearth whose inglenooks could have housed two families.

Muffins and China tea were served.

Helen looked around the vast drawing room as if something, and she couldn't quite say what, were missing.

"Anything the matter?" he asked.

"I know!" she said at last. "It's not elegant!"

"Elegant? What isn't?"

"Nothing is. Not Windsor Castle, not Chalfont Abbey, not Knightsbridge House—nor any of the grand London houses we've been to. I expected everything to be more elegant."

"I think that must be an American misapprehension. Say 'elegant' to us and we think at once of our atrocious Regency grandparents. They *lived* for elegance, barbarous, profligate potentates that they were. I suppose that's why we'd rather burn our homes to the ground than be accused of displaying anything like elegance. But it'll all come back. It always does. Things go round and round. It's all music."

"What d'you mean when you say 'it's all music' like that?"

He grinned and shrugged.

Because Charles was so easygoing, Helen dared to show him the results of some other researches she had done. "It was when I was copying out the dates of people's birthdays," she said, "from your mother's book. I wrote them American style, the month *before* the date—which I find easier."

"Because it's so logical!"

"Don't sneer. If I hadn't translated each date from European to American style, I'd never have noticed it."

"Noticed what?"

"See if you spot it—remember, we put the month first." She handed him a list. "I've put them in chronological order, so it should be easier for you than it was for me."

He studied the list:

6/4/51	Emily
12/14/51	William Bullen-Chetwynne
5/18/53	Louise
2/9/54	John B.-C.
11/9/54	Knightsbridge
8/21/55	Frances Fitzbois
2/29/56	Charles
11/6/56	George B.-C.
1/14/57	Felicity
1/18/58	James B.-C.
10/18/58	Grenville F.

"Well?" He was mystified.

"Look at the intervals between them."

He groaned at the chore. "Half a year . . . couple of years . . . best part of a year . . . best part of a year . . ."

"No! Do it in months."

"Hang on." He groaned louder and fished out a propelling pencil. A couple of minutes' figuring produced the sequence: 6, 18, 9, 9, 9, 6, 9, 2, 12, 9.

"They're all multiples of three except one." He laughed. "I say! Clever you! What a coincidence!"

She sighed. "You still don't see it. Perhaps I saw it only because the week before we came over to Europe, Blanche—she's my eldest sister—pointed out to me that our uncle, who has a mistress in Winnetka nobody's supposed to know about, has three children by her. And their birth dates are each of them exactly nine months after one or other of his legitimate children. And we were laughing about it—about the way when Aunt Sue was confined, Uncle Morgan had one sure way of relieving the tension."

"Good heavens!" Charles looked at the list again. "But you don't mean . . ." He could think it but not say it. "No. That's impossible."

"Good. I hoped it was. It's just a coincidence."

"And yet"—he was remembering now, little things—"Uncle Bull was always away . . . But, no! I can't believe it. And yet their bedrooms were always . . . and I have felt, once or twice, a certain . . . Oh, no! Not them! Not those three—the Fifth of Devonshire, maybe, but not the Fifth of Saint Ormer."

"The Fifth of Devonshire?"

He told her the story. Then it was Helen's turn to be astonished. "You mean it's possible your mother *knows?* That she accepts it?"

"It's quite possible. Just like the Devonshires. Georgiana and Bess were inseparable, too. I stayed at Chatsworth once and young Cavendish showed me their letters. Whenever they were apart they wrote to each other, most tenderly, every day. They were always seen about together—always affectionate. Bess nursed Georgiana through her last illness and was absolutely inconsolable when she died."

"And you don't find that odd?"

"What's odd about it? If two women love the same man, and he loves both of them, and they like each other—where's the mystery?" He made a discovery and laughed. "Heavens! In convincing you about the Devonshires I've just talked myself into believing it about the Saint Ormers, too. I know I ought to be shocked—but I'm not."

"Then what about Felicity and William?" Helen asked. "Aren't you shocked to think they could be half-brother-and-sister?"

"Never. The duke's a gentleman. He'd let Bull fix one undoubted heir before he . . . er . . . cut himself a slice. No, William Redvers is a Bullen-Chetwynne. Be sure of that."

"Well, I hope it's a disease of *fifth* dukes," she said, "because I'll tell you, Charles, I wouldn't share a minute of your passions with any other woman."

He, who thought it miracle enough for one lifetime to have found her—and to have won her love—laughed at the very thought that this rare brand of lightning could strike twice this even rarer piece of earth.

"I suppose you'll be watching me, too," she said, matter-of-factly.

"Good heavens, no!" He was appalled. "Why d'you say that?"

"You're a great family of *watchers*," she told him. "There's reams of reports up there on the descendants of the Reverend Lord Richard, or the early generations, anyway. The first two dukes kept a very close watch on *them*."

"Well, they were possible successors. If the main line ran out."

"D'you know anything about an Orlando Boyce?"

"I think he's the illegitimate one. You ought to ask the mater, she knows all those ancient generations."

"And so do you. Perfectly well."

He laughed. "One does like to appear ignorant on some matters."

"So I've noticed."

"Some kinds of knowledge are so *professional*."

"Hm."

"Very well," he said. "Orlando was the eldest son of William du Bois, who turned Quaker and adopted the name Boyce. William was my . . . fifth-great-grandfather. He married Margaret Champion."

"Did you know he was a Roman Catholic before he turned Quaker?"

It sounded so improbable that Charles simply laughed.

"Oh, yes! It's all there. Spying reports to the First Duke. And I'll tell you something more. He was married in a Roman church—or at least in a Roman ceremony by a Roman priest—to Margaret Champion, before Orlando was born!"

Charles wouldn't believe it. "Even William himself always said Orlando was illegitimate."

"William was obviously a very fiery, up-and-down sort of man. He had a violent set-to with the Roman Church soon after the wedding, and from that day he refused to recognize it had happened at all."

"Even at the cost of making his eldest boy a bastard?"

"Even so."

Charles sat up at that. "Good God!" He sucked in a deep breath. "But if Orlando really is legitimate . . . then his descendants are in the true line of succession—not ours."

"Well, that's not so sure. The marriage happened in Ireland, at a time when the Roman Church there was illegal."

Charles leaned back and relaxed. "Anyway, it's all music. Orlando's line was finished within two generations, when William Boyes died on a prison hulk. So we inherit anyway."

"But what narrow threads it all hangs on," she murmured. "And what twisted legal pathways."

"I'll tell you the real mystery: Since the only people who *never* lose are the lawyers, why don't they own the whole works by now?"

His dilettante detachment annoyed her. "Charles," she said after a short silence.

"Mmm?"

"You are going to take your diplomatic work seriously, aren't you?"

"Oh, I expect so, one way or another. Looking at it all round. By and large. On the whole. Taking the square and the . . . pff!"

She shut him up with a pillow.

CHAPTER FORTY-SIX

FOR THE REST of the 1880s and well into the 1890s Lord Charles and Helen lived, as he and the duke had predicted, in the great courts of Europe—Berlin, St. Petersburg, and Vienna. He was never sent to Paris, which, being republican, was no longer a great court anyway; but they spent many holidays there.

"Worst first," Charles said, when they heard it was to be Berlin.

They called on H.R.H. the Prince of Wales at Marlborough House before they left—for it had always been understood that Lord Charles would be sending private intelligence to his father, who, naturally, would share it with H.R.H.

"The key to understanding Germany," Bertie said, "is war. Over the past two centuries the Hohenzollerns have turned war into the German national profession. They've taken Prussia, which was an insignificant, sandy little kingdom, and have made it the foremost power in mainland Europe. In the past twenty years they've defeated Denmark, brought Austria to her knees, and crushed France in weeks. They are the only power in Europe who've made war *pay*."

"You see them as a threat to England, sir?"

"Not for many years yet. Perhaps never, Charles." He smiled wearily. "A lot depends on when—and if—Prince Wilhelm becomes emperor . . ." The word "emperor" sent him off on another line. "Also we must remember that Bismarck, for all his skill, could not get Wilhelm proclaimed 'Emperor *of* Germany,' only 'German Emperor.' You see, those petty German kingdoms are not as united as they claim. I hope you will be looking especially for signs of that division. You too, my dear," he added, smiling genially at Helen. "The gossip around the Kaiserin and in the Schleppen Cour may be more revealing than anything Lord Charles can discover."

"He's nice," Helen said afterward. "Like a big friendly bear. I don't believe he deserves his reputation at all."

"For?"

"For seducing friends' wives. I felt no vibrations."

"Well, of course not! He *is* a gentleman first, as I said about the duke. It's unthinkable to make advances to a friend's wife before she's produced at least one undoubted heir; but no one in the Marlborough House set cares much whose blood goes into the tail-enders, as long as it's that of a good friend. And H.R.H. is a damn good friend—ask anyone."

"He was going to say something else about Prince Wilhelm, then he looked at me and thought better of it. What was that, d'you think?"

"I suppose he feels he doesn't know you quite well enough yet to say openly that Willie—who is his nephew, after all—is mad."

"Is he?"

"Everyone who knows him believes it, even his mother. And she is English. Anyway, he's an arrogant, pigheaded fool. He nearly drowned our ambassador's wife in the Jungfernsee at Potsdam a few years ago, entirely through his own stupidity."

• •

Helen, who, despite her father's wealth, had been "reared mighty frugal," felt more at home in Berlin than Charles did. The Prussians might have turned war into a paying business, but it was the sort of business that devoured its own profits in reinvestment —and more. There wasn't one noble family, from Junker barons to petty kings, who had not sold their jewels and plate, some of them many times, to pay for one war or another.

Life within those elaborate, heavy buildings was a nightmare of cheeseparing in which Flora's "gardeners' gloves dipped in whitewash" would have seemed a scandalous luxury. After all, it was not so long ago that the Hohenzollern princesses had paraded up and down the Linden in cotton frocks and cotton gloves, and the whole royal family used to walk to the Christmas fair and return carrying presents and gingerbread tied up in *brown paper!*

Charles found it all vastly amusing, as if the inmates of a house for distressed gentry had invented an empire and were now acting out the fantasy, day and night. Etiquette was ferocious. Helen felt sorry for the lower ranks of official society, who were obliged to hold a set number of dinners for their colleagues and superiors each year. These were threadbare affairs of terrifying pomposity, where conversation—so formal that it could have been carried intact, like the plate and powdered wigs of the waiters, from one dinner to the next—flowed over, for example, a fish course composed of two sardines and a slice of rye bread.

Dinners by rich merchants were only slightly less dispiriting. A truly grand affair consisted of thirty guests—who turned up in white tie and swallowtails at the grotesque hour of five in the afternoon. The food was good but, as no one kept a chef, it was all sent in from restaurants—and as there was only a handful of good restaurants in the entire city, dinners soon became as recognizable in style as any new piece of music by a great composer. Indeed, half the conversation turned on guessing which establishment had furnished the banquet.

"There is surely a touch of Mendrzyck at the Vier Jahreszeiten in this soup," one connoisseur would claim.

"True, but I detect the hand of Hohn at Zum Franciskaner in the sauce for the fish," another would riposte.

These sparkling exchanges had to compensate for the lack of flowers and plate—and of after-dinner conversation, too, for at exactly seven o'clock everyone bowed and took his leave.

As an American, Helen, if she had not also been Lady Charles Boyce, would have ranked very low in Berlin. Bismarck, who knew all about petticoat power across the Atlantic, insisted on the immediate resignation of any German diplomat who was rash enough to marry an American woman. The U.S. Congress did its ignorant best to kill any effort to improve America's reputation in the Old World; on one occasion its pennypinching resulted in the forced sale of the Berlin Embassy. The joke went about that a foreign gentleman was arrested for loitering overnight in the Tiergarten; when the policeman told him to go home, he said, "Home! Dammit, sir, I *have* no home—I am the American Ambassador!"

Lord Charles's duties were exactly those to which he had been reared. Sometimes, if there were a heavy traffic in cables, he would take his turn at ciphering long into the night. And if there was a big crop of D.B.S.s (as Distressed British Subjects were called), he would pull his weight in Chancery—a separate building in another part of town, where all commercial business that might sully the embassy was transacted. But apart from such emergencies he was required only to hunt and shoot, to attend dinners and balls, to be seen at the theater and opera, to dine visiting members of English Society and to see they gained whatever entrée, to Berlin Society was appropriate to their rank.

German friends would often chaff Helen and Charles at the dreadfully elastic nature of English Society—especially in the circle around H.R.H., who entertained actors, merchants, and even Jews, and expected all his friends to do the same. The Germans clearly despised the English monarchy for being of the constitutional or figurehead variety; the model they admired was that of the autocratic and absolute emperors of Russia. Charles would then remind them of the oak and the reed and how they fared in the autumn gales—and of what had befallen the absolute autocracy in France and what fate was even then overtaking the equally exclusive and rigid Habsburgs.

In later years, whenever they read of an industrial or commercial baron being received at the Kaiser's court, Charles and Helen felt able to claim a small share in the achievement.

Presentation at that court, in the Alte Schloss at the end of the Linden, was a memorable experience for anyone, quite apart from the social or political overtones of the event. The building was nothing special from the outside, but the interior was one of the finest in Europe.

The rooms were modest in scale but wonderfully rich in their decoration. The way to the throne room led through an enfilade of half a dozen splendid antechambers. Their gorgeous painted ceilings were encased in richly gilded cofferwork, deeply carved, like the ceilings of the Doge's Palace in Venice, but domestic in scale. The walls were clad with silk and hung with portraits and scenes of Prussian history—all military, of course. In the Drap d'Or Kammer the walls were draped in a sumptuous cloth of gold. In the neighboring Rothe Adler Kammer the furniture and mirrors were carved in oak and then clad in beaten silver; the effect was inexpressibly ornate.

But these antechambers paled the moment one entered the throne room, or Ritter Saal, where, according to some, the rococo movement in European art reached its very pinnacle of achievement. The carving of the large central door was a masterpiece. Above it stood a minstrel gallery that had once been solid silver and had formed part of Frederick the Great's war chest, until that monarch melted it down to pay for some campaign. Now, like the furniture in the Chamber of the Red Eagle, it was of carved wood burnished over with silver. The gorgeous, incised strapwork rose to frame an arched and painted ceiling, from which hung fine old chandeliers of cut rock crystal. The walls, with all their pilasters, carvings, and moldings were gilded to form one entire sheet of gold; they framed Gobelins tapestries of the finest period, and over the side doors stood allegorical groups of statuary by Schlüter—his best work—representing the four corners of the world.

Charles and Helen were first presented there at night, when the candlelight and oil lamps made the tapestries glow and brought out the opulent sheen of those vast walls of carved gold. For sheer magical splendor there was no throne room in Europe to equal it.

"The only thing that marred the evening," Helen wrote to her mother, "was the old Emperor's dentist. He's been fitted up with teeth that not only make it impossible to hear what he's saying but even what language he's saying it in. Fortunately, when he 'makes the circle' of those who are being presented, you're not supposed to talk back anything more than a conventional phrase. The trick is to listen real hard for a nasal sound (which means he's muttering in French) and then reply, 'Parfaitement, Sire.' But if you hear gutturals, you say 'Zu Befehl, Majestät,' and all is smiles. Charles has a way of muttering back nonsense words in what sounds like a universal European tongue, but no one else can manage it."

During their first year in Berlin, Charles played very little part in the "high-policy" activities of the embassy; he was, after all, only second attaché. But then came the International Financial Conference in London, at which Bismarck, supported by Jules Ferry for France, opposed Britain's use of Egyptian revenues to pay for the military campaign in the Soudan. Charles at once received, via the duke, a bitter and violent letter from Lord Knightsbridge, written from Omdurman, complaining at the way the lesser powers of Europe were interfering in England's Grand Design for Africa. The duke added that H.R.H. was worried at this sign of a possible entente between France and Germany. He wanted France for England. H.R.H. wrote directly to Lord Charles of his worries later in the year, when Bismarck and Ferry organized the Berlin Conference on Africa.

Charles's extraordinary talent for absorbing knowledge now served him well. It amused Helen to see how Lord Ampthill and other senior embassy people would listen to him. "I'm sure in the American service," she wrote to Flora, "they admire the sort of fellow who's carrying four hefty books and looks around him for a fifth, who never relaxes and hardly ever laughs. Nothing could be further from our dear Charlie. To see him lying on cushions in a skiff on the Jungfernsee, taking turns to row idly about, spouting facts to Lord A. on Tanganyika or the Congo Basin or the charter of the German East Africa Company, all in the laziest drawl, and as if he's just so astonished at how all this knowledge got itself stuck in his head in the first place, makes me laugh. The Germans, who share the American love of seriousness, solemnity, efficiency, and all the other *Pfui* (to use the Germans' word) are completely taken in by him. They consider him a congenial but inane young fop—and so are much less on their guard than they ought to be in front of that keen mind and those lazy but all-seeing eyes."

It was Charles who managed to obtain a summary of the treaty of friendship between Germany and the South African Republic before it was signed. Later that year he got advance warning of Germany's intention to annex Northern New Guinea and the Bismarck Archipelago—which enabled Britain to be so quick in declaring a protectorate over Southern New Guinea and block any further German ambitions in that area. None of the German delegates suspected that the languid lord with whom they dined, shot, fenced, rode, and chatted so amiably had any part in it.

When Russia refused to renew the "Three Emperors Alliance," Prince Wilhelm complained bitterly to Charles that H.R.H. had written letters to the Russian emperor, Alexander III, poisoning his mind against Germany—little knowing that he was making his complaint to the very man who had supplied many of the ingredients of that poison.

Charles crowned his time in Germany by obtaining—again before it was signed—a final draft of the German-Italian military agreement, which could be interpreted as egging Italy on to fight

France, with the promise of German support. The merest hint of it, passed on to France, was enough to scotch any budding Franco-German entente. H.R.H. was well pleased.

How Charles acquired the text could have run on the stage for years as farce. It was his duty one evening to chaperone some younger English royal dukes in their debaucheries with a group of German cavalry officers. The highlight of these visits was always an all-night orgy of drinking and lechery at a café with private rooms. Charles was drinking his fourteenth cup of coffee on the terrace when he was approached by a tall, earnest man—an Englishman, to judge by his clothes.

"Have I the honor to address Lord Charles Boyce?" he asked.

Charles admitted to the name.

"Then you are the last person I ought to approach in this way, my lord—just as I am the last person you'd expect to address you, if you know my story. My name is Royston Dart." He studied Charles anxiously for a reaction and, seeing none, relaxed and smiled. "I once wrote a most stupid and discourteous piece on your family, sir. This is by way of amends." He leaned confidentially close. "I have in my pocket, my lord, a copy of a new secret treaty between Germany, Italy, and Austria."

"The devil you have!"

"Yes, my lord. And I think it's too big for my paper—too big even for the *Times*."

"Let me look at it."

Dart was horrified. "Not here!"

"Have you been followed?"

"I don't think so, sir. But supposing—"

"If we go to a private room, anyone watching will know you've got something. If you show it to me here and I laugh and throw it on the table and we talk amiably and you leave, forgetting it, and I shout after you, 'Hey, your little skit!' and you come back and collect it . . . ?"

When Dart looked only nine tenths convinced, Charles added the coffin nail: "Don't worry! To be seen with me is a guarantee of frivolity."

One paragraph into Dart's paper and he was straining all his skills to remain calm and aloof; it was the most explosive thing he'd ever read.

Soon after midnight, when his royal watch was relieved, he was back in the embassy, convincing Dart that to publish it would imperil the peace of Europe. The man needed little convincing. English reporters had long been more keen to join the inner, upper circles of power and privilege than to spread their discoveries to the masses; Dart knew his self-denial would not go unrewarded.

Before dawn the full text of the treaty was with the Foreign Office; and Dart had a letter of recommendation to the duke.

That same week the F. O. decided it was time to move Charles to St. Petersburg. Britain and Russia had just signed a treaty on Afghanistan; they needed a man of Charles's talents close to the court of the Czar.

"Don't call him 'Czar,' by the way," Lord Ampthill warned Charles. "It's a terrible faux pas there in official communications, though everyone does it informally. Peter the Great was the last Czar of Russia, and the first Emperor of All the Russias." He smiled. "You're not ambitious, are you, Charles?"

"Not in the slightest, sir."

"Good. Because the idea is to send you out as second attaché still, as if they're not very pleased with you. And you can amble along in your good-for-nothing way and repeat in Petersburg the good work—the *excellent* work—you've done here in Berlin. I wish I knew how you did it."

"It's a bit of a mystery to me, too, sir, at times."

When they first went to Berlin, Alfred, quoting Duke Augustus, had encouraged them to "go two—and come back three." They did better: They came back four, with Michael, almost three years old, and Katherine, not yet one.

CHAPTER FORTY-SEVEN

THAT CHRISTMAS saw the largest family party ever assembled at Chalfont Abbey. Everyone was there; even Lord Knightsbridge (who lost his right eye in the relief of Khartoum, and whom everyone had thought was dead) came and brought young Neville, now rising thirteen. In all there were the nine children of Flora and Hermione, all of whom were now married, with fifteen children among them. Neville and Lady Louise's Tarquin were the oldest; four of them, including Charles's Katherine, were less than a year old and so took little part in the festivity.

But there were plenty of presents for the older ones—rocking horses, lead soldiers, printing sets, dolls, papier-mâché armor, a doll house for Georgina—"An alternative household for her to turn upside down and leave ours in peace," Felicity said—and a tricycle for Neville.

When they were all opened and gasped over and kissed and thanked for, Helen said, "Isn't it a shame that the poor children in the villages can't have such lovely things?"

Felicity agreed, and then had an idea. "Couldn't we at least make an exhibition and invite the village children to look at them?"

"Yes!" Lady Louise said. "And send them away with a little packet of sweetmeats each, or an orange, or a new penny—wouldn't that be nice!"

And so began the tradition whereby on Boxing Day morning all the presents of the nobility's children at the Abbey were put on display and the poor children from all the country around filed in through one door and, being kept back by a rope, shuffled on a sackcloth drugget laid over the polished floor and carpet, wide-eyed and wondering through this Aladdin's Cave, and so out by another door; there each received an orange, a sugar mouse, an illustrated prayer, and a new penny. The duke's chief tenants were annoyed at this innovation; the house of du Bois, or Boyce, however spelled, had always been too considerate of the poor, in their view.

Hermione's hothouses had transformed the place. There were twenty-eight displays of flowers about the house, each of which was changed daily by the gardeners through the twenty days of the holidays. Everyone congratulated Hermione on the quality of the blooms and the artistic way she had taught the gardeners to arrange them, but she was even prouder of the strawberries, peaches, asparagus, and other out-of-season delicacies they were now able to enjoy. "We gave the high and mighty M. Taillefer a lesson," she said with relish. "He's the new chef, you know—arrived in November. And when Tom Archer, the head gardener, came up to the kitchens, which he does every morning, and asked what vegetables were required, Monsieur said with his nose in the air, 'Just bring a leetle of everything, my man'—which is *not* the way even the duke would speak to our Mr. Archer. So the old boy simply nodded and turned on his heel, without mentioning that we had, in fact, a hundred and thirty-seven different varieties of vegetables ready for table. He took every single gardener—all twenty-eight of them—and the boys, and he got every barrow and dog cart he could lay his hands on, and he took 'a leetle of everything' up to the chef. As commanded. Well! It filled the Great Courtyard. And not a smile on anyone's face." She laughed. "He's *Mister* Archer now in the kitchens, and no one asks his opinion more readily than M. Taillefer!"

"We even had tomatoes this summer," Flora said.

"Those new fruits?" Lady Emily asked. "Aren't they supposed to be poisonous?"

"A lot of people say they are, but we've survived the experience. And the taste is delicious."

After dinner one evening, toward the end of the holiday, Knightsbridge congratulated the duke on the appearance of the estate, especially comparing it with other estates he had seen from the train.

Alfred nodded glumly. "It's a delusion, my boy. The rents have been static for at least ten years. If we hadn't the businesses, we'd be as badly off as Bath, Northumberland, Cleveland, Verulam, Ailesbury, and dozens of other big landowners I could name. Alexander Bath tells me he's having a terrible time with the Wiltshire farms, which are all chalkland—sheep and corn. Tenants are absconding or going bankrupt all the time and their farms are falling into hand every week. Of course the dairying farms are holding their own."

"But we're all right, I take it, sir?" Charles asked.

"Only in a very narrow view. What's bad for landowners is bad for us. Most of them are clearing themselves only by cutting back on improvements."

"Isn't that common sense?" Knightsbridge said.

"Depends how long it goes on, doesn't it?" Alfred told him. "A year? Five years? We're spending a quarter of our rents on improvements, but most landlords aren't spending a tenth—and haven't done so for fifteen years or more."

"Surely, sir, they're the ones who'll suffer?"

"We'll all suffer. Everywhere I hear the farmers asking, 'What good is a landlord who won't improve his land?' And they've every right to ask it. The next question will be, 'What right do the landlords have to keep the land if they can't look after it properly?' And when farmers and town radicals make common cause, we must look to our powder."

"Confiscation?" Charles was astonished. "In England?"

"They wouldn't call it that, of course. Income tax is confiscation by another name. They'd confiscate a tenth of the estate on the owner's death and call it 'estate tax' or 'death duty' or some such folderol. But it's—as you say, of course—plain confiscation."

"Still," Knightsbridge said, "most estates could lose a tenth part and survive pretty well, sir."

Alfred laughed dryly. "Spoken like a general! But land ain't like a regimental muster, my boy. Such a tax would force so much land on the market, the price would drop like a stone—or, in our case, like a headsman's ax. It's bad enough now. George Marlborough says half the land in England would be on the market already if the price was only halfway decent. Land isn't what it was. The port is with you, Charles."

"Why are you telling us this, pater?" Charles asked, passing the decanter to his father.

"To explain why I'm selling the Cornish estates."

Both sons sat up, astonished. "But the entail?" Knightsbridge said.

Their father smiled. "Thanks to the recent acts, an entail in the hands of a good lawyer is more of a sieve than a pail. Full of holes. We'll keep Constantine Park, of course, but the Duchy of Cornwall is buying the rest. Rosevean and your thirty acres of cliff and foreshore is excluded, naturally," he added to Charles. "We're putting the proceeds toward buying some land west of London, in the Shepherds Bush–Hammersmith region."

"Do what the Grosvenors have done?" Charles asked. "Go in for urban estates?"

"Exactly. It's a question of balance, you see. Town versus country. Like the First Duke in the Civil War, we know when to go over to the other side."

A silence fell. The log fire partially collapsed; they watched the sparks, like fireworks, as two footmen rebuilt it.

"What's your view of it all, Knightsbridge?" Alfred asked.

"It doesn't really concern me, sir."

"Don't you want to say anything?"

"May I?"

"Of course you may."

"Well, thank you, sir." He turned to his brother. "I just want to tell you to tell Johnny Russki that if he interferes with us in Afghanistan, or Persia, or Turkey, or anywhere else—we're damn well going to biff him, and biff him hard."

Alfred half-hid a smile. "Well, Charles? What's that in diplomatic lingo?"

Charles grinned from one to the other. "D'you know, sir," he said, "I rather believe that Knightsbridge, in that inimitable way of his, has just condensed the contents of half a dozen embassy boxes into one succinct sentence. Dickens himself couldn't have put it better."

CHAPTER FORTY-EIGHT

IT WAS THE BEST of times, it was the worst of times to arrive in St. Petersburg. The temperature was hovering around the minus forties. The actual day of their arrival was January 18 (or January 6 in the unreformed Russian calendar); it was also the day on which the Holy Russian Church blessed the waters of the Neva.

A great hole was cut in the ice and a temporary chapel built above it. Helen and Charles, together with the rest of the embassy, had privileged seats at the windows of the steam-heated Nicholas Hall in the Winter Palace. The poor czar, Alexander III, had to stand bareheaded outside until the long religious ceremonial was over and the Metropolitan dipped his great golden cross in the waters of the river. Most of all to be pitied were the soldiers who had to stand guard until the hole froze over again, to prevent fanatical peasants from bathing in the newly consecrated waters.

That evening the Court held a "Bal des Palmiers."

"Who else would hold a ball beneath palm trees, when the weather outside is minus forty?" the French ambassador remarked to Charles. "Who else but the Russians?"

A hundred large palm trees were brought in huge heated vans from Tsarskoe Selo, fourteen miles to the south. They were set out down the vast length of Nicholas Hall; then tables, each seating about fifteen, were built around their trunks. It was an amazing contrast—tropical palms waving their bright green fronds only yards away from air so cold that spit would freeze before it landed.

The Russian love of effective display extended to the lighting, too. When the guests filed in, only a few of the candles were lighted, enough to prevent people from bumping into each other or the palms, and enough to show ten thousand other unlighted candles all in their holders, waiting for the flame that was to descend upon them in a most spectacular way. All day the moujiks had been busy dipping the wicks in kerosene before they put the candles in their sockets; then they ran one continuous thread of gun cotton, like a fuze to explosives, all around the hall, twisting it around each unlighted wick. Just before the czar made his entrance, the major-domo would touch a light to the gun cotton, which would ignite faster than the eye could follow—so that thousands of candles would appear to burst simultaneously into flame, quite by magic. The oohs and aahs of wonder rang out as people hid their eyes from the pain of so much sudden brilliance; then, as the noise fell to a hush, the czar was among them!

Before any dancing or eating began, he made a round of the tables, spoke to two or three people at each one, ate a morsel of bread or a grape, and wet his lips in champagne, just so that everyone there could say, "I dined with his imperial majesty this evening."

Although Peter the Great had built St. Petersburg as a copy of a Western European city, the splendid barbarism of an older Russia had defeated his purpose. The imperial court spoke French but breathed pure Boyar. The uniforms, above all, shouted *East!* Everyone was in uniform, even the girls. Theirs was a heavily embroidered dress of white satin and, on the head, a white silk kakoshnik, the traditional, crescent-shaped headdress of Russian women. Married women and single women "of a certain age" added an overdress of deep red, blue, green, or brown velvet, lavishly trimmed with fur and with a long train embroidered with flowers of gold or silver, or both; their kakoshniks were studded with precious stones—and nothing more plainly showed the Eastern influence than the women's preference for polished but unfaceted jewels.

The dancing and feasting went on until dawn. Charles and Helen, who had slept only fitfully on the twenty-four-hour train journey from Wirballen to the capital, had by then passed beyond tiredness and into a euphoric state in which their feet hardly seemed to exist. They drifted from group to group, table to table, saying the right things and making the right gestures entirely by rote, like automata. So when M. Orloff, the director of the Hermitage Gallery, asked them enthusiastically if they would like to see over the rest of the Winter Palace, they did not say, "We are just a *little* fatigued from our journey . . ." but rather that nothing would delight them more, and they strolled out on a dawn-lit tour.

Orloff did not tell them the palace contained over forty large public rooms. But what better frame or framelessness of mind in which to see such a monument to autocracy? Days later, when they had slept off their fatigue, they found that it was not the long succession of vast and mediocre rooms which lingered in the memory—all rebuilt after the fire of 1837. Nor was it the somewhat finer rooms that had escaped the fire, including the Ambassadors' Stair and the Throne Room itself. What had struck them indelibly were two features that had resulted from the mere whims of two czarinas.

Around the turn of the century the Empress Sophia had chosen a smallish room on the second floor as her library because it overlooked a quiet little courtyard. One day, apropos of nothing, she had said how pleasant it would be to walk out of the window and under an avenue of lime trees. When she returned next year, the entire courtyard had been filled with earth, blocking not only the ground-floor windows but the first-floor ones as well. On top of it was a floating grove of mature limes which had been transplanted there in the spring.

Several decades later the Empress Charlotte, not to be outdone, had wished for a winter garden, and for her they had contrived a vast hanging terrace that followed all the angles of the building, complete with palm trees, gravel walks, and lawns of club moss. Because they were reluctant to put wet earth against the building, the walls were clad in imitation creepers and vines of wrought iron, painted with great realism.

When Charles and Helen saw what labor went into the indulgence of imperial whims, and contrasted it with the bare, whitewashed cells reserved for mere dukes and princes in the imperial Russian household, they understood what absolute monarchy meant—and why the Prussians so admired it. Just at that moment, though, Germany was distinctly out of concert with Russia.

A month after their arrival Bismarck published the full text of the German-Austrian alliance, concluded nine years earlier and kept secret until now. This was a clear warning to the czar to curb any military ambitions he might have—a warning that Bismarck underlined in a fire-eating speech to the Reichstag only a few days later. Bismarck had got the wind up about Russia the previous year when M. Giers, the Russian foreign minister, had refused to extend the Three Emperors Alliance and had signed instead a much more limited reinsurance treaty with Germany. In Russia it was seen as M. Giers' victory over extreme Russian nationalists; but Bismarck had been unable to view it in quite that light. Now he was coughing sparks.

The embassy received copies of all the previous day's cables from Paris, Berlin, Vienna, and Rome concerning Russia and the East in general; so the wires between London and St. Petersburg glowed red for days. Charles, like everyone else, was up until the small hours ciphering and deciphering the traffic. He had learned the work in Berlin but here there was an extra twist. One of their codes had fallen into Russian hands and they had to be careful to use that code only for messages they wanted the Russians to understand.

Charles wrote to the duke saying he thought it a good time to encourage a Franco-German entente. The reinsurance treaty would be up for renewal in two years and would give a good indication of Germany's response to a French initiative. H.R.H. had reservations and delayed replying until March, when the old kaiser died and Bertie's brother-in-law, Frederick III, came to the throne. Then he agreed it was worth trying. Certainly there was no point in looking toward Austria.

A week after all the excitement died down, Charles and Helen began to go about in Petersburg Society. They started learning Russian and soon reached a point where they could quite easily mispronounce the strange Cyrillic names over all the shops. But before they could progress further, they were whisked away into the depths of the Russian forest, into a society that could have been a million miles from the glittering kaleidoscope of the Winter Palace and its steam-heated court. It began when a peasant came into town with bears to sell.

He was one of a group of peasants who made a fair living by noting the winter-hibernation quarters of the bears and then traveling up to the capital and selling them in the clubs and embassies at so much per *pood,* a weight equal to forty Russian *funts* or about thirty-six imperial pounds. For this he provided sledges and beaters, and the sum was payable only if the bear was driven close enough for a shot.

The ambassador virtually ordered Lord Charles to buy one.

"But I'm due no leave yet, sir," Charles protested.

"Leave? Who said anything about leave? One of your duties is to learn to know the country. There's no better teacher, believe me, than a bear hunt."

They left as if for the moon, armed with smooth-bore guns, a sporting rifle, furs, and good advice.

The adventure began with a five-hour train journey to a remote country station in the heart of a taiga forest that stretched for thousands of miles further east. There they were met by their bear seller, Juri Frolenko, who carried their boxes to a country sledge, which was a collection of wooden poles tied loosely together, set on iron runners, and filled with hay. The boxes, guns, and food were put beneath the hay and tied securely, except for one rifle and some buckshot cartridges.

The sledge was long enough to lie on, feet pointing backward. Side by side, in thick felt boots and heavy furs, Charles and Helen lay with their heads on pneumatic cushions, and set off on the eighty-mile journey through the forest—an all-night drive from next-to-nowhere to nowhere itself.

At first it was magical. Their heads were closely wrapped, each in a Persian bashlik—a fine camel-hair hood—to prevent frostbite. From its cocoon of warmth, snuggled up as they were beneath a thick fur rug, they stared up at the steel-gray arch of the heavens, where the stars blazed with a brilliance that almost hurt, and the conifers were pyramids of Bible-black. They were touched with awe at the vast, cold, stillness of everything—and the eternal silence, for sleigh bells were unknown in northern Russia.

Only once on that journey was the silence broken by anything other than the horses, the humans, and the sledge. There was a long-drawn howl away to their left; a few minutes later Frolenko's companion nudged Lord Charles and pointed to that side, where a phantom of a darker gray was trotting swiftly among the trees, easily keeping pace. One shot from the loose rifle and it was gone, quick rather than dead.

Sometime after midnight the track became much bumpier and sleep was fitful at best. Occasionally the driver fell asleep, and the horses grew careless and would pull part of the sledge over steep drift sides or tree stumps; then the whole lot would overturn and be tipped out into snow so cold it burned like hot iron.

But these inconveniences were overshadowed by wonder at the mystery of the gray forest and the vague but powerful sense of drawing close to some Absolute that pervaded its vast and silent emptiness. As dawn broke, a pink aura seemed to wreathe itself among the trees and the silence trembled on the edge of a new music, never before heard by man.

Their deepest sleep of the night came between that dawn and their arrival in the village, by which time the sun was climbing well up the sky. The temperature, too, had soared. At only five degrees of frost, the air felt tropical.

When they later returned to the capital, they had seen only this one village, whose name they never learned. Yet in it they saw a hundred thousand others, all identical: a single long street, defined by forty or so log houses, or *isbas,* well spaced apart on each side. Each *isba* had two rooms: a cold room, used only in summer, and a hot room, one eighth of which was filled with a five-foot-high brick stove on top of which the family—and ten million voracious little guests—all slept. An ikon shelf, a table, benches, a cupboard, a samovar, and cooking and eating utensils comprised the rest of the furnishings.

Charles, profiting from the advice of his colleagues, insisted on occupying the cold room with Helen. At five degrees of frost it was free of vermin; yet, with some hay thrown down on the floor, it was not so cold as to prevent them from sleeping. He had to insist quite strongly before he got his way, with the help of Frolenko, who had a smattering of German. They were also helped by the widespread conviction that anyone from beyond the Russian borders was a barbarian fool, a *nyemski*, a maker of inarticulate noises.

The first thing they did, even before they ate, was to unpack their rubber washstand and fill it with hot water, so that Helen was able to wash and dress again before the village had congregated around their *isba*. The few who did arrive Charles was able to keep at bay by holding the door shut. But Helen could not do the same for him; she guarded the door but people peered in the windows; and when she went outside to shoo them away, they opened the door and trooped into the room. When she came back, they (all men) made anxious signs at her to cover her eyes against the wicked sight of her husband stark naked—a sight at which they all gawped with open mouths.

"Why are they so excited?" she asked Frolenko.

"We wonder he didn't wash himself last summer when it was warm."

She laughed. "But we wash every day."

He shook his head sadly. "Russians never get as dirty as that."

Their curiosity extended to everything. Helen had no need to unpack; it was all taken out for her, passed from hand to hand, sniffed, felt, poked at, rubbed, laughed over, and laid neatly on the table or put in the cupboard. Yet nothing, not even their money, was missing at the end of it all.

Then they went into the hot room, where the woman of the house had made them breakfast of the food they had brought; porridge made with milk, boiled eggs, and ham and pickles. Next they put on skis, which they had seen some fowlers using on the frozen Neva in Petersburg but had never actually handled. Then the entire village set off, all on skis, for the bear's cave, some with horns, some with iron pots, some with flat pieces of wood to bang together. Charles carried his gun and Frolenko brought the rifle, which would be needed if the bear did not come close enough for the gunshot.

In the first hundred yards both Charles and Helen toppled off their skis several times, and everyone thought it very funny. After two miles, when they were drawing near to the bear's lair, they could manage to get along fairly smartly.

The lair was a shallow cave in a small outcrop of rock. The ground on the exit side shelved steeply down for about thirty yards and then leveled out. The beaters divided into two equal parties and formed wings down the slope about sixty feet from the cave mouth. A few climbed above the cave, ready to discourage the creature from going up that way and escaping over the ridge. Charles, Helen, and Frolenko stood alone, directly before the cave mouth, about sixty yards from it.

On a signal the beaters set up enough noise to rebuild Jericho, banging their iron pans, yelling, whistling, blowing their horns, and clapping their sticks together. A minute later the bear poked his nose out into the day. From the hang of his head and the grumpiness of his movements he was clearly in an evil temper. He made a half-hearted lurch toward the left-hand line of beaters, who yelled and hammered with redoubled vigor. He paused.

Then he must have become aware that the land before him was quiet. He slithered down the slope and set off on a line that, in about ten seconds, would put him on top of Helen. Charles, seeing how fast the creature moved, realized that even an experienced skier could never get away. He stepped off his skis, hoping for a firmer purchase on the snow.

He found it—nearly four foot below the surface.

"Are you mad?" Frolenko hissed.

Charles ignored him. He cocked the hammer of his gun, raised it to his shoulder, and waited.

His movement alerted the bear to the fact that he had enemies—just three puny little enemies—to deal with on his way out. He changed direction slightly and came straight at Charles.

"Now!" Frolenko said, when the bear was forty feet away.

Charles drew breath.

"Now!" Frolenko shouted. The bear was thirty feet away.

Charles let half his breath go and held the rest. The advantage of a smooth bore is that you don't need to aim accurately. A lead ball has immense stopping power at close quarters; but to let a large, powerful, and deadly animal like a bear get to close quarters, you have to remain absolutely calm and keep your head. Frolenko was not helping.

"Now! Now!" the peasant shrieked. The bear was twenty feet away.

"Halt's Maul, du!" Helen said icily. Frolenko was shocked to momentary silence; but it was enough.

When the bear was less than fifteen feet away, and either he or Charles no more than two seconds from death, Charles fired. Nothing seemed to happen. He began to reload at once.

From his pygmy vantage point, waist deep in snow, Charles saw the bear lurching up, up, up to a monstrous height. Its head leaned to one side. There was a wild, boarlike gleam in its tiny eyes. It danced toward Helen. Charles was still reloading when there was a sharp, almost dainty crack near his left ear.

He turned to see Helen, absolutely calm—indeed, with a little smile, part resignation, part amazement, on her lips—holding a tiny woman's pistol in her hand.

He looked back at the bear. Of course he was dead the moment the lead ball had entered him; hydraulic shock alone would have hemorrhaged every vessel in his brain. He was already falling when Helen fired. Yet the exact coincidence of the two events made it seem that Charles's shot had merely stopped the bear, while Helen's had killed him. He lay at her feet in the precise shape of the rug that he later became.

Not one of the villagers doubted that Helen had finished him off. They put her on top of the carcass, on a country sledge, and almost as an afterthought they put Charles up behind her. Then, with everyone carrying fir branches as a sign of rejoicing, they all went singing back to the village.

There about thirty of the women seized Charles and tossed him in a blanket, up and up, again and again, until they were helpless with laughter and he with giddiness. Not since he was a jew at Eton had he received such treatment; then it was bullying, now it was an honor. An honor, moreover, that Helen did not escape.

Following the custom the visitors presented the village with a cask of vodka. Within two hours there was not a sober male in the place. Some of the more pious turned the ikons to the wall, but all drank themselves to a stupor. Even quite young boys were reeling all over the place. But the women touched not a drop—or if a drop, no more. Their hostess begged for one of Helen's magic bullets, which had prostrated so mighty a creature. Years later they heard it had become a powerful ikon, with several miraculous cures to its credit.

Two days later they returned to Petersburg, not as outsiders from another hemisphere but as people who had seen, and touched, and been moved by, one small part of that great, brooding, childlike, mysteriously profound spirit at the heart of Mother Russia.

PART FIVE

1888-1900

SPERNO ME
RECIPERE AUT
MUTARI

Not Honor More

Chalfont Abbey
in the 19th century
showing the "Brighton" additions
of Duke Augustus

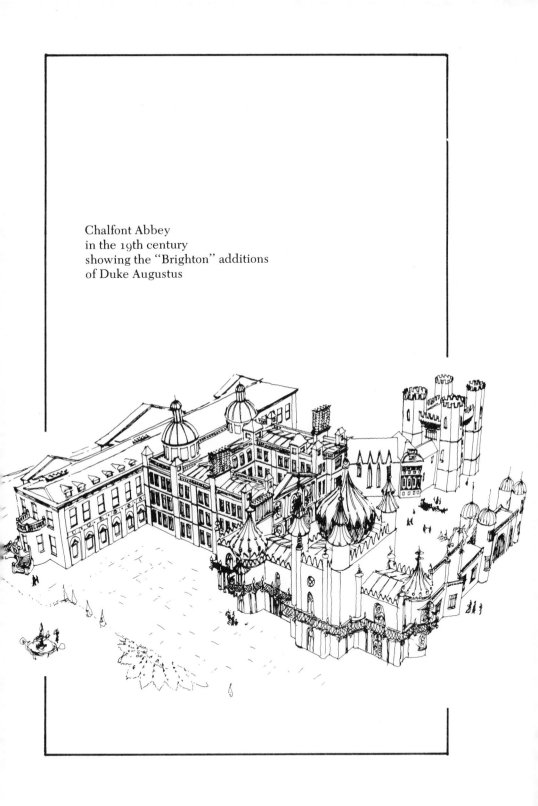

CHAPTER FORTY-NINE

"BUT IF THE GIRL was a Roman Catholic, the marriage would be void *anyway*," Alfred objected. "No member of the royal family can marry a Roman."

Salisbury stared glumly at the raindrops chasing one another down the windowpane; he nodded but made no reply.

"Is there some point I'm missing in all this?" Alfred pressed. "Have you told me everything?"

"Everything?" The prime minister snorted at the impossibility. "No one knows the whole of it—the thing's become so thoroughly out of hand. All we can do is hope we've got it back within our grip, and pray it will never get out of our control again."

Alfred digested this astonishing outburst—astonishing for a man of Salisbury's caliber. "Perhaps I oughtn't to ask any more, then," he suggested.

Salisbury turned and stared. He was a soul in torment. "If I survived a century more," he said, "and lived as a saint might hope to live, I feel I should still die"—he sought the word—"tainted. Yes—*defiled!*"

"And yet you are asking me to—"

"Good God, man!" Salisbury interrupted. "Do you imagine for one moment I'd ask it, or the prince would ask it, if there were any other way?"

"Well . . ." Alfred tried now to soothe him.

"I swear to you, if a condemned murderer stood here before me, I'd not willingly ask it of him either. Not even of such a one."

His solemnity moved Alfred. "I'll do it," he promised. "At least you may set your mind at rest on that. Whatever the prince asks of me, I'll do it. And I'll ask no questions in return."

Salisbury hardly seemed to hear him. "If Dizzy had lived," he sighed, "it would never have happened."

"It's hardly *your* fault, man."

The prime minister smiled wanly and nodded. Alfred had half-opened the door before the other spoke again: "Your grace!"

The formality of the address startled Alfred.

"It really is best to remain in ignorance," Salisbury said.

The prince was as low in spirit as Alfred had ever seen him. There were times in his life when a succession of reverses or misfortunes, each too small in itself to dent that normally jovial and ebullient personality, combined to bring the darkness upon him. This was obviously such a time. Alfred thought he might cheer the prince up by reminding him of others.

"Remember before you went to India, Bertie?" he said. "You had all that unpleasantness in Parliament—those wretched republicans? And the Baker scandal? And her majesty being very tiresome about the members of your party? And Derby losers . . . and the Guelpho lampoons . . . and Lord knows what else?"

The prince nodded morosely.

"Yet didn't you carry all before you! Didn't Chamberlain dine with you? Didn't Dillwyn come pigeon shooting? And didn't Dilke himself become your greatest champion in Gladstone's cabinet? And hasn't the rest just passed into history—who remembers any of it now?" He chuckled but there was no response.

"Cheer up, sir! Things are never so bad as they seem!"

"Seem?" The Prince stirred. "There's no seeming here!"

Alfred, having nothing left to deliver but more banalities, kept silent.

The prince turned to him. "Salisbury told you of this dreadful business? Eddy's marriage?"

"Mismarriage, rather. What can have possessed the boy?"

Bertie sighed. "The same as possessed your boy, I imagine." He made a gesture of hopelessness. "Why can't we propagate like vegetables? Why are we such slaves to it? Eddy knew exactly what was at stake, and yet . . . Trouble is, he's so soft-hearted. He'll fall in love with *anything*—woman, man, or beast—anything that's halfway kind to him. I've seen it happen."

"What does the woman look like?"

"Did. Not does."

"Why—is she dead?"

"As good as, I'm coming to that."

A terrible foreboding hung over them. The prince took out a photograph and passed it to Alfred. For the merest moment he thought it was Alix; then he saw it was of a woman who in every detail was infinitely coarser than the princess. A common laboring woman. Yet something persisted to remind him of Alix—a vile, cruel caricature, no doubt, but it was there. This was the creature whom young Prince Eddy had married.

Still he said nothing.

"I'm about to ask you," the prince said, "something that no man should ask of another, something that no prince should ask of any subject, that no degree of friendship can justify, nor claim of duty deserve. Believe me, if there were any other course, any other—"

"Sir!" Alfred protested. "Salisbury has already convinced me of the gravity of it. Please don't distress yourself—and me—by going *about* it so. I have already agreed. Whatever it is. Don't ask me—tell me."

Tears brimmed in the prince's eyes.

Alfred was as embarrassed by it as by anything in his life. "If I would not do it for my prince, if I would not do it for a fellow Mason, I would do it for friendship's sake alone, Bertie. All three of those ties bind us, yet friendship alone, as I say, would suffice. So"—he smiled—"say no more. Ask on."

The prince turned away, mastering his emotion. Still not looking at Alfred, he said, "That woman is now mad."

There was a silence.

"Mad," Alfred prompted.

"Simple-minded, anyway. She . . . she cannot earn a living, not even . . . in the obvious way."

"But how could Eddy . . . I mean, how *could* he?"

The prince drew breath and said, "She was not always so. She was once . . ." He could not finish. After a pause he added in a whisper, "She has been . . . rendered simple-minded."

Alfred heard himself say, "Good God!"

He divined that, horrible as this confession might seem, it yet was not the substance of the defilement Salisbury had spoken about.

"I meant to tell you none of this," Bertie said. "I meant to say that the woman has been unhinged by . . . events. That the best in life she can hope for is to drift from workhouse to workhouse. I meant to ask you to use your position on the Poor Law Commission to see that wherever she may turn up she will be taken in at once. No questions. No referral to her native parish. Nothing of that sort."

"Of course I'll do that, Bertie. Consider it done."

The prince gripped his arm. "But think," he said. "In the eyes of your fellow commissioners it will mean accepting a kind of responsibility for her disgrace."

"I know."

"Oh, uncle! We don't deserve you."

"Tell me," Alfred ventured. "Was it . . . necessary?"

Bertie frowned. Then a horrified understanding dawned.

"God!" he said. "You think we *knew* about it! We knew nothing until it was all over." He looked uncomfortably around him, as if the very air had become oppressive. "D'you mind if we go outside?" he asked.

Without waiting for an answer he opened a French window and stepped into the damp autumnal air. "I'll tell you everything," he said.

"There's no need."

"Oh, but there is, uncle. You've made it a matter of friendship, not duty. In honor I cannot keep it from you."

"Then I do it for duty, your royal highness."

The prince smiled grimly but shook his head. Alfred understood then that to tell the story in all its horrors—whatever they were—was a compulsion.

"There was a child to the marriage," Bertie began.

"Was?"

"*Is.* A daughter, fortunately. She's in France, being fostered there. She'll present no problem. The mother's name, by the way, is Crook. Sometimes Cook. Annie Crook or Cook."

"How on earth did Eddy meet her?"

"Through one of his bohemian painter friends. They found a way of switching carriages so that Eddy . . . well, we've all done it, I suppose. A pretty girl can turn any man's head."

"But not to the point of marriage."

"Quite. Then Eddy mentioned the marriage to someone at his Lodge. I don't know how many Masons were involved, and I've not tried to find out. But I do know that they resolved—for the sake of the royal family—to end the situation. They took it on themselves. They told no one."

"End it?"

"One of them was a surgeon—a specialist among other things in cranial surgery." He spoke slowly.

The full implications of these words hit Alfred. "Lord!" he whispered. " 'Rendered simple-minded'!"

"Exactly." Bertie watched him intently.

"I understand your distress, of course. And your disgust. But you are not to blame. Good heavens, you didn't even know about it."

Bertie shrugged as if that were small comfort. "We have taken part in covering over the tracks. We have lied. We have dissembled. The throne itself is tainted." He looked away. "But I've not told you the whole of it, uncle." He barked a harsh laugh. "Not the half. Not the hundredth!"

A gardener appeared, carrying a crail full of corms lifted to store over the winter. The prince turned abruptly and led Alfred to the middle of the lawn. He looked about before he spoke again. "Miss Crook," he said, "shared her secret with four women of her class—who, after the operation, wrote to Eddy. A letter of extortion, of course."

"Which he showed to you?"

"He didn't even know of it. No more did I. He still doesn't know of it. He knows none of this. His A.D.C. showed it to Knollys, who sent it to Scotland Yard, where—it was one of those chances that makes you say for the rest of your life, 'If only . . . if only!' I shall certainly say for the rest of my life, 'If only Warren hadn't seen it!' Sir Charles Warren. You know him, of course."

"Of course. He's a Mason, too."

"Precisely." Bertie sighed. "Precisely. And from the same lodge as the surgeon I mentioned."

"What was his name?"

"You oughtn't to know, uncle. In fact, you won't *want* to know. Warren went straight to him, naturally." He clenched his fists and shivered. "If *only* . . . ! Of course no one—least of all Warren—knew then that the surgeon himself was insane." He shook his head. "Quite . . . utterly insane."

Suddenly Alfred's blood froze. "Dear God! Are you talking about these dreadful East End murders? D'you mean Jack the Ripper is this surgeon—this fellow Mason?"

The prince was weeping. Silently, massively. "We didn't know," was all he could say.

Alfred took his arm and waited for the emotion to pass.

"We read the papers, like everyone else," Bertie went on as they began to walk back indoors. "And, like everyone else, we were appalled. Horrified! I even saw Warren about it. By God—*there's* a man I'd not like to cross! Not one word did he say, not a gesture, not a flicker of an eyebrow."

"Then who told you?"

"Salisbury. After much—"

"He had no right! Why didn't he ask me? I'd have—"

"He had every right. Heavens, if only I'd been told at the outset! People seem to think we live in aspic. They think we're made of crystal. They treat us like porcelain."

There was a pause. "It's over now?" Alfred asked.

"It'll never be over."

"I mean, there'll be no more—?"

"Who knows? We are all implicated. You too now. Wider and

wider the ripples"—he stumbled at that word—"spread. What will be in tomorrow's mails?"

"But the surgeon . . . at least he . . . ?"

"He is under restraint. He has been certified insane, under a false name. In a year or so his death, under his true name, will be published. The poor, crazed fool will live out his natural life anonymously, a threat to no one."

Alfred snorted a grim laugh. "He'll die *twice*." It was a reference to a piece of Masonic lore.

The prince nodded and looked away. Alfred's comment opened avenues he would rather not explore.

"I'm glad I know," Alfred said. " 'Glad' may not be quite the word, but I'm now enabled to tell you that I don't consider you in the least to blame. Nor, in Christian conscience, can we blame a madman. The one I blame is Warren. What on earth was he thinking of? After the first murder he must have known. From that moment onward he was in a conspiracy."

"Which I joined, uncle. And now—so have you!"

It was true. Alfred could not blink the fact. He detested what had been done. Yet he too was now as busily engaged in the concealment as anyone. Warren was still a Mason; so were all the other Scotland Yard people who had been active in "investigating" the murders; so was he.

The prince, whenever they met privately, was still under a compulsion to talk about it. "My first response," he said, "was to want to run away. There's not much in my life I've run from, but I wanted to run from this. I never wanted to see my Masonic things again. I wanted to find some constitutional way of abdicating in advance."

Alfred replied that it was more in keeping to do what they were in fact doing: continuing to set a good public example. They were not free people but slaves of a country that needed them. And so on.

"What is this 'honor,' uncle," Bertie asked, "for which we will put our immortal souls in peril? Can any kind of honor grow out of such vileness?"

Inevitably, though, the ritual and trivia of everyday life began to wash over the horror of it all. Even that first day—or the day when Alfred first learned the truth—Bertie left him to go to a country party for the children of some drowned lifeboatmen; there he had played the jovial uncle, the slave of others' expectations. He had even gone with Alix, ten miles through the rain, to the bedside of a child who had fallen ill and could not attend the party. The little girl died two days later, happy that she had entertained the royal pair.

"We must hope these things weigh somewhat on the *other* scale," Bertie said wryly to Alfred the next time they met.

As the weeks drew into months Alfred watched the prince embrace life once again, at first hesitantly, then with gusto, and finally with abandon. Alfred grew worried. It was as if the prince's belief in himself as one of Europe's foremost statesmen had been so undermined that he now saw himself only as the Prince of Pleasure. Gala balls, race meetings, baccarat parties—these filled his days.

When France floated the Russian loan, and so began openly to cultivate the Franco-Russian entente for which the prince had worked so hard, Alfred could barely get him to read Lord Charles's private dispatch from Petersburg on the subject.

"You're not letting Willie push you out of Europe now, are you?" Alfred challenged.

This was a reference to a most wounding snub that the new kaiser, the mad young Wilhelm, had delivered to the prince in Vienna earlier that year, forcing the emperor to ask H.R.H. to leave the city, at Wilhelm's insistence, while he, Wilhelm, visited it.

Alfred's rebuke worked, but not for long.

The dreadful suicide of the young Crown Prince Rudolph at Mayerling the following year had, for a time, the effect of rekindling the Prince of Wales's interest in Europe; but it did not last. He was soon immersed again in a life of pleasure.

Helen and Flora, to the great surprise of both—for neither would have admitted to deep feelings on the subject—got involved in quite an argument about it that Christmas. It began innocently enough with Helen passing on the comments their Russian friends made about H.R.H.

The Russian aristocracy was the most charming, the most childlike, the least censorious in the world; but even they thought the change in the prince's private life called for some comment. The case of Daisy Brooke was very much to the point.

She had for years been the lover of Lord Charles Beresford. And when it became clear that Mina Beresford, his wife, was expecting a baby (and no one could suspect the prim, hysterical Mina of dallying with another), it was also clear that Beresford had embraced her. To Daisy this was outright treachery. Her lover had been unfaithful to her. Even worse, he had committed the act with his own wife.

She had written a most unwise letter to Beresford, charging him with the treason—unwise because he, being a naval captain, was then and for most of that year at sea. It was Mina herself who opened the letter. The earth trembled and the skies fell in. At the very least she demanded that H.R.H. should cut Daisy Brooke from good society.

Poor Daisy, having no Lord Charles Beresford's shoulder to weep upon, wept instead on that of H.R.H. She was a fascinating woman, so full of charm you'd think there'd be no room for wit, yet so witty you'd think her beauty might pass unnoticed, and yet so beautiful that . . . well, that even H.R.H. was deflected from what plain self-interest would have told him was the proper course.

Before long it was poor Mina who found herself being excluded from Good Society—which, in her view, began and ended with the Marlborough House set. Even the tolerant, charming Russians found it bizarre.

"And what do you tell them, Helen dear?" Flora asked. "You who are sent to lie abroad for the good of our country."

"I try to generalize, duchess, on the nature of hypocrisy. From their point of view it brings the discussion so much nearer home."

"Hypocrisy?" Flora asked.

"Saying one thing, believing another. Hypocrisy, I believe."

"Hm." Flora dealt a new hand. "I have never understood this modern cant about hypocrisy. Suppose an officer about to lead his men into battle were to be overtaken by a sudden fear. Suppose he reveals his fear to his men, talks about it openly and honestly. Is that admirable? Do we strike medals for such honesty? Or suppose he conceals it. Suppose he puts on an outward show of dash and spirit, even while his innards crawl with the fear. Suppose this show puts such heart into his men that they turn certain defeat into a triumph. Is that hypocrisy? It is certainly 'saying one thing, believing another.' Do tell us."

Helen, who did not in the least want to get into an argument with her mother-in-law, smiled contritely and said, "No, of course it isn't. How wrong I was."

But Flora behaved exactly as if Helen had not just agreed with her argument. "I tell you it's not," she said. "And you can tell it to your sneering Russian friends. The values that his royal highness upholds in public are Good Values. They are a right and true and proper guide to all classes. Especially the lower classes. But if he finds it tedious or inconvenient to uphold them strictly in his private life, then I say more honor to him for nevertheless championing them in public."

"And anyway," said Hermione, the pourer of oil, "we've always known that Daisy Brooke is a much *nicer* person than Mina Beresford. How can we blame the prince?"

Everyone laughed and the incident was over.

"You were very hard on Helen last night," Charles told his mother next day.

"I'm sorry," she said, but so curtly that both knew it was not sincere.

"I'll take her side if you do it again," he warned.

Later his father said, "It's this awful rheumatism that makes her short-tempered."

Alfred knew the prince was not, as he seemed to be, managing to bury his sense of guilt in his long rounds of pleasure. Yet he envied him the attempt. He wished that he too could assuage his own continuing disquiet so amicably.

What had overcome decent, honorable people like Sir Charles Warren and those who had helped him? True, they had not known their chief agent was insane, but that did not fundamentally change their conspiracy. What had they intended? To frighten the woman? A word with the local bobby would have been enough; and the woman herself could have been comfortably set up. That is surely what Bertie, or any of the upper classes, would have done. Why were the middle classes so utterly different?

And they *were* different, it could not be denied. Priggish, stuffy, self-important, self-righteous, bland, they were also ruthless, avaricious, and quite without scruple in their dealings with the lower classes. This dreadful conspiracy and its consequences forced Alfred to bring out into the open a number of latent ideas connected with government, the state, leadership, democracy, and the hereditary principle—ideas that had hung around his mind, half-formed but unconnected, for decades.

All that winter he haunted the library of the Athenaeum, reading Plato, Aristotle, Locke, Hobbes, Rousseau, Mill, Burke, Saint-Simon—everyone who had ever written anything important on the nature of society. It depressed him acutely that the earlier writers had a far better grasp of reality than more recent ones. Everything since Aristotle had increased the obscurity and complexity of the subject. But Aristotle's theory that all societies go through cycles was not only beautifully simple, it was also demonstrably true. It was actually unfolding all around him.

The civilized world (by which he meant the European world) was passing out of the aristocratic phase of government by élites.

The next stage would be the descent into full democracy, which, inevitably, would tumble into anarchy, out of which would come tyranny, leading to a revival under a messianic leader, who, in time, would yield first to a form of legalized despotism and finally to the rule of a man-god. This absolute monarch would unavoidably create around him an aristocracy who, by some future Magna Carta, would slowly wrest power for themselves . . . and the whole cycle would revolve once more.

As soon as the middle classes were the absolute top dogs (and they were everywhere rising into the ascendancy) they would turn on the aristocracy and dismember them. It was happening already. These new county councils were nibbling away, like mice at cheese, at the powers of landowners. Soon a man wouldn't be able to do what he liked with his own estates, villages, woodlands, roads, or tenants.

"One day," he said to Salisbury, "there'll be an Employment Conservation Act, making it impossible to sack anyone without permission from some local committee, mark my words."

Salisbury laughed and said the duke was developing a good corner in gallows humor. Everyone thought him an amusing wag; no one took his ideas seriously.

He began to dislike most of his fellow Athenaeum Club members, they being stolidly—not to say staunchly—middle class. He saw their deference to him as the deference of a lackey scheming murder; their kindness was merely provisional. He did not yet risk open rudeness to those who had the temerity to greet him here and there about the club; he merely snorted contemptuously as he turned his back on them and walked away.

Naturally this led to comment and complaint, particularly to the Membership Committee, who were reminded that His Grace the Duke of St. Ormer had never actually been elected into membership. And it was quite true. Alfred, who had been advised to walk two miles a day by his doctors, had taken to dropping into the Athenaeum to use their lavatories on his walk from Knightsbridge House to the Palace of Westminster. He found the place convenient and comfortable—and splendidly free of those earnest conspirators who haunted the Carlton, or the hearty Marlborough types, or the crusty Rag types, or the lunatics who bearded one at the Savage. The Athenaeum was exactly what he wanted in his old age: dull to the point of screaming. He settled in there.

When servants asked him if he was a member, he answered, "I am the Duke of St. Ormer." Half a dozen members volunteered to have a quiet word with him and let him know that his behavior wasn't quite *comme il faut;* but each of them funked it when he found himself sitting face to face with the duke. So it was quietly and reluctantly decided to do nothing and to send him his bills as if he were a member.

And now here he was turning and biting the middle-class hands that had fed him so magnanimously. It was too bad. "I'm glad you've brought the matter up," the secretary soon found it effective to tell complainants. "I've been looking for someone to take his grace aside for a good man-to-man talk. Since you feel so strongly about it, I know you'll stand no nonsense—so perhaps you'd take it upon yourself?"

Alfred retained his uniquely privileged form of nonmembership. He continued to sit in those sumptuous leather chairs and watch the rising tide of the middle classes swell around him, feeding his impotent anger.

CHAPTER FIFTY

AS THE LAST decade of the century opened, Kaiser Wilhelm's madness rose to a new pitch. He dismissed Bismarck. Europe shuddered. No one had liked the man, but then the need to be liked is a curse in government, as many a democracy has proved. He was one of the rocks in the European landscape. A rock? No, a towering mountain, *ein fester Berg*, one might say. While he dominated Germany, other governments might grumble but they slept of nights. Now? A madman had seized the tiller.

It was exactly the shock the prince had needed. Alfred, like all H.R.H.'s more mature friends, was delighted to note that the prince's talk once again was full of European affairs. The kaiser, no doubt offended by the growing Franco-Russian entente, which H.R.H. had so sedulously promoted after Charles had obtained the text of the secret German-Italian treaty, refused to renew the reinsurance treaty with Russia. Salisbury was alarmed, thinking it a dangerous departure on the part of Germany under her new and not-to-be-trusted ruler.

But the prince, with his forty years of involvement in European diplomacy to steady him, knew better. He detested his nephew Willie; but he did not let that blind him to the fact that the kaiser had done exactly what the crafty old Bismarck would have done. The refusal to renew the treaty was a warning shot across the Russian bows, no more—a signal to alter course.

England's interest was to get the European powers falling into and out of treaties with each other until the moon turned blue. The prince's advice to Salisbury was to prevent the Franco-Russian entente from getting too warm; the last phase of this game, after all, was to be a Franco-*British* entente—and that was to be fanned as hot as all the wind in the diplomatic bellows could manage. "Time to be nice to nephew Willie," he said. "Let's offer him Heligoland in exchange for those two Arab islands, Zanzibar and Pemba. The last Arab rising will have made Germany think twice about the real value of the clove harvest."

"Time, too," he told Alfred, "to think of moving young Lord Charles to Vienna—that's the weak link in the alliance, and therefore in our strategy."

"He has got hold of copies of private letters from the czar to the kaiser asking Willie to think again about letting the treaty lapse. Alexander is trying to arrange a meeting."

"Ah, then perhaps he'd better stay another month or so."

Alfred smiled. "It's marvelous to have you back at the helm, sir."

The prince smiled and looked shrewdly at Alfred. "I suppose you think it was the sudden flurry of international activity that lured me back?"

"Was it not?"

A remote look came into his eyes. "I don't expect anyone to believe it—in fact, uncle, you're the only man who'll ever know this—but the man who put me 'back at the helm' was Lord Charles Beresford."

"Good heavens! I didn't . . . I mean, I'd heard you weren't on speaking terms."

"We aren't. He struck me."

"Struck you as what?"

"Not *as* what. *With* what. With his hands. He struck me with his hands. In the heat of the argument. He pushed me down on a sofa."

Bertie seemed to be making light of it, so Alfred said, "No *man* has ever done that to you."

Bertie laughed and then grew serious again. "But that's what righted my keel, uncle. I thought to myself, 'What sort of person have I become, what sort of figure must I be cutting in the world, if a man like Charlie Beresford, who knows to the tips of his fingers what manner of deference is due to a prince—if such a man can feel able to assault me?' "

"It's about this wretched letter of Daisy Brooke's, I suppose?"

"Yes. So I shan't be too hard on the Beresfords. They're in the right, really, except that they're so pigheaded and holy about it. I'll persuade Daisy to leave London for a bit. She can go down to Easton Lodge and give some splendid house parties. She may write *To meet the Prince of Wales* on every invitation. If Daisy gets out of London for a while, Mina Beresford will surely hand back that letter." He sighed. "Daisy won't like it, of course."

"Tell her that Society is wherever Daisy Brooke is, not the other way round. She's vain enough to believe it."

Bertie shook his head. "You wrong her, uncle. Daisy's an extraordinary woman. When she becomes Countess of Warwick, then you'll all see. She's one of the most startling women of this or any age."

"Aren't they all!" Alfred laughed.

He was remembering that the stable bell at Easton Lodge was especially rung at six in the morning when guests were sleeping in the house—and that the carpets in the corridors were thick enough to deaden even so heavy a footfall as Bertie's. H.R.H.'s reconversion to public duties was clearly to be no monomania. House crawling and baccarat would still own their places.

CHAPTER FIFTY-ONE

HELEN AND Lord Charles were well prepared for Vienna. At the Gare du Nord in Paris, where they broke their journey, there were a hundred and nine pieces of luggage bearing Charles's crest. "*Mais alors!*" the stationmaster said. "*M'en va vous donner deux camions!*" The two monster vans crawled on flat springs over the cobbled streets between there and the Gare de l'Est. Yet every single piece was safely loaded off the express at Vienna two days later.

They rented a "palazzo" (it was in fact no more than a fairly substantial house) in the Landstrasse district, not far from the embassy and very near the Prater, where they could go riding every day, as they did in Rotten Row in London. Vienna was the center of the Haute Ecole style of riding and Helen hoped to become perfect at it during their stay. The owner of the palazzo was an impoverished Italian count, Count Ursini; Vienna was second home—and often first home—to royalties and aristocrats from all over Europe. It really was the Kaiserstadt, or Imperial City, that Berlin aspired to be. (The Viennese called Berlin "Parvenupopolis.") It took a month for the house to be readied to Helen's standards, during which time they stayed at the Erz Herzog Karl Hotel. From there they were swept at once into the social life of Vienna, as narrow as the streets of the old Inner City and as brilliant as they were dark.

"It's like Peking," Lady Moffat, the "chiefess," told Helen. "Did you ever go there?"

Helen shook her head.

"They think all foreigners are barbarians—that's us. We don't count. The social life of this vast empire revolves exclusively around a mere four hundred families, the ones who can show the famous *sechsen Ahnen,* the sixteen quarterings, all royal. They and they alone are fit to be presented at court."

However, any Englishwoman who had been to a drawing room at Buckingham Palace or St. James's was entitled to a presentation at court in Vienna; naturally they turned up at the embassy in their hundreds and it often fell to Helen to introduce them before the year was out. She marveled at the extraordinary assortment of frocks these women considered suitable. One even turned up in a short red thing that showed her ankles—how Helen cringed at the anger in the empress's eyes!

At that time Her Britannic Majesty's Embassy at Vienna was still the channel through which passed all traffic to and from the ambassador in Constantinople. Turkey was the key to Europe's efforts to contain Russia, so traffic was always heavy. Lord Charles was thrown into abstracting and commenting on the flow of messages almost from the day they arrived, but his comments fell on deaf ears at home. Old habits and old enmities die hard.

After three years in Petersburg he was astonished to return to central Europe and find how mesmerized were the other major powers by Russia's supposed might. If Czar Alexander II had not been blown apart by an assassin's bomb ten years earlier, those fears might be justified. Alexander had ended serfdom and liberated those great Russian masses whose power, properly organized, might indeed make Europe, on one border, and America, on the other, tremble. When Alexander left the Winter Palace on that fateful March afternoon, he had folded up a copy of the new Russian constitution, the document that would have made mighty strides toward such a reorganization. "I'll look at that when I come back," he said.

As he was carried, dying, back into the palace, his son and successor seized up the paper and tore it in two—thereby setting the entire Russian empire on a course of internal strife that would surely one day engulf it in blood.

Now Russia was growing weaker, not stronger, with each passing year; it was folly on the part of the other powers to goad her at the edges—as with Turkey—when they should be doing everything they could to shore her up. If Duke Alfred was right, America, already far down the road of republicanism and democracy, would shortly descend into anarchy, out of which would arise a socialist tyranny. France, the republican cancer in Europe, might soon follow. It was madness in the face of these possibilities for the *civilized* powers of Europe—by which he meant those that were governed by monarchies and aristocracies—to vitiate one another's strength with all this sniping and posturing.

Three years in Vienna, among the most charming, the gayest, the most brainless, arrogant, degenerate aristocracy in the world, were to modify these views.

It was late in the spring when Helen and Lord Charles arrived in Vienna. All court functions were over until the following season, so neither could be presented until then. The first party Helen attended was an impromptu ball, or "sauterie," at the German embassy. It was such a spur-of-the-moment affair that only verbal invitations were sent out; yet all the world was there.

"How fortunate," Lady Moffat said. "Now you can meet all our colleagues and all the ladies you need to know in Vienna."

Poor Helen looked longingly at the dance floor; the band was playing the most delicious melodies, full of that Viennese sparkle and gaiety that no other music in the world could match. But it was no use. On the arm of her chiefess she sailed from one splendid room to the next, each more crowded than the last with gorgeously bedecked dowager archduchesses with names that reached back to the foundations of the Holy Roman Empire and the Hapsburg dynasty.

To each Helen made her *plongeon,* a curtsy about a third as deep as that reserved for royalty. Vast bosoms of diamonds and breastplates of emerald and topaz rose and fell in her field of view; sadly polite phrases rained down . . . and then she passed on to the next group and the next. It took all evening.

"Now tomorrow," Lady Moffat said when it was over, "you must leave cards on every one of those ladies. And be sure to remember their names and faces when you meet them again."

Helen astonished her chiefess by complying with both instructions. What Lady Moffat did not know was that Helen, being a *thorough* American, had spent the past six years amassing a photo library of *cartes de visite* and pictures from journals identifying the ladies of all the courts in Europe. She could have introduced her chiefess to more than half the women they had met that evening.

There was one room they had not entered—indeed, they kept strictly from it.

"That's the Contessen-Zimmer," Lady Moffat explained. "The unmarried young ladies of Vienna—the Contessen, as they're called, even if they're princesses—absolutely rule Society at dances. No mother would dare go in there. Princess Metternich tried it once and was shrieked back outside."

Helen noticed that after every dance the unmarried girls withdrew to this room and that the partners to whom they were engaged for the next dance had to go there to seek them out.

"Our diplomatic mothers, especially the Italians and the French, who are used to keeping their young doves firmly beside them between dances, don't like it one bit. But they have no choice. Their daughters, too, must run to the Contessen-Zimmer."

"Yet the young men can go in at will," Helen said in astonishment. "Surely that can lead to compromising—"

"Not at all!" Lady Moffat laughed. "No chaperones can be more severe than the Contessen themselves. Young Count Clam Gallas—this happened during a dance at our own embassy some years ago—young Clam Gallas was seen in a private tête-à-tête with a pretty young lady called Marie Hoyos. Between two marble pillars it was. Well, they simply had to announce their engagement before the evening was over, otherwise she would have been ruined!"

That night in bed Helen slipped her arms around Charles and kissed him passionately.

"What now?" he said, laughing.

"Oh, I'm just so glad that I married into the *English* aristocracy," she said.

"How opposite we are, you and I," he answered. "I'm glad I *didn't.*"

"Silly!" She kissed him again.

They often saw the Empress Elizabeth riding in the Prater in the early morning. The great leafy avenue was almost empty at that hour. Sometimes a thin mist off the Danube would hang among the trees, creating a setting and a scene that neither Helen nor Charles would ever forget: that immaculate horsewoman, sewn into her riding habit each morning, floating gracefully up the avenue with flecks of sunshine dancing on her hair and on the burnished chestnut coat of one of the most superb hunters ever to leave the emerald pastures of Ireland. She acknowledged no one, but cantered by in a dream, lost in silent, mysterious communion with her horse and the ride. At court she was stiff and unbending, mortally terrified, it was said, of doing anything that might cause wrinkles. She neither smiled nor frowned; her face was a perfectly frigid mask. Yet there in the Prater—or, on inclement days, in the Riding School—she was as supple as a two-year-old filly.

The truth was she hated being empress, hated anything to do with the court, did the barest minimum that duty demanded, and did it with bad grace.

When Helen was finally presented it was at a drawing room with about twenty other ladies. To the first the empress said, "Do you ride?" To the second, "Have you any children?" To the third, "Do you ride?" To the fourth, "Have you any children?" To the fifth, "Do you ride?" . . .

As ill luck would have it the tenth lady had lost her two children recently from meningitis. She had worked out from her position in the circle what question was to fall to her, and when it was asked, she burst into tears. The empress immediately turned to Helen, who was eleventh, and asked "Do you ride?"

"I do, your imperial majesty," Helen said.

"Have you any children?" the empress asked the next lady.

And so on around the circle.

"I wanted to shout at her," Helen said to Charles. "I wanted to scream: 'You *know* I ride. We pass each other every bloody day!' She knows what to do. She simply can't be bothered. I think it's dreadful. It's certainly not what I understand by aristocratic behavior."

They heard and saw many other things that ran absolutely counter to their understanding of aristocratic behavior. Baron Rothschild's house looked out on the shabby back wall of a palace belonging to one of the princes. The baron wrote asking if he might not be allowed to restore and decorate it a little, at his own expense, to be sure. The prince replied, *"Ich mache keine Juden Geschäfte"* —I'll have no truck with Jews. The story went around Vienna and he was applauded by the other 399 noble families.

Far worse was the fire at the Ring Theatre with some thousand people inside. Among the audience was an archduke, and so exaggerated was the respect given to royalty that all the other doors were shut until he was got safely out. But half way down the street he became agitated and ran back, saying he must help rescue the others. Already a cordon of troops surrounded the place, and the officers, trying to spare his distress, kept the doors shut and repeatedly assured him that everyone had already escaped. When he finally left, they opened the doors to discover that nine hundred people had died within. A stink like burned pork hung over the city for days.

"I wonder," Helen said, "if the hereditary principle is quite as wonderful as we have always supposed?"

To Charles it was clear that they were a degenerate, inbred group—this Old Aristocracy of Vienna. The women were so tall and so pretty. The men were so short and so wide across the cheekbones. Their degeneracy sprang at you. What worried him far more, as a diplomatist whose job it was to assess Austria as a potential ally, was the deep division in the officer corps between noble and common officers. The common officers knew that no matter how devotedly they worked, any glory going would, if at all possible, be given to the nobility; and the noble officers knew that no matter what a hash they made of things, the blame would, if at all possible, be placed on the commoners. It was a recipe for snatching certain defeat out of the jaws of any potential victory.

He struck up a friendship in the Rotunda of the Prater with some officers of the common variety, who were full of admiration for the English. What had impressed them particularly was the way the Prince of Wales had befriended Baron von Hirsh, one of the despised new aristocracy of Austria, the kind "not fit for court"—and worse, a Jew. The common officers were as violently anti-Semitic as the court (and most of them, being unable to live on their pay, were heavily in debt to Jews); they nevertheless admired a prince who could so unbend as to befriend someone like Von Hirsh.

"Not only that," Charles told them, "he has many friends who are radicals, and commoners. I mean real friends. And he expects everyone in Society to entertain them, too."

"No!" they chorused in disbelief.

They stared in amazement at one another. And in a flash Charles understood why the English aristocracy would survive when all the glittering and gilded butterflies of the Hapsburgs, the Romanoffs, and the Hohenzollerns had gone the way of the Orléans. And there was no doubt they would go. The smell of apocalypse was in the very air.

"Let us cherish these years in Vienna," he told Helen, "and our memories of Berlin and Petersburg. We have been privileged to see Europe at the very pinnacle of her brilliance. This elegance, this polish, this gaiety, will all soon pass away. Don't you feel it?"

"In violence? Do you mean war? Is war coming?"

"I hope not. It won't touch England, anyway. We know how to yield."

CHAPTER FIFTY-TWO

THE SERVANTS at the palazzo were inherited from the landlord, Count Ursini. In time Helen got to know all of them by sight and name. But there was one couple who walked in and out, perfectly at ease, whose function she could not discover. At last, after pressing the steward, it came out that they were Italian peasants off the Ursini estates, people to whom the Count owed some kind of favor. He had said they could live there for life in one of the cellars.

"Then he must take them to wherever he is living now," Helen said. "He may rent out his palace but not his obligations."

She went down to see the couple and discovered an entire extended family, cousins, aunts, uncles, and grandparents—nine adults and countless children—living in appalling squalor in two cellars. They survived entirely on scraps sent down from the kitchens, eked out by what they could beg in the streets.

Ursini was not the least abashed, but seemed to think the whole affair too trivial to take seriously. "Surely," he laughed, "it is a little matter for representatives of the two richest countries in the world? What harm are these people? You've had them for two years without knowing it—what harm will two more do?"

"We're not talking about harm, count, but about responsibility. They are your responsibility."

He gestured around his tiny, threadbare apartment. "I can hardly have them here."

"Of course not. But you must make other arrangements. They cannot stay on at the palazzo."

Ursini grumbled and promised to do something; but weeks dragged into months without any action.

"We must simply turn them out," Charles said, when his patience was at last exhausted. "Force his hand."

"But we can't," Helen protested. "It's not Christian."

"I don't like it any more than you. But unless we do something of the sort, there's no pressure on him to—"

"Let's just withhold the rent."

"The chief wouldn't approve of that. Besides it's not due for four months."

So, reluctantly, they agreed to turn the family out. But that reluctance delayed them two fatal weeks, during which time the family was joined by yet another Italian relative—who immediately went down with cholera, which was rampant at Naples.

The palazzo was at once put in quarantine; it became, in effect, a fever hospital. All over the city engagements and functions were canceled in a quite needless panic. The Inner City emptied as the nobility left for nearby country houses. The empress even stopped riding in the Prater. And who was blamed? The immigration official who had allowed in a visitor from Naples? No—his daughter was an archduke's mistress. Count Ursini? No—he had a dozen relatives among the Old Nobility. The ones to blame were clearly the Englishman and his American wife.

What had his father been? An apothecary's apprentice! And wasn't the fellow, this so-called "duke," still engaged in trade? And *her* father—a Chicago hog killer! *Lord* and *Lady* Charles Boyce—what sort of nobility was that! Reeking of factories and pig dung, it was too unsure of itself to do a simple thing like evicting a bunch of Italian parasites. That's what came of a parvenu, cosmopolitan aristocracy like the English—consorting with radicals and tradesmen and even Jews. "How right we are, you see," they assured one another, "to insist on our sixteen quarterings. It is the only guarantee against a menace to Society like this 'Lord and Lady' Charles."

Charles's usefulness as a diplomatist at the Austro-Hungarian court was at an end. But at that moment it was the least of his worries. For both their children had gone down with the cholera.

Sir Kenneth Macleod, one of London's greatest physicians,

happened to be in Salzburg at the time and came at once to Vienna. He owned an estate at Great Marlow and knew the duke well. By the time he arrived, both children, Michael, then just nine, and Katherine, almost six, were well advanced in the second stage of the disease. Unfortunately, the first stage had not been treated particularly wisely. The children had been allowed all the water they wanted, and they cried incessantly for it. No antipurgatives had been given, nor poultices. As a result both were now vomiting incessantly and the familiar "rice-water" evacuation was more-or-less continuous. Sir Kenneth noted the patches of stomach lining in the bowls, and hid his concern beneath a mask of grave professional cheer. "I've seen worse," he told the parents. "A great deal worse." He omitted to say that the "worse" he referred to was, in fact, the third stage—toward which both children were now deteriorating fast.

"Both have an excellent pulse," he said. "That's the very best sign. Their general health, before this happened, was good, I take it?"

"Very good," Helen said. "Though Michael always had a delicate tummy."

He answered as if she had not spoken this qualification: "Good! Very few of those whose previous health is sound actually die of this sickness."

He gave the children opium and acetate of lead, put mustard poultices on their stomachs, ordered the water to be taken away and sent for ice instead. Within hours they showed signs of improvement. The vomiting and "rice-water" discharge almost stopped, and the ice helped to convince them they were not "burning up," as they had often complained of feeling. But their pulses grew fainter and the cramps more intense.

Helen and Charles exhausted themselves in massaging the little legs and arms to soothe the muscular spasms, until the children moaned at the soreness of their skin from all the rubbing. Sir Kenneth sent for powdered ginger, which acted partly as an anesthetic and partly as a talcum, to reduce the friction.

By nightfall the two little ones had passed into the third stage. Their pulse could not be felt. They began to breathe rapidly and shallowly. It almost broke their parents' hearts to see how weak and shriveled they were from dehydration. Their faces were sunk inward on their bones and their eyes were quite hollow. Their temperature fell below normal. Sir Kenneth gave them enemas of warm beef tea and allowed them small draughts of dilute sulphuric acid in iced water. Hot-water bottles were sent for to keep them warm. Both of them complained constantly of the cold—and of thirst.

Just before midnight the steward announced that the ice company men had become unwilling to visit the house. By luck Lady Moffat, who, assuming diplomatic immunity as if it were medical too, had swept past the quarantine guards almost hourly, arrived moments later. Within the hour she had organized a fleet of English nannies who spent the rest of the night wheeling blocks of ice through the streets of Vienna in bassinets, bath chairs, and perambulators.

Charles, remembering his physical chemistry, crushed two thirds of it and mixed it with salt to make a freezing mixture, which he put in the bath. The remainder, in cast-iron pots imbedded in the mixture, remained frozen for over twelve hours.

"Mama, are Kathy and I destined to die?" Michael asked a little before dawn.

His high-flown choice of words helped Helen to smile as she answered, "Of course not, dear, but you are very ill. Do you want anything?"

"I want to sleep but I can't."

"I know. I know, my darling. Just try to rest."

Birds were singing. Horses and traffic were passing to and fro in the streets outside. A tug hooted from the Vienna Canal. It seemed grotesque that ordinary life could be starting up again so unconcernedly out there.

"I think I might like to try some extreme unction now," Michael said.

Helen could only stare at him.

"What's that, old chap?" Charles asked.

"Extreme unction," the boy repeated. "It's what they always give to people who are extremely ill. I'd like to try some."

"Me too!" Katherine whispered. "Please, please, please."

"It might do me good," Michael added.

Charles looked at Sir Kenneth. "Out of the mouths of babes and sucklings . . ." the physician said.

"You think we should send for the Reverend Dawes?" Helen asked.

"If you believe in such nonsense," Sir Kenneth told her, his irritability betraying his anxiety for the first time. "It can do no harm."

He left the room and returned ten minutes later with some coarse bread moistened in cold milk. "They can often keep down food at this stage which they would have rejected earlier." He let

Helen feed it, morsel by morsel. "I'm sorry for what I said," he told her.

"You've been marvelous," she assured him.

The children remained in that condition, craving sleep and water, and shivering with the cold, until well into the afternoon. Then Michael's temperature began to rise.

"Is that a good thing?" Helen asked anxiously.

"Most probably," Sir Kenneth said. "As long as it doesn't rise above normal."

Within half an hour it was around 100°. Sir Kenneth said gravely, "You must send for the Reverend Dawes, I'm afraid."

"Oh, no!" Helen's whisper pleaded.

"Is there nothing more you can do?" Charles asked.

His eyes met theirs and they understood how little hope there was now. The chaplain was sent for.

Michael lay in a semicoma, his breathing very shallow and rapid. His half-opened eyes seemed filmed over; the pupils were mere points and the whites so bloodshot they seemed more red than pink. His skin, too, was dusky red and clammy with cold sweat.

Before the chaplain had finished the last rites, Michael gave a series of low, rapid moans, like deliberately babyish attempts at a song; then he fell into a deep coma. Later his breathing slowed until it was—forever—still.

"No!" Helen stared at the suddenly frozen little body, so emaciated, and so *wrong* in color. "No . . . *no!*"

What had gone from him? What was different between now and ten seconds earlier? If only she could capture it and force it back into him! She wept.

Charles put his arm around her. She rose from her knees and fell into him, needing all his silent strength, wanting it to engulf her.

"Katherine's temperature is starting to rise," Sir Kenneth said.

It cut across their grief; for that moment they had forgotten they had another child. Now, for a somewhat longer moment, they forgot the one who was gone.

Minute by minute Katherine's temperature rose, though by the smallest fractions of a degree. It took over half an hour to reach 98°. Helen was surprised to realize that the chaplain was still in the room.

Katherine's breathing grew slower and deeper; by everyday standards it was still alarmingly unnatural, but compared with Michael's at the end it was like a deep repose.

After an hour there was no doubt she was sleeping at peace rather than in deep coma. "Now," Sir Kenneth said, "all we have to do is nurse her back to health. Perhaps, padre, you'd say a prayer?"

Several weeks were to pass before Katherine could be safely pronounced out of danger. She developed a number of nasty abscesses, which caused her to cry a lot with the pain; and once she passed blood. But at least the constant need to nurse her helped to distract Helen from her grief at the death of Michael. It was many weeks before she thought to ask about the Italians in the cellar.

"They've all gone," Charles told her uncomfortably.

"Gone!"

"It seems the newspapers didn't share the views of Society. They laid the blame entirely on Ursini, poor fellow. He came here one night, put all the Italians in a sealed van, and took them out to a farm near Neusiedl, where he locked them in a barn."

Helen was appalled. "No doctor? No medicines?"

"He went to get a doctor, but when they returned, the barn had burned to the ground and everyone in it had died."

He did not tell her that the wags of Vienna were calling it "Ursini's private Ring Theatre."

Helen was aghast, unable to voice the thoughts that sprang to mind.

"The doctor confirmed it," Charles added. "We mustn't speculate, not even to each other. We will have to go on meeting Ursini socially."

"Never! We shall return to England."

"I'm afraid not, my dearest. Even that has changed. Vienna is having an orgy of sympathy for us, and . . ."

Helen snorted in fury.

Charles hugged her to pacify this anger. "It is as shallow as their former condemnation. You mustn't apply *our* standards to them, darling. They are children, with all the rashness of children, all their lack of keel, all their violence and passion—but also all their gaiety and spontaneous affection and charm. We mustn't let what happened poison our judgment and the rest of our time . . ."

"We're staying?" She still could not believe it.

"We have to. We aren't free agents; we represent England here, not ourselves. To leave now would be seen as an insult. They feel guilty. Our going would throw it in their faces and deny them a chance to make amends. I know you can't contemplate it now, but when we're out of deep mourning, we're going to find a Vienna that never did so much to sweeten the visit of any other English family."

She shook her head, only half following him.

"For a month or so, at least." He smiled. "Until the next wonder engulfs them—a troupe of calculating dogs, or a ballerina in a bottle!"

When the duke and duchess and Lady Bullen-Chetwynne traveled out to Vienna, Helen understood the importance of one aspect of Michael's death, an aspect she had overlooked until now. The ducal line once again ended with Charles; after him it fell into abeyance until Katherine grew up, married, and had a son—if she did all those things. Failing that, the abeyance was between Emily, Louise, and Felicity, Charles's sisters. Fortunately, Helen had reassuring news for her parents-in-law. She had suspected herself to be pregnant even before the cholera struck; now she was certain. The child, which would be born early the following summer, had better be male. If it were another girl, Katherine could produce a hundred sons and the title would still be in abeyance, this time between her and her as-yet-unborn sister.

Alfred and Flora would have come earlier if Flora had not been half-eaten with rheumatism. Her hip, especially, was one ball of pain, whether she used it or no. She had to retire to her bed as soon as she arrived. It was, in any case, a few days short of the two months that had to elapse before any of the family could go about in Society, so no other etiquette could rule them.

Only very sketchy accounts, much garbled, had reached the English papers, and Charles, in his letters, had spared his people most of the details. Now they had to be told all.

Even to Charles and Helen it now seemed inexcusable that they had not at once got rid of the Italians. True, the very idea of cholera could not have been further from their thoughts; they had merely seen poverty and wretchedness and had tried to respond to it with a Christian spirit until they could awaken Ursini to his responsibilities. But now even that compassion seemed itself unpardonable. *Nothing* ought to have come before their duty to their own children and to the dukedom.

Charles tried to take all the blame on himself—which, perversely, made Flora assume that Helen had been entirely responsible. In no time her anger became quite ungovernable.

"She's murdered the line!" Flora shrieked.

Helen, whose anguish and bitter self-recrimination had overflowed for weeks, collapsed under this onslaught. Charles led her weeping from the room and made sure she took a draught before he returned—angry as never before in his life—to his parents.

"Lady Bullen-Chetwynne, I must require you to leave us," he said.

"Stay!" Alfred commanded.

"This is my house, your grace. I must insist."

"Charles, my dear boy! Your mother is not well, we've had a dreadful journey. The fog in the Channel was like soup—the whole of Europe was cut off—and you know how nervous it makes your mother—"

"Do not talk about me as if I were not here," Flora shouted.

"No, dear. Don't distress yourself now, please." He turned back to his son. "Her rheumatics are a torment and her hip is one unending hell. She doesn't really mean—"

"I will not have your making excuses for me! I meant every word of it. I was against that marriage from the start."

Alfred shrugged at Charles. "You see? She's rambling . . ."

Charles was shivering with anger. Hermione, who had never seen him show any kind of passion, began to grow quite worried for him.

"Your graces must stay tonight," Charles said icily. "There is now no alternative. My carriage will be at your pleasure tomorrow morning to take you to the hotel that Josef, the steward, will meanwhile arrange. Lady Bullen-Chetwynne, we have no quarrel with you so please do not feel obliged to go, too. I'll bid you all good night."

"Charles! . . . Charles!" Alfred was torn between wanting to run after him and staying to comfort Flora, who was weeping loudly, half in rage, half in dreadful pain.

But Charles was relentless. He was just finishing a letter to his father, insisting that all communication between them must be by letter only—and confined to necessary business—when Hermione slipped quietly into his study. "D'you mind?" she asked.

Charles, who loathed being angry, smiled ruefully at her, glad of a chance to smile at all. He rose and placed a chair for her.

In the candlelight the legendary beauty of her youth still seemed to cling about her. Those eyes were still large and dark, and they gleamed with a brightness that belied her sixty-three years. Her blond hair had darkened to silver but its luster was undimmed. Her skin, which the rays of the sun had never touched, was still pale and smooth, furrowed only by the lines of much laughter. It was said that to see her was to fall in love with her; Charles remembered the legends and believed them.

She looked at the letter, still unfolded on the bureau. "To the duke?" she asked.

He nodded.

"Well," she said, "I can guess what's in it. Tell me, Charles, what do they think of you in London?"

"The F. O., you mean?"

"They think you're a good diplomatist, I'm sure. Tell me what you think they'll make of this."

Charles shifted uncomfortably. He had been so sure of the rightness of his anger, as chivalrous protection for Helen, that its external consequences had not crossed his mind.

"What would they make of a public quarrel between the Duke and Duchess of St. Ormer and their son, the Second Secretary, here in the Imperial City?"

He snorted.

"It won't do, Charlie, will it?"

He could not look her in the eye. "They may have a suite here in the palazzo. We shall communicate by letter—until the duchess apologizes to Lady Charles."

Hermione smiled. "And, of course, you'll dismiss all your servants and hire blind deaf mutes in their places!"

Charles breathed heavily for a while; Hermione wisely said nothing.

"She must apologize," Charles said at last. "It was unforgivable."

"It was *almost* unforgivable. Don't exaggerate. Actually, when the time comes, you're going to find it surprisingly easy to forgive. You'll remind yourself of the terrible strain your mother's been under, and the almost constant pain she endures—like a *saint,* I may say. And you'll be astonished how easy it is to forgive. Only don't make her apology a condition of anything. Treat her with the sympathy she deserves and it will follow, I promise you."

The anger went out of him. "You make me feel so childish," he said.

"*I* do?" She mocked surprise. "I didn't imagine you'd left me anything to achieve in that line."

He mimed surrender. "I don't suppose the world will ever know what we—our family I mean—owes you, aunt Hermione."

Her eyes leveled with his for a long moment. "It's bad enough," she said, "that the recording angel has it all down. That's nightmare enough for one frail old lady, I'm sure."

Helen required more persuading than Charles had needed before she agreed to ignore what had happened—but in the end she consented. Next morning Charles decided to take the breakfast tray in to his mother.

The sight of her shocked him. In the excitement of yesterday, first of greeting, then of the argument, he had not really looked at her. How she had aged! And she had obviously lain awake in pain most of the night; her eyes were fire-red. He felt dreadful now, especially when he saw the joy in her eyes at his entry.

"Marvelous news," he said. "Helen is with child."

She laughed and cried and said his name a dozen times; tears of happiness fell down her cheeks. Then, still excited, she rolled herself out of bed, moaning at the pain, and insisted on hobbling along to Helen, who was still in bed—where she repeated the whole performance. Flora sent her son into exile for an hour and treated Helen as if she were already near to term—and with a first baby at that.

"Your mother hasn't looked so well for twelve months," Alfred told him.

As soon as their two months of deep mourning was out, the women were able to sew black silk flounces onto their plain bombazine dresses and to wear black silk gloves and shawls.

Helen breathed a great sigh of relief. "You and aunt Hermione," she told Flora, "always remained duchess and lady, even in the plainest things. But I felt so horribly classless." She laughed. "Hark at me! Now let anyone dare call me American! But it's true." She was serious again. "Is that right, d'you think? Ought I to need flounces and fine clothes before I feel like Lady Charles?"

Flora's days of being a new duchess were so far behind her that she had to think a moment. "If I saw a duchess wearing silk in deep mourning," she said at last, "I'd suspect her of not being quite sure of herself. The old Duchess of Manchester—you never knew her—she'd have done it. She never even knew when to enter or leave a room. And if I saw a cook with a black silk hat in deep mourning, I'd also know she wasn't too sure of her tenure as cook. That's the thing, you see, dear—be sure of your station, know its rights and duties, exercise both as effortlessly as possible, and you'll live a life of true ease. Hah!" She was delighted at bringing together ideas that had lodged in her mind for years without coalescing. "If you want to be unhappy, try to live sixpence beyond your income and one rung above your station all your life. There!"

Helen laughed. "You should write all these things down, duchess. You could be a Samuel Smiles for women."

"I fear not," Flora said. "D'you know, I saw John Murray only last spring. He isn't looking at all well, by the way. He told me that Mr. Smiles was proposing to write a new book to follow *Self-Help* and *Thrift* and that other one."

"Duty?"

"Yes, *Duty*. He wants to call this one *Conduct*. And Murray told me he doesn't think he'll be able to publish it. The book won't sell. There now! There's a sign. The only books in that line will be *How to Become Very Rich* or *How to Be a Great Success*. Isn't that dreadful? I think people are in for a most unhappy time. I'm so glad to have lived when I did. I envy you a little, but my grandchildren not at all. There now, hark at *me!* What a thing to say to you in your condition! Pay no attention to me, my dear. I'm getting old and I say lots of things I don't really mean."

Helen knew this was the nearest Flora could get to an apology. She put her arms around the old lady and hugged her.

CHAPTER FIFTY-THREE

THE BLACK SILK flounces were barely sewn on before the invitation came from the British Embassy and the social round began once more. The gay, incompetent nobility of Vienna who had so viciously mocked the Apothecary Duke and his duchess now came like blind archers to see if their darts had even gone near the targets.

What they saw was so different from their expectations that their later gossip could find no words to encompass it.

"He's like a terrible chief of police," said one.

"No, a judge," another said. "A chief justice."

"What an empress she would make!"

"I wonder why their companion, that Lady Bullen-*Wiewass*, is in full mourning too. Surely she isn't family—or is she?" They made a great deal of that.

Alfred represented a being so far outside their experience that their vocabulary could not cope with him: He was a *working, professional* aristocrat! True, their own emperor, the beloved Franz, was something of the same sort—but he was an emperor. This fellow was an ordinary duke, not even an archduke. So they evoked judges and police chiefs to describe the sense of authority and dedication that Alfred could not help radiating. The wonder lasted about eleven days, after which the duke and duchess could have driven in an open landau from Kaisermühlen to Schönbrunn without fear of recognition.

Word of all this soon reached the empress, who, without delay, sent them her own invitation—in effect a command to appear at the Hofburg. Alfred went in court dress but with the silver buckles oversewn with crape; the only color—unavoidably—was the enormous blue diagonal of the Garter sash. He omitted all his other decorations, wearing instead a ribbon bar slighted with black.

"Is that correct?" Hermione wondered nervously.

"Whatever an English duke chooses to do at a *foreign* court is naturally correct," he said calmly.

At the Hofburg they were told it was to be a private audience. Charles and the ladies were led away, not to a drawing room but to the winter gardens at the back of the palace. Alfred, a little bewildered, was conducted to the Riding School.

The Empress Elizabeth was unmistakable. Her immaculate riding habit hung about her as if a painter had draped it. She sat her horse, a pure Lipizzaner stallion, as if she grew out of it. It obeyed her as if her mind were its own.

For a while she did not see him. Lost to the world, she guided the horse through *piaffe* and *passage, travers* and *pirouette, passade* and *renvers*, making the animal seem born to move that way and no other. Alfred could not help applauding.

She looked up, recognized him by description, smiled, and rose at once in a levade by way of salute. "How does your grace," she said.

"How does your imperial majesty?" He bowed. This informality angered him but he did not show it.

She trotted over to him—a trot that was like a ballet movement. At once his anger melted. She had that rare, vibrant quality which Hermione had possessed in her youth, and still possessed for him. He forgot she was an empress. He even forgot she was a foreigner. She became . . . desirable.

The fact communicated at once, as such things do. Her eyes sparkled. "Do you ride?" she asked.

"Yes," he said. Then, remembering what Helen had told him, he added impishly, "And, yes, I have some children."

Suppressing a smile, she raised her schooling whip and pretended to strike him. "You mustn't tease," she said. Her English was as flawless as her riding. "If only you knew how I *loathe* ceremony. And how glad I am to meet you like this. Say you don't mind —please—or I shall be so desolate."

"I am delighted ma'am. Truly." To his own great surprise, he found he was not lying.

She beckoned to someone behind her, without a backward glance. Alfred had once watched Queen Victoria and the Empress Eugénie sit down in the imperial box at the Paris Opéra. Victoria had simply sat down, absolutely confident that her chair would be pushed beneath her; but Eugénie had given the briefest glance behind her first. Thus does the born sovereign distinguish herself from the parvenue. Elizabeth, by her gesture, placed herself firmly among the former.

At once a groom came forward out of the shadows at the farther end of the great arena, leading a stallion that might have been the twin of the empress's mount.

"Let me see you," she challenged.

He was about to protest that he was in court dress, but some merriment in her eye made the objection seem mere caviling even before he spoke it. "Very well," he said, handing his hat and stick to the equerry.

For a moment he feared he was, in essence, going right back to his first day at Chalfont Abbey, when Duke Augustus had mounted him on a mettlesome thoroughbred filly that had bolted with him up the marble staircase. But he was long since familiar enough with horses to know this was to be no such occasion. The spirit of a Lipizzaner is in its willingness and its immense strength; no fiery, nervous steed could have progressed so far through the school as this one obviously had.

Alfred had never ridden *haute école*, so he attempted none of the complicated maneuvers the empress had displayed, but he executed all the basic movements of dressage. This was the best-schooled horse he had ever ridden. There was nothing it could not do. It was equally supple and willing on both hands—something he had never experienced before. In half a pace he could ride it onto its forehand, then, with the merest squeeze, he could gather it onto its hindquarters. Cantering up the long side of the school, it would do as many flying changes as he asked. It would halt from the canter and canter from the halt.

"Well?" she asked as he trotted up and halted beside her.

"He's far and away the best dressage horse I ever sat, ma'm," he told her.

"He is yours. I make you a present of him."

He began to protest but she cut him short. "You may ride him for another ten minutes. I will be quick." And she cantered away and out of the school.

It was actually closer to half an hour before she reappeared, but to Alfred, so delighted was he with his new stallion, it passed like five minutes.

"Bravo!" she interrupted him, standing in the spectators' gallery where he had first stood. "Now you must escort me to your family."

Reluctantly he dismounted and let them lead the horse away. "What is his name?" he asked.

"It's for you to say."

"I'll call him—with your imperial majesty's most gracious permission, of course—I'll call him Elizabeth."

She laughed and took his arm. How little she needed to move her face to convey all her moods! "Silly," she said.

"Something else will come to me," he promised. "At the moment I am intoxicated by his excellence, and the only name I can possibly associate with such excellence is your own."

"Is it true that the very first day you ever sat a horse, you rode it at the gallop up a marble staircase?"

"Something of the sort. I don't know which of us was more frightened. But fancy your hearing of it. And so long ago, ma'am!"

"That story, duke, went around Europe."

"What an achievement to be known for!"

"Oh but we know a great deal more about you, sir. The Prince of Wales often talks of his 'uncle.' That's why we already feel we know you so well. And he speaks so affectionately, too. Naturally, we have caught the mood from him." She chuckled. "Will you really call that stallion 'Elizabeth'?"

"Unless I am commanded not to. I realize it's not conventional, but we are here to make new conventions."

She halted and stroked his blackened ribbon bar with one lean, gloved finger. "So I see," she answered. "This is naughty—but in a moment you'll see why I am not very angry." She smiled a secret promise and then, quite suddenly, became solemn. "I was sorry about your grandson Michael."

"Your imperial majesty is most gracious to say so."

"I know something of that sort of bereavement." She meant, of course, the dreadful suicide of her son Rudolph at Mayerling.

"Yours was a bereavement which touched all Europe, ma'am. Her grace and I certainly felt and shared it."

Just as suddenly she smiled again. The corners of her lips moved barely a quarter of an inch but her face was radiant once more. "I hate death, and talk of death." She continued their walk, still on his arm.

Her dress was a brocade of that mauve-magenta hue she favored to the exclusion of the rest of the rainbow. It was shot with silver thread so fine it seemed almost to hang an inch or two in front of the material, like a haze or something crystalline. It rustled like half a dozen unclouded invitations. He trembled to be so near her.

She knew quite well what effect her charm had on him, and she relished it. "Bertie tells us you frighten his mother. Is that true? You don't frighten me."

"I don't frighten her majesty either. He is very"—he picked the word she had used earlier—"naughty to say it."

The word evidently reminded the empress of unfinished business. "Ah, yes," she said and looked about her. They were approaching a door barred by two liveried footmen, who were preparing to open it. "Let me have that rosette off your hose," she told one of them.

He, evidently the senior of the pair, was wearing dark-blue, almost black rosettes at the sides of his calves. Without demur he knelt and removed one. It was held by a spring clasp. The other footman hastened to fetch a silver tray, which lay in an embrasure nearby. He handed it to the first, who placed the rosette upon it and proffered it to the empress. She took it and turned to Alfred.

"If you are to make a new convention, let it at least be elegant. This"—she flicked his ribbon bar dismissively—"is mere utility." She pinned the rosette to his Garter sash.

She knew her colors well. The blue of the sash killed what little blue there was in the rosette and turned it black. Nevertheless, it was the sort of thing that no one, not even an empress, did to a Garter sash. He drew breath to protest.

But she, raising a finger to her lips, forestalled him—as if to say, "Wait, and you'll see."

The walk to the winter gardens was interminable. "I'm taking you the long way around," she said. "I thought you might like to see . . . the Mirror Room."

She timed it perfectly. As she spoke the words, two footmen threw wide the doors on the magnificent baroque chamber which had played such a vital role at the Congress of Vienna almost eighty years earlier.

"I love to think of them all here," she said. "I can almost see them and hear them—Metternich, Hardenberg, Nesselrode, and, of course, Wellington and Talleyrand. All handing out Napoleon's Europe to each other like so much booty. You take Trieste, we'll have Heligoland, they can have Herzegovina . . . and what about Piedmont?" She stopped dramatically. "Here! In this very room."

"Would you like to have been alive then, ma'am?" he asked.

"To listen to such arrogance?" She made a *fui!* of disgust. Then she smiled. "No, I'll tell you when I'd like to have been here: six months later, among that ragtag of royalty who danced and feasted here for half a year and then—it wasn't in this room, it was over in the Court Theatre—all gathered to see *The Interrupted Dance.* Hah! God himself surely chose that title. And the chamberlain walked on the stage and dropped his thunderbolt: Napoleon had escaped! Napoleon had landed in France! Napoleon was marching on Paris! Yes, I would give the rest of my life, whatever it may be, to go back and witness *that* 'interrupted dance.' You knew Napoleon III, of course, duke. What did you think of him?"

They resumed their walk through the Hofburg.

Diplomatically Alfred told her of the incident at the Paris Opéra, and why, when he had seen her beckoning without turning in the Riding School earlier, he had been reminded of it. Naturally she was delighted.

"Yes, they were parvenus, both of them. You know how he got that Roman III after his name? It was a printer's error. The proclamation of his seizure of power ended *Vive Napoléon !!!,* with three exclamation marks, you see? The printer misread the handwriting and put *Vive Napoléon III* with a Roman III. And Louis, because he was an opportunist to his fingertips, said, 'Let it stand so'! He saw the value of it you see—continuity. It's what we all want."

"Good heavens!" Alfred was fascinated. "Is that true? Really?"

"No," she smiled. "It's even *more* than true."

She was just as vivacious when they reached the winter gardens. She saw at once that Flora was in pain and insisted on sending for a bath chair. She told Hermione that the Chalfont Abbey winter gardens were famous, even here in faraway Vienna. She commiserated with Lord and Lady Charles, and somehow divined that Helen was pregnant. She wished them a son and long life to him and them. She captivated them all.

"And now," she said, shooing them into a group but plucking Alfred toward her, "my surprise." She turned to Alfred. Again there was that lightning change of mood and pace; she was as schooled as any of her horses. "Your grace, most noble sir, I beg you will do me the honor of allowing me to install you in the Royal Hungarian Order of Maria Theresa. It is the only order entirely within my personal gift."

Alfred collected himself so quickly that the others swore later he had been forewarned—and so he was, though only in the general sense that he was by now attuned to her mercurial changes of mood. "Your imperial majesty, you do me too great an honor . . ." he began.

"It's a mark of my esteem," she said, conversational again. "Come and kneel here where her grace may see you clearly."

Flora smiled and nodded; at last the courts of Europe were awakening to the sterling character her duke possessed. It was fitting.

Charles, watching his father go through the ceremony as if he had been born to it, pondered on that mysterious quality which set such a man apart. He had seen the old man's effect on Viennese society; it was as if Metternich or Wellington had come back to walk among them. He knew he himself would never possess it. Sadly he reflected once again that his father would be the last real Duke of St. Ormer. He looked at his mother. She had fallen asleep but was smiling still.

Now Alfred understood why Elizabeth had not been angry at his leaving off his orders and decorations, and why she had been so insistent on slighting his Garter sash with the near-black rosette. Nothing now competed with the gorgeous brown and gold of the Order of Maria Theresa. And, he reflected, for this day alone that was proper.

"I do this also," she said when the ceremony was over, "to show the Old Nobility what I think of them. I go abroad whenever I can, but that's so negative. Now, like this, I show them who I think is a *real* nobleman, and that's so much more positive."

Alfred went to let Flora see and handle the Order. "My dear?"

As he bent toward her something in her attitude told him she was dead. Perhaps because they were in mourning and death was never far from their thoughts, the others were quick to grasp the fact too.

Dead! The word was meaningless. It suddenly filled the universe with its utter lack of meaning. Dead. For a moment he faced an almost overpowering urge to break down. Then there was a reaction, astonishing in its savagery—Flora had deserted him! She had no right to go on ahead like this. It, too, passed, leaving an intimation of the lonely years ahead, years that would be infinitely more lonely but for Hermione.

There was the swish of a dress. The empress was coming up behind him, wanting to share Flora's delight. He knew, suddenly, that she would not be able to grasp the fact of this death. He straightened and turned to her. "She's sleeping," he said. "Please let's leave her. She gets so little sleep these days. Take Lady

Bullen-Chetwynne and show her these wonderful flowers, she would so appreciate it." He looked at Hermione.

"Oh, I would, your imperial majesty," Hermione said, quickly going to the empress.

Alfred sat beside Flora and waited until the two ladies were out of earshot. "You realize what's happened?" he said to Charles.

His son nodded carefully and looked at Helen, who returned his gaze steadily.

"We'll wheel her out in the chair, as if she were asleep. And we'll pretend to help her into the carriage and then go directly to the embassy. She'll be registered as having died there."

"Oh, father . . ."

"Don't go to pieces now. Understand why we must do this—and remember who you are. We cannot indulge ourselves."

It was an effort but Charles managed it. When he was calmer he said, "We'll *have* to leave Vienna now, Helen and I. If we are in mourning and can't move in Society, we're useless to the embassy."

"Yes. They won't expect you to stay now. Come home with us."

"I think she knew," Helen said suddenly. "She told me the other day she was glad to have lived when she did. She said she'd had a happy life. D'you think she knew?"

"We all know," Alfred said. "It's the only common certainty for all of us. Hermione has the yacht down at Trieste. We can go back by sea. God, I couldn't face two more months of deep mourning in England!"

The others said nothing.

"Does that sound unfeeling?" he asked. "This death is a release for her. I'll mourn her in time, I know. Hermione and I will mourn her for all time. But at this moment, remembering her pain and her saintly endurance of it, I sing for her release."

"It's as if we're all sitting here waiting," Helen said.

They did as Alfred had asked, taking their leave of Elizabeth with smiles, even joking at how angry Flora would be when she heard how they'd let her sleep on and so breach all the rules of etiquette. But as Alfred looked back and saw Elizabeth standing perplexed and uncertain among those great banks of flowers, he knew she had guessed and was too fearful to speak. He knew, too, that he could not leave it there.

He went back to her and took her hand, pressing it to his lips. "What better place," he asked, "than here amid such beauty? What better hour than the proudest of her life, and of her husband's life, too? What better company than that of Europe's most gracious lady?" His smile was relentless.

"To die?" she asked, bewildered, needing to hear it said aloud.

"To rest."

"Ah, yes. To rest among flowers. To die among flowers. Wish it for me, too, dear cousin."

"I don't suppose we'll meet again, but if you come to England, dear empress, you know how very welcome you'll be at Chalfont Abbey."

"If not, we'll meet in heaven—or hell." That sudden radiance of her smile. "I have good connections in both places."

CHAPTER FIFTY-FOUR

HELEN'S BABY was a girl. They swallowed their disappointment, put a brave face on it, and christened her Hope.

But for Alfred hope seemed over the horizon. He began to despair of a male line. He had chosen Helen Graham partly because of the high proportion of males in their progeny—and here were two daughters to one son; it even made him doubt the wisdom of all the livestock-improvement schemes he had promoted on the estate.

One general solution occurred to him. An heir apparent to a title should be permitted to father a son on a girl before he was obliged to marry her—though of course the girls who couldn't deliver what was required would have to be provided for. He made a list of dukedoms that had become extinct during the century: Ancaster and Kesteven, Buckingham and Chandos, Cleveland, Dorset, and Gordon; five per hundred years. At that rate all the dukedoms would be extinct within four centuries. It was alarming.

One day at the Lords he outlined his scheme to the Archbishop of Canterbury—who at first thought he was joking. When it became clear that Alfred was serious, the archbishop looked around him with a caged worry that rapidly turned to fear.

"But see here, St. Ormer, dukedoms must go into extinction," he tried at length. "Or there'd be no room for new ones."

"Ah! But there is, you see, Canterbury. At the beginning of the century we had twenty-seven dukedoms and the population was—

what?—about fifteen million? Most of the people living in the kingdom could look to the protection of one or other members of the nobility."

"And a poor job they made of it, by all accounts!"

"With an unreformed church, remember. Surely you're not going to say that with the church as she is today we couldn't do a great deal better! But what's the population now, eh? Soon be forty-five million, three times as many! My question is this—why aren't there seventy-five dukes, eh? Five went extinct and we've made five more. That's no way to keep pace. There should be seventy-five dukes, sixty-six marquises, four-hundred-odd earls, a hundred and twenty viscounts, and about a thousand barons. *And*"—he dug the archbishop's ribs hard enough to make the man wince—"ninety bishops! Think of that."

"I see the principle. Three archbishops of Canterbury? We'd work eight-hour shifts. Is that it?" The archbishop had had enough.

Alfred looked at him sadly. "I had hoped for better things from you, Canterbury. The queen told me that when you were headmaster of Wellington you were the most sensible man who ever put his collar on the wrong way round. But I suppose you can rub shoulders with the nobility all your life and yet in the end the middle-class blood will triumph." He walked away dejectedly.

"Blood is all," he growled at the doorkeeper by St. Stephen's.

"It is that, your grace," the man said. "Still, it may clear up later."

That was the year in which Alfred was finally ejected from the Athenaeum, the club he never properly joined. There was one position in the lobby, just to the side of the entrance door, which in military terms was "blind country" to anyone coming in. Alfred took to standing there in ambush with a light Malacca cane. He would spring upon any member, or guest, whose writings or speeches or conversation annoyed him, bellowing, "Middle class! Middle class!" after them as they fled indoors.

They tolerated him for months on the grounds that an eccentric duke was an ornament to any gentleman's club—and hadn't His Grace of St. Ormer provided them all with dining-out stories for years? But even the English middle class, the most patient and long-suffering breed that ever lived, has its limits. In the end, they bought him a first class ticket—single, not return—to Timbuctoo and presented it to him with a round robin signed by every genuine member and all the servants.

Yet within weeks they were saying to one another, "I miss old Alfred St. Ormer, you know."

• •

"And I say you've got to give up this nonsense now. Resign and come home and do your duty by the dukedom."

"But I'm on the General Staff, sir," Knightsbridge said. "It's my life now. In the beginning, I admit, I only wanted to die gloriously, but now . . ."

"Look at you! What's the African sun done to you! You look like a bloody Hottentot. You look eighty years old. And there's only half of you left. I say twenty years is enough. Honor's even. Your pledge is fulfilled. Come home."

"I think my country is more important than your dukedom, sir."

"*My* dukedom!" Alfred roared, turning purple. "It'll be yours when I die."

"Yes—and Charles's, when I die."

"And then? The fool can't get a son—and he can't keep the one he gets. Look, my boy, you don't have to give up the army. Just marry. You needn't hobnob with her. Go back to Africa as soon as you've fixed a brat in her. I know a hundred gels who'd marry a baptized *ape* to be rid of mama. So they wouldn't think twice about you. I suppose there's enough of you left to do what's necessary, eh?"

Knightsbridge sighed. "I took a vow, sir. Over her dead body I swore it."

"Got a taste for the Hottentot women? Is that it? We wouldn't mind that. Old Eb Graham tells me the black washes out in three generations. Bring her home—as long as she's baptized and confirmed."

"I swore to be celibate for life."

Alfred, about to explode terminally, remembered that Knightsbridge was close to being his last hope; he dare not anger his son irrevocably. "That fellow who pretended to marry you and the Walberswick gel . . . ?"

"Bimbo Morgan. Yes?"

"I don't suppose he ever went on and took holy orders?"

"Of course not, sir. In fact, he's in command of the Eighteenth at the moment."

"What would he say to the notion of being ordained, eh?"

Knightsbridge stared at his father, open-jawed.

"We'd give him a good pension, of course, on top of his stipend."

His son shook his head, uncertain what line to take.

"He could have whatever he asked. Name his price. I've never known the middle classes turn down money. We'll give him a living in good hunting country, too."

Knightsbridge decided to try logic.

"It wouldn't be retrospective, sir. It wouldn't count."

"What about the Mormons? They'll baptize your ancestors as fast as the genealogists can turn 'em up! Perhaps they'll ordain backward too." He considered the idea. "Of course we'd have to pay him extra to turn Mormon on top of everything else. What d'you say? Will you ask him?"

"Of course I won't! What makes you so certain Charles won't produce?"

"Spends all his time in the House. These wretched all-night sittings. Gladstone seems intent on killing them. And when he's not in the House, he and she go gadding about with Oscar Wilde and his set. He just says 'it's all music!' whatever that means. They've no time for getting heirs." He pondered a moment. "I never thought of asking Gladstone. Now there's a fellow can get his tongue around most things."

"It wouldn't be a good idea to involve the prime minister, sir."

"Or the Walberswicks! Yes, *he* seemed a sensible, determined fellow—a barrister, too. He must have dug up something in twenty years. If anyone knows how to get Neville all patched up and legitimate, it'll be him. I'll write at once." He sniffed. "Don't fancy meeting that Gorgon of a wife again, though."

She was a frail, pathetic woman walking uncertainly across the Great Courtyard, not quite knowing which door to approach.

"What the devil!" Alfred exclaimed as from an upper window he watched the valet du jour admit her. He rang for a footman. "Ask her ladyship kindly to join me in the silver drawing room," he said. "And tell them to show our visitor in there—after her ladyship."

But Hermione, who had also seen Mrs. Walberswick approaching the Abbey, had other ideas and gave other instructions. She swept into the silver drawing room with a great basket of flowers moments before Mrs. Walberswick was shown in.

"Aren't they marvelous," Hermione said when the woman had been introduced. "It's a new variety we've been trying."

"Gorgeous, my lady," she said quickly, glad of anything to break the ice. "But I've obviously called at an inconvenient . . ."

"Not at all, my dear. You shall help me. Now how shall we arrange this, eh? That vase, d'you think? Or this?"

Alfred watched Hermione put the woman completely at her ease, and he marveled at his luck. Could even the least reasonable man hope for two such women in his life as Flora and Hermione?

What treasure trove they had been—even in the most elementary and mundane matter, like interviewing this Mrs. W. What a hash he would have made of it. And now here was Hermione making it all easy.

"I trust Mr. Walberswick is not indisposed," he said when the ladies had finished the arrangement to their satisfaction.

She looked down at her hands, folded in her lap. "My husband does not know I'm here, your grace. I have to confess that I intercepted your letter, and when I read it, I knew I dared not show him."

"You . . . what?" Alfred could not keep the anger from his voice.

But Hermione stilled him with a fractional lift of one eyebrow. "Why not, my dear?" she asked.

"Because it would give him hope, my lady—when all the hope has gone out of him and when we all know there is none to be found." She stared levelly at Alfred. "Except what is false."

He nodded, tight-lipped, unwilling to betray an emotion before her.

She went on, "I have hated you during this quest. All of you, but *you* above all, your grace. At first for what you did to our darling . . ."

"I remember."

"But then, much more—oh, so much more, how much you'll never know—was for what you'd done to us."

"But—" Alfred began.

This time Hermione lifted her hand.

"Obviously," Mrs. Walberswick went on, "I couldn't be telling you all this if I still felt that way. But the fact is . . . well, you did warn us. 'It'll ruin your life,' you said . . ."

"Did I?"

"Words to that effect. And . . . well . . . that is . . . that's what has happened." She bowed her head and wept silently into her handkerchief.

Hermione moved and knelt by her. After a while the woman grew calmer. "We had . . ." she began.

"You needn't go on if you'd rather not," Hermione said. "I'm sure we already understand what you came to say."

"I must tell his grace. He mustn't do what we have done." She looked again at Alfred. "You mustn't."

Alfred nodded and leaned toward her.

"We had such friends. But we've lost them all. Thomas became so . . . he could talk only about one thing, you see. He began to sound like a socialist. And all his work on the plants of Studland Heath, and the invertebrates, that was his special study, you know, the invertebrates. He was so respected for it. They kept a special seat for him in the library at the Natural History Museum, every Tuesday." Her smile was wan. "It's all over now. Because he could not accept what Patricia did. He had to prove her innocence."

"She was innocent," Alfred said.

"To herself. He had to prove it to everyone. And your letter, your grace . . . it filled me with such horror, because it was so exactly like the letters Thomas used to write. So sure. So *sure* you will be able to prove Neville's legitimacy. Without any reason for it. Beyond all reason."

Hermione returned to Alfred after seeing Mrs. Walberswick out. "I think that woman may have saved your sanity, my dear," she said.

He nodded glumly. "If it was madness, it was also exciting," he said. "What shall I put in its place?"

She was ready for that. She had been ready for weeks, waiting this opportunity. "Some more productive legal business," she suggested.

"Eh?"

"We must prepare for an abeyance. You should spend the next four or five years with the lawyers setting up trusts dividing the estate among all the heirs."

He stared at her aghast.

"You've talked for years about the confiscation of land. Have a word with Lord Charles. Ask him what the younger Liberal members are saying. It's all much closer than you imagine. We've got to adjust . . . adapt. We must begin to think of the *family* as the unit which inherits, not just the heir. Divide the estate among, say, twenty members—then the most that's at risk with any one death is one-twentieth."

He was intrigued but not convinced. "But ownership is power," he protested. "You can't divide power. Power is what's important."

She smiled. "Is it? Tell me, dear, who owns Ultra Chemicals? Who owns Birmingham Metal Box? Who owns London Distillate . . . and all the others?"

"I do, of course."

"And who *controls* them?"

"I do, too." But he half saw her point. "Ultimately, at least," he had to add.

"But the day-to-day control?" she pressed.

"It's the ultimate control that's important. The marionette may twitch independently as long as the puppet master continues to hold the strings."

Hermione had not considered the point in that light. She thought awhile. "Suppose," she said slowly, "suppose that doesn't quite cover the case. Give me your watch."

He looked askance at her.

"Only for a moment!" She laughed.

Warily he obeyed. She took it. "Although, in fact, it is my watch, not yours. Did you know that old Duke Augustus actually left it to me?"

"The devil he did!"

Her smile told him she was merely playing with the idea. "Oh, but he did—with conditions, mind you."

"Ah-hah!" He nodded knowingly and smiled.

"Yes. He said you were to have absolute and unfettered use of it for as long as you liked. As long as you wanted it, I could not take it back or sell it or even give it away—except on the same conditions. Now tell me, does it matter a scrap that you've never actually owned it?"

"Give it a wind, there's a good girl."

"Answer the question."

"Yes! It matters to me."

She pushed the watch back into his waistcoat pocket and dug him in the ribs. "*That's* the attitude you've got to change if you want the estate to survive." Then, to stop him from talking himself out of the idea at once, she returned to the subject of Mrs. Walberswick. "D'you know that woman walked here from Fingest? I made Mrs. Molesworth do her some pie and sandwiches and I sent her back in one of the carriages."

"I thought the Walberswicks had money."

"She says they've spent a lot on lawyers. *The* lot, by the sound of it. And him a barrister!"

Alfred sighed. "Bloody awkward, what? Neville's grandparents in Carey Street."

"Perhaps—I don't know what you think about this—perhaps you could give Neville an extra few hundred a year, to let him make them an allowance? He could hardly afford it himself on what *The Times* must pay."

CHAPTER FIFTY-FIVE

In 1894, WHEN THE YEAR of mourning was out, Alfred and Hermione quietly married; he was then sixty-eight, she sixty-four. Naturally, no children were expected. The following year Helen gave birth to a third daughter, Ada. The family was bitterly disappointed; Alfred almost reverted to his mad schemes for trying to legitimize Neville and so shunt Lord and Lady Charles onto a cadet line. If Hermione had not been there, gently keeping him on course, it would all have begun again. But he still railed against the middle classes, whom he saw as the dead heart of modern morality. He sought practical steps against them too.

Chalfont Abbey had always been open—in a limited way—to the public. Noblemen and foreigners had been welcome on any Monday to Friday; so, on application, had artists and students of the applied arts. Ladies and gentlemen in carriages had been free to come on Tuesdays, and on other days by application. They were shown around by Mrs. Mouncey, the housekeeper, Mr. Riley, the butler, and Mr. Archer, the head gardener, for a tip of five shillings to each, which these head servants pocketed. Mrs. Mouncey let them sit upon the bed Queen Elizabeth had slept in (though no history could attest to her visit); Mr. Riley let them sample the best wines in the vast ducal cellars; and Mr. Archer sold them rooted cuttings and fruits out of season. Under these arrangements as many as two thousand visitors might visit the Abbey each year.

Alfred ordered some changes. A notice went up at the gate reserved for nonnoble visitors:

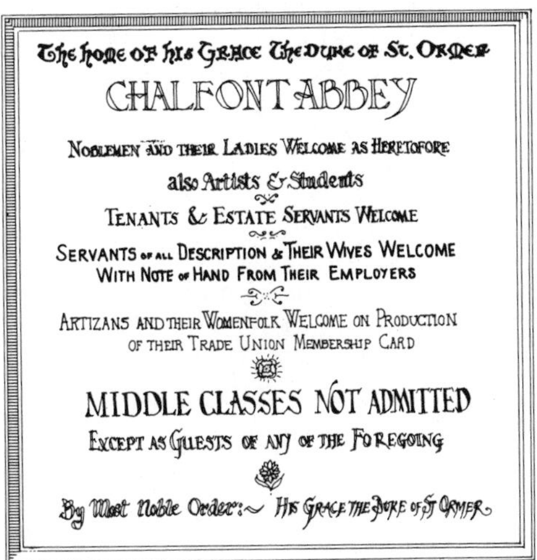

The home of his Grace The Duke of St. Ormer
CHALFONT ABBEY
Noblemen and their Ladies Welcome as Heretofore
also Artists & Students
Tenants & Estate Servants Welcome
Servants of all Description & Their Wives Welcome
With Note of Hand From Their Employers
Artizans and their Womenfolk Welcome on Production
of their Trade Union Membership Card
MIDDLE CLASSES NOT ADMITTED
Except as Guests of any of the Foregoing
By Most Noble Order:~ His Grace the Duke of St Ormer

Naturally it made not a scrap of difference to the actual pattern of visiting at the Abbey.

The other factor that kept Alfred firmly in the here-and-now was his, and Hermione's, granddaughter, the Honorable Georgina Bullen-Chetwynne. Having been "asked to leave" three schools for young ladies, she had fretted away her time—and her mother's temper—at Bullen Towers until her favorite aunt and uncle, Helen and Charles, came back to live in London. Then she announced that henceforth she would live with them.

"And what d'you imagine you'll live on?" her father threatened.

"Charity," she answered.

They thought she meant to accept it; the opposite was the case.

On arriving in London, she sent her bags to Lord and Lady Charles's house in Eaton Square and went to pry him out of the Commons. Within half an hour he had made her a loan and, far more important, promised to find her an appointment somewhere.

Her father was furious but Felicity wrote, "Take no notice of William—his anger is all for show. He's as delighted as I am to be rid of her, for, tho' we love her dearly, she can, as you will find soon enough, destroy all hope of serenity and order. She will obviously never marry, so there's no point in trying to keep her ignorant as one would a marrying girl. You may find this unconventional, but where G. is concerned we abandoned conventional ideas many years ago—when she was six weeks old, if I remember. As to her working for money, too many women of good class are doing it now for Wm. to vex himself for long. (Even Daisy Warwick in trade in Bond Street, we see!) But get her a *respectable* position."

Charles got her a most respectable position: Registrar of Births, Marriages, and Deaths in the poverty-stricken district of Limehouse in the East End. It being a working-class area, she annoyed her clerk but delighted her "clients" by staying open late two evenings a week. The cockney poor are as quick to sense a caring person as they are to sniff out a fake; they took Georgina to their hearts at once—and to their homes and clubs and pubs as well.

She saw a way of life she had, until then, merely read about. She expected to find it dismal—all work, pain, and noble tears. Their boisterous, boozy cheer and quick humor astonished her. For a time it misled her into thinking that reports of poverty were much exaggerated. Then she understood how thin was the crust of wit and good nature on which they walked; the most terrible destitution was for most of them just a sprained wrist away—or a fractional drop in the level of trade in the docks—or two pints of beer too many.

The women and girls were even more sweated than the men. She saw them sewing shirts and fine dresses for West End houses in conditions she thought had been shamed or legislated out of existence forty years ago. By way of experiment she tried to live, day by day, on the diet of one of these women. Within two weeks she was brought home after collapsing in the street.

"You goose!" Helen said as she nursed her back to strength. "Cook tells me how little you've been eating. Why? Surely you're slender enough as it is!"

Georgina explained. She had a round, businesslike face—no beauty, but lovably plain. "How can I see their condition without wanting to do something?" she asked. "And how can I begin to do anything until I know what it's like?"

"You really do take it seriously, eh?"

"So would you, Helen. You honestly ought to come and see it for yourself."

But Helen had smelled the poverty on Georgina's clothes when she came in of an evening and rejected the idea. Georgina was clever. She didn't insist. Nor did she burden Helen's dinner table with missionary talk of her East End experiences—just the odd, intriguing snippet now and then, to whet the appetite.

Then, around the time that Helen had Ada, Oscar Wilde, who had been an intimate of Lord and Lady Charles's circle and a frequent guest, was sent to gaol. The whole of Society, and certainly those immediately associated with Oscar, suddenly grew more serious. Another court case at the time, which excited a good deal of comment, was the trial for murder of a thirteen-year-old girl who had abandoned her illegitimate baby in the frost. Georgina was at the Old Bailey to see the judge don his black cap and pronounce that terrible sentence, ". . . there to hang by the neck until you are dead . . . ," on the poor creature. Everyone knew the girl would be reprieved—but had anybody bothered to tell *her?* And in any case, why go through a ritual that was insupportable even when it was in earnest? Georgina was furious. That evening at dinner the case was mentioned and Georgina, less circumspect than usual, let slip the fact that she knew the child—and that the girl's own father was also the father of the baby.

A dowager marchioness at the table thought it dreadful that a well-brought-up gel like Miss Bullen-Chetwynne should even know of such things; but everyone else was fascinated—not in a prurient or even curious sort of way, but seriously. Seeing her chance, Georgina lightly challenged them to accompany her on a guided tour of her district.

They came—partly as their great-grandparents had once gone to Bedlam Hospital, to marvel at the lunatics and see the bad ones whipped. They were impressed enough to found an East End mission and clinic by subscription from Mayfair dwellers.

Helen was impressed, too—with Georgina. "That's what you've wanted all along, isn't it?"

Georgina grinned. "I want something much bigger now," she said.

"People still think of you as the self-willed, impetuous child of ten years ago. That's how you do it, of course."

"Do what?"

"Work away like a quiet little death-watch beetle—while everyone's so glad you aren't a wasp. You know you've practically pushed Charles out of the Liberal Party with your quiet little conversational asides."

"Do you mind?"

"He had a long talk with George Lansbury last week. He's getting very interested in socialism."

"And you think I'm to blame?"

Helen shrugged noncommittally. "Your zeal and energy always fascinated him. What's this much bigger thing you're interested in?"

Again that grin. "The Vote!"

"Oh." Helen was dismissive.

"No! It's important. It's all-important—precisely because it's *meaningless!*"

That made Helen listen.

"I used to think the suffragists were wrong. I thought it was men's entire view of women that was out of joint—and ours of men. I thought we had to change that, and then everything else would follow easily—the vote, careers, work, the professions, money, etcetera. But now I can see I was wrong. The Vote must come before everything. D'you know when I realized it?"

Helen sat on Georgina's bed and looked around the room. She herself had never known such freedom—nor would she even have dreamed of it before she married. And that was just ten years ago! "No, dear. When?" she answered.

"When I saw that judge putting on his black cap for a ritual he knew, and everyone in court knew—except, I suspect, that wretched little child—was empty, meaningless. And it came to me suddenly: Men don't think like us. We're logical. We're practical. But men think in symbols. Like the black cap . . . and the Garter regalia, and the king's crown, and the regimental flag, and the school colors, and the boating song, and *Forty Years On.*"

Helen began to laugh. It was so true . . . and yet so perverse.

"If *logic* could persuade men," Georgina went on, "we'd have had the Vote in 1832. So we'll have to stand things on their head, you see. Since logic won't win us the Vote, we shall have to get it by some other means. Make the Vote a Symbol, see? Then once we've got it the men will suddenly start supplying all the logic we could want, all the logic we're going to need to break down the other barriers. With men, the symbol comes first. Logic comes limping along after, trying to hide its bruises." She giggled. "And that's why the Vote, which—if you've ever watched an election in the East End and seen the brewers' drays laden with beer and Tory Party colors at every street corner, you'll know is just about the emptiest, stupidest ritual ever devised—is also the Most Important Thing in the Universe for me now."

Helen had been trained in the lobster-shell school of diplomacy—put the knife in the soft bits. She said, "Then I'm surprised you concern yourself with Charles. Or are you just practicing on him?"

"For what?"

"Well, obviously, for the day when you start trying to manage the duke."

Georgina's eyes went as round as if she had just been picked up by the hair. "The duke! Lordy!"

"Don't say you're afraid of him, Georgie. Don't tell me there's something under heaven that scares you!"

Georgina, annoyed at letting the fact slip out, snorted. "Of course I'm not! Anyway, even the queen's a little afraid of him. I've heard you say that before now."

" 'In awe of,' not 'afraid.' "

"Yes. Well. I don't mind admitting I'm in awe of him. So are you."

Helen smiled tolerantly.

"You are!" Georgina insisted.

"But never excessively."

"So you say."

"I have an infallible little trick."

"Oh?" Georgina was curious despite herself.

"I imagine to myself he's just an ordinary man. A commoner."

Georgina peeled off a laugh. "Impossible."

"Ah! If you did but know how thin is the thread by which his inheritance once hung!"

"Oh, everyone knows that."

"Do you?" Helen was astonished.

"Yes. If old Duke Augustus had had an heir . . ."

"Oh! Yes—well—now you see what I mean."

But Georgina realized that Helen had meant something quite different, and badgered her until she revealed it.

"You promise you'll keep it to yourself?" Helen asked.

"Of course. Keep what?"

So Helen told her of the papers she had once come across in the muniment room, the papers showing that William du Bois had undergone a Roman Catholic marriage in Ireland before Orlando was born—and how William had quarreled with the Romans soon after and had thenceforth refused to recognize the marriage as lawful, thus bastardizing Orlando and ruling him out of the line of succession. "But if the marriage really was lawful . . ." Helen let the rest hang.

"Perhaps that's why Orlando took to crime!" Georgina was excited. "What stories they might tell if only we could bring them back! All those people."

"If you're interested in stories, you ought to spend some time in the muniment room. It's overflowing with them."

"D'you know, I think I shall. I'll take a long Friday-to-Monday and go down to see the duke. History might be a good way of starting on him. Family history or England's—they're much the same thing, aren't they."

The sudden irruption of Georgina at Chalfont Abbey was the other factor that kept Alfred firmly in the here-and-now (and wistfully remembering the there-and-then).

• •

"Women shouldn't meddle in politics," Alfred said. He was out riding with Georgina, who was somehow less overwhelming in the vast open spaces of the deer park.

"I agree, grandfather. But I don't think of it as politics. My interest is historical."

"Hmph!" They were approaching the grove of Wellingtonias, now tall specimens, soaring above the beeches that flanked the lakes. "Talking of history, your grandmother Flora taught me to canter properly here, nearly fifty years ago. And it seems like only yesterday both your grandmothers and I were seated just over there, wondering if your father and mother were romantically attached or not. And now here you are—telling me I'm a walking history lesson. Well, well!"

"Oh, granddad! I didn't mean—"

"Come on. What was your question again?"

"The Tories and the Whigs. What did they think of each other? After all, they both came from the same class. What was there to fight about?"

"Classes don't fight. That's a modern fallacy. It's *tribes* that fight. Us and the froggies. Protestants and papists. Town and Gown. Celt and Saxon. They're all tribes. And the Tories and Whigs were tribes, too. That's why they fought."

"But what did they say about each other?"

"I'll tell you what the Tories said about us. We were always a Whig family. The Tories said we had no principles except to stay in office. We'd mortgage the future and gamble recklessly with the present and rewrite the past—*anything* as long as we kept the power in our hands." Alfred laughed. "And I'll tell you another thing: They were quite right! That's why we're a Tory family now. Except for Charles, of course. He thinks that because Whigs now call themselves Liberals, they're different. They're not. A Liberal is just a Whig in middle-class clothing."

"It's all so confusing," she pretended.

"No, it isn't, my dear; it's very simple, really. Just remember this. If we could stand all the middle classes up against a wall and shoot them, the aristocracy and the working class together could build a paradise on earth inside ten years. If you want all history in one sentence—there it is."

Georgina's heart sank. The duke was going to be a Long Haul.

She wanted to point out to him what a terribly chancy thing "aristocracy" was. She wanted to show him that we are all brothers, all of one flesh, when artificial differences of wealth and inheritance are removed. She thought of the papers she had found in the muniment room, the ones Helen had mentioned, which showed that but for William du Bois' quarrel with the Roman Church, Orlando might have been legitimate and might not have turned to crime, and might . . . well, anyway, it might all have been otherwise. And this awe-inspiring grandfather of hers might have been an ordinary commoner.

She actually drew breath to begin. But one look at the duke and the words froze.

CHAPTER FIFTY-SIX

A YEAR BEFORE the century rounded itself out, Hermione died. She climbed into her coach to go to Ascot, and when it got there she was dead. Like Flora, she died of a heart attack or stroke. Like Flora, she did not trouble the doctors to distinguish between them. Like Flora, she had a smile on her lips when all else was still.

It was a family funeral, despite the presence of the queen. The family—Boyces and Bullen-Chetwynnes—by then numbered twenty-three grandchildren, and all the "children" were living still, so it was no small affair. The Bullen-Chetwynne grandchildren were, for the most part, in their teens. The Boyces, in their twenties, sagely joined their parents in nervously eying the duke and wondering what mischief he might get up to now that both his duchesses lay deep in the family crypt at the base of Herberts Tower.

Alfred took the opportunity to tell them of the inheritance plan Hermione had engendered just a few years earlier. It meant little to them at the time. They came away with a vague impression that each was to own a giddy portion of a vast inheritance—but without controlling any of it, or, necessarily, enjoying much of its income. It did not augur well. The air was heavy with the stench of costly upper-class litigation.

When they had all gone, and silence descended on the Abbey, Alfred at last yielded to the dark melancholy that had hung in the forecourt of his spirit all these days—kept waiting only by the press of affairs. He took a candle in his hand and wandered about the passages and rooms which, after half a century of occupation, still caged the magic of Flora and Hermione.

The queen, surprisingly, had announced she would stay the night; he tiptoed past her room, on to the end of the passage, to the small stair, with its wicket gate to prevent children from descending unaccompanied, and so down to the main door and out into the Great Courtyard.

His candle was made superfluous by a bright moon. It dipped in and out of thin, fleecy clouds, driven by a wind that extinguished his light before he was halfway to Herberts Tower. But he did not pause. He knew his way into and about the crypt well enough to touch and name each coffin, blindfold. From the moment his hand, reaching for the key, brushed the ancient toy horse, Caesar, he was in long-familiar territory.

His two duchesses lay side by side, with a space between them where his own coffin would one day fit. He stood in that blacker-than-black, seeing phantoms and miasmas of light that moved inside his skull, resolving into nothing. One hand touched each coffin as he prayed, yet again, for eternal peace for their souls, here and yet departed. He longed to talk about them. "These," he said aloud to his Tribe, "were the two noblest women I have ever known or ever shall know."

On his way back to his room and what he knew would be a sleepless night he paused outside the queen's chamber and listened. It was as quiet as the crypt had been. But half a dozen paces on, he heard the door open.

"Alfred?"

She was still in her evening dress. "I *knew* you wouldn't sleep, my dear," she said.

"You didn't wait up on my account, ma'am."

"I was *days* behind with my diary." She implied he might believe it if he wished. "What shall you do now?"

"I have political and estate duties which . . ."

"No. *Now?*"

"Oh." He had not considered it. "Walk around, I suppose. When old Duke Augustus died, Flora and I walked for hours about the house—the way country people tell everything to the bees, we told the house." He smiled apologetically at the fancy.

"May I come with you?"

"I shall be honored, ma'am."

She went back and brought a thick shawl. The night lights along the corridors gave them all the illumination they needed. In the rooms, the moonlight streaming through the tall windows soon seemed almost as bright as day. When they passed the wicket gate at the stairhead she told him that as a child she had never been allowed to walk downstairs without holding a grown-up's hand.

"That's what it was to be heir to the throne," she said. "The throne has taken precedence over me all my life."

Several times they passed in silence Old Knapman, the night watch, padding around the corridors with seaboot stockings drawn over his unstudded boots; the regular clunk of the time clocks he punched on his rounds was the night music of the house.

"Bereavements like this seem natural at our age," she said. "I often think there is a book unfolding inside each of us, making us childish, fast to learn . . . impetuous, rash . . . mature, sound . . . tired, and senile by turns—all those things Shakespeare says so much better. It prepares us for loss."

"It doesn't make it more bearable. When Flora died, only a second or so afterward I had a terrible premonition of the loneliness . . ."

"Yes! Oh, yes, one knows at once! How profoundly you see these things, Alfred dear."

"And yet . . . life goes on. My granddaughter Georgina . . ."

"Oh, that young lady!"

"Yes. That young lady. You know she's going to marry?"

"I hadn't heard. Do we know him? She hasn't been to a drawing room."

"I wouldn't keep the candles lit against that possibility. I'm sorry to say he's a Socialist. A man called Campbell Stone—an Australian."

"Horror upon horror!"

"I'd forbid them this house if I thought there was even a chance they'd come near it. I've only heard of her engagement through backstairs gossip."

"Oh, Alfred! What's happening to the world? Little Georgina—who's been at court, who's been like a daughter, who knows what's Good Form and what's Bad. Not to come to a drawing room on her engagement! Not even to announce it in *The Times!*" She hugged his arm. "I say thank heaven we've so little time left down here, don't you? Soon we'll be reunited with all those we've loved so . . ." She could not finish the thought.

"And yet," Alfred answered, "I'd always like to hang on and see if I've bred another Derby winner. Wouldn't you?" After a pause he went on, "Yet you have so much to be proud of, ma'am. Do you remember what a dreadful state the monarchy was in when you came to the throne?"

"Could I forget it! They booed me and pelted me with mud. Your predecessor, Augustus, disliked me."

Alfred cleared his throat to make a ritual disclaimer.

"Oh, yes! Not that it matters now." She laughed. "Go on. You were saying?"

"I was saying, you changed all that. You've made the monarchy loved, revered even, and honored."

"With *Albert's* help."

"With or without, *you* did it. You have made England the foremost nation of the world. You have brought *pax Britannica* and progress to every continent. The corruption and dissipation of the Hanoverians could never have achieved that."

The queen was a long time silent. Alfred realized how loudly her stays creaked. "Not I alone," she said.

Alfred insisted: "You above all. Whenever the Union Jack has unfurled over another foreign land, and savages have felt the majestic protection of British law, and peaceful trade has stilled the tribal slaughter . . . haven't you felt proud that the Crown itself was at last a worthy symbol, to put its seal on this ever-widening civilization? And not just the Crown, but all the institutions that depend on it? The nobility, the law, the army . . . Parliament. How vastly they have reformed themselves—thanks to the example from above."

Again she was silent. This time, Alfred realized, she was quietly weeping. He patted her arm until she was recovered. "Thank you, dear, *dear* Albert," she sniffed, accepting his offer of a handkerchief. She did not notice her slip with his name.

After a while she said, "I feel a little peckish, you know."

"I have some water biscuits and brandy in my room," he offered.

She grinned. "Perhaps I mean I feel more than a little peckish."

"Ah!" He was reaching for a bell pull when she stayed him.

"No servants!" she said. "Isn't it so *nice* being alone? Just for a while. One is never alone. Take me to the kitchens and we can surely find something." She chuckled almost naughtily. "I shall be Mrs. Coburg and you Mr. Boyce."

After wandering around for a while, Alfred had to admit defeat. "Knapman," he called to the night watch, "where's the way down to the kitchens?"

It baffled Knapman's powers of description; he had to lead them through the labyrinth to the head of the stairs. "I could have found it in daylight," Alfred said lamely.

He was delighted to find them spotless, all the big deal tables scrubbed and bare. He swept back a chair, one of the Chippendale ones that used to grace the upstairs rooms, like a stage gallant and said in a posh-acting voice, "If you will ever so kindly seat your good self there, Mrs. Coburg, my love, I shall see about a nice drop of something."

"Oh, ta, Mr. Boyce." Her dignity was as unsteady as the woman's she was parodying. It was an amazing piece of acting for a woman to whom dignity was like a second skin. He saw how, in a different age, she might have been quite a different sort of queen—and every bit as good at it.

He wandered over to a small pantry. "Cold quail?" he called out. "Veal pie? Some cold sausages . . ."

"English or real ones?" she asked.

"English."

"Quail and veal sound nice."

He brought them over to the table, together with an unlabeled tin, which he opened. "It smells like cocoa. D'you think that's what it is?"

She looked and sniffed. "I don't know," she said. "It smells chocolaty anyway. Let's see."

"How does one make cocoa, Mrs. Coburg?"

She laughed in astonishment. "How on earth should I know, Mr. Boyce? Put the powder in some cold water and heat it up."

There were eight cups of water and powder scattered about the table in various states of semicongealment or separation before Mr. Boyce produced an acceptable drink; but they enjoyed it all the more as an *achievement.* Mrs. Coburg cut the pie and they devoured it picnic style. As they munched away in silence, solemnity returned to them.

"I was telling you of that sort of premonition I had when Flora died," Alfred said.

"Yes?"

"I think Empress Elizabeth had one, too. There were all those flowers around us. Did you ever see her winter garden at the Hofburg?"

"Alix has told me."

"Banks of flowers all around. And I said something about its being a perfect place to end a perfectly happy life. And d'you know what she said?"

Victoria shook her head.

" 'Wish it for me too, dear cousin—to die among flowers.' "

"And so she did." Tears sprang to her eyes. "But did she also see the anarchist's bullet? Oh, Alfred dear, let's not talk of death again tonight. It's so near us anyway." She shuddered. "Tell me about Flora and Hermione, if you can bear it. Tell me of all the happy things you did. Let's remember all the good things."

When the young scullery maids came on, yawning and frowsty,

at half past five that morning, they were astonished to find the eighty-year-old Queen of England and their own seventy-three-year-old Duke of St. Ormer, looking not the least bit tired, sitting amid the ruins of pie and quail and some of the most nauseating cocoa ever to disgrace those kitchens.

CHAPTER FIFTY-SEVEN

ALFRED'S ECCENTRICITIES and his often extravagant language led many to believe that he was going, in the French expression of the day, *gah-gah*. For some it was a costly mistake. The duke's grip on the estate, on the reins of power in the county, and on his many businesses, was as firm and tight as ever. Business rivals who thought they were up against a "funny old buffer" came away looking for their shirts; tenants who thought they could get by with tales of woe and their fifth-best suits found their income set out to the last farthing, and their rents raised to exactly what the business could stand; peddlers of influence who approached the new County Council found unexpected deviations in their path—like a maze—and when they reached its center there stood, not the expected County Hall, but Chalfont Abbey. They all discovered, some too late, that Alfred was not an eccentric at all but rather a man who enjoyed eccentricity and knew the value of it.

But perhaps it could be said he was not quite cynical enough about it: He knew its value but not its *price*. The deficiency almost cost his proper heirs their inheritance.

He had a violent quarrel with Georgina about the East End mission. "They're not *our* people," he bellowed at her. "What you're doing is pure interference. Find the landlords. Find the masters. Make them do it."

She turned the other cheek and told him it was only Christian.

"Humbug! Christianity's been infested and perverted by the middle classes. They're out to destroy this country with their universal charity. The landlord must look after his own tenants. The master must serve his own servants. That's Christianity. It's also good sense. You're turning yourself into a middle-class busybody."

After the birth of the third daughter in a row, Helen began to mourn all over again for young Michael—and even more deeply. "He came to me last night," she told Charles once. "He sat on my bed with that delicate, precise way he had of doing things, and he turned his dear little face to me—and it was so *real.* And he said, 'Mother dear, I'm so happy here. You're not to worry or grieve any more. It makes me sad.' But, of course, I can't help it."

Charles and Georgina between them conspired to get her working first one and then two days a week at the mission. Now that Georgina was the Honorable Mrs. Campbell Stone she had less time for her mission, so she was glad of the help. As Helen began to immerse herself in others' desperation and misery, her own receded.

But to Alfred it was just another defection to the Enemy. "I've a bloody good mind to marry some slut off the estate and cut them all out!" he said. He stopped seeing them, which was how he failed to hear of Helen's latest pregnancy as quickly as he might have done; and they decided not to breach the barrier in case this baby, like the others, should prove to be a girl.

Not long after that he visited the Boyce Cottage Hospital, which he had given to Great Marlow. One of the patients in the lying-in ward caught his eye—a coarsely pretty girl with a slightly vacant look, good teeth, and a loud laugh. But no wedding ring. The matron, seeing his interest, thought it a good moment to mention the girl and to ask if Something could not be Done about her.

"Why?" the duke asked.

"Well, it's quite dreadful, your grace. She's nineteen years old and is all set to follow her mother's dreadful example."

"What was that?" the Duke asked.

"Old Mrs. Bucket? Surely your grace has heard of the woman? It's a wonder she's not here in the lying-in ward, too. She's produced a baby a year since she was fourteen. Young Meg here was her first. The next will be her twentieth."

"Good heavens! You'd think she'd be quite broken down."

"Not her! She's as strong as a shire mare. Never any trouble. She just comes here for the bed and the food. She hardly knows she's having them, these babies. In fact I don't believe she does know. The furnishing on the top floor, I'm afraid, is a bit rudimentary."

"What do you think should be done, matron?"

"Well, sir. I blame the men of the town. They know when she's coming out of here. They just sit around waiting. Great sniggering faces at the window. Lewd creatures. Then the minute she's out they're all running away to Harleyford Meadows or Rassler Wood and lining up for their chance. The constable doesn't know who to serve with a paternity order—it could be any one of eighty men. She's just a burden to the parish. And now, as I say, it's starting all over again with her daughter."

No solution immediately suggested itself to Alfred. "I'll have a word with the vicar," he said, "and the local Bench. We'll try to find some answer to it." He began to walk away.

"If you don't, your grace, they'll fill the St. Ormer Boys' School on you."

Alfred paused. "Boys?"

"Oh yes, they're nearly all boys. That family hardly ever has girls."

Alfred returned to her. "A possible solution occurs to me," he said. "Tell me her name again."

Three weeks later the constable himself escorted the newly nubile Meg Bucket past the lines of waiting, would-be paternalists and out to Chalfont Abbey, to the greatest would-be paternalist of all.

"But is there no way of stopping him?" Lady Emily asked. "What does Knightsbridge say?"

Charles snorted. "His first cable said CERTIFY THE FOOL. The second told us to SHOOT HIM."

"Well, what about certifying him?" Lady Louise asked.

"I know it seems insane to us, but he's not insane in law."

"Then 'the law is a ass,' " Lady Felicity said.

"What about Knightsbridge's other solution?" Georgina asked. Her mother told her for God's sake to be serious; so did the others—but not all, she noticed, were quite so vehement about it. A thoughtful glance or two passed from one to another; but none of them was willing to heed advice from a female Socialist to shoot a duke, even though he was also a relation.

"If only we hadn't haggled so long over the details of this settlement," the Earl of Roundstone, Louise's husband, said. "It wouldn't matter so much."

"Perhaps," the Marquis of Keyhaven, Emily's husband, said brightly, "he's only pretending—to push us into making up our minds."

"We can't take that gamble though, can we?"

"Has anyone at all *talked* to him?"

Lady Emily spoke. "I have. He says she's not as simple as everyone makes her out to be. No one's ever taken the trouble to teach her anything."

"How heartening!" Roundstone said.

"There's worse," Lady Emily added. "He says none of us knows how unpolished and uncouth he was when he came into the dukedom and we're all infected with the middle-class virus of conformity and respectability. In forty years' time she'll be as good a duchess as he is now a duke."

"It's to spite us. I'm sure of it," Lady Felicity said.

"Does he know you're *enceinte,* Helen?" Lady Louise asked.

Helen shook her head.

"We considered telling him," Charles explained.

"We must!" Lord Keyhaven insisted.

"Consider this first," Charles warned. "Suppose there *is* an element of bluff in this threatened marriage. Suppose he's only ninety percent set on it. And then suppose Helen and I have another daughter?" (Helen was grateful for that "and I.") "Wouldn't that, or *couldn't* it, tip him all the way and make him do what he might not have intended doing? Or not absolutely intended?"

No one could deny it.

There was a silence.

Georgina cleared her throat. "Knightsbridge didn't say kill him," she pointed out. "Only shoot him. People can be laid up quite a long time with shooting accidents."

They were mad to imagine that the duke would not get to hear of Helen's pregnancy. It was the only thing that made him postpone the wedding.

One evening, when Helen was near to term, Lord Charles left the House of Commons in company with Gladstone. They were both to dine at the Reform Club, and when Charles gave instructions to his man as to his whereabouts, in case Helen started, their conversation naturally dwelled for a while on his hopes for an heir.

"It'll be a girl again," Charles said lugubriously. "I'm sure of it."

They happened to be passing the doorkeeper at the time.

"Lady Charles Boyce is going to have a little girl baby," the man told his wife that night. "They're quite sure. The old duke won't be happy with that."

"You know that Lady Charles Boyce, that American millionaire's daughter?" the wife told her neighbor next morning. "She's been expecting for months now." Her tone implied that of course she'd known all about it from the start. "Well—it's a little girl. That's definite. The old duke's furious."

" 'Ere, that funny duke, whossname, St. Ormer," the neighbor said to the butcher. "He's got his nose properly out of joint. That daughter-in-law of his, Lady Whossname, has been and gone and had another daughter, and all he wanted was a son."

"Guess what I heard at the butcher's just now," a kitchen porter at the Marlborough Club said to the chef. "The Duke of St. Ormer, he's a member here, isn't he?"

"What of it?" The Head of Waiters chimed in.

"His daughter-in-law, Lady Something . . ."

"Lady Charles Boyce."

"Yeah, that was it. She's gone and had a daughter when he wanted a son."

"When was this?"

"Must have been yesterday."

"Leave this to me, George," the Head of Porters said when the Head of Waiters carried him the tale. "I happen to know"—he winked—"that His Grace has already fallen out with that certain aforesaid party. So I'll break the news to the poor old gentleman. There's a certain way to do these things."

Five minutes after entering the club that teatime Alfred was in his carriage and driving hard for Paddington Station. A telegram to the rector of Fingest overtook him on that journey home. PREPARE THE WEDDING, it read.

Meg Bucket had not been confirmed. The rector began to say something about . . . er . . . in certain circumstances . . . taking into account the rather particular . . . ah . . . er . . .

"Get her done," the duke commanded. "Take her to the bishop if need be. She may enter heaven unconfirmed; she's certainly not going to enter my dukedom in that state."

Riley, the butler, sent word of this change to Lords Pennington and Lambert at the Plume of Feathers in Fingest. They were almost sick with relief, just as they had almost vomited with fear when they cut cards to see who'd draw the Queen of Spades and, with it, the privilege of trying to wound their grandfather, not fatally but just enough to RAISE HIS VOICE AN OCTAVE OR TWO, as Knightsbridge had put it in a third cable.

"We must go out with him on a normal shoot once or twice, before we do it," Pennington said. "Otherwise it'd look so bally fishy."

"But then he'll ask why we're not staying at the Abbey. And we can hardly say we've got to stay here because Fingest Post Office has the only bloody telephone for miles. I'll go and see if there's any word."

There was no word. There was no word all the five days it took to get Meg confirmed. Then the morning of the wedding arrived.

This time Lord Lambert cut the Black Lady. It was a melancholy party that set off after breakfast to do that most melancholy deed.

The duke was in high spirits as he greeted them. "You don't know what a happy day you come on!" he chortled. "You can be the family witnesses."

He was delighted with their idea of going shooting that afternoon—though a glint in his eye told Lambert he intended passing an hour or so with his new bride first.

He helped them off with their guns. "No need to change," he said. "Come as you are. We're doing it up in the middle library. You're dressed a damn sight more respectably than she's used to."

He hefted Lord Lambert's ammunition bag onto the table. "Hello!" He flicked it open with his thumb. "You've left your cartridges behind, my boy. I thought it felt light. Not to worry. That's one commodity we're never short of here."

Lambert felt the blood draining from him. He too had thought it felt light—but only because he had spent the hour before breakfast taking some of the cordite out of each cartridge so that even at point-blank range he was unlikely to kill the Duke; no other cartridges would do. And he had forgotten to put them back in his pouch! He had to go back to the Plume of Feathers and get them. And he had to go now—the duke could not be allowed two minutes alone with his bride. The "shooting accident" would have to occur in the unlikely surroundings of the middle library.

"What's up, my boy? You look as if you fell in two parishes."

"Touch of the squitters, duke," his grandson said. "I suspect the egg I ate at breakfast. You go on. I shan't be half a jiff."

He ran to the stables. The groom had removed the saddle but left the horse bridled. Lambert, who was one of the best horsemen in Derbyshire, leaped onto the brute and rode him arrow-straight over great raspers of fences to Fingest, full gallop all the way.

He scrabbled up the cartridges, stuffed his pockets with them, and ran back to the street, where he almost knocked down the young son of the postmistress.

"Telephone message for you, my lord," the boy said.

"The baby's come at last?" he asked, against all hope.

"Yes, my lord. And they're going to call him Simon."

The heir to the Sixteenth Earl of Roundstone gave a yell of joy that brought every inhabitant to his door or window. They were just in time to see a pair of hooves flash over the fence beyond the pump on the village green.

"This is a trick," the duke said angrily to his breathless grandson.

The rector had just reached: "Alfred, so you take this woman . . ."

"No trick, sir. I swear it," the young man gasped. "Oh, get me a pint of claret for pity's sake!"

"But Lady Charles had a daughter a week ago. I had it on the best authority—he even told me they'd called her Alexandra."

"It was a bald lie, sir. I swear it to you. See here—bring a Bible. I'll swear on that." He looked up and saw Landseer's portrait of Flora. He ran and put his hand on the frame. "I swear it on my grandmother's memory," he said.

Alfred was impressed at that.

"Who told you this other news, duke?" Pennington asked.

Alfred cleared his throat. "Fellow member of the Marlborough," he muttered. "Never mind, now. Simon, you said."

"Simon."

"Well!" He put his arms about their shoulders and swept them toward the door. "Let's go and break out a magnum in his honor. Then we'll have that shoot."

They were outside in the passage before the Rector found his voice. "Your grace!"

Alfred stopped in his tracks. "Oh, Christ!" he said, grinning guiltily at his grandsons. "You go down and tell Riley about the champagne," he told them. "I'll settle this."

He beckoned a footman to him. "Are those laborers still digging for that drain in the Great Courtyard?"

"I believe they are, your grace."

"Go down and see the foreman. Tell him to line up all his unmarried laborers. Pick the youngest, strongest, and handsomest, and bring him up here."

"As he is, your grace?"

"Sweat, mud, beetlecrushers, and all."

The man went on his errand.

"No!" a voice cried. It was Meg. "I don't want that."

"Don't be silly," the duke told her. "I'll give you a nice cottage. He'll never want for work. And you shall have a pension. You know how well we look after our own people. And beggars can't be choosers."

"I'm no beggar."

"You will be if you say no to this."

"I want to be yours."

"You are. Everyone on the estate is mine. My people."

"No. *Yours.* Oh, God . . . please!"

Something in her desperation reached through the obscuring clouds of cross-purpose. "What?" he asked. "What d'you mean?"

"I love you," she said. "I don't want no other man. Not never again. Why was you so good to me if you don't love me?"

"But I'm not going to marry you now."

"I don't care about marriage. Never did. I thought it was silly, me being a duchess. I only said yes to be with you. I'd rather be with you and not be a duchess."

She was especially pretty that day. Her distress and obvious desire for him gave her eyes a new luster. She was young. Her body was close. Her bosom heaved with emotion. Alfred knew he had lost.

"Let's try it," he said.

The rector cleared his throat in loud distress. Neither paid him the slightest heed.

She threw her arms around Alfred and kissed him warmly, wetly, voluptuously.

The footman returned with a strapping young man, broad-chested and handsome. Alfred turned to Meg. "Change your mind?" he asked.

She shook her head vigorously.

Alfred told the man he was very pleased with the way he'd seen him working, borrowed half a guinea off the rector to tip the fellow, and sent him, bewildered, back to the Great Courtyard.

Meg hugged him again. "Oh, I do love you," she said. Then she broke half-free and looked at him. "Here! If we was to have any babies . . ."

"Yes?" He thought he knew her worry. "They wouldn't be noble."

"But they'd be mine? The Board of Guardians down Great Marlow Union, they couldn't go taking them away from me like what they did off of my mum, could they?" Her eyes sparkled. Her tongue lingered on her lip.

The Duke wondered what idiot could ever have dismissed her as simple-minded.

CHAPTER FIFTY-EIGHT

THE ONLY MEMBER of the family who was not delighted at this resolution of the Meg Bucket Crisis was Campbell Stone, Georgina's husband. "As a good Socialist," he said, "I thought it rich that a duke in one of the realm's premier dukedoms might end his tenure in such ridiculous circumstances."

"As a good Antipodean you don't realize how robust our English institutions are," she told him. "Such a marriage would have made it stronger, not weaker."

He was surprised at her. "I thought you wanted to see an end to it all. An end to privilege and—"

"So I do! Of course I do! But it must be rational. Even the aristocracy itself must see, and understand, and agree to its own extinction. The society of the future must be one in which reason is king."

He shrugged his shoulders and deferred to her.

He deferred to her quite a lot, now; but it had not always been so. A few years ago, when they first became engaged, he had been the masterful one. People had shaken their heads and said it would never last, that Georgina would never, in the Chinese phrase, *kautau* to him. But he had been the one who changed. Quite suddenly, too. It was like a religious conversion.

From the start no one in the family had liked him. They told each other it was because he was a Socialist, but that was a mere shorthand, a convenience to mask a deeper unease they all felt about him without being able to be specific about its cause. Even Georgina felt it: There was something repellent about him.

In a way, that was also his attraction—for her. She knew that she'd never marry (because nannies, governesses, parents, siblings, and friends had, all her life, insisted "you'll never marry if you behave like *that*"—and she had not the slightest intention to stop "behaving like *that*"). It is curious how such prophecies have a way of insuring their own fulfillment. Georgina knew she'd never marry; therefore she had put herself in a nonmarrying frame of mind—ceased to look romantically at men. Therefore all those fine and subtle signals by which the nubile and the eligible make clear their mutual intentions and ambitions ceased to radiate from her.

"Georgina's a good chap," men would say, or, even more significantly, "Georgie." Therefore she knew she'd never marry.

And therefore Campbell's pursuit of her was startling to a degree. It was relentless, almost fierce; there were times when she felt he had come all the way from Australia with the express purpose of finding, courting, and marrying her. She once said as much but he took it so amiss that she never repeated what she had meant as a joke but he had taken as an accusation. Nevertheless, his single-minded pursuit of her, through the thickets of her indifference, bafflement, and, finally, wonder, shook her out of that spinster mold; she fell, overripe, into wedlock.

Had he been the conventional suitor, a man so stunning in her eyes that she could but blindly adore him, he might, paradoxically, have stood no chance with her. But there was that elusive *otherness* about him which served every bit as well. Helen said he was charming, "But, Georgina dear, can he really be as charming as he seems?" George Lansbury, the Socialist, praised his many qualities, yet wondered if he could be quite as sincere a Socialist as he made himself out to be.

"All it needs," Georgina complained to Charles, "is for the Australian governor general to say, 'I agree he has an Australian birth certificate and Australian citizenship, yet I wonder if he's quite as Australian as he claims to be.'

"Nevertheless, it is a pattern, isn't it, Georgie?" Charles warned.

He knew, of course, that his warning, like those of others, merely added to Campbell's attractiveness in her eyes. This was the sort of fire she had always loved to play with. And so, half-fearing, half-loving, and knowing not where fear began and love ended, she agreed to marry Campbell.

Yet he had changed, not she. She could remember the exact moment of it—or what, looking back, came to seem like the exact moment. As a good Socialist couple with thoroughly modern views they discussed the size and timing of their family before embarking upon the Production Phase. Georgina, by then twenty-five and a veteran of many and varied negotiations, had developed a fair array of bargaining skills. She began with her ultimate hopes, knowing full well she would have to yield a little here, compromise a little there. She wanted no children until she had put the mission on so firm a foundation that her presence or absence was indifferent to its success. She wanted no children until she had established herself (in some as-yet-undefined way) in politics. She wanted no children until she had kindled a torch so bright that it would glow through the ten tedious years she would have to devote to breeding and rearing, and leap up again soon after. "In short," she said, "I want no children until I'm"—she swallowed—"thirty-three." She watched him anxiously.

He pursed his lips. He frowned. He sighed. He clenched his fists until his knuckles whitened. He raised his eyebrows. He smiled thinly. "That's all right by me," he said.

And that, she later realized, was the pattern for all their relations. He gave every appearance of being the strong man, the bluff, no-nonsense colonial, self-sufficient, self-confident, able to address a meeting impromptu at the drop of a chairman's gavel, or to star-navigate his way out of a thousand miles of wilderness; yet when put to the wall, the ultimate wall of Georgina's will, he always yielded. He would never provoke, never even risk, a quarrel.

"Sensible fellow," the family said.

But Georgina, to whom a good quarrel, and the warmth of making it up after, was like a second heart, wasn't so sure.

In one thing alone he would not yield to her: He would not go near Chalfont Abbey. His refusal was strange. In the early days of their courtship, when he had made all the running and she had been merely bewildered that any man could pursue her so ardently, it had seemed that his second greatest desire was to visit the duke and the Abbey. Daily he had asked when she would get an invitation for them. She, for reasons she could not be clear about, had not told him that she needed no invitation, and she had put off their visit to Chalfont Abbey from week to week, always finding it inconvenient.

Then quite suddenly, about the time they (or she) decided not to start a family until 1908, he changed his tune completely. It would be positively wrong to visit Chalfont Abbey; there was even a vague hint of danger in the idea. Socialists were too easily seduced by the centuries-old grace of such establishments; it needed a strong character to withstand the charm of a true aristocrat. "You're all right," he told her. "You're safe. You were vaccinated early in life. But I daren't expose myself to the infection now."

Georgina, who knew she had hurt the duke by not bringing Campbell to meet him, now cursed that inexplicable reluctance which had prevented her when Campbell had been so pressing. But it was no good. He would not go. She had to make her peace alone with the duke.

In an odd way he seemed to understand it better than she. "You always did work by opposites, Georgina," he said. "I don't suppose you ever could have settled with a simple, straightforward fellow. So why are you complaining at not getting one?"

"Because I'm Georgina?" she offered.

He smiled at that. "How pleasant it is," he said, "to agree with you once or twice each decade."

PART SIX

1912-1913

SPERNO ME
RECIPERE AUT
MUTARI

Pride and Privilege

From *Debrett's Peerage and Titles of Courtesy* (1911 edition)

ST. ORMER, DUKE OF. **(Boyce.)** **[Duke, E. 1639.]**

SPERNO ME
RECIPERE AUT
MUTARI

ALFRED BOYCE K.G., G.C.B., G.C.V.O., P.C., 5th Duke; *b.* January 14th, 1826; *s.* 1850; Hereditary Lord Marcher of the Royal Forests; High Steward of Oxford Without; Hon. Colonel-in-Chief D.St.O.L.I.; patron of thirty-five livings; Chairman of the Poor Law Board; Lord Lieutenant of Buckinghamshire; Chairman of Oxfordshire Co.; a D.L. for Cornwall; Fellow of the Royal Society; Pres. of Ox. & Bucks. Territorial Force Assoc.; Brig., Roy. Co. of Archers (King's Bodyguard) for Scotland; appointed a Member of Roy. Comm. on Mil. and Vol. Forces 1903; Hon. Equerry since 1902 to H.M. King Edward VII; K.G. 1874, G.C.B. 1880, G.C.V.O. 1904; has Order of Maria Theresa of Austria and Legion of Honour of France; elected an Hon. Member of Ancient and Hon. Artillery Co. of Boston (U.S.A.) 1882; *m.* 1stly 1850, Flora Laetitia, who *d.* 1893, eld. dau. of the late Sir Duncan Kinnaird, Bt., of Rodings Hall. Oxon. and has issue; *m.* 2ndly 1894, Hermione, who *d.* 1899, dau. of the late Sir Eric Newbiggin, Bt., of Cokeley, and widow of 1st. Viscount Bullen-Chetwynne of Staffs.

ARMS,—Argent, a chevron sanguine surmounted by a fish haurient gold. A chief sable charged with two mullets or. Over all, in the chief centre point, on an escutcheon azure, a cross argent, thereon another cross gules. CREST,—A peacock in pride proper upon a serpent nowed proper. SUPPORTERS,—*Dexter*, an heraldic goat, armed, unguled, and tufted, ducally gorged and chained reflexed or. *Sinister*, an ancient Briton wreathed about the temples and waist in laurels, holding in his dexter hand a sword, gold, resting on his shoulder proper, and supporting with his sinister hand an antique shield, silver. *Motto,*—Sperno me recipere aut mutari.
Seats,—Chalfont Abbey, Bucks.; Constantine Park, Cornwall. *Town Residence*—Knightsbridge House. *Clubs,*—Marlborough, Grillion's, Royal Yacht Squadron, Jockey, Army & Navy, Savage.

SONS LIVING

RICHARD CLARENCE FITZSTEPHEN WROTTESLEY VEITCH *Marquis of Knightsbridge) V.C., K.C.B., K.C.M.G., D.S.O., b.* September 1854; ed. at Eton; is a Maj. General, Coldstream Guards; served in numerous campaigns in Afghanistan, The Soudan, Egypt, and S. Africa, including Rorke's Drift, where he was awarded the V.C.; was A.D.C. to H.M. King Edward VII from 1880; V.C. 1879, K.C.B. 1894, K.C.M.G. 1882, D.S.O. 1890. *Clubs,*—Guards', United Services, Pratt's, Travellers', Savage.

Lord Charles Augustus *M.V.O.; b.* 1856; ed. at Eton and at Trinity Coll. Cambridge; was Attaché and later Secretary at H.B.M's embassies to Berlin, St. Petersburg, and Vienna; M.P. for Marlow since 1895; M.V.O. (Fourth Class) 1897; *m.* 1882 Helen, dau. of Ebenezer Graham of Chicago (U.S.A.) and has issue living, Simon, *b.* 1900; Katherine, *b.* 1887, *m.* 1908, Terence de Vere and has issue living, Leopold, *b.* 1910; Hope, *b.* 1892; Ada, *b.* 1895. *Residences,*—Rosevean Manor, St. Just-in-Roseland, Cornwall; 214 Eaton Sq. SW. *Clubs,*—Reform, Savage, Beefsteak.

DAUGHTERS LIVING

Lady Emily Harriet *(Marchioness of Keyhaven), b.* 1851, *m.* 1875, the 5th Marquis of Keyhaven. *Residences,*—Torridge Hall, Devon; Castle Lovat, Kincardineshire.

Lady Louise Katherine *(Countess of Roundstone), b.* 1853, *m.* 1871, the 14th Earl of Roundstone. *Residences,*—Corby Hall, Cumberland; Lochleven Tower, Skye.

Lady Felicity Grace *(Viscountess Bullen-Chetwynne), b.* 1857, *m.* 1875, the 2nd Viscount Bullen-Chetwynne. *Residences,*—Bullen Towers, Staffs; Ventless Hall, I.O.W.

PREDECESSORS.—[1] GUERINFRAY, *Count of Aumale* (Norman peerage) 11th C., built the castle of Aumale; *s.* by his dau. and h. [2] BERTHE, who *m.* Hugh II, Count of Ponthieu; *d.* 1052; *s.* by their son [3] ENGUERRAUD, who *m.* Adelaide, dau. of Robert, Duke of Normandy (father of William I, the Conqueror, of England) by Herleve or Harlotte, dau. of Fulbert or Robert of Falaise; Enguerraud *d.* at the siege of Argues, 1053; Adelaide became Countess of Aumale; she *m.* (3rdly) [4] EUDES, Count of Champagne, who was deprived of Champagne by his uncle Thibaut before 1071; Eudes acquired Holderness after Domesday; *s.* by his son [5] STEPHEN, Count of Aumalee, Lord of Holderness, who was *b.* before 1070 and would have *s.* the Conqueror if the barons' revolt had been successful; *m.* Hawise, dau. of Ralph de Mortemer of Wigmore, co. Hereford, Seigneur of St. Victor-en-Caux, and one Millicent; *d.* ca. 1125; *s.* by his son [6] WILLIAM, *le Gros,* who, being too fat to fulfil his promise to join the Crusades, founded the Abbey of Meaux, ca. 1150, also Thornton Abbey, co. Lincoln, 1139; *m.* Cicely, Lady of Skipton, dau. of William Fitz Duncan and Alice, L. of Skipton, dau. of William le Meschin, Lord of Copeland; *d.s.p.m.* 1179; *s.* by his dau. [7] HAWISE, who *m.* (1stly) 1179/80, William de Mandeville, Earl of Essex, who *d.s.p.* Nov. 1189; *m.* (2ndly) 1190, William de Forz, who *d.* 1195; *m.* (3rdly) Baldwin de Béthune, Seigneur de Choques in Artois, 3rd son of Robert de Béthune, *le Roux,* S. de Béthune and Avoué d'Arras, and Adelaide, dau. of Hugh III, Count of St. Pol; *d.s.p.m.* 1212; *s.* by [8] WILLIAM II de Forz, son of the 2nd marriage, *b.* 1190–95, was made a conservator of Magna Carta; *m.* 1214, Aveline, 2nd dau. of Richard de Montfichet of Stansted, Essex, and Milicent; *d.* 1241; *s.* by his son [9] WILLIAM III de Forz, *m.* (1stly) before 1236, Christian, dau. of Alan, Lord of Galloway, and (by 2nd marriage) Margaret, dau. of King David of Scotland, Earl of Huntingdon; she *d.* 1246; *m.* (2ndly) 1248/9, Isabel, dau. of Baldwin de Revier, Earl of Devon, and Amice, dau. of Gilbert de Clare, Earl of Gloucester and Hertford; *d.* 1260; *s.* by his son [10] THOMAS, *b.* 1253, *d.* 1269; *s.* by his sister [11] AVELINE, *b.* 1258/9, *m.* 1269, Edmund, later Earl of Lancaster, 2nd son of Henry III of England; she *d.s.p.* 1274; *s.* by her sister [12] MATILDA. (At this time all Aumale lands, which were extensive, and the title, were conveyed by fraud to the Crown. One John d'Eston falsely claimed to be descended from Avice, dau. of William, *le Gros—see* [6] supra—and was so found by jury; whereupon he immediately surrendered all his gains to Edward I of England, receiving by way of reward for his perjury 4½ knights' fees in Thornton by Pickering, co. York. The later Dukedom of Aumale, 1397–1399, granted to Edward, Earl of Rutland, son and h. ap. of Edmund, Duke of York, 5th son of Edward III of England, and extinguished by attainder for treason, was later conceded to be a usurpation of the Aumale title [*Parl. Roll* 14 Charles I, *m.* 14, *fo.* 23] on the granting of the Dukedom of St. Ormer.) Matilda *m.* 1260, Robert du Bois, *b.* 1240, Count of St. Aumer, Lord of Missenden; *d.* 1299; *s.* by his son [13] BALDWIN, *b.* 1275, who *m.* 1311, Alice du Cros, dau. of William, Marquis of Dublin; *d.* 1334; *s.* by his son [14] THOMAS, *b.* 1315, *m.* 1334, Theresa Flitch, eld. dau. of Sir Reynard Flitch; *d.* 1385; *s.* by his son [15] *Sir* CLARENCE du Bois, *K.G.*, one of the founder knights of the Order of the Garter; *b.* 1340, *m.* 1361, Anne Harley; *d.* 1412; *s.* by his son [16] CHARLES, *b.* 1410, *m.* (3rdly) 1486, Matilda Veitch, Lady of Marlow; Sir Charles was summoned to Parliament in right of his wife as *Baron Marlow* (peerage of England) 1486. His natural son was Clarence Fitzbois, *b.* 1434; appointed Hereditary Lord Marcher of the Royal Forests, 1490; cr. *Baron of Stonor* (peerage of England) 1492, he *d.s.p.* 1506, when his titles passed by Royal Favour to his legitimate half-brother [17] RICHARD VEITCH, *b.* 1490, who had *s.* his father in 1494. He commanded the English cavalry with great distinction at Flodden and was cr. *Earl of Brompton* (peerage of England) 1503. He was attainted for treason under Henry VIII of England and beheaded in the Tower; *d.s.p.* 1538. The evidence at his trial was supplied by his nephew [18]GODFREY, son of Sir William du Bois and Margaret Knowle, son of Charles (see [16] supra); *b.* 1522; was cr. *Earl of Belgravia* (peerage of England) 1539, and received all his cousin's titles as reward for his testimony. He served the 1st Duke of Somerset and, on acquiring estates in Cornwall, was cr. *Viscount Constantine* (peerage of England) 1542. He escaped Somerset's disgrace and later greatly enlarged his Cornish estate. He also acquired and rebuilt Chalfont Abbey in co. Buckingham; *d.* 1591; *s.* by his son [19] CHARLES CLARENCE VEITCH, who, falsely suspected of complicity in the Lopez plot to poison Queen Elizabeth, was attainted and forced to flee to Spain in 1594. In 1596 he supplied information that helped Lords Howard and Essex to sack Cadiz, and for this was restored to all his dignities and estates and cr. *Marquis of Knightsbridge* (peerage of England) 1597; *m.* 1578 Lady Pamela Wildwood, dau. of the 2nd Marquis of Westwell; *d.* 1621, *s.* by his son [20] WILLIAM CLARENCE, 2nd Marquis; *m.* 1600 Jane Seton, his cook; played a leading part in organizing the Hampton Court Conference, which was responsible for the King James Bible; *d.* 1624; *s.* by his son [21] CLARENCE WILLIAM HENRY, *K.G.*, 3rd Marquis, then a minor; cr. *Duke of St. Ormer* (peerage of England) 1639, the oldest surviving uninterrupted dukedom, the remainder of which, by a *novodamus* of 1641, may pass, together with the other honours, on the extinction or abeyance of the male line to the hs. of the 1st Duke's eld. dau. Lady Anne Wrottesley; *b.* 1641 (she having fulfilled the necessary condition that she marry a descendant of her uncle, Rev. Ld. Richard, by marrying her cousin, Godfrey du Bois, in 1670) [see * * * infra]; founded big estates in the American colony; he was later a patron of the consortium of London Merchants who profitably farmed the entire English customs duties until 1671 and was able to add tens of thousands of acres to the Berks. estates; he deployed the Berks. Yeomanry, of which he was C.-in-C. first in the royalist cause, later for the parliamentatians; he was a brief supporter of Monmouth's Rebellion in 1685 but in 1688 was of the Whig faction that invited William of Orange on to the throne; *m.* 1638, Jane, eld. dau. of Sir William Wrottesley of Watling Hall and widow of the 4th Earl of Farnham, thus returning the estates at Marlow and Henley to the family; *d.* 1702; *s.* by his son [22] HENRY VEITCH WROTTESLEY, 2nd Duke, Col. of the Berks. Yeomanry, who *d.* in circumstances of utmost gallantry at Oudenarde, 1708; *m.* 1700, Pamela, *Baroness Yeo* in her own right, dau. of 4th Baron Harwick of Bledlow, whose estates at Bledlow passed into the du Bois inheritance; *s.* by his son [23] WILLIAM WROTTESLEY VEITCH, *K.G.* 3rd Duke, then a minor; on his majority he was successively Lord-Lieut. of Ireland, Ambassador to Spain, and a member of most Whig administrations until his death; *m.* 1768, his cousin at one remove, Stephanie Anne, dau. of John Tainter of Bledlow Manor; *d.* 1770; *s.* by his son [24] AUGUSTUS CLARENCE FITZSTEPHEN WROTTESLEY VEITCH, 4th Duke, then in his first year of life; *m.* 1800 Lady Charlotte Emily, dau. of 5th Earl of St. Mawe, who *d.* 1821 without issue; *d.s.p.* 1850; *s.* by his kinsman [25] ALFRED BOYCE, descendant of Rev. Lord Richard du Bois [infra], the present peer, who is also Marquis of Knightsbridge, Earl of Brompton, Earl of Belgravia, Viscount Constantine, Baron Marlow, and Baron of Stonor.

* * * [1] *Rev. Lord* RICHARD du Bois, *K.G.*, Chaplain to Windsor Castle, *b.* 1622, *d.* 1685;

s. by his son [2] GODFREY HENRY of Fingest Manor, *b.* 1645; *m.* 1670, his cousin Lady Anne Wrottesley eld. dau. of the 1st Duke, to whose issue the remainder of the honours [supra] has now descended; *d.* 1707; *s.* by his son [3] WILLIAM, *b.* 1671, who later took the style of William Boyce and embraced the Quaker Faith, *d.* 1723 with issue of three sons,—Orlando, *b.* 1697 out of wedlock by Margaret Champion, who in 1698 *m.* William Boyce,—Henry, *b.* 1699,—John, *b.* 1702; *s.* by his son [4] HENRY, *d.* 1745 with issue of two daughters,—Chastity, *b.* 1732 and—Piety, *b.* 1735. The line of inheritance fell into abeyance between the lines of these daughters. Chastity *m.* 1750 her cousin Oliver Boyce, also styled Boyes, son of the natural son Orlando [supra] and had issue of William, styled Boyes, who *d.s.p.* 1770. Piety *m.* 1755 her cousin Harold Boyce, *b.* 1730, the son of John Boyce [supra] and through her [5], PIETY Boyce, the line continues, *d.* 1790; *s.* by her son [6] JOHN, *b.* 1758, *d.* 1809; *s.* by his son [7] ARTHUR, *b.* 1790, *d.* 1830; *m.* 1825 Felicity Bell, *b.* 1806, *d.* 1827, and had issue of one son [8] Alfred [supra], who succeeded to the dukedom and all other titles save the Barony of Yeo in 1850.

CHAPTER FIFTY-NINE

"WHAT ARE YOU DOING, boy?" she asked. She called them all "boy" because that was what her father called them; she used his peremptory tone, too, which did not suit a ten-year-old girl.

"I'm not 'boy,' " he said. "I'm Boyce."

"What are you doing, Boyce?" She sounded interested this time.

"I'm pushing this hacksaw back and forward against these iron bars."

"Why?"

"To saw them through. Or nearly."

"Why?"

"And then I'm going to fill the saw cuts with clay and boot-blacking so that no one can see I've done it."

"Will you be beaten if you get caught?"

"Probably."

"I won't tell anyone. Do you like my shoes?"

He looked—the price of her juvenile blackmail. "Very pretty. Yes, I like them very much."

"Mr. Starling says they're very pretty too. He lifted me over a puddle in the High Street, and"—she giggled at the memory—"he said, 'We mustn't get those pretty shoes wet, Good Queen Bess.' " She came to Simon's side and gathered some iron filings into the palm of her hand. "He says there are shops in London that sell nothing but ladies' shoes. He says the windows are full of ladies' shoes."

"I shouldn't be surprised if old Eagle doesn't wear ladies' shoes himself," Simon said.

Good Queen Bess shrieked with laughter.

"There!" Simon flexed his fingers and stretched his aching arms. "Now for the disguise."

"Why haven't you sawn them all?"

"I only want a space big enough to get out by if there's a fire. I sleep in this room, you see, and the only other way out is down two flights of wooden stairs and along a wooden corridor."

"Is there going to be a fire?" she asked.

"I hope not. But if there is, I'm not allowed to die."

"Why not?" She was impressed.

He had endured enough. She was very good at corridor football and tag, but she couldn't stop talking. He gave a wink. "I'm much too important. I'm the most important person in the whole world. If I die, I stop dreaming." He made it sound very impressive.

"What harm would that do?"

"Don't you *know?*"

She looked at him sideways, torn between childish fascination at what was probably a tease and grown-up scorn at being thought so juvenile.

"I'm a Dreamer. I'm *the* Dreamer." He shook his head sadly at her ignorance. "Everything in the world is just part of my dream. I'm dreaming this room. I'm dreaming you. I dream everything. And if I was to die, it would all stop. You'd snuff out like an electric light. All of you. Eton. England. All the stars. Everything."

"What about God?"

"He's my best dream yet."

"You're not dreaming *me,*" she assured him scornfully, and pinched her own arm.

"There!" He grinned. "That's exactly what I just dreamed you did."

She was nonplused a moment. Then, cunningly, she pinched *his* arm. It hurt but he steeled himself not to flinch. "I'm dreaming that, too," he told her. "Only you can't hurt the Dreamer."

Even more cunning, she drew back a leg to kick him.

"Have a care," he warned. "I can easily undream those shoes. You ought to be grateful to me for dreaming you something so pretty."

She paused, realizing it was a big risk to be taking. Too big, she decided. She kicked the leg of a bed instead. "I'll bet you didn't dream an unsinkable ship!" she challenged.

"The *Titanic?* Of course I did—last half. And I wasn't even trying. This Easter, just you see, I'll dream a much better ship than that."

"My aunt's going to America on it."

"So's my pater and mater."

"Perhaps you can dream they meet my aunt."

"Cut along now," he said. "Or you'll get me into trouble."

She had the last word. "Could you dream my nose just a little bit straighter and more . . . superior?"

• •

After the fire they said he must be clairvoyant; but he always pointed out that there had, in fact, been an insignificant fire started in the cupboard under the stairs only three nights before he bought the hacksaw. He had even spoken to R. R. Renouf, his housemaster and tutor, about the danger posed by the bars. "Three Arse" had agreed but said that any change had to have the approval of the bursar. Simon had passed two fitful nights, waking up every hour thinking he smelled burning, before he took matters into his own hands and sawed the bars. As his action saved more than forty lives, no one dared to tell him off.

The fire had started just after one o'clock. The first to spot it was a boy in the Upper Boats, called Beeder. He went running through Eton town to the fire station, calling fire all the way. But for his prompt action the house would have been reduced to ashes instead of being merely gutted.

Simon, who had woken hourly to nonexistent fires and phantom smoke, slept through the real thing until the lower stair was an inferno of red. He was awakened by the smell of panic rather than of smoke. Boys who had tried to get down to the ground floor were shouting that they were trapped and were going to die.

He was astonished how quickly he came awake. No sooner was he conscious than he was already walking to the window.

"Two of you fellows, come on, hold me!" he shouted.

Two boys ran to him. He pushed one each side, facing the window, threw an arm around the neck of each, and, using them as anchors, lifted his heels chest high and lashed out at the bar. It snapped at once. "One more!" he shouted as they sprang at the gap.

The second bar was just as easy to knock out. The two boys gasped, thinking it was magic. Simon didn't bother to explain. "Stay here," he ordered, "and help the fellows out. Hold them till they've got a good grip on the ivy. I'll go and tell the others along the corridor."

Within moments his calm voice and businesslike message had quelled the panic. An orderly file of boys—who had even found time to put on slippers and dressing gowns—came pouring into the one room where the bars were absent from the windows.

Simon felt that as "host," so to speak, he ought to be last one out. He even began to argue the point with two fellows in Library, Cockerell and Hasluck; but they forced him out and then made one final tour of the rapidly consuming floor. He could have murdered them.

It was Cockerell and Hasluck who heard, above the roar of

flames and the crack of disappearing timbers, cries for help from the floor below. There was now no possible way down the stairs. They made for the exit window as fast as they could.

"Someone's trapped below!" Hasluck shouted. "It sounds like Sims and Braithwaite."

"No, I'm out here," Braithwaite shouted up.

"Never mind. Get a ladder and . . ."

"All right, my boys!" It was the voice of A. C. Heygate, another housemaster. "Come on down!"

They were still climbing down when R. R. Renouf and two other seniors came running up the street carrying a ladder. Without a pause they hoisted it near-vertical just beside the window at which could be glimpsed the pale faces of two terror-stricken boys, already lit by the hellish red of the fire. It was Sims and Cartwright.

Still without pause Renouf ran up the ladder and, wrapping a handkerchief around his fist, knocked out the glass. The piteous cries of the boys were now audible to everyone.

Renouf grabbed at the bars and hurled himself as hard as he could backward; if they had given way, he would have killed himself. But they held. He shook them futilely, shaking only himself. "An ax!" he shouted. "A hammer! Anything!"

No one had such things. Boys ran off in all directions. Cockerell came up with half a paving stone but it made no impression. The two trapped boys now had to leave the window and retreat to an inner corner of the room.

"Water!" Renouf shouted.

They formed a chain and passed buckets—three in all—up to him. He dashed the water inside, but it was futile. During the long wait for the buckets to be refilled and passed back up, he—blackened, burned, and despairing—was forced helplessly to watch the two boys die, screaming horribly. The fire brigade, which came about five minutes later, saved the outer walls of the house, but no more lives were at risk. They had all been saved by Simon's freelance disobedience of the recognized process.

Dr. Warre, the former headmaster, now provost, and several other masters came at the same time—so quickly had the fire taken hold and done its grim work. The boys were parceled out among them. Warre took Simon. At the end of the street they paused to look back and Simon was disgusted to see that the provost was weeping.

Simon slept beside Warre in the man's own bed. He slept soundly, glad to have done his duty, sorry for the boys who had perished, and slightly contemptuous of the authorities who had allowed such a state of affairs to come about. The trouble with most people was that they could not think ahead.

Next morning he knew it had been no trick of the light. Dr. Warre stood shaving by the window with the tears running freely down his lined and wrinkled cheeks. Simon buried his face in the pillow and fumed.

The provost came over and put a strong hand on his shoulder, trying to comfort him, thinking he was crying. Simon turned and looked coldly up.

Later he heard the provost in his dressing room, the door of which was open, dictating the telegrams to be sent to the two dead boys' fathers. "Very grave news. Come at once. Edmond Warre," he said.

"Sir!" Simon called.

"Are you all right, my boy?" Warre's anxious face appeared in the open door.

"Colonel Sims will come from Scotland, sir," Simon reminded him.

"Yes?"

"By the time he gets to Euston, it will be in the newspapers. Everything. He'll see it."

Warre nodded gravely. "Yes, I see," he said. "Thank you, Boyce." And he went back to dictate the telegrams again, this time in specific terms.

It was a good breakfast. Simon ate as heartily as he ever had in his life. Boiled eggs had never smelled so magnificent.

"How old are you, Boyce?" Warre asked.

"Twelve, sir, last January. I was born on the first day of this century. One, one, oh, oh. My mother says I'm lucky because it's the same in the English and American ways of writing it. My mother's American."

"When you told me about Colonel Sims traveling from Scotland . . . did that strike you as soon as you heard me dictating those messages?"

"Yes, sir."

"You've a remarkable head on your young shoulders."

"Thank you, sir." Simon smiled the way beautiful women smile on being told they are beautiful. "The fact is, sir, I was talking with my uncle, General Knightsbridge, at Christmas and he said the hardest part of command is writing to the next-of-kin of soldiers who die."

"Well, it is. He's quite right."

"And he said if you send a telegram always tell them everything. Never let them find out from neighbors or the papers." Simon smiled and dug into his second egg. "So it isn't surprising I thought of it, really, is it, sir?"

"Perhaps not." The provost was taken aback at his coolness. "But I'm grateful to you for speaking up as you did. You've saved me from inadvertently causing both parents a great deal of unnecessary distress. I thank you."

"Not at all, sir," Simon said graciously.

He was put in Heygate's until more permanent arrangements could be made. On his second night there he was disturbed by a rustling sound; he had always slept lightly, but since the fire he would awaken to the sound of a mouse on the next floor. He rose and peeped outside the dormitory door.

Beeder, who had been transferred to Heygate's too, was creeping down the stairs. Beneath his arm he carried a roll of newspaper and in his hands a bundle of kindling. He did not notice Simon though he walked directly past him. Simon followed him down to the ground floor, where Beeder at once made for the cupboard under the stairs—the house was a mirror image of Renouf's. Moments later he heard a match being struck and saw the flicker of flames. He drew back into a doorway.

Beeder, unseeing as before, and night-blinded now by the fire he had kindled, ran stealthily past and tiptoed up the stairs. Simon walked quickly to the cupboard, saw that the flame, though burning merrily on the paper, had barely caught the wood, and pissed it to extinction.

He knew exactly what to do next. The unwritten Eton code said in effect, "Can you cope on your own? If so, don't bother others." Simon was never in his life doubtful that he could cope with anything. He went back to his dormitory, put on socks and a jersey under his dressing gown, took a chair, and went to sit outside Beeder's room for the rest of the night. When Heygate did his morning rounds at six forty-five, Simon calmly explained why he was there. Heygate, after looking at the evidence below the stair, came back and told him to say nothing and tell no one. Beeder was away by breakfast time, never to be seen again.

At first they said that the upset of the fire (lots of boys were sleeping badly) had made Beeder walk in his sleep and start this second one all unknowingly. But then people began to remember that it was Beeder who had raised the alarm at Renouf's fire—and that he had, even then, been fully clothed.

The following evening a message came asking Simon to call on

Dr. Warre. The fellow looked grave as he ushered the young man into his study.

"Normally, my boy," he said, "the headmaster would tell you this—as he would have sent those telegrams if he had not been away at Oxford at the time. But I have asked him if *I* may tell you this grave news, applying those precepts you yourself taught me." He drew agonized breath. They said his heart was not good. Simon worried for him.

"It is with the deepest regret that I have to tell you that the liner *Titanic* has sunk and that many people—most of those on board—have drowned. Your father was, I'm afraid I have to say, among them. He was a brave man and a gentleman. He could have taken a place in a lifeboat, yet he yielded it to others."

Simon stood rigidly before the old man. He was shocked, of course, but he knew how to take it. "And my mother, sir?" he said at last.

"She is here." He gestured toward the rest of the house. "She has come to—"

"But wasn't she with him? She was traveling with my father."

Warre was nonplused. "She said nothing of that, my boy. She has come to take you home for a while."

Simon nodded. The relief that his mother was safe helped him to master his grief at the news of his father's death. Warre, who had blubbed so unmanfully the other day, would now see that he, Simon, knew how to play the man. Was he not, after all, a Boyce? He drew breath.

"I thank you, sir," he said. "I am glad my father died like a gentleman. He would not, in fact, have known any other way. I imagine I am to go home?"

The provost, at any other time, would have delivered a stiff lecture on priggishness but, in the circumstances, let it go. "At once," he said. "I shall ask your mother to leave first and wait in the carriage."

Simon stiffened. "There will be no need for that, sir." He smiled at Warre. "And . . . thank you for telling me."

The "carriage" was a 40/50 horsepower Rolls-Royce with a Pullman body. His mother formed no more than a pale shape, sitting stiffly upright, in the back. He sank into the luxurious West of England cloth, not touching her.

"Hello, mother," he said. All his manliness began to desert him.

"Hello, Simon." Her hand found his and squeezed as the car pulled silently away. He almost succumbed. In panic he looked around the lamplit streets, seeking the familiar shades of other Etonians in their toppers and cutaways—wanting above all to show them he was not crying. Helen waited.

Past Windsor, on the Runnymede road, he yielded. Hating his childishness, he turned to his mother, threw his arms about her, and sobbed as he had not sobbed since he was half his age. Her soft, perfumed body, her strong, protective grasp, her understanding silence—these were comforts he had forgotten, indeed, had forced himself to forget ever since, at the age of eight, he had been sent away to school. The intensity of the pleasure they yielded was a mark of that sacrifice.

But what had been sacrificed was truly dead. He would make sure he paid for this childish and contemptible indulgence. For her sake he disguised his weakness by saying, "I thought you were sailing with the pater."

His mother explained that she had been on the point of leaving with his father when Hope, who was due to travel to Sweden to meet Count and Countess Cederstam, her fiancé's parents, had gone down with an appendicitis. Helen had stayed behind, intending to take the next suitable boat and join Charles in Chicago, where they were to attend her parents' diamond wedding anniversary.

"How is Hope?" he asked through his after-tears hiccups.

"Coming along fine."

By the time they reached Belgravia he was relishing the pleasure of whispering at speed through the misty, gaslit streets of London, warm and cocooned—and above all alive—in such luxury. He remembered the luxury of the *Titanic*, which his father had shown him in photographs—a jumbled memory of acres of mahogany, gilding, marble and crystal, of deep carpets and inlay, of brilliant lights, of every last refinement that money could command. He imagined his father's drowned body floating like a torpid fish in that vast, unsinkable tomb on the ocean floor, nudging the Corinthian columns and tangling with the velvet curtains. He did not shrink from the picture. His moment of weakness was past.

He asked his mother if she knew exactly what had happened. "Sharpe will tell us when he returns," she said. "He was there to the end."

Sharpe was his father's valet. Like Lord Charles he had gone down with the ship; unlike him, Sharpe had apparently survived.

Helen reminded her son that he was now the heir presumptive to the dukedom—in view of which he would spend the whole Easter holiday with his grandfather at Chalfont Abbey.

In the following days a letter arrived from Sharpe, enclosing a letter given him by Lord Charles in case he, Sharpe, survived. It was to all of them:

14th/15th April, 1912

My darlings,
The unthinkable is happening; the unsinkable *Titanic* is sinking, not very fast, but undeniably. Soon the champagne glass before me will fall over because of the tilting.

For all the care they lavished on the luxuries, it seems they forgot to provide sufficient lifeboat accommodation. I went on deck a while ago and was sickened not only at the lack of organization but at the mad scramble for places by male first-class passengers. It may not be so all over the ship, but it was certainly the case on whichever deck it was I visited. I came back below to write this, a copy of which I shall give to Sharpe. An officer told me there is little chance of surviving in the cold sea for more than a few minutes; but we are putting up distress rockets all the time and neighbouring ships are bound to answer.

If I survive, we shall laugh at this letter. If not, you will weep at it. What can I tell you in so short a time that I have not told you in long years? Be godly, righteous, and sober? Love one another? Does it come to no more than that?

You will never lack for such counsel and do not need me, five thousand miles away and much, much closer to Eternity, to add to it. Let me tell you what I now regret.

I regret the myriad ideas I rejected without testing them—because I thought I had no time. I regret the thousands of people whose company I never cultivated—because I thought I had no time. I regret the hundreds of books I bought and did not read—because I thought I had no time. Far more, I regret the thoughts I did not share with you, the kindnesses I planned and did not carry out, the compliments I rehearsed and never spoke, the love I often felt and never expressed—because I thought that time was infinite.

If in the hours of your deaths (and may they be long, long away) you feel this letter has helped to lessen for you the sting of such regrets, then I am not wasting what may be the last hours of my life. At last I have time!

> Do not imagine I am now going out in order to die. I shall take my chances with the sea, freezing though it is; but I will not do so at the expense of women and children. Nevertheless, I'll do my d——dest to survive.
>
> Thank you, Katherine, Hope, Ada, and Simon, for the gaiety and zest and life and sparkle that so enriched my middle years; your mother will need them all now so do not stint them to her.
>
> And thank you, dearest Helen, for a life so immeasurably richer and more full of wonders than I deserved or ever dared to hope for. You are a woman of rare qualities. Do not incarcerate them in my memory. Share them—in memory of me, if you will. You were not spared this death merely to impose another kind upon yourself.
>
> Your eternally loving father and husband,
>
> Charles

A week later, Sharpe himself returned, looking ill and tired. His wife, one of the upper servants, was naturally delighted at his escape. Helen offered them a holiday in a cottage on the remnant of the Cornish estate. Sharpe joked that he'd seen enough of the sea for one year; he thought he'd mend better if he got straight back in harness.

He told them the story that, from a dozen newspaper accounts, they now knew by heart; the iceberg, the annoyance, the calming reassurances that the ship could not sink, the increasing forrard tilt, the overflooding of the first watertight bulkhead, and, with it, the realization that every bulkhead was just as vulnerable and that the ship could, indeed, be sunk; then the realization that there were not enough lifeboats, the locking of the gates upon the third-class and steerage passengers, the disgraceful confusion on the boat decks and the utterly selfish and unscrupulous behavior of some first-class passengers, especially some of the men . . .

But he also told them of true gentlemen, some of whom assisted at the boats, others of whom went back below and played cards, or read the Bible, or wrote letters . . . according to their way.

When Lord Charles had finished his letters and the copies, he wrapped them in oiled silk and gave one set to Sharpe. Then he took two bottles of champagne and two glasses and, in his top hat and fur coat, went up on deck with Sharpe.

"He gave me his silk city coat with the astrakhan collar, my lady," Sharpe said. "I reckon that's what saved my life. I didn't know a good coat'll keep you warm in water like what it does in air, but I'll swear that coat did to me.

"We went up near the back of the ship where the orchestra was playing. Of course it was tilting too much for comfort to sit down, so we stood nearby, leaning against a deckhouse. He asked me to open the champagne, my lady. Bollinger '84 it was. And he held the glasses while I poured. Then he gave me one and thanked me for . . . well! I'd blush to repeat it now. I didn't deserve all the fine things he said, but it certainly kept out the cold!

"Then we toasted England and the king. Then our wives and all our loved ones, then the navy—only not so quick like this. When the band played a good hymn we joined in and sang. Still, we got rid of that bottle quick enough. Then we started on the other one.

"The worst thing was the great cracks that kept ringing out as the ship tilted. You can't describe them. It wasn't only hearing them. You felt them, too. They were so loud in the air you could feel them in the bottoms of your lungs. And through the deck, through your feet, of course. But feeling them in your lungs was worse. Each time you'd think it was breaking up.

"Then the tilt got very steep and a great wind was rushing out of everything, and you could hear a sort of boiling noise down inside. And we'd almost finished the second bottle when he looked at it and he said, I'll never forget it, he looked at it and said, 'This champagne's flat—and you're Sharpe'—he looked up at me, see? 'This champagne's flat, and you're Sharpe!' Then he laughed and he said, 'It's all music!' The way he always said it."

Helen bowed her head and wept.

"I'm sorry, my lady." Sharpe was worried for her now. "I didn't mean to cause you distress, your ladyship."

Helen waved her hand. "No, no. I want to hear." She blew her nose. "Go on."

"There isn't much more, my lady. The band had to leave off playing. We, Lord Charles and me, we stood on the side of a deck house for a bit and sang hymns. 'Nearer, My God to Thee,' I remember, and 'Lead, Kindly Light.' Only it was getting very loud now. Then he said, 'Well, Sharpe. Time to go. If you make it and I don't, tell them' "—Sharpe's voice quivered and began to break—" 'tell them . . . my last thought . . . was of them.' " Now he was weeping openly. Only Simon remained master of himself.

CHAPTER SIXTY

GENTLEMEN, YOUR HEIR, Simon Boyce," the duke growled as he led the boy into the crypt. "Our Tribe—God Almighty's gentlemen." He completed the introduction.

Simon was the first in the line of Boyces who did not look to see if this introduction were some sort of joke.

"I knew half a dozen of these people," the duke said. "Three of them intimately. My predecessor, the Fourth Duke, old Augustus—and my own two duchesses, your grandmother and step-grandmother. They were the noblest people in my lifetime. These"—he touched Flora's and Hermione's coffins—"are the remains of two of the noblest women who ever lived."

He peered at the boy. "You may wonder if you have the makings of a duke in you. I certainly wondered when I stood here, over sixty years ago now, beside old Augustus. But don't worry, my boy. It's in the blood. Blood is all. The blood of all these people flows in your veins. When it's your turn to be duke, remember these ladies and gentlemen, our Tribe. It's all you need. They'll come and stand by you when you need them."

Simon took it very coolly. He had always known these things. But when it came to placing his hand inside the coffin of the Reverend Lord Richard du Bois and touching the mummified corpse, even he felt—as his own father and Alfred before him had felt—that sudden mystic communion with the very *idea* of what the duke called their Tribe. Then it was more than simple pride that filled him.

"But remember this too," the duke said, pointing to the marble slab he had inserted on Duke Augustus' coffin. "He said it to me on his deathbed: All empire is no more than power in trust."

He took the toy horse, Caesar, which he had carried from the moment they entered, and placed it between the two latest coffins, Flora's and Hermione's. Then he pointed to an empty bronze coffin on the floor. "That's mine," he said. "It'll go up there when I'm in it. Meanwhile we'll let Caesar keep my most noble ladies company. Before I go up, put him back where the keys are kept. I want you to do that."

On the way up to the top of the tower the duke, riding piggyback on a gardener, told Simon of the mummified head of Captain Plisetski. Then from the battlements they looked out over a mere fraction of their land.

Simon found his grandfather one of the easiest people in the world to talk to. He had always got on with the old duke. In 1906, because of "health" and various other excuses, they had all gone cruising in the *Hermione* in the Aegean and had tied up in Athens. He and his granddad had spent a marvelous day souvenir hunting among the ruins. That same day they heard that the Olympic games were going on in Athens, and cousin Frederick, Georgina's brother, walked in to town in his flannels and came back with two gold medals and one silver. In Simon's world, achievements and honors were easily won. His other grandfather, the venerable Gramps Graham, always said that "success is perspiration enjoying its retirement." But he had only half the story; opportunity is the other half. And Opportunity wore the Boyce livery. The duke waved his hand over the landscape. "It's a grand thing to feel you own all that. It gives you no end of a feeling of importance. The same with our three pages in *Debrett*. You see yourself there as Duke of Saint Ormer and you think, 'I must be one hell of a fine fellow.' What I want to say to you is: Don't deceive yourself that way or you'll go down in history as a nincompoop. It means nothing. It's a snare. It's a drag-scent across your real line.

"All over England now, great families are parting from their houses and estates. No doubt they think they have their secure place in history but most of them aren't even footnotes. They're leaving because they're failures. And we're still here because we aren't. We're still doing our job." He cleared his throat. There was a moment's pause.

"Nothing new in all this, of course," he continued. "Been going on in a small trickle for centuries, but the little beck is now a great river of failure and desertion. Where are the Findernes now? The Findernes who once had vast lands in Derbyshire and fought for England in the Holy Land? Where's Lord Egremont, eh, who less than a century ago gave away twenty thousand pounds a year in personal charity? Have you ever heard of him?"

"No, sir."

"There you are! And we'll vanish the same way unless we go on maintaining our part of the bargain, the bargain that allows us to keep all that land, all those homes and lives, under our own control. It's two-sided, you see? The lands and titles are privileges we must go out and earn afresh every day of our lives. And the pensions we give our people, and the schooling we give their children, and the medical attendance . . . the libraries, the hospitals, the parks, the meeting halls . . . we spent over a hundred thousand pounds on it last year . . . all that—it isn't their *right*, either. They have to earn it by keeping their part of the bargain. It's a bargain between master and servant that goes far beyond anything in the lawbooks."

He sighed. "For me it's been easy. I lived through a time when most people understood all I've been saying. But you'll have a much harder time of it, I'm afraid, Simon. You'll have to carry the fight out to the enemy. You'll have to preach the Gospel of the Aristocracy among the Unbelievers."

"What enemy, granddad?"

"The middle classes," the duke said. "They've got the power now. So don't imagine you'll be able to fight them there. That was old Duke Augustus's battle—and even he saw it was lost. He told me the middle classes have got to set the sail and officer the ship, as long as we captain her and do the steering. That was my battle—staying captain and keeping the tiller in our grasp. We won it *here*, we Boyces, on our own estates and in our own industries. But we lost it, we the aristocracy, we lost it in the nation at large through pride and frivolity. There'll never be another prime minister from the Lords. They've taken the tiller from us and stolen the captain's hat and spyglass. They've got them for good, I'm afraid."

"What's left, then, granddad?"

"The map, my boy. We still have the map. That's *your* battle: Stop them from redrawing it. Stop them writing *Here be strange beasts* over our demesnes. D'ye see?"

"Of course, sir."

"If ever you need a guide—your mother won't like this, bless her, but it's the plain truth—if ever you need a guide about what *not* to do, look to America. They began with a good map—naturally, it was drawn up by aristocrats. But ever since then they've been led astray and polluted by raw democracy. So America will always show you the unlovely face of a land and people bereft of a nobility. Their political life is one great cesspool of corruption. Roosevelt even made idealism stink. And now—*Taft!* Their industry is in the hands of thieves and moneygrubbers. Natural gentlemen like your Grandfather Graham are June snowflakes over there. Their system of land tenure is democracy gone mad. No great estates at all. Every snout in the trough. So the country's greatest asset is in the horny hands of illiterate, unshaven, collarless cowboys who couldn't keep the job of parish hedge trimmer hereabouts.

"But they'll reap the inevitable harvest of all this. In your lifetime they'll sink in socialist anarchy, you'll see. Perhaps then our own middle classes will understand and draw back from the abyss, and restore to their rightful place in the shires those of the nobility they haven't plundered out of existence.

"That's what you must fight for—that day, my boy. That's why you must keep the standard of the nobility flying high and proud and clean. Put principles before money and it'll surprise you how the money will pour in. Think first of your obligations to our people, and you'll be astonished at how the respect and deference flows toward you in return. Now d'you see?"

"I do, sir. Indeed I do. In fact I never doubted it."

"Mind you," the duke added. "Don't make a god out of principle. That's falling into the middle-class trap. What I mean, my boy, is that I can show you the road. I can tell you it's straight. And I can tell you to go straight along it. But on the way, you know bloody well you're going to meet puddles, potholes, horseshit, dead badgers, footpads, pretty wenches, calls of nature, and ten dozen other good reasons for a little detour where the going is a sight more rough and you're rather glad no one can quite see what you're up to."

The duke then surprised his grandson by asking, "Seen anything you want to change, young man?"

Simon, feeling that a show of modesty was called for, said, "I should think I'd have a hard enough job keeping things the way they are, sir."

"You would indeed. That would be the hardest job of all—making no changes. You'll make them all right, because you're not me. All you have of me is my blood. Also that of the Kinnairds, who have all the charm of fox cubs and all the cunning of old hunting dogs. Also, of course, the Grahams. They're as fine a family as America is likely to produce under her present lamentable circumstances. So look at the influences you'd be fighting if you simply tried to follow me rigidly!

"I made changes from my very first day. I was the first duke to own industrial companies, to engage in manufacture. I was the first to promote polytechnical education. When I founded the *Vindicator* for Neville, I was the first to own a newspaper—and I'm still the only one. I'm sure old Augustus has turned in his coffin a dozen times since I became duke. So if I'm still lying supine, hands on chest, fifty years from now, it'll mean you're a great disappointment to me, I promise."

He returned to the theme after dinner as he and Simon shunted the port back and forth.

"Don't be afraid to change things," he said. "You couldn't have had a bigger change than that between Queen Victoria and Bertie. She did most royal business from Windsor, which was kept very quiet by her wishes. The whole castle used to be like a cloister. People whispered in the corridors. There was always the sense of some awe-inspiring *appearance* about to occur. Well, Bertie couldn't have been more different from his mother—accessible, friendly, not even afraid to be familiar. Also bloody frank when need arose. He knew, you see, how to discard ceremony without losing dignity. If I think of him now, I see him standing with his back to the fireplace, smoking, and two or three of us—Lord Esher, Lord Knollys, people like that—sitting, talking with him! *Sitting!* Some changes, I'm sure, he made deliberately to say, 'Mark me now! I intend doing many things differently.'

"It was a symbol, you see, my boy. A duke, above all people, should know and understand the power of a symbol. People think in symbols. They're not logical at all."

The old duke thought back over what he had said, nodded profound agreement with it, and then added, "Thank heaven."

CHAPTER SIXTY-ONE

CHARLES HAD SENSED it back in the 1890s; by the autumn of 1913 only a Highland shepherd would have sufficient excuse not to feel it in the very air: apocalypse. The powers of Europe were hell-bent on teaching one another a lesson. Hardly anyone questioned that there would be a war—only when.

Knightsbridge, professionally closer to it than any of them, suggested to his older sisters, Emily and Louise, that they, as the seniors of their generation, should set about and organize the grandest Christmas that Chalfont Abbey had ever known. Above all they should try and assemble all the descendants—children, grandchildren, and great-grandchildren—including, he stressed, his own bastard son, Neville, his wife, and their three infants.

The two old ladies protested that it had been all very well having Neville at Christmas when he was little more than an orphan; then it had been an act of charity. But now that he was a prosperous newspaper publisher, it seemed like rewarding immorality. Knightsbridge told them that the duke would certainly insist on having all Danielle's brood, so he was hemmed if he could see why Neville should be excluded. They should be grateful that their father's thirteen-year liaison with the new trollop, this Meg Bucket, was so far barren.

Emily and Louise were, of course, chiefly afraid of unsuitable attachments between legitimate daughters in one half of the family and bastard sons in the other half. Neville's three were all under eight years old and so posed no immediate threat. The two great ladies turned to their father's descendants via Danielle. She herself had been pensioned off in the 1870s and had died in 1906, but Frances and Grenville were both married, alive, and well. Too well. It was infuriating, the way immorality had triumphed and turned respectable.

Frances, now nearly sixty, had married Henry Turnbull, a well-to-do Manchester tea merchant; they had a large house and five acres on the Countess of Wharfedale's estate at Alderley Edge. Of their three sons two were married, one with three children, the other (only three years married) with one. The third, Will, was thirty years old and a bachelor. He was the danger, then.

Grenville, at fifty-five, was reaping the harvest of over thirty years of successful expansion from refrigeration to compressors, to rock drills, to mining machinery of all kinds, to compressed gases, to welding and cutting equipment—all under the *Diamond* trademark. The duke's original thousand was now worth several hundred times as much. Grenville's three offspring were, from Emily's and Louise's point of view, quite satisfactory. Stewart, the middle one, had just married. Patrick and Laura, eldest and youngest, were newly engaged.

"If they come with their affianced ones," Emily said, "they may get each other into trouble but keep us out of it."

"It only leaves Will," Louise agreed, meaning that if two old dragons like them couldn't keep him the wrong side of the blanket, then Propriety was a lost cause anyway.

The duke was delighted at the idea of the party. He had already lived seventeen years beyond his biblical span. Now, with the smell of war everywhere, this Christmas had to be reckoned as the last of his chances to assemble and see the living half of his Tribe. Even then Father Time had done his winnowing. Charles and Felicity were gone; so were John Cardigan and James Lucan. Two of Flora's fifteen grandchildren, and one of Hermione's ten, were dead. All twenty of Flora's great-grandchildren were alive, and more were on the way; but of Hermione's four, one had died in infancy only last year. Still, with Danielle's six grandchildren and four great-grandchildren, it made a respectable sixty-four descendants (fourteen of whom, Hermione's, imagined they descended from Bull). They amounted to one descendant for every year that had passed since he married Flora—plus one for luck.

It was a good thing Alfred had not married Meg, for she had produced neither son nor daughter for him—and it wasn't for want of trying. But her youth and untutored sensuality had brought new zest to what would otherwise have been his declining years. The trick that had failed with King David had put the spring back into the step and life of Duke Alfred.

The first thing the two old ladies did was draw up a list of the family as it then stood:

CHALFONT ABBEY—Christmas 1913

(FAMILY LIST)

FAMILY OF MARQUIS OF KEYHAVEN, Mervyn, Emily.
Henry, E. of Pennington, and Gertrude (37 & 25): Lawrence (3), Ellen (1);
Ld George and Amy (35 & 25): Winston (4), Beryl (2), Theresa (bia);
L. Lucy and Laurence Rothschild (33 & 40): Stephen (13), Paul (11), Edward (8), Bernice (6)

FAMILY OF EARL OF ROUNDSTONE, Michael, Louise.
Tarquin Viscount Lambert, and Edna (38 & 30): s.p.;
~~L. Fabia Wellcome (35):~~ Faith (16), Peter (15);
L. Portia and Sir Bernard Devereaux (33 & 39): Felix (4), Mary (3)

(Family of Marquis of Knightsbridge) Richard Neville Boyce and Annette (38 & 30): Paula (7), Theo (6), Veronica (3)

FAMILY OF LATE LD. CHARLES BOYCE, Helen.
Katherine and Terence de Vere (26 & 28): Leopold (3), Margaret (1);
Hope and Yngve Cederstam (21 & 29): Ada (18), Simon (13)

FAMILY OF VISCOUNT BULLEN-CHETWYNNE, William Redvers.
Hon. Georgina and Campbell Stone (38 & 48);
Hon. Frederick and Cynthia (32 & 26): William (1);
Hon. Ada and Claude Wingfield (30 & 32): Peregrine (7)

FAMILY OF LATE HON. JOHN CARDIGAN BULLEN-CHETWYNNE, Letys.
Herbert (26);
May and Henry Williamson, Ld. Malvern (23 & 49): Phoebe (1)

FAMILY OF HON. GEORGE RAGLAN BULLEN-CHETWYNNE, George and Lady Mary Peregrine (27);
Albert and Eleanor (26 & 25): Edward (6);
Rowena and Hon. Roger Bouverie (23 & 35): s.p.

FAMILY OF LATE HON. JAMES LUCAN BULLEN-CHETWYNNE, Jennifer.
Michael (27);
Fanny (25);
Florence and Frederick Cunningham, Ld. Felton (23 & 37): George (3), Mary (2)

(Family of Fitzbois)
Family of Frances (48) and late Henry Turnbull:
Claude and Marjorie (36 & 31): Alfred (10), Charles (8), Mary (4);
Bertie and Mary (34 & 23): Graham (2); Will (30)

Family of Grenville and Joan Fitzbois (55 & 46): Patrick Fitzbois (23) and Laura Pennicot (18?);
Stewart Fitzbois (21) and Alicia Enderby (19?);
Laura Fitzbois (18) and John Taw (25?)

Lady Louise picked up a thick colored pencil and drew a line through the name of Lady Fabia Wellcome, her own elder daughter —the unmentionable black ewe of the family. "That creature will *not* be coming," she said with large determination and a tight little smile. She tapped the list with her pen. "Eighteen of them are younger than six. That's absurd. Let's get everyone to agree to leave them at home."

Lady Emily was doubtful. "Gertie won't be parted from Larry

and Ellen," she said. "And will the Feltons leave George and Mary? What is happening to parents these days?"

"I know what you mean, dear. Portia's just the same with Felix and Mary. How can anybody be expected to arrange a successful house party with all that infantile indiscipline and vomit going on in the wings?"

"You know those empty rooms in the Brighton wing, the ones that aren't used as laboratories? Let's make them over into nurseries."

"A good idea." Lady Louise chuckled. "All the smells together. Yes! And the under-tens beside them—a dormitory. That'll teach them!" She ticked her savage way down the list. "Well, that's got rid of twenty-six of them," she crowed.

Lady Emily had meanwhile been counting. "Here's luck," she said brightly. "All our ten-to-fifteens are boys—"

"Coal hole!" Lady Louise interrupted.

"The two Rothschilds, Peter Wellcome, Simon—and this little Turnbull creature, Alfred, they've called him. Such impudence!"

"Definitely the coal hole."

"And all our sixteen-to-nineteens are gels: Faith Wellcome . . . Helen's Ada, Laura Fitzbois, and these two betrothed young females who (I assume) are not yet twenty—Laura Pennicot and Alicia Enderby." She lingered over the names.

"Anyway," Lady Louise said decisively, "We'll put all five gels together. And Fanny."

"Oh! D'you really think so? She's such a determined little spinster. She'll resent it."

"Serve her right for not getting married when she had the chance. An unmarried gel of twenty-five can hardly expect a room of her own."

"I'll tell you what, Louise. Let's put her in with Georgina. That husband of hers is bound to refuse the invitation."

"*If* Georgina doesn't need the extra space for storing bombs and pamphlets," Lady Louise said. But she agreed to the suggestion.

"Our great problem, as I see it," said Lady Louise, "is Master Will Fitzbois, the family's least eligible bachelor. And Ada, our most eligible young gel. She and Will are half cousins. Hmmm!"

"Hmmm!" Lady Emily agreed. "And she'll be the sister of the next duke."

"Or next but one, if what's left of Knightsbridge survives our father. It is quite clear to me that we must steer Master Will either toward Fanny or toward our five widows. And Herbert, Peregrine, and Michael must be told to monopolize Ada. Well, dear, I'm sure Knightsbridge would agree we've got that particular flank very well covered."

"What else? We have a teeny little worry about the ages. We are only thirteen over-fifties and there will be forty-one in their twenties or thirties."

"Lord! I hear foxtrots and turkey trots—the whole menagerie of trots—already."

"It isn't that," said Lady Emily, who was quite fond of dancing, "it's the greasepaint, the crêpe hair, and the smell of collodion and theatrical costumes!"

"You're so right, dear. I wonder if there's a nice quiet hotel nearby—or even in Paris?"

CHAPTER SIXTY-TWO

WHEN THE INVITATION came, Campbell—as everyone had expected, even Georgina—refused to consider it.

"But this will be a *family* affair," she pleaded. "It'll never happen again in our lives. Even the duke's bastard children will be there, and their children, too."

He gritted his teeth. "Don't," he pleaded. "You don't know how hard it is to say no to you, my darling. But I must. It's a matter of principle."

"Oh, bugger your bloody principles!"

"Georgina!"

"Well . . ." She paused. A sudden understanding dawned. She smiled. "Why did I never think of it until now? That's what it is. You're frightened."

"Nonsense!"

"It's not nonsense. You're frightened of us. And of the duke—yes, especially of the duke. You needn't be, you know," she assured him. "Aunt Helen told me a spiffing trick around that; it really cuts the duke down to our own size. Even to *his* own size."

"What?" he asked. "What trick."

So Georgina told him how Helen had discovered papers in the

muniment room proving that Orlando Boyce had been legitimate after all. And therefore, if his line had not petered out two generations later, when William Boyes died on a prison hulk, his descendants would now be at Chalfont Abbey and the duke—the present duke, Alfred—would be a humble manufacturer of lacquered boxes.

The story had the most astonishing effect on Campbell. He began to tremble. He stood up and walked about. He stared at her as if he suspected some trap was about to spring. "I don't believe it," he said when she finished. "I don't want to believe it."

"But why ever not, darling? I find it a great help."

"I won't believe it."

"Which means you won't come to the house party."

"No." He almost fled from the room, pausing only to say, "You go, though. I'd hate you to stay away on my account. You go."

Georgina, puzzled enough by this behavior, was even more puzzled a week or so later. He received a small package from Australia and, on opening it at breakfast, said in a toneless voice, "My dad's dead."

He had rarely mentioned his father. She had no idea how he felt about the old man. She watched his face intently for clues. "Oh, Campbell, dearest, I'm so sorry," she began.

"Ah, well, it happens to us all," he said, still without emotion. He was sorting through the remaining contents of the package.

She thought he was being very brave about it. "Will we have to go out to Australia now?" she asked.

But he was lost in one of the papers the packet had contained. "Mmm?" he asked at last.

"I said, do we have to think of going to Australia now?"

He shook his head, but she wasn't sure he'd even heard her. He looked at the paper again, then at her. "This family party," he said. "It means a lot to you, eh?"

"You know it does."

"You'd really like me to come?"

Her face lit up. "Oh, Campbell! Would you? Oh, would you, my dearest?"

He grinned. "Why not. You're all the family I've got now. You and the duke and the whole tribe of you. Oh, and by the way—we inherit about two million pounds. Maybe more. But it's vulgar to be precise about these things, isn't it?"

The first to arrive were Helen and her family, as soon as Eton went down. Their London house was being redecorated after a loose chimney pot had crashed through the roof. The duke had offered them Knightsbridge House, at least while they did their Christmas shopping, but Helen found it impossible to stay there because of the primitive conditions of all the toilet facilities. The only water closet in the place was intended for the servants and was put behind a screen in the kitchen. Gentlemen, even callers, were supposed to go out and use the bushes in Hyde Park; for ladies there were two rows of cubicles with chamber pots under the main staircase.

The family considered Helen excessively fussy for refusing to stay at Knightsbridge House, but she preferred at least the earth closets of Chalfont Abbey, even if it meant two hours of travel to do her London shopping. Anyway, the young people were far better off at country pursuits in Bucks than getting up to no good in London.

"Where are we? Where are we?" Ada rushed to the guest book to find what rooms they had been assigned. "You're in the green Chinese room, mother."

"Aunt Hermione's old room."

"We're in the Jane Seton room," Ada said. "Where's that?"

"The boys are in the Wrottesley room," Simon said. "But that surely doesn't include me?"

"No, Master Simon," Mrs. Mouncey, the servant in charge, said. "His grace commanded you were to have the room you stayed in at Easter."

Soon afterward the two older Rothschild boys, Stephen and Paul, arrived and Simon went with them on a great refresher exploration of the house and outbuildings. Next day was better still. Peter Wellcome arrived and, being fifteen, took charge at once, even of Simon. He led them over to Stainor Common, where they pretended to be poor boys and opened and shut the gates for passing cars and carriages, scooping up the pennies and halfpennies with exaggerated whoops of delight, shouting "Whoi, thankee zur, thankee hearty!" in broadest Mummerset. When they had collected a shilling, they reverted to being lords and masters of mankind, commandeered a ride to Great Marlow, and bought three pennyworth of fish and chips each, "and a good dollop of the scrumpy bits, too!" Peter told the man. Simon wondered if all this was quite befitting the dignity of a future duke, but didn't see why he shouldn't get the best of both worlds.

On their way back through Strawberry Grove they stalked for German spies—which was how they saw the man and woman without the man and woman seeing them.

"What is he doing to her?" Paul Rothschild asked, he being only eleven.

The others giggled and he understood he had asked a naïve question.

"Here's a caper!" Peter said and began to strip off his jacket.

"I say, don't let's lower ourselves," Simon said. "What's the game?"

"I know one place I wouldn't mind lowering myself," Peter told him. "Who's still got their fish-and-chip papers?"

All three of the younger boys produced balls of rolled-up newspaper from their pockets.

"Start tearing them up," Peter said. "Like for a paper chase."

A minute later, stripped to his vest and holding his cap full of torn paper, he rose and trotted nonchalantly over to the horizontal couple, letting a dribble of paper scraps fall from his hands. They did not notice him until he shouted, in feigned breathlessness, "Seen hounds?"

His sudden irruption upon their ecstasy precipitated a frenzy of activity to recover a decency they had abandoned quite some while earlier.

"Huh . . . uuh . . . ah . . . what?" the man asked, bending double and pretending to tie a shoelace. "What did you say, young man?"

He was of good class—a lean man with dark hair, ginger mutton-chop whiskers, and moustaches like matched scimitars hanging on the wall of his face. The girl, by her dress (which was all Peter could see of her), was more common. "Have you seen hounds, sir?" Peter asked. "We're on a paper chase. Hare and hounds, you know. I'm the hare."

"Ah! Er . . . oh . . . no," the man said. "No. No hounds this way."

"Please don't give me away, sir, if they should happen to come through this part of the wood."

"No, boy. We won't. Promise. Cut along, now—they can't be far behind."

"Your friend, sir? Is she all right?"

"Yes, she's . . . we're just . . . there's nothing wrong. So off you go."

"I can easily fetch a doctor, sir. This is only a silly old paper chase. It's not impor . . ."

"Damn you, you puppy! She's . . . we're just tired."

The woman, lying on her face in a tangled heap of her own disordered clothing, was heaving with silent laughter.

"Well, if you're quite sure, sir . . . ?"

"Absolutely sure!"

"Because, as I say, it would be no trouble to . . ."

The man, purple faced, half rose, felt the draft amidships, and subsided again with an incoherent, throttled sound.

Peter was still brightly insensitive. "Remember your promise now, sir. Tell no tales?" And off he ran, dropping the telltale litter of fat-sodden newspaper behind him.

He ran a wide circle, out of sight of the couple, and returned to the others. The man and woman had gone, obviously deciding that if the "hounds" were coming through this grove, they had better find another.

"Got to keep them in sight," Peter said, breathlessly struggling back into his shirt and jacket. "This bit of fun's only half over."

They almost ran upon the couple as they breasted a small hollow leading down to thickets of lycesteria, planted to feed the pheasants through the winter. If the man and woman had not been so interested in gaining the shelter of those dense clumps of evergreen, the game would have been up.

The four boys dropped flat and crawled awkwardly backward up over the brow of the hill. Peter alone kept watch.

"They're gone into that clump of bird food," he whispered. "We'll give them sixty seconds, then here's what we'll do."

Soon all four boys were squirming down through the mud and leaf mold, taking care to snap no twigs, until they reached the edge of the thicket. Low cries of "oh" and "ah" and nipped-off giggles told them of the rekindled excitement within. A yard or so of undergrowth made a thin screen for the boys as they poked their heads above a fallen tree trunk. They watched in fascination. What an extraordinary thing, the younger ones thought, for a man and a woman to be doing—and neither of them laughing at such business.

Soon all but Peter were bored with just watching. They crawled back to the more open woodland, Peter following reluctantly. Then, more sure of themselves, they stood and ran back to the hilltop.

"Now?" Simon asked.

For answer, Peter raised his face to the treetops and bayed like a hound. At the signal the others joined in, thinking how marvelously like a pack they sounded.

Peter nodded and, still baying, they set off on a roundabout course leading ultimately to the edge of the thicket. There, panting and trying not to laugh, they changed their tongue to the excited yelp hounds give at a find.

Peter cupped his hands and shouted: "Come on, Peter, you oozy slobber! The chase is up!"

"We know you're in there!" Simon shouted.

"Caught you! Caught you!" the Rothschilds chorused.

All four laughed until they ached at this fun.

"Little boys!" The roar from the heart of the thicket silenced them. "Little boys," the man repeated, still in his schoolmaster imitation—but quietly now, like a master who has won the upper hand and is about to exploit the fact. "If you do not instantly vamoose, and scarper, and decamp, and become scarce, I shall appear among you like the Angel of Death and tear you limb from limb."

The three younger boys looked uncertainly at Peter. He grinned. "Pretty good, Wellcome!" he sneered. "But you don't cod us, you sniveling lump of snot. Come on out!"

They shrieked with laughter and resumed their baying and calling of insults. So absorbed were they in this marvelous display of power over two compromised grown-ups that they failed to notice the man as he took advantage of that same fallen tree trunk and gained the open woodland to their left.

When they saw him it was too late; he was bearing down silently and at full speed from behind. To escape, they had to run sideways, the thicket barring the way before them. Peter and Stephen ran to the right and made it; Simon and Paul ran leftward and were borne down by a flying tackle that was surely perfected on Agar's Plough at Eton or some such green nursery.

The man, dressed only in his shirt, turned them over and looked at them. He was hairy, with a manly smell, like the senior fellows at school. His wang hung limp but was swollen and red. "You can go," he told Paul, who leaped to his feet and scooted away. The man held Simon fast. "You'll do," he said.

"You'd better not lay a finger on *me*," Simon told him, wishing his own position were more dignified.

"Oh, hadn't I!"

"No. I enjoy the protection of his grace of Chalfont. So you'd better just jolly well let me go."

The man held him as firmly as ever. "Perhaps I'd better know your name."

"Sss . . . er . . . Sandy."

"Ah? Sandy who, may I ask?"

"Heygate. Sandy Heygate."

The man smiled. "And where d'you live, Sandy Heygate?"

"Chalfont . . . er . . . *Cottages*."

"I see! And your parents, these goodly folk, the humble cottagers—they put by a bob a week, I suppose, to send you to Eton?"

"Eton?" But Simon knew he had lost.

"D'you think you can hide that accent?" The man laughed and —to Simon's surprise—released his grip. "Run, if you like," he added. "I have a feeling we'll meet at breakfast tomorrow, if not earlier. Chalfont Abbey? Christmas house party? I'm Will Turnbull, by the way. A grandson of the duke's."

He stood again and stretched his legs like a cock turkey. His apparatus, swinging above Simon, embarrassed the boy; he scrambled hastily to his feet, from which viewpoint Will's shirt front restored his modesty. "So am I," he said. "Simon Boyce." Self-assuredly he held out a hand. They shook. "Did you go to Eton?" Simon asked.

Will laughed. "Certainly not. Too damp. I went to that much healthier place on the hill. We used to thrash you at cricket."

Simon wasn't going to let a man from Harrow say things like that. "It must have been a long time ago," he answered.

Will cuffed him playfully, then became thoughtful. "But here's a pickle! You're Lord Charles Boyce's son, aren't you?"

Simon nodded. "Which makes me a future duke," he added.

Will was less impressed by this than Simon felt he ought to be. All he said was, "Still, I daresay you wouldn't be averse to earning yourself an extra pound this hols, what?"

"No." Simon was wary.

Will dashed back into the thicket and reappeared a moment later, still in his shirt but now clutching four crisp one-pound banknotes. "Here," he said.

Simon stretched out a hand, but Will surprised him by neatly tearing the notes in two. "Now, your future grace, you take these four halves and give one to each of your evil-minded young friends. Tell them that if I am disturbed again, today or any other day, or if any word of what has happened here in this covert should spread among our fellow guests, none of you will ever see the missing halves again. Is that clear?"

Simon took the notes and said haughtily, "You really shouldn't fornicate while wearing Old Harrovian sock-suspenders. It's desperately bad form, you know."

Will laughed. "And now, if my fair young companion has not fallen asleep, I'll return to her ample charms and begin once again. Remember what I say. Your friends, by the way, are watching us from behind the trees up there. They probably imagine I can't see them." He grinned and vanished among the shrubs.

"Gosh!" Peter said, looking thoughtfully down at the thicket. "It's almost worth forfeiting a quid to see them at it right through."

CHAPTER SIXTY-THREE

THERE WERE, if one included the babe in arms—and why not?—one hundred and thirteen guests at Chalfont Abbey that Christmas. Ninety-two of them were "family" and spouses descended from Alfred (all his living descendants, in fact, except for the unmentionable Lady Fabia, who was presumed to be nursing her disgrace in some dismal backwater like Paris or Cannes). Many of the others were "family" in the other sense, being colineals of the former duke, the du Bois line, come to keep an eye on the old place. The rest were political friends or people who had nowhere else to go. And Meg.

To show that, in his own demesne at least, a duke could still do anything he pleased, Alfred insisted that Meg act as his hostess. On the first night it meant that she led the field up to dinner, with the notoriously prickly Mervyn Gaspard, Marquis of Keyhaven, dragging all his seventy-five years at her side. Meg was, and always would be, a cunning, cheerful, vulgar country girl. But those very qualities, after thirteen years in the duke's company, had taught her how to deal with anyone. Mervyn was child's play.

There is nothing an aristocrat loves more than to hear his fellow aristocrats, of either gender, being minutely and mercilessly dissected by a knowing insider. Meg understood all this intuitively and played old Mervyn like a game trout. She told him of the time the late king, Bertie, had come to Chalfont Abbey on a private visit, and they had all been playing bridge after dinner and she had played one hand badly, and that had annoyed him, and he had been quite short with her . . .

"So I looks at him and I says, 'I'm sorry, sir, but 'tis my eyes, see? Sometimes I can't tell the *Knave* from the *King!*' He loved that, old Bertie did."

The marquis loved it too; he roared with laughter and ate out of her hand all evening. The talk was continuous and breakneck—among the younger set, at least. The older ones realized that the rules of precedence which had placed them beside each other tonight would place them beside each other tomorrow night, too, and every subsequent night of their visit; so they were more careful to budget their news.

Simon, the only under-sixteen allowed to be present, listened north, south, east, and west, letting the talk flow over him. The duke had spoken of their Tribe at Easter; here it was at its very growing point, making its own history!

It spoke in that wonderful, have-to-be-born-to-it, upper-class accent which sounds cold and clipped to outsiders and yet is warmth itself to those who have it. It spoke in allusions, relying all the while on insider knowledge, insider connections, insider memories. Harrovians knew what Agar's Plough was at Eton. Etonians knew what "hotting" meant at Winchester. Wykehamists understood "Ducker" at Harrow. The circle was thus complete. Not to know these and ten thousand other things was to stand forever outside it. To say *serviette* and *mirror* and *lounge,* to pronounce it pryvacy instead of privvacy, eyesolate instead of issolate, or dekkadent instead of dekaydent, was to lose the entrée.

To those outside, and those on the shadowy fringe of the charmed circle (and there were several there at dinner), an evening like this was torture on the rack; they could not know whether the appreciative smile and flattering attention of the left- or right-hand neighbor was genuine or just *noblesse* doing its duty of *oblige*ing. For in this the English aristocracy were the opposite of the Continental. An Austrian prince might write to a Rothschild wanting to decorate a dull wall, "I'll have no truck with Jews." An English duke would have written a charming note, thanking for the kind and generous etcetera, and ending, "but, to tell the truth, I've always rather liked it as it is."

Now, sitting at that dinner, listening to his Tribe, an insider himself, Simon said a fervent Thank God for being born a Boyce; thank God for being in the line of succession; thank God for being inside the charmed circle and never having to think what was right . . . correct . . . good form . . . *comme il faut* . . . but simply knowing. Thank God for being able to share so much with all these marvelous people, and for being able to express that sense of sharing in such elusive ways . . . a twitch of a smile, the fractional lift of an eyebrow, the fleeting compression of a lip, a particular inflexion of the voice. They understood such things perfectly.

There are some outsiders who, though they know they are outside, can, by talent or sheer presence, promote themselves as honorary insiders. And so it was with Campbell Stone. From the moment he and Georgina arrived at Chalfont Abbey he had won the admiration and even the affection of everyone who spared him ten seconds more than the time of day. He did not moderate his

Australian accent by one triphthong; "dance," for instance, still came out as *day-ee-unce*. And though he did not voice his socialism, he did not pretend to other convictions more in keeping with the company—and, since everyone knew his views, his silence on the subject was as eloquent as a play by Shaw. In fact he did nothing that might deliberately ingratiate himself with his in-laws; and yet they warmed to him. Even the duke was once seen to take his arm as they walked in conversation on the terrace.

Georgina was delighted. "You see!" she said. "I told you, you needn't be afraid of him. I told you Aunt Helen's way—and it works, doesn't it!"

He nodded ruefully. "Most of the time," he agreed. "Now and then it slips a bit. I'd like to see those papers, then I'd be absolutely . . . D'you think Aunt Helen would show me? I'd like to know all about your family now. D'you think she would?"

"I'll show you," Georgina said. "I know where to find them, too. But not now—it's so dusty and cold up there. I'll show you after Christmas, when we're all repenting of our excesses and looking for something quiet to do."

On the third morning the younger set rebelled. They did not see why they should sit next to the same people every night of their visit. Instead they demanded of Lady Emily and Lady Louise that they should all go up to dinner on the "Fortnum & Mason" principle. The two doyennes, who were county rather than metropolitan aristocracy, had never heard of it.

"Oh, mother!" Edna explained. "It's so simple—you just hand out cards with one name on each. Like Fortnum on a gentleman's card and Mason on a lady's, and so on with Army and Navy, Oxford and Cambridge . . ."

"And then," Katherine cut in, "Chalk goes up with Cheese, In with Out, Grace with Favor, and so on, you see?"

They saw and they thought it outrageous. The marquis, who had thoroughly enjoyed his evening at Meg's side and wanted more of them, thought it outrageous. The duke, old in the ways of politics, proposed a compromise so unworkable that the Old Guard, being the minority, relented and agreed to the "Fortnum & Mason" principle. It produced some lively dinners.

But then all the days were lively, too. They began at half past seven with tea, biscuits, and shaving water—and the morning post, if any. Modern-minded mothers could see their children at this hour and read them stories—usually, in the Boyce family, retold from the Bible.

Breakfast was from nine to ten. Three large oak buffets, with spirit warmers, buckled under the weight of molded porridge, cream of wheat, boiled eggs, coddled quails' eggs, eggs in cream, omelettes, poached eggs, scrambled eggs (all to order), bacon, deviled kidneys, braised liver, poached haddock, grilled haddock, kippers, Arbroath smokies, whitebait, smoked trout, smoked eels, poached salmon, chicken croquettes, kedgeree, grilled chops of pork and mutton, English and German sausages, York ham, cold beef, cold tongue, baked apples, Viennese croissants, fresh-baked rolls, thick toast, thin toast, home-farm butter, orange marmalade, ginger marmalade, lime marmalade, cinnamon butter, rum butter, brandy butter, crystalized honey, honey in combs, tea, coffee, hot and cold milk, lime juice, cider, Bucks fizz, straight champagne, apples, oranges, nectarines, melons, peaches, strawberries, grapes, figs, dates, and the usual variety of nuts.

Every morning Knightsbridge came down, paraded morosely along one of the buffets, flipping open the lids of the servers and naming the contents in a dour monotone, selecting nothing. A footman followed behind, closing the lids again.

"No bloody imagination!" Knightsbridge would mutter, taking some dry toast and a glass of Bucks fizz. "Wish I was at Laugstein with the Von Raegers shootin' wild boar!"

Then he would limp to the newspaper table, where ironed copies of all the London morning papers were kept, take up the *Sporting Times*—the "Pink 'Un," as it was always called—and settle in a corner, far from the crowds. Sometimes he would remember to take his own son's newspaper, the *Vindicator,* too.

There were no set arrangements for shooting parties, but around ten Alfred would sidle up to some of those who had not gone out hunting with the Duke of St. Ormer's or the Bullen and say, "Fancy a spot of shooting? Be out in the Great Courtyard in fifteen minutes." He restricted the number of guns each day, but every keen shot got in at least five days during the fourteen. A quarter of an hour after the invitation, four Rolls-Royce open tourers drew up in the Great Courtyard and a dozen or more men were lost to the house party until evening.

Straight after breakfast Meg collected all the scraps not required by the household or the kennels and set off in her own car, a brand-new Armstrong-Siddeley with a sphinx on the radiator cap. With the back seat and dickey full of leftovers, she drove herself around the local villages, handing out largesse to the deserving poor. Helen, who went with her a number of times, soon saw that Meg's notion of "deserving" did not at all coincide with that of benevolent upper-class ladies who undertook the same sort of distribution. The top of her list was the bottom of theirs: seduced women left with fatherless children. She kept almost a dozen of them from burdening the Poor Law. Next came the gossips and tale carriers. For a few scraps of mutton, people would unburden to her tales they would have carried to the grave rather than reveal them to ladies of high respectability, even for a whole plate of Beluga caviar. Only then did Meg satisfy the needs of the more traditionally deserving.

The information she carried back to the duke was invaluable. Troublemakers were dismissed from estate employment before they had caused the slightest flutter in the dovecotes; poachers stood blinking in the lockup, and not a snare set for their pains; wife beaters were encouraged, usually in dark lanes, to desist; seducers in the duke's employ were given every inducement to make honest women of their appassionatas; usurpers of unwarranted perquisites—free vegetables, free oats, free stabling, and the like—found their wages docked by amounts that were astonishingly accurate.

"Does this flow of useful tidbits of gossip to the Abbey depend on the flow of edible tidbits from it?" Helen asked.

"Course it does, dear," Meg replied. "People aren't fools. That's what the feudal system's all about—you do your part, I'll do mine. And don't let no one play the fool."

"And what when there's no one staying at the Abbey and the leavings are few? How d'you manage then?"

"I go down the kitchens and steal them." Meg laughed hugely as she swung the car about the lanes.

They were usually back for sherry and biscuits at half past eleven. A generally light luncheon of no more than four courses was served at half past twelve: sole fillets in mayonnaise, braised beef and savory jelly, dressed ox tongue, duckling fillets with pâté de foie gras, braised stuffed quail, pheasant baked in pastry, Japanese salad, rice and prunes, savory cheese fingers, cheese, and a dessert of biscuits, cakes, tarts, and sweetmeats. The choice of wines was equally parsimonious, no more than four being offered —a hock, a white Bordeaux, a claret, and a champagne.

The afternoons were for naps to aid the digestion and walks to improve it. Those who ate wisely and needed neither could rehearse theatricals, play hide-and-go-seek or real tennis, or make a selection of gramophone records for those who wanted to dance after tea. Albert and Eleanor had brought down a new gramophone with a vast, twelve-foot acoustic horn; it could fill the ballroom with its sound.

Hope and her brand-new Swedish husband, Yngve, who were in the last month of a six-month honeymoon, surprised everyone—and shocked many—with a set of records from the latest show, *Hello, Ragtime.* The notoriety this brought them led to no greater accuracy in the pronunciation of Yngve's name, but within two days most of the faster set could manage a very creditable imitation of his version of the Bunny Hug and the Chicken Scramble.

Helen, who was keeping an eye on her daughter Ada, watched the young ones dancing; she envied them their casual freedom, the loose, flowing frocks of the young women, the unaffected, natural manners of the men.

"Care to score the floor, Lady Charles?" It was Will Turnbull, the family's least eligible bachelor.

"I've never done this sort of dancing," she protested.

"You play music with the most marvelous sense of rhythm. That's all you need."

"That and joints which aren't toying with the notion of rheumatics." But she stood and "scored the floor" with him. They exhausted the weather, the success of the house party, the food, the new London shows, the coming Season, the mentionable aspects of the Tribe, and, finally, Helen herself.

"I told you you'd manage it, Lady Charles," Will said, leading her to a sofa.

"But look who guided me so well!" They sat side by side. "And what shall you do in life?" she asked.

"It's hard to decide. At the moment I'm living off the immoral earnings of three thoroughbred stallions and a couple of pedigree bulls. Everyone's so sure there's a war coming—it hangs over one a bit."

"It'll be very short. Knightsbridge says it couldn't possibly last six months."

"Oh, and I believe him. Despite similar optimism in the Boer War. Even so, exams at college only lasted a morning, each one, but they had a way of hanging over one the whole week, or even a month. That's what it feels like." He looked glumly at the dancers. "I suppose I'll enlist."

"You have no thoughts of marrying?"

He broke into a broad grin. "I am receptive to suggestions, especially from highly placed mothers with charming and marriageable daughters."

"Now, now!" She suppressed a smile. "There's one label you'll never see on the door to social success, and that's a label saying PUSH."

"Ah!" He patted her arm. "But I'm told that if one searches

very hard, one will discover a discrete little sign that reads PULL!"

She laughed. "That's very good. Oscar Wilde would have loved you for that."

They were interrupted by Mr. Riley walking through the rooms and corridors banging away at the dressing gong.

There was one thing Helen did not envy modern Society and that was its taste in evening dress. Indeed, no one who had seen and worn the gorgeous evening dresses of the eighties, with their enormous *balayeuse* trains and tier upon tier of stiff frills, their elaborate bows and ribbons, the studding of sequins, beads, transparent dewdrops, artificial birds and butterflies rising in a gush of froth to an almost bare décolletage and shoulders—no one of that day could envy the girls of 1913 their wisps of cloth, their Niagara bosoms, their commissionaire shoulders and piled-up hair.

Helen inspected herself and pulled a face. "D'you think pretty fashions will ever return, Millie?" she asked her maid.

"I'm sure they will," Millie said. "Not but what you don't do credit to this."

"Dear Millie, you always know the thing to say. I blame Miss Georgina and her friends for our present deplorable fashions."

In that evening's draw she was Scylla; Charybdis turned out to be Will Turnbull. "My guardian angel shall have a squeeze and a hug when next we meet," he said.

Knightsbridge, seated on her other hand, said, "I wish to hell I was at Laugstein with the Von Raegers. The boar huntin' there is pretty spiffin', don't you know."

Helen glanced at Will and hid her smile behind her menu, which she then pretended to study minutely. It read:

HORS D'OEUVRES		Sercial Madeira 1813
SOUP	Consommé Royal Creamed Tomato Soup	Sherry—Tio Pepe
FISH	Baked Turbot Cold Salmon	Schloss Johannisberg 1905 Scharzhofberg 1907
ENTRÉE	Quennelles of Veal Stuffed Quails	Château Lafite 1902

REMOVE	Baked Turkey à la Milanaise Saddle of Mutton Venison Cutlets en Croûte	Romanée-Conti 1876
ROAST	Woodcock Guinea fowl Pheasant	Champagne—Krug Private Cuvée 1906
ENTREMETS	Cauliflower au Gratin Marrow Fritters Asparagus	
	Savarin Trifle Kirsch Baba Ginger Cream	
	Savoury oysters Zéphires of Wild Duck Savoury Meat Fritters	Sillery 1904
DESSERT	Fruit Crystallized Fruits Bons-bons Petits-fours Dessert Ices	
	Turkish Coffee Coffee à la Russe	Port: Dow 1899

"No imagination," Knightsbridge grumbled. "Oh, for some *Rippchen mit Kraut,* or *Sauerbraten mit Knödel,* eh? Did you ever have *Aalsuppe* in Hamburg?" he asked a terrified Mary Turnbull, Will's sister-in-law.

"N-n-no, general" she stammered.

Delighted, he began a gastronomic tour of Germany with her.

"I must rescue poor Mary," Will muttered to Helen when they had reached the roast and the general was still a few miles short of Frankfurt. "What are his other topics?"

"London clubs," she said.

"Oh, Lord! Still—here goes." He raised his voice. "I see you and Kitchener are both members of the Savage, general," he began.

"Say?" Knightsbridge took long moments to retreat from *Bohnen, Birnen, und Speck.*

During that time he was appealed to from across the table by Edna Lambert, his favorite niece, who was simultaneously bent on rescuing poor Mary. "You never got on at all with Henry James, did you, uncle Knightsbridge?"

"Can't stand the fellow. He'd tell you how to build a clock if you let him."

"You'll enjoy this, then. Lambert and I went down to Sussex to visit him last month and I really set my foot in it. Lambert's only just back on speaking terms with me. James was going on and on in that interminable way of his about some rural experience he'd undergone, and at one point he said there was this scratching at the door, and he opened it, and there, he said, he saw—or *fancied* he saw—'something dark in color, something essentially feline in nature . . .' And I interrupted!" She pulled a naughty-girl face; everyone (especially those who had themselves suffered through a Henry James anecdote) leaned forward in anticipation. Edna went on: "I said, 'Don't tell us, dear Mr. James. Let us guess. Was it a black cat?' "

She shrieked with delighted laughter, in which everyone, including Knightsbridge, joined. "Very good!" he said and turned at once to Will. "The Savage?" he asked. "What of it?"

"Is it true, a fellow told me the other day, they don't wash the small change nor iron the banknotes there?"

"Of course they do—your friend's talking piffle. He needs to watch his tongue." Then he turned to Helen. "Did you know Henry James when you were in America?"

Helen smiled. "I left America thirty-four years ago, Knightsbridge. I doubt if he and I ever came within a thousand miles of each other."

Her brother-in-law had always had the delusion that the United States was just slightly larger than Yorkshire.

"You knew Oscar Wilde though, didn't you, Lady Charles?" Will asked. He was immediately aware of an uncomfortable ripple among the older people; but the younger ones, like himself, were interested. They knew there was a scandal—memories of it had been revived by Lord Alfred Douglas's recent action for libel against Arthur Ransome, but since Lord Alfred was still received in London, the scandal couldn't (they imagined) have been anything very dreadful, even though the newspapers were absolutely silent on its exact nature.

"Did you really?" several people asked. "Was he such a great wit as they say?"

Helen now had a difficult path to tread. At a more formal dinner she could have pointedly turned the conversation; but this was family—they wouldn't let her away at that. She gave a trapped smile that she hoped her contemporaries and elders would understand, and said, "Yes. Charles and I knew him very well."

"There was some great tragedy, I remember . . ." Edna prompted.

Another ripple. The policy of discreet silence, enforced by society for nearly twenty years, was blowing up in their faces.

"D'you know," Knightsbridge said, "Lord Tempest—Old Tuppy Tempest—pulled a mutton chop out of his pocket at the Marlborough the other day and asked for it to be sent down to the kitchens. And when the secretary came to see him about it, he said he saw no difference between his sendin' down a mutton chop and other members sendin' their *envois* of pheasant and grouse to the club larders. Got a point, I suppose."

What *was* the tragedy, Aunt Helen?" Edna persisted.

Helen sighed. "The real tragedy is only just becoming apparent as those of us who knew Oscar begin to thin out. He didn't take much trouble over his plays, but even so the wit in them is far more polished than his wit in life—and, of course, much less human, for that very reason. I remember we once gave a dinner for the late King Edward, when he was Prince of Wales. And Oscar was invited, too. At one point H.R.H. was telling us about his own youth and he said there came a moment when he realized for the first time that one couldn't do everything in life—he himself faced a choice between becoming a master shot and mastering the art of European diplomacy . . . Anyway, he then went on to talk about other things and Oscar called out, 'Oh, come, sir! Do put an end to this dreadful suspense: Tell us which of the two you chose!' Nobody but Oscar could have said it and made H.R.H. laugh."

Everyone enjoyed the story and wanted more. "What other sorts of things did he say?" Will asked.

Helen shrugged and smiled. "I have a thousand memories. I'll tell you one that stands out . . . because, I suppose, it was so . . . *typical* of him. We went to a small dinner at Ralph Nevill's, in Mayfair. Oscar was already there and as soon as he saw me he said, 'Ah, Lady Charles! I'm so absurdly delighted to see you. Come and sit here by me. There are a thousand and one things I want to avoid talking to you about, so let's begin at once!' He was an *enthralling* man, you know."

She looked around, a new glint of challenge in her eyes. The memory of Oscar, revived like this, also brought back the disgraceful thing that had been done to him.

"Oh, you should write it all down, aunt Helen," Annette said. "Before it all gets forgotten."

"But that's my point," Helen answered. "You *can't* write it down. The . . . the"—she sought the word—"what the Germans call *Stimmung* . . . the voice, the mood, changes when you do. The true man was in his charm, his voice, his . . . his niceness!"

There was no doubting now the challenge in her tone. Everyone, even those who disagreed with her estimate of Wilde, nodded at the immense sadness of things—things that by their very nature perished: memories, past happiness, friendship, the enrichment of life by outstanding people.

Helen, seeing that she had unintentionally cast a bit of a damper over her part of the table, forced herself to brighten. "Still," she said, "perhaps Oscar oughtn't to be remembered for his wit."

"But for what?" Will asked.

"He should be remembered for the fact that not a single one of his true friends deserted him after he was ruined. Not one!" She smiled around at them.

"He died in Paris, didn't he?" Edna said. "Did you see him there, aunt?"

"Once, yes. It was before Simon was born. Oscar was . . . well, dying even then. It was absinthe killed him. We sat on a café terrace in the Rue de la Huchette. He knew he was dying. He even toasted it in an oblique way. He said 'the trouble with Death is that He leaves one with nothing to do for an encore.' "

A tear trembled on Helen's eyelid and fell softly down her cheek. There was a sympathetic lump in more than one throat. She grinned suddenly, unashamed. "I *liked* him," she said.

Edna smiled too, and leaned across the table. "Good for you, aunt!" she said.

"Yes!" Will joined in. "I hope I have such friends when I'm gone."

Everyone smiled and relaxed. Helen felt for a handkerchief.

"One advantage of belonging to the Marlborough," Knightsbridge said, "is that the king lets members park their motor cars inside the gates of Marlborough House." Surreptitiously he passed Helen a large, freshly laundered handkerchief. "But standards are droppin', even there, now people know King George don't dine in. Last time I was there, I saw a young Grenadier puppy in a dinner jacket, a right-down regular Homburg. 'Young man,' I said to him, 'I hope you're goin' on to a fancy-dress ball!' "

Everyone laughed absurdly.

"Bless you," Helen whispered, passing back the handkerchief.

CHAPTER SIXTY-FOUR

NEXT AFTERNOON the duke happened upon the dancers in the ballroom. "Pray continue," he said when, out of respect, they stopped.

He was delighted with the gramophone and the amplifying power of its vast horn. He sent a footman to fetch the records that had been made of his own political speeches—a crushing riposte to those of Asquith, which H.M.V. had recently issued.

The dancing stopped. The echoes of the gay music died, to be supplanted by Alfred's ringing bass, now magnified by the twelve-foot horn, booming like a sergeant major, rolling in waves over the vast ballroom. He sat enraptured, only inches from the mouth of it.

After the fifth twelve-inch record Helen slipped quietly away. In the middle of the sixth she returned with Meg, who stayed at the doorway. During the applause—the increasingly strained applause that had greeted the end of each record—Helen whispered something to the duke.

He signaled to the footman not to play any more speeches and walked over to Meg. At the door he turned. "I'm sorry not to be able to play you the lot," he said. "Do continue dancing, please."

When he was alone with Meg and Helen he asked tetchily, "What is it?"

"You'll never guess," Meg said. "You know that Will Turnbull?"

"Yes."

"You know he's got his bit of stuff staying at the Plume of Feathers . . . ?"

"Yes, yes. And pops over to visit her every night. What of it?"

"It seems he's got tired of country air at three o'clock of the morning. He's asked young O'Neill, the new chauffeur, he's asked him to run over to Fingest tonight, half past two, and bring her here to the Abbey. He's going to fix a ladder up to his bedroom window."

Alfred broke into a broad grin. "The devil he is! We must turn some trick on him here."

"Send her into someone else's bedroom?" Helen suggested. "Or decoy someone into his?"

The duke chuckled. "This bit of fluff, some common merrylegs is she? Some street wagtail?"

"Not by all accounts," Meg said. "She was Lord Wortley's Sunday girl before Will Turnbull took her off him. Alfie Kemp says she's got real class. Her name's Daisy. Daisy Walpole."

"Who's Alfie Kemp?" Helen asked.

"Landlord of the Plume," Meg told her.

"And no mean judge of social standing," Alfred said. "This situation has distinct capabilities! I think *I* shall be at the top of that ladder."

"Here!" Meg complained. "I'm beginning to regret I ever . . ."

"I'm joking!" he said, placating her. "Who's in the room next to Turnbull?"

"It's the Old Library on one side, and the Wrottesley room—the young boys—on the other."

"And next to the boys?"

"It's empty—that's where the plaster needs repairing."

Alfred chuckled. "Good. We'll move the ladder and send her up there. Who's in the next to that?"

"Emily and Louise said they'd put all the undesirables along that part of the passage: Will, the boys—and Lady Fabia, if she dared come. So the bed's all made up and everything but there's no one there."

"Well, there'll be one desirable there tonight—Miss Daisy. I think I shall be in Fabia's empty room to watch the fun! Now here's what we'll do."

While he told them, Helen laughed nervously.

"Don't be so bloody middle class!" he snapped at her. "Send a footman to fetch this O'Neill to see me!"

Will slipped a half-crown to Old Knapman, the night watchman—whose pockets fairly bulged by dawn each day—and was let out by one of the French windows on the east terrace. Instead, however, of making his usual way to the stables, where one of the lads' bicycles would normally be waiting his hire, he went to the little walled garden, where he had earlier bribed an under gardener to leave him a ladder.

As he approached the gate he gave an owl hoot.

"Right you be, squire!" O'Neill, a cockney lad, was fond of parodying what he thought were rural speech ways.

Together they carried the ladder to the edge of the terrace. "It'll be fine from here," Will said. "You cut along now. Make sure she wraps up well."

He knew his own window—just before the central bay of the entire east façade and up on the first floor.

With some effort he raised the top of the ladder just above the keystones of the ground-floor windows; from there he had to jerk it awkwardly up the expanse of brick until it reached to his own sill. The length was perfect. He sighed with satisfaction and ran nimbly up to his room. Yes, he thought, a healthy, lithe young thing like Daisy should have no trouble. His innards turned over in pleasurable anticipation of certain aspects of her slender agility. As he looked out into the night he heard the scrinch of tyres on the gravel —O'Neill, leaving for Fingest. He opened his door, intending to go to the earth closet at the end of the passage.

"Why, Lady Charles!" He was surprised to see her right outside his door. "Did you want me?"

Helen had to think quickly. She wanted him out of his room until O'Neill returned with Miss Walpole. She had thought of a ruse to get him out, but if he was leaving of his own accord, she'd save it until he tried to go back in. She smiled weakly.

"Just a silly mother worrying," she confessed. "We caught young Simon climbing down the wistaria to the Wrottesley room a few nights ago. I merely wanted to be sure he wasn't still doing it. I hope I didn't disturb you?"

"No. Not at all. I was just . . ." He smiled and nodded vaguely toward the end of the passage.

"Good night, then," she said, and walked off in the opposite direction.

"Good night, Lady Charles." He hurried to the closet.

If he had stayed at his window just two seconds longer he would have seen Peter Wellcome, Simon, the Rothschildren, and Alfred Turnbull, his own nephew, scouting their way onto the terrace. They moved oddly, for they were burdened down with the fruit they had just stolen from the hothouses.

"Here's a piece of luck!" Peter said. "Your uncle Will's left a ladder for us." He put his own load of fruit against the wall and turned the ladder over and over, spinning it across the brick between Will's window sill and their own.

"Suppose he needs it?" Simon said.

"He's finished with it." Peter leered. "Lucky bastard!"

"What d'you mean?"

"Remember that piece of skirt in the wood?"

"Yes."

"She's his piece. He's got her settled in at the Plume of Feathers in Fingest. Goes for his bachelor's fare every night."

"What's bachelor's fare?" Stephen Rothschild asked.

"Bread-and-cheese-and-kisses." Peter laughed and, after gathering his fruit, shinned up the ladder to the Wrottesley room.

The others followed in quick order. Paul Rothschild, the last of the boys, climbed into the dorm at the exact moment Will shut and bolted the closet door. Less than a minute after that, the duke let himself into the empty bedroom, kept for Fabia, and warmed his hands at the fire.

Daisy Walpole—not one of the great, collected minds of the still-young century—had got the arrangements wrong. Her taxi met the Rolls-Royce, with O'Neill in the driving seat, just outside the commoners' entrance, at a place too narrow for passing—otherwise they might have whizzed unknowingly by each other. Giggling, she paid off the taxi, transferred to the Rolls, and sped toward the Abbey—where she was not expected for a good twenty minutes.

Five of those minutes later she and O'Neill were standing on the terrace looking at the ladder, which now led up to the Wrottesley room. "Is that it?" she asked.

"No," O'Neill said, remembering what the duke had told him: *Move it on two windows nearer the tower.* "Mister Will said he'd leave it, deliberate like, two windows away. I'm to move it two."

He, like Peter, spun the ladder over and over . . . to the window of Lady Fabia's room, where the duke stood watching. He was about to throw open the window and shout, "No, no, you fool, you've come one too far!" when he suddenly saw possibilities in the situation. He stepped back into the shadows and waited.

The sash window was already open a crack; she pushed it up all the way. "Will?" she whispered.

Silence.

"Will?" It was more urgent.

Alfred wondered if he should step out and reveal himself. But might she fall back off the ladder? She saved him the decision by climbing angrily in. "Will!" she said sharply.

As soon as she was inside, O'Neill, still following the duke's instructions, rolled the ladder back to where he had found it. If the original plan had been followed, Miss Walpole would now be stranded among the plasterers' trowels and scaffolds next door and Will would—after Helen's distraction had run its course—come back into his room and wonder what the hell was keeping her. And the duke would watch the fun.

Helen was beginning to delay Will's return—"I feel a draft . . . I'm sure there's a window open . . . d'you think it's a burglar . . . ?"—at the very moment Daisy Walpole said, "Who the hell are you?"

"I'm the Duke of St. Ormer. Welcome to my house, my dear. Come and warm yourself by the fire."

Warily she came to his side and did as he invited. His hands, all wrinkled and gnarled, looked so old beside hers, which were young and smooth. Still, he was friendly and had a nice voice. And there was a look in his eye that she knew quite well by now. "You really a duke?" she asked.

He grunted. "Going from Lord Wortley to *Mister* Turnbull was a bit of a social step down, young lady. How about stepping up to a duke—even if it is, as the concert posters always say, 'for one night only'?"

"What about Will?"

"He won't dare grumble. But if you could boast of a duke in your conquests, you could forget Will." He could see she was considering it. "If you did make that boast," he added, "I wouldn't deny it."

She grinned. "Righty tighty!" she said. "Where's me nightie!"

Alfred, trembling with happiness, went and shut the thick plate-glass windows and drew the heavy velvet curtains.

Will came back from Helen's diversion, looked at his hands in the gaslight, and saw they were stained with a lot of lichen or something off the ladder; in the mirror in his room he saw it had marked his face, too. Quite a lot of hard scrubbing was needed to get it off. His skin fairly glowed. He was beginning to feel excited.

He went to the window to see if she was in sight, saw that the ladder had been moved, and groaned. "Fucking boys!" He stormed next door.

They were gorging on fruit, telling smutty stories, making belches, and giggling. "Very funny!" Will said with an effort to keep his voice down. It weakened his authority. "Now go and put it back."

They laughed. "You mean you haven't *gone* yet," Peter said. "It's all right—use our window."

"Never you mind what I've done and what I haven't done. Just you put that fucking ladder back where you found it!"

"Oh!" Peter was truculent now, sensing the weakness of Will's position. "It's your *fucking* ladder is it! That puts different specs on it, I must say. Tired of doing it in the fucking woods, are you, Will? Tired of the fucking Plumes, eh? Do it on fucking ladders now, do you?"

"Just put it back where you found it," Will commanded.

"There's something *we* want back," Peter said. "The other halves of our pound notes."

"You've not earned them yet."

"Will you give them to us if we put the ladder back?"

"Yes!" Will hissed.

"Let's see them," Peter insisted.

"No," Simon interrupted. "He's got our family's blood in him and he's given us his word."

"He could go back on it."

"He won't. He went to Harrow." Simon walked to the window and climbed down the ladder.

A moment later he was climbing in again through Will's window. Silently Will handed him the missing halves of the banknotes as he passed. "Eat yourselves sick," he said, "but see you don't disturb me."

"Emily!" Lady Louise shook the warm body in the bed. "Emily!" She said it like an expletive.

Mervyn Gaspard, Marquis of Keyhaven, came back to life a fragment at a time. Even when he sat up he had to remove a cat's cradle of elastics from around his head before he could reestablish contact with the world. Out came the earplugs. Off came the patent ventilated nightcap. Off came the moustache guards. Off came the antisnoring nose clips. Off came the eye muffs—and he blinked at the world as he groped for his teeth, the only man-made items to join his head rather than desert it.

"Keyhaven!" Louise said in exasperation. "Where's Emily? I thought you were Emily."

"What an absurd thing to believe. Why d'you want Emily, anyway?"

"Where is she?"

Keyhaven waved into the dark that shrouded the farther side of the vast four-poster. "Somewhere there. But you won't wake her. She took some opium pills against her indigestion."

Lady Louise stumped around the bed and shook her sister, hard, several times, bawling her name into her ear—but getting nothing in reply beyond a small, sleepy fart.

"Don't risk any more," Keyhaven said anxiously. "We're none of us as young as we were." He looked at his watch. "Oh my god, Louise, have you any idea what time it is? Nearly three o'clock! What *are* you doing?"

"They're eloping. And we've got to stop them!" She looked miserably at Keyhaven, her only trooper for the battle ahead.

"Who? Eloping? Have you gone amok?"

"Will and Ada, that's who. Oh! *Emily* would have understood at once! That dreadful Will Turnbull is eloping with Ada Boyce, sister of the future duke. Now, d'you see! We've got to stop them, God save the mark!"

"How d'you know they're eloping?"

Lady Louise was exasperated. "Come and see for yourself!" She strode confidently in the direction of the windows, sent a jardiniere and a couple of cactuses flying, cracked her shin against a conversation piece, but plodded gamely on. "I don't know if you can see it from here. You can certainly see it from my room."

She flung back the heavy draperies. The bedroom was on the angle where Elizabethan butted onto medieval. Across the squint the ladder was just visible in the two-thirds moon. "There!" she said triumphantly.

Keyhaven hobbled rheumatically to the window and peered over her shoulder. "Where?"

"There! That's his window."

"Can't see a thing."

"You're not even looking at the house!" She took his shoulders and pointed him more or less in the right direction. "The *ladder!*" Lady Louise almost shrieked. "That's a ladder and that's his bedroom window. He's obviously going to slip down it and carry it to her window and help her down and then they'll elope."

"I can't even see Herberts Tower," Keyhaven said. "I can't see anything at night. Never could." He ambled back to the bed and raised the covers.

"Aren't you coming?" Lady Louise was shocked. "Keyhaven? We *must* stop them!"

"Go back to bed, Louise," he whined as he climbed into his own. "I never heard such nonsense. People don't elope down ladders at three in the morning. Only in books. In real life they go out and call a taxi. And they do it at a civilized hour. Good night!" He took out his teeth.

"Then I must do everything myself, I see," Lady Louise said with vehement determination. "I shall keep watch from the bay window of the Old Library."

The taxi drew into the Great Courtyard. The lady within looked out uncertainly, biting her lip. "Lord," she said. "They're all asleep."

"Looks pretty dead to me," the driver said. "You sure they've not gone away for Christmas?"

"Of course they haven't. This is where they go away *to.*" Yet again she scrabbled through her bag in quiet desperation. Yet again she found no more than a pound note and some loose change.

And the taxi, all the way from London, would be at least ten pounds. She must have been mad! Or drunk. Had she been drunk? Well, she was sober enough now. She opened the door.

"I'll go round the east side. See if there's anyone awake there. Wait here."

She hadn't gone a dozen paces before he was at her side. "My legs could do with a stretch, too," he said.

"Don't trust me, eh?"

"You might fall in the dark."

"I grew up here. If you insist on accompanying me, you could at least bring my bags."

She waited while he fetched them; the cold reached her and she pulled up her fur collar all round. They walked to Herberts Tower and skirted it until they came to the gate into the East Gardens. "There's a light on there," he said, superfluously.

They reached the terrace without mishap.

"A ladder!" she said. "And an open window—here's luck!"

They walked stealthily to the foot of it. "Coo-ee?" she said quietly.

A man darted to the window, a silhouette against the low, gaslit warmth beyond. "Darling!" he answered in a great stage whisper.

"Can't see a bloody thing!" It was Keyhaven's voice coming from the doorway. Lady Louise, at vigil by the window, cursed to herself. There was a loud clatter from the same direction. "Damn!" Keyhaven again. "Dropped me gun!"

"Gun?" Lady Louise started up in alarm.

He was scrabbling about wildly on the floor.

"Leave the bloody thing, for Christ's sake!" she said. "Stand up. Find the table. And feel your way along it."

He obeyed her first command. Then her second. And then, almost immediately—he being already under the table—her third. The almighty crack of oak on skull, the reeling fight with unconsciousness, the ferocious oath, and the collapse back upon the carpet—these for a while prevented him from obeying her fourth.

"I said leave the bloody gun," Lady Louise commanded.

"Not the gun. It'sh me teesh," his voice came out of the dark.

"Got em!" There was a cavernous rattle as his teeth slid in over their mates.

"If you can't see in the dark, what on earth possessed you to bring a gun?" Lady Louise asked bitterly.

"Good God!" He was staring out of the window. "A ladder!"

"Someone's coming!" Lady Louise was triumphant. "It's *her!* That's Ada. I'd know that coat anywhere."

"Can't see a damn thing."

"And she's got her bags with her. And a chauffeur."

"Or taxi man. People elope in taxis."

"She's come straight to the foot of the ladder and stopped. There! I said this was prearranged! She's saying something."

Each strained an ear toward the window.

"Damn this plate glass!" Lady Louise said. "You can hear nothing. I'm going to try and ease this thing open."

The words they missed were: "Can you lend me a tenner for this taxi driver and then help me in?"

"You're not Daisy," Will said.

"I never said I was. Look, the poor fellow wants to go home. Have you got a tenner?"

"Who are you?"

"I'm one of the duke's granddaughters. Can't we do all this *after* you've lent me the money?"

"You didn't see a Rolls-Royce out there? With a young woman in it?"

There was a pause. "Is that who this ladder's for?"

"Ladder?" Will was impatient. "Oh, no. That got left behind when they built the place."

"Sorry. It was a silly question. I didn't see any other car." She turned inquiringly to her driver. "Nor me," he said.

Another pause. "Look—if you can't lend me a tenner, I'll have to go back to the main door and wake someone. Only I'd rather like to be inside before my mother finds out. It's easier to refuse admittance than rescind it, don't you know."

The appeal to his chivalry won. "Come on up," he said. "If your man brings the bags, I'll pay him up here. I've only got a Scottish twenty-quid note."

The driver went back to get some change.

Lady Louise subsided in horror. "They're *not* eloping!" she said.

"That's what I told you."

"It's even worse. They are Jumping the Starter's Gun!" She left the window and stumbled over the fallen chairs all the way to the door. "We must get Helen and find the duke to stop it."

Keyhaven, crashing after her, found the shotgun he had dropped when he entered the room.

On the other side, five boys giggled and sucked in their breath as they watched this elegant angel in furs attempting a wobbly ascent of the ladder.

"She's brought some bags with her," Simon said. "Perhaps she's left the Plumes and is moving in here for good."

"No." Peter was full of worldly knowledge. "That's all her snaky clothes and feathers and jewels. And perfumes. They do a lot of dressing in silks and fondling and French tricks before they spread the gentleman's relish."

"I'm tired," Alfie Turnbull said. "I'm feeling sick."

Peter froze. The woman on the ladder, Will Turnbull's "piece of fluff," had just risen into the light—and she was the living image of his own mother! That put the kibosh on any more scarlet fantasies.

He left the group at the window. "Come on," he said. "This is silly. Let's go on with the feast. Who's got the cigarettes?"

In the next room but one a still-grinning Daisy was polishing her knees on the sheets one more time and pretending to complain. "Swipe me! I thought young men was bad enough, but you've got enough in you for half a dozen, haven't you!"

The duke pretended to growl.

In the *other* next room they had completed their introductions and had a good laugh.

"I was told you were in Paris," Will said.

"Oh dear, has everyone been talking about me?"

"No. On the contrary. Everyone's been studiously *not* talking about you. So I twigged something was up. Except Georgina. She said a word or two."

"Lord! Is she here? Yes, she would be. Without the Australian, I suppose. You haven't got a Turkish cigarette, have you? I can just imagine the sort of thing *she's* been saying."

He offered her his case. What was she? His cousin? Biologically, anyway, if not in law. You couldn't call her handsome but there was something vital and damned attractive about her. "These are Virginian, those are Turkish." He lit her cigarette for her. "Georgina's your great champion, actually. And her Australian is here. In fact he's quite a hit."

"Georgina—my great champion!" she snorted. "She was my great tormentor in the days when I was being tormented enough for one life by my dear husband. You don't know any of the story?"

Will shook his head. She had suffered; you could see that. Even when she tossed her head and drew on her cigarette and smiled, there was that wary, creature-at-a-waterhole look about her.

"Best forgotten," she said. "It was a great disappointment to Georgina when I didn't join some menagerie of feminist martyrs. Instead . . ." She broke off and looked steadily at him. Then she gave a sudden, dazzling smile. "I'm not ashamed of what I did instead. That's why I've come here, to show I'm not ashamed. My parents are the ones who should be ashamed—Georgina's right there—either for what they knew about my husband-to-be, or for what they willfully failed to know."

He barely followed what she was saying. The suggestion of looseness in her life had given her a purple aura long before this night; now the nervous angularity of her movements, the hurt appeal in her face—and, no doubt, the frustration of Daisy's non-appearance—were having their effect on him.

She noticed, but instead of being offended she smiled. "I do live in Paris," she said, looking about for an ashtray while the ash dropped spontaneously to the carpet. "I live with a painter. But if you think that those circumstances, and these"—she waved vaguely about them—"and this"—she flaunted the cigarette—"and your tenner, are a prelude to something . . ." She laughed and raised a hand to his cheek. "Poor man! I've embarrassed you dreadfully."

He clutched her hand to his face. "Not at all. You saved me from making a giddy ass of myself."

"I hope your friend in her Rolls-Royce is all right."

"The chauffeur would look after her. But what about you?" He hit his forehead. "But of course! I quite forgot. There's a room prepared for you, just along the corridor."

Being in his shirtsleeves, he slipped his dressing gown over his shoulders and, picking up her bags, led the way out. They tiptoed past the dormitory, past the room full of plasterers' scaffolding, and stopped outside the room Will thought was empty and ready for Fabia.

But it clearly wasn't empty. Someone was very quietly shoveling coal onto the fire.

"Oh!" Lady Fabia said knowingly. "An empty room, well away from the rest of the party . . . an unused bed . . . it was much too good to be left idle."

He grinned. "I think we're entitled to investigate strange noises in the night, don't you?"

She looked dubious. "Some things are best left undiscovered."

But he was already opening the door, which moved without a sound. Equally silently he crept in.

A short lobby led to another door. He pulled it quietly open. A naked woman, her back to him, was squatting beside the hearth, tipping coal off a shovel into the grate with infinite care.

For a moment he stood thus, admiring the generous anatomy

whose firelit curves and dimples were so unconsciously displayed. Then he was shocked to realize it was not the first time in his life he had adored that same sight.

Then he realized what must have happened. The boys, of course. The monsters! They had shifted the ladder. Yes! That's why it was left against their window—my God, why hadn't he thought of it at once? They were capable of anything, the little wretches. And poor Daisy had come up here and, thinking this was *his* room, was waiting for him. *Ready* and waiting.

"Hello, darling!" he said.

There was a sleepy grunt from the direction of the bed, only the footboard of which was visible to him.

Daisy looked around in surprise. She laid the shovel down on the carpet and sprang at Will, bearing him back into the lobby. "For gawd's sake don't wake him!" she hissed urgently. "I only just got him off!"

"Who?" Will's anger was boiling up.

"The *duke*," she said, unable to keep the triumph out of her voice. "What a man, eh! Is he your grandfather?" But the words trailed off as she saw Lady Fabia out in the gloom of the passageway. "Someone's there," she whispered, putting her hands over her breasts.

"Here." He draped his dressing gown around her. "See you tomorrow."

Before he turned she reached up to him and put her arms about his neck. "Sorry, Will, love," she whispered. "But I couldn't do nothing else. He was in here, waiting for me."

"Of course you couldn't." He kissed her. "Lock the door."

"The old so-and-so!" Lady Fabia said admiringly. "Castled you, eh?"

He nodded glumly. "You take my room and I'll go sleep in an armchair somewhere."

She gripped his arm. "Someone's coming!"

He peered down the corridor. "Oh, heavens, it's Lady Charles again! Does she never sleep?" He stepped out to meet her and raised his voice. "Good morning, Lady Charles."

She hurried toward him. "Oh, Mr. Turnbull, Simon's not in his room. I wondered . . ."

He smiled. "Don't worry, he's safe." He gestured at the dormitory door. "He's in there with the others. They're having some kind of a feast."

She put her hand on the doorknob but he stayed her. "Better not, eh, Lady Charles? Some things best left undiscovered, take it from one who knows from bitter experience. Boys will be boys."

Helen bit her lip. "Perhaps you're right." She frowned and peered into the dark over his shoulder. "Isn't that Lady Fabia?"

"Yes, aunt Helen. How d'you do." She came forward.

"How d'you do, my dear. It must be years since we last met. I'm so glad you've decided to come. The duke, I know, was especially sad at your absence." She walked past Will. "Was Mr. Turnbull showing you your room?" She went to open the door.

"Don't!" they both said.

She looked from one to the other with astonishment.

"It'll take too long to explain, but the fact is . . ."

At that moment a loud voice coming from somewhere down the corridor and round the bend said, "Dammit all, Louise, you know I can see nothing in the dark. I told you I can see nothing."

"Keyhaven and Lady Louise!" Will said.

Helen looked at him half undressed and herself in a dressing gown, and gulped. "They can't find us like this!" she said. It was almost a plea.

"In here!" Will opened the door to the room that was undergoing repairs. The three scooted inside and stood in the moonlit dark. He shut the door quietly.

Their relief was short-lived. "The cases!" he hissed at Fabia.

"What cases?"

"Your suitcases. I left them out there, just outside the door." He opened it a crack. A shadow moved along the floor of the passage. Silently he closed the door again. "Too late."

Lady Louise and her brother-in-law peered around Will's empty bedroom. "Sure it's his?" Keyhaven asked.

She pointed at the window. "There's the ladder."

"Well, they're not here."

"Then they're hiding. They can't be far. Where would one hide along here?" Inspiration struck her. "Fabia's room! Lombard Street to a china orange that's where they are." She picked up her lantern and the hem of her long, billowing nightdress and strode from the room. Keyhaven hefted his gun and followed.

She had actually walked past the suitcases before their oddity struck her. She stopped. She turned. She slowly smiled. She pointed at the door to the room where her daughter, Will, and Helen were hiding. "There!" her tongue, teeth, and lips said.

They squared themselves before the door, summoning all the considerable self-righteousness at their command. They were unashamed Victorians who had survived into a new, unlovely age; nothing could give them greater joy than to burst into a Room of Sin, there to confront and denounce the Monster in all his reeking

Vileness. They licked their lips. Their eyes glistened. This moment was nostalgia incarnate. "Ready?" Lady Louise asked.

"Never more so."

He threw wide the door and shoulder-to-shoulder they stumped in.

Hasty glances at forbidden books had prepared them for a confusion of crimson silk upholstery, turkey carpets, a riot of cushions, the reek of opium, numerous soft lights, crusted goblets of rare vintages, and the random evidence of slow *déshabillement.* A little bit of Paris here in Bucks.

They slewed to a halt in another world—a world of timber scaffolding, plasterers' hawks, barrels, buckets, bare boards . . . the only connection with Paris was the plaster in the bags.

And there, frozen in the lamplight, stood . . .

"Fabia!"

"Hello, mother. Hello, uncle Mervyn. I'm sorry. Did the pair of you want to use this room?"

"I . . . you . . . er . . ." her mother breathed vigorously between each word, taking stock of the situation as Fabia's question recast it.

Will and Helen, who were as astonished at Fabia's coolness as the two intruders, now fought hard not to laugh.

"It's not *terribly* comfortable," Fabia went on. "But you're welcome to it. We were just leaving to look for somewhere better."

That was too much for Keyhaven. "Dammit, Fabia," he said, lifting the butt of his gun off the floor. "You've no *right* . . ." He brought the butt down hard.

There was the most colossal explosion as both barrels discharged simultaneously. The workmen had taken three days to remove part of the ceiling. The shot now did the rest in a flash. Chunks, hunks, slabs, crumbs, and dust rained down on all five of them.

"I told you! I told you!" Lady Louise shrieked between fits of coughing.

The boys rushed in from next door. For poor little Alfred Turnbull it was too much. The fruit had made his stomach uneasy. The cigarettes had made it positively queasy. It had been only a matter of time before the flesh rebelled. And this was the time.

The condition of the others, to tell the truth, was only an inch or two behind young Alfred's. The sight of him retching against the wall was all it required to reduce the gap to zero. As the clouds of dust settled, they took the gleam off four warm pools of freshly consumed out-of-season fruit. Peter, just slightly more in control, made it back to the dorm window in time to drench two five-pound notes and the driver who was holding them.

Please don't let him wake! Please let me get some kip! Daisy was praying next door. But it was too late. The duke, chuckling heartily, had already got a leg over her.

On the floor above—literally *on* the floor, for that was where he slept—Knightsbridge had just unknowingly demonstrated yet again how charmed a life he led. It wasn't the explosion that woke him so much as the impact of hundreds of flying pellets as they imbedded themselves in the oak of the floorboards beneath him. Some came to rest not a sixteenth of an inch from his spine.

He stood, pulled the covers about him, and went to settle in a chair until first light. "Bloody place!" he said. "God, I wish I was at Laugstein!"

CHAPTER SIXTY-FIVE

HELEN HAD REMEMBERED the way the candles were lighted at the Winter Palace in St. Petersburg. Now, for the re-creation of that marvel here at Chalfont Abbey, Ultra Chemicals Industries, Explosives Division, provided a hair-fine fuze of gun cotton, and Simon organized the servants to fix it to the chandeliers and candelabra in the southern entrance hall—the great marble hall containing the staircase up which the duke had galloped into European legend sixty-four years ago.

The hall now contained marbles of a costlier kind. Donatello's *David,* Michelangelo's *St. Jerome,* and Canova's *Sleeping Shepherdess,* fruit of the Duke's judicious collecting over the past four decades, had joined Bernini's flamboyant portrait bust of the First Duke. Their undotted eyes stared universally out at the throng of family who assembled there that Christmas Day, some grudgingly, some curiously; some in the throes of boredom, others of rheumatism; some hungry, some a dyspeptic caldron of past gluttonies; some in arms, some in armor—or its modern equivalent, full-dress undress; many in perambulators. It was Lady Louise's and Lady Emily's list breathed into life, or as passable an imitation of life as any mature aristocracy might achieve.

Majestically unobtrusive, Riley, the butler, who knew each silhouette—even the shape of each ear or the droop of each shoulder—counted and recounted until all were there. A single raised finger. A nod. A hush.

They stood in the deep twilight, shadows amid shades . . . waiting.

A second nod.

By wizardry the candles burst to light and life, and to oooh! and aaaah! and the sudden howls of babies, life's conservatives, voting with their lungs. And then the applause.

Most of them had electricity at home. Most of them had long ago accustomed themselves to dark rooms that turned into solariums at the touch of a switch. But Chalfont Abbey was different. Here it was magic still.

And magic, too, that their duke, Alfred, the orphan who had won the affection and respect of monarchs, was now being carried down the stairs to the great half-landing in the open chair used by the First Duke, his fifth-great-grandfather, three centuries ago. His arrival was continuity made flesh. It had the impact of a great promise.

But the duke, as he sat in his chair, hands crossed on the silver knob of the cane whose ferrule delved between his crossed ankles—what of him? Was he then a Man of Industry, and these his wares, his manufactures? Was he the feudal lord, and this his tribe? A teacher, and these his apprentices? An apostle of a faith, and these his acolytes? He was all, and more.

The applause died away. But the pleasure of surveying them all—*all*—as they stood below, a quarter-acre of faces, was so intense that still he did not speak. He knew each one; each one recalled a thousand incidents of their growing up. The only sound was the crying of babies.

For a while he lingered there, lost in the treacherous archeology of memory. Then he tapped his cane once upon the marble. "The infants may go," he said.

As they left, there was a shuffling of feet and a clearing of throats while the remaining children and grown-ups spread outward into the spaces. The silence fell again.

Alfred rose stiffly to his feet. "Four and sixty years ago," Alfred began, "I was introduced to this house by my predecessor, Augustus, the Fourth Duke. I've often wondered what he thought of me. Looking back on what I was, I know what I, as I am now, Duke Alfred, would have made of young Mister Boyce. And I have to say—*not much!*" There was a ripple of politely disbelieving laughter.

"Oh, but it's true! Mister Boyce had never *seen* a member of the nobility. For him they were one with the grand viziers and high chamberlains of fairy tales; they belonged to a remote past—not to the future. Oh, no! *He* was the future.

"Now here's an interesting conundrum. Suppose young Alfred Boyce had not inherited this dukedom. Suppose he had built his japanning factory and turned it into Birmingham Metal Box—and so had gone on to found London Distillate, and Ultra Dystuffs . . . and all the others.

"Suppose, too, that by good works, and careful works, and *useful* works, Mr. Boyce was the first Viscount Cokeley by now—or even the first Earl of Birmingham—a new member of the nobility. Let us say that over the years our earl and his countess had five children—and that, as a widower, he married a widow with four of her own. And those nine children had thirty-odd children of their own, who, in turn, had twenty-eight of *their* own.

"And come the Christmas of 1913 they are all assembled, all ninety of them, at the earl's new baronial hall—think of it as Bear Wood, or Cragside, or some other ugly great Victorian pile—"

They laughed, glad not to belong to the parvenu nobility of such modern and unmellowed houses.

"My question to you is: How would the First Earl of Birmingham, formerly Mr. Alfred Boyce, differ from the Fifth Duke of St. Ormer, formerly Mr. Alfred Boyce?" He looked around. "Not easy, is it! The same blood flows in both—the blood of the First Duke, and all the kings and barons and ladies back to the Conqueror, back to Guerinfray, the first Count of Aumale. The same blood.

"Yet there would be a difference between those two Alfred Boyces, Fifth Duke or First Earl. Not just *a* difference, but *the* difference. In one word . . ." He stood suddenly and threw up his chin.

". . . Heritage!" He looked around, not at them but at the great marble columns, the painted ceilings, the dark, echoing dome. "Heritage!" he repeated. "Mr. Boyce the Earl would have the blood and the rank—and, most important, the money to keep it up. But he would stand in no tradition. He would have no heritage.

"To put it at its very simplest—because I want even the youngest among you to understand this—at its very simplest, if he, the earl, wanted to see his ancestor the First Duke, he'd have to come here on one of the appointed opening days, and he'd have to tip Mr. Riley five shillings or more for the privilege of visiting the family crypt, there to stand for ten minutes or so—and then back to Bear Wood or Cragside where the plaster's still drying out.

"How different for us! We guard those private catacombs of our forebears. We walk daily beneath their pictures. There, where you stand, and here too, upon the stair—here walked William, the Third Duke, the one who built all that you see around you. Where we sleep, there slept the First Earl, Godfrey. The First Duke sat in this very chair. He hunted and husbanded these lands. The people around here were his people, too, bound to one another by a feudal tie that rootless city people cannot understand—a tie that the First Earl of Birmingham would find laughable . . . uncomfortable . . . embarrassing. A tie that still binds us.

"Our heritage is to stand at the heart of that network of obligation, duty, and privilege. To keep it working. To pass it on intact. We have no divine *right* to do so. Ours is that far more justifiable right—the right that is *earned.* And we earn it in exactly the same way as the humblest ditch digger or hedge trimmer earns his place: by our performance.

"The older ones among you could each name a dozen members of the nobility who fell down on their performance these past forty or fifty years. I could name a hundred. Their titles did not save them. All the clever lawyers' entails did not save their estates. Where are those people now? The best of them are teaching Hottentots to plow the African bush. The worst spend their lives sewing on leather patches and putting out buckets to catch the drips through the roof. Nature has no mercy on failures.

"And I am talking about *Nature.* It is *natural* for men and women to belong to a tribe . . ."

From the throng below came the sound of Georgina clearing her throat of no particular obstruction.

"Even our rebels," the Duke said, "belong to our tribe. It is, as I said, *natural* for people to cleave to tribes. We, this family, this tribe within a tribe, represent an unbroken line of nobility stretching back almost nine centuries. Nine hundred years! Isn't there something in that to quicken the blood? Son to father, daughter to mother, we can trace them back name by name, date by date. Brother to sister. Cousin to uncle. We can name them all, follow back that golden thread almost nine hundred years.

"The children of those who left this hall, howling or asleep, ten minutes ago will be able perhaps to look back on a thousand years. Will they stand here to do it? Will the grandchildren of our footmen here pass among them with wine as ours now do among us? Or will that thousand years have come to nothing for us, as it has come to nothing for so many families and will come to nothing for so many more that now think themselves secure?"

He made a small motion with his hands and sat again, not looking to see if the chair were there, knowing it would be. "I am an old man now," he said. "I have outlived two of the noblest women of our times—without whom this family (and I think of us all as one family)"—Helen smiled to herself at that—"without whom this family would be as nothing. Soon I shall be united with them, and with all those others who have gone before: with the First Viscount Bullen-Chetwynne, 'Bull' as we always affectionately knew him; with Lord Charles, whose gallant death is still recent enough to cast its shadow over this gathering, and with his son, Michael; with Lady Felicity and her daughter Ada; with John Cardigan and his daughter Paula; with James Lucan and his granddaughter Mary; and with those hundreds—those thousands—of our ancestors who made this precious heritage, this most precious family.

"I want therefore to read you part of a letter written to me by Lord Charles in the last hours of his life."

That caused a sensation. Everyone had known of Charles's letter to Helen and their children; it had been copied and sent around among almost all those present. They had assumed that a similar letter to the duke had not survived, or that time had not allowed it to be written.

The duke pulled out a tattered sheet of paper but did not look at it as he quoted: " 'Thank you above all—you and my dear mother, whom I hope shortly to join—for giving me a code by which to live. That may seem a strange choice of words when the same code now compels me to face death in the sea rather than dishonour in the lifeboats, but I would not choose it otherwise; neither the word nor the course of action. I would rather have one hour more of life as you have taught me to live than half a century of mere survival in unworthiness. There is no stronger way now for me to affirm my absolute belief in our way of life than to die for it. To seek to live in the teeth of that conviction would be a far worse death than that to which I am now resigned. I am proud and privileged to have this opportunity to show it—even if these words should never reach you, and I am the only one to understand such pride and privilege!' "

The duke folded the letter, which he still had not looked at, and held it between thumb and forefinger. "Pride and privilege," he echoed. "Words that are often used in connection with the nobility—yet how rarely in"—he raised the paper—"this sense. Yet this *is* the true sense of those words." He rose again to his feet and took a glass of champagne from Riley. "And now that we all have our glasses, I ask you to join with me in drinking a toast in his memory, and using those words of his in the true and noble sense he gave them." He raised his glass; so did they all.

"Pride and privilege!"

Pride and privilege! The words rose from a hundred throats and reverberated among the marble walls. None spoke it louder than Campbell Stone.

Then Knightsbridge began "He's a Grand Old English Gentleman—Which Nobody can Deny" and they all joined in heartily—though none so heartily as Campbell Stone. The meeting broke up with three rousing cheers and everyone went up to Christmas dinner.

"I didn't know Charles wrote that last letter to you, duke," Helen said later, when they were momentarily alone.

Alfred smiled. "D'you think I don't *know,* word for word, what he would have written, my dear?"

CHAPTER SIXTY-SIX

IN THE PENITENTIAL cold of after-Christmas, on Boxing Day, when it seemed the entire party either rode to hounds or at least drove out in support of one or other of the hunts, Georgina and Campbell wandered alone through the echoing rooms and corridors.

"You obviously don't regret having come here at last," she said.

"I was a fool to have stood out so long. Oh . . . you remember you promised to show me the muniment room?"

"I suppose it'll be all right," she said doubtfully.

"Of course it will be. And today's the perfect day."

She led him along many corridors and up the narrow stairs to the old, dusty room in the attic story. For half an hour or so they pulled books and boxes out at random, struggling to read ancient and unfamiliar hands, writing as often as not in dog Latin or Norman French. Much of it was dryer even than the dust that lay so thick upon it—records of land transactions, changes in tenure, prices got for stock in the markets—the ephemera of life to which time alone gave any interest. There was the occasional small nugget: a complaint from a dairymaid, preserved, no doubt, for its glorious spellings and its unwittingly frank revelation of life in the haylofts; an enigmatic reference in a steward's day book to "a great rayne of froggs and towds and other slimey insecks in the forenoone," and so on. But in general it was unrewarding stuff.

Campbell grew increasingly impatient until finally he burst out, "Come on, old girl! You know the box I want to see!"

But when she at last put it before him his whole manner changed; it was almost as if he were now afraid to go on. He placed one hand at each side of the box as an anarchist might hold a bomb.

"What's the matter, darling?" she asked.

He looked at her and closed his eyes. She saw he was holding his breath. "Are you unwell? Shall I call someone?"

He shook his head vehemently. "I wonder if I am going to regret this the minute I've done it."

"Don't do it, then. You're not compelled to. Anyway—such a fuss about something that can't matter one way or the other!"

He began to read.

Georgina had her first misgivings when she saw what effect the old papers had on him. His breathing grew tremulous. He chewed his lips and pursed them until they were bloodless. He hardly blinked.

"What is it?" she asked before he had finished. "What do you know about Orlando?"

When he didn't answer her she put a hand across the paper he was reading, covering the words. He tipped it off as if it were a pile of pebbles. "Let me finish," he said in a new, hard voice. Then, only slightly more softly, he added, "I'll tell you everything when I've finished. I promise."

"Tell me what? What's to tell? What d'you mean, everything?" she pressed.

He gave no sign of hearing her but read on as if the words were written in fugitive ink. When he finished, he squared all the papers up neatly and put them back in the box, which he pushed toward the center of the table, toward her. For a moment he merely looked at her with a gaze she could not read. Then he lowered his eyes. "You remember you once said you thought I came to England deliberately to find you and marry you?"

"You got very angry, I recall."

"I wasn't born Campbell Stone, you know. Stone was my mother's maiden name. I took it—legally, by deed poll—before I came back to the old country."

"What was your real name, then?" she asked in a voice much steadier than her spirit.

"Boys," he said. "My father's name is—was—Bruce. He was Bruce Boys."

"Boyce?" she asked. It was clear that particular name meant nothing to her.

He nodded. "My father fought a lifelong battle in the courts to prove he was the rightful heir to Orlando Boyce. There's always been a tradition in our family that Orlando was legitimate, and that we . . ." Instead of completing the sentence he smiled and gestured all around; it was a gesture of ownership.

"No!" Georgina said.

"Yes." He was quiet and calm. "These prove it. The question is—"

"You're a scoundrel!" She was still coming to the realization of what he was saying. "It's all been a cheat. You've been living a lie—you made me live a lie."

He shook his head, radiating a confidence that when she understood all she would pardon all.

"You've tricked me into becoming a traitor." Her anger was mounting. "Everyone said you were too good to be true—"

"Georgina."

"My God! When I think of all the years—"

"Georgina!" He was suddenly quite sharp. "Just listen! I know what you must be thinking. And you're quite right to think it. I don't blame you. But just hear me out, will you?"

She fell silent but her anger remained.

"You were right, that time you said I came here deliberately to get you to marry me."

"Me!"

"Well—any Boyce female. Anyone with the entrée to the duke. Or to Chalfont Abbey. My dad knew—we all knew—the answer must be here. And . . ." He tapped the box, again leaving the rest unspoken. "So, my darling, our meeting, and the first few months after that, were . . . not an accident, and . . . not sincere. But then I changed. Didn't you notice? You must have noticed I changed."

Doubt gnawed at her anger. He saw it and pressed on. "Why d'you think I resisted every effort you made to get me to come here to the Abbey? I landed in England with only one ambition—to take away this dukedom from those who had usurped it. You were—in the *beginning*, you were only a stepping stone toward it. And then . . ." He shrugged like a man confessing to an endearing but fatal character flaw. "I fell in love with you, Georgina. I suddenly wanted you more than . . . well, if you want to know, more than all the world. I still do. My dad was livid."

He pushed the box of papers all the way across the table to her. "Now I don't know what to do about them." He laughed. "Even my socialism became sincere! There now!"

He fished in an inner pocket and pulled out some papers. "Before you say anything," he told her, "you ought to read this." He unfolded it, ironing it with his hands several times, before passing it to her.

She read: *Attested Death-Bed Confession of William Boys, Alias Boyce, Alias Bugis—19th December 1812*

"It's a copy, of course," he added. "The original is with, er . . ." The sentence trailed off as he saw how absorbed she already was in the confession.

It told how William Boyce, awaiting transportation to Australia for life on a prison hulk moored in the Thames, had come to hear of the death in a nearby cage of one William Bugis, a clerk of Northampton, whose death sentence (for forgery) had been commuted to an astonishingly mild seven years' transportation. Realizing that Boyes and Bugis were close enough in their handwritten forms to be confused if the hand were bad, and realizing, too, that seven years was better than life, William Boyes had, at first, tried to bribe the turnkey to forge his name instead of Bugis's, so leaving the way open for a later impersonation.

The turnkey refused but, after considerable "oil of angels," agreed to write the name in so slipshod a fashion as to create room for doubt. Even more—if he were ever asked which name was intended he'd "just about swear as it was Boyes as what died."

Next day, on transfer to the transportation vessel, Boyes pretended to several fainting fits—and so on for ten more days, until they were well at sea. When he "recovered" he strenuously objected to being called, or treated as, Boyes. From Cape Town, their first landfall, messages were sent back to London inquiring as to which had died in the hulk, Boyes or Bugis.

Two months after his arrival in the penal colony, word came that Boyes had died and that the prisoner must therefore be—as, indeed, he claimed—William Bugis. And it was as William Bugis that Boyes returned to England seven years later, having served "his" sentence.

Back home he married one Sarah Cotehele and by her had a son, Frederick; that was in 1780, three years after his return. But two years later he feared that his imposture was in imminent danger of discovery and, realizing that it was better to return to Australia a free man rather than in chains, he deserted his wife and infant son, "never more knowing nor hearing tell what become of them until of late."

In Australia, where he took the name Boys, it was not long before he met and married another Sarah, Sarah Jones. The coincidence led him to give his son by this Sarah the name of Frederick too. Perhaps (though his confession did not say so) he reasoned that no drunken revelation of names would give him away.

"Until latterly," his confession added, "I believed my marriage to Sarah Jones was bigamous by virtue of my prior marriage to Sarah Cotehele, my first wife. But recently I have ascertained that Sarah, born Cotehele, died in Spitalfields in the Year of our Lord 1783, the year before I wed Sarah Jones, who was therefore my legitimate spouse as our son Frederick Boys is my legitimate heir."

The final paragraph smacked even more of the attorney who attested to the confession: "As to my certain knowledge I am in the Shadow of Death, as I know I am shortly to stand before the Judgment Seat, so I will not imperil my Immortal Soul with one burden greater than those it now inevitably bears, so I swear to the foregoing as the Truth."

And there was his signature, and those of the witnesses, and the attorney's seal.

Campbell broke in as soon as he saw her reach the end. "I don't expect you to forgive me, my darling," he said. "But I do hope you may understand."

She folded the paper and waited for him to say more.

"His son Frederick, my grandfather, said that William swore a blue mountain that Orlando was legitimate and that they'd all been cheated out of a great legacy. Of course it was just a family jape until my dad read in the paper about the Fourth Duke not having an heir and all about the hunt for the Boyces."

A sudden thought struck Georgina. "But if there was a big legal battle, as you say there was, didn't all this come out then?" She waved her hand at the confession. "How can it still be secret?"

Campbell smiled ruefully. "That's what really gouged him. He couldn't use it, you see, for fear that there was a survivor of Frederick's—the first Frederick, the one he had in England when he was living as Bugis. This confession proves they had legal priority. It was a trump card and he couldn't play it."

"So nor can you."

He gestured an unwilling disagreement, as if he wished what she said were true.

"Surely you can't," she pressed.

"I think I've proved that Frederick Bugis died. His mother came from Diss in Norfolk, and when she died in Spitalfields her body was sent back there. From what I can gather, her little boy, Frederick, would have been sent back to the workhouse there at the same time. No one liked to keep the rubbish of other parishes. But there's no record of a Frederick Bugis anywhere in or near Diss. Only one Frederick of any kind—a Frederick Boyle. He was adopted by the Vicar of Diss and later took holy orders himself. So we can be as good as certain that no line through Frederick Bugis has survived. We're safe."

"We?"

"Well—now it's out in the open we have to talk about it, darling. We can't just leave it—"

"I believe that's exactly what we ought to do: Leave it! Tear it all up."

"But that would be . . ." He could think of no word terrible enough.

"What d'you imagine we'd be giving up? I'll tell you—the chance to die at the Law Courts. Much better to follow the Sixth Duke of Buccleugh. He burned his ancestor's certificate of marriage to Lucy Walter—the certificate that proved him to be the rightful heir to the throne. This would be very small ale in comparison."

He shook his head. "I couldn't do that, Georgina. It'd be like spitting on my old dad. All my life he reared me for one thing—he told me I was put on earth for just this one purpose—to bring those papers together and *use* them."

"Use them for what? To destroy my family! And why? You haven't even got one of your own. You heard the duke when he spoke to us all. There was a lifetime of service to this estate and its people in that speech—and to the country, and to all of us. What would *you* put in its place?"

He obviously had not even considered it. "Socialism?" he said, and immediately warmed to the idea. "Yes! Think of *that* in the Lords! A socialist duke! Think of our ideas getting an airing at last in—"

"Pshaw!" She was indignant. "Have you learned nothing since you've been here? All you'd achieve would be to reduce socialism to the status of an eccentricity. The aristocracy is a hundred times more durable than the toughest armor plate." Her patience was exhausted; she sent the box of papers skittering across the table to him. "Do what you like, Campbell," she told him. "I could get men up here to prevent you. I could have those papers burned. I could stop you dead. And I could never face you again. So it has to be your decision. Take the box and do whatever you think best. But understand this: If you don't burn those papers, all of them, it's the end of everything between you and me."

"But . . . Georgina . . ." he began to wheedle.

"You say you love me more than the world. Fine words! Now's your chance to prove them." She turned her back on him and put her hands over her ears to shut out any reply. It also hid from him the fact that she was in tears.

It was half an hour before she was sure that the redness had worn off enough for her to risk leaving the muniment room and running the gantlet of footmen and maids between there and her room.

When she arrived, the first thing she saw was the note on the mantlepiece. "Try to understand," it read. She looked at the glowing coals of the fire; there was no crusting of burned paper, no shreds of unconsumed parchment. And there was no Campbell.

Full of dread, she sat and composed herself to tell the duke what she had done. But there were no tears. She had shed the last of them in the muniment room.

PART SEVEN

1914-1917

SPERNO ME
RECIPERE AUT
MUTARI

Dulce et Decorum Est...

CHAPTER SIXTY-SEVEN

IN AUGUST 1914, the month that England declared war on Germany, Campbell du Bois (who had resumed his fourth-great-grandfather's name) declared war on the duke. It had taken Alfred a long time to understand why Georgina had done what she did, and even longer to forgive her; she knew she would never forgive herself.

For Alfred the two wars took a course that ran curiously parallel. Both began in a breezy confidence that it would soon be over, with the enemy routed and in utter disarray; then the first, sobering skirmishes; the dawning realization that there were big guns on the other side, too, and seemingly boundless resources; then the first lost battles and the sudden, sharp terror of the unthinkable, ultimate defeat; then, by 1917, the weariness of long attrition, the numbness of brain as old, failed ideas and strategies played over and over again in the otherwise empty theaters of the mind. What else could one do except what one had done before? It had been right—all the best talents agreed—and yet it had failed.

To be sure, in the to and fro of daily life the parallels were never drawn as close as summary makes them appear; and there were many times when one war prospered while the other seemed close to ruin. But by and large the gloom of each helped to darken both and cast a double pall over what, Alfred thought, must surely be his last years.

The Great War had taken its meed of his family, even as the private war threatened its very basis. Emily's Henry, heir to the Marquis of Roundstone, died with the first Life Guards at Saultain in the first month of the war. Louise's Tarquin, heir to the Earl of Roundstone, died at Hill 60 with the Seventh Cavalry Brigade in May of the following year, leaving the succession in abeyance between Lady Fabia and Lady Portia. Herbert Bullen-Chetwynne, John Cardigan's elder boy, died on the Somme in 1916. James Lucan's son-in-law, Freddie, died with the Prince of Wales's Own Yorkshires, taking the Messines Ridge in 1917. Florence's sister Fanny, the determined little spinster, drowned in a shell hole near

No. 19 Casualty Clearing Station at Rémy Siding, also in 1917. John Taw, Laura Fitzbois' fiancé, died on "A" Beach, Suvla Bay, during the Gallipoli landings of April 1915. And Will Turnbull, still the least eligible bachelor, died early in 1916 from wounds received during the withdrawal from that same beach in December.

These deaths were repeated blows not only at the family but at those very traditions Alfred had extolled in his "Pride and Privilege" speech. In the early days of the war, each individual death could be seen as heroic—a sacrifice made in the same spirit as Lord Charles's on the Titanic. But as the toll mounted, the grief hammered out *why, why, why* with ever greater force. The standard, obvious answers seemed less and less compelling.

And it was not just the family deaths, either. Alfred opened Chalfont Abbey as a convalescent home for those tommies lucky enough not to die, unlucky enough to get "a Blighty one"—a wound so severe it brought them home. Usually they came on to the Abbey after the acute medical crisis was over, when they needed rehabilitation more than nursing. But sometimes, when there was a big push on and the wounded spilled backward through the system—through France and Dover, through Kent and London—they arrived at Chalfont Abbey still with the mud of Flanders beneath their fingernails.

Then the Abbey air was suddenly laden with the stink of gangrene; the death wagons called daily, never leaving empty. And the War Office would add a few more "we regret" telegrams to the hundreds of thousands—ultimately there would be millions—already sent out. A new and grisly meaning was given to the medieval knight's phrase "in the lists."

When Alfred first instigated inquiries into "the Australian Claim," sixty-seven years earlier, his opponent had been the near-penniless descendant of a felon, twelve thousand miles away; and the temper of those times was undoubtedly more pronobility, and certainly more antidemocratic, than these. Now, however, the penniless Mr. Boys had made several millions (ironically, in ships fitted out for cold storage with refrigerators manufactured by Alfred's and Grenville's Diamond Refrigeration Company). And, though it must never be imagined that eminent lawyers and barristers would be swayed a hairsbreadth from the strict and impartial interpretation of the law by mere money, nevertheless, the fact that there was a goodly glint of gold on the other side had led to some remarkable moderation in the assurance with which opinions favorable to Alfred's case were now expressed. Legal niceties and doubts which had scarcely troubled anyone when nothing but the cheap clink of copper coins could be heard (and that over half the world away) suddenly assumed new and solemnly worrying dimensions, demanding months of thought, acres of parchment, and thousands of pounds.

Back in 1850, when Mr. Bruce Boys had first suggested, without proof, that his forebear Orlando was the fruit of an illicit 1696 Roman marriage, no one had even mentioned the 1829 Catholic Emancipation Act (10 Geo. IV. *c.* 7). Now it assumed a central importance, for parts of it, read in conjunction with other acts to advance the legal status of Roman Catholics, could be taken to validate illicit marriages contracted during times of repression. "Otherwise," the argument ran, "how could the Duke of Norfolk and Lords Dormer and Clifford have been permitted to take their seats just fifteen days after the 1829 Act received its Royal Assent? They, too, were the offspring of unions cemented by outlawed priests using proscribed rituals."

"What I can't understand," Alfred objected, "is why all this didn't come out in 1850. We must have asked half a dozen Q.C.s their opinions. Most of them actually sat in the Parliament that passed the 1829 Act, so why didn't it occur to even one of them to mention it?"

And it was, of course, very hard to explain, without turning to scurrilous and quite improper ideas of how the legal profession acquits itself (that is, prosecutes and defends, judges and juries itself) in cases of this potentially lucrative kind.

The illicit nature of the Roman marriage had been, as it were, the Messines Ridge—the commanding height that could not be stormed—in the war between Alfred and Campbell. Now, or so it seemed, that bastion had fallen. True, the House of Lords would still have the final say on the matter; but that was the opinion to emerge from the preliminary skirmishes. These, like their counterparts in the Great War, were far from being valiant man-to-man contests; instead they were fought over mile upon mile of legal mud, a landscape in which everything of man or of nature lay blasted and withered, with words for bullets, affidavits for mortars, writs for grenades, and depositions for shells. And if pennies had parents, both Alfred and Campbell would have sent out as many we-regrets as did the high commands of the Central and Allied Powers together; and the regrets themselves would have been decidedly more heartfelt, too.

"Either way it's ruin," Alfred began to say.

In mid-1917, while the push on Passchendaele was, by its

casualties, horrifying a public long accustomed to deaths in the hundreds of thousands, the private war emerged from the trenches of judges' and barristers' chambers and moved with awesome solemnity toward its first and final great set-piece battle before the Lords.

From an obscure seat in the Distinguished Strangers' Gallery, where he sat by choice, Alfred looked down on the gowned and wigged assembly—the judges in full-bottomed wigs, the barristers in what could have passed as skullcaps for large sheep.

Middle-class to a man, he thought glumly, already feeling certain he had lost.

Those judges might be called "Lord" this and "Lord" that but they were mere life peers all—noble, like bishops, only by virtue of choosing the right trade and advancing high enough through it; their children were all misters and misses.

What did they know of Pride and Privilege? Or care? They'd sink the lot to preserve a legal point. Once Helen had told him of an artistic friend who said he'd gladly sacrifice the whole of humanity for the sake of one correctly placed comma. Now, it seemed, the world was filling up with such unthinking zealots—generals who'd sacrifice an entire generation to establish a single strategic point . . . union leaders who would sacrifice the livelihoods of their members to win a single principle . . . Were these judges any different?

A mute witness to a crumbling world, he listened for the umpteenth time to the arguments that had punctuated these four years past. His tired old mind saw position after position abandoned—the invalidity of the Roman marriage, the lack of proper certificate, the credibility of the witnesses to it, the last will and testament of William du Bois, the felonies perpetrated by three generations of his heirs from Orlando to William, the prior marriage of William-alias-Bugis to Sarah Cotehele, the lack of proof of the extinction of that line, the value of the Dying Confession of a convicted felon and self-confessed bigamist (as William had thought himself to be), the innumerable chances for forgery at every one of these stages, Bruce Boys's suppression of the Dying Confession during his abortive claim . . . and so on.

Each had seemed so strong, yet each yielded to the relentless and pinpoint assaults of Campbell's brilliant array of legal armor. His leading Silk, in particular, the redoubtable Sir Timothy Moran, had captivated the judges by his subtle and profound knowledge of the law of inheritance and descent—always ready with an apt precedent, always able to provide the exact reference that would advance his cause and cast an ill light on Alfred's.

"Don't worry," the duke's own advisers told him. "We still have our own big guns to fire—your writ of summons and your own installation and tenure through nearly seventy years."

Having seen the damp squibs that other supposedly "big guns" had fired, Alfred was not comforted. Day by day he watched the abandonment of his territory as position after position seemed to be yielded up (for, naturally, until the judges spoke no one could be certain what, if anything, had been lost).

What did all these words—these *quia timets*, these *prout de jures*, these *ratio decidendis*, these *negatorium gestios*, these *nemo dat quod non habets* (and the endless sly digs at "Oxford" pronunciation or "the other place")—what did these have to do with the loved and cared-for stones of Chalfont and those thousands of people, masters and servants, who had done the loving and caring? How, by clever manipulation of law and precedent, could these ignorantly learned apes set all the past at nought and deliver such a heritage to a parvenu traitor whose very blood and country shrieked *criminal?*

The entire world had passed beyond his understanding.

CHAPTER SIXTY-EIGHT

ON THE EVENING before the final arguments were due, Campbell, knowing in his bones that he had won, came to make what peace he could with Georgina. Somewhat belatedly he had realized there was a dynasty to found. He was not going to found it on a divorce—not, anyway, without a fight. He knew she would be down at the mission with her war widows.

Georgina, who during those dark days had lived from one *Times* Law Report to the next, at first refused to see him. Then, thinking herself cowardly not to try one last appeal—even though she knew it would be futile—told Toby to let her husband in. Toby was her "crooked V.C.," as she called him; morally he was no straighter than a gimlet, yet he had single-handedly wiped out a Hun machine-gun post at Arras.

Campbell began disastrously; and the more he said, the worse he fared. How could she interpret his cajoling and wheedling except as an insult to both her intelligence and her honor? And then, in return, how could he see her anger as anything but a slur on his manhood and a rebuff to his patriarchal authority?

At last it was clear that there was no hope of a reconciliation on any terms. Then he changed his tune to one of sneering menace. He blurted out that she would see! He had all but won his case and would soon be the Sixth Duke of St. Ormer. "If that old baboon doesn't croak first, I'll heft him out of Chalfont Abbey before the ink on the judgment is dry. You think you're all so marvelous, you Boyces. You behave as if you were brought up with Garter Ribbons for napkins. Well, now you're about to learn you're nothing but jumped-up tradesmen; and I'm the man to teach you."

Georgina was too furious to reply. Her heart beat like a riveting gun at the nape of her neck, at her temples, and in her ears. Reality shimmered in the heat of her fury. Anyone who knew her—anyone but Campbell—would have felt the aura and have gone from the room (indeed, from London) at that moment.

"Especially you, my proud madam," he blundered on. "I'll teach you. Oh, yes! I know the Law. The felon's grandson has come home and the Law bows to him! I know how to use the Law to bring the likes of you to heel. Just you wait!"

"What do you mean?" she thundered.

For a moment, even at this peak of his arrogance, he quailed. That hesitation was, did he but know it, his last chance of survival; he passed it by. He squared himself to her and went on: "When I've put that senile idiot out on the street where he belongs, I'll sue in the courts for the restitution of my conjugal rights." He grinned. "Like it or not, my love, you're going to be the next Duchess of St. Ormer and you're going to stand to me like any brood mare and let me sire the Seventh Duke on you. And there's nothing you can do about it. If the coppers have to hold you down, they'll do it. Because I've got the Law right here."

He squashed an imaginary bug between thumb and palm. And because he looked down to admire the finality of the act he failed to notice, and thus to appreciate, the far more convincing finality of Georgina's act as she seized a heavy brass statuette of a cockatoo and placed it between his ears, literally and geometrically between the tips of his ears, only slightly off the median line.

He fell in a heap; after a short pause he gave out a deep sigh and collapsed into an even smaller heap.

Her conscious mind told her she had done an appalling thing. Her spirit exulted at his lifelessness. Her conscious mind begged for the clock to go back just fifteen seconds, to the moment where she might have pulled or redirected the blow. Her spirit staged a jubilee as her mind's eye played and replayed the moment of impact.

Her conscious mind said, "You have done what you have done. Now you must not shirk the consequences."

Her spirit sang hosanna for the duke's liberation; it was above all an atonement to him for the harm she had done.

Outside the door, Toby and Widow Tripp, who had eavesdropped with shameless glee on the argument, looked dubious and fearful at the sudden silence.

"You don't think . . . ?" Toby began.

"Course not!" the widow said, with such lack of conviction that he stretched his hand toward the doorknob.

"Blimey!" they whispered, shocked into rare unison, when they saw the cockatoo (which he had stolen too long ago to remember and she had polished ever since) peeping cheerfully out of its slit trench in Campbell's head.

"What you been and gone and done, eh, gel?" Toby asked.

A police rattle sounded in the street. A zeppelin raid was about to begin.

"You can see what I've done, Toby. I can't deny it. And now, I suppose, I must accept the consequences."

A slow grin spread over Toby's face. "Yeah!" he said. "That'll be a tidy sum, I'll be bound!"

"What?" She did not understand him.

"The . . . er . . . *consequences.*" He leered. "I never seen him down the workhouse gate."

"It's like a helmet, innit!" Mrs. Tripp was looking at the brass cockatoo, putting her head first on one side, then on the other, as women do when they judge hats.

"Don't you two realize what I've done?"

A bomb fell with a lung-shaking crunch several streets away, followed quickly by two more.

"'Ere, we'd better get down the cellar," Toby said, being first at the door.

"What about . . . him?" Georgina asked, looking back at Campbell.

"If he ups and runs off, gel, that's one trouble less, innit!"

It was the hop-picking season down in Kent; the East End was half empty and the Mission—fortunately for Georgina—was even emptier. Apart from herself, Toby, and Mrs. Tripp, there was only the cook and her sister, both Russian Jews with next to no English. Even in the cramped cellar the three of them could talk freely.

"You don't seem to understand what I've done," Georgina said.

"Course we do," they assured her.

"You had an argument . . ."

"We heard, we was listening . . ."

"He threatened you summink shocking . . ."

"Raised his voice. Shouting, he was—screamed the place down. Oh, we heard."

"And you begged him. 'Don't hurt me, don't hurt me!' Didn't you hear her say that, Toby?"

"Plain as what I'm hearing you now, old duck. Yus! And then . . . then . . ." Invention was running out.

"The fire irons!" Mrs. Tripp hit a new lode.

"Yus! Clattering like the devil in a tin shop. (Remember to put the poker in his hand)," he added in a redundant whisper to the old duck. Then he beamed broadly at Georgina. "Well, thassit, innit, gel! Self-defense. They can't skin yer fer that, now, can they!"

Georgina, mentally breathless, said, "But you still don't understand! It may have sounded like that, but it isn't at all what happened. I *killed* him. I wanted to kill him. I enjoyed killing him. It was . . ."

The word "murder" was overlaid by the massive percussion of a nearby bomb. *Very* nearby. Dust showered down from the arched vault of the cellar.

"Blimey! That felt like next door," Toby said.

" 'Ere! What if it was us?"

Toby grinned. "That'd just about end our little trouble, wouldn't it. Eh!"

"What d'you mean?" Georgina asked.

"Well—take out the brass bird, stick in a brick or a lintel." He cackled. " 'Tragic Demise of Hopeful Duke at Mercy Mission—Yet Another Hun Atrocity,' " he quoted with glee.

"But I have done wrong," Georgina insisted. "It would be doubly wrong now to shirk my punishment."

There was another bomb. Several streets away.

Toby sniffed. "Yeah, well, if it was just a couple of years in the clink, I wouldn't disagree with yer, me old love. But for murder, it's a oyster and a artichoke for breakfast!"

"Oh." Georgina vaguely remembered something about the condemned man's last breakfast.

"You don't geddit." Toby laughed. "Listen: a *hoister* and a *hearty-choke* for breakfast!" He and Mrs. Tripp threw back their heads and howled with laughter. Even the uncomprehending cook and her sister were moved to join in.

Whether it was their calm acceptance of the murder, or their bland and unquestioning assumption that she would let them conspire with her to conceal it, or the tension of the zeppelin raid, or simply their laughter which moved her, she never knew. But when the next bomb came—and was even farther away—she stood up and said, "Come on, then. Let's see if there's a handy new ruin nearby."

The bomb they thought had fallen next door had, in fact, demolished most of the façade and one upstairs room of the house across the street. The gaslight, still burning in the front room, spilled out over the rubble.

"Over there," Toby said.

"You'll have to be quick," Mrs. Tripp urged. "You won't have the street to yourselves for long."

She bent and removed the brass cockatoo; it came away with a sucking sound, like lifting a flat spoon out of blancmange. The noise was more horrifying than the sight of the dead man and for a moment Georgina doubted that she could go through with it.

But Toby was marvelous. "Come on then, gel," he said in that rich, hoarse cackle of his. "I can't do it on me own and you know Ma Tripp's weak heart . . ."

She was astonished to discover how heavy and awkward a dead body can be, especially when a large man and a none-too-small woman try to drag it through a narrow passage. They got it out through the side door; dust and burned high explosive hung on the dark, damp air of the late summer night. Sweat broke out all over her body. Somewhere someone—a woman—was shouting.

She felt every cobblestone as the vibration was transmitted through the corpse to her straining arms. Halfway over the street the woman's shouting resolved itself into a cry for help. A light rain began to fall in giant, tepid drops, well spaced as yet.

Bathed in sweat and breathless, Georgina let go of Campbell's body and stood up to restore her shrieking back.

"Please!" cried the woman's voice; it came from the rubble in front of the damaged house. Georgina walked toward her.

"'Ere!" Toby called. "What about this, then?"

She did not pause. "We'll come back to that," she called over her shoulder. "Someone's hurt here."

"Yeah . . . but . . ." he protested and began dragging the body alone.

But her cry, "Toby! Come here quickly!" forced him to drop it and run the few paces that were left.

A young woman, little more than a girl, lay pinned under the remains of a door, which, in turn, was under a heap of bricks. "Are you hurt anywhere? Anything broken?" Georgina asked.

"Bleedin' bastard!" the woman spat out.

"Bleeding?" Georgina repeated.

"Bleedin' ran off and left me here."

"Blimey!" Toby said. "Kitty Marshall. I thought you was working up West. You all right, love?"

"Get them bricks off and you can tell me."

"She said something about bleeding," Georgina said as she and Toby began to manhandle the bricks off the door. Their roughness set her teeth on edge.

"Bleedin' bastard ran off," Kitty repeated. "It's all de-dah de-dah de-dah when they want a bit and it's private. But when there's a risk of being copped you can't see the scut of their tails."

"Was there anyone else in there?" Toby asked.

"Don't fink so. Sal and Dandy was dead drunk in the back. The rest was on the beat or down the boozer. My God, I'll crack his nuts next time he comes sniffin' round 'ere."

At last they had removed enough of the bricks for Toby to be able to lift the door in one swift heave.

Georgina, who had only partly followed Kitty's conversation (and hoped she'd misunderstood even that), gasped at the display of flesh and exotic lingerie that was suddenly revealed.

Toby gasped too, but in a different key.

"Toby!" Georgina was peremptory. "Go inside and find something for her to put on."

There was no disobeying such commanding tones. When he had gone, Georgina bent beside the woman and made her try to move each limb and joint in turn. She took off her chiffon scarf and flapped the brick dust away from Kitty's body. She was badly bruised, grazed in a couple of places, but no bones seemed broken.

"What happened?" Georgina asked.

"Search me, ma'am. One minute I'm dressed in me wrap, sticking me head out the door, saying a fond farewell—next minute I'm stretched out here with the door and half the house on top of me. And no sign of dear darling 'Six o' the Best'!"

"Good heavens," Georgina said. "You mean he might be buried under all this!"

Kitty sat up, sobered. "Blimey! I never thought o' that."

Georgina helped her to her feet just as Toby came out with a multicolored wrap. He nudged Georgina. "Come on, gel! Time's wasting."

People were beginning to emerge from their houses. The pair of them ran to where they had left Campbell's body, but no sooner had they bent to pick it up than a dark-uniformed figure stepped out of the gloom and said, "Now then. What's up 'ere?"

The sight of the uniform, and all that it implied to an upper-class woman in terms of the incorruptible and reassuring majesty of the law, was too much for Georgina. At once she saw how unforgivable it was to have entered this cockney conspiracy to conceal her wrongdoing. She must own up and put an end to it. She opened her mouth to speak.

But her throat was dry and dusty, and only an uncertain little croak emerged. If it had been a calm and confident noise, it would have calmed her and fed her own confidence; but this feeble little utterance had the opposite effect and she subsided into silence. *Leave it to Toby,* she thought, feeling a wretched coward.

And then she was suddenly alert in every fiber: Toby, too, was falling to pieces! Toby, who had laughed so devil-may-care when he suggested the plot, who had begun its execution as if doing no greater wrong than stealing a sack of coal . . . Toby was melting in incoherent terror at the sight of the law. "I knew it!" he whimpered. "I said we ought to of got it done . . . over and done . . ."

Georgina saw at once that confession was now impossible. No one would believe that Toby was not party to it. She might have sacrificed her own life for the sake of her honor; but she was not going to throw his into the pot as well.

All her confidence returned—and fortunately it showed in her voice. "You've caught us, officer," she said crisply. "I hope you'll find yourself able to suppress it in your report."

"Oh, do you!" The constable was too surprised to say more for the moment.

"Don't you know me, man?" Her voice was the flick of a light schooling whip.

"Ah . . . er . . ."

"I am the Honorable Mrs. Stone. This is my husband—or *was* my husband. He's dead, as you can see."

The constable shone his bull lantern on the corpse, lingering on the large, square dent in his skull. Georgina caught a glimpse of the handcuffs dangling from the constable's belt; for a moment she was unnerved. But then—perhaps because they recalled a gallows noose—she stiffened her resolve. "He died," she went on, "in *that* house. You know what that house was?"

The constable was embarrassed; obviously he did know what that house was. Kitty Marshall, who had been standing a little way off, listening, now came limping over. "He was with me," she said.

"Ah . . ." the constable said. "Er . . . yes . . . I see."

Georgina went on more quietly now, knowing she would soon have to turn on the waterworks. "We came out after the raid and heard this young woman calling for help—trapped under a door. Then she told us to help her 'gentleman friend' and . . ." She made her voice tremble and break. "We found . . . it was . . . my . . ." She burst into tears.

Toby, now all confidence again, said, "Didn't want it reported he was found in a house like that, see?"

"Ah! Yes!" The constable was more certain of himself now. "And where was you going to take him? If I may ask, ma'am."

Through her tears she saw paralysis begin to creep back into Toby's face. "Anywhere," she sobbed quickly. "Anywhere away from . . ."

"And how was you going to explain that injury?"

Georgina let the question penetrate her grief. She caught her breath. She stared at him in bewilderment. "I don't know," she said in a straying, uncertain voice. "We didn't think. We didn't *think!*" She clutched his arm. "Oh, how providential that you came along to help us, officer! What do you suggest?"

"Well, now . . ." He was none too sure about that.

Kitty nudged him. "Go on, Alf. You know what she's done for this street—the whole neighborhood. And where's the harm, eh? You wouldn't blacken her husband's name saying he spent his last hour with the likes of me."

"Well, I don't know . . ." he said. But his eyes were already searching the street for possibilities. "That's your Mission over there, ma'am, isn't it?" he said.

Georgina threw her arms about him and hugged him. "Oh, you marvelous man! Whoever said our police aren't marvelous!"

He held her at an embarrassed arm's length. "Let's say he was just leaving when the bomb fell. He thought the raid was over, and then—bang! A brick in the head."

"Oh—genius!" Georgina said and began to weep again. Kitty comforted her while the men got on with the hard labor.

They dragged the body back to the front of the Mission and put it on the side pavement, directly in front of the doorway.

"No bricks over here," the constable said.

"We can soon put that right," Toby told him.

Moments later the pair of them, quickly joined by half the street, were standing amid the rubble, shying bricks over the roadway at the Mission, laughing and cheering.

There was a loud crash of splintering glass. A brick had gone through one of the Mission windows.

"Enough! That does it!" the constable called.

Instantly the hail of rubble ceased. He ran over the street and, picking up a brick, bent over the corpse and tried it for size in the wound. The fit was perfect. Bits of brain and skin adhered to the brick when he pulled it away.

Light flooded over him as the door opened. Mrs. Tripp, startled by the shattering of the window, stood framed in the doorway. "'Ere! What you doing?" she asked.

She herself was holding a large brass cockatoo, which she was polishing . . . polishing . . . polishing.

CHAPTER SIXTY-NINE

IT TOOK ONLY a few months to sort out the estate. Georgina, as next-of-kin, relict, and sole legatee (which made her an extremely rich woman), declined to pursue the claim on the dukedom. She paid off Sir Timothy Moran and his terriers—all of whom assured her how relieved they were to give up their lucrative daily "refreshers" and to drop this highly distasteful case against one of England's most distinguished noblemen. The papers in the case all reverted to her, "At once!" she insisted.

The following weekend she took them down to Chalfont Abbey and handed them over to Alfred. "Burn them," she said, thinking how he would relish it.

But he held them in his hands, turning them over and over, and shook his head. "Everyone's seen them," he answered. "There must be a dozen copies in London—and even more people willing to swear to their accuracy. Burning them would only add to their power, showing how we fear them."

"We needn't fear them now."

"No."

"What then?" she asked.

He sighed. "Knightsbridge will be here this evening. He'll know what to do."

She had never known or heard of his yielding decisions in that way; suddenly she divined how weary he must be.

He could still sit a horse, slumped like a small caricature of the aged Duke of Wellington seventy years earlier. That afternoon, when the day grew warm, they mounted and sauntered through the woodland rides, among groups of convalescing soldiers, down to the grove of Wellingtonias. It was now late November, but a brilliant day, as warm as summer while they stayed in the sun. At ground level there was no breeze, but a light soughing of wind among the giant treetops spread the illusion of a hot day downward. Seeds of broom and shrub lupines cracked all around like embryonic rifle fire.

Convalescents and nurses moved some way off as they approached, providing the duke and Georgina with the feeling of being alone in their own grounds. They dismounted then and walked without speaking to a bench half hidden by some low hanging branches.

For a long while they sat in silence, side by side. Her arm, linked through his, was a great comfort to him. He smiled to himself at the thought that he was both her paternal and maternal grandfather; even if Campbell had won, he, Alfred, would have left a bigger share of himself here than the world imagined.

"What would you have done with the place?" he asked.

"Done?" She was astonished.

"If he'd won."

"*I* wouldn't have come."

"Tscha! Of course you would. You'd have come here with him and fought him over every brick and tile and pane of glass. Whose granddaughter are you?"

As soon as he said it, she knew he was right. She would have done exactly that.

"And you'd have hammered him to his knees," the duke added contentedly.

After a long silence, without a trace of unease, she said, "I killed him, you know. Not the bomb. I did it."

He chuckled. "I thought as much. Or perhaps I should say I hoped as much."

"The zeppelin raid was just . . . good luck, I suppose."

"Yes. We mustn't imagine that He"—his eyes were on the heavens—"would abet us in so trifling a purpose."

"Thank God it's over."

"And good has come out of it, my dear."

She was silent, not wanting to question that statement.

But he went on. "When I faced the loss of the dukedom—we'll never know, I suppose, how near or far we came to it, but it felt very near. And when I faced it, I began to understand that a title and an estate isn't the most important thing in the world. In fact it's the ruin of some. Look at Charles Marlborough. Look at Arthur Wellington. Look at 'Bend Or.' And Herbrand Bedford. Miserable buggers every single one. They ought never to have been dukes. They'd all have been much happier as commoners. In a humane world someone would have come along and taken their dukedoms away. Someone like Campbell."

"But you haven't been a . . ." She wondered how to paraphrase him.

"Miserable bugger?" He laughed. "No. I've loved every minute of it. But it would've made Knightsbridge miserable. And Charles was much happier in his own shoes than he would have been in mine. Of course, you're a Socialist, aren't you? You probably think we all ought to have it taken away from us."

"I'm afraid I do, grandfather," she said.

He grunted. "You may be right at that. When you realize how bloody miserable most peers are most of the time, you'd probably be doing us all a great kindness. I wonder what sort of a duke young Simon will make. We both know several peers who are actually insane. I wonder what they were like when they were young? Like Simon, d'you think?"

"Surely not?" She laughed, thinking he might be joking. "Why d'you say that?"

"If they were obviously insane, you see, someone would have locked them up. There must be some kinds of insanity that just creep up, so slowly that everyone else adjusts—instead of getting worried enough to call in the alienist."

"But not *Simon*."

"Why not?"

"He's so calm . . . so collected."

"So convinced he's right?"

"Well . . . yes."

"Yes!"

A bee circled them warily, twice. Alfred yawned and, coincidentally, the bee fled as if it had stung itself. They both laughed. It changed the mood between them.

"Surely the war must be over soon," she said.

"One would think so." He sighed. "Nothing will ever be the same, you know. Even the little Boer War changed things. But *this* one! Look at the changes already. I'm afraid four-course dinners and fifth-rate service are here to stay."

"I know people who wouldn't mind a four-course dinner once in a while, with or without service."

"Well none of them works here, I assure you of that."

"I know. You're the kind we Socialists dislike the most, you know. You undercut all our arguments."

"Anyway," he said, pleased and wanting to tease her, "you'll be a rich woman now. You can hand out all the four-course dinners you want."

"Beast! I've got to think very carefully what I do with it. I've got to make every penny count."

"I've been a member of that club longer than I can recall," he said. "Welcome!" There was a long, restful silence and then he added, "I'm going to die soon."

He spoke exactly as he might have said, "I'm going to dress for dinner soon." So she was a little late in catching his meaning, and even later in her conventional response, "Oh—grandfather . . ."

"No, no. I don't mind. I don't even want to know if we're going to win next year's Derby. But I would like to do one thing more. I'd like to meet Lansbury or some of your Fabians. Do you—"

"Good heavens!"

"Do you think it might be arranged?"

"Of course. But why?"

Unable to sit still for long, he stood and took a few paces. She rose, too, and gave him her arm for support.

"I've been reading some of their papers," he said. "They've got it so nearly right. Tell me, what would you say is the Socialist ideal? The heart of it all?"

"From each according to his abilities; to each according to his needs," she answered glibly.

"Exactly!" he crowed. "And isn't that the ideal here at Chalfont Abbey? 'From each according to his abilities'—that's service, isn't it? Everyone doing his bit, pulling his weight, from the humble shepherd and mechanic right up to those born and trained for leadership—all contributing, all working, not just for money, not for personal advance or gratification, but for the common weal. The good of the Tribe. And 'to each according to his needs'—the cottage for the servant, the schooling for his children, the doctor for his ills, the pension for his dotage, the gravestone for his grave . . . and so on, right up to the leaders, whose needs include the symbols and trappings of their authority. Me and my Garter. You see! Your socialism sums up Chalfont Abbey in one neat phrase."

Georgina drew breath to protest, but he went on. "Where all you Socialists have gone wrong is in the scale of the thing. You want to put it all on a national footing. Or 'basis' as your jargon calls it. But men's minds don't work like that, my dear. A man can tip his hat to me and say, 'Good morning, your grace,' and feel respect (as

I feel, too, for him) because he gets his livelihood from me and so we've both got a bargain to keep. But how can he tip his hat to some pin-striped nonentity who probably went to the same school as himself and say, 'Good morning, Mr. State-Functionary-Responsible-for-the-Implementation-of-the-Employment-Act, 1916'! It's absurd. No! Socialism's a first-rate *idea,* but it's got to be organized on human lines. We've got to give it a human face, something the ordinary bloke can understand. Men are tribal—you can't change that."

"Men certainly don't think logically," she risked saying.

"Just so!" He was delighted to have her agreement.

"They think in symbols," she risked adding.

"There!" He was overjoyed. "I can see I don't need to explain it to you at all."

Now she was thoroughly bewildered. "Explain what, grandfather?"

"Well, your Lansburys and your Chamberlains think that because the middle class has been decimated by this war, it's going to be a chance to build a workers' paradise after it's over."

"And don't you agree?"

"I do. I do! The slaughter of the middle classes is a godsent chance for the workers and the aristocracy to join hands and put everything right again. The middle classes reduced everything to money—all the marvelous, wonderful . . . *richness* of human life—all reduced to sordid money. All human relationships are in danger of being reduced to cash relationships. I see the coming years as a splendid chance to remind the workers of all the other riches, the *human* riches, all of which they will lose if they scramble after the middle-class gods of money, personal ambition, and novelty."

She looked at him closely, afraid the excitement might have exhausted him. But he was even chirpier than before. "And what a godsent chance to reorganize the Empire along proper, feudal lines! Tribes within tribes—that's true socialism!"

"And war?" she asked. "Will it be an end to war?"

"An end to wars like this one, certainly. This is the middle-class idea of war—where men are turned into coins to be gambled by generals. We'll go back to the good old tribal wars again. Little wars. Saxons against Celts. Protestants versus Papists. Even village against village. And just a few deaths—enough to keep alive the heroism and self-sacrifice which is blood itself to the tradition of the Tribe. D'you see now?"

"And that's socialism?"

He nodded. "True socialism."

"And you want to talk to Lansbury or MacDonald about . . . that? These ideas?"

"Can you arrange it? I'd be grateful."

"I'll try," she promised. "On condition you let me be present. I'd hate to miss such a meeting."

"Historic," he said.

General Knightsbridge was delayed a few days, so he arrived after Georgina had left. He had been part of the liaison between Field Marshal Earl Haigh, G.O.C. of the British Forces in France, and the various armies that fought along the Flanders front. When Passchendaele was "won" that November, he could be spared a spot of leave.

He was despondent about the victory, which had cost a quarter of a million dead, wounded, or missing. Over forty thousand had simply vanished, buried in craters or blown to butchereens. As long ago as 1915, Knightsbridge had been a supporter of General Sir Horace Smith-Dorrien in wanting to reduce the Ypres Salient, poking out like a vulnerable blister into German-held Belgium—even though Smith-Dorrien had been sacked for the suggestion. Since then the holding of Ypres and the drive from there to Passchendaele, six miles nearer Germany, had cost 430,000 Allied casualties: forty men per yard—or ninety, if one included German losses too.

"Why d'you chaps let it happen?" the duke asked his son.

"It's too big for anyone to stop, duke. If you want my absolutely candid and confidential opinion, I don't believe Passchendaele was even a military objective. We had to put up a bit of a show in Flanders to distract the Hun from the mutinies in the French army. We had to win Passchendaele because a spectacular victory might stiffen up the Russians—and also convince the merchant navy we're getting poised to biff the U-Boats." He snorted. "And that's the sort of sloppy thinking you get out of the War Cabinet. I only hope our intelligence reports are true that the Boche are as demoralized as everyone else."

In Alfred's mind these assessments made it even more imperative for him to see Lansbury, Snowden, and the other Socialist leaders at once. If Europe was to follow the Russian example of collapse into revolution, it was even more important not to repeat the dreadful mistakes that were being made there.

On the fifth day of his leave Knightsbridge received a telegram.

"Not bad news, I hope?" the Duke asked.

"No!" Knightsbridge was grinning hugely. "No, the very best.

We've picked up the body of Colonel Freiherr von Ritter. An enormous piece of luck. D'you know the fellow?"

"Should I?"

"I should say so! He's the envy—or was—of the entire high command on both sides. They've embalmed his body but I've got to get back and see it at once, before he's buried. French wants to see him too, I know. And Haigh. They say they'll postpone it two more days."

"But *why*? What can possibly be so special?"

"You really don't know, duke? Heavens! I thought everyone knew. He has a complete set of stainless-steel teeth. All thirty-two of them, shining like new gun barrels. I simply have to see it before they bury him. You do understand, don't you?"

Before he left, Alfred handed him a carefully wrapped packet of papers. "These are for Simon," he said. "You'll outlive me. You'll outlive this war—generals always do. Give them to Simon. It's no bloody good talking to him at the moment. All he can think of is Sandhurst and France."

"But why not leave them here, sir? What are they, anyway?"

"They're the papers Campbell du Bois stole from the muniment room. Georgina brought them back to me last week. I don't want them just lying around here. I want to know it's *with* one of us. You or him."

Knightsbridge nodded and tapped the packet with his cane. "Count on me," he said.

A puzzled George Lansbury stared at the card in his hand. "The Duke of St. Ormer?" he said disbelievingly. He turned it over as if hoping to find a contradiction on the other side. " 'Workers and Peers of England—Unite!' " He read the crabbed, old-fashioned handwriting. "It's surely a joke."

"No, Mr. Lansbury," the secretary said. "Look out the window—see if that isn't his grace's car."

Sure enough, there was the Roi-des-Belges Silver Ghost, with the ducal crest on the passenger door, parked immediately outside the entrance of the none-too-imposing H.Q. of the Independent Labour Party.

"He begs you'll excuse him, Mr. Lansbury, sir, as being an old man and desires you'll attend him in his carriage." That was O'Neill, the chauffeur, back from France with more stainless steel in his skull than even the Freiherr Colonel.

"Pass me that *Debrett* a moment, would you?" Lansbury asked the secretary. A short while later he said, "Oh, I see he's the Honorable Mrs. Du Bois' grandfather. Oh, yes! She said something about this."

Alfred knew he was dying even before Lansbury appeared. The excitement of this coming union—the cymbal clash of a thousand years of English history—proved too much for his ninety-one-year-old heart. The world began to fly apart. The corners of his view tilted drunkenly. He lost touch with his body, could not feel the seat beneath him, knew not if he were breathing still.

His vision narrowed to a tunnel. Oh, Time! Steps. Columns. Lansbury. The man grew bigger. Opened the door. Looked. Spoke.

"My God!" he said. "Fetch a doctor!"

With superhuman will, Alfred reached an unseeably black hand forward into the black unseen around the tunnel. Lansbury took it. "My, but he's got a grip," he said.

"He wants you to sit by him, sir," O'Neill told him.

Wonderful O'Neill! For those words you're worthy of your life.

Words!

Words?

No time now for words, for logic, for argument. Time only for . . . a *symbol!*

Lansbury sat beside him. The fierce grip did not relent.

"Together!" Alfred said, quite clearly. "Together!" He gripped and shook the hand he held. "Together!"

Georgina, who had intended to be present at this meeting, arrived soon afterward, in time to hear the doctor tell them the duke had had a stroke. He was paralyzed below the waist and his speech was affected; he could, however, communicate well enough to insist, later that day, on being moved from the hospital back to Chalfont Abbey.

Squeezing the words out of one side of his mouth, with a great many hesitations and false starts, he also managed to convey to them his wish to see Knightsbridge once more.

CHAPTER SEVENTY

"WHERE'S General Knightsbridge, anyone know?" the colonel asked.

"He's down at Cambrai for this new show," a major said.

"Oh, dear, that's awkward. Can we get a signal down there? Where's forward H.Q.?"

"Traffic's pretty heavy, colonel. Is it important?"

"I don't know, Huxtable. What are one's priorities? How important is it to tell a general in the middle of a battle that he's just about to come into a dukedom?"

"Pretty important, I should say."

"Is he running the show?"

"No, sir. Observing. General Elles has always complained that his tanks have never had a proper trial over virgin ground—always over mud and craters. So the G.O.C. sent General Knightsbridge down to watch."

"Better get a signal off to him. Regret inform you . . . etcetera. Look all the titles up in *Debrett*."

"At once, colonel."

"Send it by pigeon, too. Just to be on the safe side."

06.20. First Light. A favorable haze was lifting off the Canal du Nord—indeed, off all the fields. It was a dry, dull, windless day, perfect for a tank attack. General Elles gave the signal for the advance.

There were four hundred of them, spread over a six-mile front from Hermies in the north to Gonnelieu, away to the southwest. Their orders were to push directly onward toward Cambrai, to their front, each with a company of infantry or dismounted cavalry in mutual support. As the roar of their engines signaled their departure, the artillery began to lay down smoke over the immediate objective, the First Hindenburg Line. The Hun had no idea what was coming.

The ironclad fleet roared forward and, to the watching party of observers from G.H.Q., the advantage of this formation was at once apparent. No man's land was a maze of barbed wire barriers with, here and there, lethal gaps on which every enemy machine gun was trained. The tanks ignored them, plunging straight through the wire, tearing out the posts in one long series of splintering crashes. Through the wide gaps thus created—far wider than the tanks—the infantry poured. Where the tanks met ditches they dropped tightly bound faggots of brushwood to act as solid bridges, hardly pausing in their amazing progress.

The dawn light played tricks of magnification on the scene, so that to the observers the tanks looked monstrous. With their trailing columns of infantry all marching in silent order through the wreaths of mist, bayonets fixed, they made a sight that none who saw it would ever forget.

At 06.30 a runner came back out of the smoke to say that the First Hindenburg Line had been secured at 06.26 and the units were pressing on toward the Second.

"Six minutes!" General Elles said triumphantly. "Gentlemen, we shall need our horses today!"

The dispatch rider took the wrong turn out of Fins but did not realize it until he reached Gouzeaucourt. There he met the first walking wounded coming back from the Twelfth Division's push toward the Banteaux Spur.

"Seen a party of generals on horseback, mates?" he asked.

They hadn't seen a party of generals on horseback.

He turned not quite full circle and set off toward Metz-en-Couture.

"Of course, you're concentrated at the beginning," Knightsbridge said. "But as you push out, north, east, and south, you'll be spread thinner. Won't that slow you down?"

"Not at all!" Elles was intoxicated at the success of his tanks. "The German defenses are only two or three miles deep. By the time we're significantly thinner, he'll be running in open country, too—and running backward!"

Knightsbridge looked at the map. He put his gloved finger on the country around Graincourt. "Let's go and test the theory up there," he said.

"Why there particularly?"

"Because the canal will impede you. Because you've got a Territorial division fighting there, whereas most of the others are Regulars. And because if I were Fritz, I'd try and get behind you there."

"Graincourt it is, then!" Elles was not shaken.

At that moment the dispatch rider was just turning back toward Metz.

"Seen a party of generals on horses?" he asked a crowd of French civilians. *"Lays generahlz? Sure lays shevalz?"*

They shrugged uncomprehendingly.

Some people! he thought, looking around at the four northern and eastern exits to the square, any one of which might be his route to the generals.

He chose the route to Trescault.

• •

The generals caught up with the West Yorkshire Territorials just as they swept through Havrincourt, carrying everything in fine style at the point of the bayonet.

Knightsbridge intercepted a company runner carrying news back to Div. H.Q. "Any trouble here?" he asked.

"Resistance from the château was a bit stiff, sir. But the tanks got the measure of them soon enough."

"And where's the next objective?"

"The reserve German trenches, sir, just beyond those trees. Then we'll press on to Graincourt." He saluted and ran for his bicycle.

"Let's cut across to Flesquières," Knightsbridge said. "I don't think these Terriers are going to meet with much."

"Seen a party of generals on horses?" The D.R. asked his question now without much hope—and so was delighted when the company runner said, "Blimey, I should just think so. Can't you smell the cigars from here?"

"Where are they?"

"Just north of Havrincourt, watching my lot."

"Where's your lot making for, then?"

"Graincourt."

The D.R. looked at his map. "Got it!" He folded it along new creases. "Thanks, mate. Spot o' luck running into you. I'd probably have gone off east to Flesquières!"

"Ah!" The cavalry colonel couldn't quite keep the triumph out of his voice. "Now here's the great drawback with tanks."

And there was no denying it. A dozen and a half of them littered the long, open slopes up to the château at Flesquières. The hill obliged them to change to bottom gear, whereupon they became easy, slow-moving targets for the well-served Prussian guns in their heavily fortified emplacements in and around the château.

They watched the fighting for over an hour. The barbed wire and the extensive walls of the château, to say nothing of the open field of fire for the machine guns, made it a hard position to overrun. Yet until it fell, the vital approaches to Marcoing would be denied—and Marcoing was their best hope of capturing an intact bridge over the Canal de l'Escault. Without at least one such bridge there was no chance of pressing onward to Cambrai itself.

"Seen a party of generals on horses?" he asked the umpteenth party of wounded. "Blimey! I'm going round in circles here!"

"I seen 'em," one said. "About an hour ago. Maybe two. When we come through that village there." He pointed.

"Havrincourt?"

"Search me! But they was there. I'd try over that way, where all that fighting is." He pointed over the fields toward Flesquières. "They love fighting, them generals. They could stand and watch it all day!"

"General Elles, sir?"

"Here, man!"

"The Sixth and the Twenty-ninth have taken Marcoing and Masnières, sir. They came up from the south and met very little opposition."

There was a spontaneous cheer among the generals.

"Well, that takes this château off the boil," Elles said with relief. "We must have them surrounded. We'll squeeze them out tomorrow. I won't throw in any more tanks today." He looked at his watch. "Eleven hundred hours. Four hours and forty minutes. We've pushed them back at a mile an hour!"

"God! I'd love to refight Spion Kop with tanks!" Knightsbridge said. He was still surveying the château through his glasses. "But here's your Achilles heel, Elles. See that gun emplacement right on the corner of the château?"

"Yes." Elles found the one.

"That Prussian deserves the Iron Cross. He's knocked out ten of your tanks with that one field gun. We've got to account for him before he can put in a report. Who's your best sniper?"

Their best sniper dropped the Prussian officer five minutes later. Knightsbridge, sitting to attention, saluted the gallant enemy. "Let's cut across these fields here to Ribecourt," he said. "See how Snow's Sixth managed to get on so well."

"Seen a party of generals on horses?" he asked the flank scout of the unmounted Canadian cavalry, who were being stood down from the assault on the château at Flesquières.

"Sure did," the man said. "Up in that stand of timber just short of the skyline. Whole bunch of them."

"Thanks!" He was effusive as he revved up; he sent dirt flying all the way up the slope.

The Canadian hadn't been lying. The cigar butts alone were evidence enough. He followed the hoofprints down to the road, noted that they faced across country toward . . . he looked at his map . . . Ribecourt. Then he made yet again for Havrincourt, from where there ought to be a road or lane.

• •

"We could hear the bullets pattering like hailstones against the tanks, sir," the Sherwood Foresters major was saying. He was their guide in a verbal replay of the battle for Ribecourt. "Infantrymen were walking on both sides in full view, and no one shot at them. The tanks drew all the fire—the Boche were hypnotized by them."

"Marvelous!" Knightsbridge said.

"We cut off one of their companies," the Foresters major went on. "They retreated into that farmhouse." He pointed at a building only twenty yards away. "And fought it out to the last man. I held up a flag of truce and went forward to offer them quarter. The officer said, 'Only I am here,' in English. Then he put a pistol to his head and shot himself."

"You know," Knightsbridge said. "There are times when you can't help admiring the German spirit. I should like to go and salute such a man!" He dismounted and walked to the door.

"We ought to push on, old boy!" Elles called after him.

"Shan't be a jiff. I'll have a jimmy-riddle while I'm at it."

The door swung drunkenly on its hinges. He went inside.

The horses pawed the ground impatiently. There was the sound of a motorcycle coming toward them through the lanes.

"Not a bad idea, actually," Elles said, dismounting too.

He was halfway to the farmhouse when the shot rang out.

The generals looked at each other and made a concerted dash toward the building. Halfway there, they halted.

A German officer staggered into the doorway, leaned against the reveal, took careful aim at Elles, who was nearest . . . and fell headlong in the dust.

"My God, that's the same fellow!" the major said. "How did he survive?"

"That'll be for the court of inquiry to decide," Elles said meaningfully.

The motorcycle drew nearer. A corporal and two Foresters were sent in to flush out the farmhouse, but no further living Germans were found.

They stood around Knightsbridge's corpse, appalled at the thought that the warrior who had survived Rorke's Drift and Lord alone knew how many other desperate hand-to-hand encounters with the enemy should die here, unarmed, after the battle was won, from a bullet in the back, fired by a crazed enemy officer.

There were no words to express the horror of it.

"Do his flies up, someone," Elles said.

None of them noticed the little packet lying about four feet away.

"I have a dispatch for General Lord Knightsbridge," the D.R. said, pulling his machine onto its stand and saluting.

"I'll take it," Elles told him.

"It's marked Private and Personal," the cavalry colonel said.

Elles looked at the D.R. "Do you happen to know the contents?" He tapped the message. "I'm afraid General Lord Knightsbridge has just been killed."

"Oh, I'm sorry, sir. The message was to tell him that the Duke of St. Ormer, his father, is dying."

Elles handed him back the message. "They'd better look for . . ." He glanced at the other officers. "Anyone know the family? Who's next in line?"

They all shrugged.

"Where's the nearest *Debrett?*" Elles asked the Foresters major. "Oh, never mind. They'll have a dozen at G.H.Q."

CHAPTER SEVENTY-ONE

GEORGINA WAS the watchdog of Alfred's room. None but she and Meg were allowed near him—except, naturally, the nurses and specialists, who confirmed what any astute fool might have suspected: the duke would die, perhaps soon, perhaps next year, perhaps later.

Another exception, once Knightsbridge's death was known, was Simon, now the undoubted heir. Georgina led him across the vast bedroom, to the great bed where the duke lay, the bed he had shared with two duchesses. The duke did not open his eye until the footsteps drew very close; he husbanded every minute of his life.

"Here's Simon, grandfather," she said. "Come to see you."

The mobile half of his mouth smiled. She wiped the drool from the other half. Successive minor strokes had robbed him of his little power of speech, but he made a gruff noise of welcome.

"Stand here where the light falls on you," she told Simon.

She plumped up the lace pillows and maneuvered the duke to where he could watch his heir with the least effort.

"Hello, granddad," Simon said, thinly cheerful.

Georgina walked to the door and then, seeing that Simon was completely preoccupied with his grandfather, she closed it as if she had departed; then she slipped behind the screen that masked her bed from the general view.

"I was very sorry about uncle Knightsbridge, granddad," the young man said. "But we can both feel proud of the way he died, I think—and of the fact that he was the only officer there who had the nobility to want to salute a gallant enemy. It makes a fellow grateful, sir, to have blood like that in his veins, what."

Simon was used to conversations with the duke that were largely one-sided—but his was usually the quieter half. This reversal was unnerving. He wanted to reassure the old fellow, so that whether he died today, or next week, he would at least know the dukedom was in safe hands. It was hard, especially when the old boy's only communication was a ghastly lopsided grin. But Simon was never one to shirk a duty, however difficult or unpleasant.

"I've been thinking, granddad," he said. "A great deal, in fact. An awful lot. About all the things you've told me over the years. I think I can remember everything you ever said to me. I remember especially that time after father died and I spent the whole of the Easter holidays here. And you asked me if I'd change anything, and you said the hardest thing in the world would be to keep things the way they are. Remember?"

The duke gave his half-smile.

"Well, that's what I've been thinking about. What do we want to see after the war, eh? That's what it boils down to. I've talked it over with some of the fellows at Eton, chaps who'll inherit a title and a few acres some day. At first we kept the circle to earls and above—the heirs to earldoms, I mean. And we decided—with a great deal of pushing from me, I may say, and all thanks to you, sir—we decided that what we want to see is a sort of feudal democracy. Once we'd got that clear, we even drew baronets and viscounts into it, because we realized that if we were going to take this democracy business seriously, we'd have to consult with people we wouldn't normally consider. No sense in provoking a new rash of Magna Cartas, what."

He could see how desperately the duke wanted to hear the rest of it. He hastened on. "The workers of England, you see—the good, honest hewers of wood and toilers in the vineyard—are going to be pretty ballsed off about middle-class democracy and the whole gang of bourgeois crooks who bungled us into this war and bungled us through three long years of it, and still no end in sight. They're going to want something different to put in its place. They haven't sacrificed themselves by the hundred-thousand just to see the same old oily cliques with the same grubby fingers in the public purse. They'll want something cleaner and nobler. And we're the chaps to give it them."

The duke's enthusiasm was by now almost breaking through his paralysis. Simon continued: "Of course, in the beginning there'll be a lot of wrongheadedness and muddled thinking to counteract. The jails won't be empty and we may even have to do a spot of shooting to set an example. But we won't shirk it, sir. Or I won't, anyway. And I'll keep the other chaps up to it."

The duke was now so visibly excited by the vision that Simon began to wonder if he had been altogether wise in saying so much all at once. He decided then to cut it short. "The key, as we see it, sir—or as I see it—is the king. The bourgeoisie in Parliament have held the monarchy in pawn too long. The king must reassert himself. And I think we know just the way to help him do it. The war is our golden opportunity. It was my own idea, actually, based on all the things you've told me over the years. So I'll put it to him at the first opportunity."

He patted his grandfather heartily on the shoulder. "You've started something, duke! You've lit such a fire in England as, by God's grace, may never be put out."

Georgina heard a growl and a gurgle from her grandfather. Then silence. Then her cousin said, "Granddad?"

A pause. "Granddad?"

She peeped out. Simon was drawing himself up to attention. Not being in uniform, he gave a vaguely Romanesque salute and said, "Farewell, most noble!"

"Simon?" Georgina stepped out into view.

Simon turned, broke into a broad smile, and beckoned her excitedly over.

The duke was undoubtedly dead. Georgina closed his eye, crossed his hands, and pulled the sheet up over his face.

"He died happy," Simon said. "He died knowing he had not lived in vain."

CHAPTER SEVENTY-TWO

THE DOUBLE FUNERAL and the interment in the family vault were kept as simple as possible; after Christmas there was to be a memorial service at Westminster Abbey. The war was too old and death too familiar for people to want much more ceremonial than that. Simon was furious at the decision. His family deserved better of the nation.

Alone, by unwritten family tradition, he went into the crypt to see his grandfather and uncle put to rest.

The Sixth Duke, he thought.

Caesar was still there, dusty between the two coffins—grandmama Flora and grannie Hermione. He took the toy down and nodded at the gardeners, augmented today, because they were old, by two local bobbies.

"Now he'll rest in peace," he said to them when the great bronze coffin had rolled into its place between the two duchesses.

"That he will, your grace," Archer, still head gardener, agreed. "They were marvelous people, all three of them. If all these others were like them, you've great cause for pride, sir."

"I'm glad you understand that, Archer. I hope there are millions more like you."

Knightsbridge's coffin was a lead replica of the Second Duke's, "Mask of Steel"—the family's other great military hero. When it had been placed, the men withdrew and left him alone with his Tribe.

He tried to feel sad but could not. Instead a magnificent sense of his own duty filled him. His life stretched before him in selfless dedication to that mission. The joy of it had ended the Fifth Duke's life; now it would fire that of the Sixth.

There was a footstep on the stair. His mother, Helen, came into the crypt. "The king and queen are waiting, dear," she said. "And the queen mother."

"It'll do them no harm. I want a word with him, anyway. I think he ought to grant you the style of a dowager duchess. It's the least he can do for this family, don't you think?"

"I wouldn't raise the subject just yet, dear."

"You should call me duke now. Not dear."

"I daresay his majesty has it in mind. It wouldn't be good coming from you so soon."

"No. Quite right. Besides, I've something much more important to put to him."

"We really mustn't keep their majesties waiting, dear."

Their majesties stayed to a late luncheon.

The hors d'oeuvres were barely served before Simon began. "Are you entirely happy with the constitutional position of the monarchy, sir?" he asked.

The king frowned, looked meaningfully at the small army of footmen and other servants all around the little table, and said, "It was a raw enough day for it."

"One always thinks of our poor men in France," the queen said. "Having to endure such weather."

"It's their duty, ma'am," Simon explained with a generous smile. "But it won't do to go sympathizing with them. They'll only get the idea they deserve some sort of special favor when it's over."

Helen interrupted with an edgy laugh. "The keenness of young people to go out and serve their country, even after three such dreadful years, is most inspiring."

"Indeed, Lady Charles." The king eyed Simon nervously.

"*King* and country." Simon corrected his mother. "Those who have given their lives did so for the king as well as for the country. It's time those who have usurped the king's power were reminded of that fact."

There was a silence, uncomfortable to everyone but Simon. Georgina caught Helen's eye and gestured a throat-slitting operation with a slight nod toward her young cousin. Queen Mother Alexandra saw it and smiled. "I probably knew Duke Alfred better than any one who now survives him," she said. "Except perhaps you, Lady Charles."

"I'm sure you knew him better, ma'am. We saw only his domestic side. He *never* discussed public affairs *en famille*." She aimed this heavily at Simon.

"Our family is more in his debt than history will ever know," Alix went on. "He was so discreet. He must have performed a thousand services for us, many of the greatest delicacy. Yet he was *so* discreet." She, too, spoke directly at Simon.

"Thank you, ma'am." He smiled back. "And you are so right to mention history. For history will remember him as the man who turned the tide. The man who started the great task of rolling back the middle classes."

"He was a magnificent horseman in his day," the queen said. "Is it true he rode up the Great Stair here at the Abbey?"

"Oh, quite true, ma'am," Helen answered. "It was his first time on a thoroughbred."

"Horsemanship was part and parcel of his vision, ma'am," Simon explained. "He was essentially feudal. He was a Knight of the Round Table."

"No, no," the king said. "He was a Freemason."

"Of course he was," Alix said. "He was a Past Zerubbabel."

"I mean, sir"—Simon was beginning to despair—"in the Arthurian sense. A parfit gentil knight."

"He was a perfect gentleman," Alix agreed.

They all agreed.

"I raise my glass to his memory," the king said. "To our right trusty and entirely beloved cousin, Alfred, late Duke of Saint Ormer!"

"Alfred!" they all said.

"His ambition was to see a feudal democracy," Simon added. "He came from the people. He was a man of the people."

"And," Alix said, "if an old and pensioned-off friend may join a second name to our toast: to our right trusty and entirely beloved cousin, Simon, Duke of Saint Ormer, and the newest, *youngest* duke in the realm."

"Simon!"

He acknowledged their toast. "He foresaw a great partnership of the aristocracy and the people," he continued.

"And Lord Knightsbridge," the queen said. "We certainly mustn't forget him." She proposed the toast and they drank it.

"Naturally, sir," Simon went on, "such a partnership would be unthinkable without the monarch at its head."

The king forced a laugh. "I can see, young man," he said, "that nothing will satisfy you but I must hear this notion out."

Simon, vastly pleased, retailed to his sovereign his gloss of Alfred's notion of that partnership between peerage and people.

Helen and Georgina listened in ferocious embarrassment until they realized that their majesties were taking it as no more than a youthful *jeu d'esprit.*

At last the king said, "You want a feudal monarch again, is that it?"

"Indeed, sir."

"Sire!" the king barked.

Simon was alarmed until the king smiled again. "I can assure you of one thing—you wouldn't like him. D'you know how many dukedoms were extinguished on the chopping block at the Bloody Tower?"

"No, sir."

"No, sir! And nor do I. But I'll wager it was more than have been extinguished by natural deaths. Think of that, your grace. And think of this, too. These little jokes and pleasantries are all very well in private—*en famille* like this. But if word of it gets out, if I hear you touting it in public, I'll turn myself into a real feudal king and I'll have you in irons in the Tower so fast your feet won't touch the ground—as the regimental sar'major says."

His grin showed he still thought it a joke—if only just. Simon, now desperate to convince him of its seriousness, said, "It's more than just me, sir. All of us at Eton, everyone who's in line for a title, we're all agreed. And we've even spoken to a few courtesy lords at Harrow. What we want to do, you see, sir, is to form a new regiment. The Peers and People, the P and P. The officers would all be peers or heirs apparent. The other ranks would be made up entirely of people off their estates. I haven't actually put this idea to the other fellows yet, but I'm sure they'll agree. The idea would be for you, sir, to be not just our colonel in chief but our actual colonel. Come out to France with us, d'you see? Lead us to a glorious victory. The monarch shouldn't be skulking here at home when there's such glory waiting to be won—or only popping over to France to witness tame reenactments of battles staged for his benefit by cooks and battalion clerks . . ."

Georgina buried her face in her hands. Helen stared aghast at her son.

The king rose, wiping his lips. "Enough," he said, dropping the napkin. "We must leave now."

Everyone rose. He was very apologetic to Helen and Georgina. "Not well," he said with a nod toward the young duke. "Bereavement, no doubt. Get him to a good doctor."

"You're very kind, sir," Helen replied.

Simon was not at all perturbed as he escorted the royal party back to their waiting Daimler. "I had my doubts about you, sir, from the beginning," he said affably. "Age shuts off the mind to new ideas, don't you know. But your son David will see it. He'll be a true King of the People."

His twinkling eyes and cheerful smile contrasted strongly with the concerned and worried faces all around.

Genealogical Table

ABBREVIATIONS

B. baron(ess)
C. count(ess)
D. duke
da. daughter
d. died
d.s.p.m. died without an heir male
E. earl
eld. eldest
h. heir
L. lord (lady)
M. Marquis
s. son
V. Viscount

NOTES: **1.** On the death of Aveline de Forz in 1274 all Aumale lands and titles were usurped by the Crown via a false but successful claim by one John d'Eston to be descended from Avice, da. of William le Gros; d'Eston then surrendered "his" lands in Normandy and England to Edward I and received 4½ knights' fees in Thornton-by-Pickering as reward for his perjury. The dukedom of Aumale (1397–99) granted to Edward, E. of Rutland, s. and h. apparent of Edmund, D. of York, 5th s. of Edward III of England, and extinguished by attainder for treason, was later conceded to be a usurpation of the title (Parl. Roll 16 CHARLES I m. 14, fo. 23) on the granting of the new dukedom of St. Ormer. **2.** Richard Veitch du Bois gained the barony of Stonor from his half-brother Clarence by Royal Favor on Clarence's death. **3.** The same Richard was attainted for treason in 1536 on evidence supplied by his cousin Godfrey, who received all of Richard's titles by way of reward. **4.** Aumale having been used for a royal dukedom (even though by usurpation), and its variant Albemarle being then in the English peerage, the title of St. Aumer was chosen for the new dukedom—the spelling St. Ormer being due to an error of transcription on the patent of creation. **5.** A novodamus of 1641 provides that the remainder of the dukedom, together with all other honors and titles, may on the extinction or abeyance of the direct male line pass to the hs. of the First Duke's eld. da., L. Anne Wrottesley, on condition that she marry a descendant of the duke's younger brother, the Rev. L. Richard du Bois, which she did in 1670, when she married her cousin, Godfrey du Bois, the direct ancestor of Alfred Boyce, who then became the Fifth Duke of St. Ormer.

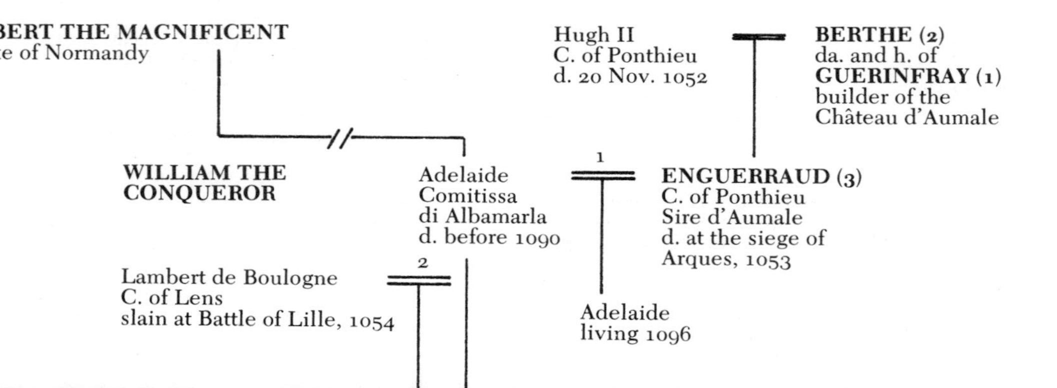

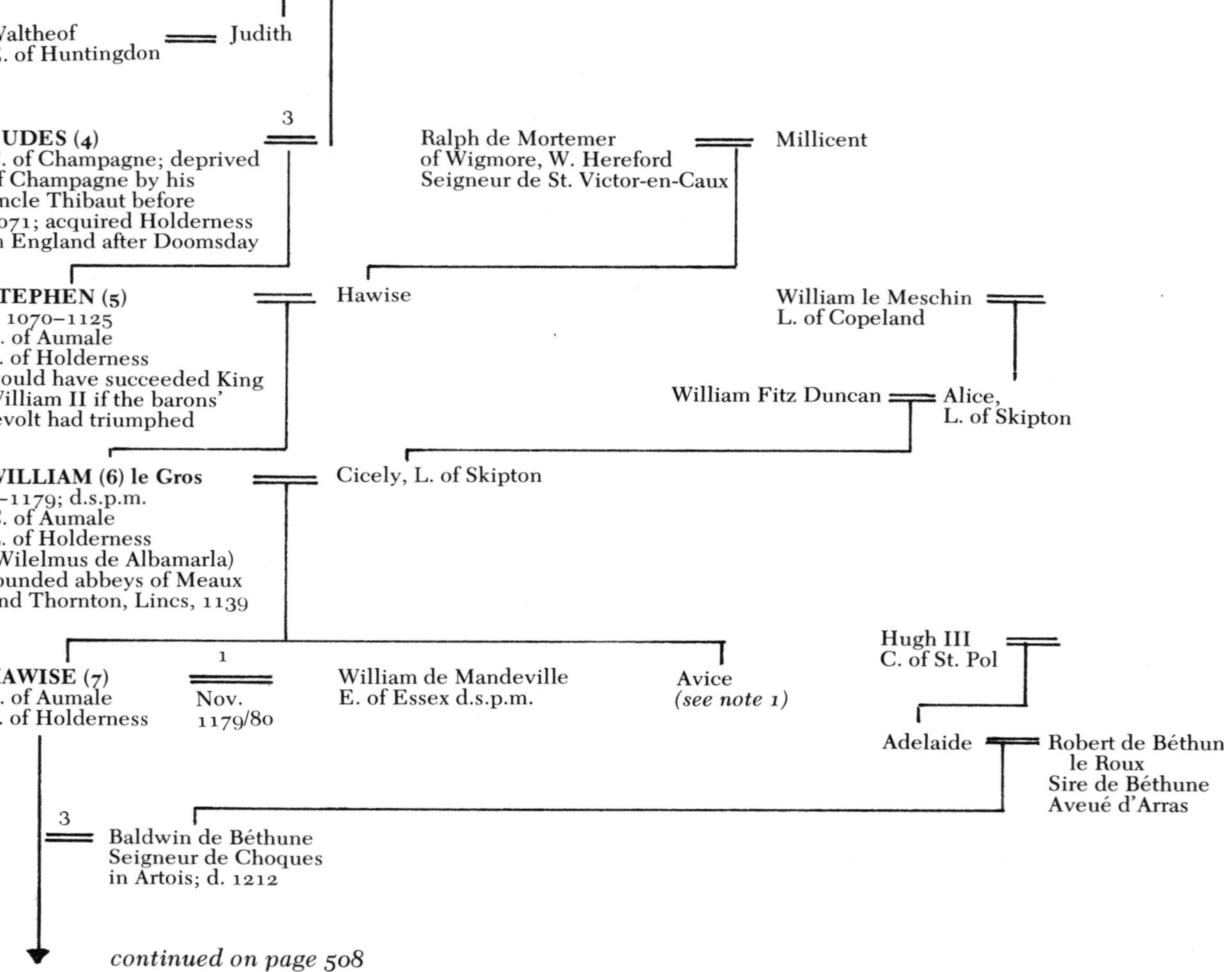
Waltheof
E. of Huntingdon
Judith
3
EUDES (4)
C. of Champagne; deprived of Champagne by his uncle Thibaut before 1071; acquired Holderness in England after Doomsday
Ralph de Mortemer
of Wigmore, W. Hereford
Seigneur de St. Victor-en-Caux
Millicent
STEPHEN (5)
c. 1070–1125
C. of Aumale
L. of Holderness
would have succeeded King William II if the barons' revolt had triumphed
Hawise
William le Meschin
L. of Copeland
William Fitz Duncan
Alice,
L. of Skipton
WILLIAM (6) le Gros
?–1179; d.s.p.m.
C. of Aumale
L. of Holderness
(Wilelmus de Albamarla)
founded abbeys of Meaux and Thornton, Lincs, 1139
Cicely, L. of Skipton
HAWISE (7)
C. of Aumale
L. of Holderness
1
Nov.
1179/80
William de Mandeville
E. of Essex d.s.p.m.
Avice
(see note 1)
Hugh III
C. of St. Pol
Adelaide
Robert de Béthune
le Roux
Sire de Béthune
Aveué d'Arras
3
Baldwin de Béthune
Seigneur de Choques
in Artois; d. 1212

continued on page 508

continued from page 507

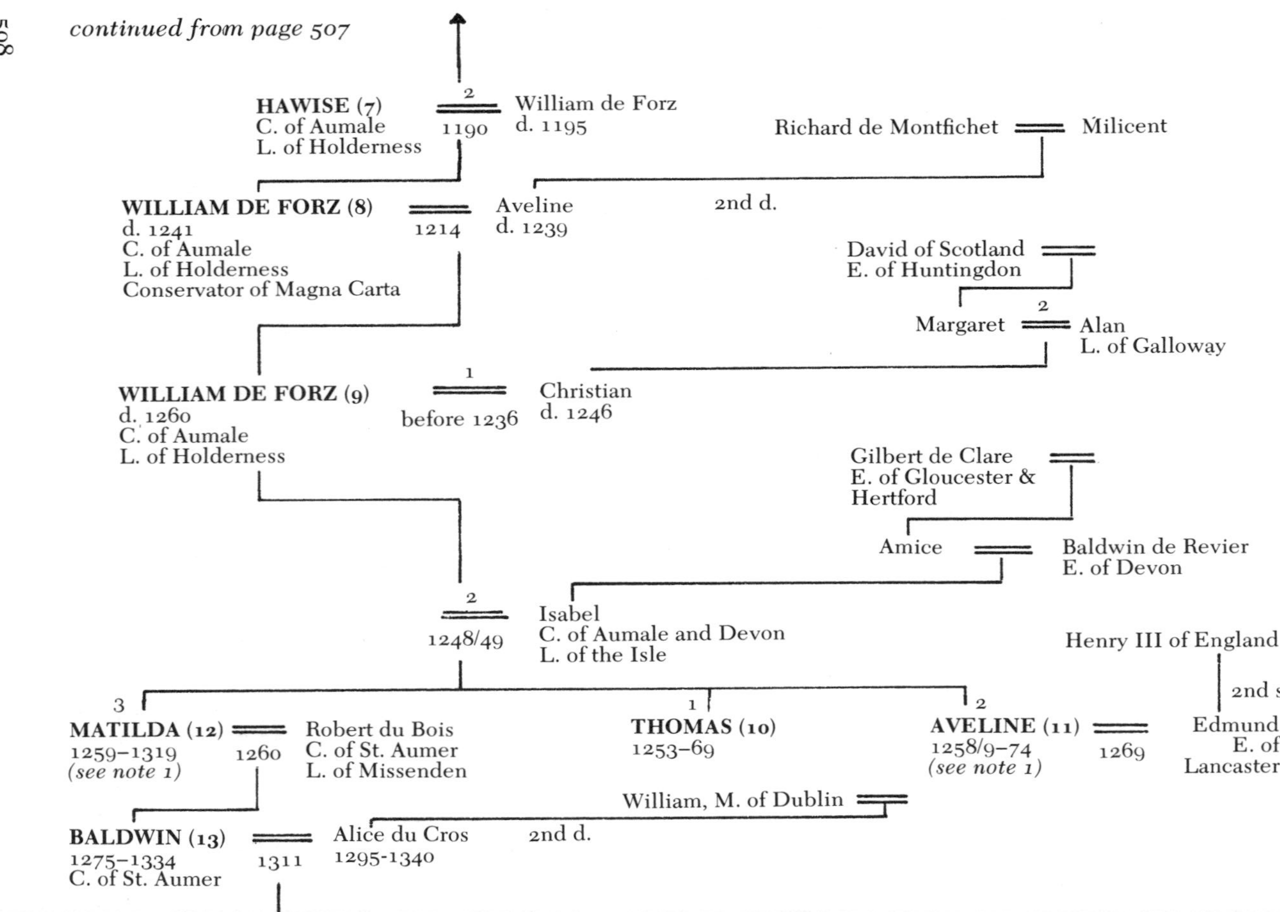

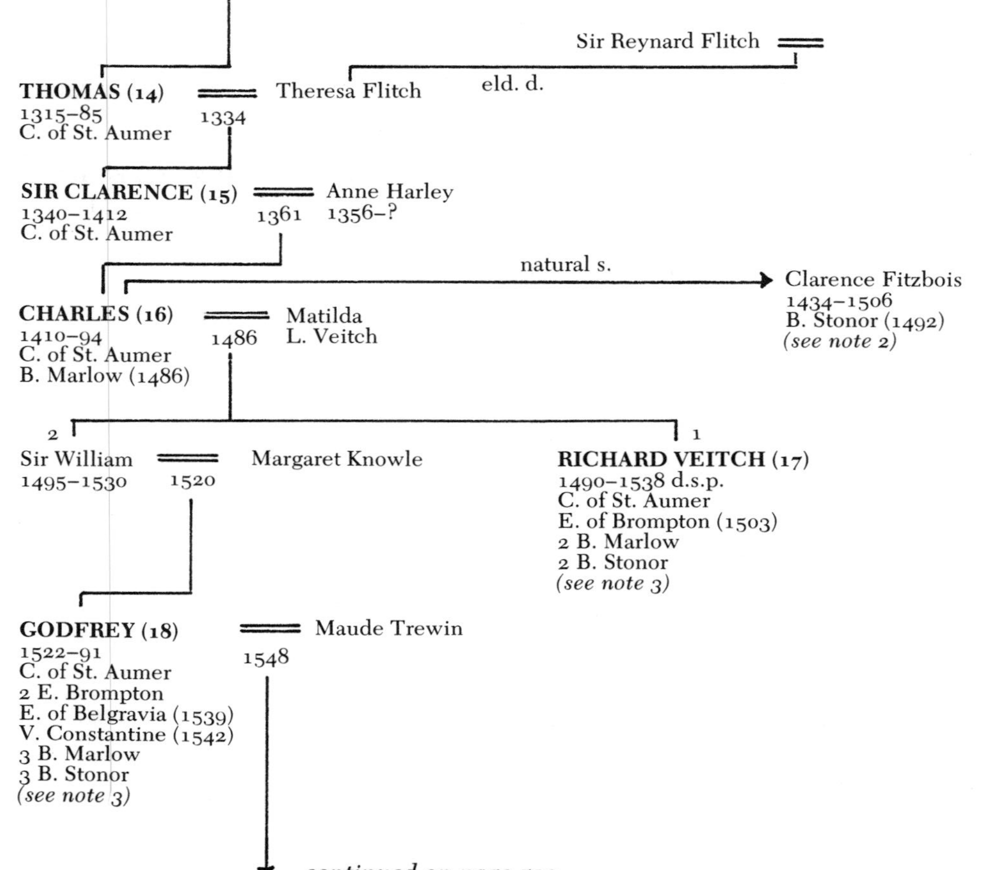
Sir Reynard Flitch
eld. d.
THOMAS (14)
1315–85
C. of St. Aumer
1334
Theresa Flitch
SIR CLARENCE (15)
1340–1412
C. of St. Aumer
1361
Anne Harley
1356–?
natural s.
Clarence Fitzbois
1434–1506
B. Stonor (1492)
(see note 2)
CHARLES (16)
1410–94
C. of St. Aumer
B. Marlow (1486)
1486
Matilda
L. Veitch
2
Sir William
1495–1530
1520
Margaret Knowle
1
RICHARD VEITCH (17)
1490–1538 d.s.p.
C. of St. Aumer
E. of Brompton (1503)
2 B. Marlow
2 B. Stonor
(see note 3)
GODFREY (18)
1522–91
C. of St. Aumer
2 E. Brompton
E. of Belgravia (1539)
V. Constantine (1542)
3 B. Marlow
3 B. Stonor
(see note 3)
1548
Maude Trewin

continued on page 510

continued from page 509

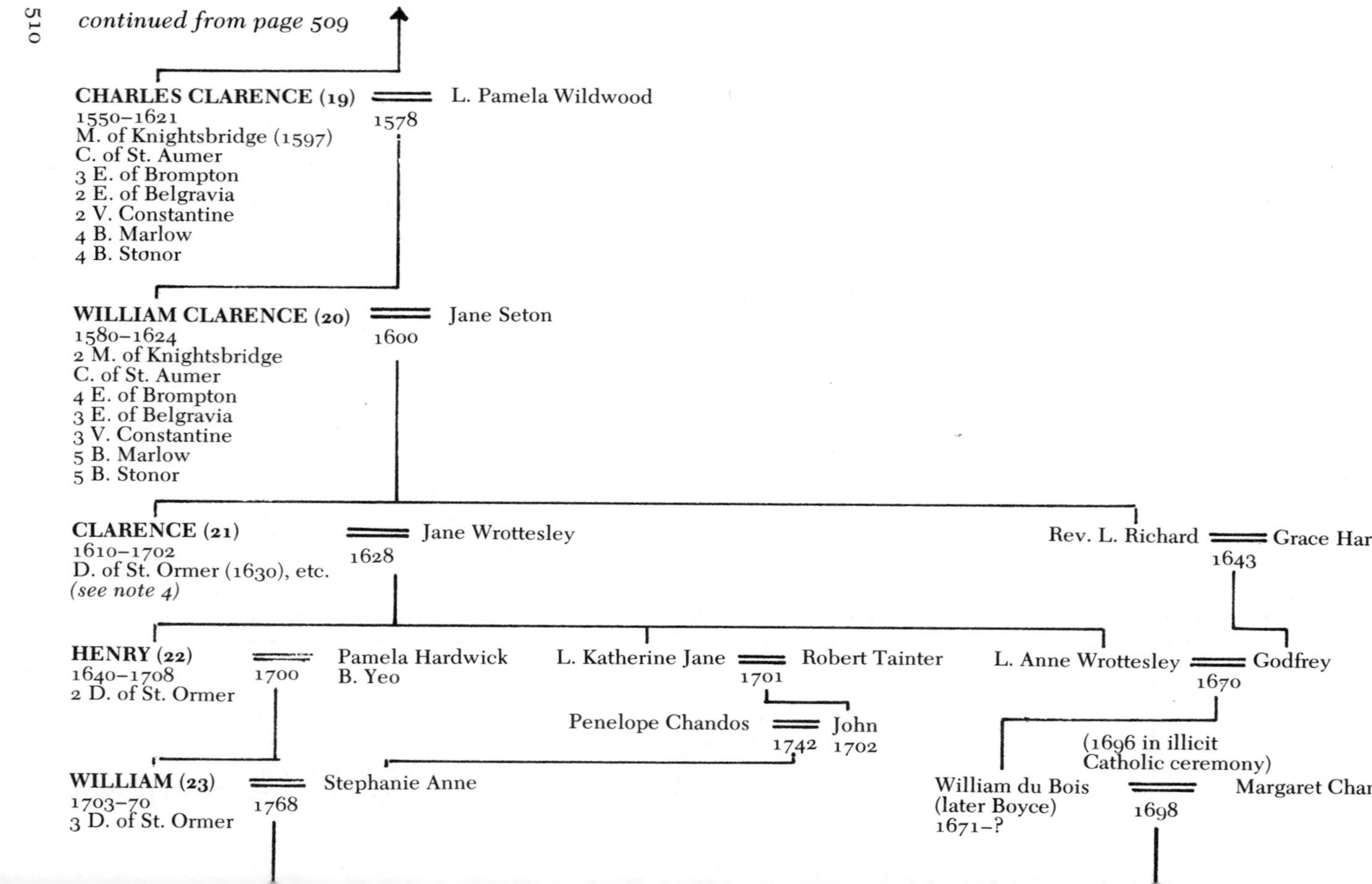

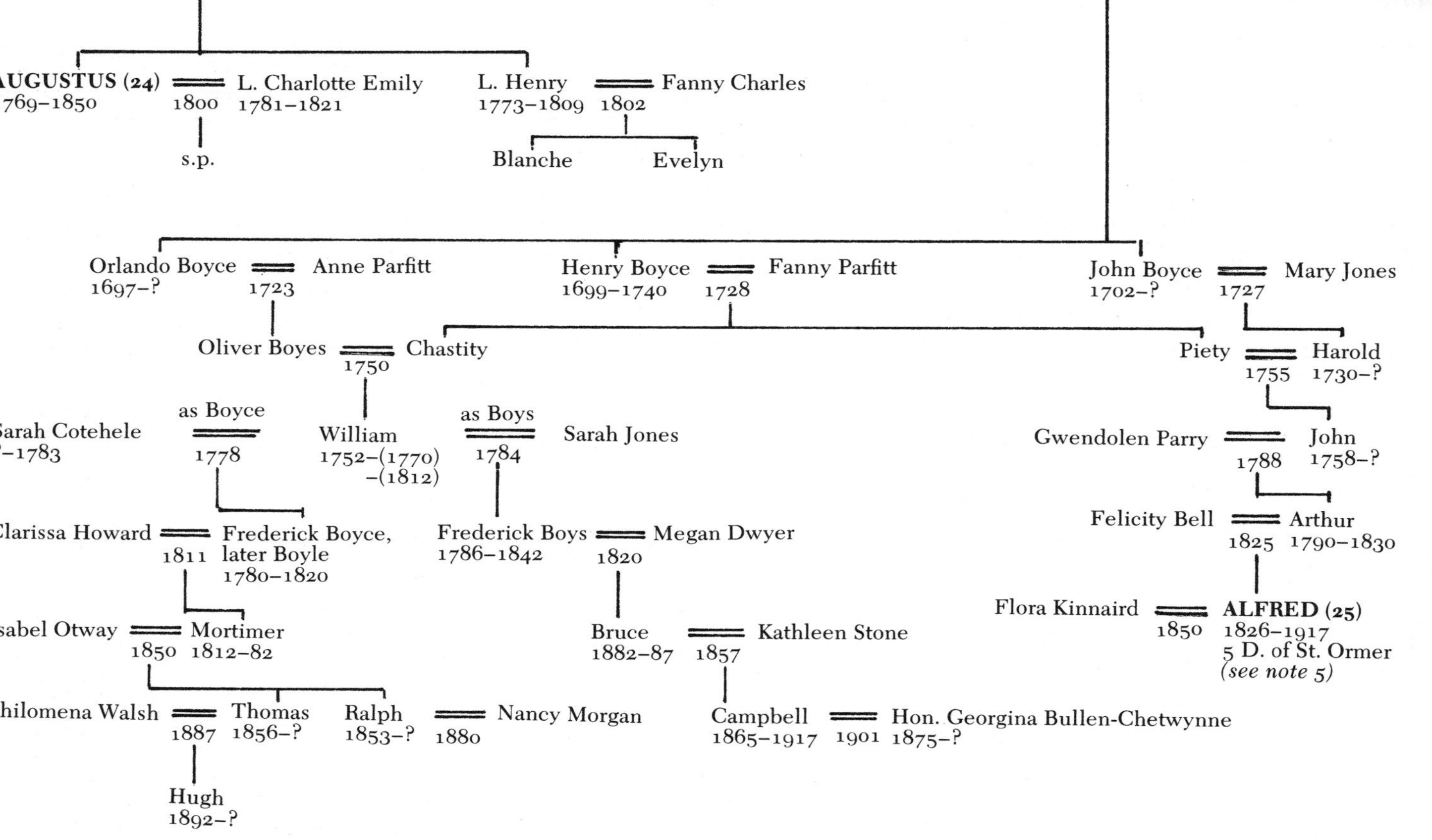
AUGUSTUS (24) 1769–1850
1800
L. Charlotte Emily 1781–1821
s.p.
L. Henry 1773–1809
1802
Fanny Charles
Blanche
Evelyn
Orlando Boyce 1697–?
1723
Anne Parfitt
Henry Boyce 1699–1740
1728
Fanny Parfitt
John Boyce 1702–?
1727
Mary Jones
Oliver Boyes
1750
Chastity
Piety
1755
Harold 1730–?
Sarah Cotehele ?–1783
as Boyce
1778
William 1752–(1770) –(1812)
as Boys
1784
Sarah Jones
Gwendolen Parry
1788
John 1758–?
Clarissa Howard
1811
Frederick Boyce, later Boyle 1780–1820
Frederick Boys 1786–1842
1820
Megan Dwyer
Felicity Bell
1825
Arthur 1790–1830
Isabel Otway
1850
Mortimer 1812–82
Bruce 1882–87
1857
Kathleen Stone
Flora Kinnaird
1850
ALFRED (25) 1826–1917 5 D. of St. Ormer (see note 5)
Philomena Walsh
1887
Thomas 1856–?
Ralph 1853–?
1880
Nancy Morgan
Campbell 1865–1917
1901
Hon. Georgina Bullen-Chetwynne 1875–?
Hugh 1892–?

THE NO THEIR GRACES TH
Ch
Herberts Tower
Northern Approach
The South Wing